2019

P9-BHS-581

5.00

RED METAL

TITLES BY MARK GREANEY

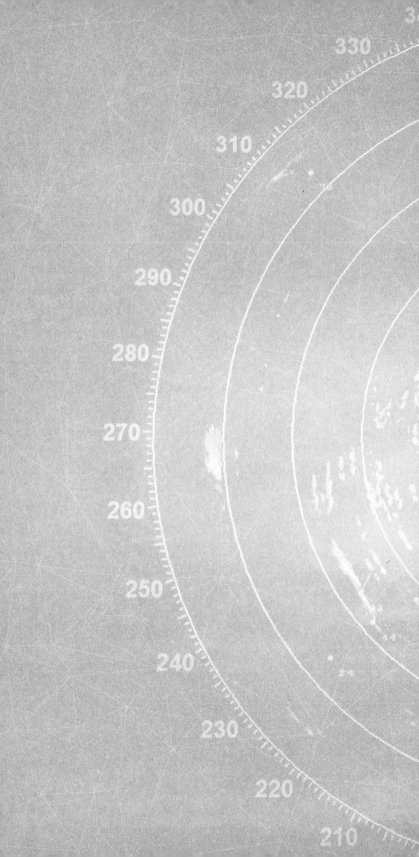

RED METAL

Mark Greaney and
Lieutenant Colonel
Hunter Ripley Rawlings IV, USMC

BERKLEY
NEW YORK

BERKLEY
An imprint of Penguin Random House LLC
1745 Broadway, New York, NY 10019

Copyright © 2019 by Mark Strode Greaney; Lt. Col. Hunter Ripley Rawlings
Penguin Random House supports copyright. Copyright fuels creativity, encourages diverse voices,
promotes free speech, and creates a vibrant culture. Thank you for buying an authorized edition
of this book and for complying with copyright laws by not reproducing, scanning, or distributing
any part of it in any form without permission. You are supporting writers and allowing
Penguin Random House to continue to publish books for every reader.

BERKLEY and the BERKLEY & B colophon are registered trademarks of Penguin Random House LLC.

Library of Congress Cataloging-in-Publication Data

Names: Greaney, Mark, author. | Rawlings, Hunter Ripley, 1971– author.
Title: Red metal / Mark Greaney and Lieutenant Colonel Hunter Ripley Rawlings IV, USMC.
Description: First edition. | New York, NY : Berkley, 2019.
Identifiers: LCCN 2019007191| ISBN 9780451490414 (hardcover) |
ISBN 9780451490438 (ebook)
Subjects: LCSH: Imaginary wars and battles.
Classification: LCC PS3607.R4285 R43 2019 | DDC 813/.6--dc23
LC record available at https://lccn.loc.gov/2019007191

First Edition: July 2019

Printed in the United States of America
1   3   5   7   9   10   8   6   4   2

Jacket art: photo of battle tank by Don Farrall/Getty Images;
photo of Red Square: Kremlin Wall, Spasskaya (Savior) Tower,
and Saint Basil's Cathedral by Max Ryazanov/Getty Images
Jacket design by Steve Meditz
Book design by Elke Sigal
Map illustrations by Daniel Lagin

This is a work of fiction. Names, characters, places, and incidents either are the product
of the authors' imaginations or are used fictitiously, and any resemblance to actual persons,
living or dead, business establishments, events, or locales is entirely coincidental.

To Erin for all her wonderful love and support as we take this next big step together (and for patching up me, and many other men, downrange)
—RIP

To all NATO forces past, present, and (let's hope) forever
—MARK

ACKNOWLEDGMENTS

The authors gratefully acknowledge the hours of research, thought, and support from the valuable community of professionals and friends who helped make this book as accurate as possible. Any inaccuracies inevitably are the authors' and not owing to those thanked here, as we use ample creative license throughout.

AIR FORCE

The whole team of the 66th training squadron at the United States Air Force Weapons School, Nellis AFB, for their support and help, specifically including: Maj. Edward "Nooner" Brady (A-10 instructor); Lt. Col. David "Chunx" Chadsey (Sqn. Comdr.); Lt. Col. Brian "Shfing" Erickson; Maj. Scott "Furball" Redmon—we will not forget our time at the Hog Trough . . . hangovers included; Maj. Travis "Fog" Ryan (USAF bombers expert and all-around GTG guy).

ARMY & MARINE CORPS

Lt. Gen. Lawrence Nicholson—for just being the best damn leader the Corps has seen in a long while, and Rip's commander in Fallujah; Brigade-general Klaus Feldmann (General der Panzertruppen der Bundeswehr)—Vielen Dank, Sir, für die Erklärung des modernen Panzerkriegs; Col. Rick Angeli; Maj. Robert "Donnie" Barbaree (USMC Air & Ground advisor); Lt. Col. Owen "Nuts" Nucci (USMC aviation); Lt. Col. Ben Pappas (USMC); Captain Anonymous (USA, Apache pilot, who wishes to maintain her anonymity but gave us the goods to create Glitter).

NAVY

CDR Scott Boros (USN and all things Navy that fly); LCDR Luke Olinger (USN Silent Service and all things nuke propulsion and weapons); CDR Lee Ensley (USN, Ret.).

OTHERS

The men and women of Conference Group-3, Marine Corps University, Command and Staff College, for putting up with an old, broken infantryman; Dr. Doug Streusand, Rip's partner in crime and a damn fine professor; the Rawlings and Felger families for their strength, love, and devotion; Capt. Josh Smith (USMC, Ret.); Lt. Col. Laurent Bonsept, French Special Forces; the Tellaria, Friedman, Hoang, Cerritelli, Dashtur/Haksar, and Westbrook families—loyal readers and friends; Joshua Hood; Scott Swanson; Mike Cowan; Taylor Gilliland; Brandy Brown; Igor Veksler; and Boniface Njoroge.

Raids are operations to temporarily seize an area, usually through forcible entry, in order to secure information, confuse an enemy, capture personnel or equipment, or destroy an objective or capability.

—JOINT PUBLICATION 3-0; U.S. DOCTRINE
FOR JOINT OPERATIONS, 27 JANUARY 2017,
UPDATED 22 OCTOBER 2018

In the absence of orders, go find something and kill it.

—FIELD MARSHAL ERWIN ROMMEL

CHARACTERS

THE AMERICANS

COLONEL KEN CASTER (USMC)—Commander, Regimental Combat Team 5

LIEUTENANT DARNELL CHANDLER (U.S. ARMY)—Assistant maintenance officer, 37th Armored Regiment

LIEUTENANT COLONEL DAN CONNOLLY (USMC)—Infantry officer, assigned to the Pentagon; former commander of 3rd Battalion, 2nd Marines; former platoon commander with 3/5

COMMANDER DIANA DELVECCHIO (U.S. NAVY)—Captain, USS *John Warner* (SSN-785)

LIEUTENANT SANDRA "GLITTER" GLISSON (U.S. ARMY)—Apache pilot

LIEUTENANT COLONEL TOM GRANT (U.S. ARMY)—Tank logistics and maintenance officer, 37th Armored Regiment, deployed to Grafenwöhr, Germany

MAJOR BOB GRIGGS (U.S. ARMY)—Infantry and Ranger officer; Army infantryman, Ranger tab; on assignment to the Joint Staff Office for Strategy, Plans & Policy (J5)

LIEUTENANT COLONEL ERIC MCHALE (USMC)—Operations officer, RCT-5

CAPTAIN BRAD SPILLANE (U.S. ARMY)—Interim operations officer, 37th Armored Regiment

CAPTAIN RAYMOND "SHANK" VANCE (USAF)—A-10 pilot

THE RUSSIANS

COLONEL YURI VLADIMIROVICH BORBIKOV—Russian Federation special forces commander

COLONEL DANILO DRYAGIN—Russian Federation infantry commander

CAPTAIN GEORG ETUSH—Submarine commander, *Kazan* (K-561)

COLONEL DMITRY KIR—Chief of staff and de facto chief of operations for Colonel General Boris Lazar

BORIS LAZAR—Russian Federation colonel general

ANATOLY RIVKIN—President of the Russian Federation

EDUARD SABANEYEV—Russian Federation colonel general

COLONEL FELIKS SMIRNOV—Deputy commanding officer to Colonel General Sabaneyev

COLONEL IVAN ZOLOTOV—Russian Air Force Su-57 pilot, Red Talon Squadron

OTHER CHARACTERS

CAPTAIN APOLLO ARC-BLANCHETTE—French special forces officer, 13th Parachute Dragoon Regiment

PASCAL ARC-BLANCHETTE—Officer in Direction Générale de la Sécurité Extérieure (DGSE), the French foreign intelligence agency; Captain Apollo Arc-Blanchette's father

CAPTAIN CHEN MIN JUN—Chinese special forces officer

DR. NIK MELANOPOLIS—Analyst, National Security Agency

MAJOR BLAZ OTT—German Bundeswehr armor maintenance officer

PAULINA TOBIASZ—Polish civilian militia member

RED METAL

PROLOGUE

The radio crackled to life and Marine Lieutenant Colonel Dan Connolly snatched up the handset mounted on the dash of his Humvee. He wiped a heavy crust of southern Afghanistan dust off his mouth for the fifth time this morning, using a corner of his desert camouflage neck scarf, and he licked his dry lips.

A swirl of dust spun around the vehicle, seeping in through the top gunner's hatch and between the nooks and crannies in the seams of the doorframes, which sagged because of the heavy appliqué blast armor. The vehicle's position, at the center of a convoy of Humvees, ensured it was constantly engulfed in a nearly impenetrable cloud of sand and dirt.

Connolly pulled his canteen off his web belt, took a sip of warm water. Into the mic he said, "This is Betio Six. Send your traffic."

A rushed and eager voice said, "Betio Six, this is Betio Main. Sir, flash, flash, flash! Report from the Deuce follows."

It was barely ten o'clock in the morning and already the temps were in the nineties. Connolly wiped sweat from his eyes with one hand as he reached over and turned up the radio. The Deuce was the call sign of the battalion's intelligence officer, and a flash report from him told the lieutenant colonel that this already sweltering Afghanistan morning was probably about to heat up even more.

Without pausing for acknowledgment, the radio operator in the battalion's operation center said, "Someone in your vicinity has eyes on you. Deuce says attack on your convoy imminent."

"Betio Main, Betio Six, acknowledged."

Shit.

Connolly was commander of 3rd Battalion, 2nd Marine Regiment, and he didn't have to be here right now. There was no operational reason for someone of his rank to go out on this mission to a neighboring town to speak with the mayor. Any of his company commanders, all captains, could have handled this themselves, but Connolly had wanted to see this town for himself because the reports he'd been getting were that the locals had begun working closely with the Taliban.

And now someone was watching his movements. He assumed the Deuce had decoded a radio intercept of insurgent chatter.

He clicked over the dial on the AN/PRC-119 radio and rekeyed the handset. "Lima Six, this is Betio Actual. Be advised: Stay tight and sharp. Betio Main just reported we've got someone with eyes on us, time now. Let's do a security halt and see if we can get inside their loop." This was Marine jargon, meaning Connolly hoped to do something the enemy wouldn't expect to make them trip a potential ambush early.

Lima Six acknowledged the order, and the convoy began slowing to a halt.

An earsplitting boom rocked the road at the front of the convoy. Connolly was shaken in his seat, and even before he could look through the dust out the front windshield, he heard the sounds of multiple RPG rockets detonating and bursts of incoming machine-gun fire.

Connolly saw huge chunks of road flying through the air ahead of him, followed by a plume of flame and smoke. The debris came raining back down amid the small-arms fire, pounding his vehicle and adding to the soundtrack of the chaos.

The twelve vehicles immediately performed a "herringbone," a well-practiced battle maneuver in which each vehicle pulled either left or right in alternating fashion. The turret gunners on each Humvee began firing their .50-cal machine guns in their sectors, churning the surrounding hills with heavy rounds.

"That sure as shit didn't take long!" yelled Connolly's driver over the heavy thump of the M2 Browning machine gun and the steady ringing of bullet brass and metal links dropping through the vehicle's hatch above them.

Connolly turned to the radioman in the back. "Sergeant Bosse, grab your rifle and get out, my side! Let's go!"

The radio operator didn't need to be told twice. Sitting in a Humvee during a firefight was a sure way to get killed. The version the Marines rolled in today was heavily armored, but a well-placed RPG could destroy the vehicle and everyone in it—and, with the firepower pouring out of the turrets, each Humvee would be an RPG magnet.

Before he could bail, Connolly heard another transmission on the radio affixed to the dash. "Six, this is Echo Six Papa." It was Lima Company's First Sergeant Perez, one of the battalion's most competent enlisted leaders, sounding as calm and confident as ever. "Lima Six's vic is down," he said. "They gotta be shaken, but I see his gunner returning fire, so I think they're good to go. He's on the platoon radio tactical net right now giving orders to attack."

The improvised explosive device was usually fabricated from several hundred pounds of iron or steel scrap, surrounding dried ammonium nitrate mixed with fuel oil. The Taliban buried these devices in the middle of the road, often using battery acid to melt pavement, then planting the weapon and covering it with dirt. The Taliban fighters liked to initiate their IEDs, launch a few rocket-propelled grenades, hammer the area with machine guns, and then leave in the confusion.

Connolly knelt outside his vehicle, his rifle at his shoulder held with one hand while he clutched the radio handset with his other. "Copy, Echo Six Papa. I'm coming to your position. Let Lima Six know he's got this fight." He tossed the handset back in the Humvee and put both hands on his rifle.

Sergeant Bosse's heavy body armor slowed down his escape, as he had to cross over from his side of the vehicle and between the machine gunner's feet, but he tumbled out of the Humvee seconds later.

"Bosse, get the damn radio!" Connolly shouted, pointing back into the vehicle at the PRC-119. The young Marine had grabbed his carbine but forgotten his primary weapon, the battalion commander's portable radio.

The radioman clambered back inside as incoming AK fire raked the armor on the opposite side of the Humvee. As he stumbled back out, radio in hand, he and his lieutenant colonel were joined by the sergeant major, and the three Marines set off down the length of the convoy at a crouched run while 7.62mm rounds whizzed overhead.

All the Humvees' turrets had pivoted their M2 .50-cal machine guns to the left side toward the attack, and they crackled off a near-constant volley of fire. As Connolly ran along, he saw the air officer firing his M4 over the hood of one of the vehicles. Connolly grabbed him by his load-bearing vest and pulled him along, knowing he might well need him.

M2 tracers pounded the hillside to the north of the column. Some of it was aimed fire, blasted at points where the gunners saw enemy positions, but other shooters were simply hosing the hills, because they were, after all, Marine Corps machine gunners, and even if they couldn't see their targets, they loved an opportunity to fire their weapons in anger.

And so far it was paying off. The Marines' heavy barrage of outgoing lead established immediate fire dominance and forced the enemy to take cover behind rocky outcroppings. Connolly knew that if he could just press this attack, he could get the Taliban retreating, caught out in the open on the far side of the hills.

Connolly, the air officer, the battalion sergeant major, and the radio operator arrived at the lead vehicle, where the Lima Company commander was positioned.

Connolly was almost out of breath when he reached the young captain. "How do you want to handle this?"

"I got a good base of fire goin', sir. I want to keep drivers here in their vics to maneuver if needed while I flank left with an assault force."

"Okay, you got it. I'll grab the air-O and see what's on station."

Lima Company began pushing up a rocky hill, maneuvering toward high ground adjacent to the rear side of the hill, where the Taliban attack had come from. Connolly followed behind. Lima's captain was the one running the fight, and even though Connolly was the battalion commander, his job here was simply to support.

He positioned his small team of four on a rocky hilltop two hundred meters away from Lima Company so he could see the battlefield. His first action was to get his air officer, a Marine pilot who'd spent the past few years on the ground with the grunts, into the fight.

"Bill, you are danger-close range to Lima, but I'll have him hold back a bit if you can get something overhead in the next five mikes."

"I have a section of fast movers itching for gun runs, sir."

"Copy. Deconflict with Lima and let's nail these fucks."

The air officer knelt behind cover and worked up a nine-line briefing. Each line of text was chock-full of data describing the target, the location and composition of the enemy, and how the air officer wanted the aircraft to attack. After the necessary radio calls, the air officer told Connolly a pair of A-10 Warthogs was en route.

Soon a distant but unmistakable whine signaled the A-10s' approach. In moments a solo A-10 blasted directly over Connolly and the rest of his small team of headquarters personnel on the hilltop, its 30mm cannon spitting fire at 3,900 rounds per minute. The blast of the low-flying aircraft's jets knocked Connolly flat as the *brrrrrrrrt* of the cannon slammed rounds into the insurgents' positions.

Some Taliban, apparently certain they would die if they remained in place, made the choice to run from their positions.

They didn't run far.

Lima Company resumed their ascent onto the small, rocky peak where the enemy held out. The fight quickly became localized as smaller platoons and squads from Lima Company coordinated with the supporting aircraft. The first A-10 pulled off wide right, giving the enemy a chance to pick up and move, right as the second A-10 began its gun run, killing more of them.

The Marines swarmed upward, closer to the enemy's remaining fighting positions.

The air officer signaled that the A-10s were moving off to get set for another run, giving Connolly and the men from his headquarters a break in the noise level. The lieutenant colonel pulled out his binos and watched Lima's maneuvers with satisfaction and pride in their skills and training, but also with a gut-wrenching concern for the Marines with each daring step they took.

Suddenly a burst of AK-47 gunfire crackled no more than twenty meters off Connolly's right side. Next to him, the air officer cried out and fell to the ground.

The sergeant major spun quickly and emptied a full magazine at two Taliban fighters firing over boulders lower on the hillside. His shots missed but convinced the attackers to drop back behind cover.

Connolly pulled a grenade from his pouch and yanked the pin.

"Frag out!"

He threw it twenty meters out, just to the left side of the boulder.

It bounced down and landed near the two Taliban fighters, but one man kicked it away, and it skittered farther down the hill before detonating in craggy rocks.

This wasn't the result Connolly was looking for, but it gave him an idea. "Bill, you still up?"

The air officer replied through obvious pain, "Yes, sir. I'll be fine."

Connolly glanced back from his position low in the rocks, and he could see Bill crouched ten meters back, blood pouring out of his right calf, but he held his radio up and was clearly still in communication with the A-10s.

"Stay put," Connolly said. "Keep the Hogs on Lima's insurgents. But I need you and Bosse to keep up small bursts of fire to keep these two guys pinned. Sergeant Major, you got any grenades?"

The sergeant major was closer than the air officer, just five meters to Connolly's left. His eyes and his rifle were pointed at the boulder that the insurgents hid behind. "Yes, sir! I'm stacked."

"On my signal, toss one at a time, three total. Let them cook off a second or two first; buy me some time to move to the south. Once the last one blows, I'll attack from the right flank."

"Got it, sir. Ready when you are."

"Go!"

With bursts of fire from the air officer and radioman preventing the enemy from maneuvering, the sergeant major threw his three grenades, keeping the two Taliban low and focused on not getting blown to pieces. The first two missed their mark, but the third grenade blew close enough to kick rocks and debris over the two men crouched behind the boulder. Connolly had shifted wide to the right, and now he put his rifle's Aimpoint sight right on the rocks. Flanking the enemy position, he saw two darkly clad forms holding AKs.

One of the Taliban saw him at the same time and swung his weapon around to his left.

The Marine dropped hard to his kneepads and fired twice, hitting the man in the head both times. The other fighter stood up and shot wildly, but Connolly squeezed off two more shots, knocking the man down. The

Taliban groaned and climbed back up to a kneeling position, but the radio operator took him out with a head shot of his own.

Connolly climbed back to his feet, peered around the boulder, and then noticed a suicide vest on one of the men.

"I see an S-vest on one of these guys! Get some cover while I give him a head shot to make sure he can't detonate it."

Connolly moved around the boulder and aimed his rifle, and then the suicide vest went off.

The lieutenant colonel was blown backward and then the steep gradient of the hill sent him rolling to his right, debris and shrapnel ripping through the air around him. He tumbled end over end twice and then went upright, but he was still falling.

With a crunching impact he landed feetfirst on a rocky footpath twelve feet down the hill.

He ended up on his back, his knees raging in pain from the rough landing, but he checked the rest of his body and was stunned to find he had not been injured by the blast itself.

Christ, he thought. *Dumb luck.*

He struggled to stand, his knees aching still, and had to pull himself upright with the help of a nearby boulder.

The sergeant major called from above. "You hurt, sir?"

Connolly limped a few steps as his knees recovered slowly. "I'm good." He took the footpath back up the steep hill to his men, still walking gingerly. He found the sergeant major standing by the two mutilated bodies.

"You keep doing young-guy shit like that, sir, those knees ain't gonna last."

"Thanks for the advice. You know of anybody around here looking to hire someone to do *old*-guy shit?"

"No, sir. I'll keep my eyes open, though."

They left the enemy fighters' bodies and went back to the radio operator and the air officer, who now had his boot off and was applying a bandage from his medical kit. Blood poured from the raw calf wound, but the dressing stanched it quickly.

"Let's call in a medevac," Connolly said.

"Lima just called one. He has a few casualties, too. None life-threatening. Shrapnel wounds and a gunshot to the arm."

Connolly grabbed the radio as he leaned in to look over the air officer's wounded leg.

"Lima Six, Lima Six, this is Betio Six, sitrep, over."

"Copy, Betio. We have seventeen dead mooj. I understand you have two of your own up there."

"We do. Keep on the alert for more. Understand medevac birds are en route for your wounded."

"Yes, sir."

"Okay. Great work, Lima Six."

"We're gonna have to thank the Deuce, sir. Pretty sure he saved our asses with that intel right before the IED."

"Copy. Make sure you buy him a round when we're back stateside. We're going to grab the air-O and climb down to your position."

Connolly handed the handset to the operator and patted him on the back.

The air officer was still talking to the pair of A-10 pilots orbiting nearby, keeping them on station as insurance. While doing this, he tried to stand, as if he wanted to walk on his own, bootless and bleeding, down the hill.

The sergeant major glared at him, then grabbed him by the arms, pulling him and his heavy gear up onto his back like a human rucksack.

As they moved down the hill slowly, the sergeant major spoke through labored breaths. "Eighteen years of fighting Taliban, sir . . . and I'd say we've finally just about got it down. What do you think?"

Connolly struggled with the pain in his creaky knees and the arduous movement down the hill. "Well, it's about damn time. But I can't help but worry we've spent too much time fighting these medieval assholes and not enough time getting ready for the next fight."

"What's the next fight, sir?"

"Well, Sergeant Major, can't say. But I figure whoever we fight next, they won't look like our enemy now. An enemy with no air, no navy, no armor, no cyber, no reach or lift or tactics beyond hit-and-runs and roadside bombs. Trust me, we're going to look back on the good ol' days with a sense of wistful nostalgia, pining for the times we were just getting blown up and shot at in the mountains."

There was a long pause on the sergeant major's side, then: "Have to say it, sir. You're a bit of a buzzkill."

The wounded air officer riding on the sergeant major's back chuckled at this, then winced in pain as his bloody calf brushed against a thicket.

Captain Raymond Vance banked his A-10 to the left and looked down at the smoking, cratered road below. The Marine Humvees had begun picking their way over the broken terrain again, hunting for remaining Taliban.

He called his wingman as he leveled off. "Hey, Nuts, what's your round count?"

"Below two K."

"Copy. I'm at eight hundred."

"We're gonna have to call off station, but they look like they've got it all in hand down there."

"*We* handled it. The Marines just got our scraps," said Nuts.

"Yeah. Hate to be those boys, though."

"Why? Livin' down in the dirt was their choice. They could've been pilots if they wanted to."

"Maybe so, but we leave theater in three days, while they have months more of this shit."

Captain Ray Vance, call sign Shank, saluted in the Marines' direction as he checked off station with the unit's air officer.

CHAPTER I

Major Yuri Vladimirovich Borbikov hated this hot, filthy, nothing part of Africa, but he was ready to die for it.

And as he looked out over the jungle and down the hill to the flatlands below, he thought the odds were stacked in favor of his doing just that today.

The forces arrayed against him were preparing to attack this very morning, and all intelligence reports indicated they would advance up the hill, destroy everything in their path, and take this position. Borbikov and his men could slow them and bloody them, but ultimately could not stop them.

Nine kilometers distant, hidden from his view by a thick jungle wood line, a coalition of French, Kenyan, and Canadian soldiers waited with helicopters and armored personnel carriers. Their artillery was in place and their multiple-launch rocket systems were ranged on Borbikov's position. The Russian didn't know the enemy's total strength exactly, but his intelligence reports indicated his small force might be outnumbered seven to one.

Borbikov's communications officer and a dozen troops stood or knelt with him on the roof of this two-story cinder-block building and peered out through narrow partitions in the wall of sandbags erected to protect a pair of 82mm mortars set up behind them. This fighting position wouldn't survive twenty seconds of concentrated shelling, but Borbikov chanced coming up here because he wanted to look out over the battlefield himself: an officer's wish for any last bit of intelligence before the commencement of hostilities.

Yuri Borbikov was in command of a company of specially trained troops, members of the 3rd Guard Separate Spetsnaz Brigade of the Armed Forces of the Russian Federation. Eighty-eight men in all, they were dispersed now in their defensive positions, manning machine guns, mortars, shoulder-fired rockets, and air defense weapons.

There was a larger contingent of Russian paratroopers here as well: two companies from the 51st Guards Airborne Regiment, five hundred men strong, and while they weren't as well trained as the Spetsnaz unit, they had spent the last five weeks digging in and preparing for the attack that had seemed more inevitable by the day, and Borbikov fully expected the boys from the 51st Guard to fight valiantly.

But he knew it would not be enough. The major was a highly trained infantry officer; he'd graduated at the top of his class from the coveted Combined Arms Academy of the Armed Forces of the Russian Federation in Moscow, and he had been here in-country long enough to have an almost perfect tactical picture of the battlefield.

And all his knowledge told him there was little chance he could defend this hill for more than a couple of hours.

The Russians had been cut off for the past three weeks and were low on food, water, and other provisions, and there was no way they could be resupplied from home, because the French had brought in significant numbers of Mistral surface-to-air missiles to prevent just such an attempt.

Borbikov knew defending this location might mean death for himself and his men, but he strongly preferred death to dishonor. He was a true believer in the Russian Federation; he'd long ago bought into the notion that the West was continuously plotting against the interests of his motherland, and he felt surrender here today would bring disgrace on himself and his troops.

To Borbikov, this fight was about honor, but to Russia and the West, this fight was about the wide, flat, and barren strip mine that lay on the top of the hill behind him.

Russia had sent troops to defend a few square miles of rocky scrubland and jungle in a remote part of Africa because something had been found under the dirt here in southeastern Kenya, and that something had been determined to be necessary for the survival of the Russian government, economy, and military.

Experts said the concentration of highly valuable rare-earth minerals here was like nowhere else on earth. Fully 60 percent of the world's known supply of eleven of the seventeen essential minerals was thought to be under the soil and rock just behind the Russian lines. Russia now held this ground because the country had discovered, purchased, and developed the mine, and even though the Kenyan government had invalidated the contract after accusations of corruption surfaced and ordered the Russians to vacate, Borbikov knew Russia would be crazy to relinquish it without one hell of a fight.

The standoff had been ongoing for five weeks when Kenyan and French authorities informed the lieutenant colonel in charge of the mine's defenses that time had run out. The lieutenant colonel reached out to Moscow and waited for orders.

The Kenyans and the French soon notified the defenders of Mrima Hill that the sovereign territory of the Republic of Kenya would be retaken by force without delay.

That call had come five hours earlier, just after midnight, and despite the fact he and his men were seriously outnumbered, Yuri Borbikov was ready to get to it. Five weeks of waiting and talking were over. He was a man of action; at this point he considered fighting a welcome diversion from the boredom of the siege.

In the distance now he heard engines, and his ears were tuned to listen for the sound of the inevitable firing of artillery as the softening-up stage of the attack began.

But it was a different sound altogether that he heard: the metallic creak of the stairwell door as it opened behind him. Borbikov turned around, ready to scream at one of his men for leaving his defensive position. But it wasn't one of his men. It was Lieutenant Colonel Yelchin of the 51st Guards Airborne Regiment. While Major Borbikov was in charge of the Spetsnaz force here, Yelchin had command authority over the entire mine and all the troops.

Borbikov caught his acid tongue before it let loose something he would regret, and instead said, "I'm sorry, Colonel, but this position is not safe. The artillery could begin at any time."

Yelchin stepped up to Borbikov's sandbagged overwatch. "Good news,

Yuri. There will be no attack. We have been ordered to lower our weapons and go to Mombasa to await transport back to Russia." He grinned. "It's over."

Borbikov leaned back against the sandbags, utterly stunned. *"Chto?"* ("What?")

"Da. Moscow has worked it out with the Kenyans. We have four hours to pack and vacate. We'll obviously have to leave some of—"

"Sir, did you explain to Moscow that we can repel the coalition attack? At least the first wave. We can hold them off, target their antiair missiles, and if we get lucky, take them out. Once we get resupply from our aircraft, additional Spetsnaz, and airborne troops, we can—"

The colonel interrupted the major. "I did not explain *any* of that, because this is a political decision, Yuri. The tactics weren't discussed."

"Sir, you *know* the Kenya Defence Forces. Even with help from the French, they aren't ready for a fight. Their tanks are from the 1960s, their artillery is unreliable shit from Serbia, and they won't expect the fury they'll face when they come up this hill."

"They aren't coming up this hill. We are going *down* it. Four hours."

Borbikov muttered to himself. "Unbelievable."

Yelchin regarded the special forces major now. "I get it, Yuri. You actually *want* to fight."

"And you *don't,* sir?"

"What I *want* is to get the hell out of this shithole and back home to my family. I want to eat real food and drink clean water." He pointed to the blazing morning sun. "I want *motherfucking* air-conditioning!"

Borbikov did not hide his disdain now. "Air-conditioning, sir?"

The lieutenant colonel softened a little. "Look, Yuri. Your passion is admirable, as is your bravery. But we do what we're told."

Colonel Yelchin turned and left the roof without another word.

Four hours later Major Borbikov sat high in the command turret of a BTR-90 armored personnel carrier, the fifth vehicle in the long column leaving the mine. His back was ramrod straight, his shoulders broad, and his head high as they passed the forward positions of the French and Kenyans.

If Borbikov had been in command, he told himself, this would have gone down differently. *Much* differently. The major would have ordered his

Spetsnaz forces and the paratroopers to fight for every last inch of the mine, they would have booby-trapped the buildings and the equipment, and they would have held out for as long as they could. And then, when the battle was lost, when Borbikov and his valiant comrades were all dead, the citizens of the Russian Federation would have known the mettle of its army, and the West would have known the danger that just a few hundred committed Russian soldiers posed.

Borbikov knew his death in battle would have brought honor to the *rodina*.

But he wasn't in command. Yelchin was in command, and Yelchin obviously couldn't wait to get the fuck out of here.

As his vehicle reached the bottom of the hill and turned onto a dirt road that would lead to the A12 Highway and the coast, Borbikov passed a large contingent of Kenyan, French, and Canadian troops sitting in or on their armored vehicles, staring down the surrendering and retreating Russians with utter contempt. A small herd of rail-thin oxen shuffled lazily among them in the heat.

The Kenyans were chanting and laughing. Hard to hear over the BTR's engine at first. Borbikov concentrated on the sound till he could make it out.

"Ishia, Russia, kumamayo! Ishia, Russia, kumamayo!" Over and over and over.

Borbikov didn't speak Swahili, but he could guess the chant was something along the lines of "Hey, Russia, get the fuck out of here."

Borbikov heard a sudden commotion up ahead, men shouting in anger over the rumble of the armored vehicles, and then he saw something slung through the air in the direction of the APC in front of him. Men riding on the BTR-90 ducked down, but no one raised weapons. Borbikov himself reached for his radio transmit key, but before he triggered it, he was slapped hard on his right side with something wet and sticky.

He looked at the soldiers standing there, right off the road. Several French paratroopers had trenching tools out, and they were slinging something in the air toward the passing vehicles, laughing hysterically as they did so.

The major touched his finger to the slop on his neck and cheek. Held it up in front of his goggles to get a better look.

Fresh, wet ox dung.

Borbikov glared back at the men throwing shit in his face, his chest still high and his chin still up, but inside he raged. He'd fought in the Caucasus and in Ukraine and in Syria, and he'd never suffered the shame of retreat, much less indignities such as this.

Looking into the eyes of his enemy here, and then into the eyes of his own troops around him, he realized something.

Everyone here thought this was over.

But not Yuri Borbikov. No . . . this was *not* over. He made a vow to himself right then and there that yet another chapter to the Mrima Hill saga would be written, and he would write it.

Yuri Borbikov would be back, and Russia would be the ultimate victors here, slinging hot shit on the vanquished Westerners and Africans as *they* retreated in shame.

CHAPTER 2

A sliver of moon slipped out of the clouds just as the dark forms emerged from the ocean, fifty meters from shore. Two dozen jet-black wet suits shimmered in the moonlight and moved forward through the low surf.

The men scanned the dunes in front of them through waterproof night observation devices, breathing heavily as they did so. The twenty-four heavily laden men were supremely fit, but they were not immune to the effects of the nearly four-mile swim from the submarine.

Once on land and satisfied their ingress had remained undetected, Captain Chen Min Jun slung his rifle on his back and took an infrared buoy from a mesh gear bag. He turned on the device, then tossed it in the water, setting it adrift in the light surf. The wet synthetic-rope shore cable slipped easily from his grasp as the buoy floated with the flotsam back out to sea. Chen pushed the stake at the other end of the long cable into the sand, then blinked salt water from his eyes, lowered his waterproof night-vision goggles, and confirmed the buoy's invisible light could be seen in his specialized optics.

Chen turned to his men. All twenty-three knelt in the sand now, still scanning the isolated beachfront with their own night-vision devices, their rifles arcing back and forth with the movement of their eyes.

The captain whistled softly, a gentle birdcall, and all eyes turned to him. He said nothing. He just raised his hand, then lowered it with a flat palm while pointing away from the water.

The team stood in unison, moved up the beach across the moonlight, weapons sweeping for targets all the way to the mangrove and palm jungle that welcomed them with the sounds of tree frogs and crickets, covering the soft sounds made by the men's footsteps.

One by one, the men melted into the foliage.

The unit found a clearing after twenty minutes' push through the triple-canopy jungle. Captain Chen knelt in softly blowing grass and looked into the dark sky as he extended the thin wire-mesh dome antenna of the radio. The instrument was equipped with a digital terminal port, and he plugged in his small tablet computer, tapped a few keys, then waited until it made its connection with the uplink. Chen then pressed the button that read "burst" and the waterproof tablet blinked red, then green, indicating it had completed its task.

Reliable Chinese computer technology, thought Chen as he folded the antenna up and looked out at his second-in-command, just a few feet away in the grassy clearing. Chief Sergeant Class 3 Liu stared back at him, awaiting orders. But Chen was in no hurry. He was calm. His training had always stressed the most important virtue of a special forces officer: patience. He took his time now, reflecting on what his team had just done.

With only two dozen men, the Sea Dragons unit of special forces of the People's Republic of China had invaded Taiwan.

The Sea Dragons were stationed in the Nanjing Military Region, just across the Strait of Taiwan from the enemy island nation. The unit was revered by other PLA soldiers and duly celebrated by their leadership. They were the only unit in China allowed to wear all-black uniforms with a patch bearing the inscription "The Front Line," due to their special mission to remain always prepared to invade Taiwan.

After a nod between the men, Chen watched Sergeant Liu and twenty others move out of the clearing in small units and slip back into the jungle. For the next twelve hours the Chinese would work in teams of three operators.

Chen himself stowed his gear, tightened his pack on his back, and stood. With a determined nod, he turned to the southeast and began walking. Two men trailed silently behind him.

Four hours after stepping onto Taiwanese soil, Captain Chen Min Jun left his two men high on a hill and continued down, climbing over a vine-blanketed stone wall, making sure to keep his profile low as he did so.

As if to bolster his assuredness in his team's success, a vibration from the computer tablet in his cargo pocket told him one of his eight teams had already completed its mission.

Moving along the edge of a second low stone wall, Chen looked out and down into the city of Taichung. As the first glow of sunrise appeared in the east, he climbed the wall, then moved along a wooden fence line. And in the dawn's rays striking the mist in the valley below him, he could now see the top of the crenellated walls of an ornate building in the distance.

Chen looked over his tablet again now; the positions of his eight teams were represented by red and green dots. One team's GPS location was about an hour old, but that was Corporal Xien's group, and Chen knew Xien and his men would now be traveling on the number 12 North public bus into Taipei via the Xinhai Tunnel.

Two of his teams registered on the pad as green dots now, two successful missions, and he was pleased to see both units were already returning to the south, toward the coast, in preparation for their long swim to the *Shang*-class nuclear submarine. The other six, including Chen's dot, still glowed red, meaning their operations were under way.

Chen began moving through the tall grass on the hillside along the fence, down closer to the large building at the bottom of the hill. As he advanced he picked out a particular building. It was the Lavender Cottage, a structure built in the center of a lush garden that was itself in the center of the Xinshe Castle Resort.

Chen stopped again, brought binoculars to his eyes, and centered them on the cottage. A crowd had gathered.

He unslung the sniper rifle off his back, a large German DSR-1, opened the bipod, and rested it on the wooden fence. He would rather have used his country's reliable QBU-88 or even the new Jianshe Industries JS-7.62mm sniper rifle. But this particular German rifle had been etched with the exact serial number of an identical weapon the Taiwanese special forces had lost a year earlier in the surf zone in an exercise off Taipei. When Chen's rifle was found after today's mission, the assumption would be that it had been fired by someone in Taiwanese SF.

Just as he settled his eye in front of the ocular lens of his scope, he felt a triple buzz on the tablet in his pocket. One of the teams was trying to communicate with him via text, but he ignored it now much the same as he ignored the sweat soaking his black bandanna and dripping onto his nose. The triple buzz, he knew, was bad news. None of the sergeants in charge would dare communicate with him unless something had gone seriously awry.

But there was no time now to think of the other teams. Through the optics of his weapon he centered on the garden to the east of the cottage. There a large group of diplomats and military officers had gathered in the center of a sea of media. Panning around slowly, he found his target, just as the man began crossing a wooden riser. Chen recognized him from his gait even before Chen steadied the aiming reticle onto the man's heart.

The target stood at a lectern and waved his hands, facing fully toward Chen's position. The crowd seemed to respond, but at a distance of one thousand meters Captain Chen could hear only the birds chirping in the brush next to his position.

Chen dialed the windage into his scope, subtracted a click from the elevation because he was a little higher on the hill than he'd originally planned for, and then secured the butt stock of the weapon tightly against his shoulder.

He took a moment to relax, to settle his breath. He pushed worry about the communication code from the other team out of his head, ignored his fatigue and his stress, and even took pains to detach his emotions from his work, blunting his adrenaline and steadying his hand.

At 8:01 a.m., Captain Chen Min Jun of the PLA's Sea Dragon commandos pressed the trigger and sent a .30-caliber round downrange, through the morning air in the valley, over the crowd in front of the stage, and dead-solid center into the chest of his target.

The man at the lectern lurched back a step, then slumped forward, his head slamming into the microphone before his body crumpled onto the stage in a heap.

With the recoil of the shot, the bipod that rested on the ivy-covered fence jumped slightly, but as soon as Captain Chen focused again through his optic the weapon was ready for a second shot.

But there would be no need.

Chen confirmed his target was down, and then he left the rifle in place and began moving toward the large wooded defile that led to the Dajia River. The two men above him had their own routes to the river, and though they were just a few hundred meters apart right now, he wouldn't see them again for over an hour. He was looking forward to getting to his next waypoint, where he could take a knee, pull out his tablet, and check his text messages to see what the problem was with one of the other teams.

As Chen approached the wood line in a jog he was surprised by movement close to him. He pulled up quickly, but not before he nearly knocked over a small girl who had stepped out from behind a tree. She was no more than six years old and held what appeared to be a frog in her hands. She looked up at him in surprise.

With no hesitation, the captain pulled his silenced pistol and shot the girl twice in the chest. Her body tumbled softly back onto the lush grass, the frog leapt from her hands, and Chen continued on, stepping over her still form and disappearing into the woods.

There were to be no loose ends. Her death, while regrettable, would fit nicely into the profile they were trying to create in the media.

The assassination of the Taiwanese party leader who had allied himself most closely to China politically would never be associated with mainland China itself. The unmistakable image the local press would run with was that the ruling Taiwanese Kuomintang Party was evil and would stop at nothing to prevent a reunification with the mainland.

Including assassination and murder.

China would not be blamed. Why on earth, people would ask, would China kill their biggest ally in Taiwan? No, this would be linked to Taiwanese special forces, working for the ruling Kuomintang Party, and as Chen ran on, he knew the girl's death would simply add kindling to the fire this mission had started.

An hour later, after Captain Chen had made it to the banks of the Dajia River and reconnected with the two other soldiers in his team, he finally had time to check his mission tablet. While the others climbed into their skin suits, Chen fired up the device and executed the swipe necessary to unlock it.

Looking at the map, he saw seven of eight spheres glowing green and moving toward the coast.

But one bubble was now blinking yellow and black. It was Sergeant Liu's team, and Chen's heart sank. A note attached to the graphic said Liu himself had been killed, but his body had been recovered by the other men with him.

Seven successful reconnaissance and sabotage operations, and one successful assassination, but at the loss of his best man.

He shook off the terrible news, slid the tablet into a small neoprene bag, and began changing into his skin suit.

Chen thought about the magnitude of what they had accomplished, and this helped him deal with his grief. Liu had died for something important. The integrity of China. This operation, he had been told, would help China reunify with the breakaway republic of Taiwan.

Yes, Chen told himself, his chest pounding with pride, his fatigue and his pain a thing of the past now. Sergeant Liu died a soldier's death, a *hero's* death, and Chen himself should be so lucky.

He and his teammates slipped into the cool water of the river for a two-mile swim back to the beach where they'd stepped ashore hours earlier. They would wait in the dense jungle till nightfall and then begin the arduous swim back to the sub.

CHAPTER 3

Lieutenant Colonel Dan Connolly shifted his Ford F-150 into reverse and checked his rearview mirror as he backed out of his driveway. A car horn and the sound of screeching tires forced him to slam on his brakes. An angry Mazda driver honked again and then rolled off up the street.

"Check the flanks!" Connolly barked almost reflexively. He looked down at himself to see if he had spilled any coffee on his Marine Corps service "Charlie" uniform.

Nope, he'd dodged that bullet.

A voice behind him spoke with even more zeal than he had at this time of the morning. "Check the flanks!" It was his fourteen-year-old daughter, Elsa, and she was teasing him.

Sitting next to Elsa, Connolly's twelve-year-old son, Jack, deepened his voice and repeated the mantra, doing his best impersonation of his Marine officer father. "Always check the flanks!"

The kids refocused their attention on their phones as their dad pretended not to be flustered by his near miss with the passing car.

Connolly checked over his shoulder more thoroughly this time, and then he backed out successfully on his second attempt. "What do I always say, kids? Mastering battlefield tactics is as much about repetition as it is about choosing the correct battlefield application."

Jack mumbled without looking up from his phone. "Backing out of the driveway is *totally* a battlefield tactic."

"At that moment the Mazda was the enemy. Stand by." Connolly took a sip of coffee from a big red Marine Corps coffee mug emblazoned with the logo of the 3rd Battalion, 5th Marines, one of his old units. He then placed it back in the cup holder. "Elsa, Mom's taking you home this afternoon."

"I know."

"And, Jack, don't forget you have baseball tonight. Mr. Marlon is picking you and Marko up from practice together. Also, you're going to have dinner at the Tellaria house tonight. I'll pick you up on the way home at about twenty hundred."

"I know," Jack said, still without looking up from his phone.

The kids were used to their dad's tendency to go over the plan of the day each morning. It was a habit he'd picked up on his multiple tours in Iraq and Afghanistan.

The Marine lieutenant colonel pulled into the driveway of the school and waved to Principal Moody as he let his kids out. Jack and Elsa shot out of the Ford and melted into the throng of preteens and teens, heading into the building without even saying good-bye.

Connolly turned back onto Arlington Boulevard, this time headed east. He put on his right blinker and watched the car in the right lane speed up to keep him from merging into his lane. He fought his way in, using his truck as a large kinetic weapon, and soon he was listening to music on the radio and thinking about the day ahead.

It was good to be back home after years of near-constant deployments in the War on Terror. It had been a drain, and he had welcomed this two-year posting to D.C. for a chance to recharge his batteries and reconnect with his wife and kids.

He and Julie had been married seventeen years and this had been the longest stretch they'd been regularly living in the same house in the past decade.

His cell rang and he put his coffee down again to snatch it up. "Lieutenant Colonel Connolly."

A computerized voice said, "This is the Walter Reed automated voice mail for the service member whose Social Security number ends in 4472 with a reminder that you have an appointment with . . . Commander Del

Rey today, Thursday, twenty-five August, at . . . zero nine thirty hours. Please press one if you will make your appointment or press three to cancel."

Connolly pressed "1" and listened as the automated voice thanked him and hung up.

These shit knees, he thought. If he didn't get the damn things fixed, he would never be eligible for command again. He'd still had enough fight in him to ace his Marine Corps Combat Fitness Test the previous November, but his knees seemed to ache more and more each day, and by the time the cold weather came back around to D.C. and played havoc with his joints, he knew he'd need to find some way to loosen them up before the CFT this year.

Too many days jumping from seven-ton trucks or hiking around the desert, chasing twenty-something Marine infantrymen, he thought. And there was that time in "the Stan" when he got blasted down a hill in full combat load and landed feetfirst on rocks.

Whatever they grow up to be, I hope Elsa and Jack don't become infantrymen.

After twenty-two years in the United States Marine Corps, Lieutenant Colonel Dan Connolly had held just about every "heavy lifting" infantry leadership position the Corps could throw at him. He had been a platoon commander in Camp Pendleton, California, in charge of twenty-six hard-charging Devil Dogs when he was just twenty-one and a fresh graduate from the Virginia Military Institute. A rifle company commander at thirty in Okinawa, Japan, which saw him deployed twice to Iraq. Then a battalion commander of the mighty "Betio Bastards" of the 3rd battalion, 2nd Marines, so named after their resolve in seizing and holding the line on a little speck of volcanic dirt in the Pacific during World War II.

At the ripe age of forty-three he had been selected by the Corps to command a battalion, but after eight deployments to Iraq, Afghanistan, and other locations, it had taken every ounce of his six-foot-two-inch frame to keep up with the youngsters under his command.

Connolly hadn't mentioned anything about his knees to anyone other than Julie, and there was good reason for that. If he told his superiors about the chronic pain, there would be some immediate benefit. The Marine Corps would do everything they could to take care of him. He would get great VA docs and all the treatment he needed.

But he would never get another infantry command. Any shot at a regiment would be blocked and the Corps would give the assignment to another man.

A fitter man, they would say, but Connolly would know it would just be someone better than he at hiding the years of built-up scar tissue and aching joints.

So Dan Connolly suffered in silence like many of his peers.

Going to the doc today would be okay, he told himself with only a little doubt. He'd minimize the chronic nature of the problem, get a couple shots of cortisone, and be good as new.

And if the treatment didn't help, he'd just suck it up as best he could, keep popping Tylenol and taking long, hot showers, and he'd power on.

The news came on the radio as he drove down the parkway, and it instantly took the Marine's focus away from his physical aches and pains.

"Shocking word out of Taiwan this morning as authorities there indicate members of the island nation's own elite special forces have been implicated in the assassination of Taiwanese People's Party presidential candidate General Sun Min Jiang. Experts agree that, if proven, the ruling party's involvement in the killing of the opposition candidate and lead proponent of improving relations with Mainland China could have a devastating effect on Taiwanese-Chinese affairs. A speech by Chinese premier Fan Li-wei will be delivered in Beijing in moments, and China watchers expect a harsh condemnation of the Taiwanese government."

Connolly shook his head in disbelief. He had been following affairs between China and Taiwan closely for his entire military career, and to him it made no sense for the government in Taipei to kill the opposition candidate. General Sun didn't have a chance in hell of winning, and the government in power getting caught in the process, as they apparently had, could lead to a shooting war with China.

A war Taiwan could not win without U.S. involvement, and a war that would claim millions of lives.

Connolly knew his week would be affected by this morning's news, and he worried he'd now have to reschedule his doctor's appointment.

He glanced at the dashboard clock and saw it was 0740. He flipped his right blinker and watched the cars in the right lane all speed up to block him from merging. *Typical D.C. drivers,* he thought. *They'd rather take a bullet through a headlight than yield to one car merging into their lane.*

Connolly squeezed his big truck behind one of the offending vehicles and made his turn into the Pentagon's south lot to hunt for a parking space.

CHAPTER 4

Connolly stood in line at the gate and finally shuffled forward to the front when a young man motioned him to the chip scanner. The Pentagon Force Protection Agency, or PFPA, had been trying to catch the security guards allowing people to pass through without the scan, but this corporal was playing it by the book, and Connolly had no problem with that.

He was a by-the-book kind of guy himself, after all.

Connolly ran his badge, stepped through the gate, and then walked to his office in the "J5," the Joint Staff Office for Strategy, Plans & Policy.

He was usually the first of his work group to arrive in the morning, but today a pair of Air Force majors was already working, half hidden by the cubicle walls. The men were with the Joint Air Plans desk and did not work directly with Connolly, although they shared an office.

After a nod Connolly stepped over to his own desk in a two-cube space that he shared with an Army major.

The major had not arrived yet, but this didn't surprise Connolly in the least. Bob Griggs usually didn't roll in till almost eight fifteen. Connolly had rebuked him numerous times for this, with no discernible effect.

The Marine officer poured himself a cup of coffee, began listening to his voice messages as he fired up his computer, and then he started reading through the rough transcript of the statement made by the Chinese president just minutes earlier.

It was even worse than Connolly feared. The president threatened war with Taiwan, to liberate it from the hold of criminals, if the far-right Kuomintang Party president was reelected at the end of December.

Connolly glanced at the calendar on the wall. *Four months till war in the Pacific?*

Just as he finished reading the transcript, Major Bob Griggs entered the office of Strategy, Plans & Policy, late but clearly unconcerned.

"Morning, sir," he said.

"Griggs," came Connolly's flat reply. He made a show of looking at his watch, not that he thought Griggs would be chastened at all.

The Army major dropped his backpack, ignoring his superior's silent scolding. When the lieutenant colonel looked up, he found Griggs holding a box of doughnuts. "The line at Krispy Kreme was nuts. Yeah . . . I'm a little late, but I *know* you want one."

Connolly sighed. "Did you really save one, or is that an empty box?"

"Eight left, boss. Two for you, two each for our Air Force pals, and two more for me."

Connolly laughed a little despite himself and wondered if he'd ever eaten six doughnuts in the same morning in his life.

Griggs put the box on the conference table behind him, let the Air Force majors know breakfast had arrived, and went back to his own workstation to turn on his machine.

As Griggs sat down, Connolly asked, "Did you hear the news?"

"About the Taiwanese army whacking the main oppo candidate?"

"Unreal, isn't it?"

Griggs shrugged. "Their special forces have always been fiercely loyal to the Kuomintang Party, and the People First Party that General Sun led has turned into a proxy for the Chinese Communists in Taiwan."

Connolly turned around to face Griggs now. "So you *aren't* surprised the military offed the main opposition candidate in Taiwan?"

"Nothing surprises me anymore. Still, it was a boneheaded move. The only thing assasinating him will accomplish is firing up China. Killing Sun has pissed off the big angry country right next door and given them an excuse to invade."

The Marine drummed his fingers on his desk a moment. "What if that was the plan?"

Griggs laughed. "To start a war? Sure, some hard-liners in China want Taiwan reunification by force, but you'd have to be one hell of an idiot in *Taiwan* to think that way. Taipei will burn to the ground if the Chicoms invade."

A colonel who worked for the Chief of Naval Operations opened the door to the office. All four men in the room stood up.

"Morning, sir." Three of the four men said it in unison, and then Bob Griggs brought up the rear with a lazier "Morning, sir" of his own.

The colonel seemed more intense than usual. "Connolly, I need you to follow me."

"Aye, sir!"

Thirty minutes later Connolly returned to the office. The Air Force guys had run out to a meeting, and the now-empty box of doughnuts stuck out of the trash can. Major Griggs sat at his desk with a look that told Connolly the man had been doing nothing but eating doughnuts and looking at the door, waiting for his boss to return to tell him what the hell was going on.

"Let me guess. They want us on the first landing craft to hit the beach when we have to retake Taiwan from the Chicoms."

"It's bad but not *that* bad. As if the assassination in Taiwan weren't enough to contend with, we now have ourselves a new disaster. A video has popped up on the Internet—a man and a woman in a hotel room"—he paused—"*in flagrante delicto.*"

Griggs cocked his head. "I don't speak Spanish."

"It's Latin, and it means, in this case, anyway, that they were having sex."

"Oh. Cool."

"Nope, Bob. Not cool. The man in the video is Lieutenant General Dale Newman, the new head of Pacific Command Intelligence Directorate. And the woman in the video is Rear Admiral Upper Half Leah Kelley, deputy commander of the Pacific Fleet. She was due for promotion to vice admiral and was their choice for PACOM chief of staff.

"Both the admiral and the general are married, and not to each other. No word yet how long this affair has been going on."

"Oh, shit."

"Newman and Kelley have already been recalled. We got word from PAC Fleet JAG that PACOM commander will relieve both of them within the hour.

"Yeah, this is going to be a huge mess for both services. More importantly, it's going to affect our readiness in the Pacific at a time when Chinese relations with Taiwan are as bad as they've ever been.

"Newman and Kelley know the Pacific, and they built cogent and competent command teams. We'll get replacements, but it'll take time, and time is something no one is sure we have with the upcoming exercises in Japan and the elections in Taiwan."

Griggs said, "What's the chance this is some sort of smear campaign? An intel hit job, like from the Chinese? God knows it benefits them directly."

"Obviously whoever posted this video no doubt was looking to stir up trouble for us in the Pacific."

"Next question," Griggs said. "What does any of that have to do with us?"

"The CNO wants to know for sure if the Chinese bugged the hotel room or planted some sort of surveillance gear on the laptops of Newman and Kelley."

"And?"

"And you and I are going to look into that, as well as the effect losing these two will have on the war plans in the theater."

Griggs nodded as he thought over the ramifications. "If this was a Chinese intel op against the Pacific Fleet, it could mean all this saber rattling from the PLA in the past several months could really be leading up to offensive military action."

"It might, but if we had a chance to get China to fire two of their top military minds and embroil their army and navy in a scandal, we'd do it, too, even if we *weren't* planning on a shooting war."

"True enough," said Griggs. Then he looked at a point across the room. "Maybe it's just me, but I can't picture PLA officers humping on camera in some hotel room."

"Chinese military officers don't cheat on their spouses?"

"It's not that. It's that we aren't lucky enough to catch them."

Connolly nodded. "Yeah, but only because any Chinese military officer caught doing this would be stood up in front of a wall and shot. Our two horny leaders will probably write books about it."

"The CNO and the Army chief of staff will have aneurysms if that happens," Griggs said.

Connolly was already thinking about the task ahead. "You know, to evaluate the war plans, it would help to evaluate China's resolve."

"I hear you. If we knew *if* they did it and *how* they did it, we might get a clue in how serious a threat they pose, their level of commitment to kicking something off now. We can look over the war plans accordingly."

"The question is, where do we start?"

The Army major thought this over, but not for very long. "We go talk to somebody who's working on the computer-hacking side of this. I know who the point man will be: a dude who *literally* reads Chinese military mail before breakfast."

"Who's that?"

"Dr. Nik Melanopolis, NSA. You know him?"

Connolly stood up from his desk. "Nope, but you do, because you know everybody. That's why I keep you around."

Griggs stood as well, then grabbed his backpack. "Road trip!"

The headquarters of the National Security Agency is at Fort Meade, in southern Maryland, and naturally Dan Connolly thought this would be their destination, since they were going to see an NSA staffer. Griggs did nothing to dissuade Connolly of this notion—not when he took the 295 north toward Maryland, and not as he drove on for over a half hour, mostly listening to BBC World News about the latest goings-on in Asia.

But when Connolly slowed to take the Fort Meade exit, Griggs said, "Probably should have told you: Nik doesn't work in NSA headquarters itself. He's at a classified location not far from BWI." Griggs was speaking of Baltimore/Washington International Marshall Airport.

"*What* classified location?" Connolly asked.

"Stick with me. I'll take you to the dark side."

———

It was nearly eleven a.m. when they drove to the end of a leafy street, then turned into the driveway of a nondescript nine-story office building. Their credentials were checked at the main gate.

"How do you even know about this place?" Connolly asked as they walked up to the security center.

"When you finally embrace the fact that you're lazy, as I have, you realize that in a sea of people doing really good work, all you have to do is fly around from flower to flower and absorb all the intelligence nectar they have to offer."

Connolly didn't look Griggs's way as he walked on. "I thank God your service is still drug testing."

"Hey, I'm just high on life, boss."

Connolly thought back to how he had had underestimated Griggs when the two first met. He'd evaluated the man exclusively on his lack of fitness and punctuality, but after several months of sharing an office he learned that hidden under the major's seemingly uncaring demeanor were an elite knack for D.C. politicking and first-rate people skills. Bob definitely knew the important faces around the intelligence community and could get some high-level info when they needed it. Plus, Major Griggs had been through some of the worst combat deployments in both Iraq and Afghanistan.

He'd paid his dues as a young man, even if he wasn't as much of a hard charger anymore, preferring to roam the halls of the Pentagon to the FOBs in Afghanistan.

Inside, they proffered their Department of Defense IDs and filled out paperwork. Both men had top secret security clearance, so they were soon ushered in, met at a steel door by a guard, and escorted deeper into the building.

In the hallway a middle-aged female stepped out of the ladies' room. "Morning, Trudy," Bob said.

Connolly noticed a deer-in-the-headlights look from the woman. "Oh, hi, Bob. You aren't here to see me, are you?"

"You're off the hook today. We're dropping in unannounced on Nik."

"He'll be overjoyed," she deadpanned.

Trudy continued on down the corridor, and soon Griggs and Connolly were keyed through a locked door. They entered a large office space with several high cubicles, and they followed the security officer through the maze for a moment, finally arriving at a large work space in a darkened corner of the room. The desk was overflowing with papers and stacked with towers of books.

The security officer said, "Dr. Melanopolis, you have visitors."

A heavyset man in his forties with thick glasses and a thin, razor-tailored beard rimming his lower face swiveled around in his chair, which creaked and groaned under his considerable weight.

Nik Melanopolis was still spinning his chair around when he saw Griggs, and he continued the motion, bringing him 360 degrees, where he again faced his monitors.

With his back again to the new arrivals, he said, "Not today, Bob. I'm slammed."

Griggs sat down in one of the two chairs next to Melanopolis's desk. Connolly moved along behind and took the other seat, but he did so self-consciously in light of what the man had just said.

"Yeah, I'll bet you're having a hell of a day," Griggs said cheerily.

"Dude, my *day* started last night at ten, *after* a full day before it."

"Let me guess. You've been working on a certain sex tape out of Tokyo?"

The heavyset computer sciences PhD nodded while he worked. "Yep. Just about have it wrapped up after twelve hours nonstop, and I don't have time for a chat at the moment."

"Even if we buy you lunch?"

Melanopolis stopped tapping at his keyboard, but he didn't look away from his screen. "Who's the Marine?"

"Nik, I want you to meet my friend and boss, Lieutenant Colonel Dan Connolly. Don't mind his Marine-ness; he's actually a halfway decent guy."

Melanopolis didn't look back. In a bored voice the NSA man said, "*Semper fi*, Devil Dog." It was delivered with less than 1 percent of the zeal most Marines used when delivering this standard greeting—so much less that Connolly couldn't tell if the man was being a smart-ass.

"*Semper fi*," Connolly repeated. "Bob tells me you're a computer analyst."

Bob rolled his eyes at this, and Nik chuckled. "And Jesus was a carpenter." He sat back in his chair, and it squeaked again.

Connolly said, "Right. Look, we don't want to take much of your time, but Bob thought you might be able to help us with something."

Now Melanopolis sighed dramatically. "It's something about General Newman and Admiral Kelley, I take it?"

Nods from both military men.

"Lunch is on you guys?"

More nods.

The doctor hefted a shoulder bag and said, "Okay, I have to pick up my laptop from my car on the way, and I'm starving, so we're getting something tasty." He pointed to Connolly. "Not one of those *Semper fit* green salads you Marines eat. Let's go."

CHAPTER 5

The three men piled into Connolly's truck and drove to a nearby Chinese buffet, where Melanopolis and Griggs stacked foam containers high with fried rice, General Tso's chicken, spring rolls, and other side items, while Connolly chose a bowl of mixed greens and white rice. With their food packed they drove to Sawmill Creek Park, a nearby cluster of baseball diamonds and tennis courts that was all but deserted on this hot day. The men found a secluded picnic table and they laid out their meals.

During the twenty minutes between leaving Dr. Nik's office and sitting down to eat, Connolly had attempted to get Melanopolis to talk about the video and any conclusions he might have come to about how it came to be broadcast to the world. But the NSA staffer seemed intent on talking to Griggs about a litany of gripes and moans regarding his job, his benefits, his cholesterol, and some sort of a beef he had with his condo's homeowners' association.

Connolly was beginning to worry he and Griggs had wasted the day on this trip. But once the big man started eating, he turned his attention to the reason he'd been invited out. "Okay, about the video. You came to the right place, because I spent the entire night tracking the hack."

"So . . . it *was* a hack?" Griggs asked.

"No question about it. You want the short version or the long version?"

Connolly said, "The short version, as long as it comes with a conclusion."

Melanopolis took a swig from his can of iced tea. "It does. Your culprit is China." He held up a forkful of food. "That cost you a load of their general's chicken, so I hope you're satisfied."

Connolly shook his head. "I'm going to need more than that. How do you know it was China?"

"I can show you better than tell you." Melanopolis took a bite from a spring roll, then put it down, wiped his hands off on his pants, and pulled his laptop from his bag. He opened it and typed on the screen. Soon a map opened with China in the center.

"This is mainland China. We track their Internet traffic constantly." He typed again, and crisscrossed tracks of red lines appeared on the map. He pulled out another spring roll and used it to point to the screen. "We call this an Internet trace-routing diagram. A depiction of how computers link up and who they talk to. It's like a real-time road map. Typically in China all public Internet is routed through the government hubs. That's because China controls all public access. They look to see what people are looking at, spying on their own people at all times. Trying to get into their computers and minds to ensure they are still thinking like good Communists." He finished his spring roll in a single bite.

"Understood," said Connolly.

Melanopolis moved the map to the east, until the continental U.S. appeared. A pair of larger star patterns of lines was clustered where the Chinese Internet intersected with the American Internet.

"What's all this heavy traffic here?" Griggs asked.

Melanopolis said, "Internet porn."

"Whoa."

"And if you are a cyber warrior, where do you hide the really important traffic?" Melanopolis began zooming in on the huge number of lines leading from China to U.S. porn servers. A few of the red lines branched out, away from the main pack. "This is nontraditional traffic from U.S. servers. We're not supposed to look at it because it's inside the U.S., outgoing to China. It represents less than one-tenth of a percent of all the traffic."

"So, what is it?" Griggs asked.

"It's probably the porn king checking his profits and changing his content to lure new people into his web." He clicked a few more buttons. "But this is net traffic on the same server from three months ago." The map centered in on the U.S. Twelve very sharp lines led from the porn sites to various points around the continental U.S., and then two led back out to the Pacific.

Connolly said, "I'm not getting what we're looking at."

Melanopolis zoomed in on one line originating from California. "This IP address is a base near Los Angeles. It's tough to tell, because your Navy and Marine Corps computer whizzes do some basic rerouting tricks to try to prevent this kind of thing from happening, but watch a minute." He typed again and the red line bounced around the States for a while, then over to Hawaii. On a base near Honolulu it ricocheted around three more times, then on to one specific building. Melanopolis punched the military base street number and building number up, and the headquarters of U.S. Pacific Command appeared with a picture of the front of the building.

Griggs said, "Let me guess. That's General Newman's office, isn't it?"

"You got it."

"So . . . they bugged his laptop somehow?"

"Better than that," Melanopolis said. "They set his personal laptop up as a mini audio and video recorder. Every night they spied on him, I guess, and then one night they got lucky when he decided to bump uglies with the admiral in a hotel room in Tokyo. The laptop was open and the cam was pointed at the bed."

"Oops," muttered Connolly.

Melanopolis said, "The Chicoms probably had the video for months, then just put it out yesterday after the assassination in Taiwan. They spread it around to topple our command authority to prevent us, or at least to slow us, from responding to this new crisis with China."

But Connolly seemed less convinced. "You figured all this out in twelve hours?"

Melanopolis ate a forkful of fried rice. Nonchalantly he said, "It's what I do."

"Any chance you're being misled?"

Now the heavyset bearded man sat up straighter at the picnic table. *"Misled?"*

"There's no way someone might be trying to get you to think it was China doing this, when the real culprit is someone else?"

Griggs jumped in now. "Who? And for what possible reason?"

"It's just . . . it's just that it's pretty convenient that China did this, and we busted them in less than a day. And the assassination in Taiwan was perpetrated by the Taiwanese government, where the rifle that was left at the scene was traced back to them in just a few days."

Melanopolis said, "I don't see your point, Colonel. Two different actors. Two different countries. How are they related?"

Connolly shrugged. "Something happens to implicate China, and something happens to implicate Taiwan. It makes each side look at the other with even more distrust. Add to that the fact that the U.S. military is degraded in the region, and it all just seems fishy to me."

"Wow." Melanopolis turned to Griggs. "This guy sees conspiracies everywhere, doesn't he?"

"Sorry, Nik. He just doesn't realize how thorough you are in your work."

Connolly shook his head. "No, I get it. You're the Jesus of computer analysts."

Now Connolly was the one being sarcastic, but he quickly reached out his hand. "I'm sorry, Doc. I'm just a suspicious guy. I appreciate all your time and the intel."

"Sure," Melanopolis said, his own voice a little unsure now.

As soon as they dropped Nik Melanopolis off at the NSA facility, Griggs turned to Connolly. "I don't get why you don't buy into the fact China did this to hurt the U.S. in the Pacific."

"Never said I didn't. I just don't like the timing of this."

"You think some *other* party is trying to foment a war?"

"Just saying we have to keep open minds. There could be someone else driving the bus."

Griggs turned to Connolly as they drove south toward the Pentagon. Before he could speak, Connolly's phone rang.

"Connolly."

An Air Force colonel from the Office of Strategy, Plans & Policy was on the line. "The president just announced he's sending Carrier Strike Group Five to the waters off Taiwan."

Connolly knew that Carrier Strike Group Five, with the aircraft carrier USS *Ronald Reagan* (CVN-76) at its nucleus, was stationed in Yokosuka, Japan, so it would arrive in theater in just days.

"Things are heating up," Connolly said.

"That's right. We need you back here."

"We're on the way."

Connolly hung up the phone a moment later and muttered softly, more to himself than to Griggs, "If this *is* a trap, then I think we just started walking up to it."

CHAPTER 6

Colonel General Boris Lazar felt like a stranger in Moscow. He was born here, had graduated from Frunze Military Academy here, and had served multiple postings earlier in his long and storied career at the Ministry of Defense building overlooking the Moskva River. But the vast majority of his forty-one years of service had been far away from the Russian capital; in the Caucasus and in East Germany, in Ukraine and in Belarus, in Afghanistan and in Siberia, and when he came back here, he always felt like he drew stares.

And he was drawing stares now. He stood at the interior security entrance at Kutafya Tower inside the gates of the Kremlin, and in front of him a half dozen armed guards in full dress uniforms gawked at him in a way that made him think he had a damn horn sticking out of his forehead.

But an instant before he asked the men what they were looking at, a colonel approached and saluted, apologized for the delay, and escorted the general out into the warm August morning toward the Troitskaya Tower.

"What's wrong with your men, Colonel?"

"I apologize, sir. They see a lot of celebrities at the VIP visitor entrance. Politicians, entertainers, and the like. But you have a special place in the hearts of the troops. Surely you are aware."

Lazar just sniffed. He'd been more of a celebrity twenty years earlier, before some of those pimple-faced boys were born, but he wasn't going to mention this to the colonel and risk appearing like he gave a shit about his fame or his legacy.

They walked on.

Lazar had no idea why he'd been asked here today. As commanding general of the Southern Military District, he lived and worked more than eight thousand kilometers from Moscow, in Khabarovsk, so he knew this was no social invitation.

The only thing in the world Lazar cared about was his army, and he worried today would have nothing to do with it. If he was being summoned to Moscow to receive military orders, those orders would be handed to him in the Ministry of Defense building just down the river, so he didn't expect today to revolve around anything he gave a damn about. The meeting would likely be with some minister of President Rivkin, it would be about politics, and Lazar would have to force himself to endure it before he could get back to his tanks and his men, and wash off the stench of the suits at the Kremlin.

He was led into an ornate conference room and immediately saw there was one other person already inside. The stranger faced away, admiring a massive painting on the wall depicting the Battle of Vyborg Bay, a 1790 naval engagement during the Russo-Swedish War.

But even without seeing the man's face, Lazar knew what he did for a living. He was wearing the exact same uniform Lazar himself wore. He was an army general, and where Lazar was short, thick, and barrel-chested, this man was tall and lean.

Just as the man turned toward him, Lazar realized who he was, and his confusion about today's meeting only increased.

"Eduard?"

Colonel General Eduard Sabaneyev looked at Lazar, blinked hard as if in surprise, and moved quickly around the table with his hand extended. "Boris Petrovitch! Wonderful to see you."

Sabaneyev was commander of the Western Operational Strategic Command, based in St. Petersburg.

"What are you doing here?" Lazar asked.

"I know nothing," Sabaneyev admitted as they shook hands. "Strange, isn't it? Stranger, still, seeing you. They brought you all the way from Khabarovsk for this?"

"Yes. Whatever *this* is."

Sabaneyev was twelve years younger than Lazar, but the men were equal in rank. They'd known each other for all of the younger officer's military career, and Sabaneyev had been a protégé of Lazar's much of that time. They greeted each other warmly.

"It's been years," Sabaneyev said.

"Too long, for certain, Eduard."

The door to the conference room opened suddenly and both generals were surprised again, because they found themselves facing a small man with piercing, intense eyes and a confident manner.

It was the Russian president, Anatoly Rivkin.

Rivkin shook both men's hands with a wide smile, asked after their families, and then paused. Lazar thought he was going to invite them to sit down at the conference table, but instead he remained standing while he spoke.

Rivkin said, "I know you've been watching the news in the Pacific. The United States is turning its attention to the Far East. China says it will invade Taiwan in late December if they reelect their leader, and since there is no other viable candidate, it appears a conflict *will* happen. The United States is trying to get China to back down by sending a carrier battle group into the area, and we are hearing talk of more movements of American military power to come.

"This was planned and forecast and it affords us a unique opportunity, right now, but only if we are willing to do everything within our power to exploit it."

The generals exchanged a glance and then returned their attention to the president.

Rivkin said, "It's been a difficult time for our nation these past few years. With sanctions from the West, with the illegal business dealings by America and its partners, the *rodina* has suffered greatly.

"But, Generals, I have wonderful news for you both. The decision has been made to fight back against this aggression, and the two of you have been chosen to lead Russia in its quest to retain its proper place in the world."

Sabaneyev nodded appreciatively. "What is our objective, sir?"

Rivkin smiled and put a hand on a shoulder of each man. "You will get your orders presently. I only wanted to drop by first to urge you gentlemen forward and to wish you great fortune."

Again the generals shared a glance. This time Lazar spoke: "I will read the orders with great interest, Mr. President."

Rivkin eyed the men gravely now. "What will be asked of all of us will require incredible fortitude. Ruthlessness. This is difficult, even unpalatable work for civilized men, I know. But the moment we accept that our survival, the survival of our families, the survival of our people, is at stake . . . only *then* can we do all that must be done."

Sabaneyev said, "We will not fail you or the motherland, Mr. President."

"I know you will not. We will strike with speed and complete surprise, and we will be victorious."

And seconds later Rivkin was gone.

Sabaneyev and Lazar looked at each other in silence for a moment; then the younger, blond-haired man said, "I suppose that means you and I are off to war."

Lazar said, "'Surprise'? Did he say '*surprise*'? Is he unaware of the impossibility of strategic surprise?" Lazar knew, as did Sabaneyev, that Russian military planners had determined that any conventional attack on Europe would take at least two years of preparations—preparations that could not be hidden from Western satellites, spies, and signals intelligence collection. NATO knew this fact, too, and a key part of NATO's defense was close monitoring of military production, training, force mobilization schedules, and the like.

Lazar could think of no way he and his army could surprise *anyone* in the West.

Sabaneyev said, "He didn't say the target was Europe. It's Africa—I'm sure of it. A small armored force to retake the mine that was stolen from us."

Lazar shrugged. "Africa by what route? Have you taught your tanks to swim, Eduard? As of yet, mine cannot."

Before Sabaneyev could reply, a colonel entered the room via the same double doors Rivkin had used and he placed briefing packets on the table next to where the generals stood.

Both men were clearly confused. Sabaneyev said, "I've never been handed field orders at the Kremlin. Why aren't we at the Ministry of Defense for this?"

The colonel replied, "Security reasons."

Lazar chuckled at what he saw as the absurdity of this. "We are being given orders, but we can't let anyone at MoD know? Can we tell our armies, or will *we* be driving our tanks ourselves? Firing them, too?"

Sabaneyev laughed, but the colonel remained professionally cool. "At this early stage, Colonel General, President Rivkin and Colonel Borbikov thought it should be done this way."

Sabaneyev started to speak, but Lazar cut him off. "Colonel *who*?"

"May I ask you to please read the orders? I believe your packets will have more answers than I am able to provide. Colonel Borbikov very much looks forward to meeting you and receiving your feedback as soon as you are finished."

The colonel left the room.

"Who the fuck is Borbikov?" Lazar asked.

Sabaneyev shrugged, and the two generals sat several seats apart at the conference table and opened the packets left for them. Each leather-bound folio was sixty pages of typewritten orders, clarifications, and charts, with a second sheaf of printed maps.

On the title page of the booklet, three words were written.

Operacyia Krasnyi Metal. *Operation Red Metal.*

Below that was a date: 24 December 2020. Less than four months away.

Sixty-four-year-old Colonel General Boris Lazar put on his eyeglasses and hunched over his papers, and fifty-two-year-old Colonel General Eduard Sabaneyev lifted his pages, leaned back, and crossed a booted leg over a knee. The men did not speak to each other; instead they just read.

Five minutes into the reading, Sabaneyev let out a loud gasp but said nothing.

Lazar caught up to the other general a minute later and he spoke under his breath: "You've got to be joking."

After Russia vacated the Mrima Hill rare-earth metal mine, they took their case to the International Criminal Court, where a hearing on the issue was blocked by Western powers.

But the Kremlin never gave up on their goal of returning to the mine.

Russian president Anatoly Rivkin had suffered a devastating hit to his domestic support after his promises to his people about the windfalls they would reap from Africa failed to materialize, and although there was some benefit to demonizing the West, claiming the Russian people had once again been humiliated by America, Western Europe, and Canada, he realized his choke hold on power was weakening by the day.

Additionally, he and his partners had lost billions of dollars. Not only were his political fortunes on the brink of ruin; his own personal fortune was in jeopardy.

The REMs meant the survival of Rivkin's regime, of Rivkin himself, and he quickly determined he *had* to use the full force of the Russian military to regain control of them.

It was no tough sell to get the military behind him. He had the support of his nation's generals and admirals, because if Rivkin needed REMs to survive, his military needed them to remain strong. Every aircraft, communications network, missile, computer, and guidance system utilized these resources, and with the West taking over two-thirds of the known world supplies, and China owning most of the rest, Russia would be at the mercy of China and the West to exist as a military power.

And this would not do.

Rivkin's Kremlin and the Ministry of Defense moved in secret but in lockstep, and they determined they needed a plan to retake the mines by force.

It didn't take long to produce one, because the plan had already been written.

Yuri Vladimirovich Borbikov, the commander of the Spetsnaz forces at the mine during the standoff, had written a proposal at the Russian Federation Armed Forces Combined Arms Academy that was immediately classified at the highest levels of secrecy in the Russian military. The proposal was a plan to retake the Russian strategic resources under the soil in Kenya using an incredibly bold strategy.

Borbikov had worked on his operation for two years, meeting unofficially with hundreds of military, intelligence, and political experts all over Russia. Using his own money and time, he had traveled to several different countries to look at the lay of the land in person.

The proposal was so audacious, Borbikov was written off by many at the Ministry of Defense as a crackpot, and the document seemed destined to cripple his meteoric ascendency in the Russian army.

Until that day Anatoly Rivkin demanded a bold strategy from his generals, damn the costs and the consequences.

Some in the Ministry of Defense wanted to suppress the paper, worrying that a desperate Kremlin might actually entertain the far-fetched plan as somehow feasible. But others saw Borbikov and his blueprint to take the mines by force as *exactly* what Russia needed in this desperate time, and they leaked to government officials the existence of the Borbikov proposal. As it was, it was just the right tactic at just the right political moment.

The president of Russia himself contacted the defense minister and demanded that the proposal be presented to him by the architect himself, and three days later Yuri Borbikov entered the Kremlin in his crisp uniform, ready to defend his plan to save Russia from ruin.

Nine months after Borbikov and Rivkin first met, and days after the assassination in Taiwan and the release of the compromising video that dealt a blow to American military leadership in the Pacific, Russia's two most iconic generals sat in silence at a conference table in the Kremlin and read Borbikov's detailed operation. An operation that had been fully approved by the president of Russia.

CHAPTER 7

It took Sabaneyev just over an hour to digest it all, but when he had done so, he waited patiently on the older Lazar. General Lazar needed an additional twenty-five minutes before he closed his packet, looked up, and then stared out the window in silence.

Lazar finally said, "One hundred and twenty days from now. Not much time at all."

Sabaneyev agreed, partially. "Not much, but enough."

Lazar turned to him. "This Borbikov. I've never heard of him."

"I remember him now," Sabaneyev said. "Spetsnaz."

"I gathered as much from the battle plan. It's certainly heavy on the special operations."

Sabaneyev said, "If I knew he was capable of coming up with something like this, I would have fished him out of Spetsnaz and brought him up in armor."

"He's got quite an imagination," Lazar said. The comment could have been taken a number of different ways, but the younger general correctly interpreted it.

Sabaneyev leaned back in his chair in surprise. "You are actually saying you aren't impressed with the operation? *Really*, Boris? A raid into Europe to destroy America's Africa Command in Stuttgart and a simultaneous mission to Kenya to retake the mines? You aren't so old that you can't appreciate creative thought, are you?"

"The creative thought *I* appreciate involves coming up with a way to fix an idler wheel arm on a frozen T-80 in the field without the proper tools. It *isn't* coming up with a way to send virtually all Russia's Western and

Southern Military District's armor into battle abroad at the same time, leaving the motherland exposed and vulnerable to conventional attack."

Sabaneyev shrugged. "At a time the threat from the West is nonexistent, and for only a short period."

Lazar continued looking out the window. "Funny thing about war, Sabaneyev. One side's timeline isn't always respected by the other side."

"Ah, here cometh the lecture."

"No lecture. You are no longer my student. You and I are equal in rank if not in experience."

"And you wear those extra miles on you as a cloak of invincibility, don't you?"

Lazar looked over the younger man now. "Invincibility? On the contrary. I am painfully aware of how vulnerable we all are, and will be."

Sabaneyev waved away the comment and picked up the papers in front of him. He waved them in the air. "On the face of it, this looks like a mission for two officers more junior than you and I, but Borbikov's genius here is that he doesn't micromanage. You and I have the freedom to organize, prioritize, and improvise. We have objectives clearly laid out, but we are left to shape our campaigns as we see fit. And you have all the advantages, Boris Petrovitch. You have the larger force and you will be attacking Africa to reacquire the rare-earth mines. These orders have me up against the most powerful armies of NATO"—Sabaneyev grinned—"while you will be fighting the Ethiopians and the Kenyans."

Lazar replied, "You read the same briefing I did, Eduard. These are spearheads that should be led by one-star generals. Not us. And, more importantly, can you really say you aren't bothered by what you are tasked to do when you arrive at your objective?"

Sabaneyev did not miss a beat. "I am the right officer for the mission, and I will fulfill my orders."

"Not what I asked." Lazar lifted the booklet.

Sabaneyev shrugged. "It is simply combat. Lawful combat."

"Only if you get away with it," said Lazar, looking intently into his protégé's eyes.

"I *will* get away with it. And so will you." Sabaneyev added, "What would you say to a friendly wager? A steak dinner for the man who achieves his objectives closest to his timeline."

Lazar looked out the window again at the warm day. A light rain had begun to fall. "The goal for both of us should be to return with the fewest dead boys. Anything else is folly and an utter waste of our focus."

Sabaneyev's smile disappeared. "Don't feign a higher purpose. You didn't become the great Boris Lazar without leaving thousands of those boys you claim to love in massive lime-sprinkled pits in Afghanistan, Dagestan, Chechnya, Georgia, Ingushetia, and Ukraine. If you've lost your stomach for the fight, then that's a new development, and a lot of mothers across the Russian Federation would be disappointed to hear that out of you now, long after *their* children's corpses have rotted away to dirt."

Lazar spoke solemnly. "I lost many men who followed my orders while I followed orders myself. That will happen again in one hundred and twenty days, I am certain. Nothing changes."

"*Everything* will change when you take those mines. The map of the world will be different. Russia will be at the center for the first time in a generation. I can see that, and you should see that, too."

Lazar replied, "The Americans and Europeans will just find new sources somewhere else. They'll develop their own mines if we take these back. Our economy won't get the boost the politicians promise."

Sabaneyev cocked his head. "You're an economist now, Boris? Something you picked up studying the microeconomics of goatherds on the steppes?"

The older general did not miss a beat. "It's common sense, Eduard. Something they don't hand out like breast medals, apparently. And experience. That's something earned by living with a head up and ears open."

The younger general nodded as if a chess opponent had made a clever move; then he said, "We're here at the Kremlin right now. What a great opportunity you have to tell the president of your concerns."

Lazar stiffened a little. "No. But I suppose you might just tell Rivkin I have reservations about the wisdom of this escapade."

The statement hung in the air for several seconds. Finally Sabaneyev said, "Of course not. I want you in this all the way. You are the second-best general in the Armed Forces of the Russian Federation; that is undisputed."

"High praise," Lazar said, a stab at Sabaneyev's hubris.

"The question is . . . do you *want* in on this fight, Boris?"

Lazar heaved his broad chest and hesitated before responding. Finally he said, "Better I lead the southern spear than someone less trained. Someone with less interest in saving every life possible."

"Spoken like a wise man," Sabaneyev said. "Perhaps not a warrior . . . but a wise man nonetheless."

The older general did not respond.

Twenty minutes later Eduard Sabaneyev sat in the back of his staff car on the way to the Ministry of Defense for his one p.m. meeting with Colonel Yuri Borbikov.

He'd spent the last five minutes giving his deputy, Colonel Feliks Smirnov, an abbreviated version of Red Metal, and he could tell the colonel was as floored by it all as Sabaneyev himself had been when he read the briefing papers.

Smirnov said, "The Kremlin was wise to give you the premier operation, sir. Their European campaign will be higher profile and more technically difficult. For twenty-five years Boris Lazar was their star, but now they finally realize you are the true warrior general."

These were the words of a sycophant, Sabaneyev knew, but he also believed them to be true. He gazed out the window, a feeling of melancholy washing over him suddenly. "Ten years ago this would have made me beam with pride, Feliks. Even five, if I'm honest. But *now*? Lazar has lost his mettle. He gave me a sermon back there about how he cares only about his soldiers and insinuated the entire endeavor would be a waste of lives."

The general added, "Besting Boris Lazar *now* is no great feat." He turned and winked at Smirnov. "You could almost do it yourself."

Boris Lazar rode in his own staff car back to the Ministry of Defense. His chief of staff was with him. Colonel Dmitry Kir would be anxious to learn what had happened inside the conference room, but Lazar hadn't yet said a word about the battle plan. There'd be time enough for that later, days of meetings in secret with Borbikov and intelligence chiefs and others before he could get out of Moscow and back to his troops, but for now he wanted only to sit and reflect in silence.

The fires of Lazar's ambition had faded, and this was obvious to him by the way he felt about this opportunity before him. He still believed in the flag for which he fought, the people he protected, and he thought it likely that if this entire affair had been over territory in the near abroad—a threat from NATO against a Russian ally, or a recalcitrant satellite government attempting to break away from the federation—he would have been as heavily invested psychologically as ever.

But not now.

Eduard Sabaneyev was a different animal altogether. Lazar had no doubt that the younger man was sufficiently intelligent, charismatic, and skilled at developing the political and personal alliances necessary to make him a successful general. But Sabaneyev's drive to fight for the sake of fighting, to acquire appointments proving his power and abilities, was something Lazar had no interest in personally.

Not anymore.

Lazar wondered if it was just his advancing age cooling his ambition, or if it was simply that he had absolutely no desire to fight for fucking African *rocks*.

He looked out at the summer rain on the Moscow streets, then shut his eyes briefly in an attempt to wipe away any doubt or lack of resolve.

He opened them and cleared his throat, then spoke up to his colonel, who was surely near tearing his hair out to learn what today's trip to the Kremlin had been all about.

Lazar spoke matter-of-factly. "It seems you and I will be spending Christmas together in Africa, Dmitry."

CHAPTER 8

Colonel Yuri Borbikov stood in a conference room on the ninth floor of the Ministry of Defense, looked out the window and down to the Moskva River and Gorky Park beyond it, and steeled his nerves for his meeting to come.

This was the biggest moment of his career, even bigger than when he met privately with Rivkin at the Kremlin months earlier.

Today was more auspicious, because today he would meet his idol, Colonel General Boris Lazar, and he would have the honor of briefing him on the operation Borbikov himself had created.

Since the day he left the Kenyan mine three years earlier, Borbikov had thought of nothing other than his return. He'd worked sixteen-hour days crafting his operation, and now he would brief the two ground commanders.

Well . . . two of the three ground commanders. Borbikov would be in command of the Spetsnaz forces involved in the operation, and they would be conducting literally hundreds of missions behind enemy lines. Even though Borbikov was no general, he knew his role in the direct action of Operation Red Metal would be every bit as important as the work he did to design the operation in the first place.

He forced himself to take a calming breath to settle down and he realized his excitement had almost as much to do with meeting General Boris Lazar as it did with the operation itself.

Eduard Sabaneyev was a well-known general as well, but he was known more as Lazar's former adjutant than as a star in his own right. Borbikov wondered what it must have been like to live a career in the shadow of another man, to always be considered the heir apparent, the underling.

The colonel imagined the younger of the two colonel generals would approach his mission as if he had something to prove, and that was just fine with Borbikov.

This conference room was normally swept for bugs twice daily, but the colonel requested another pass by the countersurveillance team. They had just wrapped up their sweep when the two generals entered.

The technicians stepped aside to let the men pass through the doorway before slipping out behind them, and Borbikov could see two separate entourages standing outside the room as the door closed. Today's briefing would be exclusively for Lazar and Sabaneyev, but today would be followed by dozens more meetings about Red Metal in the next four months, and the generals' staffs would be involved in virtually all of them.

Borbikov was careful to address both men with equal deference, be-cause although Lazar had been his idol since he was a boy, Eduard Sabane-yev was Lazar's equal in rank.

"It is a great honor to meet you both," Borbikov said as he shook the two generals' hands.

Sabaneyev looked like an actor. Handsome, with high Slavic cheek-bones and a well-defined jaw, gray-flecked blond hair that was slicked back off his high forehead. He had a smile full of straight teeth and his tall, fit frame was just a few centimeters shorter than Borbikov's own.

Lazar, by contrast, was short, big, and soft jowled. His round face was weather-beaten and wrinkled, and his eyebrows were full and low on his forehead.

The three of them sat down in a small sitting area and Borbikov poured tea for them all. "I understand you've just read the briefing packages that were prepared for you regarding operation Red Metal?"

Sabaneyev spoke first, and this surprised Borbikov. "You are being too humble, Colonel. We know you are the architect of this. You've found that rare thing, that balance between firm direction and not overcontrolling those aspects better left to the man on the ground."

"Thank you, Colonel General. I've been that man on the ground many times, as I know you both have been." He hastened to add, "More than I, of course. As you are well aware, it's best to know your orders but to retain enough autonomy to achieve them in the best manner possible."

Sabaneyev said, "I've spent the last hour asking around about you. I understand you were there, at Mrima Hill, during the standoff."

"And prepared to fight," Borbikov said. "Unfortunately we were ordered to stand down." He smiled. "But now . . . now the time is right for this. We are seeing a confluence of events I didn't even dream of when I wrote up the proposal. The U.S. has turned its eyes to Asia. The scandal in the Pacific with the general and the admiral is causing a shake-up at the top of the Pentagon and throwing the American military into crisis.

"Gentlemen, if those natural resources in Kenya, which are the rightful property of Russia, are *ever* to be reclaimed, it has to be *right now*. I firmly believe, and President Rivkin agrees, that Red Metal is the way."

Borbikov turned to General Lazar now, finding himself anxious that the older man had not yet spoken.

Finally Lazar said, "I will execute my orders to the best of my ability. I have some nits to pick, but they center around the logistics end of the operation primarily, so perhaps we shouldn't get into the weeds with it right now."

"I am available to you or your chiefs of staff at any time, day or night, Colonel General Lazar, if you would like to pursue your concerns."

"*Spasiba.*" ("Thank you.") And then: "There is one thing, conceptually, that I'm not yet clear on."

"Please, sir. Tell me."

"If the operation fails . . . if I make it to Mrima Hill without the armor and the men to wrestle it away from the forces protecting it, or if I manage to take it but find myself unable to hold it with the remaining forces at my disposal . . . what then?"

Borbikov cocked his head. "I'm certain that was laid out in the briefing papers."

"Yes . . . but indulge me. I want to hear it from you. The architect."

"Certainly, sir. If you are unable to achieve your mission in full, you are to render the mine incapable of producing rare-earth metals."

Lazar just said, "Go on."

Sabaneyev rolled his eyes a little while Borbikov shifted in his chair.

Finally the colonel said, "Yes. General . . . as it states in the orders, you will carry six special artillery shells. When you and your retreating armor are a safe distance away, you will fire the shells at the mine."

Lazar made no great reaction. "And . . . what's so special about these shells?"

"As written, General, they have nuclear warheads. Also, if you are able to seize the mine but unable to hold it from counterattack, I have specially trained Spetsnaz troops who can wire the shells into a stationary device. In this case, you will place the improvised nuclear device in the center of the mine, leave, and then detonate it."

"So . . . to clarify. If we fail to hold our objective, we are to . . . *nuke* the entire location."

"Correct."

"And . . . why is that?"

Sabaneyev muttered under his breath, but loudly enough to be plainly heard. "Oh, for fuck sakes, Boris."

Borbikov looked back and forth between both men uncomfortably, then said, "For the purpose of denying the West the prize they did not earn. Control of the technology sector of the world's economy for the next generation. Please remember that although the force you will be taking into Africa will be more than enough for the job at hand, there is no way to ensure Russia could repel a protracted siege when the Americans finally do get their act together. One month after you arrive, two months, three months . . . at some point there will be a response, and you need to have an ace in the hole. Your possession of the nukes at Mrima Hill will keep our enemies at bay."

The colonel continued. "But I'm sure when the West learns any attack on the mine will not only kill all the attackers but degrade the world's future technology prospects . . . they will back down, and they will make both peace and beneficial economic deals with Russia." Borbikov smiled. "The weapons are merely a fail-safe. A peacemaker."

Sabaneyev jumped in. "This is all a moot point, because Boris Petrovitch will succeed. He's the *Lion of Dagestan*. The possibility of failure is not worthy of consideration."

Borbikov turned to Sabaneyev. "I'm certain of it. But, nevertheless, the Kremlin has approved the full scope of this operation, so I suggest we continue with the operation as written.

"Colonel Generals . . . the *rodina* called for a military solution to a problem it was unable to solve by other means. The operation you have been charged with is the one that's been approved and assigned. In one hundred and twenty days it will begin . . . and I feel quite certain our leaders have chosen the right men to lead it."

Lazar placed his hands palms up on his knees, a show of contrition. "Of course, Colonel. As I said, I'm a nitpicker. I've been around a long time, so I've seen every sort of mess one can dream up. I will question . . . That is what I do. But on the day my armor begins to roll south, I'll be leading the way, and I'll be ready."

Borbikov smiled, but his impression of the great Boris Lazar had been irrevocably damaged.

CHAPTER 9

The Pentagon's pressing concerns about a possible war between China and Taiwan meant more work for Marine Lieutenant Colonel Dan Connolly and Army Major Bob Griggs. They had been moved out of J5 and up into the director's joint plans cell in the E ring, in the chairman's old office space, where they were tasked with supporting the planners of each of the military services as well as operating as a de facto war command post for the admiral running the office.

In the three months since the assassination in Taiwan that kicked off the initial conflagration in the Pacific, Connolly had left early for work each morning and he hadn't been home before nine o'clock most nights. Even Griggs had picked up his game, rolling into work closer to "on time" than Connolly had ever known him to.

Connolly had missed multiple soccer games, music recitals, and even a birthday party for his daughter, and the situation was playing havoc on date nights and family time with Julie. She'd been through this all before, of course, during Connolly's multiple deployments into war zones, but when she learned a year and a half earlier that her husband would be coming to the Pentagon to ride a desk, she thought his absences would become a thing of the past.

It was just past six p.m. now, Connolly and Griggs were going over some new intelligence about several Chinese landing dock ships that had left port in Zhanjiang two weeks earlier. The vessels had steamed to within miles of the Strait of Taiwan and then, according to satellite photos, stopped just outside of Taiwanese territorial waters. They were already being resupplied with fuel and food, which made it look like they had no plans to go anywhere for a while. China had threatened to invade only after the December 29 elections in Taiwan, and this was still some time away, so it was presumed at the Pentagon that the Chinese were merely demonstrating their resolve in hopes of both affecting the election results and dissuading a massive buildup in the region by the Americans.

On the latter front, things weren't going as planned for the Chinese. Carrier Strike Group Five had arrived in the area, with the USS *Ronald Reagan* as the hub of the wheel. Around it were seven *Arleigh Burke*–class destroyers, three *Ticonderoga*-class cruisers, and several support ships.

On top of the CSG-5's movement into the contested area, the USS *Kearsarge* (LHD-3), an amphibious assault ship, was docked in Okinawa and ready to deliver a battalion of Marines into battle if the Chinese invaded Taiwan. Another LHD, the *Wasp* (LHD-1), was also repositioning to Japan so that two more battalions of Marines could be lifted into Taiwan.

The Americans were not backing down, but instead of this causing hesitation on the part of the Chinese, they simply sent more PLA ground forces to Xiamen, a Chinese port directly across the strait from Taiwan.

The Chinese and the Americans both moved forces around, endeavoring to influence each other's actions.

There was no question that China was threatening war with Taiwan, whether or not someone else helped foment mistrust on that front, but in the back of his mind Connolly was bothered by everything going on. He still wondered whether some other actor might have been trying to turn Western eyes in that direction.

In the past month Connolly had been looking into the latest news out of Russia, and he'd discovered military movements well inside the nation's borders that were out of the statistical norm. Fuel consumption had decreased and repairs had increased.

The knee-jerk assumption around the Pentagon was that Russia was planning on a possible foray into Ukraine. The goings-on noticed so far weren't of the obvious magnitude to indicate a major offensive, such as one necessary to invade the Baltic States, another potential target for Russia.

No, most analysts' suspicions were that Russia was preparing for some limited action, and this likely meant a heavier fighting season in eastern Ukraine.

But Russia wasn't Connolly's problem, so for now he got back to work on the conflict in the Pacific Rim.

Just as he returned to his papers, Griggs called out from his desk: "What do you say we knock off for dinner?"

Connolly didn't even look up from a new report from the National Reconnaissance Office as he rubbed his eyes. "Yeah, probably a good idea. Could go for a beer, too."

"Siné?" Griggs asked. Siné Irish Pub in nearby Crystal City was a watering hole for Pentagon workers. It was close and it was good, and for two guys who didn't want to do any more thinking today than they had to, it was an easy pick for dinner.

As the two men entered the pub, Griggs got a series of text messages that he replied to before sitting down. Since Griggs was a bachelor without many friends away from work, Connolly noted the activity.

"Why are you so popular all of a sudden?"

Griggs said, "It's Nik Melanopolis. He says he's been at the Pentagon all day, and he just swung by our office and found it empty."

Connolly cocked his head. "*He* came to see *you?*"

"Yeah. That's weird. Anyway, I told him we were here, so he's on his way over. He wants a Guinness waiting for him."

"Of course he does," Connolly said with an eye roll, and ordered a Guinness for himself and another for Melanopolis, while Griggs ordered a Harp and a basket of fried cheese.

A few minutes later the heavyset bearded man entered, scanned the room, and saw Connolly and Griggs in a booth halfway down the length of the establishment. He shook his head and pointed to the back corner. Both men looked in the direction he indicated and saw a darkened booth far from any other customers.

The NSA analyst began marching over to the out-of-the-way table.

Griggs said, "I guess he wants us to move," and he snatched up his Harp and started over.

Connolly sat there for a moment, then muttered, "Computer guys." He grabbed his beer along with Nik's and followed.

All three men sat down together, and Melanopolis hefted his Guinness and took a foamy swig before saying, "I've got something I need to show you guys."

Connolly noticed suddenly that the doctor appeared tired, drawn, and stressed.

"Dude," Griggs said, "you look like death warmed over. How long since you slept?"

Connolly added, "How long since you ate a vegetable?"

Melanopolis waved their comments away. "Look, this is serious. And this is bad."

"If it's as bad as you're making it sound," Connolly said, "should you really be telling a couple of midlevel guys in an Irish pub? Why aren't you telling your superiors?"

"I *did*. They know. Now, I'm telling you, because . . ." He looked up to Connolly. "Because you were right."

"Right? Right about what?"

Nik grabbed his pint of Guinness, took another long sip, and then put the glass back on the table. He pulled his laptop out of his bag and opened it, then moved around and slid into the same side of the booth as the other two men.

"Okay, check this out. This is data from an FBI server."

Connolly said, "Wait. *What?*"

Griggs added, "Are you literally breaking into the FBI?"

"Of course not. Not right now, I mean. I did this yesterday. This is a report I made from the metadata."

The two military officers just stared at him.

"Oh, grow up, guys. We do it all the time when they refuse to share stuff with us. We're covered under an old law that says we're allowed to as long as they don't know we're doing it and it's vital to national security." He looked back to Lieutenant Colonel Connolly's dubious expression. "You straitlaced Pentagon stiffs really have no idea, do you? There's a war going on in the cyber world—has been for some time—and guys like me are on the front lines."

He added, "We get a little callous to the public's sensitivity to these kinds of things."

Connolly finally just shrugged. "Well, *I* didn't do it, so my conscience is clear. What did you find, Doc?"

"This is a list of government computers that have been compromised in the last year. The ones we know of, anyway."

Connolly looked at the long list as Melanopolis scrolled down. One device listed was highlighted in red. "That's General Newman's laptop," the NSA man said.

Each listing noted the machine's operating system, and Connolly saw there was a wide range of OSs present. He looked at the Internet operating system reports of all the listings and again noted that many different applications and service providers had been compromised.

Besides the fact that they all worked in spheres that touched the Pacific, Connolly wasn't seeing any connection between the computers listed. "If you want me to see a pattern here, I don't."

"Let me help you out." Melanopolis zoomed in to the manufacturer's name on each of the reports of the hacked devices. "All the hardware is from the same two manufacturers."

"Interesting," Connolly said.

Nik typed up a few more items and the first manufacturer's website appeared on the screen. "All these computers originated from China."

Griggs said, "And they had some kind of latent back door in their programming allowing the Chinese to break into them?"

"Not their programming. That would never do. People scrub their software all the time. Plus, most operating systems are made in the U.S., and we have our own back doors built into the OSs."

Griggs said, "We do?"

"Like I said, there's a war going on. Anyway, the Chinese had latent back doors built into the *hardware*. That comes in handy for them, especially considering the fact they build ninety percent of the world's computers and seventy percent of the world's cell phones."

Connolly was confused. "But this is just more proof China was behind this, right?"

Melanopolis shook his head. "I've been digging for a while. For some reason this seemed a bit out of place to me. So I started pulling older and older data: three months back, six months back, nine months." He typed a moment and brought up a diagram. "This is trace routing from about a year ago. Do you see anything strange?"

"This?" Griggs asked, pointing to a single line between two points in China.

"That's it." Melanopolis turned the laptop toward Connolly. "See this odd ricochet between these two servers? That's one server taking instructions from another. The server on the right is the one that I tracked sending the code to the Chinese computer in Hawaii activating the hardwired back door. But it's that other server that puzzled me." Nik opened the link and it displayed the actual code that was transferred between the computers. "The code is lengthy, but this server on the left is an old part of Unit 61398, China's elite government hacking group. They moved to a bigger, better facility a while ago, which is the server on the right. So it looks simply like the old server sending some data to the new server. However, the old server, on the left, actually made the right server, the new Unit 61398 server, its slave for about three hours while it downloaded some code. That in itself wouldn't usually be a big deal, except Unit 61398 was no longer operating in that old building. I don't think their old server even existed, as far as I can tell. But the new server didn't know that yet. Someone set up what we call a 'doppelganger site' at the old server warehouse and made the new server believe it was just its old buddy communicating with it.

"I know I'm getting technical with you boys, but I looked through everything I could find to see who is in that old building."

The NSA analyst stopped talking, and the two officers spoke in unison. "*Who?*"

"In 2014, Russia's new version of the NSA came online. They bought a brand-new, shiny 1.2 petaflop server. China loved the idea and asked if they could tap into its computing power from time to time to crunch numbers. You know, yesterday's Commies helping today's Commies, I guess. Moscow asked for a server in China to put in their downlink station and China let them take over a floor in the old Unit 61398 building."

Griggs understood. "The Russians ran this entire hack through China and then broadcast it to the world?"

Nik said, "China unwittingly became Odysseus's sheep."

Connolly was astounded. "So this whole thing—all the smearing of our military officers to look like a surreptitious and advanced computer hack in advance of a possible Chinese invasion of Taiwan—was, in truth a full-blown Russian plot meant to both weaken us in the Pacific and implicate China in the process?"

"It looks that way," Nik said. "I've checked this data out. It was brilliantly covered up, but not brilliantly enough."

Griggs said, "And you've told everyone at NSA?"

"Yesterday afternoon. They sent me over to the Pentagon to brief the intelligence heads of the Joint Chiefs today."

"And?" Griggs asked.

Melanopolis looked deflated. "And . . . from what I gathered from their body language, nobody really gives a shit."

Connolly understood immediately. "The Joint Chiefs are already predisposed to see China as a threat. I know our leadership in the Pentagon. We've been waiting for China to make a muscle movement toward Taiwan. Our own plans lead us to believe China has just been waiting to create an opportunity like this. I'm not sure we can back out."

"Why not?" asked Nik.

"China's motive is clear and fits all our assumptions. But what's Russia's motive? If we knew what their game was, then maybe we could ring the alarm bells. But we don't. All these cyber bread crumbs are interesting, but they don't counter the fact that right now the PRC's invasion fleet is massing off the coast of Taiwan."

"What do we do?" Griggs asked.

Connolly replied, "We brief it anyway. Just pound the point that the Russians have manipulated us in some of this, and we need to proceed very carefully until we know why. This is a huge blind spot in our operations, and we can't let our guard down in Europe. We need to at least ensure that the Joint Chiefs have the information in their hands as they make decisions."

Griggs shook his head. "Dan, *I* need to be the one to brief this to the admiral. Not you."

Connolly cocked his head. "Why?"

"If you go before the admiral and tell him Russia is trying to lure the U.S. into the Pacific, and nothing happens, then it could hurt your career. Me, on the other hand . . . no one cares if I brief some harebrained theory. You can stay clean and work the inside angles."

Connolly knew Griggs was right, but he worried what this might do to his subordinate's career.

Griggs saw his unease. "Trust me, this isn't going to hurt me at all. I topped out years ago."

CHAPTER 10

The skipper of the USS *Stethem* (DDG-63) sat in the wardroom, his breakfast in front of him and a copy of *Proceedings*, the U.S. Naval Institute's professional magazine, open on his lap. Three other officers dined at the same table and at the next table over a pair of junior officers, or JOs, ate quickly and quietly, as was their custom. Most JOs ate fast, then departed the wardroom. On top of all the duties expected of the young officers while under way at sea, eating, studying for advancement, more eating, then sleeping came in an orderly but relentless pace.

"John?" He said it without looking over at the deck officer on his left. "You see this thing about the new laser aboard the *Puller?*"

"Did, sir. That's the same one that was aboard *Ponce* before, right? They're using it to shoot down drones."

Captain Fulton said, "They're going to need a lot more than one laser if the Chinese do what we think they will. If a drone swarm approaches and—" The captain stopped speaking suddenly and cocked his head. "You hear that?"

"No, sir. Hear what?"

"We just changed engine speed." Fulton knew the bridge crew would *never* change speed without asking him first. Either someone had made an error or something was drastically wrong.

He dropped his magazine on the table and stood up, then started heading over to the nearest captain's phone, a direct line to the bridge.

Before he could take more than a step, a high-pitched wailing siren sounded. Captain Fulton took off in a sprint for the bridge, followed by the deck officer, but both men slowed to listen when an anxious voice on the 1MC, the ship's intercom system, began speaking.

"General quarters, general quarters! Man your battle stations! Man your battle stations! Damage control parties, stand by. Set condition Zebra throughout the ship. Torpedo in the water. Captain to the bridge! Captain to the bridge!"

The two men raced off again through the narrow passageway.

It took Fulton no time to arrive, but his executive officer was already there, and he read the captain in on the situation as fast as he could. "Sir, enemy torp in the water, coming fast. We have three noisemakers deployed and are hitting an active ping to find the sub. We're going up to full speed and changing course. Do you want direct attack profile or running profile with Nixies?"

Why the hell the Chinese had decided to attack was something Fulton told himself he'd figure out later. Right now he needed to save his warship.

"Attack profile! Change course to aim directly at the torp."

The first decision for all battle maneuvers was either to run or to chase. A torpedo's max speed was generally double that of a warship. If a ship's captain chose to run, the torpedo would still close in on it, but the bet made was the ship would have enough time to make it outside the limited range of the weapon. Running also bought time for other defensive systems on board the ship to distract or destroy the torpedo.

If a ship turned toward the torpedo, the captain was betting he could confuse the weapon with noisemakers while trying to locate and attack the attacking submarine, which should still be somewhere along the same bearing from which the torpedo was fired.

The trouble with "turning in" was that you couldn't use the Nixie system, the most proficient torpedo defense. The Nixie was the ship's towed noisemaker, designed to distract or lure away a torpedo. But the thinking went that the submarine was the bigger threat, as she could launch more weapons, and defeating just the one torpedo wasn't going to end the threat. "Turning in" gave you the advantage of going on the offensive, hoping to destroy or at least antagonize the enemy submarine and cause it to break off its attack.

Captain Fulton spoke with a calm voice. "What do we know about the fish? Acoustic? Magnetic? What's the sonar profile?"

The XO said, "Gotta be Chinese, sir. Could be a Yu-6, based on the noise characteristics."

The sonarman spoke up from his station in the corner of the bridge. "Three minutes to impact. She's going for us, not the noisemakers. Sir, profile *is* the Yu-6; she's acoustic and wire guided." Sound traveled over four times faster in water than through air, so listening via sonar was still the best detection method for both submarines and torpedoes.

"Okay," said the captain. Easily twenty-five calculations were going through his head simultaneously. "Prepare to launch SSTDs."

The SSTD (surface ship torpedo defense) was the destroyer's anti-torpedo torpedo. A smallish swimming drone with a warhead, its job was to blow an enemy torp out of the water. A torpedo had no defenses of its own, and while it could home in on a noisy ship, the weapon itself was loud and therefore could make an easy-to-find target for the SSTD system.

"Two minutes to impact," said the sonarman now. "No change in course. She's still not going for the noisemakers."

"Any bearing at all on the Chinese submarine?" the exec asked. If they could spot the submarine on sonar, they could launch their own array of weapons.

"I have *nothing*, sir. Just a bearing from the torpedo's direction when we picked it up in the water. Sonar is sweeping on that back bearing now."

"Captain, requesting permission to fire SSTDs," said the officer of the deck.

"Fire them," Fulton commanded.

The OOD pointed to the men who initiated the system. Two loud pops followed by a long whoosh indicated that a pair of drone torpedoes had just been launched from the *Stethem*.

The sonarman said, "Sir, one minute to impact," and then, seconds later: "Sir, I have a noise. Could be the enemy submarine."

"I want to fire on that noise. Let's get our own fish in the water. XO?"

"Yes, sir. Agreed."

The officer of the deck spoke up now. "Permission to fire two Mk 32s, sir."

"Do it, OOD."

On the deck, two more pops were followed by a louder whoosh as the triple-tubed, deck-mounted Mk 32 launchers fired a pair of torpedoes into the water.

Seconds later the sonar operator said, "Sir, the sub's heard our torps and she's turning away. I've got screw noises—she's picking up speed. Three nautical miles bearing zero-zero-five degrees." The sonarman then piped acoustic noise through the bridge loudspeaker. The sounds of underwater propellers told the crew that, in their dangerous game of chicken, the Chinese submarine had just blinked. The torpedoes immediately gained acoustic signature and started homing in on the Chinese submarine.

The small joy that erupted on the bridge of USS *Stethem* was immediately replaced by shock as the sonarman called out again. "Sir, thirty seconds to impact. The enemy fish is *not* decoying; she's on us good."

"Combat? Any results with SSTDs?"

"No, sir, neither has acquired the enemy torpedo." The Navy's newest technology was not flawless, and it looked like the SSTDs were not going to get the job done today.

Fulton knew he'd have to fall back on other methods.

"Conn, prepare to divert course radically on my mark."

"Conn, aye!"

"XO, call out a brace for impact. Have all stations confirm condition Zulu. Here goes one last chance." Condition Zulu meant all the watertight doors were closed, minimizing the possibility of sinking if the ship was hit.

"Conn, pull a hard turn, then back once the torp is on us."

In a last-minute endeavor to redirect a torpedo, a ship could steer sharply away, then reverse course again to cause it to run past the ship.

"Combat, fire off barrages of noisemakers every three seconds. Keep it up as we turn."

"Combat, aye!"

With the clock ticking down till impact, the mood aboard the bridge of USS *Stethem* was just below panic.

Another two seconds, another new pop, audible up in the bridge as the noisemakers flew up from their launchers, then dropped into the water, where they began their work. Some of them broadcast a whooshing sound, a recording of the *Stethem*'s own wake noise, while others blasted out the ship's actual power plant and propeller sounds.

The most advanced torpedoes locked onto the specific sounds made by a specific ship and wouldn't let go once they locked on. They could quite literally ignore all the other vessels in a convoy or a crowded harbor and go just for the one ship acoustically printed in the torpedo's miniature computer brain.

The newest U.S. noisemaker countermeasures used by the *Stethem* were manufactured with actual recorded sounds of the warship's propellers and wake. They could even be coded with some of the most common sounds of vessels she escorted. Antisubmarine destroyers like the *Stethem* could then decoy advanced acoustic torpedoes away from their commonly undefended cargo or oil counterparts.

The bridge crew pulled the *Stethem* hard left rudder, steering the vessel to port. The crew felt fifteen degrees of heel, meaning the ship's deck tilted away from the turn precipitously, and the whole ship leaned over hard. Pens and coffee cups flew from the plotting boards and chart tables, and crewmen scrambled to stay on their feet or in their chairs.

More pops above as more noisemakers fired off the deck and into the water.

The sonarman pulled his earphones away and looked up to the *Stethem*'s captain. "Sir, ten seconds to impact . . . The enemy fish is *not* diverting."

"Copy. Helm, last hard turn now!"

The helmsman spun the *Stethem*'s wheel to the right in a blur, forcing the destroyer immediately hard to starboard. Everyone hung on again and waited as the vessel heeled over in the opposite direction.

The *Stetham* was still in the turn when a massive boom resounded, jolting the ship and her crew violently.

The men and women on the bridge watched a blast of blue-white water erupt from the bow and rise above their sight lines. The lights of the destroyer flickered off as the water came crashing down. They came back on briefly, then almost immediately went off again.

Captain Fulton had been thrown back a yard in the explosion, but he kept his feet under him. "Bring the ship to bear on the contact! Put engines to full stop!" His calm demeanor had been replaced by an anxious tone.

Fulton had pictured this moment many times, ever since his youth when he dreamed of joining the Navy and going to sea. For the moment, he would remain on the bridge and then he would go check out the damaged spaces personally. Right now he needed to let the crew do their jobs.

He sat down in his captain's chair. "XO, get me damage and casualty reports."

"Aye, Captain." The XO got on the sound-powered phone. "Damage Crews Six and Nine, report to the bow section and report to Damage Crews One and Two there. Combat, get me accountability. Engineering, get a damage assessment and give the call again to ensure all watertight doors are dogged down and verified."

Damage reports filtered in after several minutes.

The sound-powered phones worked during a loss of power but severely distorted voices, so the report that came in from the damage department a few minutes later was heavily muffled. "Early estimate is sixteen feet of bow bulkhead ripped open. Three watertight compartments sealed. Casualty numbers unknown."

The sonarman butted in with a shout. "Sir, two underwater blasts! I lost sonar with the power, but the hydrophone is working. I hear the unmistakable noises of the Chinese sub breaking apart. We got her ass!"

This was news that might have elicited a cheer earlier, but given the circumstances the crew remained concentrated on their duties and did not exhibit much emotion.

A voice from Engineering came in next, explaining that power would be returned soon after the engine crews took one main engine off-line to use as a power plant.

The *Stethem* would survive. For now.

"Sparks," said the captain now, using the old term for a radio operator.

The man manning the satellite and high-frequency radio looked his way. "Aye, sir?"

Fulton stood from his chair. "Once we have power, call *Reagan*. Ask their crew to get Admiral Swift on the net. I'll give him a report personally. I'm going forward to look at the damage. XO, you have the bridge."

"Aye, sir."

The captain stepped off the bridge and down the ladder well toward the bow of his ship. He would not admit it before his crew, but he certainly was going to report to the admiral that this was his fault.

He had made the decision to attack. To steer toward the Chinese submarine instead of running away. Ultimately he recognized he now bore the responsibility for all of this, and it wore heavily on his shoulders.

He also knew his immediate duty was to keep the *Stethem* afloat and account for his crew.

CHAPTER 11

President of the United States Jonathan Henry was the last man to arrive in the situation room. In front of him was the Principals Committee of his National Security Council: the vice president, the national security advisor and the White House chief of staff, the directors of national intelligence and the CIA, the secretaries of state and defense, the chairman of the Joint Chiefs of Staff, the attorney general, the U.S. ambassador to the United Nations, and the secretaries of homeland security, treasury, and energy.

The emergency meeting began on a somber note from the chairman of the Joint Chiefs. "Thirteen sailors killed, twenty-nine wounded. Some of the injuries are horrific. And the *Stethem* is dead in the water. She'll have to be towed in to Taiwan, which the Chinese will crow about incessantly, no doubt."

President Henry said, "The Chinese say there *was* no attack. No directive from Beijing. They are claiming our destroyer fired first."

The chairman of the Joint Chiefs replied, "A provable lie, Mr. President. We have deck recordings that clearly indicate the *Stethem* was responding to a torpedo attack from a Chinese sub."

Henry said, "When I spoke to the Chinese president, he asked me to tell him why on earth they would launch an attack with one torpedo and not follow it with anything else when they have dozens of warships in the area. I couldn't answer him. It doesn't seem to make sense as a rational strategy."

The chairman said, "Maybe the Chinese sub fired in error. Or their captain got trigger-happy. The fact is, they're all dead. It's doubtful any recordings will be recoverable from *their* bridge, and highly unlikely the Chinese will ever release them if they are. We'll probably never know for certain if that attack was sanctioned or not."

The president said, "So either they planned to scare us off, or their sub commander screwed up." He clearly was not satisfied with this, and he let out a long sigh.

The secretary of defense interjected, "Mr. President . . . to me this looks like the Chicoms made the calculated decision that the average citizen in the U.S. has no stomach for war in Asia against a superpower. The Chinese figure they can just hit one of our ships, kill some sailors, and wait for public opinion to turn sharply against our deployment over there."

The president took this in. "The question is, what do we do now?"

The secretary of defense replied, "We can't let Taiwan fall after the December twenty-ninth elections. The only way to prevent that without war is by absolutely convincing Beijing that we are more than ready to fight."

The chairman of the Joint Chiefs chimed in. *"Si vis pacem, para bellum."*

President Henry turned to him. " 'If you want peace, prepare for war.' That's what Renatus said back in the fourth century. Fundamentally, not much has changed."

The discussion went on for ninety minutes. The secretary of state pushed for a diplomatic response, which was no great surprise, but Henry was surprised to see that both the secretary of defense and the chairman of the Joint Chiefs made the case for a diplomatic response as well, albeit one with teeth.

War with China would be devastating for everyone, and *everyone* in the room understood this without reservation.

The president finally said, "I'm leaning toward mobilization and deployment. The chairman assures me he can have the forces to provide a reasonable deterrent to the Chinese before the election in Taiwan, but only if we start moving everything over there right now." He paused. "I want to hear once more from anyone who thinks this is a bad idea."

The secretary of state leaned forward and put his forearms on the table.

"Dale?" the president said. "Let's have it."

"The concern, obviously, is that by deploying forces from all over the globe, we end up inflaming the situation: that the Chinese look at this as a further provocation, and this turns their threats into action."

"*Threats?*" bellowed the chairman of the Joint Chiefs. "I've got thirteen dead sailors, for Christ's sake!"

The secretary of state nodded solemnly. "Yes, but at this point we don't know China's intentions."

The secretary of defense all but barked at this. "We *do* know their intentions. They have thousands of marines in landing ships within half a day of the coast of Taiwan. Their president point-blank declared they will intervene if the election doesn't go his way. What other possible clues do we need?"

"Threats, Rob," said the secretary of state, waving his hand over his head. "They could all be threats. Look how war with the U.S. would hurt China's economy. It would be madness for them to actually land troops."

The director of national intelligence came down firmly on the side of the secretary of defense now. "China isn't thinking about their economy at present."

Treasury said, "They're *always* thinking about their econ—"

"This is bigger," the DNI snapped back. "Reunification has been Beijing's goal since 1949. And I don't believe China's economy would suffer in the long term, especially not with a reunified Taiwan adding to their coffers." He turned to look at the president now. "No, Mr. President, it is the assessment of the U.S. intelligence community that the leadership in Beijing is very serious about this and focused on the upsides of reunification. Not the war itself."

The president looked down to his hands for nearly a minute.

And then he looked back up. "I'm one hell of a poker player. Right now, on this issue, I don't have much of a hand. I can win without a good hand, but only if my opponent doesn't know that I have no cards. President Lao knows good and well I'm bluffing when I talk tough, because right now we have less than ten percent of the forces in theater we need to repel a Chinese invasion of Taiwan."

The secretary of defense said, "Mr. President, a full, robust deployment like the one I've laid out will provide you with the decision space you need, putting the forces where they can be used so you have that card to play."

No one spoke up during the short pause that followed, but the secretary of state looked down at the table, knowing full well he'd lost the argument.

President Henry said, "I need a better hand. Until we get forces over there, we won't be in a position of strength to do anything." He looked to the secretary of defense. "Do it, Rob. Push forces to Asia. I don't want a shooting war with the Chicoms any more than anybody else, but once the steel hand of the U.S. military is on the scene, *then* I'll be able to negotiate with authority."

The secretary of defense said, "Deterrence through strength, Mr. President."

The president nodded solemnly. "Deterrence through strength. Damn right."

The subsequent orders from the Pentagon were as decisive as they could be, given the circumstances.

In the early-morning hours of November 24, an e-mail was received simultaneously across all the "yellow" machines, those coded as top secret, from the secretary to the chairman of the Joint Chiefs of Staff:

Deploy all ready forces; allocate them to the PACOM AOR to be employed as a deterrent to ongoing Chinese aggression.

This one-sentence guideline was followed by several pages of more specific instructions.

Most nations in Southeast Asia welcomed the U.S. buildup. The Philippines temporarily restored U.S. basing rights at three of their busiest ports. Australia stood up their reserve and mobilized all active forces.

The Japanese president called POTUS and canceled all the U.S. base closings in his nation, and he called for his nation's "American partners" to return in force to the Ryukyu island chain, Okinawa, and mainland Japan.

The job then fell to U.S. Transportation Command to figure it all out. The movement of men and equipment from locations all over the U.S. and abroad was a monstrous task, but USTRANSCOM had the air- and sealift to get the job done.

The first of the PACOM deterrent forces to arrive would be a second Navy Carrier Strike Group to join the *Ronald Reagan* and CSG-5. CSG-3 was led by the USS *John C. Stennis* (CVN-74), and it began moving within days from Naval Base Kitsap in Washington State.

The carrier strike group used submarines as its outermost ring to serve as the eyes and ears of the task force by venturing out from the CSGs to find enemy shipping.

The next ring was an array of frigates. The workhorses of the fleet, they screened for enemy submarines. Then came the formidable cruisers and destroyers. If the subs and frigates were the eyes and ears of a CSG, then the cruisers were its shields. Networked through advanced communication devices, the ships were linked together to provide an almost impenetrable blanket of antiair fires. The cruisers and destroyers integrated the machines to work in synchronicity to compute advanced firing solutions in the blink of an eye, with or without input from their human partners.

And then came the core of the CSG: the aircraft carrier, the teeth of the group, able to sling the nation's most advanced electronic platforms from its flight deck to any position hundreds of miles in any direction.

Two Marine Corps expeditionary units were also ordered into the region. Each MEU consisted of three ships, each carrying a full infantry battalion. Also called a rifle battalion, this was the backbone of the Marine Corps, trained to fight in forcible-entry operations.

USTRANSCOM began a twenty-four-hour air-operations cycle to send U.S. ground forces to the Pacific. Working some miracles in aviation readiness and management, they successfully flew the Global Response Force, which consisted of the 18th Airborne Corps, to Australia, Japan, and Guam. Known as the GRF and pronounced "the Gerf" by insiders, it included whatever four Army divisions were on rotation with orders to remain in a status in which they could be "wheels up" in eighteen hours or less. The list included some of the U.S. Army's most famous and most storied units: the 3rd Infantry Division from Fort Stewart, Georgia; the 10th Mountain Division from Fort Drum, New York; the 82nd Airborne Division from Fort Bragg, North Carolina; and the 101st Airborne Division from Fort Campbell, on the Tennessee-Kentucky border.

The 82nd was currently the unit on ready, and they began preparations to load up immediately.

The movements and coordination to send all forces was a testament to America's superior ability to lift its forces when a crisis happened. But with all the men, machines, and matériel moving into the Pacific, along with the vast majority of the U.S. strategic lift capability being drawn into the job, the European theater was now virtually on its own.

CHAPTER 12

General Eduard Sabaneyev and his staff rolled in a motorcade through the countryside east of Moscow. Potato and rye fields, bare with the coming winter, stretched all the way to the burnished orange and brown woods in the distance. Sabaneyev gazed out the window, lost in his thoughts. Ordinarily a drive out through the Russian farmland relaxed him, put him at ease. Seeing the Russian farmscapes gave him faith, showing him again that Russia remained a strong and productive nation, despite all the problems brought on by the West.

But now he ignored the symbols of Russia's power and organization and focused only on the thick forests in the distance beyond the farms, imagining the coming meeting with Colonel Borbikov.

General Sabaneyev had demanded to see the trains that would be at the center of his raid into the West, because, simply put, there was no operation without them. Cutting into the heart of NATO in the dead of winter with nothing more than an operational-sized assault force, he needed the capability to rearm, refuel, and reequip his fighting elements, and he needed mobile antiair missile batteries to keep the skies overhead clear.

When he'd first read the operational plan, he was surprised to see there would be trains crossing into Poland just behind the armor attack. Instantly his mind came up with one hundred things that could go wrong—a lingering effect, no doubt, of being the protégé of General Boris

Lazar. But he tried to push his concerns out of his mind and commit himself fully to the mission, because boldness was *exactly* the reason he had skyrocketed through the ranks of the Russian armed forces throughout his career.

Still, for the past three months his concerns about the trains had persisted because the concept of rail in combat seemed anachronistic to him.

Yes, to get men and matériel to the front, in the "interior lines," certainly rail lines were employed, but operating in "exterior lines," beyond the front and within the enemy's battle space—inside another country, even—train travel seemed foolish. The risks were manifest: enemy airpower, enemy ground forces, even sappers and civilians intent on causing damage. Trains weren't exactly hard to find, their routes were all but obvious to predict, and it took just a few men or women with explosives that could be carried in a lunch pail to derail them and stop all forward movement.

General Sabaneyev continued looking out the window as the farmland passed. He couldn't help but remember the discussion he'd had with Colonel Borbikov a few weeks earlier at his headquarters. He had asked Borbikov at the time, "What will stop the West from just striking the train? The train cannot maneuver; it goes in a straight fucking line. Even the most junior officer in NATO's underprepared armies will know to simply bomb the track."

"Not when the lights go out," Borbikov answered with a satisfied smile. "Not when NATO has no communication. Not when my teams of Spetsnaz, already infiltrated into enemy territory, simply switch the trains to tracks of our choosing. Not when the assault train looks *nothing* like a military train."

He added, "Western armies won't chance hitting a commuter train."

Sabaneyev found himself intrigued, but he was still infected with remnants of Boris Lazar's natural skepticism. "You place too much emphasis on these special forces of yours. One wrong rail yard switch and off we go in the wrong direction."

"My men will guide you, sir. And I will be right out there in enemy territory with them."

"It sounds too good to be true, Colonel," General Sabaneyev had said at the time, but he kept an open mind, and now the general finally found himself driving to the rail yards to see the damn things for himself.

The secrecy of the rail construction project meant it had to be located in a remote location an hour from Moscow and surrounded by checkpoints with armed guards. The motorcade slowed at the first of these, pulling the general from his thoughts.

Colonel Borbikov was there, already waiting to meet the motorcade. They exchanged a brief greeting, and Borbikov climbed into the general's car, squeezing into the backseat between Sabaneyev and Colonel Dryagin, the operations commander of the Western spear.

As they rolled along over a long gravel driveway Borbikov said, "The train will allow you to hide in plain sight behind the advance. The assault force will travel fast on roads parallel to the tracks, overland in some areas. The trains will carry heavier antiair missiles, radar, and indirect fire munitions. Not to mention they continue to serve their original purpose, hauling personnel and cargo: extra ammunition, fuel, troops, and supplies."

Sabaneyev made no reply.

The motorcade pulled up to a cluster of massive brick buildings, one of them the size of a small soccer stadium. The old-looking structures and the overgrown tracks leading into them made it clear that long ago this had been a massive Soviet railhead, a staging and marshaling area.

Borbikov confirmed this by explaining these facilities were left over from the Cold War, when using rail to transport heavy tanks into Europe had been a very real part of the Soviet strategy.

The motorcade stopped in front of the largest building, and two huge metal blast-protected doors slid open with the squeals of old hinges. The three staff cars rolled in and parked by a group of mobile offices. Sabaneyev and his colonels and majors stepped out from the cars, stretched their legs, and looked around.

Heavy floodlights lit the expansive space, but only dimly. The vaulted ceiling rose more than three stories high, the rafters crisscrossed by metal gangways and gantry cranes to service heavy rail and construction loads. The building was unheated—it was barely above freezing, Sabaneyev determined—and there was a chill in the damp warehouse air that made him feel like he was standing in a meat locker. Punctuating that notion, he turned around, startled, as the heavy metal doors slid closed behind them with a thunderous clang that seemed to echo forever through the cavernous space.

As his eyes grew accustomed to the gloom, Sabaneyev was able to take in more and more of the huge building. In the corners and nooks of the space, spiderweb-covered rail cogs and old Soviet-era train parts lay discarded in piles.

This facility had clearly lain abandoned for decades.

But now it seemed to have gained a new life. A massive, gleaming civilian train was parked on a set of tracks that ran through the building, and clusters of men moved around it, feverishly working.

Sabaneyev said, "*That's* the assault train?"

Borbikov led the way closer. "Yes, sir. I proudly introduce *Red Blizzard 1*, virtually indistinguishable from the Russian civilian express train called the Strizh. The actual Strizh is one of the latest and fastest additions to high-speed train travel in Europe, connecting Moscow to Berlin in just over twenty hours, traveling at speeds of up to two hundred kilometers per hour."

General Sabaneyev's men began to climb about the train freely, loosely following the general and Borbikov as they walked along the tracks.

Borbikov kept up his briefing. "A total of twenty cars, exactly like its real counterpart. All mocked up to appear civilian, right down to windows painted with passenger silhouettes behind curtains eating in the dining car and able to be lit with LEDs or to go completely dark and blacked out if needed."

Sabaneyev reached out and rapped his gloved knuckles on the aluminum exterior. "Is this supposed to stop a bullet, Colonel?"

"No, sir, it is not. We will make sure no bullet comes within ten kilometers of you."

The general grunted, unconvinced.

"The concept of *Red Blizzard 1* is to take advantage of three things. First, due to track problems in Poland, the actual Strizh regularly makes all manner of scheduled and unscheduled detours. This makes it easier to divert the assault train onto any lines we see fit without much notice from Polish rail stations. My Spetsnaz teams will ensure the right tracks are open at the right times.

"Second, in preparation for the 2018 World Cup, Russian Railways bought twenty-four special Spanish-manufactured Talgo trains. Central and Western Europe use different-sized tracks from Russia, but the Talgos have variable gauges, so they can change the width of their wheel gauges automatically without the usual slow and extensive gauge switches required of many other trains transiting the same stretches of rail.

"Our military appropriated three Talgos after their use during the 2018 FIFA championship to create this mock Strizh train with variable gauges."

"And the third thing?"

"Third, and possibly most important to you and your men: these Talgos are wider-body train cars that can fit more ammo, fuel, and every other thing you will need during your journey. No one will notice the difference in size unless your train happens to be parked next to an authentic Strizh."

The general was impressed so far, but he hid it well. "Tell me about the layout."

"Yes, sir. The first five cars make up your command center and officers' quarters. Fully outfitted with map boards and targeting computers, they also hold the radar masts and communications towers that will rise when the train slows to support Colonel Dryagin and his assault regiment. The next five cars hold antiair batteries, plus three complete 240mm autoloaded mortar systems and their ammunition. The next five cars will hold a company of motorized rifle troops, ammunition, and food. And the last five cars will be loaded with diesel fuel and ammo for the tanks."

Borbikov turned to the general. "For the operational level raid I've designed, this will be sufficient to support the frontline troops."

Borbikov pressed a button on a door and it slid open. He and Sabaneyev climbed up the steps.

"Your command car, Comrade General."

Walking around the car, the general ran his hands over a series of flat computer screens bolted to the bulkhead of the train and still covered in plastic. He pulled one cover off and looked at the manufacturer name.

"Sony? We couldn't find reliable Russian technology?"

"These Sony monitors are lighter than other brands, and they come prehardened to endure the jolts and bumps you might endure on your journey."

"The systems are on standby. Turn them on," Sabaneyev said.

"They come on in an instant. Observe." The colonel nodded to a technician sitting at one of the swivel chairs, who took his cue.

In moments twelve computer screens, two of them well over two meters wide and dominating the center of the car, all came to life.

"Bring up the rail route," Borbikov ordered.

A Google Earth three-dimensional image of their current rail station showed on the screen. The technician pressed a few more buttons and the rail path from the warehouse to Moscow lit up and flashed.

"Your initial path, General," Borbikov said. "It will bring you to the Moscow station on the same timetable as the actual Strizh train, which will be removed from service. From there you will travel to Smolensk. All following the exact route and virtually indistinguishable from the actual civilian train, except you will not stop. My Spetsnaz forces will switch you onto tracks to your advantage. Europe and NATO will have their hands full with other matters, and one train traveling down unauthorized tracks will not even be noticed, let alone fretted over."

"You are beginning to impress me, Colonel. Let's continue with the tour."

Borbikov then led the general and his entourage to the next train.

Red Blizzard 2 was fifty-eight cars, with four engines, which made it a particularly long European cargo train. But otherwise it looked relatively normal. On closer inspection, though, Sabaneyev saw unconcealed radar masts and communications antennas and two cars had obvious antiair batteries featuring the S-400 Triumf, a beast of a missile with a four-hundred-kilometer range.

Borbikov said, "This one was designed to follow on behind the assault train with enough fuel and ammunition for the assault element, and to be called forward if necessary to refuel, rearm, and replace losses in the assault force. Under tarps we will conceal tanks and armored personnel vehicles."

Red Blizzard 3 was another cargo train, longer than *Red Blizzard 2*, and for now it was all but empty. But on the day of the invasion, Borbikov explained, it would hold an entire regiment of additional tanks and armored personnel carriers. Its purpose would be to provide full replacements to the assault element. At a whopping sixty-eight cars long, it needed eight engines to pull it, and it had already been outfitted with numerous Pantsir-SM surface-to-air missile launcher batteries and twenty stanchions for man-portable 9K333 Verba antiair missiles.

At the end of the tour, Borbikov and Sabaneyev sat in a heated trailer in the center of the rail yard and toasted the trains with vodka.

Borbikov said, "Our next drink together will be a celebration in Moscow. You and I only, unfortunately, because General Lazar will be stuck guarding those mines in Africa for some months."

Sabaneyev chuckled at this. He was in good humor now, more confident than ever in Borbikov's plan. "Don't you worry about Lazar. Old Boris is happier in a shit-filled foxhole with pimple-faced privates than he is swilling vodka in Moscow with well-heeled senior officers."

The two men toasted again, and then they drank to Red Metal.

CHAPTER 13

THE PENTAGON
ARLINGTON, VIRGINIA
17 DECEMBER

Lieutenant Colonel Dan Connolly and Major Bob Griggs sat next to each other in the "plans cell" weekly coordination meeting, listening to each officer in the room give a quick review of the projects they were working on. Connolly's turn came up, and he delivered his review, detailing the work he and Griggs had been doing regarding the order of battle of the forces arraying in the Pacific.

The chief of staff for the director of the plans office was a Navy captain, the rank equivalent to a colonel in the Army, Marine Corps, or Air Force. The admiral was in attendance as well, but he normally didn't speak up until the end, when he'd deliver some last words of wisdom before the plans cell carried on with the day.

Griggs had been waiting for the end of the meeting to speak up. He and Connolly knew they had to try one more time to convince the admiral to take a closer look at Russian involvement in cyberespionage in Asia.

"Last thing from me," continued the chief of staff. "Don't forget—flu vaccinations are mandatory DoD-wide, so don't put the shop in a bad spot. Get your shots on time to keep us off the director's shit list." There were bored nods of ascent around the room. "Okay . . . anything else?" The chief of staff scanned the room now, pointing with his pen in the direction of each man sitting around the big table. When the pen reached Connolly and Griggs, the major raised his hand, and the chief raised his eyebrows. "Major Griggs, you have something for the group? Make it quick."

"Yes, sir, will do. Sir, I'd like permission to pull a few more facts and figures on the Russia thing."

"*What* Russia thing?" asked the chief, clearly perturbed.

"Sir, myself and Lieutenant Colonel Connolly . . . we think we may have found a connection."

"Connection to what?"

The admiral interrupted. "I've got this, Chief." He pointed to Connolly and Griggs. "You two were brought on board to review the requirements and order of battle for our deployment to the Pacific, not to worry about a completely different combatant command. We already heard from NSA about this supposed Russia hack involving the admiral and the general, and there are plenty of folks looking into it. Right now you two are to focus on your assigned mission. Is that clear?"

"Check, sir," Griggs said.

"Roger, sir," Connolly added.

The captain closed his notebook. "Okay, shipmates, I have nothing else to pass to you this afternoon. Have a super week. Keep up the good work."

The admiral stood and the room came to attention.

"Dismissed," said the admiral as he walked out of the room.

The chief of staff called out as the others were leaving. "Griggs, let's take a walk."

"Copy, sir."

"Me, too, sir?" Connolly asked.

"No. Just Griggs. Follow me, Major."

Griggs fell in next to the chief and they walked out of the briefing room and into the E ring, headed toward the "bullpen," the cubicle farm where Connolly and Griggs worked.

The chief of staff said, "Major Griggs, something's buggin' me."

"Yes, sir? How can I help?"

"You can help by cutting out the shit." On the last word the chief of staff pivoted to look directly at Griggs. "I'm tired of you digging around into a bunch of crap not assigned to you. Do you and Lieutenant Colonel Connolly really think we don't have all of the European desk officers focused firmly on Russia? How stupid do you think the chairman's staff is? Do you think J3 Ops and J2 Intel are just fartin' around?"

"No, sir," said Griggs, but he couldn't contain himself. "But we've already talked to J3 and J2, and no one is really looking at this specifically. They now admit the Russians were at least partially involved in the hack on the computer, but they don't think it means the Russians are up to anything. Dan . . . uh, Colonel Connolly feels—and I have to concur—that the Russians went to a hell of a lot of work just to make things harder for us in the Pacific. Add that to the fact they seem to be ramping up repairs of equipment and increasing fuel stores, and it's troubling. The PACOM folks are fixated on the Taiwan issue and see this all fitting nicely into their profile for Taiwan invasion precursors, and the EUCOM folks are just fixated on the NATO exercises we have coming up after the new year. I just thought we needed to make sure the admiral took this up to the vice chairman for his SA."

The vice chairman's situational awareness was the responsibility of the chief of staff.

The chief said, "All right, Major Griggs, you've told me what you wanted to say. Now I've got a few things for you. First, were you aware that this morning Russia announced war games in Belarus next week that will last through Christmas?"

Griggs shook his head slowly.

"War games that will account, I'm pretty damn certain, for the uptick in their repair tempo and fuel storage."

Griggs said nothing.

"Russia is just going to their client state for exercises; they're not invading anybody, *anywhere*, and you picking up some cyber scrap from NSA about Russia doesn't mean a goddamn thing."

The captain continued. "We've already got dead sailors off Taiwan, and we might well be just weeks away from war with the Chicoms, so get your *fat ass* back to the job you were brought over to do! Got it?"

Without waiting for a response, the captain turned and walked away.

Connolly pressed Griggs when he returned to the bullpen. "So, how bad was it?"

"Just wondering at what rank the ass chewings stop. I've had enough to last a lifetime."

Connolly poured Griggs a cup of coffee. "Bob, they get less frequent, but they also get more vitriolic."

"Guess I should be happy my military career is in the tank, then. Hey, did you know Russia just announced war games in Belarus?"

"*What?*"

"Since you and I have been working on PACOM planning since first thing this morning, we didn't know about it, and to the chief of staff that means neither of us knows jack shit about Russia."

"These war games—when do they begin?"

"Next week, running through Christmas."

"Why the hell would they hold war games at Christmas?"

"No idea," Griggs said, "but I sure as hell hope it doesn't give *our* president any ideas."

Connolly looked off across the bullpen for several seconds. "You know much about a General Lazar?"

Griggs nodded. "Yeah, he's that old-school Russian colonel general, as high ranking as they come. One of their best, follows kind of a Soviet doctrine. He was, like, the head instructor at their war college for a few years. His most recent big combat command was Chechnya and Dagestan, like, ten years ago. What about him?"

Connolly turned to his computer. "I was poking around, saw something on an INTSUM."

He clicked around a moment looking for an intelligence summary file in his saved classified e-mails. "Here it is. This struck me as odd. J2 found out that Lazar put his dacha up for rent. When I saw that, I thought that might have meant he had money troubles or something. But now . . ."

"Now *what*?"

Connolly read the intelligence summary. "DTG 2019-09-16, Moscow North West. Gavrilkovo, Tverskaya Oblast, Russia. Today the *Moskovskij Komsomolets* newspaper showed an advertisement for Colonel General Boris Lazar's dacha. The rental value was placed at 70,000 rubles a month. Leninskaya Ulitsa number 133, Novozavidovsky, Tverskaya Oblast, Russia."

Over his shoulder Griggs said, "You know the spooks are going to go nuts when they see us looking up Russian cabins for rent on our government computers."

"Better we do it on the government machines so your buddy at NSA's comrades don't see it on our personal laptops."

After a few seconds Connolly said, "Found it! It's online at intermarksavills-dot-ru." He began scrolling through images of the place. "Pretty sweet pad. Log cabin, lake view. Well appointed, and sits on a peninsula among pine trees next to the Zavidovo National Park."

"How long is the rental?"

"Looks like it's offered for up to nine months."

"That's a weird term, isn't it? I usually see rentals on a month-to-month, or six months, or a year."

"Maybe he's involved in this war game and they are training and gone for that," Connolly said.

"*That* would be the longest Russian war game in history. Let's look up who is in charge of the exercises in Belarus. They usually announce it."

Griggs typed this into his machine. "Not your guy. Looks like a fella named Sabaneyev. He's also a colonel general."

"Maybe Lazar's gotten command somewhere else."

Griggs said, "Hold up. Found something."

Connolly left his computer and headed over to Griggs's cubicle. The Air Force guys were putting on their coats, preparing to leave for the day. Connolly checked his watch: it was past 1800 hours. Julie was going to have his ass. He was supposed to be picking up the kids in a half hour, and with D.C. evening traffic he was already pushing it.

"Shit, Bob, I might have to head out soon."

"First, take a look." Griggs pointed to an article about Colonel General Eduard Sabaneyev leading upward of thirty thousand troops in the Belarus military training exercise. Moscow was bragging about his credentials in the article, which Griggs had translated to English using Google Translate. The exercise over the Christmas holidays, the Russians claimed, was for the purpose of validating several newer pieces of equipment, including the Bumerang armored personnel carrier and the T-14 Armata, Russia's newest tank, to "demonstrate the effectiveness of superior Russian technology and the spirit of partnership with the people of Belarus."

Connolly said, "Well, *that's* a load of bullshit."

Griggs agreed. "No kidding. Belarus doesn't want the Russian army pounding around their nation at Christmas, but they can't tell Moscow no. And as far as the Russians go, they've done small-scale exercises over the holidays before, but always to test some poor-performing unit's readiness. Something of this magnitude . . . I'm pretty sure it's unprecedented."

Connolly said, "Let's look at Intelink," he said, referring to the government's own classified version of Google.

Griggs and Connolly both spent several minutes looking through the files on Eduard Sabaneyev. He was clearly one of Russia's premier generals.

The reports detailed his schooling, military history, and profile, and—Connolly found this interesting—the files said he had been second-in-command to Boris Lazar for many years.

"Should we try Intelink-TS?" Connolly said, referring to the top secret version of the portal.

"We'd have to go to the vault to get on top secret." TS intelligence could be accessed only at a sensitive compartmented information facility, a special locked and protected room. The Pentagon had many SCIFs, but getting into one took some time.

Connolly looked down at his watch.

Griggs saw this and said, "You get home, boss. I'll stay and check out the top secret intel on this joker." He added, "Hey, you want me to check with NSA or CIA?"

"No. If we do that, we'll just skyline ourselves. The chief will shit his pants if we send over a special intel request that has *anything* to do with Russia."

Connolly put on his Marine Corps "tanker's jacket," the coat worn with the Marine Corps Class B and C uniform that was meant for rain or cold. "Don't stay too late, Bob. Need you bright and fresh in the morning."

Griggs waited for Connolly to leave; then he sat alone in the office for several minutes thinking over his next move. Finally he clicked on the "Intelligence RFI management" button on Intelink and then "Customer request for information." A fresh screen opened with a reminder that requests for intelligence were prioritized and might not be met in a timely fashion unless the user clicked "Urgent."

Griggs clicked "Urgent."

What the hell, he thought.

Another box opened with a pull-down menu asking under which authority he was making the request. He scrolled down to "Director of the Joint Chiefs for Planning and Operations and/or Vice Chairman." A warning popped up stating, "Please have written authorization from your staff primary member, chief of staff, or a general officer before proceeding." The major hesitated but not for long. He clicked the "Yes" box and filled out the information needed to request that the CIA provide all intelligence on one Colonel General Eduard Sabaneyev.

Then he powered down his computer, pulled out his military ID card, grabbed his coat, and headed out of the Pentagon for the night.

CHAPTER 14

Pascal Arc-Blanchette shuffled along the Boulevard de la République in a manner that made him appear decidedly older than his sixty-four years. He'd always seemed older than his actual age, in presence and mannerisms; at the Sorbonne he'd worn tweed jackets and pleated wool trousers when his classmates wore turtlenecks and bell-bottoms, and he'd had the same slow, shuffling gait back then.

The coat he wore today was ten years old—one of his latest finds, and in Pascal's mind it was practically brand-new. He wore his clothes to exhaustion, something else he'd been doing his entire life.

It was almost eleven a.m., which was like dawn for Pascal, because he was no early riser. He made his way along the sidewalk on his way to his favorite café, and on the way he stepped into a small kiosk. He skimmed over the Somali-language newspapers but picked out that day's copy of *La Nation* in French. He also grabbed an Arabic-language newspaper and a pack of Gitanes cigarettes.

The clerk behind the low wooden counter was new, Pascal noticed, and the man asked for eight hundred Djiboutian francs. The Frenchman fanned out six hundred and put them down, then shook his head as he scooped up his papers and cigarettes, scolding the clerk for trying to subject him to the "foreigner tax." The man behind the counter sneered at him but took the six hundred anyway.

Pascal's white face here in Africa used to cost him a lot of money, but he'd long since learned his way around the markets and street stalls, and now he paid like a local.

As he climbed the steps toward the doors of Restaurant L'Historil, his trousers began to slip and he had to grab them to prevent them from falling. He stopped and adjusted his belt—it was three times as old as his coat—then tucked in his wrinkled dress shirt.

Pascal stepped out onto the crowded terrace of the café but scowled as he sighted a group of young, white-faced tourists sitting in his favorite spot.

Nadal, the maître d', spotted him and glanced to the corner where the tourists had set up shop. They had taken up almost half of the outside seating, their heavy backpacks filling many of the other chairs and tables, and effectively cordoning off the side that offered the cooling relief of the overgrown vine trelliswork.

Nadal shrugged and pointed to the opposite side of the terrace. Pascal headed to an open seat there, but he wasn't happy about it.

The outdoor dining space was bustling and the Frenchman maneuvered through, then sat down on the hard metal seat. He shielded the sun from his eyes as he nodded to Nadal, who nodded back and went inside to assemble his usual order.

The Frenchman looked longingly across the terrace to his favorite wicker chair, now cushioning a gray rucksack in the middle of the group of white tourists.

Pascal pushed his frustration away and opened the newspaper, skimming down below the fold to a section detailing the ongoing crisis in Taiwan.

The latest report quoted the Chinese minister saying, "America shall not cross the Pacific and pretend to magistrate or officiate a political process that is uniquely between the people of China. America, you are not needed. Go home!"

As he thumbed through the paper a moment more, a piece on page A3 caught his attention. The headline read, "Kremlin Announces Large-scale Christmastime Snap Military Drill in Belarus."

Typical Moscow, thought Pascal. *The Russians see the Americans pivot to*

Asia, so they decide to up the tension in Central Europe with a massive military exercise near the border with Poland. It would scare everyone from Estonia to Hungary, but he did not consider the drill to be any real threat against Europe.

Nadal arrived with orange juice and a croissant and then went to fetch Pascal's coffee. The Frenchman took a break from reading his paper to butter his pastry, and as he did so he looked at the big group of young tourists on the terrace, yammering away across the veranda.

Nadal was nowhere to be seen with his damn coffee.

The Frenchman sighed. He didn't miss Paris often, but he missed it now.

Pascal Arc-Blanchette worked at the French embassy here in the capital of the small East African nation of Djibouti, which meant his career wasn't exactly flourishing. He'd been put out to pasture by his office—this was a posting no one, but *no one*, wanted—and still he'd been lucky to secure it, because the alternative would have been forced retirement.

Pascal thought sometimes that even though this was considered an exceptionally lowly job for a man with his experience and seniority, he'd probably nevertheless still be "retired" soon enough, and they'd just pull him out of service totally. If they did this, he knew he'd leave scratch marks from his fingernails at his desk, because he had nowhere else to go and he loved the intrigue of Africa with all his heart.

Pascal's cell phone in his pocket rang.

"Allo?"

"Allo, Papa. It's Apollo."

In a heartbeat all the Frenchman's problems—the lousy seat in the café, the old belt jacket, the dead-end job, the grim reaper of forced retirement—all melted away. He smiled into his phone, and smiled wider still as Nadal appeared over him and placed his coffee on the table.

"Hello, my son. Nice to hear from you." He caught his breath suddenly. "Everything is all right, isn't it?"

"Bien sûr, Papa. Just thought I'd call to see how you were coming along with your suntan."

Pascal laughed at the joke, because his son would know that his father was as pale as ever. He lived and worked in East Africa, true, but the work Pascal was engaged in involved sitting at a desk or slipping out into darkened bars, hotels, and back alleys, often late at night.

The elder Arc-Blanchette was a spy. An officer in DGSE, Direction

Générale de la Sécurité Extérieure, the French foreign intelligence agency. And while the men and women who had joined the service at the same time in the early eighties and come up the ranks with Pascal were now running the entire intelligence apparatus of the French Republic, Pascal himself walked the alleyways behind the markets of the former colony of Djibouti, desperate to pick up scraps of intelligence that might be of some slight value to his nation eight thousand kilometers away.

He enjoyed his coffee while he chatted over the phone with his son, a French army captain now stationed in Belgium. As they talked, Pascal sat facing the group of young backpackers across the terrace, and he could not help but eye them as a curiosity. Something from his training, his occupation: he wanted to determine from some little clue where they were from and what they were doing here in Africa.

There were nine of them—seven men and two women—and they all seemed to be in their twenties or thirties. Most of the men had beards; young people had given up on even maintaining their facial hair these days, and Pascal thought this was yet another indicator of the coming end of the world. From the gear around the entourage, he thought at first that they might be American adventure travelers. Americans spent a lot of money on backpacks even when they weren't traveling any distance at all, and this equipment all looked topflight.

Pascal could pick up some snippets of the conversation, enough to hear they were speaking English, but he detected some sort of accent.

The women had their hair pulled back tightly in ponytails tucked through their ball caps. Pascal caught himself glancing at their physiques. They looked exceedingly fit.

But again, what caught his eye most of all was their gear. The rucksacks, the Gortex-outer-shell jackets, even their ruggedized cell phone cases, were all brand-new, smart-looking, and pricey.

"Apollo, hold on one moment." Pacal switched to the camera function on his phone, zoomed in as tightly as he could go, and balanced the phone on his table. He then nonchalantly centered the lens on one of the big rucksacks and took a picture. When he looked at it on his screen, he zoomed in tighter on the manufacturer. "Random question: Are you familiar with a backpack called Peak Design?"

Apollo did not hesitate. "Of course. They make good stuff, but you pay for it. One of their bigger bags can run six hundred euros, easy."

"Interesting."

"Why, Papa? Thinking of getting me a nice Christmas present?"

"Maybe so," Pascal said with a laugh. "Although, on my salary, six hundred euros is pretty steep."

"Yeah, well, the ones you find for sale in the market down in the Horn of Africa won't be six hundred euros, and they also won't be anything other than cheap knockoffs."

"I'm sure you're right about that." He changed the subject. "I just read in the paper about the Russian exercises. Hope that won't ruin your Christmas."

"*Pas de tout.* ("Not at all.") No worry for us, but I imagine my counterparts in the Polish and Lithuanian militaries are pretty unhappy. The leadership here in Western Europe assures us we'll have ample warning if the Reds decide to invade."

"No such thing as strategic surprise anymore," Pascal said.

"*Oui.* That's what they say. Let's hope they're right."

Soon Pascal said good-bye to his son and put his phone back in his jacket, then motioned to Nadal. The maître d' stepped over and leaned down to the older man.

"Our new friends over there," Pascal asked softly. "Who are they?"

"No clue, monsieur. They arrived just minutes before you. Haven't seen them before."

"Did you hear how long they were in town? Where they were staying? What they were doing?"

"Nothing at all. I don't understand Russian."

Pascal cocked his head. "*Russian,* you say? I hear them speaking English."

"I heard some Russian. Softer, as if they didn't want me to hear." Nadal winked at Pascal. The maître d' knew the old white man was French intelligence, and Nadal had made a little money in the past passing on tips.

"Very interesting," Pascal said as he looked at the group.

"Really?" Nadal said with a smile. "*How* interesting?" He was asking if he'd get paid for this, and Pascal snorted out a laugh.

Pascal had run into Russian visitors to Djibouti countless times. They worked on ships that docked in the harbor, or for geological surveys or multinationals, or sometimes they were budget adventure tourists.

This group dressed and acted more or less like tourists, but from the looks of their gear there was nothing budget about them. Odd, because they were relatively young to be blowing six hundred euros on a backpack. Still . . . Russians eating lunch in a café in East Africa didn't add up to much of an intelligence coup.

"Sorry, my friend," Pascal said. "Not *that* interesting. But if they come back, do see if you can find out more."

Pascal left the café, crossed the street, and entered an alleyway where a small cluster of kiosks formed a small market. The shadows were high and he began looking through a large plastic bin full of cigarette lighters for sale while keeping one eye across the street at the new visitors to *his* city.

The foreigners left a few minutes later, and Pascal Arc-Blanchette set off behind them.

He was a spy, it was in his blood, he was curious about them . . . and, as much as anything, he saw a foot follow as something that would be a fun diversion for his day.

CHAPTER 15

Dan Connolly was the first man in the bullpen this morning. He fired up his computer just before seven, stuck his ID in the machine, and headed for coffee while he waited. When he returned he was surprised to see the bottom of his computer monitor flashing red. When it flashed green he knew there was a Pentagon alert—usually a snowstorm or a burst water main or the like.

But a red flash meant a classified message.

He clicked it and it opened up.

"Thanks for your intelligence support request. CIA European Desk was able to compile the Vice Chairman's request. Please open your Intelink-TS account for a link to all files related to the matter you requested."

Connolly started to sweat. He whispered, *"Bob, what have you done?"*

Major Griggs strolled in at seven thirty to find Connolly staring at him as he entered.

"Morning, sir."

"Did you put in an intel request to CIA?"

"I took the initiative."

"You told them it was for the vice chairman?"

"I may have clicked that box, but it's only because they didn't have a box for 'Vice Chairman's lackeys.'"

"We're going to get our asses kicked when the chief finds out."

"*I* will. *You* weren't involved. I put *my* name as the point of contact; *you* were just listed as an alternate contact when I filled out the request. Did you look at the data?"

"Of course I did."

"Don't keep me waiting."

Connolly heaved his chest and let out a long sigh. "General Boris Lazar, the guy who put his dacha up for rent, is in Azerbaijan, and he will soon be departing to Iran."

"*Iran?*"

"Yep, a joint exercise between the Russians and the Iranians."

"He put his dacha up for nine months. Is he on a *nine-month* exercise?"

"Doesn't sound right, does it?"

"Not at all. Anything about the general running the exercise in Belarus?"

"Yes. Sabaneyev has two dogs. Russian wolfhounds. And he put them in a kennel."

Griggs cocked his head. "For nine months?"

"No. He paid for two. Still . . . the Russians are planning something more than Christmastime war games in Iran and Belarus. I don't buy it."

Griggs agreed. "Yeah, but we don't know what it is, so convincing others around here is going to be impossible. What do we do?"

The lieutenant colonel spun back to his computer. "We keep digging."

The door to the bullpen opened, and an Air Force major leaned in.

"Chief's looking for you, Bob, and he does *not* look happy."

WARSAW, POLAND
21 DECEMBER

The twenty-year-old blonde with the ponytail was the only employee working the counter at House Café Warszawa for the eight-hour morning-through-lunch shift. The place had been nearly packed through the first half of her day, but the blonde kept working, blotting sweat from her brow with a washcloth from time to time, simultaneously making drinks and manning the register, pulling cakes from the display case and rushing through the small sitting area whenever she could to keep the tables clean.

The lunch hour was as busy as the morning, but she knew she was lucky: the weather in Warsaw this December day was especially sloppy; every time she stole a glance through the windows, she saw the driving sleet, and this kept the traffic through her door manageable, if only barely.

Around two there was a lull in the action, and Paulina took the opportunity to brew herself a quick double-shot espresso, which she drank down lava-hot. As she put her cup in the sink and leaned against the counter for a breather, a tall, beautiful, and young brunette came through the door, her hair askew as she pulled off her knit cap and unwrapped her scarf from her neck.

Urszula and Paulina had been best friends since grammar school, and it was their custom to kiss on both cheeks before speaking whenever they saw each other, but Paulina had not yet begun stepping around the counter before Urszula called out to her from the doorway.

"Why aren't you answering your phone?"

"Crazy day, girl. It's just me alone till three. Julia and Leo got called up by the Polish Rifles. Thank God the weather's shit, or I would have dropped dead before lunch."

Urszula put her bag down at one of the many empty tables in the little coffee shop, looking wide-eyed at her friend as she did so. "You really don't have a clue to what's going on, do you?"

Paulina moved around the counter, wiping her hands. "I don't know anything but coffee and sore feet today. What's up?"

"*We're* being mobilized, too. Our first deployment ever, and it's just days till Christmas."

Paulina put a hand on the counter to steady herself. This was the last thing she'd expected to hear. "Please tell me you're joking."

Paulina and Urszula were both in the same section of the same civilian militia unit. Their organization wasn't nearly as hard-charging as the Polish Rifles, who were a more elite volunteer corps of citizen-soldiers, so when Paulina learned the night before that her coworkers at the coffee shop had been called into immediate service, she didn't assume she'd be affected other than by the tripling of her duties at work until her boss could find replacements.

"We leave tomorrow morning."

Paulina let out a groan. "*Tomorrow?* But why? What's so different about the Russians in Belarus this time compared to all the other times?"

"Dunno, girl. All I know is that I have an art history paper due as soon as school starts again in January, and I haven't even started on it. This really sucks." She looked up with a smile. "I guess I'll get more time to study, although I'll be doing it squatting in some muddy trench."

Paulina reached back over the counter, struggling to grab her purse, which was tucked onto a shelf with a row of coffee syrups. She retrieved her phone and saw she'd received four calls and thirteen texts. As she began scrolling through them Urszula said, "I'll save you the trouble. We're to muster at Centralna at six a.m. We're being bused south somewhere."

Paulina looked off into space. "My boss is gonna literally freak out."

She had studied for a year at Warsaw University, just like her best friend, but she'd dropped out the previous spring because she hadn't been focused enough to keep her grades up. Since then she'd worked for the coffee chain, both here in the Old Town and at another location, in the Centralna train station.

She thought she might make assistant manager before too long, and while drawing espressos all day wasn't exactly Paulina's dream career, she figured she'd stick it out while she decided what to do with her life.

And she had also joined the Territorial Defense Force, the national civilian militia. She had friends in the group, Urszula included. It seemed cool, and she was aware of her patriotic duty, even if she didn't give a damn about politics, guns, or the scratchy, ill-fitting uniforms.

And joining the TDF meant an extra four hundred zlotys a month. A hundred bucks U.S. a dozen times a year would help Paulina buy a used car before long, and if she were honest with herself, she'd acknowledge that this was the main reason for her service.

But she sure as hell hadn't joined up to deploy during Christmas.

The Territorial Defense Force was most definitely "military light." Paulina served two weekends a month, training with her company in camps just outside of Warsaw or in high school gymnasiums around the city. Often the training would amount to little more than exercise, marching, and watching films produced by the Polish Land Forces about how to operate weapons, including some weapons Paulina had yet to even see in person.

An actual mobilization of Paulina's unit had seemed unreal for the past year, even in the last week, when other Polish paramilitary units had been getting call-ups in different parts of the country in response to Russia's war games in neighboring Belarus.

No one in her group, least of all Paulina, had any belief they would ever be called on to fight in combat. Even if the Russians did come pouring over the border, the Territorial Defense Force would most likely be utilized to organize trucks of retreating civilians, build tent cities, guard train stations in the west of the country from looters, or ferry equipment to the national army, the Polish Land Forces. And if Russia *did* take the nation, the TDF would, in theory, serve as an instrument of hybrid war: thirty thousand civilians trained—to one degree or another—in military tactics.

A middle-aged couple entered the coffee shop and shook rain and ice off their coats inside the door, and Paulina gave them some stink eye for it, but she kept talking to Urszula. "Why the hell are we leaving Warsaw? If the Russians invade, they are coming straight here."

"The army is staying here, ready to put tanks in the streets if it actually happens. We are being sent south somewhere."

"What do they want us to do?"

"Same as ever, I guess. Stand around in a field."

Paulina cocked her head now. "Will Tytus be there?"

Tytus was a lanky, good-looking DHL driver who served in a different section of her company. Paulina had a serious crush on him; this Urszula knew well.

The brunette just rolled her eyes. "It's the whole company, girl. Maybe you'll get lucky and Russia will attack so you can dive into a foxhole with Tytus."

It was a joke, but neither laughed.

Paulina made drinks for the middle-aged couple and they left; then the girls sat down at a table in the now-empty café. They looked out the window at the decorations all over the town square. The big tree wouldn't be put up till the evening of the twenty-fourth, but the holiday feel was impossible to miss.

"It *really* sucks that it's at Christmas," Urszula said.

Paulina's greatest worry at the moment was telling her employer she was following Leo and Julia out the door during the holiday season. She said, "Didn't they always say that if the Russians invaded, it would be in the spring or summer? They aren't going to do anything in the winter; even *I* know that."

Urszula just sighed. "I swear to God. They should put us in charge." Her chest heaved; then she launched back to her feet. "I've got a million things to do. Call you tonight."

CHAPTER 16

The 10:35 train from Moscow was only eight minutes late as it stopped at Minsk-Passazhirsky Railway Station in central Belarus. The passengers climbed out, their bodies stiff from the eleven-hour journey, but one man moved more quickly than the others. He wore a Russian woodland and winter uniform with the rank insignia of a Spetsnaz major, and on his back he hauled a massive pack that must have weighed forty kilos.

He passed through the midmorning crowd in the large and modern train station, stepped out the main exit, and scanned for a taxi stand. It was a gray day; the temperature here in central Belarus this morning hovered just above freezing, and several inches of snow had fallen the night before, blanketing the walkway to the glistening street and the rooftops beyond.

As he started forward again, a booming voice called to him from behind. "Mitya!"

The major spun around, smiled, and embraced a bearded man in a Gore-Tex winter parka and ski pants. He carried a huge pack of his own, but it was from a civilian manufacturer. "Lyosha! Good to see you, my friend!"

"You have time for a drink?"

"Always!"

The men mounted the steps to the train station's outdoor café and pulled the metal chairs from the tables, cleared the snow off, and sat down.

The outdoor portion of the café was closed due to the cold and sloppy conditions, but the major waved to a waiter through the glass, and he began quickly heading their way.

Lyosha laughed. "He sees your winter 'war god of the north' uniform and he knows to move his ass!"

"What about you? You look like a stoned tourist! What have they done to you, my poor Lyosha?"

"We get to grow full beards and we get to wear comfortable and stylish clothes. The girls in Germany will think we're Austrian Olympic skiers."

Now Mitya laughed. "Can your troops even wear a straight face and follow your orders when they see you in that bright blue jacket?"

"Mitya, you were not selected for my special assignment because Central Headquarters knows you hardly have a hair on your ball sack, let alone the ability to grow one on your chin!"

The waiter, who was now within earshot, was obviously startled by the coarse discussion between the two men, but he recovered quickly. "Coffee?" he asked as he handed them menus.

Lyosha waved the menus away. "Hell no. Vodka. Two glasses."

"The bar is not open yet, sir," said the waiter with some trepidation.

"Then you will open the bar for us. Right?" It was hardly a request. The waiter nodded and scurried off. Lyosha said, "How are your men? Are they ready for this?"

Mitya nodded. "They are. I've got Sergeant Utkin with me. You remember him?"

"The beast who won the regimental competition at Hatsavita in 2016?"

"The same."

"He's a bear."

A frigid wind blew snow around them in swirls, but the two men seemed immune to the cold. As the drinks came, they scraped a small area clear of snow on the table. Two full shots of vodka were placed in front of them. The waiter waited a moment to see if they would pay, but they ignored him and began a toast.

"To the 2nd Brigade! Anytime, anywhere, anything!" shouted Lyosha.

"To the 45th Guards Regiment! Only the strongest of the wolves will win!" Mitya roared.

The men downed the clear liquid in one gulp and only then looked up to the waiter.

"Two more vodkas, two pilsners, and two strong black coffees," said Mitya.

The waiter shuffled off again.

Lyosha said, "The other teams are already in Africa by now."

Mitya nodded. "I heard. Nice and warm. Bastards. We're leaving for the border at midnight. Crossing over through the woods into Ukraine, then passing over the river just north of Sobibór, Poland."

"You have a big group to slip over the border?"

Mitya shrugged. "Forty-eight in total. But the river is all but unguarded there. Just some acoustic sensors that we can get around. How are you guys infiltrating?"

The man in the ski outfit said, "We're leaving tonight as well, but we take civilian trains and buses. We've been given documents for travel into the EU by the spooks. All perfectly legitimate and civilized. Thirty-nine men and ten women."

"Women? Any good?"

"Good enough. All Spetsnaz trained. They'll help us blend in."

"What about the laser navigation equipment?" Mitya asked.

The wind died and a light snow began to fall. Big, heavy flakes drifted down among the morning auto traffic adjacent to the train station.

"Some was shipped and picked up by teams already in Poland and Germany; we'll carry parts in ski bags and backpacks when we board the trains. It's designed to look innocuous, like camera equipment. GRU operatives have rented helicopters in the Czech Republic and brought in good Russian pilots so we can get around," Lyosha said.

"What happens if you are captured in all this ridiculous civilian clothing?" asked Mitya. "You can be shot as a spy, you know."

"We'll have our uniforms under our ski suits."

"Good. You boys will set up the nav equipment that will allow the column to find its way to the objective. You'll be heroes of the *rodina*."

"And you and your men will control the path for the trains. You make it back home and you'll be promoted to colonel by President Rivkin himself," Lyosha said. "Where will you be during the action?"

"In the middle of the route, east of Wrocław, near some small cities where the rail junctions meet. I'm with Team Zhenya. How about you?"

"To the end of the line, my friend. The highest peak in Germany with

Team Gregory. Teams Anna through Vasily will be in the Elbe Sandstone Mountains. I am saving the really good action for myself. I want to be the one to place the last of the lasers to guide the assault column to its final objective."

"Cool. Then what? You just walk back home in that silly winter gear?"

Lyosha laughed. "Probably." He looked down and ran his hand over his Gore-Tex jacket. "Maybe they'll let us keep it. We have many routes back. Some through Czechia, some south to Austria, and some north to Kaliningrad. We disappear, then meet again for the next step. I'm off to Africa in just over a week to support Lazar's attack of the mine."

"You know, Lyosha, I thought I was the lucky one. I thought, since I was leading the uniformed forces, which will probably get to shoot, we had the best mission. But now I think maybe it is you. You get to do the truly undercover stuff and you get to play in phase two, in Africa, as well."

"Yes, but I will be honest with you: I have nightmares of being captured out of uniform."

"I can understand." Mitya grabbed his beer and held it up. "Don't get captured."

The men clinked glasses. "To your health and success, my friend. I will see you in a few weeks back in Moscow."

"I look forward to it, brother."

They clapped each other on the shoulder and each man placed a Belarusian thirty-ruble note under a glass on the table.

WARSAW, POLAND
22 DECEMBER

Paulina stamped her feet on the sidewalk in a futile attempt to stay warm outside Centralna. The northern side of the train station was a flurry of activity bordering on chaos: there were thousands of TDF volunteer militia members mustered both inside and outside the massive building, all to be sent to different locations around the nation. Old-school buses, modern travel coaches, and canvas-covered military trucks picked up individual units, but a seemingly endless supply of volunteers continued to arrive, and the crowd appeared to be getting larger, not smaller, by the minute.

Wherever the buses took her company, Paulina figured they'd all just go sit in a cold barrack building or a *freezing* tent and eat canned food for a couple of weeks. Then the Russians would finish their stupid showing off as they'd always done before, and she'd be back making espressos for the morning commuters.

Still . . . Christmas would be ruined, and she'd never forgive those old assholes in the Kremlin for this.

On a leather sling hanging from her shoulder, Paulina carried a long wood-grain rifle that looked like something from the Second World War, because it *was* something from the Second World War. In fact, the very weapon on her back was a 1940s-era Mosin-Nagant, a five-shot wooden rifle designed in Russia in the 1890s.

It had been state-of-the-art once, but that was more than a hundred years ago.

The brand-new battle rifle of the Territorial Defense Force—in theory, anyhow—was the Polish-made FB Radom MSBS "Grot," but no one in Paulina's company had ever even held one. Most of the riflemen in the outfit carried AK-47s, and Paulina had been trained on the AK, but she wasn't a rifleman, so she'd been issued a Mosin that had been pulled from ancient surplus inventory from the Polish Land Forces. She was adequate with the weapon—she'd even shot one a few times as a kid, because her father owned an even older model—but she'd never once gone boar hunting with her dad and brother, preferring to stay home and read books or go to the lake in the summertime with her friends.

Urszula appeared out of the crowd, and the two young women greeted each other with kisses and hugs. Urszula was head to toe in her green-and-brown camo uniform, which, with all the snow on the ground, appeared to Paulina to be rather ineffective camouflage. Paulina wore an identical uniform, but her backpack was the same one she'd worn to the university back when she was enrolled, and it was bright purple in color.

Not exactly general issue.

Her company's two buses arrived twenty minutes late, due to all the traffic around the station, but eventually Urszula and Paulina loaded in with the rest of the unit, and they were out of the capital by noon.

Paulina's Territorial Defense Force company consisted of ninety-three men and women; the youngest among them were eighteen, of whom there were many, and the oldest was fifty-seven: a baker who had served as a cook in the Polish army back when the Soviets called the shots. They were commanded by Lieutenant Robert Nowicki, a twenty-three-year-old active-duty Polish Land Forces infantry officer, one year out of the General Tadeusz Kościuszko Military Academy of Land Forces, as part of a program where junior officers rotated into the militias in an attempt to improve them. Paulina could tell that Nowicki would much rather be back with the PLF instead of leading citizen-soldiers, but he carried out his orders without obvious disdain for the men and women under him. She figured this wasn't always easy, because Nowicki normally saw his company for only a few days a month, and they were free to quit at any time.

They were not free, however, to talk back to their commanding officer or refuse lawful orders, but this happened sometimes. Nowicki was half the age of several men in the company, and it wasn't uncommon for the rough older guys to mouth off a little or question the young university man.

Paulina did what she was told, however. Not because she had any great respect for Nowicki. She was a diligent worker, whether she was brewing coffee or training for combat, because she didn't like getting in trouble.

Nowicki sat just behind the driver of Paulina's bus, and he talked on his mobile phone for the first part of the journey. A half hour after leaving Warsaw, he climbed to his feet and took the handset of the driver's PA system.

"Listen up. We're heading west of Radom, where we'll be tasked with guarding"—he looked down to some notes in his hand—"Expressway Twelve. It's a direct route between Radom and Piotrków Trybunalski."

A thirty-five-year-old store clerk called out, "Why?"

Nowicki looked up in annoyance, the microphone in front of his face. "Because that's what we've been ordered to do."

"I mean—"

Nowicki cut him off. "I know what you mean. I can't answer that, and if you were regular military, you'd know not to ask."

Nowicki continued for a few minutes with details. Still the questions continued, called out from the bus passengers like they were unruly students addressing a substitute teacher.

"Why did we get deployed?"

"Who says Russia is going to invade?"

"What the hell does Russia want with Expressway Twelve, Radom, and Piotrków Trybunalski?"

Nowicki had no answers, so Paulina tuned out the exchange quickly.

Instead, she and Urszula whispered to each other about Tytus, the DHL driver Paulina had a crush on. He'd climbed aboard the other bus, and Paulina worried that meant something bad about her chances with him; but Urszula did her best to assure her that the object of Paulina's affection was just oblivious to the fact Paulina had been trying to flirt with him, and as soon as she rectified this, he'd probably fall head over heels in love.

Paulina had no intention of letting the Russians interfere with her plans to get Tytus to notice her during the next couple of weeks.

At three p.m. the civilian militia buses arrived at their first destination, a lumber mill on a flat piece of frozen ground just west of Radom.

As soon as the buses were parked, everyone climbed out to find several TDF trucks in a row. The trucks were full of ammunition, food, water, tents, and the crew-served weapons issued to those whose specialty required them.

Everyone in Paulina's company had a specialty. She served on a two-person RPG-7 crew. The rocket-propelled grenade launcher fired a finned grenade up to five hundred meters. The launchers assigned to Paulina's company had been manufactured some ten years before her birth, but it was still a good and effective weapon.

Paulina and her teammate on the crew, an acne-scarred nineteen-year-old boy named Bruno who worked at his uncle's tire shop just west of Warsaw, had been assigned one RPG-7 and one crate with four rockets in it. Paulina and Bruno had each fired exactly six actual rounds from an RPG-7 in their lives, all at the Land Forces training grounds the previous summer. Bruno had been slightly more accurate with the weapon, so he'd been charged with fielding and firing it, while Paulina's job was to help him reload and to clear his backblast area. She was also tasked with carrying the ammunition in a big bandolier, protecting Bruno with her old rifle, and being ready to take over if Bruno was unable to continue fighting.

Paulina and Bruno hefted their crate of rockets out of the back of a truck, and Paulina loaded them into her bandolier. Bruno took the launcher itself from a wooden box of six, while the five other RPG gunners of the company grabbed theirs.

As they were organizing their gear at the back of one of the trucks,

Tytus walked by with his Dragunov sniper rifle in a drag bag over his shoulder.

"Hey," Paulina said with feigned nonchalance.

"Tobiasz," Tytus replied with a nod as he passed.

Now she wondered if he even knew her first name.

Tytus was the section's sharpshooter. Calling him a sniper would have been overselling his skills, but for a boy from Warsaw he could shoot well. He'd told Paulina once that his uncle had a farm an hour north of the capital and he'd gone there on weekends as a boy. Together they would hunt rabbit, and Tytus had been a natural shot.

With their packs and weapons and other gear, the militia company climbed onto the old civilian trucks driven by locals, and soon they bumped off the paved road and began heading along a winding muddy forest track that led through a farm.

As Paulina bounced around in the truck and wondered if she'd have to eat military rations for dinner, Nowicki came over the radios. "All units. We're stopping at a rail yard to pick up some wood for fortifications, and then we're going to set up camp in a bean field off Highway Twelve."

Urszula turned to Paulina. "*Now* we need wood? We just left a lumberyard."

Paulina replied, "They weren't going to let us use that stuff. We get the cheap shit, girl. We have to scrounge for scraps."

Urszula said, "Seriously, could this possibly get any worse?"

CHAPTER 17

It took four days of diligent work to find out where the Russians were staying in Djibouti City, but sixty-four-year-old French spy Pascal Arc-Blanchette was nothing if not a persistent man. The first afternoon of the tail he lost them when they climbed aboard a bus heading to the Balbala neighborhood. There weren't many tourist hotels that he knew of in that area, so he wondered if they might be staying with locals. He quietly asked his contacts around the area about boardinghouses, hostels, people with enough property to take in a large group, and the like.

With no true leads, he began driving around the neighborhood at different times throughout the day. This was slow, arduous, and boring work, especially because the air-conditioning wasn't working in his filthy, beat-up old four-door Renault. This December was typical for Djibouti, weather-wise, with highs in the eighties and nighttime lows barely dipping below seventy. But Pascal was used to sweating—he'd been doing it profusely his entire life—and he much preferred the heat to that sudden rush of bone-chilling cold he felt whenever he found himself somewhere outside of Africa in winter.

To the extent there were any centers of tourism in the city, the area around the Balbala bus station wasn't one of them. It was on the outskirts of town: row after row of ramshackle warehouses, shanties made from corrugated metal and even rusty old conex boxes, and the wind-whipped dust and sand that encroached from the south and permeated all life here on the edge of the Third World capital.

There were no hotels, but there were a few warehouses converted into housing for laborers. Pascal drove by these with a local friend and fixer who went in to have a look while the Frenchman sat outside in his Renault.

After two days of scouting around for the mysterious strangers, he'd decided the Russians had likely moved on. A dozen or more white faces in this neighborhood would be hard to conceal, after all. But late in the day he fell in behind a brand-new Toyota Hilux pickup truck that rolled north of the bus station and into town. He wasn't even following it intentionally at first. Its tags were local, it didn't stand out with any features, and he couldn't see the driver or the passenger, because they were hidden by the headrests.

But when the truck pulled into a gas station and both the driver and passenger climbed out, Pascal saw they were two large, bearded Caucasian men. He couldn't be certain they were from the group he'd seen a week earlier at Restaurant L'Historil, but he decided to back off a couple of blocks and follow the truck when it left.

The Hilux soon drove five minutes further to a dilapidated warehouse surrounded by a stalwart-looking chain-link fence. Pascal didn't have his fixer with him this day, so he couldn't send someone in to find out what was going on. Instead, he drove to an overlook nearly six blocks away and parked but remained in the car lest anyone take too much interest in a white man wandering around in this neighborhood.

Pascal Arc-Blanchette didn't spend money on nice clothes, nice cars, or nice anything, for that matter. But he did have a few nice toys, courtesy of French intelligence. He pulled a pair of Vortex Kaibab high-definition binoculars from his shoulder bag on the passenger's seat next to him and brought the fifteen-power optics to his eyes, focusing on the warehouse in the dusty distance.

Instantly he saw a white man on the roof, himself with a pair of binoculars. A moment of dread swept over Pascal as he worried he might have been compromised, but quickly he realized the man was scanning the roads closer to the warehouse and wasn't looking this high up on the hill.

Next to the man was a cheap plastic lawn chair, and propped on the chair were a rifle and a high-quality backpack.

Pascal's unkempt gray eyebrows twitched a little. Providing security for one's property was a good idea here in Djibouti—there was nothing off in in that—but the fact it clearly wasn't a local security service doing the work was a bit unusual.

Pascal wasn't sure who these Russians were, but he was now certain they weren't the international vagabonds they were portraying themselves as.

No, this was definitely some sort of organized affair. Corporate spies? No: based on their appearance and, noticeable to Pascal's trained eyes, their attempts to hide their military precision, they were more likely a clandestine military unit.

He could think of no reason a dozen or so Russian soldiers would be skulking around a Djibouti warehouse district unless the soldiers were here to protect whatever the Russian government was doing inside.

He saw no other activity on the grounds of the property for nearly an hour, but eventually a metal garage door slid open and two Toyota Hilux pickups rolled out of the main building. They passed through the front gate and turned south, and six blocks away Pascal rushed to get his Renault started.

In the late afternoon's fading light, a beige sedan drove down the RN5, two hundred meters behind a pair of gray Toyota pickups. Behind the wheel of the sedan, Pascal squinted through the dust and grime on his windshield, doing his best to keep his aging eyes on his targets.

The RN5 was the main highway out of town that led to the south and then into Ethiopia. It first left the sprawling shantytowns of the southern outskirts of Djibouti City and then rolled through the southwestern portion of Arta, one of six regions in the nation. Here the terrain switched to rolling hills almost completely devoid of vegetation and intersected with streambeds, most dry this time of year, but some flowing with brown water.

It was at a bridge over such a streambed where the pair of pickups pulled off the highway. Pascal himself slowed and veered off to the side, stopping once his car was below the crest of a long, gentle hill. He was still two hundred meters back, but he pulled his binos, stepped out of the car, and went around to the front to lift the hood.

Faking car trouble wasn't exactly the newest trick in the book, but Pascal Arc-Blanchette had been pulling this stunt around the world for some four decades, and it had worked for him almost every time.

With his hood up, he retreated back behind his open driver's-side door and lifted his binoculars to his eyes.

Half a dozen white men climbed out of one of the Hiluxes; they all appeared to be military-aged males, and they walked along the bridge, leaned over the side and looked down, and even took pictures with their phones. The men seemed relaxed about all this, nonchalant, but they were most assuredly there for a reason.

One of their number went to the near edge of the bridge, climbed over the side, and walked down the dirt embankment.

To Pascal, this seemed to be part of some sort of engineering survey. He thought they might be interested in the strength of the bridge, which meant they had plans to move something heavy over it at some point in the future.

But it was clear to Pascal they were operating covertly, which meant they were not here with the full blessing of the local government.

That's a new one: Russian special forces units working in advance of geological survey missions.

Geological survey teams from around the world had come here to hunt for minerals: gold and rare-earth metals. He knew all about the Russians losing their hold on the REM mine down in Kenya, and he assumed they were here doing more sight surveys, obviously in a clandestine fashion.

He didn't think they'd find what they were looking for. France itself had scoured the land around Djibouti looking for potentially profitable minerals and petroleum under the sand, and hadn't found much of value.

He'd return to the embassy to write a secure cable back to Paris. This was something they could hand off to the locals if they wanted, but Pascal hoped they'd ask him to keep looking into the matter and find out who, exactly, these men from Russia were and what sort of secret mining operation they were thinking about conducting to the south of the city.

It was just a hope, not born out of any real expectation of acclaim from Paris for his work, but rather simply because Pascal Arc-Blanchette so very much wanted something interesting to do with his days.

The cable was written and sent, and the next morning the response from Paris was in his hands as he sat down at his desk.

It was official-speak, as usual, but Pascal could read between the lines.

It was clear they simply didn't give a damn.

There was an acknowledgment of receipt but no request for more information, no offer of resources.

Pascal sighed, but then his mobile phone rang. Instantly he brightened, because he realized it was time for his weekly call from his son. *"Allo?"*

"Hi, Papa. Happy early Christmas."

"Same to you, my boy. How was your week?"

"Same old thing. How about you?"

"You won't believe it. Something damn interesting is going on down here."

"Oui, you are right. I don't believe it."

"I've bumped into some new visitors to town. Foreign chaps. All wearing adventure wear and carrying the best rucksacks and boots. A group of a dozen."

"What about them?"

"My guess is they are in the same line of work as you."

This piqued Apollo's interest, but only a little. "You say foreigners?"

"From the land of Kalashnikovs and caviar."

Apollo understood his father was telling him he thought plainclothed Russian Spetsnaz were operating in Djibouti, and now he was genuinely curious. "You're joking."

"Not about this, no."

"What are they doing?"

"Looking over bridges and highways, securing warehousing. They've been here for days, and from the looks of where they are staying, they plan on hanging around for a while."

"They aren't some privately contracted force? There to protect Russian civil engineers or something?"

"Doesn't look or feel like a private firm, and I haven't seen many civil engineers that are built like judo champs."

"Would be odd. You've told Paris, I assume."

"And they could not care less."

Apollo said, "Have you heard of this happening before?"

"Never. Not in the years I've been in country. I'm going to look into this riddle a little more. I'll tell you what I learn."

"Be careful, Papa."

"Don't be silly. I'm sure you're doing something more dangerous than me today."

At this the younger man laughed. "Papa, half the battalion is on leave, and I'm getting caught up on paperwork."

"Good, then I can sleep easy tonight for once."

CHAPTER 18

Thirty-two-year-old Captain Apollo Arc-Blanchette of the 13th Parachute Dragoon Regiment hung up his cell phone, then rolled his chair back and put his boots up on his desk. His tiny office here at his barracks was spartan, but he had certainly made do with worse setups in worse locations, so he didn't complain.

His battalion was winding down its six-month rotation as the duty unit at NATO's Very High Readiness Joint Task Force. He and his men would return to France, and Germany's Kommando Spezialkräfte unit would take over.

He'd been deployed in combat in Afghanistan multiple times, and he'd seen significant action during all his tours. He and his men had the battle scars to prove they were among Europe's most elite unit of special forces, and even though they'd done nothing more than train here in Brussels over the past six months, he was proud to have served NATO.

A rotation with NATO's VJTF was not the coveted Afghanistan deployment his men had wanted; they were hoping for a chance to fire real lead at a thinking enemy who fought back. But it was better than sitting at home at Camp de Souge, where the ammo was scarce, the live-fire training was hampered by constant fire danger ratings, and Apollo spent the majority of his time writing reports and filling out requisition forms.

But Apollo wasn't thinking about any of this right now. No, he was thinking about his dad.

He didn't know what to make of his father's assertion that something weird was going on down in Africa. It was not that he doubted his father's *conviction* that something was up; it was just that he worried his dad had been out in the field so long, he might have started to see ghosts.

Apollo and his sister, Claudette, had dealt with Pascal's erratic and often spontaneous world traveling for their entire lives. The kids had thought their dad to be a commercial trade representative for the French Foreign Ministry, and it wasn't until Apollo had received *très secret défense* clearance, the French version of "top secret," that he discovered his father had spent the past forty years working for the Direction Générale de la Sécurité Extérieure.

The younger Arc-Blanchette tried not to worry about his dad too much. Pascal had been taking care of himself for quite some time on his own in many foreign lands. He spoke eight languages with near perfect fluency, although he could be flighty, forgetful, and as unconventional a father as ever existed.

Pascal's defense to his son's accusations that he was "an absentminded old fool" was always to quote the French author Voltaire: "How pleasant it is for a father to sit at his child's board. It is like an aged man reclining under the shadow of an oak which he has planted."

His dad was too smart for his own good, Apollo always thought. And in his own way, by joining the French special forces, Apollo was following in his father's footsteps, since they were both servants of the French government, although Apollo employed guns and helicopters, while his father used dead drops and encrypted phones.

Apollo's mother was a society woman from Paris who had left Pascal for another man when Apollo was too young to remember her. As a boy, Apollo had strayed away from his sister's and father's inclination to read and write, and had instead gravitated toward organized sports and physical activity. He was the total opposite of his father, who had never engaged in a minute of nonmandatory fitness in his life.

The elder Arc-Blanchette always wanted his son to become a writer or a teacher, but Apollo instead joined the military and then the special forces. He loved the action, gravitated to the danger, and had flourished in the physical challenges and demands of the 13th Parachute Dragoon Regiment well enough that he had gained high regard from his French Army superiors.

And Apollo knew that his father worried about him because of the dangers of his job.

These and other thoughts gathered in his mind, as they often did just after he talked to his father. But today he couldn't let go of his dad's strange ramblings.

"Russian Spetsnaz in Djibouti," he said out loud at his desk, as if hearing it might help him understand.

Apollo decided to use his position as team leader for NATO's Very High Readiness Joint Task Force to see whether there was anything amiss down in Africa that might impact his father. He climbed out of his chair, left his office, and walked across the small Belgian special forces helo landing pads toward the ultra-classified areas of the base.

Soon he stepped into the VJTF's joint intelligence center. A perk of being assigned to the duty squadron meant unlimited access to classified information. The downside these days meant fighting off his men's boredom, since everything interesting going on seemed to be happening in the Strait of Taiwan.

Ah, good, thought Apollo on entering the JIC. His friend Lieutenant Luca Scarpetti, an Italian intelligence officer, was on watch.

"Hey, Luca." Apollo scanned the place; the usually bustling highly classified intelligence center for NATO was all but empty. "I see they have you working over the Christmas holiday."

"Yes, but it means I get days off for the . . . how you say, La Festa Degli Innamorati. The big festival of sexy."

"I'm not sure that means what you think it does."

"No, no, my friend, it is the day—how you say, the day for the lovers?"

"Oh, St. Valentine's Day."

"Yes, this. Now, how can I help you?"

"I heard a rumor there were some Russian Spetsnaz guys down in Africa. Djibouti City. You wouldn't know anything about that, would you?"

"The United States AFRICOM headquarters put out a bulletin and asked all NATO allies to look out for any Russian-tagged cell phones and satellite phones broadcasting from Africa. We are monitoring, but no one is making a big deal. Russia is always, how you say, making little plans. *Tutto a posto*—it's all okay?"

"Do you have a way to see Russian sat phones in Africa?"

"*Sì.*"

"Okay, can you pull them up?"

"I can show you the ones that we know about—you have the clearance—but you must, you know, *keep the water in your mouth.*"

"Keep it to myself, you mean? Yes, of course. I just want to see if my old man is crazy."

"'See if my old man is crazy'? French expression. It's like . . . 'Check it out'? See, even in your country some things don't translate too well."

Lieutenant Scarpetti pulled up the brief on North Africa off of the NATO intelligence system called CENTRIXS. Checking through a few briefs, he found the one he was looking for. Several signals intelligence units had put it together and it showed a map slice of the European and African hemisphere. Colored dots in Africa and a few in Russia denoted individual satellite phones and their usage over a period of time.

Scarpetti said, "The Chinese build back doors into the cell phone, and the Russians buy all their secret sat phones from the Chinese. We exploit the Chinese back doors. Someone built a batch intercept and tagged all the Russian sat phones in North Africa."

"What are the dots still in Russia?"

"Probably Russian sat phones that *were* in Africa but have returned to Russia."

Apollo noticed that one of the red dots was in Western Europe. "So, what's this?"

"A stray cat? Perhaps a Russian general is on vacation, skiing." Lieutenant Scarpetti laughed at his joke.

"If they are Chinese-made sat phones given to Spetsnaz, they are probably using them for a specific purpose. Did all these phones show up at the same time?"

"I can fish up the raw data. You wait." Luca set a search for the original raw intelligence on the CENTRIXS system and a moment later pulled up a collection matrix. It was basically a chart with times and dates and lists of the units, or asset tags that helped identify each of the phones, even if someone switched the SIM cards or changed to a different satellite phone provider.

Luca cocked his head. "Here. This is unusual. They are all turned on in the same week. In the last ten days."

Apollo saw that two of the tagged sat phones were in Djibouti City.

"Are you sure?" Apollo asked.

"Very sure."

"So something new and Russian is happening in the Horn of Africa . . . The old man was right."

"Again with the old man. But look here, this one, the one stray cat you saw on the master slide. It was yesterday. And it was in the German Alps."

"Where, exactly?"

"I pull up the JIC intercepts. We can see the same data they do at the signals intelligence branch." Luca punched up a map of Europe on the combined intelligence common operating picture. Like Google Earth, it showed intelligence collections in different zones of the world. He cleared away all layers but signals intelligence, then cut and pasted the asset code for the Russian satellite phone being used in Europe. A pulsing red dot showed up in Germany. "This one is radiating right now."

"Someone is using it *now*?"

"Yes. Looks like they are talking on the phone."

"Can you zoom in on the location?"

"But of course. Here . . ." Luca used the mouse wheel to scroll in, zooming ever closer to the red dot. Then the dot disappeared.

"Wait—is it lost?"

"No, they just hung up. But I can still see where it was. We had the position from the satellites. Sometimes we use several satellites and fake out the phone. This one was tasked to European signals intelligence; they do good work, so they at least should be able to give us a location. There— you see, it is in the German and Austrian Alps. Right on this mountaintop here, called . . . Zugspitze. Are you going to check it? You are still the alert force, are you not?"

"Yeah," Apollo said, looking at the screen. "I might go take a look. It's really curious that a Russian Spetsnaz sat phone tagged for North Africa has ended up in the Alps."

"You think the higher-ups will have trouble with you trooping around the Alps?"

"It's within my authority. No harm in going to just check it out. The German KSK guys aren't fully ready to launch for contingencies yet."

"Okay, Apollo. Hey, let me know if you want to go to *the sexy festival.* It would be so much fun, and we melt the girls' hearts, you and me both."

Apollo nodded and smiled. He patted his Italian buddy on the back, then stepped out of the JIC, still thinking about the odd connection between his father's observations and the stray Russian sat phone in the Alps.

CHAPTER 19

Colonel Danilo Dryagin left his assault element's staging area in the snowy Belarus countryside just after midnight and reported to the headquarters tent for a meeting with General Eduard Sabaneyev outside the railway station in the town of Pažežyn.

The general and his colonel shook hands standing next to a Bumerang, an amphibious wheeled armored personnel carrier and the newest addition to Russia's ranks of powerful armored troop vehicles. It was a twenty-five-ton monstrosity with a 510-horsepower engine, heavy armor protection, and a remote-controlled turret that carried an array of weapons, including a cannon, an anti-tank missile launcher, and a 7.62mm machine gun.

In addition to its crew of three, the APC could be loaded with eight combat troops, giving the vehicle more firepower through its ability to dismount soldiers to bring them into a fight.

There would be 170 Bumerangs involved in Red Metal's Western Spear attack into Europe, and this meant the entire operation relied on the success of this new piece of equipment.

Colonel Danilo Dryagin was a tallish man with thinning brown hair. Wiry, lean, he looked anything but the part of the assault force commander and the subordinate of the dashing General Sabaneyev. But what he lacked in appearance, he made up for with experience and single-mindedness. He treated his orders like they were a complete certainty, a foregone conclusion, then worked tirelessly to see them properly enacted. Dryagin was a true believer of Sabaneyev, and this made him invaluable.

They had worked together for more than eight years of Colonel Dryagin's twenty-five-year career, and the general had carefully tracked Dryagin's progress along the way. Six months earlier Sabaneyev manufactured a reason to visit the colonel as he trained his men in the field. What he saw was a quiet professional, not one taken to fits of anger or outbursts of emotion. He had an inherent understanding of tactics and was a natural with the men. Just the kind of well-loved, charismatic leader Sabaneyev needed.

Sabaneyev knew he had little rapport with troops himself—not that he cared. He had a larger sense of the battlefield, understood the "operational level of war," the in-between ground where few tacticians could translate their experiences at the company or battalion level and where few of the higher headquarters strategy and policy makers could effectively plan.

Sabaneyev asked, "Where do you sleep tonight?"

"Sir, I'll go to the reconnaissance element directly following our meeting. I will spend the night among them."

"Why not with the assault wave commanders? I'm counting on you to direct them proficiently."

"The reconnaissance elements, the GAZ Tigrs, they are where I place my bid for success. What path they forge, the rest will follow."

Ah, again he proves his worth. He wishes to stay with the frontline troops, thought the general.

They walked together to the headquarters tent and sat on folded chairs. Several gas lanterns and a camp stove burned brightly, and smoky haze gave a warmth to the glow. An unsecured tent flap occasionally blew open, stirring the smoke and making the flame flicker.

Sabaneyev's headquarters personnel with him were not used to the cold like their infantry and reconnaissance brothers, and someone grumbled for the latest intruder to close the flap. Several men on watch were bundled in their cold-weather gear manning the radios and maps. Those off watch slept, huddled up in groups against the edges of the tents, not willing to brave the cold outdoors, their sleeping bags wrapped around them like cocoons.

Sabaneyev said, "Ensure you stay in constant touch with my headquarters. I cannot support you if you try to go it alone. My train will try to stay with you, but in several phases you will be at the edge of my radios . . . and, more importantly, my fire support."

Sabaneyev stared into the fire now as he reached over to grab a worn leather map case next to his chair. He opened it and pointed to a checkpoint on the Polish-German border. "What's this?"

"Checkpoint twenty, sir."

"You have it memorized?"

"I have them all memorized, sir."

Sabaneyev stopped himself from his urge to quiz the man further; he didn't need to check his subordinate's knowledge. The man knew his orders; that was why the general had selected him. If anyone could lead the crucial Western Spear of Red Metal, it was Colonel Danilo Dryagin.

"Do not forget the prisoners," the general commanded. "They are critical. Your men must know the NATO ranks by heart."

"We do, sir."

Sabaneyev stood, and Dryagin followed. "Good luck, Colonel. I will see you in Stuttgart for a drink before the trip back."

"Yes, sir," Dryagin said with a salute.

Fifteen minutes later Dryagin's driver delivered him to the front ranks of his troops. A company of armor, T-14 Armata tanks, was staged in and among the trees. They were not enforcing nighttime camouflage, but that was by design. Let the West count their numbers by satellite. Let them underestimate them.

The T-14, the latest-generation Russian main battle tank, included explosive reactive armor (ERA) and a new composition of layered steel alloy, called 44S-sv-Sh. The ERA was called *Malachit* in Russian and consisted of bricks of explosive that detonated incoming missiles, a part of the Russian fourth-generation defensive systems intended to mitigate what was seen as the West's obsession with antiarmor missiles fired from aircraft.

Dryagin walked through the woods toward the reconnaissance forces now. They were in a spot specially chosen just kilometers from the Polish border. The music and the large campfires of the tankers behind him were replaced by the relative silence of the woods and his quiet reconnaissance forces.

"Who walks?" came a commanding voice from within the woods, startling the colonel out of his thoughts.

"It's Colonel Dryagin," he said, realizing he had walked farther than he'd expected.

"Very well, sir. Advance to be recognized," said the voice from the trees.

Colonel Dryagin continued forward, and when he was within ten paces of where he supposed the voice was coming from, he saw the outline of a camouflaged machine-gun nest. Movement close on his left in the dark startled him. A sniper climbed out of a snow-filled gully along the farmers' road.

"Colonel, do you not sleep?" asked the soldier.

"Not yet. Where is your commander?"

"Sir, the lieutenant colonel is with the Bumerang maintenance men going over some last-minute repairs. You'll find him one hundred paces down this road. You cannot miss him."

"Good. And nice work on this ambush. Don't ever let your guard down."

"Yes, sir."

Colonel Dryagin walked the requisite pace count and still almost missed the vehicle staging area. The area was silent except for the sound of some chains being dragged as a vehicle was being rigged for towing by another vehicle.

"Reconnaissance force commander, report!" he exclaimed, a little louder than necessary, refusing to go looking for him in the freezing December night.

"I am here, sir," came a voice next to the towing vehicle.

"Do we have a downed vehicle? I saw nothing of this on the headquarters report."

The reconnaissance lieutenant colonel stood from where he was kneeling with the men, hooking up the tow latches. He wiped his bare hands with a grease rag. "Sir, we are towing it over to the tank maintenance section. It needs new batteries and we must replace two of the wheel drive assemblies. It will take no more than two hours. We will still be ready at the appointed time."

"Let your men handle it. I wish to take a walk with you in the field.

Inform your men so we are not shot. They are particularly alert tonight, a testament to your leadership."

The lieutenant colonel beamed. "They are cold, sir, and nothing keeps men more alert than the possibility of lying down and never getting up."

A freezing sleet began to fall. Dryagin looked up at it. "This weather will work to the advantage of Russia." He nodded. "Very good."

CHAPTER 20

Captain Apollo Arc-Blanchette stood in the cold morning and watched as the two French special forces H225M Super Cougar helicopters taxied toward him and his ad hoc squad of soldiers.

He was glad to get the newer French Eurocopters today. They had a much better range and could carry more weight than the older and more common AS532 Cougars.

The skies were gloomy and gray, as were some of his men's looks. They were all fresh off leave, and there had been a promise of no alerts, since the German KSK commandos were already "in the hopper" to take over the NATO Very High Readiness Joint Task Force. But Apollo had thought this Russian sat phone intriguing enough to check it out for himself and to ask for volunteers from his unit to join him.

Virtually his entire second squad had mustered, and this made him proud as hell.

"You've gotta love 'em," said Apollo to the leader of his second squad, Sergent-Chef Lucien Dariel.

Dariel adjusted a strap on the backpack resting at his feet. "Good men," he agreed.

Ten minutes later, the twenty-three men of the 2nd Squad, 1st Platoon, 2nd Squadron, of the 13th Parachute Dragoon Regiment were loosely assembled under the helos.

Apollo said, "Listen, boys—it's Christmas Eve, and I know you'd all rather be enjoying your leave, but we have some intel tidbits we need to go check out. And since our German colleagues in the KSK are not fully up to speed, I asked our buddies over in the 4th Helo Regiment to lend us some lift today.

"We're going into the German Alps on a recon mission. The good news is, if this turns out to be a wild-goose chase, I'll ask the pilots to take us somewhere near the target site to do some skiing."

The men let out a cheer and Apollo couldn't help but smile, but soon he got serious. "NATO has tracked a suspicious cell phone to this area."

Apollo signaled for the intel officer. The intelligence lieutenant laid out acetate maps on the ground that showed two peaks marked with red crosses.

"First we'll fly over near Zurich and land at Dübendorf Air Base. The ops center is getting clearance for that layover and refuel now. Then we'll get back in the air. Our ultimate destination, and today's objective, is right here"—Apollo pointed to the German mountain peak called Zugspitze—"the highest point in the German Alps."

Within minutes the rotors were spinning, and the twenty-four men and their gear were on board. The helos lifted off into the gray sky, and Apollo told himself that, whether or not they found a Russian soldier with a sat phone on a mountaintop, at least this Christmas Eve wouldn't be boring.

IRANIAN-AZERBAIJANI BORDER
24 DECEMBER

General Boris Lazar looked out across the open desert. The vast sands south of the Zagros Mountain range greeted his gaze in every direction except back north from where he had come.

He was from Leningrad, which was now St. Petersburg, and he missed the salty Baltic air from time to time, but he was here now, by this brown river instead of his beautiful Baltic coastal streets. *What is the name of this dirty thing again?* He looked at his battle map and oriented himself: the Aras River. *A shit little stream,* he thought.

The ocean would be a welcome sight soon enough.

He looked over to see Colonel Dmitry Kir, his right-hand man, chief of staff, and the de facto chief of plans for his brigade task force. Lazar grinned his big, dirty, coffee-and-smoke-stained teeth at Dmitry, who was too busy talking on the radio to notice. General Lazar hadn't trained the colonel; he didn't have the skill to teach a man like Dmitry Kir. But he did have enough street smarts to recognize a spark in Captain Kir twelve years earlier that hinted at his work ethic and his ability to plan down to the minutest detail. General Lazar immediately sent the young captain off to the best schools and, more important, protected him and hid him from others, never mentioning the man's obvious talents to his superiors or his fellow generals lest Kir be stolen away.

Lazar had kept and cultivated Kir like a prized possession.

Throughout his career Lazar had always known he didn't possess the intelligence necessary to plan the really important operations, but he had surrounded himself with the best men and then bullied and politicked to keep them in his ranks. And now General Lazar had one of the most finely tuned military units in the Russian army, and he had Colonel Kir and his other staff to thank for it.

He sat down heavily in the wooden folding chair and raised his feet onto an empty green plastic case that had housed three 125mm shells in foam. The shells had already been loaded into one of Lazar's T-90 tanks.

Colonel Kir looked up from the radio and back toward his boss. The general liked that Kir always had an honest demeanor. The general mistrusted almost everyone he met, including all of these Iranian fucks around him, but Colonel Kir was as trustworthy a man as lived anywhere on earth, Lazar was certain.

Kir said, "General, the men are ready to move out; the Iranian Guards Armor are lined up to provide the escort down Route 12 all the way to the border. We are at your command."

"Fine. Put your boots up for a moment and have a Turkish coffee with me. You've worked hard, friend. Relax a moment before we go back to work."

Colonel Kir sighed a little on the inside, but he didn't let it show. Instead he just nodded and sat in a wooden folding chair that was covered with a colorful local woven rug. He took one of the small cups of thick, sludge-like Turkish coffee that, in Kir's estimation, looked more like pudding and tasted more like a lump of coal.

He didn't have time for this shit, not even for Lazar, the Lion of Dagestan. He had units to organize for the next big phase: Colonel Klava never filled his tanks with fuel when he was ordered to do so, and he was sure to stop the column halfway through the journey. Colonel Glatsky always had stupid questions just before they began their road marches, which delayed his departure. Colonel Nishkin never said anything but needed the latest maps and data spoon-fed to him or he would just start making shit up once they drove off.

Colonel Kir would have to admonish them all on the radio, as usual.

But the host of concerns vanished as he looked across the makeshift table at his boss.

The general already looked the part. His bald head and pronounced chin were features that struck Kir as old-school Soviet. Lazar had already localized a bit: his heavy Russian greatcoat was augmented by an Azerbaijani animal-skin undercoat he'd bought in one of the markets up north. His new thick boots were a replacement for the thin fake-leather Russian issue and were much more practical for the cold desert winds they had all come to know so well. It whipped through a person, the air caked with brown sand that whirled around them and got into everything.

Lazar stared back at him as he sipped his Turkish coffee.

His boss was always at ease. The general loved to say, "I *cause* great stress, but I have none personally." Kir seemed to bear the brunt of his boss's stress, and it was at times like this he wished the general would show some, just a little, at least to demonstrate that he had a clear understanding of the multitude of uncertainties that lay ahead.

But Lazar showed nothing but supreme calm, so Kir was reduced to sitting here and pretending to be relaxed.

Dmitry Kir drank his coffee, burning his lips as he gulped it too hastily, eager to get back to work and out from under his boss's grim gaze.

Finally, Lazar turned to his colonel. "Give the order, Dmitry. Let's go to war."

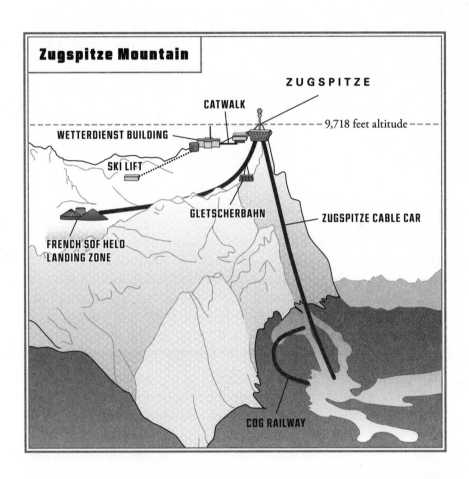

Zugspitze Mountain

ZUGSPITZE

CATWALK

9,718 feet altitude

WETTERDIENST BUILDING

SKI LIFT

GLETSCHERBAHN

ZUGSPITZE CABLE CAR

FRENCH SOF HELO
LANDING ZONE

COG RAILWAY

CHAPTER 21

The two H225M Super Cougar helicopters kicked up white vortices of snow as they lowered to the glacier. Their chosen helicopter landing zone was becoming obscured by frosted ice clouds as the French special forces soldiers looked out into the cold from the open side door.

Apollo had trusted the Escadrille 3, 4th Special Forces Helicopter Regiment pilots with his life on many previous occasions. The pilots were true pros. Their specialization in landing the Dragoons in exceedingly poor HLZ's, while occasionally under fire, had already earned them a very solid reputation.

Apollo saw an easing in the men's faces when they felt the craft sink down onto its five huge wheels.

He climbed out of the Super Cougar, leading his men twenty meters distant, where the sergeants would pause to take account of their gear and equipment. Above them, two tall columns of snow spun overhead from the five composite rotor blades.

These new Eurocopters were equipped with special deicing systems, but the experienced pilots, who were still used to the old AS532s, didn't like to take any chances with frozen engines. They would keep the birds warmed up and spinning until Apollo and his men were ready to leave. Unfortunately, seeing the rising plumes of snow above the helos would also serve as a reminder to Apollo that he was burning NATO fuel, and doing so on an only somewhat legitimate mission, what amounted to little more than a search for a curious phone signal.

Caporal Konstantine stepped up to him. "Sir? I don't see any obvious enemy forces or spies here, but I would like permission to check over the *Schneehasen*, just to make sure."

Apollo cocked his head at the German phrase. "Snow bunnies?"

Konstantine pointed to the gathering crowd of mostly females in brightly colored and tight-fitting ski suits watching them from the railing of the Zugspitze Gletschergarten, a high Alpine "Glacier Garden" bar and restaurant that now overlooked the team's landing position from higher on the snow-covered mountainside. In the midafternoon, even on Christmas Eve, there was a flurry of activity.

Sergent-Chef Dariel broke into their conversation, having just come over from the other helicopter. "Sir, you can damn well believe everybody on this mountain knows we're here. Did we plan on landing right in the middle of the ski slopes, or was it the 4th SF Helo flyboys' idea?"

"No choice. We have no authorization or clearance to land here any-how, so they picked a spot off the rescue HLZ that wouldn't annoy the skiers too much. I'll take a small contingent up to the peak. We'll get better reception for Caporal Konstantine's electronic detection equipment to search for that phone signal, assuming it's even transmitting."

"Copy, sir."

Apollo detailed the plan to the troops. One Team, led by Apollo him-self, would take the gondola to the top of the Zugspitze to look around for anything amiss. Two Team and Three Team would remain by the helos with the gear but were given a broad radius to send out teams of two to scout everything from the two restaurants and the three ski runs serviced by two ski lifts down here a few hundred meters below the peak.

The lower lift took skiers to the most popular and more basic slopes. The other, higher lift went all the way to the buildings on the very peak of the mountain, four hundred meters higher than where Apollo stood now.

Captain Apollo Arc-Blanchette, Sergent-Chef Dariel, Caporal Konstan-tine, Caporal Garron, and two other men selected by Dariel couldn't have looked more out of place in this Alpine ski resort as they hiked to the base of the gondola. Their white snow camo uniforms, the silenced Heckler &

Koch UMP45 SD submachine guns on their chests, the FN SCAR-L carbines on their shoulders, and the Glock 17 side arms strapped to their hips just added to their menacing appearances.

The six men rode from the glacier upward toward the top of Zugspitze. The cable car rose high into the Alps while skiers and snowboarders merrily shot by below them, white rooster tails of snow crystals in their wake, crisscrossing down the ever-white frozen landscape.

The cable car swayed gently in the persistent alpine winds.

Apollo looked at their destination as their gondola neared the top. The peak had been intermittently obscured by clouds from below, but now he could see it clearly.

"*Mon Dieu,*" said Apollo quietly, gazing at the beauty of these astral surroundings. " 'He makes the clouds His chariot,' " he said, remembering a long-forgotten Psalm his father had taught him.

At the gondola's terminus, a massive concrete structure was built astride the ancient rock. He could see a gift shop and a restaurant inside the huge glass windows. Outside, the building was topped with an observatory platform and capped by a weather instrument tower.

The mountains glimmered in the winter morning's sunshine around the windswept structure.

The gondola locked into the bay at the top with a loud clang and the men disembarked, some unsteady from the swaying. Apollo flashed his identity badge at a German security officer at the entrance, then explained that they were there to check out a suspicious mobile phone signal.

"This is highly irregular," said the portly fifty-something guard, speaking English with a thick German accent. "I must call this down to my superiors."

Apollo answered in English. "Sure. Call anyone you like, but we need access and for you to remain with us as we inspect the top. It shouldn't take long, but as I mentioned, we are on NATO's special response force and we have the authority."

"But . . . why all the guns?" the security guard asked. "Is there danger?"

"We never travel without our full kit. It's the rules."

Apollo rightly assumed the German would appreciate rules, and the man just nodded.

"At least he's packing some heat for a plump little piggy," said Caporal

Konstantine, speaking in French and referring to the 9mm Glock pistol strapped to the security guard's hip.

"Bet he's never fired it," Caporal Garron responded, also in French.

Dariel admonished his men. "Watch your mouths."

The small entourage of seven—six large French special forces men in winter camouflage uniforms and laden with weapons and packs, and one out-of-shape German security officer in a heavy winter coat and a knit cap—continued up the multiple stairwells to the top observation deck. Once there, they stepped outside with a sea of clouds dancing below them. The sun above shone brightly, and at this moment, anyway, their view of the surrounding peaks was crystal clear. They could see to the valley floors in Bavaria and Austria below with the glacier to their backs.

"You can practically see back to the HQ in Belgium from here," said Caporal Konstantine, again in French.

"Not so far. But you can almost see Stuttgart on the clearest days," replied the German, in perfect French. The Dragoons traded embarrassed glances.

Apollo tasked Sergent-Chef Dariel with directing the men to pull out their binos and begin to look around. He then turned to Konstantine. "Use your equipment and see if you can hunt down that signal. Get us closer than the one-kilometer radius the JIC was able to provide."

Konstantine pointed to the weather tower. "I'd like to climb this to get an even better reading. If anyone is transmitting from up in these mountains, even an additional ten or twelve meters can make a difference in direction finding."

"Okay," Apollo said, then turned toward the security guard, speaking French now. "Would you be able to allow my compatriot access to this tower?"

"My name is Herr Schneider and, yes, I can let you in. The tower is for the—how do you say?—Deutsche Wetterdienst."

"German Weather Service. I'll instruct my men to be careful around the equipment."

Schneider took the keys from his belt and unlocked the steel gate in the chain-link fence that surrounded the small tower, and Caporal Konstantine stepped in. The ladder up the tower was covered in icicles, and this made his ascent especially slow.

While Konstantine climbed, Sergent-Chef Dariel directed his boss to the railing overlooking the Alps to the north. The view was incredible and every now and then the peak became totally whitewashed as snow flurries passed overhead.

Dariel said, "It's a pity, but even if there is a Russian spy skiing the slopes and coming on to the girls, there does *not* seem to be any great threat to the NATO alliance up here."

Apollo agreed. "Yeah. Looks like a dry hole."

A shout from behind took their focus to the weather tower. One of the men was racing toward them. "Sir, Konstantine is yelling that he's receiving something."

The three ran across the iced-over metal decking to the base of the ladder inside the weather tower and peered up. They could see the top hatch was open and Caporal Konstantine was looking down.

"Sir," he said, his tone bright with excitement. "I've found it. The signal."

"Can you tell what direction? How far?"

"Sir, it's coming from this tower, right here. You better come up here and look at this."

Apollo and his other two men, followed by the German guard, climbed the frozen ladder up to the top. The wind whipped against them, and while the soldiers wore their goggles, Schneider had to squint as another snowy gust passed through and around them, momentarily obscuring their vision down to a few meters.

At the top they huddled together as Caporal Konstantine shouted above the wind.

"Sir, look here, on this big weather mast." He pointed to a metal pole that extended four meters up from the base of the weather tower. "That equipment about one meter from the top looks brand-new, and it's like nothing I've seen. There's a satellite dish, a few radio antennae, and . . . *that* thing."

Apollo saw a metal box the size of a microwave oven, with one side made of glass. Inside appeared to be a large lens facing toward the north. A red light glowed in the center.

"The hell is that?"

"Sir, that looks like a big laser. From the lack of ice accumulation, it was put up in the last day or two."

Schneider said, "A Wetterdienst crew arrived yesterday and worked here. They said they'd be working on other peaks on the mountain for the next few days."

"Where are they now?" Apollo asked.

"I think I can answer that." Caporal Konstantine pointed to a small unidirectional antenna. "That thing is too little for anything but point-to-point comms. Whoever is talking to that antenna is doing it from that peak over there." He pointed to a smaller peak four hundred meters farther along the range to the northeast.

Karl said, "There is another small weather station over there. The Wet-terdienst guys have clearance to that one and a bigger one on that peak." He indicated a rocky outcropping just fifty meters to the southwest.

Apollo scanned the closer peak. A concrete-and-iron outbuilding was built into the rock, an antenna array rising above it. A group of four men in heavy winter coats stood by the antenna, and they seemed to be looking back in the direction of Zugspitze.

Apollo eyed them for a moment, then waved. Cheerily they waved back. He then looked over his shoulder and was surprised to see Konstan-tine climbing up the steel beam of the mast, a slow process with the accu-mulation of ice on every surface.

"Just want to get a better look, sir."

In moments Konstantine had made his way up to the white box.

Dariel said, "If you fall, Caporal, I'll kick your ass where you land!"

The men laughed, and Konstantine leaned over the metal box and reached into the wires coming from it. He had to shout to be heard over the wind. "Sir, the cables connecting this thing to the battery have Cyrillic writing on them." He pulled one of them loose from the metal mast and unfastened it from the back of the box.

He dropped it down, and Dariel caught it and looked it over.

"It looks like military-grade equipment to me," said Sergent-Chef Dariel.

Suddenly Apollo realized this had not been a wild-goose chase after all. "Looks like some sort of Russian signal-intercept operation is going on here. Spy shit, I guess. Call the men. I want the rest of One Team and Three Team to get their gear, including skis, and take the ski lifts to the top of the slopes. That will put the men within five hundred meters of that other weather tower. Tell them I want HF and SATCOM up immediately. In-form HQ we are investigating further but we may have found something."

"Copy, sir. On it," said Sergent-Chef Dariel. He began passing the or-ders to the men down below on the glacier.

Apollo added, "Let Two Team come up from the glacier, put on their snowshoes, and climb up the east side of the peak. It will put them right at the base of that building."

"Sir, what if it's nothing? Just some weather service people stringing up some new equipment."

"With Cyrillic lettering?"

"Dunno. Maybe they use Russian weather equipment."

"Broadcasting radio satellite on a Russian phone tied to Spetsnaz?"

"Yeah . . . you're right, sir." Dariel got on the radio to send Two Team up to check them out.

Minutes later Dariel listened to his radio and then turned to his captain. "Sir, Two Team is trying to make contact with the German weather guys. They said they are about fifty meters from the station. They are hailing the men up top."

Apollo, Dariel, and Konstantine went over to the northern railing and from there they could see Two Team snowshoeing across the snow and up the peak's slope. Apollo peered through his binos at the six men trudging up the steep snow-covered mountainside just twenty-five meters from the rocky outcropping where the weather station was positioned. Apollo could tell Two Team's element leader was struggling to communicate with the men at the building over the noise from the high winds. He held his hand to his mouth and shouted as he walked closer.

Now Dariel said, "Two Team says the men at the station are all wearing legitimate Deutsche Wetterdienst jackets and they are speaking back to them in German."

The wind blew large swirls of snow around Two Team, obscuring Apollo's view. But when the snow cleared, he focused again, and his eyes widened in shock at what he saw.

Two men of Two Team had dropped flat in the snow. The other four were down on their knees. Guns were raised toward the weather station.

He heard the crackle of gunfire through the whipping wind and saw snow kicking up around the Dragoons as bullets struck the glacier around them.

CHAPTER 22

"Merde!" shouted Caporal Konstantine.

Apollo saw the yellow flashes coming from the adjacent peak. The wind played hell with the sound, but he could hear the staccato pops of semiautomatic fire.

Dariel, Apollo, and Konstantine all unslung their rifles, but they had no line of sight on any of the men at the weather station now.

Konstantine had his headset in his ear. "Two Team reports casualties, sir! One man is dead and one wounded."

Apollo looked over to the narrow catwalk that crossed to the other peak. "Dariel, we're going down to cross that pipe bridge. We need to engage them on two fronts or they will pin Two Team down in the open. The machine-gun section will lay down some suppressive fire; then you and I will cross together along with Caporal Konstantine."

Now Apollo turned to the security guard, who was lying on his stomach on the steel decking, covering his head.

"Schneider, how do we get down to that catwalk?"

The sounds of intermittent battle on the next peak over continued as the four raced down metal stairs and then through a small employee access hallway in the observatory. Schneider led them to an oval steel door, unlocked it with a key on a chain, and then pulled.

The door was difficult to open; ice had intruded into the little engineering room that led out onto the catwalk atop the pipe. An immense gale of wind blasted them as they looked out into the snow-driven haze. Apollo led the way out onto the slippery, grated metal surface, which was no wider than half a meter.

A soft *whump . . . whump* met their ears as one by one they started to cross the fifty-meter gap. Below them they knew there was an immense drop, but a mini-blizzard of snow raced around them, and they could see no farther than five meters in any direction, including, mercifully, down.

"Hey!" Apollo shouted back to Konstantine. "Make comms with the teams! That sounded like mortars."

"Right, boss, on it!"

The snow blew past and a moment later they stood in bright sunlight. Dariel moved farther out on the catwalk now.

"Sir, Two Team is taking intermittent mortar fire from the weather station!" said Caporal Konstantine.

"What the *fuck* is going on around—"

Before Apollo could finish the thought, he jolted to the sound of a high-pitched scream of a bullet striking the metal pipe just below his feet.

"*Shit!* Back! Back!" He and Dariel turned and headed quickly back in the opposite direction.

Another round ricocheted just above the metal hatch. Apollo dove inside just after Dariel, landing in a heap.

"Caporal Konstantine, get me all teams up on the net. We're going to coordinate our attack."

"Got it, sir! Do you want the bird commanders from the 4th on net, too?"

"Yes. They are going to have a play in this offensive as well."

As the senior man between Two Team and Three Team, Sergent Coronett called in everyone from both teams to fall in on his position.

"Captain Apollo wants us to initiate the action with a ground offensive. We're going to use the intermittent snow flurries to hide our advance. Once we move, Captain is going to hit these bastards in the flank.

"It's just like our battle drills—a fix and advance. Basic and textbook, understood?"

"Hey, Sergent Coronett, any idea who these fucks are?" asked one of the more senior corporals.

"Captain says he thinks they're Russians."

"What the fuck are Russians doing here?"

"They'll be dying in about ten minutes."

Apollo peered through the cracked door that led to the catwalk over the chasm. The catwalk looked like a metal tower on its side—a narrow span that crossed the deep chasm, steel girders wrapped in thick ice. It ended at a door in a metal wall built into the rock, which, presumably, was part of the weather station. He'd seen the four men on a ledge high above it, but now they were out of sight.

He looked for the sniper on the rocky peak, above him but only fifty meters away.

He saw nothing but whipping snow now as another squall blew through.

"Sir," Schneider said. "The other side of the catwalk. It's in *Österreich* . . . Austria . . . I have no jurisdiction in Austria. I cannot go with you."

To Apollo, this was asinine, but he knew Schneider and the other security officers here would keep civilians out of harm's way, and that gave Apollo the freedom to go do what he needed to do.

"No problem. You just watch our backs. If any of those guys make it over here to Germany, they can be your responsibility."

"Of course," the heavyset German replied.

Just then, a rapid succession of 40mm grenades could be heard impacting in the Weather Service building fifty meters across the catwalk and one hundred meters of jagged rock above them.

The attack had begun.

"Here we go," said Apollo, stepping out from the door and onto the icy grate of the catwalk, resuming his movement over the precipice.

Caporal Konstantine followed close behind with the radio, then Sergent-Chef Dariel.

Apollo made the mistake of looking down below the catwalk and the pipe. The air had cleared of clouds, so he could see a straight drop of about two hundred meters to a rocky cut between the two peaks. He continued to do a forward shuffle with one foot gliding in front of the other, his weapon elevated and pointed at the small oval door on the opposite side and the rocks above it.

A huge alpine blast of freezing wind almost blew the trio off the narrow and slick catwalk. It was accompanied by more blinding snow whipping against their faces, sweeping almost vertically past them. Their visibility closed in to less than ten meters and they shuffled even more slowly.

A rifle round ripped the air past the three exposed men. Clearly the Russian sniper hidden somewhere in the rocks could not see them in the near-whiteout conditions, but he was also smart enough to know the opposition force would use the snow and the attack as an opportunity to move closer. He knew that even a few blind shots across the bridge would make things more difficult for Apollo and his men.

Another round slammed into the side of the catwalk, knocking chunks of ice off just ahead of Apollo's position.

Apollo forced himself onward, moving faster now, almost to the point of recklessness. He didn't want to fall, but he *really* didn't want to catch a round to his head and *then* fall.

And then the wind receded, taking the violent but useful whiteout conditions along with it. Apollo moved faster still, and he hoped the two men behind him had the good sense to do the same. He slipped and skidded over the icy grate catwalk even faster now, the wall of the building only meters away.

Another rifle shot, this one behind the captain and just in front of Dariel. Apollo began running on the narrow catwalk now, because he couldn't imagine his luck lasting much longer.

Suddenly Apollo heard gunfire behind him. He was confused by it at first but quickly realized it was Schneider, who was firing his pistol toward the opposite peak. There was zero chance he would kill a sniper well hidden in the rocks fifty meters distant and far above him with a handgun, but Apollo appreciated the suppressive fire nonetheless.

He skidded the last few feet to the oval door, which was surrounded by a small metal wall built into the rock face. Apollo hoped the opposing room was no different from the side they'd come out from and they wouldn't be lost in a maze of ladder wells and antechambers as they made their way to the top.

Another rifle shot boomed, and he glanced behind him to check on Dariel and Konstantine. Thankfully the other two men were right there with him, weapons up and dividing their watchful gaze between the oval door and the top of the weather station wall, which was clearly visible.

Konstantine said, "Sir, it's Caporal Garron on the net. He says that sniper just put his head over the wall to shoot down on us, but he nailed him. Bastard is down."

Apollo just nodded, put the key in the door lock, and turned the latch.

He found himself in a narrow stairwell, and after a short trek up two flights of stairs they entered a small room full of equipment. Spread over the floor were small gas stoves, sleeping bags, winter clothing, military equipment, and lots of empty 7.62mm ammunition boxes. All of this was spilling out of some heavy civilian Peak 99 backpacks.

Lying in one corner was a man in a black Russian uniform, blood pooled beneath his body and running in small rivulets, mixing with melted snow, and forming a little pink stream toward the drain in the floor.

Apollo realized the Russian team had been operating on Zugspitze undercover, but knowing the Geneva Convention codes as well as Apollo, they had hastily taken off the Wetterdienst overalls and heavy coats once they began to fight. Besides the possibility of being captured out of uniform, which was still a hanging offense, the dishonor of fighting out of their nation's uniform, especially one they had expended many years of sweat and tears to earn, was too much for any warrior to bear.

"Fucking Spetsnaz!" said Apollo. "I know the uniform: the patch with the parachute and inverted dagger. These are Group B personnel. The Russian version of us. Small-unit operators who go in deep. They are using this room as shelter and ammo storage and first aid. This guy must've been killed in the first exchange of fire with One Team."

Apollo added, "Officer's shoulder boards. This guy was a major. Something big is going down."

The *whump whump* of helicopter rotor blades came out of the wind. Apollo said, "Fourth Escadrille helos, right on time."

Now a tremendous hail of gunfire rang against the metal Wetterdienst building.

The door flew open and a man still in a German weather service overcoat crashed through, a rifle in his hands. He'd obviously been fleeing the gunfire from the helicopters, and was stunned to see the three men in alpine military uniforms standing across the room. He made to swing his weapon up at the threat, but Apollo shot the man twice in the face with his HK UMP45. The silencer muffled the shots, and with the bullet storm firing from the two helos above the building, there was no way anyone could hear them. Apollo knew One and Three would be using the helos' fire to close the final hundred meters to the weather station.

Apollo turned to Konstantine. "Call all teams—tell them we've made it inside. We're going to hit the Russians from behind."

After the transmission was sent and acknowledged, the captain led the three-man team out of the building. He dared to look around the corner and saw the helicopter's guns shredding the thick stone-and-brick bulwark at the front of the weather station's perimeter.

Apollo counted six men in their black Spetsnaz uniforms spread out under the bulwark, keeping low as they received fire from the French on-slaught. There were three others crumpled against the wall, clearly either dead or wounded.

The volume of fire from the Dragoons overmatched the Russians, and now they were just hunkering down, trying to figure out how to get back into the fight.

Apollo turned back to the men and gave them a series of hand and arm signals: *Six enemy, around the corner. On my mark we move into position, with each man to take down two enemy.*

Nods from Konstantine and Dariel told him they understood. On cue, all three rounded the wall and opened fire.

Apollo took the high side in a standing firing position while Caporal Konstantine fired from one knee just below his boss's elbows. The Russians swung their silenced VSS rifles on the three Frenchmen. Apollo dropped two with bursts from his HK at five meters. Sergent Dariel didn't let off the trigger, just held it down and raked from his left to his right, eating up the two Russians standing adjacent to each other. It wasn't the controlled-fire discipline they had always practiced, but at this range it was damn effective.

Konstantine's two men slammed against the bulwark; the young capo-ral had shot both men in the face before they managed to return fire.

The three Frenchmen ducked back behind the wall to take stock. The gunfire from the teams on the slopes and the helo door gunners continued outside.

Apollo grabbed Konstantine by the shoulder. "Tell them to cease fire!

They can advance, but do it carefully. There could still be others up in the rocks outside."

In minutes the rest of Apollo's squadron of Dragoons had assaulted up to the stone wall and were yelling to Apollo for permission to ascend the last few feet. Apollo chanced it and stuck his head back around his wall. One of the Russians crawled slowly along the floor, leaving a bloody trail behind him, but the rest lay still.

"You are all clear. On to the objective!" Apollo yelled as he and the others stepped out now, weapons up and at the ready, trained on the Russians lying by the wall and the one crawling slowly away. The smell and sight of warm blood oozing out of the Spetsnaz men bore ghastly witness to the firefight.

Konstantine found a satellite radio, but it had been destroyed. Likely the Russians had been given orders to smash all their sensitive equipment if they became compromised.

Apollo climbed a ladder and looked up at the top of the weather station. Positioned high on the mast there was another laser device, identical to the one on the mast at the observatory. He found it interesting that this device had been left intact when all the other equipment had been destroyed.

"Caporal Konstantine, I want you and whomever you need to get onto that tower and dismantle that Russian laser. I don't know what the hell it is, but I don't like it. Then send a team over to the other one on the German side of the peak and dismantle it. Take the long way around—*nobody* goes back on that damn catwalk!"

"Yes, sir."

Apollo turned to the wounded Russian lying on the cold concrete. One of the Dragoon medics was evaluating his condition. "How bad?" Apollo asked.

"He'll survive."

The French captain smiled. "Well, then, let's see if this Russkie has enough juice left in him to talk. Grab Konstantine—his mom is Ukrainian; he speaks a little."

Apollo went back inside to the Russian major's body. He opened the man's coat and looked through his blood-caked uniform under the Wetterdienst overalls. A wallet, some keys, and some papers. Apollo looked at one, a hand-drawn diagram. The words were all in Cyrillic, and they looked like notes in Russian. With it was a small acetate map overlay.

Konstantine arrived, his eyes wild with the adrenaline of combat. "Hey, boss, that was insane. You heard about Pierre? Took a round through the forehead."

"I heard. I need you to translate while I interrogate the prisoner. But first look at this."

Apollo handed him the acetate overlay and the notes. The young man looked over them as wisps of steam rose from his sweat-soaked uniform.

"The overlay, what do the markings mean?" Apollo asked.

"Just letters, sir. Letters and dots. Looks like it would fit maybe a one-to-one-hundred-thousand-scale map."

"I had the same impression, but without the original map or some datum markers, it'd be impossible to find out any locations on it."

"Yes, sir, but this word on the far left next to the dot is Russian for 'mine.' Like 'my position,' maybe? If that's true, and we have the scale right, all these points to the east just might show where other teams of Russians are operating."

Apollo grabbed his own map of the same scale and put it on the table next to the cryptic Russian one.

"I think you're onto something." Apollo lined the last dot in the string of other Cyrillic-lettered dots on the Russian acetate map overlay.

"Look, men, if the last dot corresponded with the Russian position here at Zugspitze, then the next one over is at this spot." Apollo pointed to a location in the Elbe Sandstone Mountains, on the Czechian-German border.

He looked to Dariel. "Tell the men to load up. Ensure the wounded are successfully evac'd, and then we go to Czechia."

Around him, the high German Alps drew their cloak once more over the ancient peaks, the living, and the dead in a heavy, raging shroud of snow and wind.

CHAPTER 23

A pair of Russian Su-57 fighter jets stood wingtip to wingtip on the airport's service apron directly adjacent to the runway. A light snow had fallen during the night and a fog of frozen ice crystals hung in the air. The old Russian enclave here in Smolensk called this kind of winter fog "the Nun's Veil," but the pilots of the two aircraft wouldn't be sticking around long enough to learn any local phrases or even to see the snow melt off in the morning sun. They had an exceedingly exact timeline to meet and needed to be airborne in under two minutes.

The Su-57 was one of the world's newest and most advanced all-weather fighter/attack aircraft. The Russian air force colonel in the cockpit of the jet on the left and the officer in the other jet—himself a full commander in the Russian navy—were a perfect match for the three-billion-ruble planes, as they were two of the world's premier pilots.

There were twenty-six Su-57 aircraft in tonight's action, each paired with similarly elite men. All the other planes had either already launched or soon would be launching from remote bases like this one, and all were to converge on their separate targets at exactly the same time.

The Su-57 was equipped with three rearward-facing HD cameras, two capable of locking onto pursuing targets so the pilot would not need to "check six." But Russian air force colonel Ivan Zolotov ignored the cameras now, flexed his shoulders to pivot and look first back left, then right. The aircraft seat's gray nylon quad-harness straps strained at the unnatural motion. He released his grasp from the flight stick and throttle as he turned, then instinctively regripped them as he turned forward again after checking aft with his own eyes.

Zolotov's many years of experience had taught him to release and regrip anytime he checked the three, six, or nine o'clock positions or the aircraft would respond to the tiny, involuntary muscle movements caused by straining his torso. Many pilots had learned that mistake in the air, which was to say they learned the hard way. The momentary disorientation caused them to grip the stick or throttle and pitch the aircraft unpredictably, sometimes cracking their heads on the glass canopy in the process.

Colonel Zolotov was still on the ground, but his recent experiences hopping from airfield to airfield across the Russian Federation had also taught him to look back to ensure both engine cowlings and the tail fin stabilizing lines had been properly removed by the ground crew.

The Su-57 was, after all, a fifth-generation aircraft, one like no other in Russia's arsenal. These new Sukhoi had different safety protocols from other Russian fighters, and whenever Su-57 pilots of the 14th Fighter Aviation Regiment, nicknamed the "Red Talons," took off from any airfield not native to their parent squadron, the ground crew was sometimes so unfamiliar with the modern aircraft that they failed to do their jobs properly.

But today's crew at the almost-defunct Smolensk-Severnyy Aerodrome in far western Russia proved to be different. It was clear the airport's military section had been briefed on the importance of Zolotov's squadron's mission, although he was certain they had no idea of their ultimate objectives. Zolotov had noted a doubling of the ground crew, including a large group of guards patrolling the air base.

This mission would not be one for prying eyes.

Confident the engine cowlings had been removed from the intakes and the rudder tie-downs had been unfastened from the tail fins and stowed, Colonel Ivan Zolotov, commander of the elite Red Talon Squadron of the 14th FAR, centered his shoulders in the cockpit seat in anticipation of the final go from the ground crew.

He held the throttle with his left hand lightly, eyes fixed on the sergeant on the ground who indicated "All okay" with the final flight and engine check. The sergeant rendered a long and formal salute.

Right on time, he thought.

Colonel Zolotov flicked the thruster ignition, then cracked a quick return salute.

The young sergeant with the 12th Aviation Support Squadron wouldn't be able to see this pilot's face, only a mirrored visor, further shrouded by the darkness. The only identifiers on the aircraft were his rank painted on the fuselage: *Polkóvnik*, which meant "Regimentary" in Russian, corresponding to full colonel in the West.

And there was one more, unusual marking on the aircraft: the red talon on the tail.

Colonel Z's control panel read, "Green across the board," with some slight variations on the digital gauges, all of which the colonel took in with his highly trained eyes.

And he looked over the gauges with pleasure, because the Su-57 did something revolutionary for a modern jet—even, *especially*, for a fifth-generation fighter.

It trusted the pilot.

The 57 had full instrumentation. Each gauge, indicator, marking, and annunciator was perfectly calibrated and not dumbed down to prevent pilot error or information overload. Sukhoi Design Bureau, the new premier conglomerate aircraft designer, had gotten it right as far as the pilots in the Red Talon Squadron were concerned.

Colonel Z looked over to his wingman, Commander Tatiyev. With a slicing motion of his hand, he signaled the order to take off. Tatiyev raised his Nomex-gloved hand in his fighter's bubble canopy, making a fisted O with his thumb and fingers, the Russian sign for "Ready and okay."

Zolotov gently throttled up, and the twin NPO Saturn Izdeliye-30 jet engines obeyed his commands, responding with a hissing that quickly increased to a smooth roar. The engines sounded clean and new, and felt truly impressive in their responsiveness, with none of the hesitancy or the gravelly whine he was used to in his older Su-35S.

He flicked the switch releasing the arresting gear on both wings' wheel brakes and then the hydraulic braking system control, fully opening the engine's air intakes.

The aircraft both had a full weapons loadout hanging from their pylons, so Colonel Z knew they'd have to use the full length of the airstrip to compensate for the heavier takeoff profile.

The two Su-57s streaked down the pristine Runway 26, building speed in front of long plumes of flame.

In moments they lifted off into the black, cold December night.

Colonel Z watched the wheels fold up into Commander Tatiyev's jet on his right as his own did the same below him.

He has the knack, thought Colonel Z as he glanced at their wingtips, only two meters separating them. *Perfectly level and not an ounce of stick too much.*

As the overall mission commander he noted with interest that he would not give one order for the rest of the flight, because they were not to break radio silence for the entirety of their mission.

He settled back in his seat and thought of the hours ahead.

CHAPTER 24

Forty-four-year-old Colonel Ivan Glowski paced slowly behind his men, watching them work, although there wasn't much to see. Like robots, the three rows of computer cyberespionage specialists sat still and silent at their computer workstations in the darkened room, their eyes focused on their screens.

The twenty-six hackers were soldiers in the Russian military's GRU, the Main Intelligence Directorate, but they hardly looked the part. Not one man in the unit wore the requisite black tie with his gray-green dress uniform. Half didn't wear their tunic jackets at all, opting instead for just their military-issue T-shirts and uniform belts and pants. Many were in flip-flops, and their workstations were no more orderly than their attire.

But Colonel Glowski didn't care. He had recruited every one of these computer specialists, selecting them based on their dossiers of successful hacks, plucking them from various other units in the army and navy. In his grueling assessment interviews he'd personally grilled each of them to determine their skill level.

Glowski himself wore a uniform, in contrast to his men, but it didn't fit him at all. Unlike colonels in other Moscow commands, who wore custom-tailored finery, Glowski wore a jacket that was too short in the sleeves and his collared shirt pinched his thick neck, so he left it unbuttoned and wore his tie only for official functions.

But his troops loved him for his lack of prim and proper military decorum. It made them feel special and indicated that they weren't really in the strict, regulated part of the Russian military forces. The hackers were a rebellious group. The men appreciated Glowski's treatment of them, and they called him "Papabear" as a term of endearment.

But even though they enjoyed freedom from basic military discipline under Colonel Glowski, things were far from lax.

The unit's designation, officially speaking, was APT28. This was what was on the rosters of the GRU. But to the Americans and the rest of the West, they were known by another name.

"Fancy Bear." The name came from a coding system ascribed to the Russian unit by the West when they were still unidentified. The Russian hackers themselves enjoyed the name, so they now referred to their control center as "the Bear's Den."

They were Russia's most elite hacking arm, and Colonel Glowski's countdown clock, hanging above the front 162-centimeter computer screen, told them they were twenty minutes away from their most important operation ever.

Colonel Glowski peered over his military-issue spectacles at the big monitor. He and the men had nicknamed it "the Pageantry." It served very little real purpose, but visitors to the control room were unable to understand the hackers' universe without some kind of visual representation. Because of this, "the Pageantry" had become APT28's showpiece. Their main attraction. The data regularly displayed on the central screens was portrayed in flickering, changing colors that looked like a row of Christmas trees.

In reality, each "tree" represented an "enemy," a NATO or U.S. mainframe computer or critical terminal or junction. A mini-forest of sorts, the trees displayed a cascade of icons colored yellow or green, with a few switching occasionally to red.

Ivan "Papabear" Glowski turned away from the monitor and looked at the personal computer screens of his men now. Needless to say, Glowski was a master cyberespionage expert in his own right, known to stop his relentless pacing and rush to his own workstation to assist his men when things got intense.

And right now he had every expectation that such intensity would be called for in exactly nineteen minutes.

NORTH ATLANTIC
KAZAN
25 DECEMBER
00:12

The *Kazan* was one of Russia's newest *Yasen*-class nuclear fast-attack submarines. She was a sleek and modern vessel, powerful, stealthy, and incredibly deadly. Named after the capital of Tatarstan, a republic in the Volga District, she had been lurking for days in the North Atlantic, but now she hung in the dark, cold depths west of the northern tip of Ireland.

The K-561, as her hull number designated her, barely moved and made hardly a sound. Descending slowly, with only two degrees down bow-angle, the massive vessel's screw turned just one revolution every five seconds, narrowly defeating the ocean currents as she sank lower.

The red battle lanterns were lit inside the seafoam-green-painted bridge of the *Kazan*, giving off eerie light. The shiny copper instruments, pipes, and valves shone with a ruby-colored glow in the half darkness.

Captain 2nd Rank Georg Etush looked over the control stations in front of his men around the bridge. He knew every gauge, switch, and button by heart. He had personally served at four of the positions in front of him on other subs in his two decades of service.

Every few seconds one of the men would look up from his work and glance at the captain as he stood at the railing; the men's eyes reflected the battle lights, but Etush knew they were looking past him at the nuclear chronometer on the wall to his right.

Etush liked this spot on the bridge; it would give him the opportunity to look into the men's eyes and read their moods. And right now he could tell they were anxious. He surmised every one of their stomachs, like his own, was churning as silently but as powerfully as the ship's engines several decks below their feet.

He was pleased with the men's performance so far. In just the past few hours they'd passed close to three opponents: an *Ohio*-class ballistic missile submarine, a *Virginia*-class fast-attack submarine, both of the U.S. Navy, and a Norwegian *Ula*-class patrol sub. It had taken hard work and skill, but the *Kazan* had evaded all three.

Etush thought of the other Russian subs in his pack. Only a few people at the Admiralty Building in Saint Petersburg, and perhaps a few more at the Ministry of Defense and the Kremlin, knew exactly how many vessels were being employed in this operation. His own understanding of the threat his nation would face soon enough made him believe all four *Yasen*-class subs in service would be tasked, and surely vessels of other classes would be employed as well.

Etush didn't know the full scope of the operation, but there was an energy back at Flotilla HQ like nothing he'd seen before. Many of the boat captains he'd seen passing in the halls were electrified, switched on. Despite the fact they'd all been ordered not to breathe a word of any of this, he felt he could almost tell by sight in the mess hall who had been selected for this mission.

He'd told himself now not to worry about anything outside his control. He and his men owned one small piece of the undersea puzzle, and they would do their jobs.

His stomach continued churning as he looked back across the bridge.

More red glowing eyes on the clock.

More red glowing eyes on him.

The United States and other NATO powers kept a close eye on Russian submarine traffic out of Sayda Inlet, home of Russia's Northern Fleet. Analysts had noted the pattern and distribution of Russian submarines leaving port and being detected around the Atlantic to be more or less normative of Russian fleet actions for this time of year. In fact, if there was anything suspicious, it was that most all the vessels left port on schedule with nothing much amiss in the Russian naval yards. This improved efficiency wasn't lost on the NATO intelligence experts, but it was briefed as a new high point for Russian fleet operational readiness. Just one more reason to keep an eye on them.

It followed ten years of continuous progress for the Russian navy, after all, so it was no surprise.

The item NATO never could have determined from their surveillance, however, was that a select portion of Russia's undersea fleet was, in fact, coordinating their actions on separate targets across the Atlantic seafloor.

While the West remained oblivious, the submarines involved in the opening salvo of Operation Red Metal converged on their targets in near-perfect synchronicity.

Captain Etush squeezed the brass railing in front of him and said, "Level on the bow. All ahead three-quarters speed. Come to course."

The men on the bridge sprang to action, moving like clockwork in harmony with the vessel. The two planesmen both pulled the sub's yoke control, carefully watching their gauges to keep the boat level as the engines churned up. The men at Ballast Control bled a slight air differential from the forward trim tanks to the main ballast tanks. The navigator reaffirmed his plot both digitally and on the large seafloor map in the center of the control room.

"Sir, navigation reads target designated: *Midgardsormenan*. Distance: two nautical miles. Target attack run in three minutes."

"Very well. Helm, steady. Weapons cross-check, then weapons free; Dmitry, you may launch when ready."

"Aye, Captain," replied the weapons officer.

"Navigator?" Etush said quickly.

"Aye, Captain?"

"You own the time."

"Aye, sir." The navigator reached over near the captain and set the ship's red digital timer to twenty minutes. He would start the clock the instant the weapons officer fired the first of their torpedoes.

The entirety of the men's conversations, including the strict issuance of vital commands, was passed between them in tones that did not rise to a level above the low chatter in a coffee shop: more than a whisper, but certainly below normal conversational level. Their time beneath the waves made them superstitious of raising their voices lest any sound be heard by their enemies.

And right now, those enemies could be anywhere, perfectly silent themselves but listening for signs of a Russian sub.

Etush said, "Sonar, last American contact?"

"Captain, last contact with the *Amerikanski* was an *Ohio*-class, verified as USS *Georgia*. Eighteen hours ago. Her bearing: two-two-zero degrees, eighteen nautical miles. Plot had her as steady and on course. That would place her bearing one-nine-one degrees at one-six-three nautical miles distance. Nothing further."

"Very well," said Captain Etush. "Anything more on the *Ula*?"

"Sir, no acoustic, but she still plots on course."

"Very well." The captain wasn't overly concerned about the Norwegian submarine, but he didn't like not knowing exactly where she was. "Keep updating estimated range and bearing."

"Aye, sir."

The weapons officer called out now. "Sir, notifying the bridge of weapon one ready now. Timing set and confirmed by all weapons. Twenty minutes to complete full attack run on all three targets."

"Very well. Navigator, any replots?"

"Negative, sir. Current plot and attack run holds. Recommend steady as she goes."

"Understood. Helm, maintain course and speed."

Seconds later the weapons officer called out, a little louder than usual, which Etush knew was due to adrenaline. "Sir, launch on target one. Torpedo is in the water."

As he said this, the navigator touched the clock and it began its countdown. If their timing and plot were perfect, their mission would finish exactly on time.

There was no shudder, no whooshing sound, nothing really above the noises of the sea slipping by outside the ship to indicate that the *Kazan* had just fired the first naval salvo of the next war.

In spite of the cold air in the boat, Etush noted the two helmsmen had broken out in a sweat. *It's all in the hands of a couple of twenty-year-old boys at this point,* he thought, and he realized he'd be sweating, too, if he were in their shoes.

But he was the captain, and a much greater responsibility befell him. Even a sign of perspiration or nervous mannerism would make some of his men doubt his conviction. From his twenty-three years at sea, he had learned at times like this to minimize his movements across the bridge and to focus on the minute principles of navigating and steering his boat.

He stayed perfectly still, standing under one of the sub's downdraft ventilation systems, which blew cold air through his graying brown hair.

The sonar operator called out: "Bridge, sonar reports contact, bearing six-three degrees. Sir, it's the Norwegian *Ula*. She is twelve nautical miles and closing, speed nineteen knots."

If Etush had not been under the ventilation system, he, too, would have burst out into a sweat. Still, it brought a prickle of fresh perspiration to the back of his neck. He was an experienced enough seaman to do the calculations in his head even before his navigator spelled out the equation. At bearing sixty-three degrees and the ship driving at three-quarters speed, the Russian and Norwegian vessels would converge in about six minutes. The Norwegians would have no idea what the Russian *Yasenevo*-class was up to, but they would certainly be able to detect them.

Navigation soon completed the calculation the captain had done in his head in two seconds. "Captain, on this heading and speed, we will intercept the *Ula* in five minutes forty-nine seconds."

"Understood, Navigator. Sonar, confirm all data. Navigator, replot for full speed; veer angle on target as necessary. If we can't lay a clean row, we can still bomb all our cables at an intersection. Prepare and lay a new course to run the next two targets. We have a mission that takes priority."

"Aye, calculating."

Captain Etush watched the clock in silence for a moment: sixteen minutes remained. Speeding up meant the weapons crew would have to reset the timers on the torpedoes. He knew he'd have to trust them to just figure it out, but he couldn't resist the urge to state the obvious.

"Weapons, reset all torpedoes to zero and stand by for new timing data."

"Understood, sir," answered Dmitry. Deep down belowdecks, five sailors and one officer would be furiously scrambling to zero out the SMDM-2C tube-launched torpedo mine. The SMDM-2C series of sea mine was new, vastly improved over previous generations, but the modernized version still required the weapons officer to unscrew a plate on the cavity and reprogram the timing. With the *Kazan*'s first target properly laid, there remained two more, and the next target was only five minutes away.

"Navigation, status?" he demanded, still trying not to step on his men but watching his navigation section as they furiously computed the data.

"Captain, triple confirming now, sending initial data to torpedo room. We have the timing updates. One moment for final confirmation." Dmitry looked back at one of his men, who gave a thumbs-up. In the same monotone, but with more edge of adrenaline kicking in, Dmitry turned back to his captain. "Sir, navigation update. Recommend speed to flank, thirty knots, course change to zero-three-zero degrees magnetic."

"Bridge, Helm, do it."

The new plot, course, and speed would have already been digitally transmitted to the helm. But Etush had been in the navy long enough to follow sea protocols even in his sleep.

Three minutes to target, Etush noted. *Thirteen minutes on the clock. Still a full ten minutes to the last target. Barely enough time to reload the second torpedo into its tube.*

"Sir, weapon reprogram successful," said Dmitry.

"Very well. Inform the bridge once launched."

"Aye, Captain. Launch in on target two, designated 'cable AC-One,' in twenty seconds."

Etush glanced at the helmsmen. The two bald-headed boys held their yokes in a death grip.

The weapons officer chanted off the seconds until launch. "Ten . . . nine . . . eight . . . seven . . . six . . . five . . ."

Etush looked at the panel showing the status of the second torpedo tube and saw that it still indicated red. It was not ready to launch.

". . . four . . . three . . ." The tube coded from red to green. ". . . two . . . one . . . Launch on target designated 'AC-One.'"

The reply came instantly, with a twinge of relief from the weapons officer. "Torpedo is away."

"Helm, recommend new heading, zero-one-eight degrees magnetic, thirty-three knots."

Damn! thought Etush. They were almost at maximum speed.

"Do it."

"Sir, Sonar reporting. Target zero one, the *Ula,* now bearing three-two-two degrees from bow. She will slip behind us in two minutes at this rate. She has picked up an active ping and has us locked."

Etush kept his voice calm. "Inevitable. Keep the boat steady on final target. Work up a continuous solution." There was a hesitation in the acknowledgment of the order. Etush read the pall of nervousness permeating the bridge and attempted to alleviate it. He said, "She has no cause to fire on us. Our mine torpedo has slipped silently to the bottom by now. Our Norwegian friends could not have detected the launch."

Sonar spoke hesitantly. "Sir . . . calculating her sonar radius, the *Ula* will be within range to detect the launch on the final target."

"Yes, likely, but I am banking on her not wanting to start hostilities unless provoked."

"Sir, the *Ula* is directly abeam of us bearing two-six-three degrees, four nautical miles."

"Very well." Etush looked at the torpedo panel. Of the ten torpedo tubes, tubes one and two showed yellow for "launched and in recovery" mode, and number seven was in green, or "launch" status. Only tube three showed "red," or "unable to launch."

"Weapons?"

"Yes, sir. We're on it. Message from the torpedo room . . . The third torpedo-mine panel will not open. They report the screws are stripped."

"Then they have six minutes to figure it out." Etush said it calmly, although his insides were screaming.

CHAPTER 25

In the Bear's Den, the men of APT28 all kept their eyes on the clock above the big screen on the front wall. They were seconds away from the first cyberattack of *Operacyia Krasnyi Metal*, and the criticality of perfect timing had been pounded into their psyches for months.

Colonel Glowski knew they were ready, because most of the work had already been done. They'd spent the past two months feverishly perpetrating cookie theft attacks, turning on the Trojan horse packets already embedded in their NATO hosts, opening latent back doors, dry hacking, and launching watering hole attacks.

Now it was time to exploit all of their attack paradigms at once.

Glowski looked at the digital clock, his heart racing like a submarine commander's while cruising just over the Atlantic seabed or a highly decorated combat pilot's while streaking through the sky in a fifth-generation fighter.

Thinking of himself now, his responsibility in this operation, caused him to harken back to a time just ten weeks earlier when a pair of VIPs entered the Bear's Den. He'd been informed that the two generals in charge of ground operations in Red Metal would be visiting, and he and his team prepared the space accordingly. Cleaning up, donning ties, forcing chronically slumped shoulders back just as the door opened.

His men were truly intimidated by the arrival of the two visitors, even the young guys who didn't recognize them.

But Glowski recognized them, and he knew he was in the presence of giants. Sabaneyev, who appeared markedly young to be a colonel general, looked and spoke like a national television newsreader.

And Lazar . . . *the* Boris Petrovich Lazar. The Lion of Dagestan. Burly, weathered, and round-faced, but also the most storied general in the Russian military in a generation.

True field commanders, Colonel Glowski had thought at the time.

And intimidating as *fuck.*

The generals surveyed Glowski and his men as they performed one of the important preparatory attacks on a Polish air defense radar chain. They watched in silence, mostly, but they asked two of his lead hackers some questions.

What a day that was, Glowski thought now.

Papabear pushed the commanders out of his mind and redirected his thoughts to his own battlefield. *What a day this will be.*

Looking up at the Pageantry, he saw a green light blinking at the top of each of the ten "Christmas trees," meaning they had pinged previously discovered back channels, and they were open. This left enemy networks exposed; the only thing left to do for APT28 was to flip some switches to fire the activation codes into them. This would be done manually, because it was more covert than placing initiation times on the intrusive codes already embedded in the system. Glowski had deemed that too dangerous.

So the codes were left waiting for their triggers.

Other of the "Christmas tree" hierarchies required his men to actively hack the network and then inject a code. Of course the twenty-four cyberespionage specialists here in the Bear's Den had seeded hundreds of other government, industry, and military targets with ruse codes for months to prevent these ten hierarchies from being noted as unique.

It was all part of the cyber game.

Team Black Bear was the group of hackers responsible for Germany. As the timer over the Pageantry clicked off to the exact second of their attack, each man began tapping his keys.

The rest of the room remained silent, all staring at their monitors. Black Bear's work began to show up on the 162-centimeter screen, the German hierarchies filling from bottom to top.

The top changed from green to red as the Russian computer code just shut all German NATO terminals down.

BELARUS

25 DECEMBER

0028

As Colonel Ivan Zolotov flew west over Belarus, he looked down to his A. Lange & Söhne wristwatch. A much-loved heirloom that had belonged to his great-uncle, a tough old bastard who eventually died from cirrhosis, but not before giving young Ivan the wristwatch and the story of how he acquired it.

Leningrad, Zhukov's 3rd Shock Army. October of 1943. Colonel Z's great-uncle had described in detail the look on the German officer's face as he hacked the man's forearm off using his bayonet while two of his privates held him down.

The watch and the great-uncle had both survived the brutal war, and Colonel Z thought of it as his good-luck charm.

For the next hour, every altitude adjustment, every kilometer he and his wingman traversed, was completely scripted. He would check the timing against the timepiece on his wrist, and his great-uncle's watch would see battle again.

Looking at it, he saw they were exactly two minutes from crossing into Poland.

The Red Talon fighters had taken off in pairs from six Russian and Belarusian air bases. Each pair would fly dangerously close to each other along preplanned courses, making broad, sweeping turns at predetermined locations. Their flight profiles—for this stage of their mission, anyway— were designed to appear to NATO air defense technicians like those of Russian tankers or routine passenger jets.

Colonel Z checked the A. Lange & Söhne once more, then glanced at the cockpit's chronometer.

One minute to go.

He pushed the throttle forward a touch and noted that Commander Tatiyev responded, syncing his own speed almost instantly. He flicked a switch and opened a view below the left wing on his HUD camera.

Shatskyi National Park passed ten kilometers to the south. He was certain Ukrainian antiair gunners would be monitoring him now, but that was fine, because in less than one minute the Poles to the West would not be. Or at least their daisy chain of radar would not be. He was confident that their computer systems would turn off right on schedule . . . seconds before he crossed into their territory.

The independent AA stations were another story, but speed and altitude would prevent any danger from the ground; of this he was also confident.

Pora! *Time!* He said it to himself, looking once more at the time as he pulled a hard right bank.

He saw the lights of the Polish city of Włodawa racing below.

He was over the border.

With the easy but hostile act of crossing into Polish airspace, his airframe and that of the rest of Red Talon Squadron had just opened air hostilities with the West.

KAZAN
NORTH ATLANTIC
25 DECEMBER
0031

On board the *Kazan*, Captain Etush and his crew had less than three minutes to fire their third and final torpedo mine.

But the mine wasn't cooperating.

The whole mission in jeopardy over a few shit machine screws, Etush thought. Tough to fault the torpedo's designers. The SMDM-2C panels were not meant to be hurriedly removed and replaced as the torpedo crew had just done. Program them once, then fire them—that was the manufacturer's intended design. Not take apart, reprogram, then take apart again.

But things always went wrong in combat.

Etush turned to his veteran weapons officer. "Dmitry?"

"Sir, we will launch on target cable TAT-15 on time."

Etush looked at his old comrade. The man seemed cool right now. Etush had to admire Dmitry's confidence in his weapons, though he himself was worried.

"Bridge, *Ula*-class contact is now five nautical miles bearing one-nine-seven degrees. She's outside torpedo range, Captain."

Etush grunted in acknowledgment. Well, that was one thing off his mind, although he recognized that if they were unable to connect their last torpedo mine, he'd have a lot more to worry about than the little Norwegian submarine.

"Thirty seconds to target," said the helm. Etush looked at the weapons console and saw tube three was still glowing red.

"Twenty seconds."

Etush fixed his stare on Dmitry, although the man had his back turned . . . one hand with the weapons phone to his ear, the other hand steadying himself as he looked at the panel.

"Ten seconds."

Etush looked beyond him at the panel, and torpedo tube three remained red.

"Sir . . . five seconds to target," and then: "Captain, we are on target now."

Dmitry lowered the phone from his ear and turned to Etush. "Sir, weapons reports launch, on time, on target. Third fish is in the water." A slight smile drew across his face. The third tube showed red still, although the number seven tube showed it had just launched and was now indicating "yellow," recovery mode.

"Dmitry . . . ," said Captain Etush. "How the hell did—"

"Sir, the men left the damaged torpedo in tube three and reprogrammed the device loaded in tube seven instead. Faster this way."

Etush couldn't help but repress a smile, and the bridge released a collective sigh.

"Sir, Sonar. *Ula* will pass near the target during detonation. She will likely catch some of the blast."

The entire bridge looked up at the ship's clock. The chronometer still ticked, but now, instead of counting down, it was counting up. It showed one minute till detonation.

"Bad luck for her," said Etush.

More than a minute later an undersea explosion could be heard through the hull of the *Kazan*, and a wave shuddered the boat. It was soon followed by two softer thumping sounds.

Seconds passed before sonar reported, "Sir, *Ula*'s been hit: she was caught up near the mine. She has launched. Three torpedoes in the water. Sir, we are being fired upon. They must have assumed we attacked her. They are well outside of range, though. Those fish will drop off well before reaching us."

"Okay . . . He must've gotten a good blast, a crippled boat, and he's mad." Etush smiled.

The sonarman spoke again. "He's turning to starboard, sir. Hull popping sounds. He's surfacing! He's out of the fight!"

Etush nodded. "He's had enough of us, but be ready for other threats."

"Aye, sir."

The captain turned to Dmitry. "Weapons, I presume you have some more tricks up your skirt?"

"Aye, Captain, five other tricks are loaded and will be ready with Nav's latest solutions."

"Very well. Gentlemen, the first salvos of war have begun. And may God have mercy upon the men of the sea for what's about to come."

APT28 CONTROL ROOM
MOSCOW, RUSSIA
25 DECEMBER
0032

Colonel Glowski continued pacing the floor of the Bear's Den, keeping an eye behind all his teams of cyberespionage specialists.

"Sir?" one of his analysts from Team Grizzly Bear, the U.S. hacking team, called out. "Confirmation on all channels; all U.S. and NATO transatlantic fiber-optic cables just went off-line. Our mimicry systems are established and already taking and faking NATO classified Internet traffic. Transfer mainframes systems are broadcasting and pinging returns. Poisoned watering holes continue to distribute Trojan horses downstream. All systems are up and running in Europe and America."

"Good work, team," said Glowski. He looked around and was met with smiles and grins. He couldn't help grinning a bit himself, but soon his smile disappeared. "Let's not get cocky—the next ten minutes are vital. Back to work."

POLISH AIR RADAR CENTRAL HQ
POZNAŃ, POLAND
25 DECEMBER
0033

A young Polish radar technician looked at his screen in confusion for nearly ten seconds before activating his intercom link to the watch captain.

"Sir, I think I have an intrusion. Sector Peter-Victor-King, Southwest. Vicinity Lublin."

"What do you mean, 'think'?"

"Well, sir, it *was* there; then it was gone. The border towers sent a signal; then they all blinked out. All systems are reporting green now. Everything seems to be in order."

"Are the other outstations reporting normally?"

"Yes, sir, all stations are showing green on my board. It all looks good, sir. Must be another glitch like that one that happened last Saturday."

The captain paused, then asked, "When have we ever had *all* stations indicating green?"

The radar operator cocked his head, eyes still transfixed on his screen. "Never. There's always one or more of them malfunctioning or not reporting."

The captain turned to the communications officer. "Alert NATO immediately."

The radarman questioned this. "But, sir, the systems are actually pinging back to us really well. All the daisy-chained radars are intact."

"I don't care—it doesn't feel right. Just do it."

The radioman was already tuning to the NATO frequency. "Copy, sir. I'll send the alert message now."

CHAPTER 26

NATO AIRBORNE EARLY WARNING & CONTROL FORCE (NAEW&C)

OPS AND RADAR INTEGRATION CENTER

GEILENKIRCHEN, GERMANY

25 DECEMBER

0035

In a dark room in Germany full of American military personnel, a young Air Force technical sergeant keyed his microphone to contact his watch officer, who now sat just seventy-five feet away. "Sir, I just got a second alert from Poland. This one from Poznań. The first one was recalled as an error, but this one is being reported as a potential single radar contact that is now lost."

Captain Watten was in his nearby office, looking at pictures on his unclassified computer of his daughter's eighth-grade Christmas pageant. With a sigh he looked over to his in-box and began shuffling through the night's MCS, electronic classified message traffic. After a moment he settled on the right page. "We had another overnight memo from the Pentagon. Here it is. 'There is concern from COMUSEUCOM that Poland might exaggerate the war-gaming in Belarus to increase the number of future NATO pre-position forces.' We're supposed to avoid getting pulled into anything while the Russians are active in Belarus. The Poles really want us as scared of the Russians as they are.

"So . . . there are no reports of incursions from any other stations?"

"No, sir. Likely somebody hit 'send' too quickly on the alert."

The captain thought a moment. He didn't think there was anything to this report, but he also knew he had to cover his own ass. "Okay, check down with Integrated Radar Team Sierra to be sure. I'll call it down to the war room and have them send a message back to Mons," he said, referring to the NATO HQ in Mons, Belgium.

Watten then said, "Watch station. Message the NMCC." The National Military Command Center was the Pentagon's version of an alert center.

A voice in his ear replied, "Yes, sir. On it now."

Captain Watten went back to the pictures of his daughter's pageant on his unclassified computer. "Let me know if you hear anything back."

He clicked a few more times, but the pages wouldn't load. "Great," he said. "Does someone know if the unclass network is down? I can't get on Facebook."

Just then the tech sergeant called over to Watten in his office again. "Sir, AC Ramstein is calling on the landline. They say they've been hacked."

Watten refreshed his browser continuously on the unclassified network, still trying to get onto Facebook. "What do they want *us* to do about it? They need to call tech support or NSA or something."

"Copy, sir. I'll let them know."

POLAND
25 DECEMBER
0041

Two Su-57s flew two hundred meters over Poleski National Park at Mach 1.1.

Colonel Ivan Zolotov glanced to his right, outside his canopy, and looked through the darkness toward the blacked-out plane next to him. He could barely make it out but was pleased to see the naval commander was flying directly level with Zolotov's aircraft, their wingtips only a meter apart now. Their close, disciplined flying pattern would make them look like one aircraft if they were even picked up on radar at all.

The pilots had flown this route nearly sixty times in the flight simulators, always careful to remain low, fast, and together. This part was vital to their mission's success. They could not, even for an instant, fly too high and risk getting picked up on the independent Polish radar systems as they traversed the nation.

The other pilots on the mission would be doing just the same as Zolotov and Tatiyev right now, flying farther to the south in southern Poland and across Ukraine and into Czechia.

In minutes Zolotov oriented himself on a highway, and his two-ship flight passed over snow-covered wheat fields near Puławy. They remained low, sometimes no more than fifty meters above the gently undulating landscape.

On cue, both pilots throttled back and made a slight course correction, still somewhat hand holding the DK-12 east–west road. At their new speed, their carefully computed formula predicted they would reach their objective waypoint in less than thirty-five minutes, just as planned.

Just like this old German watch on my wrist, Zolotov thought, *I always run on time.*

POLISH AIR RADAR CENTRAL HQ
POZNAŃ, POLAND
25 DECEMBER
0047

"Sir! Radar and missile Defense Batteries Q, R, and T are all calling downstairs to the duty hut on landlines. They say our classified phones aren't working. Battery Q-12 says they confirm an overflight of two Russian fighters."

"Why didn't we pick up anything on radar?"

"They didn't pick it up on radar, either. They *watched* them fly directly over. Said they were supersonic, heading west."

"Gówno," ("Shit") muttered the captain; then he tried but failed to force calm into his orders. "Right. Okay . . . call Land Force Headquarters and inform them immediately."

"Sir, how? The phones aren't working. And the Internet says we are connected, but we're not getting through to anyone."

"Go downstairs. Call on the pay phone if you have to. Just call Warsaw! The *fucking* Russian air force has penetrated the border!"

POLISH-GERMAN BORDER
25 DECEMBER
0054

Colonel Zolotov and Commander Tatiyev crossed the border into Germany near the hamlet of Ostritz as pine trees glistened in silvery moonlight just five to ten meters below their full weapons pylons. The light from the moon made it easy for Colonel Z to see his wingman now, and he held up one finger to notify the naval commander they had one more minute to go.

Colonel Z looked back to his gauges, then heard a barely audible noise above the hum of the jet.

Colonel Z checked to his right just in time to see Tatiyev's aircraft rock unsteadily and then begin to fall back. He shifted his eyes down to his rear HUD rearward-facing camera and saw a cloud of snow burst high into the air behind the other Su-57.

Commander Tatiyev had clipped a treetop.

His airplane began to recover its level flight, but it had lost a few hundred meters to Zolotov.

All this way, and a last-minute accident, thought Zolotov. He maintained his own aircraft fast and level, kept the majority of his attention forward, but continued checking his rearview camera as Commander Tatiyev tried to creep back to parallel with his plane.

The colonel looked again at his watch. *Less than twelve seconds to go. Come on, sailor,* he thought, mentally urging his partner to get back in formation.

An audible beeping tone and a blinking panel light meant a ground-to-air missile had locked onto his aircraft.

Here we go.

The German batteries operated more self-sufficiently than the Polish air defense batteries. Here they could fire independently if the aircraft they queried did not respond or was visually identified as enemy.

Now Zolotov saw and heard the indicator that a missile had been launched at his aircraft, but from far to the north and behind his current position.

No matter: he wouldn't be sticking around here for long.

With his attack profile, the missile would fall well behind them in a few seconds when they began their next maneuver, so he found it unnecessary to apply countermeasures.

He turned to look back over his shoulder, releasing the stick and craning his neck to do so. Through his canopy he could see Commander Tatiyev struggling to catch up, but he was unable to see the condition of his aircraft. Clearly his wingman wouldn't have been able to continue flying if his ship had been badly damaged, but Zolotov worried about any slight issues with the airframe, especially in light of the aerobatics this flight of fighters was about to undertake.

NATO AIRBORNE EARLY WARNING & CONTROL FORCE (NAEW&C)
OPS AND RADAR INTEGRATION CENTER
GEILENKIRCHEN, GERMANY
25 DECEMBER
0059

"Sir, the Germans just fired antiair missiles at targets near Dresden!"

Captain Watten looked up from his frozen desktop computer in astonishment. "Wha . . . *What?*"

"Their radar defense network is all off-line . . . The duty officer in the liaison office just reported in. He said they have radio and some landline comms. Everything else is down."

Tech Sergeant James was now looking at the NAEW, a closed-loop computer that linked the building and all the NATO country liasons, called LNOs, within. "Sir, this might be the real deal. The German LNO downstairs reports radar defense batteries have shot at five different pairs of unidentified aircraft intruding into German airspace. I think we have to assume our computers are compromised. I'm getting nothing whatsoever from Poland, the other NAEW stations, or even the airborne early-warning stations."

"What the *hell* is going on around here?" Captain Watten stood from his desk, then said, "It's fuckin' *Christmas*, for Christ sakes! Alert all NATO. I'll personally call SHAPE and the NATO Response Force. Put *everyone* on alert."

"Copy. Sir, how do I call—"

"Try the STU line," he said, referring to the classified phone system.

"Not working, sir," replied an NCO a few desks away, holding up the STU receiver.

"How about satellite comms?" Captain Watten now asked.

Another tech said, "They are up but severely overloaded, sir. Looks like everyone has shifted to satellite. I'll try to send a priority message."

DRESDEN, GERMANY
25 DECEMBER
0100

It was time.

Colonel Z gave a hard pull back on the stick, rocketing his aircraft higher. He pushed his throttle forward, maintaining supersonic flight, traveling almost two hundred meters per second. He didn't even need the afterburner but he kicked it on to ensure a consistent rate of climb.

He checked his rear monitor once more. Commander Tatiyev was there, about eight hundred meters below him, but he was also climbing rapidly.

Solid flying, he thought. *Good man.*

He looked back out the front of the aircraft; the view through the canopy in front of him showed nothing but starry sky.

The pair of Su-57 fighters continued ascending, nearly vertically, firing up over Germany. In no time they hit 18,000 meters, so high now that, in spite of the g-forces, Colonel Z could feel the forces of the earth's gravitational pull easing slightly as he reached the stratosphere. The aircraft's engines burned fuel at a rapid rate in the ascent, and its acceleration slowed as the aircraft had less atmosphere with which to work.

He made a quick mental calculation; he still had almost 6,800 kilograms of fuel left, over half a tank. He had enough for the last minutes of the mission and then the return, as long as he didn't have to maneuver too much on his egress to avoid enemy forces.

The two aircraft were now almost at their attack position, a specific three-dimensional plot in the sky. This mission required flying to a point 21,000 meters over Germany and launching missiles. From there the smart weapons they carried would do the rest.

The colonel's eyes shot from his HUD altimeter to his GPS, and then to the time on the display.

He even checked his great-uncle's watch, feeling an intense pride as the second hand struck the minute.

Now.

Colonel Zolotov pressed the launch button. Waited a split second, switched the weapons control lever, and pressed the launch button again.

The special ASAT, or anti-satellite missiles, were called OKB-12 and STR-14, and they had been developed in complete secrecy, hidden from the West's knowledge. A first-strike option to be used only when the *rodina* was threatened and the decision had been made to take out one of the West's most important capabilities: its global network of satellites.

The two missiles were actually quite different from each other. One was a short-range satellite killer. The other was designed for longer and higher missions, to travel into space and hit high-earth-orbit satellites, like geostationary GPS platforms.

The Western GPS satellites were easy to kill; they transmitted location data down to earth, without concern that their own signals could lead the STR-14s directly to them. But these GPS satellites orbited at a much higher altitude than the communications sats: nearly 20,000 kilometers. It would take the warhead exactly one hour and twelve minutes to arrive at and destroy its target.

Zolotov watched for a brief moment as the missiles streaked away from his aircraft, vaulting toward space, their solid-fuel rocket motors specially tuned to these conditions. At this altitude and atmosphere there was virtually no air resistance, and the faster and smaller OKB-12 was already approaching speeds of 18,000 kilometers per hour.

The weapons' exceedingly advanced guidance packages would get them close; then they would use the target satellites' own transmissions to home in the last few kilometers.

The flames of the motors flared only slightly as they broke free of the atmosphere by which Colonel Z and Commander Tatiyev were still bound.

All across Central and Western Europe, Red Talon Squadron Su-57s launched missiles against other Western satellites, all timed to hit at the same instant. All satellite communications in Europe, both civilian and military, would begin to fail within minutes, and then all global positioning information would fail just over an hour later.

Europe would be deaf and mute soon, and in an hour it would also be blind.

Zolotov nodded to himself as he saw Commander Tatiyev's missiles streak past on their way to their targets, but there was no more time to enjoy the show. He inverted his aircraft and pulled back on the stick, grunting against the forces his body was subjected to, and then the forces ceased, but his stomach rose into his chest when he experienced complete weightlessness. Soon his canopy was facing nearly vertically and then he began his long descent, nose-diving toward Dresden at Mach 1 and gaining speed.

Colonel Zolotov pulled the aircraft to a heading of zero-eight-zero, back toward Poland. Certainly he and his wingman would have a few more antiaircraft missiles to contend with, but the loss of NATO command-and-control computers, the onset of cellular and landline jams, and soon the loss of satellite communications would make any NATO coordination almost impossible.

As Colonel Z rocketed toward earth, Commander Tatiyev pulled into formation off his right wing. He signaled an O with his hand, and Zolotov gave him one right back.

MOSCOW
APT28 HEADQUARTERS
25 DECEMBER
0125

Colonel Glowski moved behind the Polish team, nicknamed Brown Bear. "Are they discovering the bots?"

The team leader conferred with his men a moment more, then stood up. "No, sir. They are moving over to landlines, though. I am working around their data centers, but Poland's aren't like the German centers. Some are actually old hardwired systems, so we can't hack them. I've pushed into line-two botnets from the North America team. I'm counting on them not having shared any data intrusion tactics with their civilian call centers."

"Ponial," ("Got it") Glowski replied, and moved back over to Black Bear, the German team.

Here the team leader said, "Sir, Germany is blind; they are trying work-arounds every minute. Seems like an automated fail-safe. Their civilian telecom is really advanced, but it can't overcome the DDoS on their call centers. I have a ton of bots working from uncovered, badly guarded

NATO-partnered systems, like Turkey, overloading their STU and classified phone systems, too. Looks like it's holding."

"Good," said the colonel, and he moved to the NATO team.

The team leader here stood and said, "Sir, NATO is in complete disarray, and they are cut off from the United States."

Only now did Glowski grin. He pumped his fists in the air. "We've done it, boys!"

A wild cheer rang out in the room.

CHAPTER 27

Děčínský Sněžník is the highest peak in the Czech Republic's Elbe Sandstone Mountain Range, with an unobstructed view across hundreds of miles of Germany's Elbe Valley to the north. The vista was so commanding that 150 years ago Prince Franz of Hohenstein erected the Děčínský Sněžník Tower on the summit to use as a triangulation point for mapping and navigation through the region. Now the old tower served as a restaurant and rest stop along romantic bike trails used by many German and Czech tourists.

This area was alive in the summer with hikers and bikers who explored the trails through the cliffs and forests of what was locally known as "Bohemian Switzerland." In winter, however, the station and its restaurant were closed, although the manager and his wife lived on the grounds, and they opened the kitchen whenever a small group of brave souls weathered the elements and hiked to the top of Děčínský Sněžník.

The previous day the middle-aged Czech couple had been astonished to look out the window of their kitchen into the fresh snowfall and see well over a dozen heavily laden hikers marching up the road toward them. Both husband and wife excitedly put on their heavy coats and boots, ready to greet the travelers. They then stepped outside the front door, waved their hands at the group approaching some hundred meters away, and were promptly shot dead.

The architect of Red Metal, Colonel Yuri Borbikov, had himself given the order to dispatch the hapless locals. As he neared the tower with the rest of his Spetsnaz troops in civilian clothes, he saw smoke rising from the chimney in the main building, and he knew there would be no way to keep his mission covert with civilians on the property. No one would believe the ruse that he and his sixteen soldiers were just tourists here on a hike. They could fool someone passing by, but once they pulled out their weapons and commandeered the tower to place a laser navigation aid at the top, it was a safe bet that their cover would be blown.

So Borbikov had ordered the compromise removed.

The colonel didn't have to be here; Spetsnaz could have accomplished this objective in northern Czechia without him. But Yuri Borbikov saw himself as a soldier as well as a leader of soldiers, and he wanted his own boots and his own weapon involved in this operation. Right now he had over two dozen teams taking over railway switching stations, finishing the last details of calibrating the lasers, and monitoring airfields and military bases for aircraft and troop movements. Borbikov knew he could not expect his men to brave any dangers he wasn't prepared to undertake himself, so he had chosen this mission to Czechia at the beginning of Red Metal to demonstrate his willingness to lead from the front.

He planned on doing the same in Africa in a few days' time.

After their late-morning arrival at the tower, the team had spent the entire afternoon and much of the evening setting and calibrating the laser navigation aid. To their surprise they did not encounter any more civilians, in large measure due to the sleet and freezing rain that had persisted throughout most of the day. It was past one a.m. now, and the work was complete other than maintaining the team's security while they waited for their helicopter extraction.

They spent their time availing themselves of the warm fireplace inside the building and the meat and cheeses in the larders meant for weary travelers who happened by at the wooden two-story overlook restaurant. And even though the colonel had forbidden them from doing so, some of the men had snuck mugs of beer from the open tap system.

What the hell? they thought. *We're homeward bound now.* The remaining work would be that of the Spetsnaz teams at the railroad junctions.

For this group, the European part of Red Metal was coming to an end. They knew they'd be heading for Africa in just days, so they'd have to clean their weapons, reload their magazines, and pack their bags with warm-weather clothing.

The colonel walked through the snow off the road one hundred meters in front of the tower. Around him the Spetsnaz soldiers carried the last of their gear into the clearing, and there they stacked their packs and equipment cases for easy loading once the helicopters landed.

There was no longer any pretense that they were anything other than a military unit. Although they still wore civilian clothing over their uniforms, AKS-74U carbines hung from slings around their necks, NVGs hung in front of their eyes, and the men carried bandoliers of rifle ammunition and grenades over their shoulders.

Borbikov looked at his watch and saw their extraction wasn't due for another ten minutes, but just then one of his men called over to him from where he sat with his radio.

"The tower watch says he hears helos inbound, sir."

"Very well," Borbikov said. "Tell them to break down the tower watch. I want everyone here at the LZ."

"Yes, sir."

Borbikov flipped down his NVGs, looked up at the big looming tower at the top of the hill, and thought about its history. He hoped to revive the ancient purpose of the structure, this time with some vastly updated technology compared to his nineteenth-century cartography and topography counterparts. The colonel scarcely understood the science behind the ytterbium rare-earth lasers he'd ordered deployed along the route Dryagin's armor would take, but he knew what they did. They allowed the Russian assault forces to "see" their way without the aid of global positioning satellites.

This would give the Russians an incredible advantage over NATO, which by now should be totally blind.

He next scanned the night sky with his NVGs for the three helicopters, knowing they'd be flying without their lights. Just as he heard them in the distance, his radioman said, "Sir, the birds are not responding on the air mission frequency. The coded network IDs show either we or they are not on the correct cryptographic radio band."

Borbikov sighed. He'd punish someone severely for this stupid mistake. "All right. Deploy flares."

Two sergeants moved away from the pack and pulled the pins on four flares. Each flare ignited with a loud pop that echoed crisply against the wood line of the dark forest all around them. The light flickered eerily against the snow-covered pines, casting ghostly dancing patterns onto the old stone tower.

It sounded like the helos were less than two kilometers away now, but the engine noise seemed to emanate from over the cliffs, on the German side of the mountain. They were supposed to approach from the direction of Czechia, masking themselves by flying through the low valleys there.

"Get those assholes on the radio!" Borbikov commanded.

Suddenly the helos came into view in Borbikov's NVGs. There were two of them when there should have been three. "Where is the other bird? Who the hell at Central Command is fucking with my mission? I will have some asses when I get back!"

A massive spotlight flicked on from the lead helicopter, drenching them in bright light and causing the men to frantically flip up their NVGs.

Borbikov's fury gave way to the realization that these were not, in fact, his helicopters after all. "Cover!"

Men leapt to their feet and lunged for their weapons. Borbikov stumbled back over a stack of plastic equipment cases as he drew his own GSh-18 9mm pistol.

He righted himself quickly, shouted the order to fire, and began squeezing off rounds from his handgun at the approaching helos. As he did this, green 7.62mm tracers blazed upward from the clearing, fired from the AKs and targeting the approaching aircraft. The spotlight arced away quickly as rounds met their mark and the pilot of the lead helo took evasive action.

The response from the second helo was immediate. A fusillade of cannon fire from its 20mm pods slammed into the middle of the clearing. Explosions, spark showers, and flying shrapnel sent the Russians sprawling in all directions, the clearing offering them no protection from the incoming rounds.

The spotlight raked back into the clearing as the first helo sighted the area with its cannons. The light jerked and danced around the area—the gun pods shook the aircraft as they fired, making it difficult to keep the spotlight in place. More explosions rocked the center of the Russian force, demolishing equipment, fraying fiberglass cases, tossing bodies through the air like rag dolls.

But the gunfire from the ground continued as well, and both helos had to break off the attack.

Three Russian soldiers sprinted to the edge of the forest and turned around to face the enemy in the air, and soon three RPG-30 "Kryuk" rocket grenades streaked skyward. Two missed their target, but the other struck home. A blast and a small ball of flame in the night sky encouraged the missilemen, and all three reloaded quickly.

The aircraft pulled pitch and roared back, barreling left as it did so. It was followed by the second helo, which weaved wildly through the air to hamper the enemies' aim. One more rocket from the Russians narrowly missed the retreating aircraft, both of which dipped below the escarpment of the distant Bohemian cliffs.

"The one in the rear was smoking!" yelled a soldier.

"I have wounded, over here . . . I have dead!" said another.

Borbikov climbed back to his feet, surprised to be both alive and uninjured. "We'll *all* be dead if we don't prepare for action! Those helos that hit us could be carrying troops. Captain, send teams to cover the area from the forest, and more men up into the tower. Our extraction will be here soon."

The captain and the rest of his men began collecting weapons and gear. The wounded who were able to move under their own power dealt with their injuries on their own and then joined in. Those too badly injured to get up just lay there alone, unattended in the snow.

The 20mm cannon rounds had damaged much of the Russian equipment. Small arms and a few machine guns were quickly amassed and divided as the team split into two groups. The captain took four men with him to the tower, and Borbikov led five men into the forest to the west of the tower to set up a defensive position.

French special forces Captain Apollo Arc-Blanchette moved up the hill through the forest, shrouded by the darkness, the trees, and a heavy winter mist that crept down from the mountains. The men with him moved as silently as their captain, using their night-vision equipment and throat mics to stay together.

They'd been dropped off by one of the French Super Cougars fifteen minutes earlier, and they'd climbed silently but quickly the entire time.

Apollo pulled the NVGs back and looked at the sergeant and the other men gathered there in the woods, three hundred meters below the tower. "Sergent-Chef Dariel, we'll take your team and flank the tower off to the right."

"Yes, sir."

"Anything from Escadrille 3 on their second aircraft?"

"She's down hard, sir, but there were no serious injuries. Sergent Coronett has his team coming up a small deer trail. He says he's five minutes out."

"Good. Make sure he doesn't unmask himself and walk into the clearing. You can bet the tower and even the woods will be filthy with Russians. I want him to set up a machine-gun support section at the edge of the wood line while we flank from the right. Also, place snipers in the trees. We'll stay in touch on the squad radios and connect our attack as they provide suppressive fires."

"Got it, sir. Relaying now."

Apollo crept forward to see what else was visible in the night. Small flames flickered on the far side of the clearing, near the road that led down the mountain. The light made the tower ahead on his right appear to shift demonically, twisting in the spitting flames of the flares. In moments the fires petered out, and the tower, the clearing, and the restaurant were once again plunged into total darkness.

This gave Apollo an idea. "Hey, Dariel."

"Yes, sir?"

"I have an addition to the plan. Collect 40mm grenades from the men here, leaving each man with one. Give the rest to Coronett when he arrives to distribute to his team."

Ten minutes later Apollo knelt in the snow at the edge of the forest, held his throat microphone, and spoke in a soft whisper. "I have mark in two minutes. All teams roger up that you are set in your attack positions."

"One Team, ready," said Dariel.

"Two Team, ready," said Sergent Coronett.

"Three Team, ready," came the call from the mortar section.

Apollo and the men of One Team hunkered lower and awaited the start of the fireworks.

Twenty seconds before the timeline, a soft *whump . . . whump* could be heard. Then three seconds and another five *whump* sounds. One Team knew these were the sounds of the support team's mortars firing off. They had perfectly calculated the time of flight of the 47mm mortars and their own hand-launched 40mm grenades to land simultaneously.

Apollo and his men stood quickly from the snow and swept back their NVGs, replacing them with their darkened snow goggles. Right on cue, three French 47mm mortar shells exploded in bright light on the grounds on the far side of the tower. Forty-millimeter grenade flares joined their bigger brothers, bathing the back and sides of the tower in an impossibly brilliant white light.

Apollo and his men advanced rapidly in the shadow of the tower on the opposite side of the light. The flares would blind the defenders, who were likely scanning the area through their NVGs. The French captain knew Russian Spetsnaz prided themselves on having the latest fourth-generation gear, but it would be to their detriment now, enhancing the flares' light and robbing the men of their night vision.

The effect would be fleeting, but it allowed Apollo and his men enough time to advance more than two hundred meters in darkness. They sprinted across the clearing and the driveway in front of the tower, aiming for a wall near the tower's base.

A single sniper shot rang out through the cold night from the top of the tower, and one of Apollo's men fell in the snow. While two dragged the wounded soldier toward the cover of the building, the rest of the group hammered the tower with suppressive fire.

The flares burned out one by one, fizzling as melted snow extinguished them, once again enshrouding the scene in darkness.

Apollo and his men arrived at the wall, lowered their goggles to their necks, and replaced their NVGs over their eyes. Knowing most of the Russians would still need a few minutes to regain sight in the darkness, even with the aid of their night vision, the French now owned the night.

The Dragoons wasted no time; a breacher hammered the hinges off the frame as six men waited stacked behind him. The door crashed in and one half of One Team, led by Dariel, entered through the tower door. They surprised two Russian troops inside, killing them both with their suppressed submachine guns.

Apollo and the other half of the One Team men moved cautiously around the sides of the wall, closely scanning the opposite wood line. In moments a fusillade of fire illuminated the dark pine forest as the Spetsnaz men positioned there opened up.

Apollo and his men dove for cover while his own support unit in the trees, back on the eastern side of the tower, identified the location of the enemy in the forest. French FN Minimi light machine guns opened up, blazing fire onto the Russians' position.

CHAPTER 28

ELBE SANDSTONE MOUNTAINS
CZECHIA
25 DECEMBER
0159

Rounds ripped through the trees, red tracers making laserlike lines in the air as they zipped over and around Borbikov, forcing his head lower into the snow and rocks.

"Captain, you must shift fire to that wood line!"

"Yes, sir!" yelled the captain, who knew enough to shift his guns without being told, although he didn't dare talk back to the colonel.

The team radioman shouted over the incoming and outgoing gunfire. "Colonel, Captain, I have our extraction team up on the net. They are en route; they report they are five minutes out. They want to know where it is safe to land."

"Give me that radio," demanded Borbikov, seizing the handset. "You are to land no more than one hundred meters away from our position! There is a logging trail to the south. You *will* put all three aircraft there."

"Yes, sir!" came the response.

A battle between snipers had begun. Two Russian marksmen, using the open fifth floor of the stone tower and the crenellated walls, fired down on the French machine-gun forces two hundred meters away. In turn, three

French snipers in the trees kept up slow but steady return fire, rushing the men in the tower and keeping them cautious and inaccurate.

Apollo and his portion of One Team used the cover of a low wall alongside the driveway. From this position, they were able to keep up a deadly cross fire on the Russian position in the woods.

"Hand me the hook." Apollo reached up as the radioman inched around the stone wall to give him the radio handset.

"Three Team, stand by for polar fire mission for the mortars. Adjustments will follow." Apollo used the tactical radio, not wanting to chance the mortar team being outside of squad radio range.

"Copy. Standing by," came the swift reply.

He gave them a simple call for fire based on the flares they'd launched moments earlier. The mortar team would have to make a fuse adjustment to fire high explosives, but the ranges would all be tight.

Seconds later Apollo heard a soft *crump* as a high-explosive mortar crashed in the woods. The impact seemed well beyond and far to the left of the Russian machine-gun position, but the fire momentarily skipped a beat.

Good, Apollo thought. *We're inside their heads.*

"Drop one hundred, right one hundred. Three rounds." He hoped like hell this adjustment would put the next rounds on the sweet spot.

A moment later three mortars slammed, one after the other, just left of the Russian machine guns at the woods' edge, spraying them with shrapnel, dirt, and debris.

Apollo keyed the mic again as he looked at the impact area in the distance. "Right fifty! Fire for effect."

A sniper round passed just over Apollo's head with an angry crack, and he ducked back down.

Inside the tower, Dariel and his men advanced through the rooms, clearing them one at a time. Three Russians had been killed in this manner before the French soldiers reached the tower's wrought-iron spiral stairs.

At first Dariel didn't know if the Russians up in the tower could tell they were coming, but when a grenade bounced down the stairs, slipping between the metal railings and then onto the floor at the bottom, he got his answer. He and his men dove out of the stairwell an instant before it exploded. Still, the echoes off the stone walls all but deafened the men.

Dariel and his men lobbed grenades of their own up the stairs, each time diving back out of the stairwell in case their throws were off.

After a minute of this there was no more response from the men in the tower, and soon blood began dripping through the ironwork of the stairway.

Apollo radioed 4th Escadrille and a minute later the Super Cougar lit up the wood line with withering 20mm cannon fire from six hundred meters. Quickly the Russian machine guns fell silent and Apollo signaled his men to advance, closing the distance rapidly, using every snow-covered rock they could find for cover.

Some small arms met their advance, but Three Team renewed heavy bursts from their light machine guns to provide suppression as Apollo and the others closed the distance, picking off targets as they did so.

With the French helicopter covering, they advanced on the wood line.

One of the corporals from One Team came over his squad radio: "There's another helo . . . Behind their position, about three or four hundred meters."

In the distance above the trees, Apollo could just make out one, two, then three helicopters.

Apollo called his helicopter. "Shift your fire onto those aircraft!" He then radioed Three Team. "I don't want to get shot in the back by those Russian snipers. Make sure our snipers keep them off of us."

Apollo and the men had all but closed the gap and were within meters of where the now-silenced Russian machine-gun nest had been positioned.

"Switch to grenades. Toss on the count of three. Then we'll see what's left and close in."

Apollo pulled the pin on one of his own grenades and on the three count tossed it toward a clump of brush and felled logs. A few seconds later, eight high-explosive grenades blew clumps of frozen earth, snow, and debris, and destroyed the remainder of two Russian machine-gun positions. Apollo looked through the optic of his UMP45 SD. Crouching low, he advanced in a tactical shuffle. Through the smoke and flying debris he could see four figures running off into the forest.

There were several dead and wounded Russians lying around him now.

"Leave two men here to check and disarm the wounded. The rest of you, follow me. We're not letting these assholes get away."

Apollo didn't wait. Trusting his orders were being obeyed, he took point, bounding over the remnants of Russian equipment, snapped tree limbs, and bodies.

They were still well behind the fleeing Russians, but in case the survivors were attempting to draw them into an ambush, Apollo slowed his advance as soon as he exited the clearing.

Soon he found footprints and a distinct trail of deep red blood that almost glowed against the white snow in the advancing moonlight.

"This way." Apollo pointed to the blood and tracks. "They've left us a path."

The men pushed through the trees. The snow was deep in drifts, slowing their progress, but they had the advantage of being able to pick their way through the woods more cautiously than the Russians.

Soon they neared the enemy helos. Apollo and his men had next to no visibility, such was the obscuration from the rotor downdraft. It seemed to him that the Russian pilots were purposely kicking up as much snow as possible to mask their departure by not letting off their collectives.

This would blind the pilots as well. A gutsy move, one only really ace fliers would attempt.

Apollo raced from tree to tree for cover. He could see only dark shapes and the faint blur from the enemy helicopters' spinning blades.

Quickly he realized he was putting his small force in unnecessary danger. Into his radio he said, "*Merde!* Hold back, men. Grab some cover. He's going to lift off and then rake the trees with whatever he's got on board." A few men rogered up on the throat mics but the rest likely couldn't hear a thing, given the noise coming from the Russian aircraft.

In moments the aircraft's engines changed pitch and the flying debris increased. The NVGs did nothing to cut through, so the men put their goggles back on to deal with the whipping snow and forest debris in the air. As soon as the helicopter rose ten meters, a burst of rifle and machine-gun fire from the aircraft lit up the whole forest. Most of it was spray and pray, but a good deal of it shredded the forest near One Team's position. The Dragoons stayed down behind boulders and trees, pushing themselves flat against the frozen ground, and suffered what felt like an eternity of enemy gunfire until the helos were just above the treetops.

Then the French Super Cougar hanging back five hundred meters opened up with its 20mm.

The throaty *thump-thump* sound of the heavy cannon fire caused the Russians on the helo to concentrate all their fire on the other aircraft, realizing it was the greater threat. Once the Russians stopped peppering the woods, Apollo and his men rose from cover and fired every weapon they had.

Sparks and then flame shot out from the engine of one of the enemy birds. The aircraft pitched violently forward, then dipped sideways, tracing a wide upward and outward arc before finally slamming at speed into a rocky mountainside six hundred meters away from Apollo's position.

The Dragoons slackened their fire, the flaming helo blinding them from acquiring the second and third aircraft, which had used the cover of the other helicopter's death throes to escape the battlefield.

Apollo called his helicopter, which had closed to one hundred meters above his position now. "Can you see the enemy and pursue?"

"Negative. The downed bird flared our night and thermal vision. We are flying blind and trying to hold hover. We've taken hits. Leaking hydraulics. We'll set down at the tower when we get our eyes back. See you at the objective site."

"Copy." And then to his team Apollo said, "Hold all fire, men. We'd be wasting ammo. Nothing survived that inferno. God help those sons of bitches," he added as he made the sign of the cross.

The crunch of snow announced Sergent-Chef Dariel at Apollo's side. "Boss, we need to get the wounded out ASAP. Me and the radio operators will handle it. SATCOM is down for some reason, but we'll get the HF radios ready." He paused, looking at his commander. "You should get back to the tower. You'll never guess what Konstantine found."

"Let me try: another one of those laser things."

"Yes, sir. And this one is active. Konstantine says it's pinging up and down a line to other lasers, just like that map at Zugspitze showed."

"Laser navigation," Apollo said. "You can bet those things are directing something or someone onto a target."

"Guided missiles? Attack helos?"

Apollo didn't answer. Thinking, he stared for a moment in the direction of the Russian helicopters, their engines still audible even though they'd dipped below a distant mountain. He then turned to Dariel. "We're shutting that laser down, too. Get that long-haul radio up so I can report all this to HQ."

Still looking into the frigid dark skies, he said, "Something bad is coming this way."

BELARUS

25 DECEMBER

0330

The camouflaged assault train designated *Red Blizzard 1* departed from Brest, Belarus, right on time. For all intents and purposes this *was* the civilian Strizh train, as it looked nearly identical and traveled through the exact same stations, keeping, at first, to the same timetable. Only it did not stop. This fact caused some initial confusion, needless to say. Travelers waiting early on the platform to head west for Christmas Day watched the train pass through the Brest station at a fast clip. With the unrest and general unreliability of the track, the weather, and even just the newness of this Strizh train service, the stranded passengers were easily placated by rail personnel and booked onto other trains. Even the Polish central rail control thought nothing was out of the ordinary. A message had been received about an hour before its transit that it had maintenance problems and would be bypassing several stops on its way to Germany. Besides, the main track engineers at the Terespol station on the Polish side of the border opposite Brest, Belarus, had signaled the okay.

Central Rail Control had no idea this was only because Spetsnaz Team P-6 had already paid them a visit.

At 3:50 a.m. the lead attack elements of General Sabaneyev's spearhead, led by Colonel Danilo Dryagin, began crossing the bridge over the Bug River at Pto Kozlovichi. A platoon of T-14 Armatas approached the small border crossing station on the western side of the bridge, moving along at a brisk thirty-five kilometers per hour.

A platoon of PLF troops manned the crossing along with a pair of Polish PT-91 Twardy tanks. They had been placed there by the PLF, pulling holiday duty with orders to keep an eye on the border during the Russian winter exercises in Belarus.

Playing cards with the Polish border agents, sipping brandy passed around for this Christmas morning shift, the men were hardly expecting what came next.

"Vehicles approaching!" shouted one of the Polish sentries.

A veteran watch officer replied, "Just truckers returning to Poland. The idiots always forget where the border crossing station is. Hit them with the floodlights." The watch officer turned back to his poker hand; he was on a straight draw, after all.

The floodlights came on but the headlights continued advancing.

A few seconds later one soldier said, "Hey, sir, I really don't think these guys are stopping. They look like . . . like . . ."

The watch officer looked over his cards. He'd just picked up a straight on the turn. "Like what?" He put the cards down, let out a long sigh, and turned toward the road as the first two T-14s fired their main guns, blowing the Polish tanks to pieces before they even turned their engines over.

The cannon fire was instantly followed by coaxial machine guns as the lead Armatas shot out the spotlights.

"Raise the barricade!" yelled the border control agent. One of the men flipped a switch and raised a steel barricade while simultaneously a wooden swing arm lowered.

The lead Russian vehicle was a BREM-1M wrecker tank. It drove through the metal barricade and wooden swing arm like they weren't even there, the thick metal tearing away and then flying like shrapnel through the air. The rest of the T-14s followed, each spraying machine-gun fire into the small border post and the burning PT-91 tanks.

The boys in the tanks laid down on their guns, so high was their adrenaline now that they were finally being given the chance to fight.

The surviving Polish troops had the good sense to run, through the snowy fields and into the nearby hamlet of Kukuryki. They were not pursued by the Bumerang assault vehicles or the GAZ Tigr all-terrain infantry mobility vehicles that rolled in directly behind the tanks, because the Russians didn't give two shits about a half-dead platoon on the border.

The column had someplace else to be.

Colonel Danilo Dryagin sat in his Bumerang command-and-control vehicle, the sixteenth piece of Russian armor to cross into Poland. His position was carefully chosen for a man who wanted to see the battle, smell it, but not have to worry about the up-to-the-minute actions. Not too far forward to need to fire constantly at targets, and not too far back to be just a spectator. He remained constantly on the radio, giving orders and receiving situation reports as his vehicle raced past the checkpoint, small fires burning holes in the dark on both sides of the road.

He ordered the force to continue westward, demanding they make fifty kilometers an hour, because he had a very aggressive timetable to meet. Behind him, dozens and dozens more armored vehicles sped past the demolished checkpoint, under cover of both the darkness and a total blackout of the Western satellites above.

Thirty minutes later *Red Blizzard 1* crossed the river bordering Belarus and Poland a few kilometers south of the armored column crossing point, rolling without contest through the Polish town of Terespol. Eduard Sabaneyev sat in his command railcar, communicating from time to time with Colonel Dryagin, and poring over his maps of the route ahead.

Things are moving exactly according to plan, he thought.

CHAPTER 29

FALLS CHURCH, VIRGINIA
24 DECEMBER
2114

Dan Connolly looked across the dining room table to his wife, Julie, and gave her the thumbs-up. She returned the gesture with a tired smile. Between the two of them was the detritus of a small dinner party: empty plates, half-empty glasses of wine and soda, and a batch of tired, turkey-fattened family members who had eaten well this Christmas Eve.

Their dinner for eight had gone off without a hitch. Tomorrow the meal would be taken care of by his mother-in-law, so Dan and Julie Connolly were basking in the glow that came from the knowledge that their time in the hot seat this holiday season was over.

Dan's mother; Julie's cousin; the Connollys' kids, Jack and Elsa; and Julie's parents all sat at the table satisfied, chatting about family issues. Just now the topic of discussion was one of Dan's cousins who'd spent a fortune on a new swimming pool while ignoring his kid's college fund.

Dan tried to tune out the gossip and appreciate the moment. He'd spent his entire adult life in the military and a large portion of it at war. He'd missed more holiday dinners than he'd made in the past fifteen years, and he knew he had to enjoy himself while here, especially because he wondered if he'd be fighting in Asia this time next year.

More than anything he appreciated the fact that all the family members present seemed to be getting along, with no drama. *A Christmas miracle,* Connolly thought.

He was about to usher everyone into the living room to sit in front of the fireplace, when his cell phone buzzed in his pocket. Julie gave him a death stare when he pulled it out, but his intention was just to send the call to voice mail.

Until he saw it was Griggs. He looked up to Julie. "It's Bob, hon. Let me tell him merry Christmas. You take everybody in to get them started on charades. I'll come in and light the fire in just a sec."

Connolly answered. "Hey, Bob. I figured you'd be diving into dessert about now, not calling me."

But Griggs's voice was serious. "You watching the news?"

"Of course not. It's Christmas Eve. I'm sitting with the family having dinner and—"

"Turn it on! *Now.*" Connolly launched from the table with the phone to his ear. He began heading for the den, because whatever the hell was going on, Griggs wouldn't have called him and spoken like this unless it was damn serious.

As he reached for the TV remote he said, "China's not supposed to do anything till after the election next week."

"Not China, Dan. It's Russia."

The Marine felt an icy chill down his spine.

The TV came on and Connolly flipped to Fox News.

The network anchor sat at her desk, reading the teleprompter. "While experts encourage calm, they say the loss of virtually all fiber-optic, satellite, and Internet communications to Europe is unprecedented. Once again, for those joining us, Europe is experiencing what some are describing as a *total* communications blackout."

A split screen came up and the reporter was joined by a Fox engineer standing in front of a bank of dead monitors. "Jim, you've worked in telecommunications for over twenty years. What's your assessment? Could this be holiday grid overload, or something more sinister?"

"I've never seen anything like this, Stacy. We aren't getting through to our bureaus at all, and can't even raise them on landlines. Even individual private cell phones are down. No single malfunction could cause this. I can only imagine that this indicates that some kind of coordinated communications attack is under way."

"How long?" Connolly asked into the phone.

Griggs said, "Just a few minutes, apparently. CNN also says they lost their feeds into all their European bureaus and can't reach them any other way. There is *nothing* getting in or out of the Continent right now. It's as if Europe just went dark."

Connolly said, "There's no way that this is anything other than a Russian comms attack."

Grigg's agreed. "And there's no way that screwing with TVs and cell phones was their end goal. They blinded NATO. Something's coming. Something *big.*"

Connolly looked at his watch. "It could already be happening. It's just after oh three hundred in Central Europe. They wouldn't just turn out the lights. They'd move as soon as they flipped the switch. This is synced with something else."

Griggs said, "But *what?* How could Russia invade? We haven't seen the buildup. The troops in Belarus aren't enough to take and hold Poland or the Baltics. Our Russian intel desks said they had a firm count on all the Russian rolling stock, and it wasn't enough to even get through Poland, let alone break out and fight off the rest of NATO. Hell, their best general is down running drills in Iran, for God sakes."

Connolly said, "I don't have the answers, Bob, but we need to find them."

"You gonna go in?"

Connolly looked back to the dining room. Julie was sitting in her chair, but looking his way. "Yeah. I'll be there in thirty."

"See you then."

Dan Connolly went back into the living room, and all eyes turned his way.

CHAPTER 30

Paulina Tobiasz was woken by a hard shake to her shoulder. She opened her eyes and saw Tytus in her tent, looking down on her in the dark. Behind him, through the open flap at the entrance to her tent, she could see that it was still pitch-dark, and a light snow was falling.

Before she could speak he said, "You up, Tobiasz?"

"*Dzień dobry,*" ("Good morning") she replied with a surprised smile.

But then she noticed Tytus had a hard look on his face. He was all business.

"We're leaving. The trucks are coming for us in five minutes."

"*Leaving?* Back to Warsaw?"

He shook his head. "Another road. Nowicki said we've been ordered west."

Paulina sat up quickly. "We spent all yesterday filling sandbags and building wooden fortifications here. Why are we just leaving all that and—"

Tytus turned away. "The Russians are in Poland."

"*What?*"

The young man exited the tent without another word.

On the cot on the other side of the small tent, Urszula lay in her sleeping bag, rubbing her puffy eyes. "What did he say?"

"Some shit about Russians in Poland, I think."

Urszula laid her head back down. "He's screwing with you. He likes you."

Paulina pulled off her knit cap to organize her dirty-blond hair. She didn't believe the Russians were in Poland, but she *did* believe she'd have to go out into the snow, climb onto a truck in five minutes, and go to *another* area to dig *another* fortification.

The women took longer than five minutes to get ready, but so did most of the company. Nowicki finally got everyone loaded and the trucks moving, but he hadn't said a word to anyone about where they were going or why.

Tytus had been wrong about the Russians, Paulina was sure; but if Urszula was right and that had been an attempt by him to flirt, it wasn't much of one.

The trucks drove west along a two-lane paved road until they climbed an incline, significant because this was a very flat part of the country. They left the paved road suddenly and Paulina's vehicle bounced over depressions and through ditches, throwing everyone in back around and against one another, sending gear bags flying with each bounce. After five minutes of this, the trucks pulled into a clearing and stopped.

Paulina jumped from the back of the vehicle with the rest of the occupants and found herself on a gentle snow-white hill, a grazing pasture that overlooked a two-lane road two hundred meters to the south. A wet, thick snow fell steadily, meaning she could see no farther than the empty road, and she wondered if this was what they'd been rushed to protect before dawn.

The section sergeants mustered the ninety-three members of the militia company on the hill. The volunteers lined up in six fifteen- or sixteen-person sections, but they were in no way as orderly as actual soldiers. The men and women shuffled their boots in the shin-deep snow and waited to hear what the hell was going on. Nowicki remained in the cab of one of the trucks for several minutes, then leapt out and began stomping through the snow back to his waiting troops.

Instantly, Paulina could detect an expression she'd never seen on the man's face. It was almost as if the normally confident lieutenant looked . . . *scared*.

"Listen up! I don't have any more information than what I'm about to say, so don't pester me with questions. PLF comms are completely down, and the TDF net is coming in broken. But before I lost communication, someone there claimed Russian armor crossed into Poland this morning from Brest. Further civilian shortwave reports claim the Russians have engaged military targets inside Poland."

Everyone stood in bewildered silence until Nowicki spoke again. "If this is true, it means our nation is under attack."

The lines of young men and women gasped as one, and then everyone began speaking at once.

Nowicki shouted over them. "Intel reports suggest the Russians are moving west. The Land Force is rushing to get in front of them, and we are trying to get NATO to get their shit together and move forces stationed up north over to the border, but something is wrong with the NATO communication network, too. In the meantime we've been moved off Expressway 12 and ordered here to watch over that road down there, Route 740. We have received absolutely no intelligence that says any Russian is going to come up that road." Nowicki looked around—as best he could with the heavy snowfall, anyway—and put his hands on his hips. "*I* sure wouldn't come this way. Still, we have to be ready."

A thirty-year-old woman from Section F asked, "Ready for *what*? We have six RPGs, two small mortars, a dozen machine guns, and some rifles. We're going to stop a Russian invasion?"

Nowicki just looked at her. "You have to be ready to fight for your country. Whatever the odds."

The speaking turned to shouting.

A man in his forties yelled out, "My family is in Warsaw and I'm here? I have two kids. I have to go to them." He started to break rank and head back over to the trucks.

Nowicki was twenty years younger than the militiaman. "The PLF is in and around Warsaw. They will protect your family."

"Yeah, right. While I protect that *fucking* nothing road down there? I'm leaving!"

Nowicki's voice trembled as he spoke. "As of right now, your service in the militia is no longer voluntary. Anyone who runs will be shot in the back by your section sergeant. If your section sergeant fails to shoot you, I will shoot your section sergeant, and then I will shoot *you*."

The hill fell silent as that sank in; only the hissing off the snowfall continued, but only for a moment. Then a twenty-eight-year-old natural gas pipeline technician named Jerzy threw his rifle in the snow. "Fuck you, college boy. I'm getting an Uber back to—"

Next to him, his section sergeant racked a round into the chamber of his AK-47 and leveled it at the side of the man's head.

Now a roofer who'd joined the militia for extra cash shouted, "I'm not a motherfucking *soldier!*" and others agreed with him. The crowd devolved over the next several seconds; the protests grew louder.

Nowicki pulled his pistol from its holster and fired a round into the snow next to him, and everyone fell still again.

The twenty-three-year-old lieutenant's voice cracked again as he spoke. "We are going to be fine. Your families are going to be fine. Just everybody calm down and do your jobs."

The lieutenant cleared his throat. "Let's get to work. It will be light soon. I want everyone digging trenches by section."

Paulina was in Section E and, along with the men and women in the five other sections, she dug into the soft snow, then into the hard earth, doing her best to scratch out cover from the road and to the east.

The different sections all tossed dirt in front of the fighting positions, slowly building up loose earthen berms.

As Paulina fought with the frozen ground, an overweight high school soccer coach slammed his pick into the hole next to her and spoke over the sounds of the digging. "Why would the Russians come along this road?"

The young section sergeant was a few meters away. He was a hard charger in everything he did, at least as compared to the rest of Section E, and he dug twice as fast as anyone else in Paulina's trench. Still, he didn't slow or look up from his work to respond. He said, "You can ask them their plan if they show up, Jerzy."

Paulina and Urszula worked next to each other. Within minutes the beautiful brunette complained about blisters on her hands despite her thick gloves. Five minutes after this Paulina's own hands were blistered and burning.

The six trenches were sprawled out on the snow-covered hillside, each at a different angle to the road at the bottom of the hill, with all trenches more or less angled to the east. The military vehicles that had brought them there had been moved back into the woods to the west, and to the east it was an open view as far as the weather would allow, which was half a kilometer or so. The snow fell even more heavily now, and dense fog covered the road below and floated halfway up the hill.

Paulina and Bruno were set up behind the earthen berm in the second trench from the top of the hill. Their launcher lay on a backpack, already loaded, and Paulina's rifle was propped next to a bandolier of extra grenades.

Urszula and her RPG crewmate, a fifty-three-year-old with a bald head and thick glasses who'd only recently given up on hitting on her after nearly a year, knelt in the dirt directly next to them, with nearly a dozen riflemen filling out the rest of Section E's fighting position.

Lieutenant Nowicki squatted just above the southernmost trench with his cell phone. Paulina could see by his occasional frustrated gesticulations that he was still having trouble communicating with his command.

Finally, just after six a.m., the lieutenant began moving from one fighting position to the next, talking to each group of fifteen or sixteen.

Everyone in Paulina's trench stood in silence as they waited for the uniformed officer to move to them, as if their fate lay in what he would say.

Urszula moved over to Paulina now and hugged her close, seeking comfort in her best friend. They stood there, arm in arm, while Paulina scanned the trenches Nowicki had already addressed. It was hard to get a read on what he'd told them, especially with the fog and snow, but it was obvious none of them were packing up and leaving, so she knew this wasn't over yet.

Finally he made it to Section E's emplacement, and now, up close, she could see the fear on his face, in his eyes. Instantly her heart began to pound in her chest.

Nowicki said, "Listen up. No talking. As of twenty minutes ago the Russians were east of Radom, moving west on Twelve with heavy armor and scout cars."

"*Gówno!*" the roofer shouted.

Some in the group leaned against the berm or sat down in the ditch. Urszula shuddered in Paulina's arms, and her knees started to give out before her friend pulled her back up.

Nowicki continued. "There's a full battalion of PLF on the way, but they are fifty kilometers out. No one that I've talked to has been in comms with any NATO forces as far as I can tell."

Urszula spoke softly, almost to herself. "We're dead meat."

Nowicki pointed at her angrily. "No! Their main force is down on Twelve. That's fifteen kilometers south. If they do send some scouts up on Route 740, we will engage them. We will slow them down, hold them back. When we punch them in the nose, they will be so surprised, they'll stop and think over their plan, and that will give the battalion time to get here and finish them."

The heavyset soccer coach named Jerzy spoke up now. "A *battalion*? You think a *battalion—twelve hundred men*—will stop a Russian invasion?"

Nowicki was already up and moving to the last trench. "We can't control the Russians, or the PDF, but we *can* control our own actions. Listen for my commands on the radio."

He took off in a jog for Section F's trench.

Paulina looked down the trench line toward Tytus now, who lay on the meter-high earthen berm with his eye in the scope of his Dragunov. She hadn't heard him say a word since first thing this morning, and she wondered if he was as scared as she was. She thought about moving down to his end to talk to him, and had just committed herself to this when someone in the next trench over from Paulina shouted for everyone around him to shut the hell up. Heads turned to the comment, but only for an instant, because it was immediately apparent why the request had been made.

A soft, persistent rumble rolled over the hillside, and it came from the east.

"What the hell is that?" Bruno asked.

Kluk, Urszula's bald-headed, lecherous RPG gunner, said, "It's too faint to be armor."

"What's over that way?" another man asked.

Tytus scanned through his scope. "Just houses and buildings along Route 740. I don't see any movement. Maybe some semis or larger trucks are passing. I don't think there is—"

Tytus stopped talking when a new sound filled everyone's ears. It was the low, rolling rumble of what was obviously a distant explosion.

Urszula muttered softly, "Oh my God."

Paulina put a hand on her friend's shoulder. "That's kilometers away. There are lots of roads they can take."

Bruno said, "They'll stay down the main highway."

Tytus heard this, and he called from the far edge of the trench, "That's closer than the highway. That's the 740. Someone is—"

Two distant booms. Then a third. The soft but persistent hum of engines grew louder.

The sounds of explosions continued for the next four minutes, the constant reverberations gaining in volume as each minute passed.

Nowicki stepped out in front of the trenches with his handheld radio at his ear now. He pushed the transmit button and Paulina's section sergeant's handheld squawked in Section E's fighting position.

"I don't know who's coming, but heavy equipment is clearly on the way up Route 740."

While Paulina watched him from the trench, Nowicki started to say something else into his radio but then he stopped and looked around.

The hillside began to vibrate. The snow one hundred meters in every direction was dirty and churned up by footprints and truck tires and now it began to move, vibrating with the approaching engine noise. In Section E's trench Paulina watched clods of dirt roll off the berms and down into the frozen hole.

Nowicki turned around and faced his militia, a look of near panic on his face, and Tytus called out from behind his Dragunov, "Armor on the road! Armor on the road! Approaching fast!"

The lieutenant in the open turned and stared at Section E's sharpshooter in disbelief. Paulina could tell Nowicki had no idea what to do, and this brought her to the verge of panic. A man a few positions away from her vomited into the trench. She looked to her right now, past little Bruno, and her eyes met with Urszula. Her friend blinked and tears ran down her rosy cheeks. Her gloved hands shook violently.

Paulina reached behind Bruno's back and took Urszula's gloved hand in hers, then let go as both women moved to their weapons.

A flash of light appeared in the east now, a ball of flame that rose and disappeared in the gray morning. The sound of a shock wave came, and then the boom of an explosion. A second flash and a subsequent boom came just after.

Tytus looked through his scope. "It's tanks! T-90s. No, wait! T-14s, I think."

Nowicki turned to him. "Dismounts?"

"No, sir! Just the tanks. Multiple tanks."

Jerzy shouted now. "We're all gonna *fucking* die!"

Nowicki remained in the open. He shouted into his radio so all the positions could hear him. "Everyone hold positions! Do *not* fire unless fired upon!" Clearly he saw the folly of taking on main battle tanks with their impotent force.

The lieutenant ran through the snow and dirt now and leapt into Section D's trench.

A man on Paulina's left cried out in fresh alarm. She looked over and saw men in Section F's fighting position all peering along the hillside but not down to the road. Tracking their gaze to the east, she saw four big armored vehicles with black tires approaching out of the fogbank. They barreled through the snow on the hill, parallel to the road, heading right for the trenches. To Paulina they appeared to be less than three hundred meters away and closing fast.

Paulina was no real soldier, but in her training weekends she'd spent a few hours looking through books of photos of Russian military equipment, and she instantly recognized the Russian-built Bumerang armored personnel carrier. She knew everything relevant about the weapon. It had robust armor in the front; an RPG would be next to useless against it unless Bruno could strike it perfectly from behind. The APC had a 30mm cannon and a PKT machine gun, a crew of three on board, and it could carry up to nine fully laden troops into battle.

She never in her life thought she'd see a Russian APC on Polish soil.

In an instant Nowicki's plan to sit quietly and let the enemy pass fell apart. They'd been spotted, either through infrared cameras or by a drone overhead, but *someone* had seen this ragtag force through the snow.

Section sergeants in the trenches called out over their radios, begging Nowicki to surrender to the four approaching armored vehicles, and Paulina waited to hear the lieutenant's reply to this, but a sudden cacophony of automatic-weapons fire cut over the loud rumble of the passing column. A Bumerang opened up with its PKT machine gun; snow and dirt kicked into the air just forty meters in front of Section E's trench.

And just like that, surrender was off the table as quickly as it had been suggested.

CHAPTER 31

Lieutenant Nowicki's voice came over the walkie-talkie now. "Fire! Hit those APCs!"

Return gunfire chattered all around Paulina. Instinctively she looked around her, left and right, and saw men and women with weapons aimed and firing to the east.

In the span of a few seconds she also witnessed men and women just kneeling, sitting, or even lying down in the dirt and covering their heads. Beyond this she saw the camouflaged outline of a big man running out of the next trench, west toward the wood line behind them.

Paulina's and Bruno's eyes met now: they were both terrified and unable to hide it from each other. After less than a second the young, acne-scarred boy spun away, hefted the RPG-7 onto his left shoulder, and rose up to his feet. His upper torso and head were exposed over the earthen berm as he aimed.

Paulina rose up on her feet behind him. As the loader she had to prep the next round, but it was also her responsibility to help him with the firing of the weapon. She braced him with her right hand on his back, her arm stiff, turning away from him and checking the area behind the weapon's tube to make sure no one was in the way.

Around her in the trench, the sound of ripping gunfire was maddening.

"Backblast clear!" Paulina screamed, looking at the snow to the wood line in the opposite direction and anticipating the jolt, noise, and flash of the launch.

But the hot blast of the launch never came. She started to shout again that the area behind her gunner was clear, but before the words came out she felt Bruno lurch back against her hand, and where she'd expected to see the flash of a rocket launch she instead saw a dark red spray.

Blood shot over the back of the trench and into the snow, a scatter path of crimson four meters long.

Bruno went limp and fell against her, and now she tumbled down into the trench over her bandolier of rockets. As she turned around and pushed him off, all around her guns fired, men and women screamed and shouted and fell and fought, and she looked at her crewmate and saw that his helmet was off and the back of his head was gone.

It was his blood that had sprayed like the backblast of the weapon he never even fired.

Paulina screamed but she did not freeze in terror. With reflexes spurred on by the primordial desire for survival, she grabbed the RPG-7, hoisted it onto her shoulder, rose to her feet, and looked for a target over the berm.

The nearest APC was much closer than she expected, sixty-five meters away now and racing right at her. She focused on the big armored vehicle, lined it up in the ring-and-post sight, and pressed the trigger.

As in training, the weapon shuddered and flashed.

The rocket streaked across the open ground, slammed into the turret of the armored vehicle, and exploded in a fireball.

But the APC did not slow down at all; it just rolled through the flame and continued on, closing by the second.

Lieutenant Nowicki's voice came over the radio lying in the dirt in E Section. "Troops! Dismounting troops!" The terror in the young officer's voice coming through the speaker only added to the chaos in the hole around her.

Russian troops wearing all white and carrying black rifles poured out of the fog behind the armored vehicles. Some dropped to their knees to fire, some dove to the ground and fired from a prone position, and others continued advancing toward the trenches in a run, firing all the way.

Nowicki screamed, "Riflemen, engage the dismounts! Dabrowski, Borowicz, stay on those PKs! Rake that hill!"

The four vehicles ground to a halt in the snow; then the main guns began thumping automatic fire. Almost instantly Paulina heard cracks in the forest behind her as tree limbs and trunks were struck by the heavy machine guns. Close fire snapped over Paulina's head, angry, amplified wasps buzzing beyond the speed of sound.

Icy tears ran down her cheeks and her arms shook as she reloaded and then leveled her grenade launcher at the same vehicle as before.

Next to her Urszula hefted a rocket-propelled grenade with one hand and slapped Kluk on the back with the other, letting him know the area was clear behind him. He fired his RPG at the same time Paulina fired hers.

Kluk's grenade hit the Bumerang but did no damage. Paulina's explosive overshot the approaching assault vehicle and detonated in the hill two hundred meters behind it.

"*Gówno!*"

Nowicki's voice came over the radio. "Again! Lower your aim! Hurry!"

Just then, new blasts rocked the hillside around Paulina. Her ears began ringing and her heart seemed to slosh left and right in her chest. Frozen earth rained down all over.

Jesus, please protect me.

The earthen berm in front of her kicked up, dirt clods rocketed ten meters into the air, and Paulina dropped the launcher and dove to the trench floor. She heard screams and grunts around her, and she instinctively looked over to her right. Urszula lay there in the dirt facing away, unmoving in the fetal position, as if she were asleep. Above Urszula's still form, Kluk leveled the RPG launcher alone, but then he lurched back as a machine-gun round caught him in the chest.

He tumbled back over Urszula and lay still on top of her, eyes wide open.

Something snapped in Paulina Tobiasz upon seeing her best friend lying there. She reached out for the closest weapon, her long wooden Mosin-Nagant. She climbed out of her hole with the bolt-action rifle, then stood on the berm, searching for targets in the heavy weather.

Dismounted soldiers moved in the near distance, their rifles spitting fire, revealing themselves in the snowfall. Paulina began to level her weapon on one of the figures, but then, like wraiths in the fog, two white-clad Russian soldiers materialized in front of her, out of the whipping snow, just fifteen meters away.

She spun her big weapon toward them, and they both saw the movement at the same time.

A seventy-one-year-old pensioner stood in the hamlet above the battle, using the Nikon he'd bought to photograph birds to record the unbelievable sight before him on the normally placid sheep-grazing pasture. He saw a blonde with a ponytail raise her head out of a trench, not three meters from where a brunette just fell. There was something about the blonde's movement, the certitude of it, the decisiveness of it. In a half-minute battle in which many of the overmatched Poles cowered and hesitated to reveal themselves but died just the same, the blonde climbed completely out of the trench and onto the berm in front of her. In her right hand she held an old wooden-stocked rifle, and to the pensioner she looked like a young partisan from the Second World War. He centered his 500mm lens on the girl. The snowy ground just a few meters in front of her exploded with fire and smoke, brown earth kicked up with the detonation of a grenade, but she took no notice. Instead she took one or two steps out of the trench toward the approaching Russian troops and shouldered her weapon, leveling it at the men coming her way.

He held the button on his Nikon down, snapped dozens of photos as the young woman almost a kilometer away ignored the branches of the trees rimming the berm exploding into the air and rocked back a little while firing her rifle. The closest Russian was not fifteen meters from her, and he spun into the snow with her shot, falling to the ground. The girl worked the bolt, the pensioner kept shooting pictures, the girl raised the weapon again to fire, and—just when he tried to capture perfectly the fire and smoke from her long wooden rifle—she lurched back again.

But this time it was not the recoil of her weapon that sent her to her heels. She spun around on the dirt and stumbled backward, her right arm jutting out, holding the weapon fully extended as her legs weakened and she fell back, all the way back.

She dropped the rifle as she dropped face-first into the trench.

The gun remained on the dirty snow at the edge of the earthen berm, but the girl was gone.

He kept taking pictures, but his mind was on the girl even as the man she'd shot climbed back to his feet, lifted his rifle out of the snow, and resumed his advance.

She'd clearly hit him in his body armor, and he'd suffered no lasting effects.

And off to the south, just two hundred meters beyond the battle, the unceasing column of Russian armor rolled on to the east as if they were wholly unaware of the fight.

Paulina Tobiasz felt an incredible jolt against the stock of her rifle, and it spun her back into the ditch, where she landed hard on her chest on the frozen ground.

It took her a second to realize she was not dead—not yet, anyway—and once she understood this she reached out with her right hand and grabbed like mad for a new weapon among the dead and wounded around her. Her Mosin-Nagant hadn't made it back into the trench with her, so she was determined to take hold of any lethal device she could find.

She saw a wire-stocked AK just two meters away, half under the body of a dead twenty-six-year-old truck driver named Radek with eyes so bad that the Land Forces had refused to take him. His thick eyeglasses lay broken next to the weapon, but it wasn't Radek's rifle; he'd wielded an SKS in the fight.

She didn't worry about the Kalashnikov's provenance now. She just wanted to take it in her frozen hand, climb back out of the trench, and fire one last burst before the Russians killed her and every one of her friends.

On the far side of poor Radek, the forty-five-year-old soccer coach from Warsaw named Jerzy pulled himself to his knees, his face covered with dirt and streaked with blood, and he looked at the AK himself. Seeing Paulina crawling over Radek, Jerzy lunged for the weapon, scrambling over her. Even though he was gushing blood above his right ear from a vicious shrapnel wound to his scalp, he had more fight in him, just as the girl alive in the trench did. But Jerzy crushed Paulina with his weight as he crawled on top of her, smashing her down on top of Radek, and he got the AK in his right hand. He spun around with it, lying on Paulina's back and knocking the breath fully out of her. Although Paulina couldn't see what he was doing because she was pinned facedown in the broken earth, she heard close-in gunfire now, so she squeezed her eyes shut.

The pensioner on the top of the hill caught several groups of white-clad Russians running up the berm in front of the trench where the brave blonde had fallen. As he looked through his powerful lens, the young soldiers began aiming down into it. They sprayed into the pit with their AKs, some unslinging their weapons and, holding their guns high, not bothering to aim, pointed them straight down as they shot round after round, emptying their magazines.

The Russian troops were massacring the wounded.

The main column had continued rolling up the road for the entire duration of the fight, and now down on the road below him the photographer could see supply trucks and other vehicles among the tanks and assault vehicles. He photographed what he could, looked down at his screen, and saw he had taken more than five hundred images in the past three minutes.

He decided he needed to get the hell out of there.

CHAPTER 32

Lieutenant Colonel Tom Grant was in a particularly foul mood already, and he hadn't even started his workday. He'd gotten up a half hour earlier to FaceTime with his wife back in Boulder and wish her a merry Christmas only to find he had no Internet connection on his phone. He then tried to call her and, after sitting there with the phone to his ear for over a minute, realized his cell service was down as well.

His wife would be going to bed pissed at him.

Some Christmas morning this was shaping up to be.

Grant had been here at U.S. Army Garrison Grafenwöhr for the past month, preparing equipment for Broadsword, a massive NATO exercise to take place in Germany in late January. As commander of a tank maintenance regiment, he was ultimately responsible for the function of every single American Abrams tank in the operation, so he wasn't able to spend Christmas with his family.

Broadsword was a NATO exercise, but the Poles, Germans, and Americans were the most heavily invested in terms of troops.

The other member nations were involved, but the three countries that would maneuver the vast majority of the regiments of ground power and wings of airpower remained the three most committed to the defense of northern Europe.

His job was tough enough without communications problems first thing this morning. He'd taken a shower while cursing Apple and Deutsche Telekom and various other vague, undefined forces conspiring against him, then dressed in his BDU and laced up his boots. He tried to dial home again as he walked down the hall, past the doors to the giant tank maintenance bays.

A former University of Minnesota tackle, Grant had been a muscular six feet back in the day. It had helped him immensely as a young tanker, hefting rounds and changing tank tracks. Now some of the muscle had sagged to his waist, and his auburn hair had thinned in front and given way to gray. He still maintained a blocky, solid appearance, but as with most driven men, he regretted that his duties gave him less time to concentrate on his fitness.

"Sir?" a voice from an open doorway called out, interrupting his attempt at a phone call that wasn't going anywhere anyway. He turned to Lieutenant Darnell Chandler, his assistant logistics officer. "Morning, sir. There's a call for you in the Layette Room."

"At least one damn phone is working," Grant said.

"Yes, sir. Couldn't connect with my girlfriend this morning on Skype. Internet is down. Guess that's gonna be my fault when I finally do talk to her."

"No, Chandler," Grant said as he passed him. "Not until you marry her. Then *everything's* your fault."

Grant had a personal rule about not getting his first good whiff of engine oil and hydraulic fluid until after breakfast, but he and Chandler headed out into the maintenance bay on his way to the room where the tools and other equipment were kept.

As he passed through the door, he was happy to see that several German soldiers and U.S. Army tankers were paired up and working hard. Inside the maintenance bay was a pair of massive M1A2 SEP Abrams tanks, and all of the men working on them were coated with different amounts of grease.

"Lieutenant Colonel Grant, Lieutenant Colonel Grant," repeated the PA system as he walked along between the big tanks. *"Phone call, line one."*

Tom Grant hastened his stride and glanced at his cell again. The damn thing still said *Keine Verbindung.* (No connection.)

He nodded as he walked by two senior enlisted leaders, Master Sergeant

Kellogg and Oberstabsfeldwebel Wolfram, who was the German army equivalent of a master sergeant.

"Sir, they're calling for you in the maintenance office," said Kellogg.

"Yep, heard." He kept walking, with Chandler right behind him.

After the major was out of earshot, the German turned to his American counterpart. "How's your new boss?"

"He's good," said Kellogg. "I've been breaking him in slowly. But I think he gets it. He's been around the block a few times, mainly at the tactical level. He finished ABOLC, the tank officer basic school, so he's a legit tanker. Tank commander, even. But something got screwed up along the way."

Wolfram wiped grease from his hands with a well-used rag. "What do you mean?"

"He got sent on a military training mission in Iraq, and they only send guys there as a punishment when they fuck up. It's not pretty when an officer falls from grace. They give them the worst shit duty they have, and if they survive—shine, even—only then do they have any chance of saving their career."

"You Americans are so much too hard on your officers. One mistake and all washed out, no?"

"Well, not exactly, but Grant won't make it past lieutenant colonel no matter what he does." He shrugged. "Anyhow, they sent him to mainte-nance officer school and he's now a really damn good one. The troops love him. He's got a nonstop work ethic, though—I'll give him that. Dude even sleeps in the maintenance office some nights."

The German said, "This sounds like my boss. I think maybe your lieu-tenant colonel and my major are stressed about the exercise next month."

LTC Grant's voice came over the PA. "I need Major Ott, Master Sergeant Kellogg, and Oberstabsfeldwebel Wolfram in the Layette Room immediately."

The German and American master sergeants exchanged a look. "Shit," Kellogg said. "Gotta teach the boss to not sound so high-strung on the PA. Dude sounds like there's a damn war goin' on."

Three minutes later the two senior enlisted men stood in the Layette Room with Lieutenant Colonel Grant and Lieutenant Chandler. Grant hung up the landline phone and turned to the three men as Major Blaz Ott, commander of the German contingent here, came in to join them, looking worried.

"Blaz, grab a seat. I have something hot."

A U.S. sergeant walked in with a clipboard of paperwork and interrupted. "Hey, Top, I can't order that code 'oh-three' you wanted. The Internet is down again and—"

Kellogg snapped his finger and shouted, "Go away, trooper!"

The sergeant backed out and shut the door.

Grant said, "I got a call on the landline from our bosses, who, as you know, are up in Belgium on Christmas break with their families. They say cell service is out across all of Europe. So is all Internet. A few landlines are still working—they got through to me for a minute, but we got cut off.

"But here's what I *do* know. The Russians have launched an attack in Poland."

Every man in front of Grant sat up straighter, eyes wide.

"Fuck me," muttered Kellogg.

"We don't know yet what their exact composition is, and we have no idea what their intentions are."

Ott asked, "How did they cross into Poland already without anyone knowing about it? It's not as if you can hide the Russian army."

Grant said, "No idea. We're on alert status as of right now. Our bosses want us to grab the regiment and get on the move. We have to pull everyone we can muster from the battalions and line companies, man every tank that can drive with whoever is qualified."

"To do what, exactly?" asked Kellogg.

"We'll form a hasty blocking position, and the bosses will join us and take over command."

"Sir, we don't have the actual tankers," said Kellogg. The main body of their unit, the 37th Armored Regiment, was still in the States. None of the maintainers had ever considered the possibility they might actually have to maneuver the line elements in the regiment, their M1A2 Abrams main battle tanks, in battle.

"I understand and the brigadier does, too. But we don't have time to wait till the main body arrives. The rest of the BCT is not scheduled to depart the States until after the first of the year. It's us and our German brothers or no one."

Chandler spoke in an incredulous tone now. "Sir . . . this makes you . . . regimental commander?" Maintenance men, even those with a tank background, were *not* tank regimental commanders.

"Just for a few hours. I want to talk to the men in ten minutes. Then I want tanks staged within the hour."

The consternation was visible on Grant's face as he surveyed the small group of senior leaders. He knew as well as the others assembled here that not one of their men was a fully trained 19K, the military occupational specialty of armored crewmen. The Americans here at Grafenwöhr were mostly 91As and 45Es, system maintainers and turret mechanics.

"Gentlemen, I know what you are thinking, but almost all of our 91As have been to basic driving school. Hell, most of them get more driving time than the actual tank drivers. And we are all proficient in gunnery."

Wolfram spoke up now. "But what happens if they make it into Germany before the rest of the regiment's tankers make it in, sir?"

"We do as ordered: we *are* tankers and we execute the move until directed otherwise."

Chandler said, "Sir, we'll need to get you some headquarters vehicles and communications equipment for command and control."

"Yes, get me the headquarters vics. Everything we have for radio communications. The satellites are all out and I want long haul comms to talk to the battalions."

"Three tank battalions!" interjected Major Blaz Ott. "We are under your command, sir."

CENTRAL IRAN
25 DECEMBER

Colonel General Boris Lazar was so used to the noise, the dust, the vibration, and the constant rubbing against sharp and unyielding surfaces that came along with riding in the turret of a tank that he didn't notice any of it anymore. He just looked out at the long line of sand-colored armored vehicles in front of him, rumbling down the Hamadan-Bijar Road, some six kilometers northwest of the city of Zanjan, and listened in to the radio chatter in his headset.

Lazar had a headquarters vehicle, but he wanted to ride in a T-90 tank for this part of the journey. He could still get information over the radio and was in constant contact with his second-in-command, Colonel Dmitry Kir, who was buttoned up in the HQ vehicle only fifty meters behind him.

The command vehicle was one of only a few of the new Bumerang APCs in his force. Sabaneyev had scored the majority of the Bumerangs, while Lazar's main troop carrier was the venerable but trusted BTR-82A. Lazar had spent over thirty years in variants of the BTR and he had no great desire to work with anything else, but the communications suite in the Bumerang HQ vehicles was second to none, so he'd begrudgingly added five of the latest-generation APCs to his force.

Sabaneyev could have the majority of the new shit: the Bumerangs and the T-14s. Lazar was an old-timer and he'd fight his war with the tried-and-true.

Lazar knew he had his work cut out for him, even here in friendly territory. He had to move his entire combat force, his entire headquarters and supply force, over nearly 1,300 kilometers of unfamiliar terrain. He'd never been to Iran, and even though the politicians in Moscow and the politicians in Tehran had worked out this movement of thousands of Russian troops and one hundred pieces of armor across the north-south axis of Iran, it was still one hell of an endeavor.

Lazar's force moved with a large mass of Iranian armor and troops, not because they needed protection, but rather because to the lenses of the satellites still operational over the Middle East this was supposed to look like a joint training exercise between the two nations. Lazar's force racing alone down toward the southern coastline would be looked at quite differently from the joint force heading south, at least for a day or two, and that was all Colonel Borbikov determined they would need to make Lazar's mission a fait accompli.

Thirty-two hours of travel would put Lazar at port before the Americans figured out what he was doing—*that* had been Borbikov's bet. A Russian-Iranian training exercise thousands of kilometers from either the Asian or the European theater would be the least of their worries.

Until the moment when Lazar and his force set sail for the Horn of Africa, when he would would suddenly turn into their greatest worry of all.

CHAPTER 33

Connolly and Griggs worked through Christmas morning sitting at their desks, searching for information about what the hell was going on in Central Europe.

Intelligence had been all but nonexistent in the first few hours; the two men spent as much time flipping through the news channels on the TV in the bullpen as they did querying DIA, CIA, and NSA networks.

Griggs pointed out he could pull up more real-time info about what was happening in East Timor or Paraguay than he could about the goings-on in Europe.

About one a.m. Pentagon time a shortwave radio operator near Kraków was picked up reporting Russian armor moving north of the city. This would have been the first solid nugget of a land invasion, if not for the fact that shortwave operators in Tallinn, Estonia; Dagda, Latvia; and Rudamina, Lithuania, also reported that the Russians were pouring over the border. No one knew if one or all of the reports were part of a Russian disinformation campaign or not, but no one believed the story of a thousand-mile-wide Russian invasion when no great buildup of forces near the borders had been detected.

Griggs brought Connolly his sixth cup of coffee around eleven a.m. He sat down next to the Marine and said, "If this was a real invasion of Europe, there is no way General Lazar wouldn't be running it. He's spent his whole life preparing for just this thing."

Connolly said, "I don't get it, either. Unless they are trying to pull a Patton with him."

Griggs understood the reference. George Patton was America's most storied general during the later part of World War II. The U.S. sent him to England, ostensibly to train his force for the upcoming Normandy invasion, but it was all a ruse. When the invasion came, he was very publicly still in England, causing many Germans to believe nothing important was happening on the Normandy coast.

The major said, "That would be a shrewd move, but I don't buy it. Even if they didn't use him in the attack on NATO, moving him out of Russia at a time when Russia must know it's in danger of a counterstrike just seems crazy. If Sabaneyev is sending a massive invasion force to Europe, Russia is exposed."

Connolly spun around to face his colleague. "But what if there *is* no invasion force that we missed? NATO has spent seventy years watching out for and preparing for the red tide pouring over into Western Europe. But something much smaller than a total Russian mobilization could punch through, especially if the Russians sowed enough confusion with satellite and communications interruptions."

Griggs thought it over. "Holy shit, Dan! A raid. An operational raid!"

"It's the only thing that makes sense. Several hundred pieces of frontline armor racing into Europe could punch a hole, especially at Christmas, when NATO's guard is down, and especially when NATO can't see or hear what's happening."

"But . . . but *why?*" Griggs asked. "They want to race around Europe blowing shit up just to show they can? What are they going to do, take Berlin and turn it into an enclave?"

"I have no idea," Connolly said. "You want to call Nik over at NSA and ask him if he wouldn't mind poking around at the exercises in Iran?"

Griggs whistled. "You don't think he's got enough going on with the invasion of Europe and the impending invasion of Taiwan?"

"Think about it. He's been working on the Taiwan thing for four months. As for the European attack, there isn't enough intel coming through for him to evaluate. The satellites over Iran are working fine. Give him a call."

Griggs nodded. "Okay, can't hurt."

HOF, GERMANY
25 DECEMBER

A twenty-one-year-old from Utah was the first American to see the Russian invasion, although it had begun sixteen hours earlier.

Three feet of snow blown into drifts made trudging through the heavy woods north of the hamlet of Hof difficult to nearly impossible for the lone reconnaissance scout, but he'd been ordered forward to take a look into the distance.

A team driving in three cavalry scout vehicles—Humvees with .50-cal mounted machine guns—had parked well inside the trees, enshrouded by the evening's darkness and low clouds.

The young man from Utah fell more than once on the thirty-yard journey to the edge of the wood line, and each time he felt the embarrassment of knowing his mates and his sergeant were probably watching him.

He crunched through the snow, then finally dropped to his knees on a spot of ground with only a foot of accumulation, and began scanning with his NVGs along the autobahn in the distance. He saw nothing at first, but then his trained eyes picked up the faint outline of a row of vehicles proceeding at a steady pace to the southwest.

He'd watched civilian traffic all afternoon and evening long without alarm, but the unique aspect of this particular line of large vehicles was that none of them had their lights on.

He waited for them to come a little closer; then through the clear and frigid nighttime air he began to make out the individual shapes. Scout cars; long, fat, and low armored fighting vehicles he could not identify.

And then he saw the tanks.

A *lot* of tanks.

He launched to his feet, spun, and lumbered back to his Humvee as quickly as possible, where his sergeant first class was standing by the front passenger door.

"Armor and heavy recon vics, Sergeant. Definitely Russian. No lights. Heading southwest."

A radio call immediately went to Lieutenant Colonel Tom Grant, a kilometer behind with the tanks in their hasty blocking position.

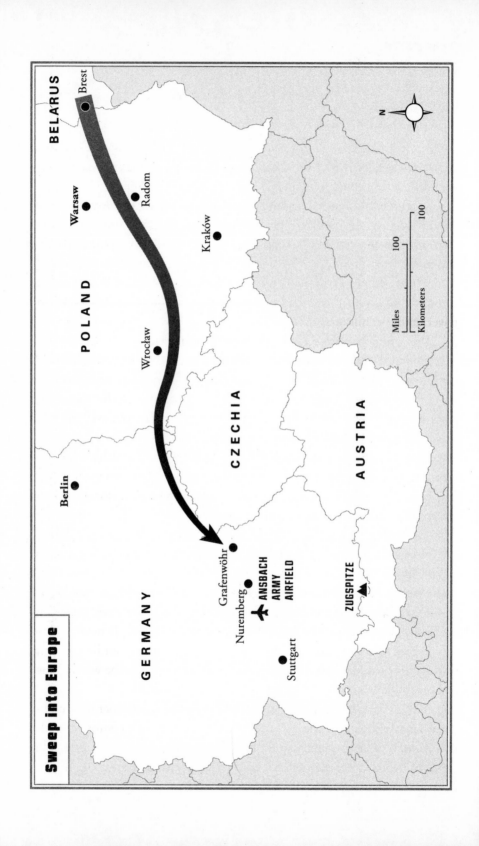

Before setting off from Grafenwöhr, Grant had been able to field forty tanks per battalion for a total of eighty M1A2 SEP Abrams tanks and a sizable reconnaissance troop of dozens of Humvees and dozens of Stryker armored fighting vehicles.

This made Lieutenant Colonel Tom Grant, a U.S. Army logistics officer, the commander of the 37th Armored Regiment, composite.

And German major Blaz Ott was now technically the commander of the 203rd Panzer Battalion. He commanded forty-four Leopard 2s, Germany's heaviest and mightiest tank. At the height of the Cold War the German army had fielded over two thousand Leopards, but they now had fewer than two hundred fifty. Still, the Leopard 2 was a marvel of German precision engineering and a force to be reckoned with.

The good news for Grant and Ott was that they both had plenty of munitions. Because both the U.S. European Command and German Bundeswehr HQ had been planning heavy participation in the upcoming live-fire portion of Exercise Broadsword, all the vehicles were well stocked with tank rounds, machine-gun rounds, and rockets.

Grant was looking at a map spread out on the hood of his Humvee when he took the call letting him know the Russians had been spotted. He and his XO, Captain Brad Spillane, quickly found the location and checked the direction of the road.

Grant said, "They're coming this way. We've got ten minutes to figure out how we're handling this, but America's war with Russia is going to start right here."

Grant had put the most experienced men into his operations and headquarters element, guys who were about to retire or had already served in command and had just been awaiting their orders for their next assignment. That left tank commanders who were less than the best he had, but if he didn't have the best directing the battle, things could be worse. Way worse.

The headquarters section, led by Captain Spillane, a former tank company commander, consisted of several radio Humvees, a command-and-control vehicle, and several camouflage command tents.

And it was from this perch that Tom Grant thought he could best command and control the battle.

The ambush Grant and Ott set up for the Russians was mostly linear, focused on what they estimated was the enemy's most likely direction of travel. By positioning themselves on a ridge overlooking German routes 9 and 72, they had hedged their bets pretty well. A separate force with only eight tanks was dispatched to cover the intersection of routes 93 and 72. It wasn't enough to do much damage, but he and Ott had decided at the last minute not to split their forces in half and instead to weight their western ambush, as it was the most likely avenue of approach.

3RD AVIATION BRIGADE, REGIMENTAL HQ
ANSBACH ARMY AIRFIELD
KATTERBACH KASERNE, GERMANY
25 DECEMBER

The landline to the 1-3 Attack Reconnaissance Battalion pilot ready room rang a second, a third, then a fourth time, but Army 1st Lieutenant Sandra Glisson found herself reluctant to put the PlayStation 4 controller down to answer it.

The battalion's classroom doubled as a lounge and was all but vacant on Christmas Day. Almost all the officers were out on leave except those here in the ready room: the two playing video games, the one filling out his flight logs with tunes from his iPhone blaring in his earbuds, and the one sleeping on the couch in front of the big-screen TV—which, while on, hadn't broadcast anything but a blue screen all day.

The regimental commander had left two gunships and their crews on ready alert status. He was brand-new and made a point of mentioning that his motto was "Train as you fight." But to the officers on watch, it was more top-brass bullshit. The G2 briefed everyone that Poland's alert status was "high," so they all needed to ensure their recall info was sound; then the regiment's intelligence officer, executive officer, and commander all took off on vacation back to the U.S.

"I've got your ass now!" shouted First Lieutenant Allen Thomas over the noise of the ringing phone and the video game. "You might as well grab that phone—you're dead either way!"

"Pause the game and I will!" replied Glisson.

Thomas kept playing, so Glisson reluctantly stood up, continuing to work her controller as she walked toward the phone.

The support battalion platoon leader finally paused the game, so Lieutenant Glisson dropped the controller on the sofa and snatched the phone off the cradle.

Thomas then unpaused the game with a laugh and resumed playing.

Glisson saw this as she spoke with an eye roll. "Hello?"

A voice boomed on the other line. "Fucking *'Hello'*? Is that how you answer the ready room phone? Who the *fuck* is this?"

She recognized the voice of Major Cussard; she'd forgotten he was even on duty. "I'm sorry, sir. This is First Lieutenant Sandra Glisson, 1st Battalion."

The phone hissed and clicked, but she could make out the major's words well enough. "Listen up, Glisson! The attack weapons team just got activated. You're to grab your wingman and launch immediately. I'll brief you on your company's internal when you are up on comms."

"Sir . . . ," said Sandra incredulously, "is this a joke?"

"Does it sound like I'm *fucking joking*, Lieutenant? Get your ass to your aircraft—*now!*"

There was a pause as Sandra looked at Lieutenant Thomas.

"Why are you still on the phone?" screamed Major Cussard.

Sandra hung up and stared at the three men in the room.

And then: "We're launching!" She slammed her hand against a button on the wall, activating red "whoopie" lights across the battalion's building.

The two aviators on the couch jumped to their feet but just stood there staring at her in bewilderment.

"Does it look like I'm *fucking joking*? This is *not* a drill! Get your ass to your aircraft *now!*" she yelled.

Three minutes later, two officers ran through their checklist in Apache aircraft number 42, right next to Sandra's own Apache gunship, number 41. Sandra's weapons officer hadn't shown up yet, but she'd climbed into the front seat of her aircraft. In her haste she had forgotten her coat, and the freezing German winter air chilled her as she worked.

Red and white rotating lights flashed on the helicopters as they powered up, illuminating the night and adding to the sense of urgency. The ground crewmen scurried around both of the fifty-eight-foot helicopters, checking systems and pulling tie-downs off the rotors and control surfaces.

Three ammunition dollies screeched to a halt as a pair of handlers prepared to strap missile and gun pods onto the aircraft.

The ground chief clicked his headset into 42's Fox-Mike connector on the outside of the fuselage so he could talk to Sandra as his men readied her helo.

He began with an apology. "Ma'am, I stripped all your armament off a few hours ago to run it through a maintenance cycle. I . . . I didn't think you'd be launching today."

"Chief, it's okay. Me, either. Just get me all the shit you can ASAP."

Sandra's UHF radio crackled to life now with Major Cussard's voice. "Viper One-Six, Viper One-Six, this is Griffin Three. Do you read me? Over."

She keyed her mic. "Griffin Three, this is Viper One-Six, Lima Charlie. Standing by for your orders. Over."

"Tell your wingman to get up on this net and listen in. I'm going to brief you as you take off."

She waved at 42 and pointed to her headset, indicating the pilot and weapons officer in the other ship needed to listen in on the battalion's tactical net.

Both men switched on in time to hear Cussard say, "We have no satellite communications whatsoever. Once you take off, we'll try to keep you on the UHF guard net, but we're expecting to lose comms. Your weapons officer was over here in the TOC, so I'm sending him down with maps. He'll be back to you any second. Over."

"Roger. Request to know what we're looking at here. Over." As the operations officer was speaking Sandra had been looking out the window, watching as the ground crew removed red flags from each of the weapons as they loaded them.

"Confirm your number two man is listening."

"Wait one, sir," said Sandra as Chief Warrant Officer 2 James appeared out of the building and sprinted through a light freezing rain toward the aircraft. He handed a sheaf of maps to Sandra as he climbed into the backseat, several feet higher than Sandra's position. He quickly put his helmet on.

"James is here and listening, sir." CWO2 James immediately began his preflight. As pilot in charge, his duty was to run up the aircraft while she, as Air Mission Commander, completed the weapons and comms checks from the front seat.

The major said, "The Russians have mounted an attack. We don't know the full composition, but we understand they have tanks, T-14s, as well as Bumerangs. Heard something about scout cars—those will likely be their GAZ Tigrs—and various supply and logistics vehicles. Strength unknown. Their last known location was vicinity one hundred fifty kilometers south of Dresden on Route 72. Direction of movement is generally southwest. SAM threat is unknown at this time."

"Ho-ly shit, sir!" Glisson exclaimed into her mic.

Cussard kept talking. "Be advised, the friendlies on the ground are call sign Courage. They are a mix of U.S. M1A2s and German Leopards out of Grafenwöhr. They have spotted the Russians in the vicinity of Highways 9 and 72. Courage will conduct a linkup with you on their unit's UHF radio network, net identifier two-one-three-decimal-one-two. The last we got from them was on the landline, and now their HQ is silent. Cell phones are out, too.

"You are to conduct hasty reconnaissance of this enemy column in support of the ground attack element from Grafenwöhr. Do *not* get decisively engaged until we get more ammo out and your company commander is up with you. Just provide the ground guys with as much data on the composition and disposition of the enemy column as you can. Acknowledge."

In the green glow of the cockpit, Sandra looked over the coordinates on the map CWO2 James had given her. She fought through her shock upon realizing she was about to enter combat in Europe and said, "Sir, I'm clear."

Now she looked out at the ground crew chief, who gave her a thumbs-up.

Sandra pulled down her helmet-mounted display and flicked through the flight profiles, setting up her targeting computer. Her face glowed green from the digital map and targeting sight as she copied down the regimental operations officer's information onto her kneeboard and punched the new frequencies into her communications panel.

Behind her, CWO2 James flicked the two switches labeled "IGNITE" to fire up both engines, then eased the throttle forward until the engines let loose a loud *whumph* and then a steady roar. The rotors spun and the ground crew unconsciously ducked lower as they continued to check over Sandra's helo.

Cussard said, "Weather is shit. It's clear, but low fog up north. I'll send you METOC, but I'm authorizing you to fly. Snow later tonight about zero-three hours. I can't think of a greater emergency than attacking Russians, so your reconnaissance takes precedence over basic safety limitations."

The radio transmission paused briefly as the brigade's operations officer thought for a moment, then continued. "Glisson, you have the fight until I can get your company commander back to base. I'll send him out as soon as he and enough of the company return so he can get forward and see what's going on up north.

"What questions do you have? Over."

First Lieutenant Sandra Glisson and her wingman were now being towed out onto the tarmac.

"Are our forces engaging with the Russians now, sir?"

Cussard said, "I have no idea, and I'm pretty sure you're going to know before I do."

"Roger that. Viper One-Six requesting permission for takeoff."

"Granted, Viper One-Six. You are clear for takeoff. Remain on the UHF net throughout the mission. Even if you lose us, we'll continue to monitor it."

The ground crew towed them to their takeoff points and backed off. The crew chief's men saluted. Glisson and her pilot saluted back.

"Copy, Griffin Three, this is Viper One-Six. We are in takeoff, time now. Over." Viper One-Six lifted and then tilted forward, began moving along just a few feet above the ground, then quickly began gaining altitude.

"Good luck, Lieutenant. Griffin Three out on this net."

CHAPTER 34

PANZER HULL NUMBER 71
37TH ARMORED REGIMENT (COMPOSITE) AND
 PANZERBATAILLON 203
MÜNCHBERG, GERMANY
25 DECEMBER

Sweat streamed from twenty-two-year-old Obergefreiter Oliver Lutz's hairline, leaving clean white vertical streaks in the grease, carbon gun dust, and mud that covered his face and neck.

Ninety minutes after the first salvo came in from the Russian tanks, the battle had been nonstop, and Lutz worried it would continue on until his tank was blown to bits.

Lutz's clear plastic ballistic goggles had broken almost in half. One of the eyepieces had fallen to the metal deck of the Leopard 2 main battle tank amid a clutter of brass 140mm case bases, chow wrappers, pine needles, and empty packets of Jacobs Krönung instant coffee.

The moment he'd smacked his face against the turret, the goggles had earned his appreciation, even though they'd been damaged in the process. Lutz had been too busy furiously loading his L/51 tank cannon to bother with the half-destroyed goggles, so he'd left them on. But now his tank commander, Major Ott, seemed to have stopped firing on the Russians for a moment to maneuver, so Lutz took the opportunity to pull the goggles off of his face and toss them down onto the discarded remnants of war under his and the crew's feet.

And Lutz's thick elbow-length leather-and-Nomex gloves were still covering a part of his sleeve that had been ripped off his body when it got caught on the breech.

Better than my hand or arm, he remembered thinking.

His ears rang, and there was an unrelenting buzzing sensation in his skull. *Did we get hit?* He found he couldn't remember everything that had happened through the exhaustion and stress.

Major Ott broke in over the intercom. "Target! Twelve hundred meters. APC." The momentary lull was over, and Lutz snapped out of his stupor and back to full awareness.

"Identified. Load HEAT," said the gunner in a loud bark.

Lutz pivoted sharply in his seat, tapping the metal pedal with his foot, opening the ammunition storage compartment door, grabbing a high-explosive anti-tank round, and jamming it into the breech. The main gun mechanism closed itself automatically when the round entered, slamming upward with a sharp *clack.*

"Up!" Lutz yelled hoarsely into his mic, knowing his voice needed to be louder than what his crew members could hear over the malfunctioning intercom.

More sweat poured down into his eyes.

"Fire!" ordered the commander. Lutz looked over at Ott, his hands cupped over the thermal sight system as he peered intently through the darkness.

"On the way!" yelled the gunner, and with a resonating *boom* the huge tank's 130mm main gun fired. The breech roared back, ejecting a metal disk called the base case, and a thick knot of gray smoke entered the turret as the gun locked open.

There was a delay of a few seconds, and then Ott spoke again. "Target destroyed. Gunner, pick up a scan."

The noise of one flat blast, followed by a succession of distant explosions, entered through the tank's two open top hatches.

Secondary detonations, thought Lutz. *Must've nailed their ammo magazine.*

The crew of the tank had ceased calling one another by name. Their minds were so focused, they reverted to the language they used at tank school and only referred to one another by their position in the machine. Any pretense of life outside the tank, along with any niceties over the intercom, had been dropped the moment that first Russian main tank round came sailing into the trees.

Every second and every decision meant death or life, so each man was all business.

Lutz's fingers felt like thick, fat sausages. Pain lanced across his back from pivoting to the ammo ready rack and then back to the main gun to load it. A thick fog crept about his head whenever he paused in between ramming the twenty-five-kilogram depleted-uranium A4 penetrator tank rounds.

He had one luxury the other tank crew members didn't: he couldn't see anything outside. He relied on their commands, his instinct, and the urgency he ascertained in every voice, the pitch of the engine, and the rapidity with which the turret pivoted. Faster meant trouble; slower meant a steady, cautious scan by the gunner or the commander.

Some recent moments had been more intense than others. Drastically more intense. He could feel it in the others' voices, how they stiffened their bodies up against the sight's eyecups, the shrill and distinct whine of incoming enemy shells. The loud *pop* when a round flew overhead.

Fear pervaded the tank, but none of them had time to acknowledge it.

Lutz moved at the pace his gunner and commander demanded. When they had targets, he was committed to action. When they hunted for targets or moved the tank to a new position, he sat, held on, and tried to imagine what was happening outside the eighty-two-centimeter-thick armor of their Leopard 2's turret.

The numbness that clouded his brain crept in again. A fatigue-induced exhaustion was beginning to swarm all around him.

Then he heard the memory of his old tank instructor, an *Oberfeldwebel*, or staff sergeant, yelling at him again: "*Idioten!* What is the third rule in tank combat?" He was referring to the German tanker's Platinum Rules of Armored Warfare.

The young students would then answer in chanting unison, "*Go ahead, let your attention drift. Now your enemy receives his gift!*"

It hadn't meant much then. Just memorize the eight rules and you didn't get yelled at—as much.

But now he fully understood the *Oberfeldwebel*'s meaning. If he fell asleep at his gun now, the enemy T-14s would rip them open, just as they had several other German and American tanks in the composite regiment.

The secondary explosions came again. They were lighting up the night and a glow flickered into the turret, shadows cast around, waving gently back and forth. Lutz's tired eyes lazily followed them.

Just like Mutti's Weihnachten candle, he thought, remembering Christmas at his mother's house.

She still uses real candles, he remembered, energy fading from his body. His eyes tracked the darkening shadows, and then another *pop* made him smile, as it sounded like the fire his father always lit in the fireplace during the holidays.

His eyes shut themselves.

Lutz shook his head. Tried hard to break through the haze and not to think about the Christmas candles' sweet scent.

A sickening smell inside the turret filled his nostrils and broke him out of the stupor. Wet sweat, excrement, gunpowder. Grease and diesel fuel.

Burning rubber from the war outside.

Fuck these Arschlöcher. *Have to stay awake.* At last, anger and adrenaline returned in a quick but small rush, and he sat up straighter, stretching his back.

Early on, an enemy tank round had glanced off their turret's sloped armor and knocked their intercom out of whack so that he could now only hear the other crew very faintly.

That's why my ears are buzzing.

The more recent history, maybe the past half hour, was kind of a blur.

A short while ago the driver hit a deep ravine and Lutz slammed his head against the side of the turret, splitting his helmet and goggles. The driver himself had been knocked unconscious, and Ott had yelled for him over the intercom to wake up. The gunner even crawled outside and banged on the nineteen-year-old's hatch, to no avail.

Lutz eventually climbed through the tank himself and shook the boy until he woke.

Then they drove on, sprinting to a new position. Advancing on the enemy, who, Lutz had heard from Ott's play-by-play of the action, was retreating through the forest and onto the autobahn.

Lutz's only awareness of the tank's whereabouts was from tidbits of intercom traffic and from the chunks of snow and the pine branches and needles that rained into the turret. Lutz had thirstily eaten the snow chunks that fell inside.

Then a succession of rapid explosions erupted close to the tank and, at least as far as Lutz could tell, the gunner had diarrhea in his tank suit, but no one had had the energy or humor to mention it.

Next their engine had taken a direct and apparently partially penetrating hit from something. No one knew what, but they were only getting about 50 percent power now. They slowed significantly but continued fighting and, from what Lutz gathered from the radio cross talk, remained abreast of the rest of the tanks attacking south as the enemy withdrew.

Lutz had never really believed a night like this was possible.

But here he was, in the middle of it.

Lutz backed himself momentarily against the cold metal hull of the tank and away from the hot breech of his Rheinmetall 130mm smoothbore L/51 tank main gun. Steam rose from his suit. Sweat and heat mixing with the cool air coming through the gunner's top hatch.

"Gunner, this is loader. Three AT rounds remain," Lutz said into his headset, using a mundane task of reporting his ammo count to keep himself awake.

"*Klar!*" was the only response he got from the tank's gunner.

The gunner, Feldwebel Herbert Kanst, peered into his gunsight system. Lutz took a moment to look him over. If Kanst even noticed his own diarrhea, he didn't show it. The gunner's hand gripped the turret joystick with white knuckles, locking the palm switch down to control the turret as he scanned through the dark, trying to spot more Russian tanks or other vehicles before his own tank was detected by the enemy. He was absorbed in his task just like Lutz and the rest of the crew were absorbed in theirs.

From the new chatter Lutz was only partially able to hear on the intercom, he gleaned the driver was asking for permission to sprint toward a copse of trees about two hundred meters to their front.

"*Halt!*" yelled Feldwebel Kanst now. "Dismounts! Two hundred meters in front . . . looks like the crew from that BMP the American tank just destroyed. They are lining up in the trees . . . I see RPGs."

"Engage. Use coax," Ott ordered without hesitation.

"Engaging!" replied Kanst, and Lutz listened to the muffled thumping sounds of the 7.62mm rounds pouring from the Leopard 2's MG3A1 coaxial machine gun. Lutz immediately shifted his body to the machine gun's feed chute and "escorted" the four-hundred-round belt. He instinctively put his hand out to hold the rapidly moving rounds over the small bump between the ready box and the machine gun's top cover, where the gun typically malfunctioned during their training exercises.

The weapon fired unerringly. When it stopped, he heard Major Ott's voice over the intercom again. "Rake that cluster off to the left side. Give it a Z pattern. *Sehr gut!* Continue firing there. Russian dismounts, that vicinity.

"*Panzer links und vorwärts marsch!*" Ott said once Kanst stopped firing.

Lutz braced himself against the turret as the sixty-five-ton beast lurched toward the copse of trees the driver had spotted.

Ott spoke again. "Tankers, take out your small arms and prepare to kill any stragglers. I'm up on the pintle." The major was referring to the pintle machine gun on the top of the tank.

Lutz grabbed his Heckler & Koch MP7 submachine gun and waited for the gunner to get out first so he could climb through the hatch.

Seconds later Obergefreiter Lutz stepped on the sticky, wet mess that covered the gunner's canvas seat and crawled out of the turret for the first time in over ten hours. He sat down on the turret next to the gunner, who was already scanning the wood line with his NVGs, his own MP7 at the ready, aiming toward the trees that they were slowly entering.

The freezing December air burned at Lutz's exposed nostrils and eyes. The sweat soaking his Nomex tanker's suit instantly chilled, a relief from the unbearable heat in the turret. Major Ott was above him, on the machine gun, scanning the trees ahead.

In the distance, Lutz got his first view of a dozen brightly burning vehicle hulks, some of which had been killed by the 130mm tank rounds he had loaded into the Leopard 2's gun. To his left he saw an American M1A2 battle tank lurking in the woods parallel to them. It rumbled slowly through the dark and stopped just short of the edge of the woods, the huge turret scanning slowly and methodically. One of the Abrams crewmen sat on his turret, an M4 carbine tight against his shoulder; just like Lutz, he was scanning for enemy dismounts.

Obergefreiter Lutz of the Bundeswehr's Panzerbattailon 203 inhaled a deep breath of the crisp winter air, and for a second it reminded him it was Christmastime. Then the smell of burning flesh mixed with oil and fuel entered his nostrils. They were new smells to him, but instinctively he knew what they were. He gripped the MP7 tighter and peered into the dark, deep woods and the white snow-covered hills and fields, looking for enemy movement.

The rest of the Russian tanks appeared to have vanished, for now.

CHAPTER 35

Lieutenant Glisson and her wingman had flown hundreds of missions in the area, but due to political sensitivities and protests against U.S. bases in Germany, they had reduced the number of night flights to next to zero in recent years. It felt weird and disorienting flying through her NVGs here, but she'd done it enough stateside and in Afghanistan to trust her abilities.

The horizon came up in her helmet-mounted display as she tried to update their digital 3-D map with the last-known reported enemy and friendly positions being read over the radio. The "last knowns" were mostly just speculation at this point, but would give Sandra a basic forward edge of the area where she could revert from traveling at air speeds down to reconnaissance speeds.

"Copy, Glitter," replied CWO2 Sean "Jesse" James.

Lieutenant Glisson's moniker had been cast in stone on a practice safety mission, when she'd accidentally dropped six sticks from her M130 chaff and flare launchers directly onto the gunship of the squadron commander, who was observing each pilot's safety protocol check flights from below. The metallic chaff looked like glitter. Her only comment as she withdrew from overhead and looked back at her handiwork of fireworks dumped onto the boss was "Oh, pretty!" Worse, she had forgotten to un-key her radio and had broadcast her inner monologue to the whole squad-ron by accident.

In a drunken call sign–naming ceremony she was knighted "Glitter," or sometimes "Princess Glitter," because she hated that even more.

She didn't let it bug her. She would have thought it intentionally provocative against her as a woman, but her male counterparts' call signs in the same naming party were worse. Much worse. And besides, her scores on the gun range were higher than 92 percent of her male counterparts'.

She realized the boys were more than happy to take her into the ranks so long as she played by a few rules. The first one, kind of a rite of passage, had turned out to be taking a lot of shit and pretending not to care about it. Not a bad rule, and it served to keep everyone tight and humble in a community of pilots that didn't tolerate egos.

"Fly your bird, support your wingman, finish the mission, help the grunts, and get back to friendly lines with your chopper in one piece." The rules to make it in the boys' club were simpler than society had led her to believe when she joined the Army.

She called to her wingman on her radio now. "Badfinger, Jesse sees a spot on the map about two clicks northeast on our general attack heading. I'll check the field with thermals, then clear us for a gun test."

"Copy, Glitter. Uh . . . are we allowed to do that?"

"Don't know, don't care. We're doin' it."

The quiet snow-covered land below them lit up in a fiery red burst as the aircraft shot off cannons and guns.

Her wingman came over the radio almost immediately. "Glitter, this is Badfinger. Be advised, I've got a damn rocket pod malfunction. Neither one is working. Looks like they didn't connect the master arm connectors or forgot to take out the arming tags. Either way, I do have eight Hellfires, which are keying as operational. Guns tested fine with one thousand rounds remaining."

"Copy," said Lieutenant Glisson. "We are continuing on to the target."

A minute later Jesse said, "Glitter, I have Courage on the net, the American tank regiment. They gave me the lead trace on their position. They are on a linear frontage loosely east to west facing at thirty-two Uni-form Papa Alpha, 9979. I'm putting it on the IHADSS now."

"I see it. Just north of a town called . . . Hof on the map."

"That's it."

"Okay, tune me in to his frequency. Do you have their actual?"

"He says he's not their actual. Didn't catch why or where their commander is."

"Copy," Sandra said, then flicked over to the radio net ID Jesse had selected. "Courage, Courage, this is Glitter. We are a two-ship Apache section coming up from south to north along the niner-zero easting approximately twenty-two klicks out from your poz. We are locked and loaded and on a recon mission, ready to support you as needed. Over."

There was a brief pause; then a crackling transmission came through Sandra's headset. "Copy, Glitter. We are facing a regimental-sized Russian force of mixed BTRs, Bumerangs, and T-14 main battle tanks. We have established battle positions along the seven-nine-five easting oriented southwest. My vehicle is at 32 Uniform Papa, uh . . . break . . . Alpha 9948 7976. Be advised, we *are* in contact at this time and have taken losses. We don't know if this is a main body or an advance guard, but they are attempting to bypass us and proceed south on Route Nine."

Glitter said, "Okay, Courage, we copy your location and situation. We are coming from south along Route Nine. I can get flank shots as your enemy column proceeds and I'll stay outside your GTL until we can develop better situational awareness of the enemy." The gun-target line was an obvious no-go zone for the helos. If Sandra flew her ship into the line of fire of the heavy main guns of the American and German tanks, she could most certainly fall victim to what they called the "big bullet, little sky" theory, where converging on the same targets could increase the chances for fratricide.

Courage replied, "Copy all. Bad fog here." In the background she could hear an occasional dull roar of tank main-gun fire, audible even at more than twenty kilometers. Then came the thermal images of several bright spots, unmoving in the distance, but flickering and glowing above the trees, illuminating the starry darkness above the German hills and fields.

Jesse spoke from the rear seat. "Hey, Glitter, those what I think they are?"

"Burning armor. Hope it's theirs and not ours."

"Yeah." He paused. "You ever figure we'd be in combat with the Russians? Because I sure as *shit* did not."

Sandra had been thinking the same thing. The past hour had been utterly surreal. "I guess America didn't send us over here to play video games and drink mulled wine, after all."

"Right," said Jesse.

"And it's motherfucking *Christmas*, too," she said as she flew on toward the raging battle ahead.

HOF, GERMANY
25 DECEMBER

The reports from Lieutenant Colonel Grant's commanders were not good: their limited higher-level tank-command experience, coupled with the bleak environmental effects of fog, night, and cold, was taking its toll—along with the Russian invaders. A fair bit of confusion and emotion was on display in their radio broadcasts as the individual tanks fought it out over hectares of snow-covered grain fields.

But at least now Grant had a couple of Apaches to work with.

Listening in on the broadcast between his radioman and the Apache, Grant jumped off the tank, leaned into the C2 Humvee, and said, "Troop, hand me the hook. I'll talk to her."

He sat down in the front passenger side of the Humvee. Mounted in the front of the vehicle was an SPI-IR 360 infrared targeting device; he looked through it as he brought the handset to his ear. With it he could use the highly advanced and accurate infrared sight system to cut through the thick German fog to try to identify targets.

Against a trained and talented Russian tank unit, Grant and the men would use any and all advantages available to them.

"Viper One-Six, this is Courage Six actual. Be advised, we have taken accurate Russian 120mm tank fire. They've hit about six of my tanks and are continuing through my position. Any and all supporting fires are appreciated." He slewed the SPI-IR 360 out across the battlefield and was able to make out at least some of the fighting while he spoke to the Apaches. Two of his tanks were in a full-bore engagement a kilometer away. He couldn't see their targets, but he *could* see the tracers from their main guns arcing through the fog.

A million things were going through Grant's head simultaneously. Some of the thoughts were pertinent to the here and now; others he knew he couldn't deal with till later. His force found itself expending ammunition at a rate that would necessitate a resupply, and soon, but he knew he could do nothing about it until he broke contact with the Russian column.

"Viper One-Six copies," the female Apache pilot responded. Grant could hear her rotor blades thumping in the transmission; she was obviously heavy-sticking it, flying hard and fast to get into the best position to support Grant's regiment.

He said, "We'll fire up IR strobes so you know where we are in the fog, but I need you to give me 'danger close' once we're able to get a good hand off. We need all the support you've brought tonight. Any chance we have another section en route?"

"Courage Six actual, we copy and will give you all we've got. Interrogative: Is one section of Apache gunships not enough for you, sir?"

Grant smiled. This pilot did what pilots did best: use humor to try to keep the ground pounders calm.

"Viper One-Six, I'm not greedy. I'll take whatever you've got."

"Copy, Courage Six. We are just the lead element. Should be more soon."

Good, thought Grant, because the night had just begun. He pointed to Captain Spillane, who instantly understood what needed to be done.

Spillane told the tankers to get out IR chem sticks and put them on their antennas. Glitter would not attack a target she could not identify, but with the order "danger close" from the one scene commander, she'd fire on almost anything that even smelled like an enemy.

"Sir, you worried the Russians will spot our IR?" interjected Lieutenant Colonel Grant's tank gunner, Sergeant Anderson, who had popped his head up from the turret and was listening to his commander issuing orders. A good gunner was always in touch with what the commander was up to and could often answer on the radios on his behalf.

Grant got the impression that Sergeant Anderson, and in fact the whole crew, probably wished he were not on the regimental commander's tank but instead in the middle of the action in the fog, noise, and gunfire down below. Grant, too, wished he were in the middle of the clash of steel, but if he had been, he'd be focusing on firing his gun and not supporting his battalions.

"Last reports are our IR strobes are specially designed to be out of sync with Russian NODs. Basically, they can't see us unless they are using *our* night-vision devices." Grant paused. "Guess we'll know really quick if the intel is right about that."

Two medical Humvees roared past LTC Grant's command vehicles. He watched them shoot off into the freezing darkness on the thermal imager. The medical section's drivers drove wearing night-vision goggles instead of using headlights, so Grant made a mental note to keep an eye on them and an ear to the radio to ensure they made it to the hospital safely.

His communications sergeant indicated that the Apaches had relayed his requested transmission via HF radio back to their base. The Apaches, at a higher altitude, had better air-to-ground communications and could act as a relay when they weren't running and gunning.

Next, German major Blaz Ott's voice came over the radio, relaying his position report. Grant leapt out of the Humvee, pulled his map board down from where he'd left it on his tank, and corroborated his position with Captain Spillane.

Major Ott and a section of tanks from his 1st Battalion had linked up and were asking permission to advance. Grant gave them permission as long as all their IR strobes were activated. He didn't need Glitter and her wingman hitting German tanks as they tried to maneuver onto the Russians' flank.

Grant's radioman called out again. "Sir, you've got Major Ott back on channel four asking for you."

Grant ducked back into his C2 Humvee and switched his radio over to the regimental net. "Blaz, are you still seeing movement?"

"Not anymore, sir. We've advanced about as far as I feel comfortable. We've lost contact with the enemy and I'm also out of touch with some of my own unit. We've all gotten disjointed because of the fog and dark. I can hear the Apaches overhead and to the south. I can't get them on the radio. They might be able to maintain contact with the Russians. We counted about forty or forty-five enemy vehicles in total. Almost all Bumerangs, BTRs, and Tigrs, but there were a couple of T-14s. We count eight enemy vehicles killed between me and your 1st Battalion. 1st Bat is with me at grid Uniform Papa 994 692," he said, reading off the map coordinate.

"Copy, Blaz. Good work. No use trying to pursue. Need to bring everyone back to a tight perimeter so we can take stock of the situation. What's your slant report?"

"Not good: red across all systems. Your Lieutenant Chandler has been *wunderbar*. He did some resupplies of my men while they were in contact.

Dropped off machine-gun ammo and fuel cans. We need a Lieutenant Chandler in the Bundeswehr."

"Well, he works for both of us right now. Kid's a born leader."

Grant had brought the lieutenant up personally: he'd been attached to his maintenance and supply section for a time and seen the young man thoroughly take charge, jumping at every opportunity for leadership.

The medical Humvees arrived at Grant's command post on the hill, and Lieutenant Chandler ran over to them. The kid had been all over the battlefield tonight, Grant thought, popping up wherever he was most needed to provide logistical support.

Chandler helped off-load a stretcher. Then one of Major Ott's officers came over to him, they consulted the map for a moment, and the German climbed aboard the lead Humvee with Chandler in the passenger seat. They were gone in seconds, on their way to the hospital, the medical Humvees following behind them.

Smart bastard just got one of the Germans who knew the area to give him guidance to the local hospital, thought Grant. That should cut the time it would take to get there, increasing the men's likelihood of survival.

Clear thinking for a junior support officer.

The medical evacuation team had a complicated drive ahead of them. There was no telling if this battle would stir up a lot of civilian traffic or cause people to button up in their homes. Plus, many of the German cities had reservist men who had standing orders to cut signposts if there were declared hostilities with the East, but Grant didn't know if the locals knew enough about the situation to make good on that plan.

At least I'm fighting with the home team, he thought.

Grant listened to another report from Ott on the radio. "Okay, Blaz, once you're back in our perimeter, maintain one hundred percent alert on all your tanks. Battalions One and Two, you are to do the same. I want actuals back at my position in one-five mikes to go over the situation."

Ott, along with each of the battalion commanders, rogered up on the radio that they had received and understood the message.

The radioman immediately said, "Sir, it's Viper One-Six on the radio again. She says she has the enemy in sight now. She wants to know if we have anyone south of the 74 grid line."

Grant looked over at his map carefully. "Tell her no. She is clear to engage those fuckers. Tell her to let 'em have it."

CHAPTER 36

Viper One-Six flew through the night, with Sean "Jesse" James on the stick. In the front seat, Glitter confirmed receipt of the transmission from the Courage communications sergeant, then called over to the other helicopter in her flight. "Two-Six, this is One-Six. You are clear to engage targets."

Badfinger said, "Okay, Two-Six, but I'm having difficulty spotting through this fog. Can't lase targets in these conditions."

Glitter told Jesse she had the stick and took over flying the aircraft.

"Two-Six," she said, "I'm going in low to see if I can get better visibility and engage with rockets. Watch to my south, my left side. I'll paint anything I can see."

Glitter maneuvered the Apache down to an altitude of two thousand feet and slowed to twenty-five miles per hour. The crystal clear night sky meant the three-quarter moon and the stars lit up the fog, turning it into a white blanket across the terrain. Patches of trees on higher ground protruded from it here and there.

Suddenly several bursts of fire from heavy weapons lit up the fog. The Russians had clearly tracked the Apache's approach. Fortunately the fog was having the same effect on them as it was on the two Apaches, and although the fires were heavy, they were uncoordinated and wide.

"Badfinger, you seeing this? Every time they fire, it lights up the fog." The Russians' heavy gunfire and tracers created a quick but unmistakable yellow-red glow surrounded by a bright white aura where it illuminated the mist.

Now they had the Russian armor pinpointed.

"I got 'em," Badfinger replied. "But Courage says they are no longer in contact. Who are they shooting at?"

"Everything in their way, I guess."

Badfinger came over the net with anger in his voice. "Let's fuck 'em up."

"Copy."

She slewed her gunship onto the closest of the many flashing gunfire halos in the fog, and Glitter lined up the light in the center of her target reticle. She pressed the trigger and pounded out twenty 2.75mm rockets from her Hydra rocket pod.

The rockets streaked down toward the target for several seconds, and then she was rewarded with a massive explosion and several flashes of bright light.

Secondaries and fire immediately caused the fog to glow constantly over the area.

Nailed him, she thought.

She and Jesse shifted her gunsight instantly to the next Russian vehicle shooting blindly at them in the fog, and she unloaded another twenty rockets. Another explosion. Another fireball. This time the fire rose in a great plume of flame, partly burning open a hole above and through the fog. The perfect outline of a T-14 tank was now clearly visible, flames roaring out the top hatch as its ammunition cooked off.

"Two-Six, get in here, stay left, and line up with Route Niner. They are traveling at a high rate of speed, maybe forty kph, down the road."

"Roger," came the response.

Sandra and her wingman fired at the Russian muzzle flashes until they were out of rockets, then switched to their 30mm guns. Eventually the Russians clued in to what was happening, becoming aware that the fog was protecting them, but only if they maintained fire discipline to remain unseen from the attack helicopters.

Sandra slewed the 30mm M230E1 chain gun to her right eye and raked the burning enemy vehicles with heavy cannon fire, giving each one "a good squirt" of about twenty rounds for extra measure. The vehicles erupted in brighter flame, and on her next pass she saw them all glowing in the night, oil and gasoline burning steadily, with occasional firework shows when ammo stores cooked off in the vehicles.

Glitter swiveled her head, tracking the hot spots on her thermals. The big chain gun below her slewed to her movements as she scanned and concentrated her cannon on the vehicles most likely to be the infantry personnel carriers.

She picked a target and opened fire.

Bra-rak-rak-rak. The gun caused the helo to shudder as it hovered just above treetop level.

A new voice came onto her net now. "Viper One-Six, this is Viper Six actual." It was her company commander, and she felt an instant wash of relief. He said, "I am coming into your zone from the south. I am at the nine-eight and six-four grid square and proceeding along Route Nine. Give me a read in on the current sit."

"Copy, sir. Glad to hear your voice. We have engaged roughly a regiment-sized element of Russian armor proceeding on Route Nine, moving south at about forty-five kph. They are not stopping. The tank unit we are supporting says they believe it to be an advance guard. Its composition has been consistent with that. Looks like mainly frontline armor: Bumerangs and the new tanks, the T-14s."

The company commander replied quickly. "Here's what I want. I will have clear visibility once the Russian column comes south of Münchberg on Route Nine. I will strike them as they pass. I'll hit lead vics; you will then hit them in the flank. You two start your attack run offset from Route Nine along—"

The transmission was abruptly cut short, as all aircraft heard an air threat indicator in their cockpits. Sandra spun her head to a new light at her nine o'clock, and she saw a hellish streak of flame lifting from the earth, just above the blanket of fog but miles away to her west.

The streak of yellow and red soon passed far behind her, racing to the south.

It had not been gunning for her.

The speed of the ordnance took Glitter by surprise. This was no shoulder-fired missile. This looked like an SA-21, which, she knew, traveled an incredible 4,500 miles per hour.

The company commander's voice came tight and anxious now. "Viper Six actual, evasive!"

Coursing from north to south, the missile traveled at just under Mach 6. It connected with its target in six seconds, and the commander of Viper

Squadron's AH-64 turned into an aerial fireball that traced a bright descending arc until impact with the ground. Sandra could still see the flames as Jesse yawed her aircraft right and the other aircraft with her did the same.

"*Fuck*, Jesse!" Glitter said. "That was a fucking *SA-21*!"

"*Shit, shit, shit!*" said her pilot. "How the *fuck* did they get mobile SA-21 launchers into Germany this fast?"

"No idea. It's not even possible. But it did *not* come from the force we've been engaging! There's something else out there. We need to rearm back at Ansbach, then get back up as quickly as we can."

17 KILOMETERS SOUTHWEST OF MÜNCHBERG, GERMANY
25 DECEMBER

General Eduard Sabaneyev clapped his fire direction control officer on the shoulder. "Good hit, Major. We don't want to use too many Triumf missiles on the enemy's helos, though. Save the big stuff for the jets."

Sensing that he needed to reinforce the latest decisions made by his inferiors, he nodded approvingly and added, "But we have ensured that the *Amerikanski* and German aviators will now spread the word that there is an antiair missile defense shield around the assault column. If any of those other bastards get inside the missile radius, they'll feel our wrath."

He amplified his last point by clapping the fire direction control officer again on the shoulder in an attempt at a fatherly manner.

General Sabaneyev was known to be anything but fatherly, and the Russian major flinched visibly.

The major said, "Yes, sir. We would have locked onto them earlier if we hadn't been masked by those hills. We're getting reports of other American attack helicopters over there, but they are too low and we can't engage."

The general forced another smile. "Stay on it." Turning toward a row of officers at their computers on fold-down desks, he said, "Operations, what is Colonel Dryagin's casualty count?"

"Sir, Colonel Dryagin reports eight BTRs, catastrophic kills," the senior operations lieutenant colonel answered. "Five T-14s also knocked out. Colonel Dryagin wasn't sure if all his T-14 losses were full kills. He left them behind so he could continue his mission. He reports he has successfully bypassed the enemy ambush point as ordered, but he was raked by aircraft-delivered gunfire as they moved on. Three support vehicles were abandoned with mechanical issues, but his rate of march has resumed its pace."

General Sabaneyev turned abruptly from the operations men to look at the maps. Five interlinked map boards were hung against the bulkhead of the train. Adjacent to these, a network of digital radar screens emanated a light greenish glow. But these were clearly not the off-the-shelf new tech that was used throughout the command car. As much as the vehicle held state-of-the-art technology, it also contained pieces of standard Russian military hardware that had been adapted to the train out of necessity.

The Russian air-sweep radars were each tuned to different altitudes and zones around the train. The screens now showed a few blips, high-flying jets above the tactical area. All were coded as routine high-altitude passenger flights. Their tracks were lettered and numbered in accordance with known flight plans. If any deviated drastically from the high, steady trajectories—if their profiles looked like there was even a 5 percent chance they were NATO bombers ready to enter the combat area—they would be shot down without question.

The general was certain all commercial air travel in Europe would be ground-stopped by now, since there was no GPS, so he assumed the few blips were longer-haul flights: from the U.S. to Africa or the Middle East, most likely.

Everything was going well, Sabaneyev told himself. The attack column and the two support trains had made it this far into Germany with what the general considered to be minimal contact.

This meant that Red Metal had achieved both strategic and operational surprise. A few local NATO commanders, as ill prepared as they were, would certainly come out to play. But that was nothing Dryagin couldn't handle with his speed, surprise, and violence of action.

And the Russian casualties? Sabaneyev considered them regrettable but expected, and far below anyone's best expectations, considering the operation's progress.

He now had a virtually clear shot from here to Stuttgart and no other enemy contact reported.

He steadied himself, grabbing an overhead handhold as the train jostled and shook while rounding a bend. The tracks clacked and the car bounced and vibrated.

Still smoother than Russian rail, he thought.

He dialed up the command net and broadcast a digital report back to attack headquarters in Belarus. The assault train had an HF long wire attached that allowed the Russians to communicate in the absence of satellites in excess of 3,000 kilometers. They couldn't send large amounts of data, but the pipeline was just large enough to send back basic messages.

> RED BLIZZARD: AHEAD OF SCHEDULE.
> ENEMY ARMOR VICINITY MUNCHBERG.
> MINOR LOSSES TO RAID FORCE.
> ATTACKING AMERICAN AIRFIELD ENROUTE.
> ATTACKING AMERICAN SUPPLIES ENROUTE.
> WEST MOVEMENT CONTINUES.
> SUCCESS IS ASSURED.
> ON OBJECTIVE IN 3-HOURS.

Above him he heard the sounds of the radar whirring in its housing. One omnidirectional 29YA6 radar and the 42S6 Morfey active electronic array gave them a radar envelope of more than twenty-five kilometers. The radar dome popped up and out of the train, but when they passed into a tunnel or wanted to remain covert, it could be retracted into its housing.

Red Blizzard 1 had four radar systems total to detect incoming air threats. As long as the switching stations captured by Spetsnaz forces were kept open, and the train remained within twenty kilometers of the assault column, the systems on board could detect and fire on any air or ground target within that bubble and keep the path clear all the way to their objective.

The rail and roads are open. There is no one left to oppose us. We are steps away and NATO was unprepared for our smaller, faster, smarter force.

Fools, he thought. The West always believed they would have time to react to a full-scale Russian invasion, the long-assumed "pizza slice" movement from Belarus into Germany. A wide border crossing into Poland with the Russian invasion route narrowing and strengthening on its way toward Berlin. But NATO never even considered a classic operational raid. Small-scale but intense, lightning fast, and brutally efficient.

A scalpel through the heart of Europe, slipping effortlessly through flesh to cut out the cancer AFRICOM, so old Boris Lazar could hold his target in Africa without worrying about America.

CHAPTER 37

3RD AVIATION BRIGADE, REGIMENTAL HQ
ANSBACH ARMY AIRFIELD
KATTERBACH KASERNE, GERMANY
26 DECEMBER

Parked on the tarmac just outside her ready room just after one a.m., Sandra clicked through the navigation systems on her Apache but found nothing but blank screens.

Into her mic she said, "Still no GPS, Jesse."

"Roger. That blows."

She cycled through the electronic maps, none of which could sync up, then finally pulled out old paper maps from the flight case next to her. She quickly penned in map checkpoints of known friendly and enemy positions, then triple-checked the grid coordinates, trying to stem the fog entering her mind now that it was momentarily at rest.

Pausing in her task, she looked out the left side of her aircraft as the ground crew pumped fuel into her tank. Despite the chill night's gloom, she could see some of the young troopers' faces. They looked utterly focused on the job at hand. The crew chiefs had kept the men up to date on Sandra and her men's exploits, no doubt, and these boys knew how important their usually mundane duties of refueling and rearming were tonight.

She watched two boys racking missiles on her wing pylon hardpoints. In the strobe lights they looked like characters in an old black-and-white movie.

Not boys—men, she corrected herself.

Old enough to do their duty for God and country.

Old enough to die. *How many young men have died on the battlefield tonight already?*

She didn't know, but she *did* know for certain she had sent some Russian boys to their graves.

Fiery, smoke-choking, burning deaths.

That's enough of that, she thought. *The Russians chose their fate when they crossed the border.* And there was the life of her captain—her commander—and his second seater, and many more in the U.S. and German tanks to consider.

Her absentminded musing was shattered as Lieutenant Thomas's unmistakable shape came up on her right, climbing up the rungs to her cockpit, then knocking on the windscreen. She opened the hatch and pushed back her flight visor.

"Jesus, Glitter. I heard you guys were in the shit! The major wants an update and your recommendations on where he should send Echo Company once they're all assembled. About a third of them are in now. They're with the major in the ready room getting briefed on your contacts. He says he'll talk to you on the radio as soon as he can break free but to get airborne immediately. He says *you* are in command of Delta Company now."

Sandra just nodded absently, looking down at her maps.

Thomas continued. "Anyway, the men are gonna paint three kills on the side of your bird. How 'bout that?"

Now Sandra reached up to her windscreen hatch. "It's five . . . bitch!" she said, then closed the hatch abruptly and turned back to plotting waypoints on her paper map.

Glitter updated the Brigade S3 and flew away from her base at Ansbach, heading northeast toward Nuremberg. She clicked over to UHF and began briefing her three wingmen.

"We need to link up with our armor on the ground. We fly recce as long as we can and help them pick off any targets of note. If able, I want to identify enemy numbers. Once the rest of our squadron can get some more platoons up here, they can go help out the tankers to hit whatever main body might be coming through next."

She was quiet for a few seconds, then said, "Still doesn't make any sense to me why they're going south and not up toward Berlin. That's the pattern of attack we always studied back in school. If the Russians went into Poland, they would be heading for Berlin . . ." Glitter trailed off, trying to remember Russian Cold War tactics.

She didn't know this enemy nearly as well as the one she'd expected to fight in Afghanistan, and *that*, she recognized, was a problem.

NEAR NUREMBERG, GERMANY
26 DECEMBER

Colonel Dryagin looked at his map and ticked off the most recent checkpoints with a jittery hand due to the high speed his command vehicle traveled along the German autobahn. He stood in the open top hatch, a stiff, icy breeze blowing around him and down into the vehicle. His command and operations personnel were used to the cold wind; the colonel believed it kept everyone awake, and he liked to look out frequently to get a better idea of the terrain, the weather, and his forces in action.

The ops personnel below him listening to the incoming radio traffic moved the pins on the analog map board in front of them, updating the position of the lead Bumerang in the column.

Dryagin noted the lead elements were about thirty kilometers ahead of schedule and just south and west of Nuremberg.

"Hey, Viktor?" said the colonel, lowering his torso back inside the command chassis. He took off his goggles and pulled the ice-vapor-encrusted white face mask down to his neck to speak more clearly, his face windblown and red. "Besides the next target set, now we know there is at least one tank battalion out in the woods. Our egress will not be as easy as the ingress. I know the predictions, but now we know for certain who is out there. This enemy tank commander will not sit idle. He was trying to pin us down into a direct fight. I want you to work with the general on planning to take alternate route C back. Start making calculations on fuel consumption and determine where we must intersect with the assault train to refuel after the raid on Stuttgart."

"Yes, Colonel."

"And make sure you're on top of mechanical issues for my whole raid force. I want to be able to resupply from the support train down to every last vehicle. Understood?"

"Yes, Colonel."

"Good. Template that American tank battalion. I had a thought," he said, drumming his gloved fingers on the metal hull. "I expect them to go back to Grafenwöhr to pick up supplies. I want to intersect them. Take out one of their supply columns."

"Yes, Col—"

"And request permission from the general to pull a section of BTRs from the support train immediately."

"Yes, Colonel."

Dryagin stood up again, scanned the frosty morning distance for threats, just as he knew the eyes of another two hundred vehicle commanders and gunners were doing.

The colonel and his assault force didn't want any surprises, because this Russian force *itself* intended to be the surprise this morning.

37TH ARMORED REGIMENT (COMPOSITE) AND
  PANZERBATAILLON 203
MÜNCHBERG, GERMANY
26 DECEMBER

Tom Grant and Blaz Ott stood in shin-deep snow in front of Grant's Humvee. It was three a.m., and they'd been frantically loading and maneuvering, and even more frantically fighting for over six hours straight. The American and German officers stared at the map laid out in front of them on the hood and tried to figure out just what the hell they were in the middle of.

Grant knew the tankers and maintenance men of the 37th Composite just didn't have the skill to mount a dogged pursuit of the Russians. With Russian doctrine in the forefront of their minds, and absolutely zero incoming battlefield intelligence, he was under the assumption that the regiment-sized force they'd encountered was an advance guard for a larger Russian force that had not yet been identified. With no higher headquarters feeding them information, that was the most likely explanation.

Grant said, "If the enemy is fighting the way we expect them to, the next attack will be a massive wall of Russian armor. They will have identified our locations and our strength through their reconnaissance in force, and will hit us from some flank if we are not working actively to get a step ahead."

Major Blaz Ott looked out over the rolling, moonlit German winter landscape. "I agree . . . but something else is going on."

"Yeah, I get that feeling, too. They had a purpose. They didn't probe our ambush positions or even try to find our flanks. There was some objective more important than destroying our armor."

"*Ja*," said Ott. "They had orders to get past us and continue on to the west."

"But . . . where are they heading?" Grant asked.

"No idea," the German captain admitted.

"I want to pursue them, but we don't know what else may be barreling toward us. And we're not going to get very far with just the two refueling trucks. The last slant report from both our units wasn't good. We've fired more than eighty percent of our ammo." He sighed. "We can't attack anybody right now. We'll stay here, improve our defensive positions, and go to fifty percent manning so the men can get a few hours rest while we wait for resupply."

"*Alles klar,*" Ott said. "When do we expect more ammo and fuel?"

"Chandler is on his way to Grafenwöhr now to pick up a supply convoy. I'm waiting to hear that he's heading back. We need everything." Grant stared out into the dark, cold distance.

"Sir? Something wrong?"

"I still can't shake my suspicion that the Russians have something else up their sleeves."

BAYREUTH, GERMANY
48 KILOMETERS NORTH OF GRAFENWÖHR ARMY TRAINING CENTER
26 DECEMBER

The twenty-five support vehicles had already been loaded by the time Lieutenant Chandler arrived back at Grafenwöhr, so he immediately got the vehicles on the road toward Münchberg.

Virtually everyone stationed at the base had rushed in to help with loading, even if they normally worked in some other support position. Post exchange clerks, administrative personnel, even food service—all had gotten involved.

Without satellite radio, long-distance comms were suffering terribly, but a few men remembered how to use the old Vietnam-vintage HF radios, which employed a technology that dated back to World War II. Too many units had fallen in love with the ease of push-button and uninterrupted satellite comms and didn't train with HF frequencies anymore, so the men who *could* operate the HF sets became instant hot commodities.

An hour into the return trip the mixed convoy of German and U.S. supply and support vehicles stopped at a crossroads north of Bayreuth so Chandler and some of the lead drivers could confer about the best route forward. As the men formed up on the hood of a truck and laid out a paper map, a sudden series of rapid explosions ripped through their middle, catching them utterly by surprise.

Boom—boom—boom!

Lieutenant Chandler and the others dropped flat to the highway.

Boom—boom—boom!

A burst of heavy automatic-weapons fire blasted up the road behind them.

Chandler looked back and saw four Russian Bumerangs racing up the long line of his vehicles on Highway 9, firing as they went.

A German ammo truck was the first to go up. A direct hit—hard for anyone to miss at that range. It high-order detonated, blasting everything in its area, including two adjacent fuel trucks. Chandler felt the wave of heat wash over him, the snow in their area vaporized into water, and the men closest to the blast were ripped apart, then cooked by the bath of flaming fuel.

Chandler ran to his M88 recovery tank and hastily scrambled on top of the vehicle, his bare hands sticking to the cold armor and metal rungs as he climbed. He jumped into the commander's hatch and swung the .50-caliber machine gun around to face the advancing Russian vehicles. He pumped rounds furiously at the armored personnel carriers as they came into view.

Amid the explosions, smoke, and fire, he trained the heavy gun on the lead Russian vehicle and he didn't let off the gun as it approached. Forty meters, thirty meters, twenty meters. He unloaded all two hundred rounds in the machine gun's ready box.

In the darkness, several of Lieutenant Chandler's column of support vehicles burned. The rounds shot in the direction of the passing Russian vehicles simply bounced off thick armor, while the Russians continued to rip shells into the unarmored trucks.

Chandler knew there was no hope. He and his column had been caught unawares and unprotected by a superior force. There was only one thing to do.

Die fighting.

He reloaded his machine gun and resumed firing, watched the tracers and white-hot rounds slam into the lead vehicle over and over. It looked like some of his rounds penetrated the heavy front ballistic windshield. The lead Bumerang slowed from its breakneck assault pace. The driver of the Bumerang, obviously dead or wounded, lost control and nosed into one of the burning fuel trucks, pushing it off the road and into the woods.

Instantly, the APC was engulfed in flames as fuel spilled out of the burning truck and down onto the Bumerang.

Undeterred, the rest of the Russian vehicles bypassed their downed comrade and continued to pound their cannon fire at everything in their path. Lieutenant Chandler watched as another Russian APC took the lead and spun its turret, training its deadly 30mm cannon right at him.

His brain hardly had time to register the danger before the cannon fired, and Lieutenant Chandler's torso was cleaved in two at the chest, his fingers still clutching the .50 as he died fighting.

CHAPTER 38

The Apache flown by Lieutenant Glisson, rearmed and refueled, raced one hundred meters over the sharp, snow-covered rooftops of the German town of Bayreuth. She looked down at the map on her kneeboard and was checking the distance to the last known sighting of the Russians when Jesse came over the intercom. "Glitter, I have Courage back on the net. They say they lost contact with the Russian tank column and need us to look to their southwest."

After another glance at the map she said, "Roger. Pull hard left and let's pick up a reconnaissance formation. I'll click over and talk to Courage's commander."

Glitter switched the radio over from their squadron net to the one the Army armored regiment had been operating on.

"Courage Six, this is Glitter. Do you have a general location for that Russian armor?"

"Glitter, Courage Six. Negative. We lost contact and we're red status on fuel and ammo. We're hearing explosions to the southwest, though. Can't judge the distance in these hills."

"Copy," Sandra said. "We'll take a look to your southwest and advise."

"Good deal. We also believe that if this is an advance party, some kind of heavy reconnaissance, there *will* be a larger follow-on force, and we need to be dug in for that. So far none of our spotters have picked up anything, though. We have resupply en route to us now."

"Copy all. You guys hang in there."

"Roger. Courage Six, out."

Jesse flicked two flight controls with his left hand, then pulled the heavy helicopter to the northwest. The aircraft responded quickly in the cold winter night. Viper One-Six and Viper Two-Six were now on a hunting mission, but given that the enemy had shown they had teeth, Glitter knew she'd have to stalk her prey with caution.

RADOM, POLAND
26 DECEMBER

Paulina Tobiasz was confused to find herself lying in a bed in a bright, clean room, an IV in her arm and her uniform replaced by a hospital gown. Her left forearm was bandaged, and her head and left shoulder hurt, but it was a dull ache, nothing like what she'd felt lying in the snow back . . . *whenever* that was.

She scanned the room till she found a clock, and saw it was 4:51. There were no windows in the room, but she knew she'd passed out in the early morning, so she assumed it was now afternoon.

A doctor entered the room through the open doorway to the hall, and he smiled when he saw she was awake.

"How are you feeling, Paulina?"

She just shrugged a little. She didn't feel good; she didn't feel happy to be alive; she didn't feel much of anything right now.

She'd seen Urszula die, and Bruno, and so many others.

She said, "How many . . . how many were killed?"

The doctor gave a pained smile now, and he sat on the edge of her bed. He was gray-haired, thin, fatherly. "Maybe you should wait to—"

"Tell me," she demanded, surprising herself with a power in her voice that made her head throb even more.

The doctor looked down at the floor. "They told me there were ninety-three militia and one PLF officer in your company. Seventy-four are confirmed dead, including the lieutenant. Ten are wounded, including you. Nine are unhurt."

At this Paulina cocked her head. *"Really?"*

The doctor said, "Only because they threw down their weapons and ran away into the forest to leave the rest of you to die."

She stared off into space. As far as Paulina was concerned, the ones who ran should all receive promotions to major. Running from that meat grinder showed a certain tactical prowess that had not been demonstrated by the rest of them, herself included.

The doctor said, "Phones are out now, but when they come up, I can try to call your mom."

"My father. You can call my father." Paulina began weeping openly now. "Please tell him I'm okay."

"Of course, dear. And I will tell him that you are a hero."

She looked through her tears. "A *hero?*" There had been no heroes on that field; of that Paulina was sure. She had been the lucky survivor of a massacre, nothing more. One more casualty of a tornado that had swept over the land before racing on.

"You *are* a hero. There were pictures taken of the battle," the man said.

Paulina cocked her head. "That was a *battle?*"

"You're right. It wasn't a battle. But still, you stood up in the face of all that armor. All those soldiers. You shot a Russian, even. You are very brave."

She remembered now. She *had* shot a man. One man out of an army. Paulina felt none of the pride the doctor clearly expected her to feel. She had not been brave; she'd been terrified, nothing more. Her body had taken over and she had wielded her gun in her panic.

I am no soldier, she thought to herself.

"How am I alive?"

"You were pulled out of a trench with a body on top of you. This man had been shot four times, but the bullets did not pass through him to you." The doctor looked down at the clipboard in his hand. "You *do* have a concussion. Probably from grenades. You took a round through the forearm, left side, but you were lucky there, too. It's superficial, already stitched and bandaged, a quick, simple surgery. We gave you some medicine, so you've been out for sixteen hours."

It was after four in the *morning,* she now realized. She looked outside in the hallway now. "Where are they?"

"Where are who?"

"The Russians. The invaders."

The doctor smiled a little. "Oh . . . of course, you don't know. They didn't take over Poland. It was a blitzkrieg, a small unit that raced across the southern part of our nation to get to Germany. We've been waiting for a larger invasion, but nothing else has come after a full day."

"*Germany?* Why are they in Germany?"

"Nobody has any idea, because communications are so bad. But whatever they are doing, they are no longer doing it in Poland."

Paulina thought a moment. "Well . . . they might want to go home someday, and to do that they'll have to come back through."

"That's true," the doctor allowed. "But you've done your part. You need to rest."

She sat up. "No. I have to be ready for them." She winced as the IV bit into the back of her hand with the movement.

"Young lady, you need another day in the hospital to—"

A captain with the Polish Land Forces walked into the room from the hallway. He wore a fresh camouflage battle uniform and had a serious, intense look on his face. "Doctor, if Tobiasz says she can fight, we're going to let her fight." His face broke into a slight smile. "You are a hero, young lady."

Paulina wished like hell people would just stop saying that, because if she *were* a hero, Urszula would still be alive.

37TH ARMORED REGIMENT (COMPOSITE) AND
   PANZERBATAILLON 203
MÜNCHBERG, GERMANY
26 DECEMBER

Grant knew he had to come in person, but even so, it was hard leaving his unit, even just for an hour.

He thought of his boss, the brigadier general in charge of the tank regiment. *Where the fuck is he?* He'd been wondering this for going on twenty hours now, always when he worried about his own skill. Or lack thereof.

All he could think of was that if the Russians attacked his regiment right now, Major Ott would have to figure it out, because Grant had appointed the German officer to take command in his absence.

Grant and the small pack of Humvees had been vectored toward the site of the carnage by the female Apache pilot. When they got within a couple of kilometers, they were further directed by the red cast of flames across the clouds that dotted the early-morning skies.

As they pulled up to the outskirts of the slaughter, they could hear the sound of a few rounds of ammunition cooking off, so they parked and walked closer along the frozen ground next to the autobahn. As others hung back, Tom Grant walked on toward the still-burning column, the ground under his feet going from icy and hard to slushy and muddy, due to the heat from the explosions and resultant fires. *When the fires burn out, this highway will be a damn sheet of ice,* Grant thought.

He and a dozen of his men walked among the burned column, inspecting the site. The damage was horrific. He saw a single downed Russian Bumerang, but the rest of the detritus of the battle was American equipment. He recognized the hull numbers of some of the destroyed vehicles, while other vehicles were unrecognizable, just twisted hulks of metal.

It wasn't difficult to find Lieutenant Chandler's M88. It and several other vehicles, including three refueling trucks, were relatively intact because of the Russians' haste.

Somehow they got behind us and they're navigating in our rear. There's no real frontage to this thing. How the hell am I supposed to make sense of this? He glanced over at shadows in the trees. More men from his headquarters group were there, skirting the wood line adjacent to him, wary of the cook-offs.

But Grant wasn't thinking about his own safety now. At the moment he couldn't have cared less if he lived or died. This was his fault. He should have known this enemy would go directly for his supply lines.

If I were a real tanker, I would have sent escort vehicles, at least some anti-tank vehicles or gun trucks. If I were anything but a fucking logistics puke in charge of fucking tank maintenance, this would never have happened.

But he knew why he hadn't sent armor to the rear with Chandler. Everything he'd ever been taught about fighting in Europe against the Russians told him the worst was yet to come. He was certain a massive wall of Russian tanks would slam through Poland into Germany at any moment. How could he divide his tiny force to protect a resupply convoy that was supposedly well behind the lines?

But his reasoning did not alleviate his self-loathing.

In the flickering light he came across Lieutenant Chandler's severed torso. He closed his eyes hard for a moment but soon he forced them back open. The Russian 30mm rounds hadn't penetrated the M88. The armor had been too thick. They had instead burst against the huge hull and its front glacis. This sprayed shrapnel like a fan up the sloped armor in front; thousands of tiny razors had sliced the young African American in half.

He crouched down and cradled the top half of Chandler's body. He lifted him up and carried him along, looking for a clear spot to lay him out for the recovery personnel. He tried not to look at the ooze coming from the young man's torso, his entrails spilling out.

He'd pieced bodies of his friends back together in Afghanistan after IED explosions, so he was accustomed to sights and smells that few humans ever encountered. Yet now he felt true revulsion. An urge to retch, to purge this fear and anger that had haunted him along with the MRE he had halfway wolfed down when the call came that the resupply convoy had been wiped out.

Hold it together, he thought. *The men cannot see me weakening.*

Through some internal strength he was able to hold back his vomit. He looked down at his lieutenant's face. It was ashen, lifeless, gray, but it was still his. *A good officer,* he thought. *Full of promise.*

This is my mess. It's up to me to make it right.

Fuck this! Grant thought. *No more waiting for the general to arrive. This is* my *fight until I'm properly relieved. For better or for worse. These are* my *people. This is* my *war. This is* my *unit and* I *give the commands.*

I own this battle space.

Five minutes later he walked back to his Humvee with a renewed sense of purpose and stepped up to his driver. "Back to my regiment. We're gonna grab some ammo and fuel, and then we're goin' on the motherfucking *attack!*"

CHAPTER 39

The first impact came before dawn and sounded like a soft thump in the darkness. Perhaps a door closing. Maybe a backfire from one of the many trucks that had been scurrying around the airfield toting ammunition out to the flight line in preparation for the companies that were assembling and prepping for takeoff.

A few combat vets stopped what they were doing and looked up, because while the sound seemed familiar, it made no sense, given their surroundings.

Lieutenant Thomas turned away from the work at his desk. His maintenance chief had stood up from his cubicle on the other side of the logistics office and was now gazing out the window.

"What's up, boss?" he asked.

"Hang on a sec, sir," came the response.

The next thump was closer now. Then a third, and then, in rapid succession and ever closer, a fourth and a fifth.

The maintenance chief spun away from the door now. "Incoming! Get down!"

By the time the sixth round landed, a siren in a distant part of the airfield began a low, angry wail.

A clatter of machine guns followed. First it came from the northeast; then more guns opened up, seemingly from the farms due east of the base.

Thomas was in disbelief.

His maintenance chief cautiously opened the second-floor steel door that had a clear line of sight to the flight line.

Two long rows of Russian Bumerangs raced into the artificial light around the air base; they had crashed through the outer-perimeter fence and were now storming toward the runway at an incredible speed, firing as they moved. Their 30mm main guns lit up the predawn sky as they mercilessly pounded away, and machine guns on the turrets spit lead across the field.

One after another, helicopter gunships went up in balls of fire in front of Thomas's and his chief's eyes. Fuel trucks exploded; ammo stores crackled off.

It all happened so fast.

EIGHTEEN KILOMETERS NORTHEAST OF ANSBACH ARMY AIRFIELD
GERMANY
26 DECEMBER

Worry grew in the pit of Sandra "Glitter" Glisson's stomach. She'd tried and tried, but had not been able to establish comms with Ansbach. She and her flight increased their speed and kept on the radio, and when she got within ten miles of the base, the morning light grew bright enough to make out the plumes of inky-black smoke in the distance.

"Jesse, look left. Is that Ansbach?"

Her pilot did not answer at first, but after a few seconds she could make out the glow of a distant fire.

Jesse said, "Oh shit."

As they closed in, the familiar landmarks around Ansbach became unmistakable.

"Yeah," Sandra said softly, still looking at the smoke and fire. "That's us."

She was mesmerized, transfixed by the idea that the enemy had somehow made it all the way here and attacked their base while they'd been out searching for them.

Jesse said, "What do you want to do?"

Sandra wanted to burst into tears, but she fought it. She was a warrior;

immediately an overwhelming urge to fight, to kill, to destroy her enemy, welled up in her. She cleared her voice of any hint of sadness, fear, or indecision, and then she transmitted. "We pick up an echelon left, attack formation, and do a few pop-ups to see if we can catch them. Bastards can't have gone far."

"Roger, boss. I'm scanning with thermals." Jesse switched to a wider scan through the gun camera, and Glitter could see the same view in one of her own multifunction displays.

As she raced south, indecision crept in. *Where will I refuel? Who is hurt? Who is dead?* She shook her head, clearing her tired mind. *No, no time to think it over, trooper. We go. Now!*

Glitter clicked over to her radio and called the other three aircraft in her platoon. "Okay, listen up. We have to find ourselves a safe airfield so we can stay in this fight."

SIX KILOMETERS EAST OF STUTTGART
26 DECEMBER

The condensation from the young lieutenant's breath whirled around his face and between his gloves. His elbows dragged across the turret as he scanned through his binoculars, leaving marks in the snow accumulated there and exposing the bare steel below.

He had hard cheekbones and a small tuft of blond hair that stuck out from under the white Gore-Tex hood that covered his crew helmet, and his young face was the only part of his body that remained exposed to the elements. As the vehicle below him sat still and quiet, positioned on a rise over the distant city, steam rose from the Russian officer's heavy winter coat.

He exhaled. His breathing was slow and heavy, his focus totally on scanning through the binoculars. He knew his job. In minutes they would begin the final assault. Their targets lay ahead, unaware of his presence or his motives.

I am an instrument of the rodina*!* He sang the lyrics from his unit's song in his mind, one sung by the last Russians in uniform to invade Germany, some seventy-five years earlier.

Thundering with fire, glinting with steel. Victory, onward to victory. By the power of my gun turret. To my front, the enemies of my people. To my sides, the men whom I trust. Let the fire rage around us. We've lived through the harsh winter, now onward, to the sting of battle. Comrades, us all!

He squinted, then widened his eyes in order to better discern the objectives at a distance. His mind registered familiar landmarks. The binoculars, still warm from being inside the heated vehicle, quickly fogged over.

Below him, inside the turret of the Bumerang attack vehicle, his sergeant picked out the skyline through his gunner's sight, and the vehicle's turret turned slowly. The gunner scanned the sparse trees, the four-times magnification allowing him to see details of the city. Rolling hills, smoke rising from chimneys, snowcapped rooftops . . .

He called through his headset, "Lieutenant, sir? I can see the Fernsehturm."

The reply came quickly. "I see it, too, *Serzhánt*. Our objective is about twenty degrees to the left of that TV tower. You can't see through the intervening terrain, but once we get on Route Eight and begin heading west, we'll run right into it."

He pulled his binoculars back to his chest and tried to rub them on a dry spot on his heavy winter gloves. He failed—his wet gloves left streaks, but that was better than fog. Heat from the vehicle crew heaters blasted up around him and out of the turret hatch. *It will be better once we're back on the move,* he thought.

Onward, comrades of the rodina, *onward!*

The song in his head stopped instantly as the radio crackled to life.

"Strike One, Strike Two. Begin your attack."

Still holding the binoculars in his right hand, the lieutenant keyed his microphone with his left. "Roger." He then clicked a switch on a control panel attached to his coat and transmitted his next call to his platoon of APCs. "Strike One, I lead. Column out and follow me."

Eight Bumerang engines roared to life as one. The small hillock adjacent to the road was suddenly alive as the few men who had dismounted to smoke or piss raced back and scrambled aboard their vehicles.

The young Russian lieutenant clicked over to the intercom again. "Save your ammo until we make it to Kelley Barracks. Doubt there will be much resistance here. Driver, forward, onto the highway. Speed: sixty kilometers until we are all up and on the move; then take it to one hundred." His body warmed, he gripped the hatch while the Bumerang's eight wheels bounced steadily over the snow-covered grass.

In less than a minute they were accelerating on the autobahn.

DEPUTY COMMANDER OF EUCOM'S OFFICE
HEADQUARTERS, U.S. EUROPEAN COMMAND
PATCH BARRACKS
STUTTGART, GERMANY
26 DECEMBER

Even though the door to the office was open, the watch officer knocked on it, then stood silently, waiting to be acknowledged. He looked in and found the general typing on his computer. Even without Internet, there were still reports to be written and filed.

Behind him were draped the three stars of his appointment as deputy commander of European Command.

The general looked up from his work after a few seconds. "Captain."

"Sir, I have a new report for you." He waited until the general motioned him inside.

"Whatcha got, Bennie?" The general looked dead tired after twenty-four hours of dealing with bad comms and bad intelligence, along with the strain of knowing the Russians had conducted some sort of attack on Poland the day before that had moved all the way into Germany near Dresden.

The watch officer said, "The airfield at Ansbach was hit. No real details yet; we just got pieces the Army AH-64 unit operations officer was able to relay through a German landline that got cut off. The word is that we had the majority of our forces destroyed by ground assault."

The general stood up slowly, his eyes wide. "Ansbach? *Ground* assault?"

"Yes, sir."

"Do we think that's accurate? Any idea of the size? Composition? This can't be a full frontage; must be a smaller unit that probed through. A recon force, maybe?"

But the captain had no more information.

The general said, "Get all leadership in. Get the war council over to the war room and, for *Chrissakes*, find me a working line back to the Pentagon!"

KÖNGEN, GERMANY
FOUR KILOMETERS EAST OF STUTTGART
26 DECEMBER

No one driving along the autobahn this morning was too surprised to see a military convoy rolling southwest on Germany's Highway 313. There were a lot of rumors about an attack in Poland, but the widespread communications problems around the continent had left most people in Germany in the dark. The 313 was one of Germany's many roads marked with few or no speed limits, and traffic, even on this snowy December winter's morning, was brisk.

The far right lanes of the 313 were designated for military traffic, so the civilian vehicles on the road, in typical German compliance and efficiency, pulled to the left, the same practice Germans had followed since the Second World War.

The wheeled and turreted combat vehicles, some forty in all, raced along the autobahn at one hundred kilometers per hour. They were speckled white and reddish brown, not the digital pattern of the German Bundeswehr or the U.S. Army, but no civilians even noticed.

The convoy slowed and turned off the 313, heading west into Stuttgart. A few motorists cursed from inside the warmth of their heated cars as the military equipment jammed the exit ramp.

Soon ten vehicles broke away from the column and turned south to the Frankfurt airport. The remaining thirty turned north onto Filderhauptstrasse and into Plieningen, a small suburb of Stuttgart. The town was mostly empty, as the students of the University of Hohenheim were away enjoying their Christmas break.

The fields surrounding Plieningen were bare, having been plowed down like razor stubble in the preceding months. A resident farmer on the northern edge of town, hearing the noise of heavy engines, came out to look at the vehicles as they left the roadway in front of his home and began churning directly across his field. The man glared, his tobacco pipe flaring red, smoke billowing around him as he stood on his porch in his pajamas.

Right before his eyes the heavy military vehicles left their traveling column formation and spread out in a neat fan, leaving massive furrows across his neatly laid-to-rest strawberry fields.

It must be those goddamned Americans again. They have no respect. He watched until the vehicles all passed his house and he could he could hear only their engine noises; then he closed the old wooden door with a thud and puffed his pipe angrily as he returned to the warmth of his fireplace.

HEADQUARTERS, U.S. EUROPEAN COMMAND
PATCH BARRACKS
STUTTGART, GERMANY
26 DECEMBER

From a distance the waves of machine-gun fire sounded like someone ripping a blanket. Loud and continuous, it echoed around the buildings of the American outpost that housed the headquarters for all American activity in Europe. One of the USAF men on watch in the combat information center turned to one of the soldiers and asked if there was something wrong with the HVAC system.

The first true indication of real trouble was when bullets impacted the brick wall outside the headquarters. Heavy rounds hit with an unmistakable violent, smacking sound.

The explosive 30mm rounds came next. They penetrated the headquarters building, showering the eastern-facing office spaces with sparks, brick dust, and bursts of small shards of metal shrapnel. Merciless, constant, concussive waves ripped through the headquarters. Those not killed in the first blasts were knocked off their feet.

A female Army warrant officer raced down the hall and dove through a doorway and into a briefing room in an attempt to escape the rounds tearing apart the building. There she crawled under the heavy wooden conference table, joining a small group who had been caught by surprise in the middle of a meeting. She saw a two-star general in the group tucked tight against a chair and desperately trying to take hold of a telephone lying on the floor just out of reach.

The warrant officer was there with a team to work on the phones, so she knew his efforts would be in vain. No calls were getting in or out right now.

More blasts outside, followed by the sounds of supersonic metal zipping through the air. The long fluorescent lights flickered and one broke loose, crashing to the ground by the table as another fusillade slammed into the wall and through the ceiling above them. Uniformed men and women dashed down the hallway outside the door.

The warrant officer was considering making a run for it, when the general turned away from the phone.

"Listen up! On my command, we're going to get up, and move toward the—"

The first main tank gun round slammed into the HQ building, shaking the room, dropping anyone up on their knees and elbows back down flat.

The next cacophonous explosion ripped a huge hole in an adjacent room. Wires, soundproof panels, and chunks of insulation rained down onto and around the table. The sound of countless steel fragments ricocheting off the concrete floors and walls added to the din.

The third round blew another hole in the roof directly above the group under the table, exposing the building to the gray daylight. Steel support beams collapsed, followed by roofing material and accumulated ice and snow. The table split under the weight of a girder, crushing the general and two others. The rest of the group, their breath knocked out of them by the shock wave like a gut punch, looked at one another, struck dumb by the hopeless devastation all around. A man stumbled in from the open door clutching his head, blood pouring from an open wound over his eye. His mouth appeared to be screaming, but no one under the destroyed table could hear a sound, since their ears all rang from the last tank round.

The young female warrant officer squinted into the thickening smoke. Through the hole that had opened into the adjacent room, she saw two men lying in pools of blood, dust and debris cascading down on them still. The floor shook again from a strike on some other part of the building, and then another; she was aware of the blasts, but she still couldn't hear anything, her senses were so dull and slowed.

With a reserve of adrenaline, she tried to rise up and crawl.

Somewhere else. *Anywhere* else.

Then the floor shook again, and she felt a sharp blow against her chest. She sat back and looked down to see a small red spot the size of a quarter on her dress green uniform next to her military ribbons. It expanded rapidly as she watched, but her brain could just not make sense of what it was.

She turned to a soldier squatting next to her and managed to mouth the words "I think I've been hit" while pointing to the growing red spot. The man stared back at her blankly, uncomprehending; he was numb from the chaos and carnage and suffering his own shock and disorientation from the tank main gun blasts.

In seconds the warrant officer's sleeve and chest turned an ugly black-red. The thick, ink-colored stain felt wet against her chest and arm. She experienced a brief and odd moment of anger: her uniform and the hard-earned ribbons would have to be tossed. Blood poured out of her sleeve like a faucet turned full force, gushing over her knees and onto the concrete floor.

The young warrant officer's face turned gray, her eyes rolled back into her head, and she fell back among the others lying amid the heavy debris as the Russian tanks continued their pounding, punishing attack.

HEADQUARTERS, USAFRICOM
KELLEY BARRACKS
STUTTGART, GERMANY
26 DECEMBER

"Son of a bitch!" said the U.S. Air Force police officer to his German Bundeswehr partner at the front gate. "The hell is that?"

A glow followed by a rumble came out of nowhere in the gray morning. They watched through light snowfall for a moment as a plume of smoke rose in the distance.

"Looks like a car crash on the other side of the base," the German finally responded.

But when nothing came immediately over the radio, they waved through a few more vehicles from the line waiting to have IDs checked.

Then came the gunfire. The low, cyclic rumbling of machine guns. Then something heavier.

The steady stream of morning traffic through the gate had been a cavalcade of officers recalled from leave. The traffic had been constant in the past twelve hours, and the men at the front gate had been told that, with the crisis erupting in Poland, they had to speed the top brass onto the base quickly.

Something was brewing way up north, and from the urgency of everyone on the various staffs coming back from leave, the gate guards speculated that Poland was having one hell of a time.

But no one knew anything about Russians *anywhere* near Stuttgart.

Both MPs drew their pistols as they cocked their heads at the distant noise.

"Better call it in," said the American to his partner.

The German *Feldwebel* reached for his radio, his eyes still on the distant smoke.

CHAPTER 40

Bob Griggs was asleep just after two a.m., his head on his desk, when the phone rang. He didn't jolt up; in fact, he let it ring awhile till he reached out a hand and, with his face on the table, answered sleepily.

"Yeah?"

"Griggs, it's Nik. This is just a courtesy call; I don't have much time. You've got Connolly there with you?"

"Nah. Poor guy was falling asleep at his desk, so I made him go home for a few hours. Can't have that shit at the Pentagon." Griggs still had not lifted his head.

"Well, I'm calling to blow your mind. I've been monitoring the Russian exercises in Iran."

"I know," Griggs said. "Because Dan and I asked you to."

"Well, right. I agreed it *was* curious they would send their most veteran general out of the country with a sizable force of armor if they knew they would be attacking Europe. But, looking into it, it appears Lazar moved his entire reinforced brigade the length of the Islamic Republic, north to south, and arrived at the southern coast of Iran after midnight local time. We didn't have coverage of the area, but when we took another look, we found the Russians are loading onto civilian flagged container ships at the port in Chabahar Bay."

Griggs shot upright, phone tight to his ear. "Container ships? What the hell for?"

"Looks like Lazar plans on doing some sailing. The ships are Singapore-registered dry goods haulers. An analyst looked into their history and didn't see any ties to the Russian government, but there is no question that they are now serving as troop transport ships. We also detected three other container ships registered to the same company—might be related to the Russians. They are already in the Gulf of Oman, heading toward Chaba-har Bay, after setting sail from Bandar Abbas yesterday morning. There are Russian warships in Bandar, by the way, but they weren't on the water last we checked."

Griggs said, "Lazar's exercise is a ruse! Just like Sabaneyev's was!"

"Exactly," Melanopolis said.

"What's your leadership over there doing about this?"

"Dunno, but here's my guess. I run it up the flagpole, and my boss runs it up his flagpole. Four or five others will get their meat hooks into the intel, they'll come back asking for clarification, have meetings about what meetings to have before the meeting where they tell the big shots they need to have a meeting with POTUS to figure out what to do."

"Jesus," Griggs said. "This is fucking *huge*."

"If Europe wasn't at war and China wasn't on the brink of war, it would be huger. As it is, it's a brigade of Russians doing something shitty in the Gulf of Oman. A big deal lost in a cloud of bigger deals. Look, man, I gotta run."

Nik hung up, and the door to the bullpen opened.

Griggs saw Dan Connolly leaning in.

"Hey, boss," Griggs said. "Thought you were getting a few hours' rest."

"I got called in by the admiral."

"Shit."

"It gets shittier. *We* got called in by the admiral. He wants you and me in Conference Room Two. Now."

Griggs stood and headed for the door. "I bet we're getting raises and promotions."

Connolly didn't smile. "Yeah, Bob. That's it, for sure."

———

The Tandberg video teleconference devices were staged on a large oak table in the middle of the conference room. The space was perfect for collaborating with their Pacific cell.

And it was also perfect for private ass chewings.

Connolly and Griggs stood at attention. Admiral Herbers stood in front of them, a scowl on his face.

Connolly looked back in silence, so Herbers switched his stare to Griggs. "No more running around over there at NSA; no more of you two ferreting out matters better left to the intel folks. You are to get back to working Pacific plans for me and the vice chairman. Am I clear?"

The men nodded.

The admiral softened his tone a degree. He wiped his face with his hands, exchanging his earlier anger for a strained grimace. "Now, look. I get it that you feel some obsession—some propriety, even—over this Russian computer hacking piece. You earned your place in the sun with some good analysis. But Russia is not your domain at the moment, and we have that situation in hand. Our boys on the deck took the fight right back to the Russkies and the reports from EUCOM do not lie. We beat them. Nailed them hard, says General Miller. His words, not mine.

"No more reports of Russians crossing into Poland since the first wave. We blunted their assault, stopped them from staging a major invasion, and we'll beat back the ones that made it through. Europe and NATO will be working on getting comms and sats and such back up for days or weeks, and only then will Russia's true intentions be obvious; but that's not my problem, and that's not your problem.

"Our problem, gents, is Asia. I need you both back on PACOM. Stat. You got me?"

"Yes, sir," they replied in unison. The admiral nodded at their acknowledgment of orders, then turned around to look over the big charts of the Pacific that adorned the walls of the meeting room.

Then Griggs cleared his throat, clearly unable to remain silent. "Sir, shouldn't we at least consider—"

Connolly sighed softly.

The admiral turned back to face the two, stared Griggs down, and said, "Major Griggs, sometimes you gotta know when to just shut the fuck up.

Maybe Plans just isn't the place for you." The admiral came closer. "Maybe we need to get you back to big Army. I hear they are still waiting for you to get a weigh-in to determine your fitness to continue this sputtering career of yours." He pointed a finger at Griggs that nearly touched his nose. "Step sideways one more time and you get tossed back to where you came from. I'm sure Colonel Richter could find some use for you."

Griggs's face twitched at the sound of the name. His voice came out more meekly this time. "Yes, sir. I understand."

"Good. I'll expect progress. I want a brief on your and the team's findings on Taiwan tomorrow at zero-six. And, Colonel Connolly, square away your partner here—you still have a few shreds of credibility left. Clear?"

"Yes, sir. Very clear."

The admiral turned and walked out the large wooden double doors.

Both men's shoulders slumped, and Connolly turned to Griggs now. "You're fucking *killing* me. We need to do what the admiral is telling us to do. It's more than our careers on the line. We do have a whole other theater we are responsible to the vice chairman for."

"No."

"No *what?*"

"No, sir, Lieutenant Colonel Connolly, sir. We will *not* do what the admiral told us to do."

"Bob . . . I swear to God."

"Hear me out."

"I'm not listening to another word. You are going to get both of us—"

"You *have* to listen."

"There's nothing you can say at this point."

"What if I say 'Chabahar Bay'?"

"*What?*"

"Chabahar Bay. It's a small coastal harbor in southern Iran. Excellent roads leading to it."

Connolly spun toward Griggs and grabbed him by both shoulders. "*So . . . fucking . . . what?*"

"General Boris Lazar just loaded his entire brigade onto civilian cargo haulers in that port. He's heading to sea."

Connolly released his grasp, took a half step back, and leaned against the conference table. "You're kidding."

"He managed to get a whole brigade through Azerbaijan, into Iran, and aboard ships all while everyone was focused on first Taiwan and then Europe. This was the Russian plan. Like a boxer: first a jab. That's the Taiwan crisis. They didn't orchestrate it, but their plan is obviously piggybacking on our distraction over there, exacerbated by the effects of their hacking of the admiral's laptop."

"Then a right cross. That's Europe. Caused us to swing back."

"And now that we're even more distracted, they bring the uppercut."

"Bob, spare me the metaphors and tell me where the *fuck* Lazar is going."

"Africa. Where else?"

Connolly slowly nodded. "Of course. Kenya."

"Yep," Griggs said with a smile. "My bet is they are making a move for that resource-rich rare-earth mine Kenya kicked them out of three years ago."

"Has to be it, Bob. Holy shit."

Griggs said, "And if we can't stop them from taking the mine, we probably can't stop them from fortifying the mine's defenses. It will take a month or two for us to get any real force to try to retake it, maybe longer."

Connolly replied, "You're right, but we'll still do it. We won't let them get away with this."

"What the hell?" Griggs said. "We're either at war or almost at war on two continents right now. Why not make it three?" It was sarcasm, and Connolly nodded in agreement, then cocked his head.

"So the plan in Europe was to just do a feint into Poland all the way to Germany so Lazar can sneak down to Africa. No other objective? That doesn't make sense."

The men stood silently a moment, and then, at the same time, they said, "AFRICOM!"

Connolly jolted back upright. "They are going to Stuttgart!"

Griggs nodded. "They figure that if they kill or capture all our military experts on Africa, who are all stationed in Germany—destroy our command and control there—then they will be able to roll across Africa with little to no response from us. We won't even be able to help orchestrate a coalition of African militaries to stop them, since we have nothing to offer and our military liaisons will be out of the picture."

Connolly said, "And it will take a year to set AFRICOM back up—a year Russia can use to bolster their defenses at the mine. Make it fucking Russian territory."

Now the lieutenant colonel had a new thought. "Wait. If you knew this about Lazar, why didn't you just tell Herbers while he was tearing you a new asshole?"

Griggs smiled broadly and winked. "Because we aren't going through Herbers on this. The admiral won't make the case that needs to be made. We need to go to the director of plans himself to explain everything."

Connolly said, "But Herbers will kick our—"

"This is too important, Dan. Getting the Pentagon to turn its attention to Africa is worth us risking our careers."

Dan Connolly nodded slowly, then said, "I hate it when you're right, Bob."

The two men spent the next hour poring over raw satellite images of Lazar's force on the highways in Iran and the cargo ships in port. The work involved three calls to Nik Melanopolis for clarification on aspects of what they were looking at, although the NSA man answered only one of the calls and gave them only about three minutes of help before begging off to get back to his own frantic work.

But Nik called the men back twenty minutes later and, in an about-face, asked if he could drive down to the Pentagon for a meeting.

Dr. Melanopolis had brought paperwork. Lots of paperwork. "The Russians have amassed quite a bit of gear, and it's all apparently with permission of the Iranian forces. Look here . . ." Melanopolis drew up a set of overhead imagery. A small grouping of Iranian naval vessels was tethered together off the Chabahar pier facility.

"How can they draw enough water to get anything into that port? Looks like all fishing vessels there."

"That's the beauty of it. No one would suspect you could load a deep-draft vessel there. But there is this narrow channel. Enough room to fit one, maybe two wide and deep cargo or oil boats. Not the massive super-tankers, but a large enough ship to carry fuel for maybe a brigade for several months, maybe longer, depending on how far they intend to road march once they hit land."

Griggs asked, "Why don't they just send it all via unmarked cargo vessels? Better chance of staying below radar. Why the armed escort?"

Connolly answered this one. "It's still a time of war. If they are heavily escorted—you know, big cruisers and stuff—we'd notice. But with the smaller Iranian escorts, they hedged their bets. If we don't know and aren't looking, they slip under our proverbial radars. If we are looking, they buy themselves some reaction time and some fine tools to keep curious Yankee destroyers and subs well away. Not a bad plan. Not too big and not too small."

Connolly turned back to Dr. Melanopolis. "Now, tell me, what's all this other stuff? The rows of things in that harbor you have on the other screens?"

"It took me a while to figure it out. You see how they all have these massive metal cases?" Both men nodded as Dr. Melanopolis tapped his pen on the screen. "Those aren't cases. They are tubes. Missile tubes. And these things I thought were shipping crates aren't crates at all. These are Chinese Hóng Qí-9 upgrades, or HQ-9B for short. Hóng Qí literally means 'Red Banner.' This is the latest generation of Chinese phased-array antiair missiles. These babies can simultaneously identify six different targets and launch and track six different missiles. I count four of them total."

"Is that enough?"

"It's enough to keep America's proud, shiny air forces at bay. And do it all from more than two hundred kilometers over the horizon."

"Son of a bitch," Connolly said. "So the Russkies bought themselves some missiles from China. Smart, too. They shipped them all to Iran, and it just looked like some basic Iranian modernization. It also prevented us from seeing Russians transferring advanced weapons to Iran. Wonder if the Chinese even knew who they were selling these things to."

Griggs then pivoted to researching the ships themselves. He looked at MarineTraffic.com to pull up both current and historical information on one of the ships, and from this he could determine the average speed of this flotilla.

He spun around to Connolly.

Griggs said, "Lazar is on the water now. If he's going to Kenya, the closest African port to the Mrima Hill mine is Mombasa. It's only about thirty miles away. At present speed, I calculate he can reach it in fifty hours."

Connolly thought about this. "Two whole days on the open ocean? That's risky for him, isn't it?"

"Yeah, but his problem, not mine. If we can impress the need up the chain of command, two days is plenty of time to respond to this attack while they're still on the water. We can have subs, bombers, and cruise missiles in place to pound them with time to spare."

Connolly was incredulous. "But . . . but Lazar would know that already. He knows our satellites and comms aren't degraded in the Middle East or Africa. Why would he sail into the trap he has to assume we'd have waiting for him?" He sat there silently for a moment. "No . . . there is another piece to the puzzle. *Has* to be."

"Like what?"

"Don't know. The Russians know what they're doing. They've been a step ahead of us through this whole thing. I don't believe *we're* suddenly a step ahead of *them*."

Griggs said, "Even if we don't have all the answers, we have to brief the director."

"Yeah," Connolly said. "About that: How are we going to do that without Admiral Herbers knowing?"

Griggs said, "I have a plan. I think we should call it 'Operation Sacrifice Fly.'"

Connolly sighed. "I fucking hate it already."

CHAPTER 41

The inside of Glitter's cockpit was muggy from heat and perspiration. She had to keep wiping off her windscreen and her helmet's visor. It was better than the alternative: opening one of the small hatches and letting the cold winter wind inside. It was probably twenty degrees out there, and flying at 120 miles an hour would only make the whipping wind worse.

She could always turn off her heater to cool down, but she knew doing so wasn't the right call. Chances of getting it going again were iffy. A few months earlier, on a cool September afternoon, she'd shut down her heater and then spent the last hour of her flight freezing her ass off.

Doing it today would be idiotic. Much better to swelter for a little while longer.

The voice in her headset gave her something else to think about. "Glitter, I calculate maybe thirty more minutes of fuel left," Jesse said. "That's at this burn rate. If we do any tricks, we're going to lose more time."

"We have to stay on these guys. Whatever their objective is in Stuttgart, I'm not hearing a lot of other units up on the net. They have a clear shot directly downtown."

"What do you think? Are they taking out the airport? On their way to hit Ramstein? Going after EUCOM?"

"Hell if I know, and with only a half hour of flight time left, I'm not sure we're going to find out."

"What's your plan, boss?"

"Find them fast and hit them hard."

"Roger, but if we do, we're landing in a field somewhere. I don't see a way we get back in time."

"There *is* no back, Jesse. Christ, who knows who's even alive back at Ansbach?"

Glitter reached out and wiped the windscreen again with her glove. "Work up an attack vector on the last known location of the lead part of that convoy. We're going to make one more attack run. Two passes, tops. Then we haul ass out of here and find a safe parking lot to put down in."

"Roger that." After a moment Jesse said, "If they keep going the same direction, I'd say they are moving toward EUCOM headquarters. But, hell, they could veer onto a new road and hit Ramstein or . . . Paris."

Glitter said, "We can make it to EUCOM HQ, but that's probably it. Put the plot on the chart and I'll just fly that line." She concentrated on controlling her big, muscular bird of prey.

For the next fifteen minutes the two Army officers flew low through the morning, south toward Stuttgart. There was nothing on the radio, which gave them the impression they were the only NATO assets in the air in the vicinity. Their fuel tank was in its war reserves, called "bingo" flight status. They were not supposed to fly inside that limit without express permission of the first O-6, a full-bird colonel, in their chain of command. Considering that he was likely dead back at Ansbach, Glitter had given herself the okay.

Just as she reached to wipe her fogged-over windscreen again, Jesse called over the intercom. "Glitter, you see that smoke in Stuttgart?"

In the snowy morning, four columns of smoke and the glow of fires were just visible on the horizon.

"Yeah, I see it," she said. "Plot us an attack cone onto the largest of those fires."

Glitter focused on the glow through the snow. It appeared that several buildings were completely engulfed.

As they approached she said, "The enemy *has* to still be in the area. Right in the city. I fly; you gun. I'm going to try for three passes." The fuel-warning alarm began to sound in the cockpit right as she said this. "Scratch that. Two passes. We're going to have to go in fast. Make sure of your targets, and make sure you hit them."

"I'm ready."

The helo's rotors chopped through the icy air as it raced along at building-top level at over 160 miles per hour. Glitter kept the down angle as steep as she dared. The flames ahead occupied their whole windscreen now.

In seconds they blasted into the area, Glitter taking them literally through the smoke and flames of the biggest burning building, providing them the best chance for cover from ground fire. The rotor blades parted the flames and smoke and they found themselves above a ruined warscape.

Jesse immediately went into action. On the other side of the glowing fires, as they had guessed, the Russians rolled along roads in an urban section of southwest Stuttgart. They saw ten Bumerangs and three T-14 Armata tanks. The tanks were silent, but three of the BTRs were pounding cannon fire into adjacent buildings.

Jesse picked a line of fire and laid on the trigger of the 30mm cannon, barely taking enough time to aim as the Apache raced by. His rounds chopped up dirt and pavement, split trees, and then shredded into a cluster of Russian troops diving for cover from the strafing run. Sparks flew as his gun line intersected with a Bumerang. Then another, then a third. The concentration of fire wasn't more than four or five rounds per vehicle, but it was all he could do as they roared behind another line of buildings.

At the end of the first run, when Glitter felt sure she'd passed over the Russian forces, she cranked her Apache in a hard left turn. "Goin' for one more," she said, "but we're flying on fumes."

As they turned to again face the neighborhood where the fighting was going on, an incredible amount of tracer fire arced into the air, sweeping back and forth in front of them, as hundreds of Russians realized they were under attack from the air. Flying back into this spray of lead was nearly suicide, but Glitter pressed on.

They made it halfway to their target zone before Glitter felt the stick slacken and the aircraft begin to slow. The aircraft responded sluggishly to her inputs. She put both hands on the cyclic to try to control it, but she could feel the last of her gas, the helicopter's lifeblood, slipping away.

The engine coughed. She kept racing forward, hoping to give Jesse one more clean shot at the concentration of attacking Russians. There wouldn't even be enough fuel left for a controlled descent.

They were crashing at the end of this attack run, if not before.

"Make this one count, Jess."

"Damn right," he replied.

Jesse saw a row of Bumerangs moving rapidly down a road alongside a park. He slewed the gun onto the first vehicle and pressed the trigger. He could see the impacts in and around the group, chewing up the dirt and smacking clusters of troops running out of a building.

Glitter kept her aircraft flying in a straight line, but she was losing both altitude and speed by the second.

"Jesse," Sandra said through gritted teeth as she fought the stick with all her strength, "we're going to crash!"

"I know," he said, spraying cannon fire into the Russians as the aircraft angled toward earth. He fired at a rate now that would melt the barrels of the Gatling gun in seconds, but he figured he'd probably be dead soon, so he wouldn't get in too much trouble about it.

The Apache received a huge volume of return fire, and a few rounds slammed into the fuselage, but soon they were over a row of buildings that masked their view of the Russians.

Only then did Jesse let up on the trigger.

Their descent accelerated. The engine was silent now and the aircraft electronics flickered on and off as they switched over to battery power.

"Goin' down, Jess!" Glitter shouted.

The aircraft's tail was the first to impact, crumpling as it smacked the top of a two-story building.

Glitter could feel her big aluminum beast shudder as the fuselage collapsed up and into itself. The force of the impact pitched both of them forward into their harnesses, then back into their seats as the cockpit collided with the building. Glass shattered all around, the sound mingling with the gut-wrenching noise of the twisting, torquing metal of the aircraft pulling itself apart. The top rotors struck the rooftop and disintegrated, sending chunks of prop spraying in all directions.

Fortunately, there was no fuel left to ignite, so there was no explosion.

All was quiet in the wrecked cockpit, but only for a moment.

Then the roof of the building gave way.

Jesse and Glitter felt themselves falling backward through space as the helicopter dropped down into the top floor, flipping over and then back upright. Two huge holes were ripped open as the cockpit was sheared away by exposed steel girders.

Jesse, still strapped to his seat and with his section of the helo torn off, fell through the hole in the bottom of the aircraft and plummeted into the building.

Glitter remained strapped into what was left of the cockpit. She bled from multiple wounds, and her left arm and left leg were twisted at ugly angles, caught in a mass of wires and cables. She faced skyward, lying on her back, held immobile in what was left of the cockpit, which had come to rest, oddly enough, next to a broken window on the second floor of the three-story building.

The last of the falling glass and metal and other building materials around her settled, and it became deathly quiet.

Glitter felt numb as her body moved toward shock, but she spoke. "Jess . . . Jesse?" she called out. She didn't know if her intercom worked. She didn't even know if the mic was in front of her mouth or even if her helmet was on her head anymore, and she sure as hell didn't know if Jesse was still behind her or even if he was alive. "Jesse?" she called again, then switched from his call sign to his real name. "Sean? Sean! Wake up!"

Nothing.

Just then she heard a rumbling to her left, and she struggled to turn her head. Through the mass of wires, smashed panels, and unidentifiable objects all around her, she realized she could look right out a shattered window and down on the street below.

She was one flight above an empty four-lane parkway with a median running down the middle. Snow covered the ground. She looked up the parkway and saw an intersection one hundred meters distant.

The rumbling intensified for several seconds. She closed her eyes because she knew what it was, and when she opened them again she saw a T-14 tank rolling onto the parkway at the intersection. As soon as it came into view it stopped; then the turret began turning in her direction.

The hair stood up on the back of her sweating, bleeding neck. She wanted to climb up and run for her life, but not a muscle in her body fired at that moment. She just lay there.

A scratching sound in her headset startled her, and then she heard an unfamiliar man's voice. It was calm yet businesslike, and it comforted her somehow.

"Any station, any station. This is call sign Shank. We are a flight of two A-10s over Stuttgart to provide support. Uh . . . we are rollin' into the zone at this time."

She was glad the A-10s had arrived, even if she *did* think they were a little late to this party.

Glitter couldn't move her arm to hit her radio button. She just lay there and stared at the tank. The massive gun barrel was slowly trained on what remained of Viper One-Six.

As she began fading, she was surprised to see two big gray crosses blazing through the sky in tandem as two jet aircraft passed low and slow above her head, with the lead ship firing on the Russian tank.

There was an incredible sound of 30mm cannon fire ripping from the A-10, and Sandra watched as the road in front of the T-14 exploded. A second later depleted-uranium shells slammed into the Armata itself, exploding the massive tank in the middle of the intersection one hundred meters away.

And then twenty-eight-year-old Sandra Glisson fell into unconsciousness.

Racing over the exploding tank, thirty-four-year-old Captain Raymond "Shank" Vance clicked the transmit button on his radio, calling his wingman. "Zoomer, there's an AH-64 crashed in a building back there. Did you see that shit?"

"Roger that. I'm noting the coordinates. I don't have a fucking clue where we're gonna find a medevac or pararescue to get to that wreckage, but at least we can mark the site. All of Stuttgart is a mess."

Shank thought about it a moment. "We're almost bingo fuel. Let's RTB. When we get back, we can try a landline to the nearest hospital. Sure hope the crew of that Apache doesn't have to wait that long, but it's the best we can do."

CHAPTER 42

Three hours after stopping in Stuttgart, General Sabaneyev moved himself and his headquarters element from the covert *Red Blizzard 1* Strizh train over to *Red Blizzard 2*, the unmasked, overt attack train that had followed along a few hours behind the assault.

Red Blizzard 2 was similar to the assault train that led the way into Stuttgart in many regards, but it was bigger and able to pack a more powerful punch. A military train, it offered no pretense of camouflage or stealth. Relying on the strength of its arsenal of defensive and offensive weapons, it wasn't looking to hide and could destroy most anything thrown at it.

With a total of fifty-eight railcars of different types, the train was loosely divided into thirds. One-third of the cars was filled with logistic items, like ammunition and fuel to resupply the thirsty tanks, Bumerangs, scout vehicles, and so on. Another third of the train was set up for command and control and troop transportation. Much like the assault train, the C2 had a battle-control detachment with a full communication suite including satellite and radio, antiair missiles, multiple-launch rocket systems, and another set of 120mm mortars.

The last third contained a fully mechanized armor battalion, bringing more fight to the assault task force should Dryagin need it.

It had been a gamble to send the overt combat train in just hours behind the trailing edge of the main invasion force, but Borbikov had counted on the Poles and the Germans in the area where the invasion already passed to be shell-shocked and disoriented, and his gamble had paid off. *Red Blizzard 2* would serve as the center of the Russian raiding force for the rest of this invasion.

An hour after moving to the new train, Eduard Sabaneyev stood in a troop transport car looking over a group of twenty: nineteen men and one woman. They were seated or lying on the floor next to the wall; most were handcuffed behind their backs, but a few were wounded and left unrestrained.

These were his captives.

The attack on AFRICOM had taken less than an hour, a fourth of the time Borbikov had allotted for it. The Americans had relied too heavily on their communications systems and satellites giving them real-time pictures. With hoods over their eyes, they were bumbling fools, Sabaneyev had noted to subordinates when the fighting was over. He'd fought foes in the basements and rubble of Chechnya more stalwart and competent than what he'd faced from NATO in the past thirty-six hours.

He looked over a wide mix of uniforms and ranks on the prisoners: U.S. and German army and air force, over a dozen colonels and four general officers, including the deputy commander of AFRICOM.

Russian soldiers guarded the twenty, but Sabaneyev could see there was no fight in this group of officers. Most of the prisoners looked dazed by the power and shock of the Russian lightning raid. Russian doctors worked over the wounded, administering medicine and bandages and assessing which of the captives would need to have shrapnel removed or bones set. The deputy commander of AFRICOM was the highest prize and he received the most ardent medical attention, although the injuries to his back and shoulder were not grave.

Still, he would be taken into the train's surgical suite and sewn up first.

Eight Russian soldiers also sat in the passenger cars, bandaged and bleeding from their own various wounds. They'd have to wait on treatment, because the prisoners were more valuable than a few kids from the farms around Moscow and Yaroslavl' and Yekaterinburg.

Red Blizzard 1 had to be abandoned here in Stuttgart. It was no longer practical, and turning two trains around would require extensive labor and time that didn't figure into their blitz assault into and back out of Germany. Besides, their attack had been successful and they didn't need to remain covert any longer.

Red Blizzard 1 had been taken to a set of tracks east of the Hauptbahnhof along Rosensteinstrasse, carefully loaded with explosives, and destroyed in a ball of fire.

Sabaneyev hated to see it go, but he knew *Red Blizzard 2* held everything he needed to get home, from fuel to ammo to fire support. In fact, the second train had more antiair missiles and mortar systems than the assault train. The Russian flag had been painted on the side just an hour earlier, and its dark camouflage pattern gave it a potent and ominous appearance.

The general turned away from his prisoners without a word, and headed for the headquarters car. He stepped to a window and looked outside.

The train was parked near the Hauptbahnhof, and central Stuttgart was quiet in the afternoon gloom. He saw Russian soldiers and armor around the station providing a protective security cordon for him and his train, but he saw no German citizens or soldiers anywhere. They'd cleared the streets quickly when the fighting had begun this morning, and they'd huddled in their homes and apartments throughout the day.

Smoke hung in the air still, black just below the low gray clouds.

The general stood with his hands on his hips for several minutes, impatiently waiting for word from Dryagin. The colonel had directed part of his attack element to Ramstein Air Base and a few smaller airfields in the area. They would crater the runways to prevent landings and destroy any combat aircraft they could find, and then they would return to Stuttgart. The general was happy to degrade NATO further. It would hamper the West in their ability to launch any potential counterattack, and would only serve to provide more proof to NATO that Russia was in the driver's seat in this conflict, which would help with the negotiations to come.

Finally, Sabaneyev's aide stepped up to him. "General, Colonel Dryagin reports all objectives met at Ramstein. He has smaller units still prosecuting the attack at other airfields but will begin his return to Stuttgart within the hour. ETA: twenty-one hundred hours."

"*Khorosho,*" ("Good") Sabaneyev said. A feeling of pride washed over him. He'd done it. His war was over, other than the return to Russia.

Now it was up to the politicians and that old goat Boris Lazar.

He walked on through the train to the command car, which he found to be a hive of activity. Soldiers passed into and out of the operations center car to the command car, and the antiair missile defense battery men were alert at their radar screens, reviewing the status of each of their missiles. The fire support officers had all their firing batteries listed as "green" and ready on the coordination boards posted in the middle of the car.

General Sabaneyev walked over to the communications officer, who was seated in front of the high-frequency radio. The HF could not reach all the way back to Moscow but could certainly reach as far as the Russian headquarters in Belarus.

The officer held up the handset and the general took it.

Sabaneyev yelled out to the room now. "Operations officer? Quiet down the ops center." The room wasn't that loud, but he was making a show to get all attention focused on him. The radio transmission he was about to make was important and he wanted everyone listening as he made it.

The officers in the room instantly hushed to low tones and the general began speaking over the radio. "Attack Headquarters, Attack Headquarters, this is *Krasnyi Metal* force commander. How do you read me?"

After a moment, a crackle and a *ping* noise came over the speakers. This was the first response, indicating an electronically encrypted transmission was coming through. Soon a distant but audible voice responded: "This is Attack Headquarters, *Krasnyi Metal*. We are receiving you. Send your transmission."

Sabaneyev said, "I am now ready to report the raid on the headquarters in Stuttgart has been successful. We have minimal casualties and damage. We have twenty prisoners, including the deputy commander of AFRICOM and much of his staff. Names and ranks of the prisoners will follow this transmission. I am pleased to report we have destroyed all communications systems as well as both AFRICOM and EUCOM headquarters buildings. We continue to attack all tertiary objectives. Those attacks will be complete within the hour. Begin the diplomatic process."

He smiled as he concluded the transmission, looking around the railcar at his proud headquarters staff.

The reply took several seconds, coming from just inside the Belarusian border. "This is Attack Headquarters. We understand all. All primary objectives met, all secondary objectives met, and you are prosecuting all tertiary targets. We will send the code that Moscow can begin the process for your safe return."

A cheer roared through the train. None of the prisoners could speak Russian, but those who hadn't been deafened by the attack well understood the meaning of the jubilant tones of the men.

Whatever the hell had just happened, Russia had won.

General Sabaneyev handed the radio back and walked to the operations officer to confer on the next moves. He wanted to have this train heading east by the time Dryagin made it back to the city. Hopefully the prisoners would serve as sufficient bargaining chips. The Americans could have their people back as long as they allowed his raid forces safe passage back into Belarus and ultimately Russia, and NATO could avoid even more destruction by staying out of their way.

THE KREMLIN
MOSCOW, RUSSIA
26 DECEMBER

The Kremlin sent the coded message through the one direct Moscow-to-D.C. undersea cable they had left intact for just this purpose. An administrative team had worked day and night to craft the perfect words, taking great care that their English translations could not be misunderstood. They added some of the data from General Sabaneyev's transmission, the number of prisoners and their names and ranks, so the veracity of their claims of captives would not be in dispute.

The message was lengthy, boisterous, and highly fictionalized. According to the Kremlin, the advance guard force of a massive invasion had made it as far as Stuttgart, but the attack's progress had been sluggish due to NATO's combined armor and air forces, so the decision had been made in Moscow to hold the main invasion force in Russia. Claiming the situation to be a stalemate, they offered terms for the Russian withdrawal from Europe, but declared that if their advance guard force was not allowed to return to Belarus unmolested, Russia would press their general invasion of Europe, further imperiling Poland and Germany.

The cable mentioned Western crimes and recent military buildups in Central Europe as the justifications for going to war but nevertheless requested an immediate cessation of hostilities and a return to preinvasion borders.

In the Pentagon the message was met with confusion. First, no massive buildup of Russian forces had been detected before the loss of satellite coverage over western Russia and Belarus. Second, even though the reports from NATO units in the combat area of Poland and Germany were only coming through in a spotty fashion, no one at the Pentagon had the impression that NATO was doing much at all to slow the advance of the probing enemy. So why the hell were the Russians so reluctant to commit their larger forces to battle? They had, after all, caught NATO with its pants down at Christmas, and the great majority of U.S. forces were now in the Pacific.

Many suspected the entire attack had simply been a way for Russia to flex its muscles, to bolster support for the nationalist government domestically, and to weaken the NATO alliance by showing all how ineffective they had become.

But others at the Pentagon drank the Kool-Aid offered by the Kremlin. After all, the talk of a larger Russian invasion had followed their expected pattern of attack: a small but decisive vanguard action, followed by a massive invasion. The Pentagon officials celebrated the fact they'd stopped the Russians even while blind and deaf to their forces in Europe. They praised their local commanders' quick decision to counterattack, feeling this had given the Russian advance force a bloody nose, one they seemed unable to recover from and continue their intended advance across Europe. It was a "stalemate" victory as the Russian communiqué suggested, to be sure. As far as some generals in the Pentagon were concerned, this proved without a doubt that NATO's strategy of frontline defense with a massive fly-in retaliatory response to a Russian attack had worked definitively to prevent an all-out war.

It didn't hurt that this same notion underscored the shortsightedness of years of congressional cuts to European and NATO defense pact budgets. Nearly two decades of fighting in the Middle East and a general lack of belief that Russia was capable or even willing to enter back into armed conflict. It was as if the idea were so remote that the West had placed all its bets against it.

The decision to ultimately accept or reject the cease-fire from the Russians was officially in the hands of NATO, but with the degraded communications infrastructure in Europe and the fact that response forces from America would be necessary to fight off an invasion, NATO leaders in Brussels deferred to the American president.

Privately, not publicly.

THE WHITE HOUSE
WASHINGTON, D.C.
26 DECEMBER

President Jonathan Henry sat at the conference table in the White House Situation Room reading the cable for the fourth time. Around him his National Security staff, all well versed in Russia's proposal, sat quietly while he did so.

When Henry was finished, he rubbed his tired eyes and then went around the table seeking the informed counsel of his advisors. All in the room were incensed about the attack in Germany, and many thought it madness to accept the Russians' terms, but no one could paint a rosy picture of the United States and NATO continuing the fight while still nearly deaf, dumb, and blind.

The president most wanted to hear from his secretary of defense and the chairman of the Joint Chiefs, but he saved them for last. When he finally got to them, to Henry's surprise both men recommended accepting the cease-fire.

The secretary of defense put the Pentagon's reasoning clearly: "You accept, Mr. President, and we've won. Just like that. You will have *personally* thwarted a full invasion of Europe. We took a gut punch but prevented a knockout blow, and we delivered a few jabs of our own. Better still, we won while facing war on two fronts with world powers. That's a win, Mr. President. A *big* win. We sell it as such and immediately return our focus to containing China. We beef up Europe with our reserves and then draw up some sanctions to impose on Russia—punish them severely. Plus, no one in Congress but the whack jobs is going to fight us for a renewed increase in military spending in the next fiscal year.

"But if you reject the cease-fire, and either Europe is subjected to an invasion of forces we haven't even identified—or else this attack element that, in a day and a half, made it all the way from Belarus to near the French border . . . well, then we'll have to fight a dangerous, bloody campaign that we cannot win quickly or easily. We will lose more American and European lives, and our ability to repel any subsequent Russian attack, should it come, will be degraded."

The secretary of defense added, "And if we reject the cease-fire, you essentially will be laying down a welcome mat in front of Taiwan for the Chinese to walk on in. They will see that America's forces are split, and they will know that their time to reabsorb their breakaway state has come."

Henry pushed back that once communications were fully restored, the media would spend weeks showing the devastation wrought by Russia, and he would look weak for letting them get away with it; but he was promised by everyone in the room, especially the secretary of state, that Russia would be held to account for their crimes.

The secretary of state said, "Anatoly Rivkin threw a Hail Mary to save his regime by attacking Europe. It didn't work as planned. Let him lick his wounds for a couple of months while we deal with this crisis in Asia, and then we'll hit him with our economic might. Russia is poor and getting poorer. When we pushed them away from that rare-earth mine in Kenya a few years ago, we started a clock ticking on Rivkin's political survival, and that clock is winding down, sir."

The secretary of state then added, "Mr. President, I don't like letting Russian forces kill our people and then just walk away, but the bigger issue is China, Taiwan, and the stability of our Pacific Rim allies."

Henry put his head in his hands. "Give me a second, ladies and gentlemen." Then he sat quietly for over three minutes. His national security advisor started to make another point, but Henry held up his hand, appealing for silence.

Finally he mumbled, "Shit." Looking up, he addressed the table. "Two adversaries, both world powers, threatening at the exact same time. *That's* the angle in all this. Like Hal said, America needs to focus on what happens in Asia next week; we can't afford to build up to go on the attack in Europe right now.

"I'll spend the rest of my years in office making certain Russia pays for what they've done over the past two days. But we need to show nothing but strength and resolve in the Pacific now to prevent a war. Europe can defend itself. They have NATO. On the other hand . . . Taiwan, Japan,

South Korea, our Pacific partners, don't have a strong mutual defense treaty like NATO. There's nothing there to balance the region. SEATO was dissolved years ago."

The Southeast Asia Treaty Organization had been a diplomatic failure, and that was never clearer than right now.

He stood up and then addressed his secretary of state. "Okay . . . here's my decision: Notify Brussels that they should accept the cease-fire and allow the Russian forces currently in Germany safe return to the Belarusian border, under armed escort. They'll rue the day they decided to fuck with us, but we'll give them the next couple of weeks to gloat and think they bested us."

"A wise decision, Mr. President."

Three hours later, two a.m. Stuttgart time, Colonel General Eduard Sabaneyev received the message from Moscow that the terms had been agreed to and that he should effect his immediate return to neutral Belarus with haste. Colonel Dryagin and his force, now augmented with armor and troops off-loaded from *Red Blizzard 1* in Stuttgart before its destruction, started off to the east soon after.

Red Blizzard 2 stayed in Stuttgart long enough to off-load some of the tanks and Bumerangs from the railcars, to further bolster Dryagin's firepower.

"If the NATO bastards decide to renege on the agreement, it will be in Poland," he said.

Sabaneyev knew that he needed to get back over the border before America realized that what Lazar was doing thousands of kilometers away was directly related to Russia's actions in Europe, and the "cease-fire" was really nothing more than a ploy to get Russian forces home with their unequivocal win in Europe before Red Metal entered its final phase.

CHAPTER 43

Lieutenant Colonel Dan Connolly had spent a half hour briefing the vice chairman and his staff about the actions of General Boris Lazar and his brigade. Everything from putting his dacha up for long-term rental, to the movement to southern Azerbaijan, to the surprise announcement of the Christmastime snap drill that didn't look like a snap drill at all but instead a purposeful race across the length of Iran to the southern coast.

Then he outlined the loading of the brigade into the container ships in Chabahar Bay, the formation into a flotilla with Iranian warships, and the cruise south out toward the Gulf of Oman.

Most of the people in the room had begun listening to the lieutenant colonel from Strategic Planning with frustration. They were trying to deal with the crisis in Europe and the other in Asia, after all, and this joker was talking about war games in Iran. But in minutes he had everyone's rapt attention. This wasn't a new crisis . . . This was an expansion of the existing crisis in Europe.

Before Connolly was even finished, someone at the conference table said, "They are going to the REM mine in Kenya. The bastards are going to take it back by force!"

Connolly nodded. "I don't see any other possibility, sir."

The vice chairman thanked Connolly for his work and asked him to have a seat at the table. The Marine did so, pulling out a notebook and a pen.

The vice chairman said, "We'll go to the president with this. He won't want to expand this conflict with Russia, but he sure as hell won't allow them to invade Africa and retake Mrima Hill, either. I'll suggest we attack Lazar's forces while they're still on the water."

A Marine general on staff said, "I concur, sir, but I do think we have to have a plan B: some forces on the ground in Africa in case Lazar gets through."

"Absolutely," said the vice chairman. "A MEU at least. How quickly can we make that happen?"

"We have a task force on board USS *Boxer*. Amphibious Readiness Group, a three-ship unit, and they're within a day of port in Tanzania. That's south of the mines but close enough to beat the Russians there, assuming we don't stop them first."

The admiral nodded and said, "I need a man on the ground, someone aboard the Navy and Marine Corps amphibious task force who understands this thing from the start and can decompress it if it goes supernova." He scanned the room quickly. "Connolly?"

Lieutenant Colonel Connolly looked up from where he had been furiously scribbling notes on the admiral's usual rapid-fire stream of ideas, worried he'd miss a tidbit and be held accountable for it later.

"Sir?" he said, wondering why the hell he was being called on.

"It's you, ace."

"It's me . . . *what*, sir?"

"It's *you* I want aboard *Boxer*. I need someone from my office. Someone who understands the whole issue at stake. Someone who knows how to author a plan integrated into our national will."

There was a long pause. Connolly was dumbfounded, but he finally found the words. "*Me?* Don't you want an intel type? Someone who can contribute to the mission? The battalions, the regimental commander . . . I mean, they won't be too pleased having a 'spy' from the Pentagon along for the ride."

The admiral said, "Colonel Connolly, you are to report to the commander, RCT-5, once aboard *Boxer*. Colonel Caster. Know him?"

"I know him well, sir. An old friend."

"Good. You can tell him you are there as a lead planner, or a headquarters liaison, or whatever . . . Just remember, you still report to me. I'll do my part back here as long as you keep me informed. We can stay abreast of any political maneuvering by the Russians that way, and if they sue for peace or some other shit like they pulled in Europe, I've got you there to send me a direct feed of ground truth."

Connolly had recovered from his initial shock. "Copy, sir. I'll gear up."

"Hey, and one more thing: I need *Lieutenant Colonel* Connolly, the strategic planner, reporting and advising a successful *Boxer* Expeditionary Strike Group. I don't need *Lance Corporal* Dan hiding behind the bushes, taking AK fire from the Russians, trying to earn himself another combat action ribbon. Leave the firefights to the grunts."

"Apologies, sir. I *am* a grunt."

The admiral smiled a little. "The *younger* grunts, Dan. Let them pull triggers. Not you. You got me?"

"I got you, sir. Not a problem."

"You worthless motherfucker!" Spittle flew from the mouth of Admiral Herbers as he roared, splattering Major Bob Griggs on the chin. "You are the absolute worst piece-of-shit officer I have ever known!"

"Yes, sir." Major Griggs did not blink. He stood at attention, looking straight ahead.

The admiral's tirade had been going on for thirty seconds already without any details as to why, exactly, he was mad. Griggs had strong suspicions, of course, and these were finally confirmed by Herbers in his next outburst. "Did you *really* think you would get by me and get in to see the vice chairman without me knowing about it? I can read his digital calendar, you idiot! You thought I wasn't going to notice the name Major Griggs on the daily meeting update?"

He went on: "I just *knew* you'd try to go behind my back. I find it telling that Connolly obviously knew better than to attempt the end around. Didn't see him on the schedule with you."

Griggs answered flatly, "No, sir. I did not put Colonel Connolly on the schedule."

"Do you *honestly* believe the vice chairman of the Joint Chiefs has time for your harebrained concoctions?"

"No, sir," Griggs said again.

"You're damn right he doesn't! Now . . ." The admiral lowered his volume and said, "Good news. I got ahold of an old pal of yours. Colonel Richter is coming down personally to collect you right now."

Griggs's eyes widened briefly, and then they returned to their impassive stare.

Herbers said, "You won't be a pain in *my* ass any longer. Instead of getting paid to make my life difficult, the Department of Defense just might get some work out of your lazy ass before you retire."

A knock at the door halted the admiral's tirade. A stiff and businesslike full-bird Army colonel wearing a starched white uniform shirt and crisply pressed blue slacks entered from the corridor.

Based on the impressive array of ribbons on his chest, the colonel had clearly seen a great deal of combat, and his face was deeply tanned. It was a given around the Pentagon that when you saw a man or woman with a heavy suntan, they probably weren't just coming back from vacation in Florida or Hawaii.

No, around here that meant they'd been downrange.

The man's name plate read "Richter." "Admiral, am I interrupting anything?"

"Not at all, Colonel. I was just adjusting Major Griggs's attitude."

"You'll find that's a difficult thing to do, sir. You see," said the colonel, closing the door behind him and striding into the room, "ol' Griggsy here just knows more than everyone else around him." He turned to look at the admiral. "Admiral, Major Griggs and I have worked together on several occasions. He *really* doesn't like being out in the field much. Seems he believes the Army life in the field is beneath him. He belongs behind a desk at some big think tank in the sky. He's just too smart to be among the riffraff of us rank-'n'-file soldiers."

Colonel Richter stepped into bad-breath range of Griggs's face. "I've had enough of you embarrassing my service up here in the director of plans's office. It's time for you to get back into the trenches. And since you're getting close to retirement, that leaves me just about enough time to get your ass deep into something vital. A crap ton of manuals I need rewritten. You're going to be my best paperwork monkey. Ain't that right, Major Griggs?"

"Yes, sir." A thin bead of sweat rolled down Griggs's forehead and onto the bridge of his nose. He let it hang there unattended.

"Because if you don't fulfill your role, even in these last months of service, I think we'll find that you are just not fit enough to make retirement. It would be a bitch to serve nineteen and a half years just to be bounced out on a profile before you can formally retire with benefits, wouldn't it?"

The colonel turned toward the admiral. "Sir, I'll relieve you of the burden of the major. I'll take it from here."

"Thank you, Colonel." The admiral smiled and turned toward the door.

But before he could leave, the executive assistant to the vice chairman of the Joint Chiefs walked in. Elena was in her fifties, sharp, stunning, and as shapely as a fitness instructor. She was as much a power broker around the office as she was a peacemaker. A lifelong civilian who had worked for more than eight chairmen in thirty-two years of federal service, Elena had remained the constant in this office for more than twelve years.

Anyone who didn't know Elena wasn't worth knowing.

"Hi, Admiral. Was hoping I'd find you here." She smiled broadly. "The deputy sent me. Seems he had a productive meeting with your man just now, Lieutenant Colonel Connolly, but he's disappointed you and Connolly's partner had to miss the meeting." She leaned to one side, looking past the admiral to catch sight of Major Griggs, who still stood bolt upright at attention in the middle of the room.

"Oh, *there* you are, Bob. The vice chairman said the intelligence data these two men put together is the tops. Wants to go hot with it ASAP. Needs you and your men to tee it up to brief the chairman himself. He passes along his sincere compliments to you and your planning staff. Your team finally got us one move ahead of the Russians."

All three men stood in silence.

Elena cocked her head. "I'm sorry. Did I interrupt something?"

"No. Thank you, Elena," said the admiral softly. "I'll have Lieutenant Colonel Connolly ready to brief the chairman by this afternoon."

Major Bob Griggs remained at attention after Elena departed, but he couldn't conceal the edge of a slight smirk.

"Wipe that fucking smile off your face," said the colonel, squaring up on Griggs again. "Admiral . . . is he still going with me?"

Herbers was still fighting off the shock. His face cleared and he said, "Hell yes. I've got Connolly. You get Griggs."

Colonel Richter said, "Be in my office in fifteen minutes, Griggs. Clean out your desk here. Your ass is mine now."

Without another word, the colonel and the admiral walked out, leaving Griggs still standing at attention.

Griggs's little smirk faded and more sweat rolled onto his collar. His shoulders fell, he relaxed his posture, and then he headed back to his brand-new, comfortable office to empty his brand-new desk into a cardboard box.

For Bob Griggs, the big leagues hadn't lasted long, but he and Connolly had successfully achieved what they'd termed "Operation Sacrifice Fly." Griggs forfeited himself so Connolly could slip in to brief the vice chairman in his place.

It had worked perfectly to plan, and now all that was left for Griggs to do was pay the price.

CHAPTER 44

Lieutenant Colonel Tom Grant's face had never been this cold in his life, but he was so intently focused on scanning the horizon through his binos that he couldn't be bothered to duck down into the warm insides of his M1A2 Abrams tank. The temperature was in the low teens, but the frigid air whipping across Grant's face was due to the fact that the tank he was riding in was blazing down the German autobahn.

One of the advantages of leading a unit comprising mainly techs and mechs was that Grant's order to remove all the governors from the engines had been obeyed and put into action in less than two hours. Now the Honeywell AGT1500C multifuel turbine engines cranked out a speed of over sixty miles per hour.

Grant's driver had the pedal to the metal, as he'd been ordered to do, and the lieutenant colonel worried that the young Army specialist might drive off into a ditch or run over a civilian car.

Sergeant Anderson, the tank's gunner, had climbed over to Grant's seat while Grant stood up in the turret, and the young man scanned through the commander's independent sight system. The M1A2 SEP had two sight systems, both thermal and both very high-tech. With the flick of a switch Grant could designate several targets and the gunner, Anderson, could then kill each one in succession.

But at the moment Grant was searching for any sign of Russian forces in the dark through his binos, and his gunner was using Grant's sight to look for long-range targets and to keep the driver out of trouble.

The voice of Grant's operations officer, Captain Spillane, came over the headset: "Sir, relay from an AH-64 pilot over the UHF. He says he's got comms with one of the ground stations on the guard nets."

"Copy, Brad. Read it out loud on this net," said Grant, his eyes still in his glass, hunting for enemy armor ahead.

"Sir, the traffic is as follows. 'Cease fire, cease fire, cease fire. All NATO forces, cease hostilities. Acting EUCOM commander is designating a cease to all NATO combat operations.'"

Only now did Grant lower his binos.

Sergeant Anderson spoke over the intercom. "You have got to be *fucking* kidding me!"

"Anderson, get off—I can't hear the operations officer," barked Grant; then he rekeyed his radio. "Brad, confirm what you just said. Acting EUCOM commander has told us to halt all actions?"

"That's an affirm, sir. I'm picking it up on the NATO frequencies now as well. It's not as clear as the relay I have to the Apache, but it confirms the cease-fire."

Anderson came back over the intercom. "This has to be a Russian trick. A ruse, sir."

Grant was too preoccupied to tell his gunner to get off the intercom again. He climbed back down into the turret, and Anderson moved out of his seat and back to his own. Wiping his face, Grant got on the intercom.

"Anderson, I want you to use the Blue Force Tracker, or a map, or *something*—just get me to the eastern half of Stuttgart. Copy?"

"Got it, sir."

Grant rekeyed the radio. "We might be able to catch them as they depart Stuttgart. We'll move into position."

Spillane replied with, "Uh . . . roger, but . . . *then* what, sir? Are we going to just blow off the cease-fire?"

"It could very well be a spoof operation from Russian radios. But at the least we'll be in position to reattack the Russian forces as they depart if we can't confirm the EUCOM orders. If there is a cease-fire, and I do say *if*, I at least want to be in a position to observe that *they* observe the cease-fire and get the hell out of Germany. I'll follow their asses all the way across Poland if I have to.

"Keep trying to contact EUCOM directly by any means to seek clarification and guidance. Got it?"

"I got it, sir. I'll plug the directions in and navigate the regiment. Permission to ask our German buddies for help with any shortcuts?"

"Do what you gotta do. Just get us there before the Russians get too far away."

An hour and a half later Lieutenant Colonel Grant and fourteen M1A2 SEP tanks of the 37th Armored Regiment sat outside the German city of Göppingen.

Grant looked through the commander's sight, and through it he could clearly see a massive military train with the Russian flag painted on the side. It rumbled along a track through sparse trees two kilometers distant, with several Bumerang escorts driving along an adjacent road.

Anderson was watching, too. "Trains, sir? Did anybody say anything about trains?"

Grant said, "It's not like we've been getting much intel, Anderson."

"Sir," the young man continued, "I could dump a thermobaric round right up that train's ass, kill all them Russians. Hell, I can see four or five of them set up as air sentries on the roof, watching those Apaches in the distance."

Grant felt the same emotions as Anderson but said, "We're not doing that. If this cease-fire is for real, then the time for us tankers to make an impact has passed." He spoke with obvious frustration.

Spillane came over the radio. "Courage Six, Courage Three."

"Go ahead, Brad."

"Sir, I have a colonel over at Panzer Kaserne on the radio."

"The Marine base?"

"Yes, sir, but he has a landline back to Patch Barracks. He confirms what we heard and offers to tank us up if need be. He relays that someone—he wasn't sure who it was—directed us to stay in contact with the Russians, to escort them right out of Germany and into Poland. We pass them off to the Poles, who will take it from there. He said there would be more to follow by radio, but our regiment is the most 'unfucked'—his words, not mine. Guess there's a lot of chaos in the city right now. Hell, all over Europe. But we're the closest and best to task with the job of armed escort right now. Orders for ROE will follow."

During the radio pause Anderson said, "Sir, if I plop a round through that engine, those fucks would be trapped here."

"You have your orders. Sit here and watch. Then we'll follow them and keep watching."

"Watch them get away with it, sir?"

Grant closed his eyes. He wanted to be sick. These Russians had killed his men and now he had to babysit them part of their way back home.

He keyed his radio. "Copy all, Brad. Ask the colonel to relay that we acknowledge and understand our mission."

Tom Grant slammed his head back into the unyeilding steel ammo magazine behind him in frustration.

CHAPTER 45

Polish president Konrad Zielinski made the decision unilaterally and knew it would make him, for the majority of the population of his nation, the most despised man in Poland.

But the calculation was not hard for him. He would not—*could* not—allow the Russians to kill, maim, and destroy their way across his country, then just return home in peace.

Like nothing had happened.

No. There would be repercussions. Despite the cease-fire NATO had declared, Poland would attack the Russian column with everything they had.

Unilaterally.

He knew the Polish armed forces did not have enough firepower to destroy the Russian invaders; there was too much Russian airpower to protect the column, they were moving too fast, and the Russian forces on the ground were too well equipped, too well trained. The surprise against his Polish Land Forces had been too complete. But the president felt his military had to try to deliver the hard lesson to Moscow that there would be a price to be paid for any invasion of its neighbor.

And it was abundantly clear to President Zielinski that the Poles would have to do this themselves. NATO did not support them. They would not help them, and had negotiated the Russian assault forces a clear withdrawal, almost as if Poland were just some middle ground for other, bigger countries to bargain over and transit at will.

No, not again. Russia would learn something of Poland's strength, and NATO would as well.

A meeting was called and the generals arrived quickly and quietly at the Ministry of National Defense on Klonowa Street in central Warsaw. President Zielinski himself came to the meeting, the lone man in the room out of uniform, and after a brief but impassioned speech harkening to World War II and the Polish history of agonies and wrongs from Russia, he sat down at a chair behind the officers.

The officers next talked over the military options, and the immediate consensus was that there were precious few. The lieutenant general who commanded the Polish Land Forces admitted he was firmly against an attack. These Russians were exiting Germany of their own accord, under an umbrella of peace, and it was assumed they'd file back quickly through Poland and end this affair. The general of the Polish air force agreed. He'd lost a sizable portion of his most advanced aircraft during the Russian lightning raid two days earlier. A coordinated and concerted Polish attack on the Russian invaders with what he had left would be very hard to pull off. The military term was "penny packeting a response"—cobbling together a mishmash of forces on an unknown timeline. It was likely he would only lose more of his air force in another round of fighting and all but invite future threats into Poland when the Russians realized Polish air had been so badly degraded.

And what would the repercussions be from NATO if Poland violated the cease-fire? The PLF might take a few bites out of the raid force, but if there was no NATO to support them after the initial attack, what more might come over the Belarusian border? This threat was real and the stakes were nothing less than the very existence of Poland.

Some sort of surprise attack was the only hope for, if not parity on the battlefield, then at least a fighting chance for the Poles to strike a solid blow, to damage this raid force without destroying their nation in the bargain.

But the Polish Land Forces could not plan on any surprise, because there was no way they could move into position to cut off the Russian armor without the Russians knowing about it from their intelligence collection. It was assumed spies and drones had poured over the border with the raid. In the past two days multiple shoot-outs and killings had taken place in and around train stations in the southern part of the nation, and bodies of dead fighting-age males in civilian clothes and carrying Russian weapons had been recovered.

The officers stood around a table and looked over maps of their nation. It was clear that the easiest, quickest, and smartest move for Sabaneyev to make would be to roll his force back across Poland along the major highways that passed closest to his original invasion route. If he did this, he'd be back in the safety of Belarus before nightfall of the following day. The flat farmland around the motorways and almost completely rural landscape would make the possibility of any ambush by the Poles remote and ill advised. Even by air they would be forced to play by Russian rules.

The generals were getting nowhere with their attack plan, and President Zielinski was becoming visibly irritated, when a colonel in Wojska Specjalne, the Polish special forces, spoke up. He pointed out that even though the motorways wouldn't take Sabaneyev through any urban areas, there were two major cities close to his assumed return route: Wrocław and Kraków. One of these cities, he suggested, could hide an irregular force with SF support that just might be able to avoid detection by the Russians until the column was too close to avoid rolling into a trap.

A general in the mechanized cavalry dismissed the idea brusquely, saying no force of any size would be able to get out of the city and into fighting positions along the motorway before the well-defended Russian column could destroy it, even if the motorway skirted right alongside the urban center itself.

But the Wojska Specjalne colonel boldly pushed back and offered up a plan that, at first blush, left some of the officers in the room questioning which side of the fight he was on.

"We have to trick the Russians. We have to let them think they've gotten what they want. We have to let them do what Russians do best . . . believe too much in their superiority.

"They are set up for sleek, fast-paced-maneuver warfare. They have enough tricks to fight back against everything we've got. So we place them where they should not be. We mire them in a city." He paused and saw confused faces looking back.

"And *then* what?" asked the cavalry general. "We fight a battle with Russian armor in the congested, civilian-filled streets of Kraków or Wrocław?"

The colonel nodded solemnly. *"Tak."* ("Yes.")

The room was silent for several seconds. And then President Zielinski said, "Colonel . . . you have the floor. Lay out the full plan. No great speeches, now. How does this work?"

The colonel turned to Zielinski. "Mr. President, please understand. I believe an attack will be successful in damaging the Russian wheeled force, ideally down to the last man, but it will be similarly devastating to the population centers. You have two choices, Kraków or Wrocław. From the map it appears they would both be well suited for my idea."

The president knew what was being asked of him. He needed to choose which city would live and which would die.

He thought it over, but not for long. He had spent the last two days steeling himself to lead his nation in war. He had forced out his old mindset, removed compassion and care for anything other than battle.

His calculation was made dispassionately but with a slight nod to potential civilian casualties.

"Kraków is the second largest city in Poland. Wrocław is the fourth. If we fight in a city . . . we fight in Wrocław."

A quick call was made and an orderly brought a detailed map of the city, which was unfurled, and after another hour of discussion, the outline of the colonel's plan was set.

The Polish Land Forces would move elements of the 12th Mechanized Division, the 18th Reconnaissance Regiment, and the 10th Armored Cavalry Brigade into Sabaneyev's assumed route along the A8 Motorway that ringed the city of Wrocław to the north. This would be a force of roughly 5,000 troops, and steps would be taken to mask the movements of these men and their equipment. These steps would fail, of course; the Russians would identify the rushed buildup.

To Sabaneyev, it would appear as if the Poles were planning a massive ambush.

If the Poles did, in fact, fight in the fields along the motorway, they would lose in a rout. But the Russians would trust the intelligence reports, and they would expect a day's delay, and sizable losses of their own.

But the colonel's plan was not to put the Polish Land Forces north of Wrocław so that they could fight the Russians. No, it was to put the Polish Land Force north of Wrocław to force the Russians to take another route—to take them out of tank country, the open fields of Poland, and into infantry country, special forces country.

The city.

So far everything Sabaneyev had done had been to avoid a pitched fight with frontline Polish, American, and German army troops, to use speed and maneuverability to bypass his enemies' strengths and to look for weaknesses. To search for gaps and move—fast.

The Poles would use this tendency against him.

The officers in the Ministry of National Defense building agreed with the Wojska Specjalne colonel when he postulated this would continue on the column's inevitable eastern return. A large enough Polish force arrayed in front of Sabaneyev might get the Russian colonel general to seek an alternate route.

He could turn north, but this would push him into the interior of the nation, not the open, flat south, and it would force him to pass close to the bulk of the Polish military, which was still arrayed near Warsaw awaiting what they assumed would be the main invasion force from Belarus. It would send him near several Polish air force bases, which would decrease the time his column and his air support would have to respond to any threats from the air.

Heading north would both slow him down and expose him to more danger. He wouldn't do that.

But there was another maneuver Sabaneyev could make to avoid the direct encounter with the Polish Land Forces. He could bypass the 5,000 soldiers dug in in front of him along the motorway, peel off into the streets of Wrocław, and drive right through the city itself. In this way he would be delayed no more than four to six hours, not twelve to twenty-four; he could re-form his column on the A8 Motorway on the other side of the dug-in Polish positions; and he could once again race across poorly defended southern Poland and make his way into Belarus.

If there was nothing but Polish civilian militia defending Wrocław, he would see the way as clear and would be drawn by the opportunity to strike a quick blow against a token force.

Sabaneyev would not take the decision to move through Wrocław lightly. No military force, mechanized or otherwise, wants to get bogged down in a major city with tight streets, civilian traffic, and high buildings on all sides, but if the way through the city looked easier and more assured than the way *around* the city, the Polish special forces colonel suggested that the brash and confident General Eduard Sabaneyev would choose this route.

Sabaneyev would surely send reconnaissance to look for evidence of traps in Wrocław; to check the bridges over the Oder River, which ran through the city, to ensure they had not been wired with explosives; and to gauge the citizenry for evidence the civilians had been moved out or warned.

But if he found no evidence of major conventional forces positions, he'd almost assuredly take the risk.

And if Sabaneyev could be steered into moving his armor directly through Wrocław, they would trap him in the spot that armor and in fact all conventional forces in the modern age detested and dreaded: fighting street to street, house to house. They would litter his route with a relatively small force of Wojska Specjalne, perhaps four hundred strong, augmented by a few thousand militiamen and -women in civilian clothes. They would make Sabaneyev pay for every block with an armored personnel carrier, every street with a tank, every kilometer with a company of dead Russian soldiers.

The Russian drones wouldn't pick up a few hundred men and women moving in small groups into Poland's fourth-largest city over the next twelve hours, and if anyone *was* tracking the militias, the fact that a couple thousand of their personnel moved along with their old, outdated equipment into the city would just look like a repositioning, moving the B team out of the way of the egressing Russian army, so the PLF could execute their ambush.

When the plan was put forward, there was arguing on all sides, especially when it became clear there would be no way to both preserve the element of surprise and evacuate the city. The historic old town, one of Europe's most beautiful, would be ground zero for some of the most intense fighting on the Continent since the Second World War.

The Polish people of Wrocław were clearly going to suffer.

But President Zielinski had urged the military men to give him something that would work, damn the costs, and it looked like they had.

The key to the attack would be the simultaneous destruction of the five bridges over the Oder River in the center of town. They would need to be dropped to force the Russians along a path of the Poles' choosing.

And this would have to happen without the Poles mining the bridges and therefore revealing the ambush to Russian forward reconnaissance troops.

An air force general solved this equation. After conferring with junior officers, he said a dozen of the nation's thirty-four remaining F-16 aircraft could take off and deliver bombs directly onto the bridges, and even though the inbound aircraft would be detected by the Russians, if the fighters took off from the 32nd Tactical Air Base at nearby Łask, the Russians would have little time to knock them out of the sky before they dropped their payloads and turned away.

The F-16s could then, with luck, retreat back out of the Russian column's air defense cone, up into the north of the nation, rearm with more bombs, and return for more action—not in the city itself, but on any targets of opportunity at the rear of the column that managed to escape the trap.

The Polish president knew hundreds—no . . . thousands—of his citizens would die in the carnage and confusion of city fighting, and he would forever be the one who had condemned them to this fate. But ultimately he decided his very nation would not long stand if the Russians believed they could invade Poland without consequences.

He was the one who would stick out his political neck and be sacked if not hanged by his own countrymen when it was all done. But as far as the president was concerned, it was NATO that had condemned the city of Wrocław to destruction by forcing his hand.

The president signed off on the plan, signed away his political career and legacy, signed the death certificates of an unknown number of his citizens and military.

He himself had friends and family in the city, but he did not pick up the phone to tell them to get out. He instead returned to the Presidential Palace, the seat of the brief Polish breakaway from Russia in 1918, itself a symbol of Polish pride and independence in their first attempts at democracy before once more falling under the boots of Russia and Germany. He picked up a hot coffee from the blissfully ignorant secretary in his outer office. He entered and sat down in the old, heavy leather chair.

The December morning sun glared through the huge floor-to-ceiling glass windows of the old palace. Out front he could see the tall, prominent statue of Prince Józef Antoni Poniatowski mounted on his horse, his saber drawn, frozen in bronze in a perpetual cavalry charge. Outside were the lush gardens, green in summer, their joy diminished by the winter's harsh cold and brown colors.

Beyond the statue he could make out the top of the tomb of the unknown soldier, with earth from every Polish battlefield in large stone urns, and the barely visible gates to the eternal flame.

He realized for the first time that the tomb was placed there to remind all Polish presidents past and future of their precise duties in times like these.

A great dread washed over him.

He thought of the men and women down south, the soldiers and civilians who were about to die, and he thought about the beautiful city he had doomed so that Poland itself might survive.

He quietly put his head down on the huge wooden desk and wept uncontrollably.

CHAPTER 46

United States Navy commander Diana DelVecchio peered at the monitors in front of her with a rare look of surprise, given her experience.

She called out, "XO, come take a look at this."

Lieutenant Commander Tad Jenkins, the ship's executive officer, pivoted away from the navigator's depth and right-of-way charts on the plotting board. He turned to the periscope displays on the conning tower and worked the zoom controls in and out as he did so.

"That's a fleet, Captain," he said, looking at the large cluster of unmarked dark shapes in the rainy gray gloom of the Gulf of Aden.

On an older boat, with an older-style periscope, submariners called the funny back-and-forth movement the officers made while looking through the periscope "dancing with the one-eyed lady." The *John Warner* had a new state-of-the-art digital periscope system, technically called a UMM, or universal modular mast, which provided constant video feeds, was visible to everyone on the multiple screens, and had enhancements far beyond its fragile glass-and-mirrors predecessor.

Jenkins flicked a switch engaging the enhanced night vision, then tried thermal to see if they could pick up any heat from the ships. Commander DelVecchio always wanted the scope low in the water to avoid detection, so

Jenkins had to pause between waves as they crashed over the specially coated digital lenses.

"That's a fleet with a purpose," he added, squinting through the scope. "Civilian ships in there, but that's a military convoy. I see escorts, and they are arrayed in a battle plan."

He turned the UMM to the right, looking thoroughly over the convoy, pausing briefly on each distant gray ship. Then he zoomed all the way out and turned the scope slowly left, trying to better appreciate the full size and composition of the fleet.

"XO, send it in," DelVecchio ordered.

"Down scope," said Jenkins, retracting the photonic mast. "Radio, get an SSIXS transmission ready. I want to send Fleet Headquarters images and audio. Wait for Sonar to send you waveforms. We should have gotten enough video panoramic, both night and IR."

"Aye, sir," replied the officer of the deck.

The XO turned to the OOD. "The scope is yours if you need it, but maintain the captain's preferred interrupted search and get pictures and laser ranges in the meantime. Get that transmission ready, then one last-up mast for a sat burst."

The USS *John Warner* was a *Virginia*-class submarine with Block-III upgrades. This meant her passive sonar included some of the latest tech, like the new large-aperture bow (LAB) sonar array and an enhanced active array of "chin-" and "sail-mounted" high-frequency sonar to hunt the enemy.

And hunting the enemy in the most guileful fashion, using all the boat's technological advances, was what Commander Diana DelVecchio did best.

Her larger-than-life approach to leadership was such that she seemed a lot taller than her actual four-foot-eleven height.

She had been born as a first-generation Italian American, and sometimes a slight Italian accent was audible, but only when she was angry or felt like her back was against the wall during fleet meetings. She also flared up when her crew or their performance was questioned, and this caused her accent to reveal itself.

The crew loved her and treated her with a deep but almost friendly respect, which she allowed. She knew every single crew member's full name, as well as the names of their wives and kids. Most of the crew worked hard for ways to get a word of praise from her, such was their respect for her naval professional skills, care for the crew, and fair treatment of them in a pinch.

In minutes they would extend the UMM again, this time to zap their new intelligence up to the sky and all the way back to Fifth Fleet head-quarters. The intelligence experts at Fifth Fleet would then go to work and dissect each ship in the convoy with known and recorded sonar data and images. If things went according to plan, they'd share the data with the rest of the fleet and also transmit some analysis to the *John Warner*.

DelVecchio stared at the bulkhead a few seconds, thinking, then turned around and walked off toward the operations center. There she watched the video of the convoy and tried, with the help of audio and her sonarmen's practiced ears, to discern who was who in this odd assortment of ships.

Colonel Borbikov paced the tiny bridge of the Iranian frigate *Sabalan*, watching the downpour outside. This time of year was called the "short rains" by local fishermen for the brief but frequent squalls here in the Gulf of Aden. The season was tapering off, but tonight the intermittent spots of light rain reduced visibility. It did have the benefit of cooling things considerably from the daily highs of ninety degrees Fahrenheit, a fact not lost on the troops in the sweltering heat belowdecks.

Borbikov peered through the glass as the bridge porthole wipers wicked away the rain. Two more infantrymen had wandered up on deck to refresh themselves in the squall. They climbed out of a hatch in the bow and faced skyward, relishing the fresh air and gentle rain.

Even though Borbikov had threatened their superiors with court-martial, a few soldiers still appeared on deck about every half hour to escape the heat and stench common to troopships belowdecks. His own Spetsnaz soldiers generally maintained good discipline, but these were General Lazar's troops aboard *Sabalan*, and the regular army guys *always* tested his boundaries. It didn't help that Lazar himself and most of his other senior officers were aboard other vessels in the convoy, leaving Borbikov as the most senior Russian officer aboard *Sabalan*.

He had taken to using the bridge's bullhorn to scare Russian infantry-men back down to their cramped quarters.

The Iranian frigates and cargo vessels loaned to the Russians came with several obligations. One was a requirement that no Russians be visible outside the skin of their ships until they made landfall. Another was that Iran would benefit from the last phase of the overall Russian campaign with a percentage of the income generated at the REM mine. It was a gain that might take several years to realize, but Iran was nothing if not patient when it came to profit.

It had been clear to Borbikov from the beginning that the Americans would understand Russia's true objective by this point in Red Metal. There was no way 5,000 Russian soldiers and their armor could be loaded into ships on the Iranian coast and then put to sea without it being noticed, and it wouldn't take too much deductive reasoning to then determine that the aim of the military movement was the disputed rare-earth-metal mine in southern Kenya.

But Borbikov had another feint to pull. He determined that all the other obligations of the U.S. military at present would slow their detection, analysis, and reaction times, and then when they *did* determine Russia was after the mine, they would reasonably assume the ships would be landing in Mombasa, less than fifty kilometers from Mrima Hill. Transit time from Chabahar Port in Iran to Mombasa Port meant the West would have two full days to execute a naval or aerial military response before the Russians landed and off-loaded.

Of course, the United States and NATO would want to engage Russians at sea. The destruction of AFRICOM in Germany meant America would have a difficult time organizing and mounting an in extremis attack in Africa, but American bombs and missiles fired at the Iranian ships could end the Russian invasion of Kenya before it even began. Once on land, the Russians would have all their ground-to-air assets up and running, not in storage several decks below the surface.

But the West would *not* have two days to mount a defense. Borbikov's plan instead sent his flotilla out of the Arabian Sea and up the Gulf of Aden, where they would go ashore at Djibouti City. This would necessitate Lazar making an arduous 1,300-kilometer armor movement through Djibouti, Ethiopia, and Kenya, but it would also mean shaving by half their vulnerable crossing over water.

Sure, Borbikov allowed, if there were U.S. ships or subs in the Gulf of Aden, the Iranian and Russian escort ships and submarines lurking below the surface would have to deal with them, but this was a far better match than the premeditated and coordinated ambush they would receive if they tried sailing all the way to Mombasa.

Colonel Borbikov lifted the bullhorn, barged out onto the bridge wing, and stood in the afternoon rain. "Get your fat, lazy fucking asses back down that hatch, soldiers!"

CHAPTER 47

Tom Grant, his crew helmet on, sat on the top of the tank, tethered to the turret through the radio cable. His gunner was locked on the Russian armor staged on the far side of the river with the tank main gunsights.

"Hey, sir," said Sergeant Anderson, his eyes still pressed up against the sight's eyecup, "how long since you slept?"

"Couple of days, Anderson. Same as you. Same as all of us."

"Yes, sir, but we aren't the ones making the decisions."

"You'd better be. You'd better have your sight on one of those enemy vics out there and you better have decided on your next five targets if it comes to that."

"Hooah, sir. Those fucks deserve a few parting shots."

Grant nodded imperceptibly. To the twenty-year-old African American from Pittsburgh he said, "You can think about it all you want, Sergeant. Just don't do it. And keep your finger off the trigger while you're thinking. We don't want to be the ones starting this thing up again."

Grant had said what he needed to say to the young man, but in truth there was no one in his regiment who wanted to open fire on these bastards more than he did.

The lieutenant colonel zeroed his binos in on a Russian Bumerang in the column. They were preparing to cross the bridge and resume their withdrawal from Poland. A Russian soldier in the back top hatch of the

Bumerang leaned forward and dropped his pants, showing his bare ass, which he began to smack with his hands.

"Sir, you see that?" young Anderson shouted. "I have his ass cheeks right in my sights . . . Just give me the word."

Grant sighed. Being in this position was bad, but being in this position surrounded by testosterone-filled twenty-year-old American heroes—men who had proven themselves over the past two days serving as the American bulwarks in this conflict—made it all better somehow. He'd been one of those kids once, fighting in Iraq, and he remembered the frustration with the rules of engagement then.

Not much had changed, he realized. He hated his ROEs now as well, and wanted to give Anderson and all the other gunners the command to start blowing up enemy armor again.

Instead he just keyed his mic. "Major Ott, bring your lead tanks up to the left of the crossroads."

"Copy," said the German commander.

The Russian vehicles began to move slowly to the bridge. As the first vehicle came alongside Lieutenant Colonel Grant, a Russian lieutenant stepped off a BTR-4. Late twenties, dirty-blond hair, he looked out of place, except that the snow-patterned uniform designated him a reconnaissance officer. Grant knew he was probably one of the assholes who reconned his fighting positions in Münchberg and likely Stuttgart, too. The officer arrogantly motioned to them and without any words made it clear Grant needed to move his tank off the road to give them more room.

Without looking back to get acknowledgment, the lieutenant mounted up on his GAZ Tigr and radioed something back; then the long column of Russian equipment rolled over the bridge. First a reconnaissance element of Bumerangs and mixed small vehicles, including the Tigrs and even some motorcycle scouts. Then a battalion's worth of T-14 Russian main battle tanks.

The Russian vehicles and equipment looked mostly unscathed. A few Bumerangs showed some battle damage, but they were all moving under their own steam.

It was an hour later when Grant and his tank crew watched the last pack of rearguard Bumerangs cross the bridge. With their passage through his location, Grant would now follow the Russians over the bridge and into Poland. The plan, as he understood it through the relayed messages he'd received, was to stay behind the Russians and ensure that they didn't resume hostilities.

"Courage main, this is Courage Six. You got the count?"

"Yes, sir, we have them. Forty-two Bumerangs, ten BTRs, and thirty-one tanks. All T-14s. I count an additional thirty-eight service and support vehicles. One hundred eleven total."

Grant thought to himself. He'd be shepherding an enemy force much larger than his, even without taking the damn train, wherever the hell it was, into account.

As much as he wanted to heed the wishes of Sergeant Anderson, restarting hostilities would mean one hell of a nasty fight.

By late evening on 26 December, the massive array of PLF had begun to arrive in position north of Wrocław. Their reconnaissance and headquarters elements immediately drew their battle lines and set their quartering parties. Next, advance guardsmen began the grueling effort of digging through the rock-hard Polish dirt, building rushed camouflaged anti-tank emplacements.

Once again, the dark, hard, frozen earth, even in this modern age of technology, was the last refuge of the forlorn infantryman.

Any sound, any noise above a whisper, annoyed the senior men to no end. They assumed Russian observers were in the area, knew they would detect thousands of soldiers no matter how much or how little light they used and how much sound they made, but the Ministry of National Defense had directed this action. *Keep it quiet, but know you will be observed at all times.*

The top, "tier one," unit of Polish special forces was called Group for Operational Maneuvering Response, the acronym GROM in Polish, which is also their word for thunder. The three squadrons of soldiers, A, B, and C, had been in Warsaw, but they flew into Wrocław just after ten p.m. They were driven in buses to several hotels along the Oder River, all in sight of the five bridges.

Other Polish special forces units arrived in the city over the next few hours, and by midnight more than four hundred GROM men were in

Wrocław, all in civilian dress, having traveled in by truck, train, or helicopter.

Multiple individual units of the Territorial Defense Force, the civilian militia of Poland, began getting orders to reposition to Wrocław proper. They were not told why, and they brought only the equipment they had with them. Coaches, trains, and old army trucks delivered the units to their designated locations in the city throughout the night. They did not arrive as a single massive force but rather in company-sized elements.

A motor coach or two here, a convoy of three school buses there.

By two a.m. the special forces and militia in place had quietly begun erecting fighting positions along the anticipated path of the Russian troops. In apartment windows, in stores and offices and government buildings, anti-armor rocket launchers, machine guns, and even rifles and grenades were positioned.

Civilians all around the city asked what was going on, but they were told nothing more than that the forces were there purely for their protection.

It would be a long night of work, and those involved wondered if it would only end after a long morning of fighting a far superior and better-equipped force on the innocent and vulnerable city streets of their own nation.

WEISSWASSER, GERMANY
27 DECEMBER

Colonel General Eduard Sabaneyev woke in his private quarters in *Red Blizzard 2*. He sat up in his sleeping berth after a jolting ninety minutes of rest, looked at the real-time map on the notebook computer in front of him, and saw they were about to pass over the border into Poland.

The map indicated Dryagin and his column had crossed forty kilometers or so to the south and were already in Poland.

It was all going to plan.

The general entered the command car and reached for a thermos of tea offered by Colonel Smirnov, when a flash intelligence report came over the radio. A headset was passed over to him.

"Sabaneyev."

"Colonel General"—it was Major Orlov, his intelligence officer—"I'm sending some files to you right now, sir." A map flashed up on the display above Sabaneyev's workstation. It was the southern Polish landscape, with thermal heat registers clustered north of the city of Wrocław.

"What is it?"

The colonel spent five minutes relaying all the information he had on the rapid Polish military buildup under cover of darkness along the column's route.

Sabaneyev confirmed the details with Orlov. "Two mech brigades, an armored brigade, and a recon regiment?"

"Yes, sir."

"Any change to their air posture?"

"Negative, sir, but they know at our present speed we won't reach their location until eight hundred hours tomorrow. They appear to be trying to set up an ambush of some sort."

Sabaneyev found himself surprised. He'd actually doubted the Poles would want another fight after the thrashing they got from his force on the way in.

But now it looked like that was just exactly what the Polish president was instigating.

"Fucking fool."

Colonel Orlov hesitated, then spoke over the command net. "Sir?"

"Zielinski. Wanting to stand and fight. Idiot."

"Yes, sir."

Smirnov leaned over Sabaneyev to look at the display. He had a headset on himself, so he'd heard Orlov's warning. "We can defeat a force of Poles three times that size."

The general shrugged, sipped the hot tea. "With time, yes. But just moving the column into fighting position will take more time than I want to spend in the flatlands of western Poland." Sabaneyev then addressed Orlov through the radio. "What's going on inside Wrocław?"

"We have a pair of Spetsnaz teams on the ground: one up near the A8 Motorway positioning to monitor this new Polish troop concentration, and the other in cover near the A4 and A8 junction, which is to the west of the city."

"I want to know what's happening *inside* the city."

The intelligence officer replied, "A UAV flight a half hour ago showed nothing irregular, sir. A normal night. Activity on the highways but nothing that looks like troop movements inside Wrocław. There are some militia in the city, but they aren't in well-fortified positions."

Sabaneyev turned to his XO. "Smirnov, bring up the plans for a movement through Wrocław."

Colonel Smirnov spun back to his computer, and soon pages of text alongside maps appeared on the center display screen.

The idea that the Poles would set up a blocking force on the egress route had been considered by the Russians, of course, and a number of contingencies had been planned. If there was a large force on the A8 Motorway in the vicinity of Wrocław, one of the possible alternatives was to drive right through the city.

But while the Wrocław contingency had been drawn up, Sabaneyev hadn't expected to utilize it.

He sighed now. This would slow him down a few hours no matter what he did. But then a new thought occurred to him. If he *did* go through the city, there was no doubt but he would face the Polish militia. The poorly trained Territorial Defense Force wouldn't be disciplined enough to hold their fire, and there would certainly be clashes along the route.

The Russian general was already thinking of his memoirs; in truth he'd been thinking of them since that day in the Kremlin when he and Lazar received their orders. Any fight in a NATO nation on his return to Belarus would be another feather in his cap. Even if it was nothing but a few skirmishes between his scouts and the militia, if it happened in a major city, the "battle" could be dressed up with literary flair to provide an exciting last act to the story of his heroic actions during Red Metal.

Sabaneyev suddenly liked the idea of moving through the city, but he wasn't a fool. To Smirnov he said, "Push a reconnaissance force ahead of the column. Send them into Wrocław. Support them with two . . . no, three mechanized companies held just to the west. Have the recon element locate any militia strongholds along our path. Order them to find the most open routes to the bridges over the Oder. Send the Spetsnaz units already in the city to the bridges, have them get under them, and make certain they aren't wired."

He shrugged. "If we can get our equipment through, and there's no funny business from the Poles, we'll move around the PLF on the A8 by going straight through downtown Wrocław." He smiled. "We rule this country now—we can do whatever the hell we want."

CHAPTER 48

Eight GAZ Tigr all-terrain infantry mobility vehicles rolled outside Wrocław just after five a.m. They parked along a trail barely wide enough for one vehicle but remote enough to remain hidden. After thirty minutes of gathering brush and shoveling snow atop their vehicles, their crews took an accurate map reading and confirmed it using the still-working Russian laser system placed on hills and mountains to the south; then they moved out on foot toward Wrocław, the lights of which twinkled in the distance. At eight men per vehicle, there was a total of forty-eight soldiers and officers, all from the 45th Guards Detached Spetsnaz Brigade.

Dressed in civilian clothes, they carried heavy packs containing communications gear, weapons, and rations. The eight-man sections worked as groups using devices that looked like civilian smartphones but actually contained sophisticated military software.

All moved as teams to different parts of the city and to different, vital infrastructure. Bridges, key road intersections, larger highways, and especially rail bridges.

One by one they sent their reports over HF radios; all appeared to be normal. There was an exceedingly light defensive presence from the Polish military—some built-up militia positions, nothing more. The entire city seemed completely clueless to the fact the Russian army was probing its streets.

One team rode through and around the Old Town on tram cars in the early morning. Efficient and visible, the team was the perfect form of reconnaissance. They arrived at the Oder, crossed the bridges, and continued east. They reported no unusual activity around any of the five critical bridges.

Another team had the central train station as their zone of reconnaissance. They reported back that light commuter trains were coming and going through the early-morning hours. A few buses were parked in front of local hotels around the Old Town, a normal enough occurrence, not an unexpectedly large amount of civilian traffic for predawn in a European city.

After less than an hour and a half they'd successfully navigated across all parts of Wrocław that Sabaneyev's planners had listed as key terrain.

The way looked clear to send the column.

RED BLIZZARD 2
WESTERN POLAND
27 DECEMBER

Nearly one hundred kilometers to the west, digital reports were coming in one after another to the support train *Red Blizzard 2*'s command operations center. The computers processed the data and plotted points of interest. The central digital map screen was now zoomed in to Wrocław.

Sabaneyev looked over his operations officer's shoulder and read the raw reports from the Spetsnaz reconnaissance men as they came in. Some of the men were verbose, others brief and to the point, but in their entirety the first reconnaissance reports revealed nothing to indicate any real danger. The colonel general began to weigh his options.

"I want to know for sure before turning south," he said. "If we continue on our course, we run right into what reconnaissance says is a growing Polish defensive belt. What say you, Ops-O?"

"Sir, maybe it's time to ditch the support train. It's done its job, just like the assault train. We have our armor off-loaded and the column is full up on fuel and ammo. Plus, we can count on full resupply nearer the center of Poland from *Red Blizzard 3*. At this stage, we should consider evolving back into assault formations. Quicker, more decisive, and adaptable to whatever the Poles try to toss at us."

General Sabaneyev looked over the map. "We have not seen all of the NATO air, or even Polish air, they might throw against us, and I want the train to help mitigate that.

"And keep the special teams in Wrocław watching for military activity. And one more reconnaissance at first light to check those bridges to make sure they're clear. If I am right, the Poles will put something on the outskirts of Wrocław to let us know we shouldn't go that way, but they'll also believe we'd be mad to attempt to take an armored column through a city."

"Sir, even if they do get forces in town, they won't have enough time to get much in the way of defenses up and established," said the assistant operations officer, drawing a scowl from the operations officer for speaking out of turn and above his pay grade.

"Yes . . . I like the way you are thinking, Lieutenant Colonel."

The operations officer, Colonel Feliks Smirnov, sat down hard in the metal chair in front of his maps. Sabaneyev loved playing his officers against one another. It worked to keep them in line, and it worked as they tried to outdo one another to find solutions, he believed.

WROCŁAW, POLAND
27 DECEMBER

Paulina Tobiasz sat in a second-class compartment as her train slowed in Wrocław's central train station. She looked down at the white sling holding her left arm up and felt the tight bandages on her forearm. She scratched at her wrist because she couldn't scratch under the bandage.

I'll have a wicked scar, she thought. Then she caught a glimpse of her reflection in the window. Her eyes looked tired, sad.

She wasn't a young girl anymore.

But what *was* she? A toughened warrior? More like a scared little wretch. She had always glamorized female warriors in legends. Tough ladies who persevered and showed the world what women could do. Maybe they weren't real, either. Maybe they just got lucky, just like her. And maybe it was universal; perhaps male warriors relied on nothing more than luck as well.

The train lurched a few times and began to slow. They would arrive at the station soon.

She removed the sling, and this hurt her arm. She moved it around slowly. Pain pulsed into her shoulder, but her range of motion was fair.

She looked again out the frosted window glass as the faint glow of morning appeared.

She wondered why they were being sent here to Wrocław. Everyone on the train was militia, and all they talked about was fighting, about *wanting* to get into combat.

Idiots, she thought. They had no idea what they were asking for.

Almost none of those on the train had faced any combat during Russia's strike through Poland, and she didn't think her combat experience made her in any way more competent than the others. She wondered if they were just being sent to escort old ladies crossing the street or to set up some rudimentary barricades.

A male militia soldier who appeared to be in his thirties sat across from her. He'd been looking her way for the past ten minutes, and she'd been trying to pretend she didn't notice. Finally, as the train came to a stop, he said, "You're the one that got shot in Radom the other day."

"About a hundred of us got shot. I'm just one of the few that survived."

"I saw your picture. Thousands have been printed out. They are up all over the place in Warsaw. In cafés, on lampposts. You were awesome. You fought bravely."

She did not reply.

He nodded appreciatively. Pointing at her injured left arm, he said, "You don't have to be here today."

Paulina looked out the window at the platform as the train stopped. "Actually . . . I do."

She tossed the sling on the floor and stood, pulled her small purple backpack off the shelf above her with her right hand, and then slung her rifle across her shoulders. Around her in the car, forty more men and women, all in civilian clothing, began making their way to the exits, and she moved along with the group.

A team of eight Spetsnaz watched as the Polish militia disembarked from the train. A quick check of the timetables told them this was not a scheduled stop, and they all moved discreetly into positions to observe. Their suspicions confirmed, they watched the mismatched-uniformed Polish defense personnel exiting the train. They counted each man and woman.

They watched as the militia leaders struggled just to take count of their forces. A few had to go back onto the train and collect the rifles they'd accidentally left behind.

The covert Spetsnaz team took photos. Surveyed closely the militia's weapons and equipment, then sent back their report:

> -POLISH MILITIA ARRIVING NOW. WROCŁAW
>   CENTRAL TRAIN STATION.
> -COMPANY-SIZED ELEMENT.
> -BASIC INFANTRY GEAR AND EQUIPMENT.
> -1ST GENERATION. NO/LIMITED ANTI-ARMOR
>   EQUIPMENT.
> -FORCE IS ILL EQUIPPED AND LOOKS UNPREPARED,
>   UNTRAINED AND POORLY LED.
> -ASSESSMENT: LIMITED TO NO THREAT.
> -P-8 FORCE REPORTING

Just two kilometers to the east, the Oder River snaked north to south through Wrocław, rimming the eastern side of the medieval Old Town. It had frozen over several weeks prior and remained that way, and now it was covered in day-old snowfall.

Hundreds of footprints visible in the snow revealed where kids, ice fishermen, and other strollers had walked along and across the surface of the river, and the tracks of some hearty cross-country skiers who'd passed earlier in the morning ran under the Pokoju Bridge and disappeared to the north in the early-morning fog.

Just to the south, the Grunwald Bridge was the only one of the five main river crossing points in the city that had any automobile traffic at all this early. With twenty-meter-high double-brick pylons on each side holding up a steel-supported span, it was connected to a major east-west thoroughfare through Wrocław, unlike the bridges to the north that supported smaller roads.

A blue four-door Daewoo pickup truck pulled to the sidewalk on the southern side of the bridge, near where a brick pylon disappeared into the western bank. Three men in their thirties climbed out, zipped their heavy coats up to their chins, and raised their fur hoods. The men walked to the railing and peered over. Soon they took the concrete steps down to a footpath that ran along the Oder and looked up under the steel bridge, shining flashlights briefly because the light down there was still poor.

They piled back into their car and drove to the other side of the bridge, repeated their check of the structure, and radioed in to their superiors that the way was clear.

Back in their Daewoo, one of the men twisted the wires under the dash of the hot-wired vehicle, and they drove off to the north to check the next bridge.

Ten minutes later Sergeant Anton Mikhailov climbed out of his warm pickup and stepped up to the Pokoju Bridge.

He looked it over, then walked back to the truck and climbed into the front passenger seat. He pulled a device from his pack, and texted a message on an encrypted tactical data device: *The Peace Bridge is clear. No explosives or obstructions noted.*

He waited for the response and then turned to his officer in the back of the truck. "They want to know what civilian traffic looks like."

Mikhailov looked around. Even though it was a frosty six thirty a.m., a few people were about, heading to early shifts.

The Russian sergeant got out and looked around some more, taking note of the cold, fresh air. He lit a cigarette and peered back inside at his officer. "Looks like a boring town. There's not much going on here. They don't have a clue the Russian army is on the way."

The captain climbed out of the back, took the radio from Mikhailov, and reported that there was no irregular civilian traffic in the Old Town area.

As he finished his transmission, a taxi pulled up next to the Russians standing around the Daewoo.

The balding, overweight cabbie rolled down his window and shouted to the three men.

"Hey! You can't just stop here in the middle of the road." The man said it in Polish, and the junior officer being addressed did not understand. Instead he angrily waved the cabbie along, not wanting to speak and reveal himself as a foreigner.

It was early and the cabbie had not had a fare and was in a bad mood.

He put his Honda in park and shouted again. He switched to English. Again no one responded; they just waved at him and gave him the fist gesture, the European sign for "Fuck you."

The grumpy cabbie had had enough of the younger generation always trying to make up their own rules on the streets. He reached into his coat and pulled out his mobile phone.

Sergeant Mikhailov reached into his coat as well, but he withdrew his silenced 9mm GSh-18 pistol. He shot the cabbie point-blank three times at three meters' distance. The man's face exploded, coating the back of his car seat with skull fragments and brain matter; blood gushed from the open cranial wounds.

The captain's eyes went wide. "Mikhailov! Are you fucking *insane*? Get that body out of here. You senseless peasant. I'll charge you with every rule under the sun if you endanger the whole *fucking* mission because of a nosy taxi driver!"

Two men moved the dead cabbie into the backseat of the cab and one of them climbed behind the wheel and drove it to the other side of the bridge, with the Daewoo rolling behind them.

They parked the cab in a vacant space and the soldiers climbed out as the captain continued to chew Sergeant Mikhailov out in the back of the truck.

75 KILOMETERS WEST OF WROCŁAW
27 DECEMBER

Sabaneyev made his final decision just twenty-five minutes before the front of the column was to take the off-ramp for Highway A8 north around the city.

He gave the order via radio to Dryagin, who was at that moment standing in the top hatch of his Bumerang command vehicle, looking out to the east as a hazy dawn broke. He and the column were stopped just west of Wrocław, but all the engines had been running as Dryagin's force waited on his command.

The colonel acknowledged his general's order, then climbed back down into the hatch. Inside, in addition to his radio officer, were his company commanders as well as the Spetsnaz major serving as the liaison between the armored force and the special forces. They'd climbed aboard for instructions, pushing Dryagin's other headquarters officers out, and now looked at him intently in the glowing red lights of the cramped space.

Dryagin didn't like his general's decision but did his best to hide it. With a confident voice he said, "All right, it is to be Wrocław. We will have a clear advance through the city. We rush through just as we did in Stuttgart. The local militia will have no idea what is going on and we'll have a clear path across the Oder. The Bumerangs will divide on four routes through town to cover the column's flanks. I want all the tanks in the center. We drive through at full speed with the Bumerangs opening up the highway like they are traffic cops. Anyone gets in our way—militia or regular troops or police or something—we destroy them and keep moving."

One of his company commanders asked, "Sir, what do we make of these reports of militia arriving?"

"Polish factory workers with guns. Doubt they have any idea which side of the stick goes *boom*. We pushed them aside on the way in. We push them aside again on the way out."

"Yes, sir."

The Spetsnaz major asked, "Should we wait for more of my teams to report in? The partisans could pull up the train tracks, mine the routes."

"If there were two divisions of militia in Wrocław, we could still take the city route with little difficulty."

Dryagin looked at the side hatch, where his intelligence officer had been poking his head through. "Razvedchik, what's the report on enemy air? Still nothing in either Łask, Poznań, or Kraków?"

"Negative, sir. And we are monitoring everything they have in the sky. Spetsnaz are watching the airfields. NATO air remains out of Poland per the peace agreement. The PAF has birds up near the Belarusian border east of Warsaw, and they are running sorties in the northern part of the country, just circling. It appears they do not have a firm idea where we are, or else they just don't want to come close enough to get fucked up." He cleared his throat, realizing what he'd said. "Sir."

"Very well," Dryagin replied. "Advance elements will move out immediately."

CHAPTER 49

Lieutenant Colonel Tom Grant had fallen asleep in the turret of his M1A2 Abrams, but only for a few minutes. His driver braked abruptly to avoid a Porsche 911 whipping off an on-ramp onto the autobahn, and Grant popped his head up and looked around.

The commander wiped sleep from his eyes and had just reached for his canteen, when he heard Captain Spillane over his headset.

"Hey, sir? Good news for a change. We got GPS back!"

"Hot damn!" Grant said. "You're sure it's working?"

"Yes, sir. The Blue Force Tracker is showing our position accurately."

"It's a Christmas miracle," Grant joked.

To this Anderson said over the intercom, "Uh . . . I think it's the twenty-seventh, sir. Time flies when you're havin' fun, huh?"

Grant smiled a little and keyed his mic. "Brad, we're going to stop at the next exit. We'll keep the rear of the Russian column in sight, then catch up. Radio to the HQ section and tell them I'll need them to throw up a satellite net. Let's see if we can actually get comms."

Ten minutes later Lieutenant Colonel Grant stood in the middle of a small circle of Humvees. A few black satellite antennas stuck up from the vehicles. They each looked like a combination spiderweb and three-foot-high ray gun, but they functioned to talk to another tiny object, a DSCS

III satellite 22,000 miles in space. As he approached, the communications sergeant raised the flap in the rear of the high-back Humvee.

"Hey, sir, I have a familiar voice for you on SATCOM."

Grant picked up the handset. "This is Courage Six."

The response sounded distant, but the voice was clear enough. "I'm pretty sure this is *not* Courage Six, because *this* is Courage Six actual."

It was the true commander of the regiment, Colonel James Fenton. Grant said, "Damn, sir! Can't tell you how good it is to hear your voice!"

"Likewise, Tom. Me and the XO are headed your way. Heard you guys have been in quite the fight."

"Yes, sir."

"You still following the Russians?"

"Affirmative."

"They playing nice?"

"So far, but I'm hoping one of them tosses some litter on the road so we can blow their asses to hell."

The colonel laughed into the radio. "Not sure that's covered in your ROEs. Just hang close to them; we'll be there in about two hours and you can brief me then. The XO and me are both sorry to have missed all the action. Nothing left to do now but follow those fuckers back to the Belarusian border."

"Escort duty isn't as cush as it sounds, sir. Especially when you've seen what these bastards did on the way in. Killed a lot of good men."

"Roger that, Tom. You've done a helluva job. No one could have been fully ready for this. And loss of life is one of the burdens of command."

"Copy, sir. See you in a couple of hours."

WROCŁAW, POLAND
27 DECEMBER

Paulina and the five militia members assigned to her arrived at their prearranged point, the third-floor offices of a bank across the street and half a block down from the town hall, in Wrocław's Market Square. She and her team found an RPG-7 leaning against the wall near the window for them, and two canvas rucksacks each holding three PG-7VR anti-armor rockets for the launcher. This, along with the rifles of the six militia members, was the full extent of the firepower at this position.

She hefted the weapon, ignored the stinging pain in her left forearm, and settled it down on her right shoulder. Aiming the unloaded weapon down at the street, she found herself comforted by the familiar weight and feel of it.

Paulina had been here in the center of the Old Town once on a school field trip when she was twelve, and she remembered walking around on the streets below. Her impression at the time was that it wasn't as nice as Warsaw, but now she found the center of Wrocław to be idyllic and quaint.

As she peered through the sighting mechanism of the launcher, everything looked so normal out there in the crystal clear morning, but she knew there would be militia and possibly special forces preparing in all the buildings in sight, and this area would become a war zone if the Russians decided to roll down the street down below.

She'd been told to expect some Russian forces passing through the city on their way to the several bridges spanning the Oder River, and this did not surprise her. Unlike many of the militia she'd encountered today, she'd come here fully expecting a battle. But this didn't mean she was any less scared. Considering what she'd already seen, she was, in fact, *more* terrified than those around her. She and her little team would comprise just one fireteam of many, but as far as she was concerned, the Russians were coming here, now, just for her.

She put the weapon back down, turned to her little group, and nodded toward a big kid who appeared to be about nineteen. He wasn't particularly strong looking, but he seemed to be the fittest of the bunch. "Have you fired an RPG?"

"Yes. I am trained as an assistant RPG grenadier for the TDF in Kraków. I fired eight rounds last summer."

That was more than Paulina herself had fired, during both training and combat, but she wasn't going to let anyone else operate the RPG. *She* would be shooting rockets at the Russians today; there was no way she would delegate that.

Paulina looked over the rest of her squad. Two were women; one appeared to be thirtyish and the other was about Paulina's age, a pretty brunette who reminded her instantly of Urszula, except she was much shorter. Paulina asked her, "What do you do?"

"I just joined last Monday. I haven't really done anything."

Paulina sighed.

The other team members—two rather overweight men—said they had been trained as riflemen, but neither seemed terribly confident in their abilities.

She looked back at the big young man. "You will be the assistant grenadier. I'm the grenadier." To the others she said, "You will use your rifles to defend us from any dismounted troops, and you will shoot at Russians exposed through the open hatches of their tanks and APCs. When he and I fall, you will pick up the launcher and continue firing."

Eyes widened at this, but the group remained silent.

She showed the women and the two older men how to operate the RPG-7, but she didn't lift it again to do so. Her shoulder and arm were still complaining about hefting the metal tube earlier.

When she finished, she told her small team of amateurs to move a cluster of file cabinets to the windows to create some measure of protection; then she knelt down, pulled the six rockets from the canvas bags, and began positioning them next to her RPG-7 by the window.

There was a tremor in her heart, and just as she noticed it, a voice behind her said, "I'm so fucking scared. How do you do it?"

Paulina looked up. It was the pretty young girl on her team; she didn't know her name and she didn't want to know. The girl wore jeans and a University of Kraków sweatshirt. She didn't look like a fighter, but she had an old SKS rifle on her back and a small bandolier with extra magazines on her shoulder.

Paulina shrugged. "It's easier for me. I should have died two days ago. I'll die today probably—we all will—but I got two days that I had no right to."

This only made the other young woman more terrified; she waited for more explanation, but none came. Paulina just turned away and began loading the launcher.

She wasn't going to make friends with this girl. That would just make this horrible situation even worse, and it would only give Paulina more pain if she somehow managed to survive again.

Normally she carried a cheap radio—most everyone in the Territorial Defense Force did—but the officers had gone around and collected them on the train before they arrived in Wrocław. The rank-and-file militia couldn't be trusted not to use them. The radio silence meant the Russians wouldn't pick up transmissions that could tip them off to the trap closing around them, but it also meant no one in the militia had a clear picture of the tactical situation right now.

She felt a low rumble in the bottoms of her feet, and then it passed up to her ankles, her knees, and then the rest of her body. She knew she was scared, possibly shaking a little from fear, but this wasn't the reason her knees quivered.

Russian armor was approaching from the west.

"Everyone to your positions," she said, doing her best to sound detached and unafraid.

The young man whom she'd chosen to help with the weapon spoke to her now. "My aunt lives four blocks from here."

Without looking up she said, "Well, pray for her when you're done praying for us."

Just then, a young uniformed PLF lieutenant leaned into the little corner office. "I need a volunteer. Someone not in uniform."

No one in Paulina's group wore a uniform now, but no one volunteered, either. One of the two fat men said, "What for?"

This regular army officer wasn't used to working around militia, so he bristled at the way he was being spoken to, but only for an instant. "I need somebody to take some RPGs across the street to the town hall. There's a position there with a launcher but no rockets."

The other of the two older militiamen asked, "Who the fuck sets up an emplacement and forgets to bring any ammo?"

"Polish SF has spent six hours building fighting positions for themselves and the militia in the dark. They couldn't even use flashlights. Give them a break."

They could all hear the distant rumble and grinding of the armor now. It sounded like it was coming right up the street outside.

"I'll go." It was Paulina. She turned to her team and looked to the tall boy. "You are the grenadier now. Pick one of these guys to assist. Good luck."

"Wait," said the younger girl. "You are our leader."

Paulina shook her head. "You're probably safer without me." She pointed to the boy. "He is your leader now. Just shoot at the Russians when the shooting starts, and if you die today . . . well, congratulations, because the war is over for you." And with that, she followed the lieutenant out of the room.

CENTRAL POLAND
27 DECEMBER

The runway at the 31st Tactical Air Base at Poznań, two hundred kilometers due north of Wrocław, had been cratered by Russian bombs, and it remained unusable. The taxiway had been hit as well, although it had been repaired the previous evening and would have been able to accommodate aircraft heading to the runway if there had been a runway to take off from.

There had been next to no activity anywhere outside the hangars of the base for the entire morning, but slowly the massive doors on two large hangars on the southeastern edge of the airfield slid open simultaneously, both under the power of several men.

And then, one by one, eight F-16s rolled out into the early-morning light. The sound of their engines grew, rumbling low across the flat ground.

The Russians had the airfield under constant observation by UAVs, and within seconds of the nose of the first F-16 appearing, calls went out on the Russian tactical air network.

The sergeants watching the UAV feeds wondered if the Poles were going to test the runway with a takeoff attempt, and the young men made quick bets with one another whether the aircraft would crash in the first crater, 500 meters down the runway, or the larger one some 250 meters farther.

But the first Fighting Falcon in the row did not head toward the damaged runway. Instead, it oriented itself in the center of the narrow taxiway, and then a five-meter plume of flame shot from its single engine and the aircraft lurched forward. The sergeants realized at the same time that the pilot was attempting to take off by using the repaired taxiway as a runway.

Five seconds after the first craft went to full afterburner, a second F-16 shot flame and launched up the taxiway behind the flight lead.

The rest of the flight followed suit.

Four of the eight aircraft were loaded with air-to-air missiles, both radar and infrared, as well as pairs of five-hundred-pound Mk 82 bombs.

The other four F-16s each had one air-to-ground munition on its center axis pylon.

It was the JASSM, the joint air-to-surface standoff missile.

GPS satellites over Europe had been operational for only a couple of hours, but it was enough time for the Poles to take the "dumb" iron bombs off their weapons pylons and replace them with these sat-guided standoff munitions. The JASSMs could strike from much farther away than the bombs, increasing the chances for both the success of the mission and the survival of the crew.

At the same time eight F-16s took off from Poznań, ten identical model F-16s rolled out of three partially damaged hangars at the 32nd Tactical Air Base at Łask, two hundred kilometers to the southeast of Poznań, and less than that northeast of Wrocław.

Four of these aircraft had JASSMs, and the other six were equipped to fight off Russian attack aircraft with air-to-air missiles.

The Łask Air Base flight of multirole tactical fighters was not forced to use the taxiway as a runway, although the one runway at the airfield was still damaged. They'd determined beforehand that they could safely take off in single file by using the northern lip of the runway, using the runway edge marking line as the center strip. It was a dangerous tactic, but one by one and in as quick succession as the flight from Poznań, the Polish pilots pushed their throttles past the full power indent and sent their engines to afterburner. All ten aircraft raced down the runway, their tires missing deep holes by less than a meter, and they rocketed into the air, one after another, soon after.

From the moment the first aircraft in Poznań appeared to enemy drones until the last of the F-16s at Łask went wheels up, only 151 seconds passed.

All eighteen F-16s immediately banked toward Wrocław on their afterburners.

Eduard Sabaneyev showered and shaved, then headed back up toward the command car in a positive mood. Still, the general expected another two hours of mild tension as Dryagin's force moved through Wrocław.

The last report he'd received, just before stepping into the shower, was that so far not a single round had been fired in anger from either side. There were reports about police cars swerving out of the line of advancing armor, shocked citizens staring in horror, and some chaos at busy intersections, but it seemed to be going better than either he or Dryagin had imagined.

Soon enough he knew he'd get the call that his lead elements had reached the few militia barricades and made short work of the weekend warriors manning them. He caught himself hoping the militia would put up something of a fight, still thinking about his memoirs and how he could characterize his return from Stuttgart as some sort of a perilous journey where success or failure hung in the balance.

As he entered the command car, his communications officer looked up from his console. "Sir! Air defense reports multiple fighters taking off from Łask and Poznań simultaneously."

Sabaneyev raised an eyebrow. "How many?"

The young man conferred over the radio a moment, then said, "Ten at Poznań, eight at Łask. All appear to be F-16s. We have Su-30s and MiG-29s closing to engage now, sir."

"Very well." He turned and addressed Colonel Smirnov. "Our fighters will be on them in minutes. The Poles got word we're moving into Wrocław, and they are going to posture a little because they know we've slipped their ambush."

Sabaneyev was correct that the MiGs and Sukhois in the Russian arsenal would close on the Polish F-16s quickly, but he did not yet realize that the ground-attack portion of these two flights wouldn't need much time in the air before fulfilling their mission.

The F-16s were in the air less than four minutes when the order came to release the JASSMs.

Soon the big GPS-guided weapons raced across the sky to the south, from both the aircraft from Poznań and the others flying out of Łask. Some of the pilots crossed themselves, knowing they had likely just condemned fellow Poles to death by their actions, but they understood their mission, which was to say they understood the ramifications of doing nothing and letting Russia traverse Poland with impunity.

And within moments of launching his munition, the first F-16 pilot received a warning in his headset telling him that air-to-air missiles had been fired at his aircraft.

Paulina Tobiasz pushed a baby carriage down the sidewalk, away from the incredible sound coming from the multitude of vehicles approaching from the west.

There was no child in the carriage, only three long, fat RPG high-explosive anti-tank rounds covered by a blanket. She wore a bright green puffy coat, a white knit cap with a tassel, and thick mittens, and she kept her gaze ahead of her, not on the Russian armored personnel carriers rumbling closer and closer behind her as they moved into Market Square.

The RPG rounds weighed twenty pounds each, so Paulina struggled to push the carriage through the fresh snowfall on the sidewalk, and her left arm hurt like hell, but she did her best to appear relaxed lest the Russians grow suspicious that she wasn't pushing a baby.

Paulina kept trudging along until she found herself across the street from her destination. By now the cacophony of engines was painful. She looked to cross and realized the lead vehicle in a group of five was rumbling closer. It was a Bumerang, the same type of armored personnel carrier that overran her position two days earlier. She knew there was little chance this was the same vehicle, loaded with the same troops, that she had encountered on the low hill near Radom, but that made it no less psychologically damaging to see it here. It was thirty meters away when she pushed the carriage in front of it, heading toward the main entrance of the town hall.

She looked to her left, eyeing the approaching vehicle as she crossed the street. A man about her age wearing goggles and a helmet looked down at her from the open hatch. He gave her a smile.

She forced a smile back, then looked away, pushing the carriage to the other side. The Bumerang rolled on toward the town square, obviously heading to one of the bridges that crossed the Oder, three blocks east.

The second of five vehicles passed by just as Paulina entered the town hall through the front door, and there she was met by two militiamen, who quickly hefted the rockets out of the carriage and started for the stairs.

"What about me?" she asked.

One of the men turned back to her. "Can you fire the launcher?"

"Yes."

"Then come on. Hurry!"

CHAPTER 50

RED BLIZZARD 2
WEST OF WROCŁAW, POLAND
27 DECEMBER

In the command car the comms officer spoke above the din of conversation. "Sir! Air defense reports multiple missile launches from the Polish F-16s!"

"Air-to-air?" General Sabaneyev asked.

"Negative. Too slow." After a pause he said, "They appear to be JASSM 158 cruise missiles."

"*Cruise* missiles?" He looked around the command-and-control vehicle. "Launched at what possible targets? We're on the move; there is no sane reason to fire a cruise missile at a target that won't be where it was when you launched."

The comms officer said, "I . . . I don't know the targets, sir."

Now the fifty-two-year-old general let his concern show. "Those are GPS guided. Should have kept the European satellites knocked out for a bit longer. Well . . . I trust we're going to shoot them down."

Colonel Smirnov said, "*Da*, General."

The communications officer added, "Current course has the first missiles arriving in vicinity of Wrocław in two minutes twelve seconds, if they don't terminate before."

This was not much time to knock them out of the sky before impact.

The general looked around at the command car; baffled faces looked back at him. After several seconds the general shouted, "Halt the train!"

An order was given, but before the train began to slow the general said, "Tell Dryagin to disperse his elements from formation and get off their routes until I put them back on. The Poles might be trying to get their cruise missiles to hit the train and the column."

Now the train slowed quickly, and the order was passed to Colonel Dryagin.

Sabaneyev sat quietly thinking for several seconds, still trying to figure out what was going on. Then it hit him. He realized suddenly these missiles had not been fired by Poland at him. No, they'd been fired by Poland *at* Poland.

As the colonel began relaying the order to disperse over the radio, Sabaneyev grabbed the communications officer by the arm. "The *bridges*! They are going to blow the fucking bridges over the Oder!"

He took the radio from the man and repeated this to Dryagin. The colonel's reply came over the net quickly. "That's madness, sir. We'll wipe out their militia positions in minutes. Why would they want us stuck in the middle of their city?"

Sabaneyev barked back. "We've missed something! This is a trap!"

"What are your orders, sir?"

Sabaneyev looked at the plotting board on the wall, indicating the location of both the train and Dryagin's force. He keyed the mic. "We can't back the column out of the city; you're in too deep already. You must advance! We need armor on the eastern side of the Oder—*now*, to protect a river crossing!"

WROCŁAW, POLAND
27 DECEMBER

Junior Sergeant Bogdan Nozdrin ordered his driver to floor his Bumerang APC toward the nearest bridge over the Oder River, following the order that had just been passed on to the forward elements of the column to get armor over the bridges as fast as possible.

He was five back from the lead vehicle, having just passed through Market Square in front of the town hall and trailing two more Bumerangs and two GAZ Tigrs. Behind him were another four APCs and two more reconnaissance utility vehicles.

This small convoy was on the left flank of the main column passing through Wrocław just to the southwest, but Nozdrin and his section had been sent ahead to scout the bridges before the tanks arrived. This put them closest to the Oder when the call came, so Nozdrin's driver was pushing his heavy vehicle forward to stay close to the big green hulks in front of them.

Just as Bumerang Roman One-Four reached Swietego Ducha, a street only a block from the river, an explosion in the distance shattered glass out of the buildings around Nozdrin, rocking him hard onto his heels and sending him ducking for cover back down under the lip of his hatch.

His headset came off as he crashed down into his station, so he rushed to put it back on. As he did this he heard another explosion, smaller but much closer. He called his driver, five meters away up a narrow crawl-through, past the vehicle's engine and at the front of the Bumerang. "What's happening?"

"RPGs, sir! Roman One-Three took a turret hit right in front of me, but he's still moving."

"The first explosion sounded like—"

Another impact rocked Nozdrin's vehicle from behind. "Shit!" he said, scanning with his camera to try to orient himself. "Gunner, return that fire!"

There were more loud booms to the northeast, and Nozdrin just scanned on his camera, desperately trying to find information about what the fuck they were driving into.

An instant later the turret in front of Nozdrin's station swiveled to the left, and 12.7mm cannon fire began pulsating from it, a painful sound even down here inside the armor covering the vehicle.

Over the radio he heard from the lead vehicle in his column. "This is Ambal One-Two. We're at the river, but the bridge has been destroyed! Part of it is in the water and smoking. We will turn left to cross at the—" A few seconds later: "Two! Two bridges are down!"

"Three bridges left standing?"

There was no answer.

"Ambal One-Two, how do you copy?"

"Ambal One-Two. A third bridge has been hit. Assessing damage." A pause. "It's partially down. I can't see the other two from here. We'll have to get closer to—"

Nozdrin heard the explosion through the microphone. Seconds later he heard the same boom outside his vehicle as the sound waves reached him from Ambal One-Two's position.

Over the mic a voice said, "This is Ivan One-One. Ambal One-Two is hit. Anti-tank rocket fired from across the river. Vehicle destroyed. *Nobody* could have survived that!"

Nozdrin ordered his driver to continue to the Oder, although it was the last place in the world he wanted to be right now.

Sabaneyev could hear the action five kilometers to the east from where he stood in the command car of his parked train. He looked through his binos out the window at smoke pillars rising over the city in the icy but sunny morning.

Behind him Smirnov said, "Sir, I'm getting reports that Anna Company is being engaged from ground positions near the Grunwald Bridge."

"The bridge? That's not near the known militia positions."

Colonel Smirnov said, "This is an ambush. In flagrant violation of the NATO cease-fire!"

The general brushed his comment away. "Calm down. We aren't the only ones who can play dirty. I was expecting this."

He was expecting *some* action from Poland, true, but he had not been expecting it *here*. His brigade thick in a city coming under fire from multiple positions was the last thing he wanted or needed.

"Tell the lead elements to blast their way through. Get over the damned river; I don't give a damn how!"

MARKET SQUARE
WROCŁAW, POLAND
27 DECEMBER

Paulina stood in the window of a municipal office next door to the town hall, shouldered the RPG-7 launcher, and felt the arm of one of the two militiamen with her on her back.

The explosions on the river, half a kilometer off her left shoulder, had been her signal to open fire. Even before she aimed her weapon she heard the chattering of machine guns, the whooshes and booms of RPG launchers, and other rockets firing onto the Russian columns, both below here in Market Square and on other, parallel streets leading toward the Oder.

But she pushed it all out of her mind, along with the searing pain in her left arm, and she concentrated on her task.

"Backblast, clear!" her assistant shouted over the sound of gunfire.

She aimed the weapon's sight on a Bumerang one hundred meters to the east. There were other Russian vehicles much closer to her position, and a GAZ Tigr armored car was directly below her window, but she'd picked this Bumerang because she could hit it at a vulnerable point, the lower rear.

She squeezed the trigger, the weapon lurched, and the backblast sent a wave of warmth behind her. The rocket raced from the window, shot over three other Russian vehicles, and slammed into the rear portside tire of the Bumerang at the northern end of the square.

The explosion wasn't impressive to Paulina; there was a small flash and black smoke and debris. No fireball, no secondary detonations.

But the Bumerang APC immediately veered to the right and impacted a brick wall, and there it stopped.

As the smoke cleared she saw that two of the four big black tires on the port side of the big armored carrier were gone, and smoke poured from a third.

A mobility kill. *Good enough,* thought Paulina.

The rear hatch opened and troops began to climb out, but a Polish machine gun hidden in a car rental agency farther west in Market Square raked the area, dropping most of the men before they made it more than a few meters.

Paulina spun out of the window and knelt to reload her weapon with the help of her assistant gunner, and then heavy machine-gun rounds tore into the room right above her head. A man next to her had been churning the street below with his Kalashnikov; he was lifted off his feet as he tried to turn his weapon toward incoming fire, and he was dead before his eviscerated body slammed down onto the floor.

Paulina lay flat and shoved the second HEAT round into the hot launcher while all around her bullets pocked the walls and ceiling.

Burning bits of office debris blew around her, ignited by her backblast, but she ignored all the danger and prepared to rise back up and fire again.

But clearly the gunner of a GAZ Tigr below had seen the smoke trail of her rocket leading away from her window, and its auto cannon kept up withering fire on her position.

She tried to crawl out of the room with the RPG to get a new position down the hall, but her shoulder and arm wouldn't allow it. She grabbed the man closest to her and pulled his face to hers so she could be heard over the incredible noise. "Carry the RPG! We're moving!"

She dragged herself along the tiles with her right forearm, her tennis shoes grabbing the flooring as she used her feet to push her along, low and flat.

Four of the bridges over the Oder were down, but both JASSMs fired at Milenijny Bridge missed their target. One fell a thousand meters short, impacting a row of unoccupied warehouses, and the other plowed into the roof of an apartment building fifty meters beyond the bridge and detonated, blowing out the top three floors of the structure.

Junior Sergeant Bogdan Nozdrin, commander of Bumerang Roman One-Four, had been informed on the battlenet that all the nearby bridges save one had been knocked out and that his mission was still to get across the Oder as fast as possible. He sat buttoned up in his commander's station at the rear of his vehicle, watching the screen in front of him as he swept the camera around outside, looking both for targets and for a way out of the kill box he had been ordered into by his commanders.

The armor of his APC took continuous hits from small arms, which would do nothing more than scratch off some paint, but all around him he could hear the sounds of streaking rockets and exploding ordnance, and he knew a well-placed anti-tank round could either disable the vehicle or kill him, the other two crew members, and the nine infantry troops in the back of the vehicle with him.

He saw on his moving map display that his Bumerang was just coming to the end of Plac Uniwersytecki, and he ordered his driver to turn left. A block later they were on Grodzka Street, which ran along the western bank of the Oder, and here he got his first look both at the narrow frozen river down a slight concrete embankment and at Uniwersytecki Bridge, which had been severed in two places by what he gathered to be a pair of Polish-fired missiles.

There was one bridge left undamaged, but it was the farthest away from Roman One-Four, and the realization that the Poles were blowing up their own damn bridges made Nozdrin disinclined to drive onto it.

The 7.62mm machine gun on his vehicle began firing long bursts; his gunner had identified a target on the far bank of the river that apparently didn't warrant rounds from the 30mm auto cannon. This meant it was likely a soft-skinned vehicle or even troops in the open.

A new sound erupted from outside the vehicle: heavy explosions, impacting both the street and the walls of a building nearby.

The driver called over the intercom, his voice nearly wild from panic, "Mortars!" A massive detonation rang Nozdrin's ears, and then: "Direct hit on one of our Tigrs. Blew it to hell!"

Shit! Shit! Shit! Nozdrin thought. *The fucking Poles are dropping mortars on their own city now?* He was exposed to all the buildings up and down the opposite bank of the river, the enemy was shelling his position, and he had nearly a kilometer of this to endure before he even had a chance of crossing the lone remaining bridge.

"Okay," he said into his mic. "Here's what we're going to do."

Seconds later Roman One-Four broke ranks with the other three Bumerangs and the three remaining Tigrs from his scout column, turned to the right, and rolled off Grodzka Street and up onto the sidewalk. It then crashed into the railing alongside the riverbank, bending the ironwork like soft clay as it rolled over it. The lumbering beast tipped down, dropped onto the icy white surface of the Oder River, and cracked it easily.

The massive green armored vehicle crashed into the river through the ice and snow.

Once all eight tires had disappeared below the surface, the Bumerang's two massive hydro jets turned on, and the APC pushed forward, high against the twenty-centimeter-thick ice sheet over the Oder. The vehicle moved slowly and with great effort, but Roman One-Four did advance as it churned up the hard river surface and motored like an icebreaker toward the other side.

The 30mm automatic cannon chattered now, tearing up a building on the opposite bank where the smoke trail of an RPG had been spotted by Nozdrin's gunner.

The steel hull shattered the ice in front of it as it moved along, and in the thickest parts of the frozen river the front tires even rolled out of the water and up onto the white expanse, only to crack through and crash back into the dark, icy water. This Roman One-Four did, over and over, as it clawed its way across the frozen river.

Two more Bumerangs followed the first, and as Nozdrin scanned behind him through his camera for additional threats, he saw dozens of dismounted Russian troops racing from the museum, crossing through the smoke and haze hanging over Grodzka, and leaping over the railing. These men tumbled down snowbanks and onto the frozen river, where they began pouring fire on the northern bank and moving over the ice as they crossed on foot.

In seconds, mortars began raining down on the river, blasting foamy water, ice, and snow high into the air.

Nozdrin called his superiors to let them know Bumerangs were making their way across the Oder, and soon the order came from other APC companies to follow suit.

He alternately yelled at his driver to make the crossing faster and at his gunner to keep pouring fire on anything he saw, while he rotated his camera around looking for new targets. He was just panning across the Hotel HP Park Plaza on the northern bank when he saw a flash and then the smoke trail of a large rocket fired from a top-floor bedroom. The round raced over the footbridge to Słodowa Island and slammed into Roman One-Three, just to the left and slightly behind Roman One-Four, which was now halfway across the Oder.

Nozdrin was almost knocked out of his seat by the nearby explosion. He panned over to check the vehicle and saw that an 84mm high-explosive round had hit the underbelly of the Bumerang just as its front wheels rose out of the water and onto the ice, detonating against the thinner armor under the engine.

The front-engine design of the Bumering protected the vehicle's crew from the explosion of the rocket itself, but the engine was torn to pieces, and the vehicle stopped moving forward. It smoked from multiple points as it slowly sank back into the water in the center of the river.

As Nozdrin watched, the men inside One-Three began pouring out of the rear exit, falling through the broken ice and into the water.

The river was only five meters deep, but it was easy for a man wearing steel body armor to drown in the icy water. Those who did scramble out and found the hard ice to the left and right of the vehicle's trail faced automatic fire from multiple weapons on the northern bank and Słodowa Island, which chased the men as they tried to find some cover.

Russian soldiers caught in the open ran to their left, searching for a place to hide near the wreckage of the shattered University Bridge, just fifty meters away.

Nozdrin keyed his intercom mic again, calling to his driver. "Faster! Get us across, damn you!"

CHAPTER 51

Paulina had found a new shooting position, a few offices down on the third floor of the municipal building. The window there had been shattered, either by gunfire from the street or else by the vibrations of the explosions all around, so she didn't have to break it out before standing and leveling her sights on the rear of a Tigr scout car, the last Russian vehicle still moving within her line of sight. She watched it spraying 30mm grenades from the remote control launcher on its top turret as it moved, but she couldn't see what the vehicle was firing at.

"Backblast is clear!" shouted the man beside her, and she began to press her finger against the trigger; but just as she did so, a grenade from another Tigr slammed into the wall right below her perch in the window an instant before the distant Tigr suffered a catastrophic kill.

The RPG-7 on Paulina's shoulder discharged, but she was falling back on her heels as it did, and the rocket raced over the Tigr and exploded against the wall of a bank up the street.

The twenty-year-old blonde found herself on her back, the room filled with gray dust and choking black smoke. The men with her coughed somewhere nearby, which told her they were alive. The ceiling had partially caved in around her, and the twisted wreckage of aluminum ceiling beams hung low.

She fought her way back to her feet, lifted the now-empty launcher, and stumbled back up to the demolished window. Looking out into the street, she saw death, destruction, the chaos of frantic civilians, vehicles raging with fire and smoke, and Polish militia and soldiers running toward the river.

But she saw no more targets.

Two disabled Bumerangs littered the road below her, both with their rear hatches open, which meant the crews or infantry had disembarked. Along with this, three GAZ Tigr scout cars were utterly destroyed.

Mangled bodies lay around all the vehicles in sight.

The fight continued raging over by the river; this was plain to hear. Paulina turned to the men in the room with her as the dust and smoke cleared, and she found both to be unhurt and only now getting back to their feet.

"We will reset in another window. They might come back, or other vehicles in the column could pass this way."

Ten minutes earlier and fifteen kilometers west, Tom Grant dug into a cold beef patty from an MRE pouch, shoveling it into his mouth as he looked up toward the cloudy sky. He had spent the morning following the Russian column to the east with his regiment, but he'd sent a company of Leopard 2 tanks to take the lead so he could halt to meet his commander at the helicopter LZ set up for him in a large, broad field on the northern outskirts of the town of Jawor. This halt by the headquarters section spread his force out on the highway a little more than he liked, but this escort duty was supposed to be nothing more than rolling along behind the enemy anyway; so whether he was personally one kilometer behind them or ten kilometers, he could close the distance at will if necessary.

Interestingly, a platoon of Russian BTR-82 armored personnel carriers was lagging far behind the Russian exodus out of Poland. The Russians had explained in the cease-fire talks that their unarmed medical train would be departing Germany and Poland behind their main assault element, and the BTRs were therefore needed near it for its defense.

It was obvious to Grant that this was a bullshit story. The Russian train was armed, it was likely their rolling headquarters, and the BTRs were back here because they'd been ordered to try to keep the Americans away from the main Russian column, assuming with a little muscle they could force the U.S. forces to simply bring up the rear behind them.

But Grant wasn't falling for that. He'd sent his tanks on beyond the BTRs so that they could be within striking distance of the main body of the Russian force if the Russians broke the cease-fire. The BTRs still lagged behind the main column, just ahead of the headquarters section of Grant's regiment, but they'd caused no trouble, and right now they were over a kilometer away and out of sight beyond a nearby forest.

He was glad his colonel was due back any minute: Grant was exhausted from the constant requirements of command during combat. He wasn't sure how long it had been since he'd gotten any real sleep, though it felt like a month.

He climbed out of his Humvee and stood with Major Ott and Captain Spillane. A security team of soldiers fanned out into the field and faced away from the landing zone, most taking a knee, hoisting their weapons to the ready.

Within moments helos could be heard overhead.

As the men looked up into the gray sky to try to spot the helicopters, the radioman sitting in the Humvee spoke up in a rushed voice. "Lieutenant Colonel Grant? Forward scouting elements report sounds of tank fire coming from the vicinity of the Russian column near the city of Wrocław."

Grant looked to Ott. "How far are our tanks from the Russians?"

Ott replied, "I have a company of Leopards about five kilometers west of the rear of the main body."

Ott's radioman spoke to him in German now, and he looked up at the American commander. "Our Leopards are seeing aircraft overhead. Hearing the tank fire, too. Explosions seem to be coming from inside the city itself."

"Son of a bitch," Grant said. "Either the Poles or the Russians violated the cease-fire."

Ott added, "And it doesn't matter who at this point, because our forces are close enough to get stuck in the middle of it."

Grant asked Spillane, "How far is that trail column of BTRs from us now?"

"They are just up the road, sir." Without being asked, Spillane got on his own radio and ordered all units to be on guard for potential enemy action.

Now Grant looked up at the sky again. The two Chinooks ferrying the colonel and the rest of the command staff of the regiment were in sight, approaching from the northwest.

"Shit! Wave them off. This LZ is too close. We'll move back west ten klicks where we are out of—"

Suddenly the sound of gunfire erupted on the other side of the field. Assuming they were the targets of the fire, Grant, Ott, and the others outside their Humvees hit the dirt, burying their faces in the cold, hard ground. They lay flat and tried to look for the source of the shooting. The *zing* of a few stray rounds passed overhead, but to the men's newly trained ears they were likely not the targets. The section of BTRs that had been detached from the main group of Russians was exchanging fire with someone else.

"What the hell?" Grant shouted, and then he saw the Russians. The BTRs drove fast, out of the woods, turrets reversed and firing in the direction from which they were coming.

Grant yelled to Ott, "Something's chased the Russians out of the forest!"

Ott said, "It's not us. Must be the Poles."

There was precious little they could do in the middle of the field but watch. The BTR crews had obviously seen something other than small arms that had spooked them. As they drove over the bumpy plowed fields, blazing away as they went, several streaks of fire and smoke came out of the wood line.

RPGs, thought Grant.

Then another salvo, this one better timed and better aimed than the first. Six rockets in total, and one found its mark, slamming into the rear of a BTR. The impact and destruction were nearly instantaneous: fuel ignited and panicked Russians dove out of the hatches of the burning vehicle. The second BTR halted and hastily returned to pick up a soldier, using the conflagration as cover from the continuous incoming small arms directed at it from the woods. With the Russian soldiers mounted on top of the second BTR, it took off, back to the road, to get away from additional salvos of RPGs.

As it bolted in haste, the BTR drove right toward Grant and Ott, still prone on the ground. The Russians must have assumed the Americans were working with the Polish fighters who had killed their partner vehicle. They opened up on the American and German forces, 30mm explosions rocking the earth, sending giant clods of frozen dirt flying around the two trapped men.

Three well-placed 30mm rounds caught a nearby Humvee, blasting dinner-plate-sized holes in and through the vehicle.

And then: *Boom!*

A single tank main gun round whizzed over Grant's and Ott's heads and smacked into the advancing BTR.

In milliseconds, the M830A1 high-explosive anti-tank HEAT round's shaped charge melted through the vehicle's hull, then burst into a white-hot jet of flame inside the crew compartment, setting everything on fire. Men, equipment, and ammo all went up, vaporized in a mere fraction of a second.

Grant pushed himself to his feet and watched the BTR burn a moment; then he ordered his men back aboard the Humvees and tanks so they could move to some cover.

Grabbing the radio out of the damaged Humvee, he called up to the helicopter on the tactical air net.

"Hot LZ, hot LZ!" He watched the helos turn away quickly.

Still listening to the tactical air net, he heard his commander's voice.

"Grant? What's the situation?"

"There's new fighting in Wrocław, fifteen klicks east of my poz. The trailing forces of the Russian column just got into a firefight with an unknown group on the other side of a wood line from us, then came our way shooting. Two of the Russian scout BTRs just got killed. The Poles got one. We got the other."

"Understood. We're going to find us a better LZ and link up with you on the ground. We are heading—"

Grant heard a sound through the radio that made his heart sink. It was the unmistakable Klaxon warning of an inbound missile.

The colonel said, "Shit! We've got missiles inbound. Looks like air-to-air, long-range, radar-guided."

Grant watched with horror as the two big Chinooks weaved in the gray sky, chaff and flares firing frantically from their sides.

Seconds later one Chinook exploded into a ball of flame and spun toward the ground. A second missile hit the other helo and it, too, nosed toward the ground, leaving a trace of fire in its path.

Both helos exploded over the low rise of a hill not more than two kilometers to the west.

The commander of the 37th Armored Regiment and his second-in-command had been killed right over Tom Grant's head.

Grant got on the radio. "Air defenses! Eyes open for any MiGs or Sukhois!"

"Sir?" came a shaky voice from atop the nearby M1A2 tank. It was Sergeant Anderson. "I fired the shot that took out the BTR. I *had* to. Is it my fault?"

"Enough of that shit!" shouted Lieutenant Colonel Grant, his blood boiling. The fear, the loss of his commander—all of it slipped away, replaced by the thoughts he next gave voice to. "You did what you were supposed to, trooper! Those fucks were going to kill us. Now mount up. We'll check the crash sites for survivors; then we're going to pursue these Russians all the way to fucking Moscow if we have to."

THE WHITE HOUSE
WASHINGTON, D.C.
27 DECEMBER

The Poles had broken the cease-fire, but the Russians had attacked American forces, and this was the news that made it back to the Pentagon. Within minutes the president of the United States was notified at the White House, where he'd just gone to sleep after working in the Oval Office until well past midnight.

President Henry had had it with the Russians, and he did not hesitate in his response.

By now he knew Russia's attack on Europe had been one part feint and one part the disabling of AFRICOM so that Russia could take and hold the rare-earth-mineral mine in Kenya. The entire cease-fire had been a trick, and he, President Jonathan Henry, had fallen for it.

His anger was reflected in his orders.

Speaking to his secretary of defense over the phone, he said simply, "Under my authorization, all military forces of the United States of

America are ordered to engage hostile Russian forces inside Poland until they quit Poland entirely. If they fire on U.S. forces from Belarus, U.S. forces are authorized—no, *ordered*—to return fire."

The secretary of defense understood the clear message, and he passed it to the Pentagon.

The Pentagon, in turn, transmitted it to Europe via the newly working communications links.

CHAPTER 52

A flight of four A-10 Thunderbolt II aircraft flew east in formation, the pilots focusing on the sporadic radio traffic in an attempt to get a clearer picture of what lay ahead of them.

From the reports they'd picked up from both the ground unit and English-speaking Polish Land Forces analysts doing their best to understand the action, it appeared the Russian column had been hit hard in the center of Wrocław, and it was now fighting its way out in company- and platoon-sized elements. They had placed plenty of rearguard forces to block any American attempts to advance on their main line of withdrawal, which was back to the west and hampered by narrow streets, debris, destroyed vehicles, and, amazingly enough, some civilian traffic. The Russians also seemed to be offering up enough counterfire to keep the American tank regiment pursuing them at a healthy distance. Clearly the peaceful withdrawal mandated by the cease-fire agreement was dead and buried now.

And somewhere down there in the middle of all this, there were rumors about a big train with enough ground-to-air missiles to knock anything out of the sky that threatened it.

Captain Ray "Shank" Vance was the leader of the flight of four, and he spoke into his microphone while scanning the blue-gray skies ahead. "Okay . . . we should see U.S. positions soon." Shank squinted, looking through his visor and his canopy. "There, on the edge of the woods . . . just to our east."

Zoomer, the lead pilot in Shank's second section, called out: "Antiair missiles fired! Right front side. Radar lock. We're taking evasive maneuvers."

"Copy. Looks like MANPADS. Shake them and get back into formation. I want to hit that Russian armor." The Man Portable Air Defense Systems were shoulder-fired antiair missiles, deadly to any aircraft in the area.

"Copy. I'm seeing a lot of SAF-fire." The pilots pronounced the abbreviation like "sapphire" but it was short for "surface-to-air fire" and was not specific with regard to the types of munitions used. They could have been guns, rockets, or missiles, but SAF-fire was the catchall word to put everyone on the alert.

But this alert came too late for Zoomer's flight, and their altitude was too low to maneuver. Four missiles rocketed up, fired in unison from under a canopy of trees. One missile detonated close to Zoomer's wingman. A small red pop and a brown burst of shrapnel erupted just in front of his left tail section near the engine. Smoke flared out of the engine and the aircraft immediately lost half its power and went into a shallow dive.

"Shit!" the wingman shouted into his mic. "I'm hit. I gotta turn out." The pilot was focused on shutting down the stricken engine and powering up his remaining engine to counter his immediate loss of speed and altitude. His instincts were to turn away from the formation so he didn't crash into one of his buddies, but he was so low that he was in real danger of losing control and impacting terrain.

Shank said, "Focus on recovery. Radio if you have to punch."

The wounded aircraft drifted out and away from the pack as the others carried on the hunt.

"Leave him, Zoomer," Shank instructed. "He'll be okay. Focus on . . ." He stopped speaking as he squinted into his windscreen. "Bogeys! Two of them! Two o'clock high and coming in fast! Circle the Hogs on me. Do it now!"

"Circling the Hogs" was a well-practiced defensive maneuver Shank had taught at the weapons school at Nellis Air Force base in Vegas, back when he was an instructor at the 66th Squadron.

The three A-10s entered a tight circle, flying parallel to the ground.

The tactic allowed one of the aircraft's deadly 30mm cannons and its anti-air missiles to be pointing outward at all times. Turning practically on their wing, pivoting so tightly that the Russian aircraft, which had now closed to less than three kilometers, couldn't get behind any of them without having to worry about another A-10 right on his tail and getting him in his sights.

Shank said, "Drop ground munitions; get ready for some dogfighting." The A-10s needed to remove their outboard stores, because the heavy missiles and bombs slowed their acceleration and inhibited the tight turns needed for air-to-air fighting.

Each pilot mentally noted his position, then pulled a release on his Maverick missiles, dropping the unarmed munitions harmlessly into the snow-covered woods below.

It took Shank some time with his tight turn, but he soon came back around and saw the enemy aircraft's profiles clearly against the pale blue sky. To his astonishment, they were Su-57s, Russia's newest fifth-generation fighter, purpose-built for dogfighting.

The A-10, in contrast, was primarily a ground-attack weapon; it was *no one's* first choice for an air-to-air combat platform.

Well, that sucks, Shank said to himself.

The three A-10s might outnumber their opponents, but they were outclassed in a fight with them and needed every edge they could take.

The Russian fighters seemed to quickly recognize the threat of the circle maneuver, and the two fast Su-57s jetted up to a slightly higher altitude and adopted a wider circle, trying to get a good angle at the tail of one of the A-10s. A dance of death between the fast and sleek Sukhois and the old and slow Warthogs began.

Shank said, "Call out any gaps in the enemy approach."

One of the Su-57 pilots decided to test the Americans' tactics. He pulled a hard left stick, breaking away from the Russians' loose concentric formation around the Hogs and firing a precision Izdeliye-170 missile.

Called the R-77 by the West, the Russian missile was one of the most formidable active radar-homing munitions in the world.

"Fox Three! Fox Three! Hit chaff now!" said Zoomer, flying the point aircraft at that moment in the circle. From his position he'd seen the launch before the others and was also the first to detect the missile on his active radar.

All three A-10s began dumping chaff and flares. Ten pops from each of their RR-129 tinfoil chaff dispensers and half a dozen flares apiece in case the missile carried a heat-sensor backup.

The Russian fighter's aspect angle on his target and the three A-10s releasing their haze of chaff into the circle did the job and the missile was unable to maintain a lock on its target. It flew harmlessly right through the middle of the circling American aircraft, detonating in the snow-covered trees below.

But the Su-57 pilot kept his nose on his target and followed his missile with a hail of accurate gunfire. Several rounds did the job the missile failed to do, tearing three fist-sized holes in Zoomer's left wing. His position in the circle broke slightly as he fought to regain control of the damaged aircraft.

His alarms wailed. He looked out his canopy to check the damage and saw fuel spraying out behind his portside wing.

Checking the gauges, he realized he was losing hydraulic fluid as well.

"Shank, I'm venting fuel and fluid. I can stay in the circle, but not for long."

"Copy that," said Shank. "Gonna have to make something happen. If we sit here, they are going to pick us off one by one." Shank kept trying to discern the enemy pattern of attack, weighing a multitude of variables. He struggled to come up with relevant tactics against the superior Russian fighter aircraft. If they ran, he and his cohorts would immediately become more vulnerable; the Su-57 could outrun and outfly the A-10. If they stayed, Zoomer was already proof that eventually they'd all get hammered.

The second Su-57 dove on the Americans and fired a missile.

Again the A-10s simultaneously dropped a cloud of chaff and flares, which spread outward from their circle, obscuring them from missile lock.

The Su-57 followed up with guns, and this time two rounds impacted Nooner's tail. Then the Russian pulled up and outward while his wingman lined up for his next attack.

Shank could see that they were now going to coordinate individual standoff attacks, each aircraft closing in, firing, then pulling away.

But this opened up an opportunity for the Americans as well.

Shank broke out of the circle, pulling his stick hard back and left. His aircraft's nose slewed onto the tail of the climbing Sukhoi.

"Shot!" said Shank over the radio as he launched a missile, then held his angle a second longer to fire two bursts of 30mm cannon.

The Russian pilot juked left, then right, releasing his own battery of flares. The American missile failed to lock, but the blast of cannon fire, eight rounds total out of the two long bursts of twenty rounds apiece, punched into the broad open wing and canopy of the Russian fighter.

Unlike the heavily armored A-10, which could take a beating, the more sophisticated Russian jet came apart in midair. Flames and sections of the aircraft peeled off. The left wing broke and fell from the stricken modern jet as it pitched violently up and then began to flutter toward the earth, spinning out of control like a leaf falling from a tree.

The remaining Su-57, likely the flight leader, saw his chance as Shank fell outside the circle. The Russian lined up behind the A-10, and two missiles left the Russian's aircraft, tracing across the sky for Shank's tail.

He looked back and saw what was happening. "Chaff and flares! Breaking hard left! Let him come for me. Then you two nail him!"

Both Zoomer and Nooner broke out of the Hog circle to attack with missiles and cannons in an attempt to protect Shank.

The quick thinking in rolling out of the circle had meant two aircraft could threaten the Su-57 from two different angles, and the Russian could threaten only Shank.

Shank worked his finger switches rapidly to fire chaff, and then his hands and feet deftly controlled the stick and rudder in perfect harmony. It took three full banks of chaff and flares, but as he prepared to launch his fourth and final bank, the missiles chased the flares and Shank pushed the stick down, then rolled left to ensure he lost the Su-57's lock. Pulling the stick back hard and advancing the throttle all the way, he pulled an Immelmann, an ascending half loop and flip of the aircraft to turn 180 degrees.

Now at higher altitude and pointing back toward the enemy, he could assist the other two pilots.

The Su-57 pilot realized he had drastically underestimated the capabilities of both the American ground-attack aircraft and its three pilots. He kicked on his afterburners and climbed rapidly. Zoomer fired an antiair missile at the fleeing Su-57, but the weapon failed to lock onto the stealthy state-of-the-art fighter.

Seconds later the Russian pilot had disengaged completely, and the A-10s let him go.

"Zoomer, you are cleared to go look for your wingman," Shank said. "Keep us on the net while you search. Nooner, you've got to get your crippled bird back to base."

"Shank, I'm stable, and we're almost to the Russian armor. I can take a couple passes before returning, and I can loiter at distance while you make some runs. Then we'll go back."

Shank thought it over. The transmissions from the Army guys on the ground sounded desperate enough for him to decide to risk it.

"Okay, we'll do that. We can pound armor with our cannons and then RTB. Come to heading oh-seven-five."

Nooner asked, "Did you get close enough to catch the tail art on those guys?"

"Yep, looked like an eagle talon painted in red," replied Shank. "That pilot who made it out of there knows his shit. We got lucky today."

CHAPTER 53

Captain Diana DelVecchio paced the control room, hands on her hips.

"Captain," her communications officer said, "we're not getting any real uplink to SATCOM. Radio Division says it's not us: our equipment tests fine. There are one or two birds that seem to be responding, but they are too far on or over the horizon to get a decent handshake."

"Do we think we got *any* data out about the flotilla?" DelVecchio asked.

"Possible, Captain, but no guarantees."

DelVecchio nodded. She pointed to the LCD screens on the navigation officer's briefing table, where newer, better images of the flotilla were on display. "XO, Nav, what do you think of that?"

"Ma'am . . . looks like three fuel ships."

"Yes, but look in between these two."

"That's an Iranian frigate and an Iranian corvette. *Sabalan*-class, and the other . . . tough to make out."

She scrolled with the mouse and zoomed in on the image captured by the UMM. "Look at the bow profile. The side-strapped torpedo rockets. The forward gun."

The Nav said, "Is that what I think it is? A *Tarantul*-class corvette?"

"No, it doesn't have a slanted masthead," countered the executive officer.

DelVecchio said, "The newest modification is the *Tarantul III*. It has a straight masthead."

"But Iran doesn't have the *Tarantul III*."

DelVecchio looked up at the XO now. "And that's my point."

The XO blinked in surprise. "You're right. Ma'am, that's a Russian *Tarantul*-class—I'm sure of it! When I was in PACOM, we tracked a ton of *Tarantuls*. They're also all over the Black Sea and we saw a bunch in the Pacific, escorting convoys."

DelVecchio asked, "But what's she doing here in the Gulf of Aden? Russians don't have any *Tarantuls* this far south of their Southern Military District."

DelVecchio pointed to a ship near the back of the convoy. Another gray hulk, this one with a more pointed bow, sailed along with the merchant ships, nearly blending into the gloomy, rainy weather.

"That's her—that's their flagship. My guess is that's the *Sabalan*. One of Iran's newest *Moudge*-class frigates. But why is she hiding in the back and not leading from the front? Why is there a Russian escort craft in her midst? What's their destination?"

The navigation/operations officer said, "Ma'am, escorting oil maybe?"

"Too big a convoy for that. Also, most of those are cargo ships, not tankers," she said.

"Maybe the Russians sold Iran some more nuclear material. The last few times they assembled fleets outside the Persian Gulf, they were trading with our pals in North Korea."

DelVecchio shook her head. "No, usually the nuclear material is going the other way. Into Iran, not out of, and the Russians just send it across the Caspian Sea. No reason to go under everyone's noses through the Strait of Hormuz, the Suez Canal, and all the way past Europe. No, this is something else."

The navigator said, "Russians are fair targets after what happened in Europe, no?"

"No," she answered, perhaps too bluntly. "That conflict remains localized. We're not at war with Russia per se. But having said that, we don't know their intentions, so they are definitely a threat."

"Track them?" asked the XO.

"Yes, let's follow them. They're up to something—that's for sure . . ."

NEAR GÖRLITZ, GERMANY
U.S. AIR FORCE EXPEDITIONARY RUNWAY
27 DECEMBER

Captain Ray "Shank" Vance stepped down the small retractable steps on the left side of his aircraft and dropped the last three feet onto the S127 highway northwest of the town of Görlitz, Germany. The Fairchild Republic A-10 Thunderbolt II required more than a kilometer of runway when fully loaded, so this straight stretch of the S127 had been selected by the Air Force tech, radar, and munitions quartering party as the best location to serve as an expeditionary runway.

The hills around the area were filled with several huge, spinning turbines that provided power to the town and were initially assessed to be a big risk to low-flying aircraft, and therefore the highway was deemed unsuitable. But no sane enemy looking to hit the expeditionary airfield would risk low passes in and among the windmills to drop bombs.

The ground crew still hadn't established any antiair missile batteries, but Shank could see those were being trucked in now.

Both Zoomer and Nooner had landed before him while he provided air overwatch. Zoomer's wingman, Furball, had bailed out in western Poland, but he'd already been picked up by locals and had called back to his squadron.

Shank, Zoomer, and Nooner entered an Air Force general-purpose medium tent. The expeditionary team had rigged up electricity to power some heaters and radios, and the men, steaming cups of coffee in hand, tuned out the sounds of the pop star Pink blaring outside the tent. It wasn't the only loud noise they could hear; it sounded like fifty men and women were pounding hammer-driven impact tools here at the expeditionary airfield.

The noise of the construction work was more music to the pilots' ears than Pink; but if the sounds of pop rock blaring got the ground guys to turn wrenches, then Shank had no problem with it at all.

The men looked over the maps on the table, and their colonel pointed out the latest known locations of the Russians as they worked their way out of Wrocław and tried to push again to the east.

The discussion was short and to the point. The squadron was bringing up more fuel, and two more A-10s would be here within the hour. They were to link up with the two operational aircraft, Shank would take the lead, and together they would hit the Russian armor with everything they had.

The cease-fire was over. Russia and Poland were fighting, and the U.S. president knew he'd been played, so the U.S. was fighting, too.

This was war.

Senior Master Sergeant Hernandez walked over to the planning meeting, looking for an opportunity to break into the conversation. He waited till the men paused to refresh their coffee from the big steel pots.

Hernandez addressed the colonel. "Hey, sir, I needed to talk to Major Vance." He turned to Shank. "Sir, we've got pretty much everyone turning and burning, but a few guys were looking for some way to help. We're a little overmanned until the rest of the squadron arrives. You want us to paint a kill on your bird? And we can put some tiger's teeth on your planes. We have enough red, white, and blue to paint a whole unit."

The colonel squinted, clearly thinking about the fallout and weighing the risk of some general seeing an unauthorized paint job. Then he just shrugged and nodded assent to Shank.

"Thanks, Senior. That'd be great."

"Heard you all ran into some enemy aircraft with a red eagle claw painted on the tail. I figured we could use something to let those guys know who they were up against."

"Everything else in order?" Shank asked.

Hernandez said, "Just need you to try to bring them back the same way we gave them to you next time. No BS or hot-dogging out there. Just do your jobs so my men can do theirs. Deal?"

In the maintenance team's minds, planes were only on loan to the pilots; the maintenance crew were the ones who actually owned them.

Sarcastically, Shank said, "We'll keep trying to dodge those pesky missiles."

On the other side of the map table, the colonel said, "Every minute that Russian convoy slips closer to Belarus. I want to spank their asses all the way to the border."

"Copy that," Shank said, and looked to the other pilots. "Back to work."

WEST OF WROCŁAW, POLAND
27 DECEMBER

Three hours after the shooting down of his regimental commander and the resumption of fighting in Europe, Lieutenant Colonel Tom Grant received official orders to close with and engage the Russian forces. The order made him smile a little, because at that moment the lead elements of his brigade were already doing just that, west of Wrocław proper. Leopard 2 tanks had just picked off a platoon of GAZ Tigr scout cars that had made it out of the Polish ambush in the city and back onto the main road.

Ott was forward with his men, but he relayed back to Grant that five scout cars had been blown to bits in the past ten minutes, and three more were racing for their lives away from the long-range German Rheinmetall tanks' cannons.

The fight was back on, and Lieutenant Colonel Grant was damn sure he'd make Sabaneyev and his men pay for every single inch of Polish ground they crossed.

Grant's radio in his Humvee crackled to life. It was his lead reconnaissance team, a couple miles ahead of him on the highway that led around the big Polish city of Wrocław. "Hey, sir, we're seeing a lot of combat in the city."

"Confirm *in* the city? Still?" asked Grant.

"Yes, sir. There's one hell of a battle goin' on, from the looks of it."

"Can you tell who's fighting?"

"Uh . . . I'm pretty sure it's those Russians we've been chasing."

"No shit, it's the Russians. I mean, who are they fighting *against*? Militia, PLF, some random NATO unit that got caught in the middle of this?"

Grant thought for a moment. Who the hell did he have on the lead reconnaissance team? Someone particularly thick, obviously. Then he remembered it was Lieutenant Macarter, who was a brave and hardworking young man but not known for his intelligence.

Macarter said, "Oh, roger that. Wait one." Grant heard the young man call his lead scout. "Hey, Davis, they need to know who the Russkies are fighting. Do you have anyone close enough to assess?"

"Yes, sir, I have an element that's entered the city and is engaging and observing now."

Lieutenant Colonel Grant turned to Captain Spillane, his acting operations officer, who had heard the exchange and was reddening with fury.

"Did you authorize anyone into the city?" Grant asked.

"No, sir. Would be stupid, given the circumstances. Likelihood of getting blown up by either side, let alone figuring out who's who, is pretty high. Macarter must've done it on his own initiative."

"Well, shit," Grant said. "Get on the net and find out why Macarter thinks taking initiative for the first time in his life was a good idea today." He thought for a moment. "On second thought, just tell him to get his ass out of there. I'm going up. Tell Bandits to send a company's worth of tanks to reconnoiter with me and to send his own reconnaissance element forward. I'll go with him to the edge of the city and see things for myself."

"Sir, you think that's a good idea? Macarter has gotten himself into something now. It'll be tricky."

"He's not reporting enough for us to get a clearer picture. I'll go forward and see if I can pull him back and make some kind of linkup with the Poles in contact with the Russians. Anyway, I'm not exactly sure Macarter has any clue who he's engaging. Do you?"

"No, sir."

"I'll be back. We'll skirt the suburbs a bit and see if we can make contact with the Poles."

"Check, sir. I'll be here on the net when you get your ass killed."

Grant gave a half smile. "Way to dish out the enthusiasm. Organize security for the HQ element and prepare all the command-and-control functions we'll need. Have 2nd Battalion set up a hasty perimeter and push up whatever they need for resupply. Get the German battalion to pull into our perimeter and support HQ. They need to prepare to be a ready response force. Meanwhile, tell everyone I want them topped off with fuel and cross-leveling all ammo. Major Ott is in command in my absence. I want him to ensure we have a tight perimeter, and you all have to remain hidden from any possible enemy air attack."

"Wilco, sir. Good luck. Make sure you let 2nd Battalion commander run his own battalion. Try to remember that you, sir, are the regimental commander."

Lieutenant Colonel Grant mounted up on his tank, thinking about that last statement. Spillane was right. He would have to be more careful about stepping on his commander's toes. They were all in this together, and there wasn't a lot of time for egos, but he could still learn a thing or two from his subordinates on *how* to lead.

Meanwhile, he was going to show them his style on *where* to lead: from the front.

When Grant got his headset on, he heard his gunner Sergeant Anderson's voice. "Where to, sir?"

"Keep heading east, toward the fighting. Link up with 2nd Battalion." He sat down in his seat and closed the hatch above him. "We're gonna start killin' Russians again."

"Hooah, sir!"

CHAPTER 54

The pilot turned to his copilot. "Tom, take the stick. I'm going to grab some coffee."

"I've got it. Might be a bit burned by now, but that just concentrates the caffeine, right, boss?"

The pilot unbuckled his harness, grabbed the seat back, and pulled himself up, sliding between the cramped seats of the big bomber, carefully ducking to avoid the huge array of switches on the bulkhead above. He filled his cup, and smelled it. The scent alone put a smile on his tired, weathered face.

Yup, definitely burned, crap coffee, but it's still coffee.

The Rockwell B-1B Lancer was one of America's most advanced bombers. Stealthy, sleek, and modern, it could deliver a payload of Mark-84 "dumb" bombs or the current payload on this aircraft, the AGM-154 missile.

They had gotten an update via radio on the enemy flotilla concentration in the Gulf of Aden, and the defensive combat systems officer, doubling at the moment as the radio operator, radioed the information to the three other bombers in the squadron to confirm and deconflict their target designations. The update had come via a ground radio retransmission site in Greece, and the new location data for the spot report of the enemy fleet came from a submarine somewhere in the Gulf of Aden. It was a small shuffle of the deck from the original flight-attack plan they'd been given, but nothing the four B-1B Lancers of this flight out of Dyess Air Force Base in Texas couldn't handle.

After all the fire and fury they had been briefed about happening in the European theater, they were sorry not to be hitting targets there, but hitting something the top brass had deemed *a big deal* here off the coast of Africa was a good enough second.

The motto of the 7th Bomb Wing was *"Mors ab alto,"* which meant "Death from above" in Latin, and that was their intention tonight.

The copilot checked the aircraft's FOG, or fiber-optic gyroscope, part of its inertial navigation system. "Fix is certain, sir. Course correction is point-eight degrees. Negligible. No need for adjustment, just need confirmation."

Since passing the mid-Atlantic, they'd had no GPS. It was still spotty in places, as the U.S. had retasked several satellites over the European theater. The Lancers were navigating by map and the FOG system.

The B-1B Lancer still had a digital map that could be updated by the crew as they took very careful instrument readings and tracked their course corrections and speed over land. It was difficult work, but it did allow them to input target-direction data and read terrain.

Their last "tank," or midair refueling, had been off the coast of Egypt via a KC-135 from Italy. Fortunately they had been able to coordinate the linkup via radio and gassing up had not been an issue.

Their orders were to strike the target, then continue east to the island of Diego Garcia in the middle of the Indian Ocean. After a night's stopover in Guam, they would return home. The trip back would be easier without any bombs on board.

As they said in the Air Force: "Lighter aircraft, longer legs."

The copilot called off landmarks for the next few minutes as they followed their course, changing directions. Once they hit a predesignated imaginary point above a piece of water in the Red Sea, the 2nd Combat Systems officer hit a button indicating they were close enough to prepare for their bomb run. It sent a transmission to the other three aircraft, syncing their bombing computers.

He called over the radio to the aircraft commander, a lieutenant colonel.

"I've got IGS lock. I have co-response from the flight. We're ready to launch, sir. About twenty-two more nautical miles and we'll be at the release point."

"Copy. Fish in a barrel, Major. Update the targeting computers and keep feeding location data. I want my missiles to get deep inside their locking envelope with good coordinates."

The aircraft shifted to the left as the bomber took over navigation. The first combat systems officer flicked the switch labeled "Master Arm." Almost forty feet behind him, three banks of eight AGM-154 Joint Standoff Weapon (JSOW) cruise missiles in rotating carousels armed themselves.

The next procedures were simple, unchanged since aircraft had been purpose-built for delivering bombs: Close the distance, open the bomb bay doors, and hit the launch button. Then all three carousels would rotate, out of sequence with one another, and one by one they would launch twenty-four JSOW missiles at their targets.

Overkill, the pilot thought, but orders were to "wallop the enemy," and the B-1B pilots aimed to please.

IRANIAN CRUISER *SABALAN*
GULF OF ADEN
27 DECEMBER

The Iranian ship's captain called to the admiral, standing at the rear of the bridge near the Russian colonel. "Admiral, we have a report from our westernmost picket ship. A flight of four large aircraft, possibly American bombers, just crossed the Egyptian coastline and are headed in our direction. They are two hundred eight kilometers from the task force and closing. They will be within our antiair radius in minutes. Permission to fire?"

The admiral looked over at Colonel Borbikov, who stood next to an Iranian translator. After the translation was finished, Colonel Borbikov nodded.

"Fire." Seconds later, the deck-mounted, upgraded HQ-9B Chinese missile launchers pivoted to the northwest.

There was enough moonlight to see all the ships in the fleet, and Colonel Borbikov looked out the side portholes as blasts of red rocket flame followed by plumes of smoke erupted from six ships. Each ship had been equipped with two missiles. Bolted on, their mountings were not as solid as if they were fully integrated into the ships' hulls, but they served their purpose just fine, launching twelve of the expensive, state-of-the-art Chinese missiles.

Borbikov watched as the missiles arced skyward, long, slender smoke trails heading to the northwest, disappearing in the distance.

OVER THE GULF OF ADEN
27 DECEMBER
1720

Inside the lead craft of the four-ship flight of B-1B Lancers, the defensive combat systems officer's voice was tight with tension over the radio. "Captain, I have missile launch. There are multiple . . . I count twelve inbound missile systems headed our way."

The two pilots looked at each other quickly. The commander said, "What the *hell*? There's *nothing* in the Iranian navy that can launch from that far out. How close are we to the maximum engagement distance?"

"Sir, we're still way outside the radius of our missiles."

The copilot flicked his seat belt nervously. There were only seconds, not minutes, to make the decision.

The commander keyed his headset to transmit to all four aircraft. "Abort, abort, abort. Come to heading two-eight-nine. Increase to maximum speeds. Take evasive action. Maintain altitude, but individual actions are authorized. We'll have to get them another day.

"Okay," he said, turning back to the crew. "Tom, pull us to that heading. Weapons, give me a report."

"Sir, these things are fast. Tough to tell without GPS, but they'll be on us in less than two minutes—I say about a minute and a half. We'll add a little time once we're running from them."

The Air Force officers all turned back to their duties and listened to the aircraft's weapons officer as he ticked off the distances. In each of the other three bombers, their crews would be doing the same thing.

"One hundred fifty nautical miles and closing."

Sweat formed on the men's foreheads. They didn't dare glance at one another; they remained focused on their individual duties. The commander had resumed control of the aircraft, and he looked out the windshield at the Egyptian coast as they retreated.

"One hundred nautical miles," said the combat systems officer, his tone now ominous and dire. The missiles were approaching, streaking at more than four times the speed of sound.

"Copy. Prep countermeasures," replied the commander. "We can spoof them and see if they are too fast to turn around. Chaff and flares ready?" It was an unnecessary question.

The defensive combat systems officer said, "Yes, sir. We're ready."

"Use everything. I'll radio the split."

The captain got on and relayed to the other aircraft to split. By splitting up they would stand a better chance of confusing the missiles. If they all released a cloud of chaff and banks of flares, their distance from one another would force the missiles to choose between the maximum number of targets, hopefully overloading their puny brains. The tactic was designed for Russian-style weapons and counted on the warheads picking the hottest and surest of the targets.

Unfortunately for these pilots, that was not how the Chinese missiles screaming toward them operated.

"Sir, distance thirty nautical miles and closing."

"Copy. Coordinate that release of CM."

"Releasing countermeasures *now*!" The four airplanes, now separated by over ten nautical miles apiece, each released the tiny tinfoil strips along with beads after beads of flares. The flares fanned out below the aircraft, tracks of fire and smoke following as they fell slowly.

One missile turned toward the flares, but after a moment it corrected itself and again began tracking the bomber it had been pursuing.

The bombers tried another round of flares and chaff, to no avail. As the missiles closed within three nautical miles and the aircraft fired a constant stream of flares and chaff, the missiles remained undeterred.

"*Fuck!*" shouted the commander. "I'm slowing to two hundred miles per hour. Stand by to eject! Check harnesses!"

Out their right window a bright flash of light signaled the destruction of one of the other bombers. Another flash outside their left window indicated a second hit.

The pilot realized he would not be able to slow down before they, too, were blown to bits.

"Eject! Eject!" They were flying at nearly five times the recommended ejection speed.

Each of the four officers punched out at about the same time. Their ejector seats were not designed to eject at speeds so high, and they failed to fire them clear. Three crew members were killed by the speed of the jet and their impact with the skin of the airplane. The fourth crew member survived for a brief moment, but the explosion of three HQ-9B Chinese missiles, each with over four hundred pounds of polymer-bonded HMX explosive, blasted apart thick chunks of the American aircraft and spun shrapnel through the air. Among an enormous amount of flying metal, a five-foot section of intake fan blade of number three engine blew out of its housing while still spinning like a commercial blender, slicing through the plane's copilot and killing him.

WROCŁAW, POLAND
27 DECEMBER

Shank pulled left pitch and looked through his canopy down at the large Polish city of Wrocław. He could see tracers, explosions, and smoke. It was tough to discern who was who, but he was pretty clear that the armor he could make out was all Russian. The Poles seemed to be attacking with anti-tank weapons, using buildings for cover, and a thick pall of gray hung low in the air.

A platoon of Russian tanks advanced across an open square in front of a set of high-rise apartments. Behind them, Shank could see another company of tanks and a company-sized element of infantry in and around some BTRs. He took their stance to mean they were being held back, waiting for the right moment to be called forward.

Armored reconnaissance in force, thought Shank as he watched. A classic Russian tactic.

He saw damaged and destroyed Russian armor, but the different columns of tanks and APCs now seemed to be moving out of the city with authority. He suspected the Poles had expended their biggest and best anti-tank weapons, and they had little way of pestering the Russian armor further.

The fleeing Russians hammered the militia, dropping entire buildings in the process. From his vantage point up here he got the feeling they were minutes away from crashing through the remnants of the militia on the eastern and northern sides of the Oder, and from there they would be able to race out of the kill zone and continue their push back to the safety of neutral Belarus.

Shank was certain the Poles did not have any tanks down there in the city, so all the armor below him was fair game, but without someone on the ground to clear him hot onto Russian tanks, firing on them would be going against procedure.

If there even *was* a procedure. Manuals didn't cover situations like this: a mix between conventional and nonconventional forces in close contact.

Shank knew he'd have to do what the A-10 community did best: improvise.

Through his mic he called the other pilots in his flight. "Here's the pattern of attack. We're going to set up a round-robin. Loiter with our battle position as the center. Give me a wide, seven-craft Hog circle. Keep spotting and IDing the enemy ground targets. Keep the net alive with chatter; we're all responsible for everyone's situational awareness. I want to hear you all cross-talking every new item you see on the battlefield."

The other pilots rogered up.

"Then we go in one at a time. One dive-bomb run, one missile, one gun. Rinse and repeat. I want to keep up a continuous pressure on the armor, hopefully force them to withdraw and relieve the Poles. As you come off the target, you call your shot away and ID the targets; then immediately the next man in the stack peels off and attacks. We've got the fuel to keep us drilling armor targets for up to an hour. Watch the MANPADS. Copy?"

In quick succession, the other pilots in his understrength squadron confirmed their readiness to commit to Shank's plan.

Shank searched for his first victim.

He spotted a set of high-rise apartments and a broad courtyard, but it was an explosion on about the tenth floor that caught his attention. A Russian main tank round pounded the building, and he could see an armored company moving up to the edge of the courtyard opposite the high-rise.

Shank circled back and skyrocketed up to 8,000 feet; then he entered into a stomach-lurching dive directly onto the square. He couldn't make out individual tank targets yet, but within a few seconds he saw white puffs of smoke as two Russian T-14s fired in rapid succession. Diving rapidly below 5,000 feet, he locked his Maverick onto one of the hot spots at the edge of the square and flipped off the gun's safety.

At 4,000 feet, he continued his dive, the g-forces pinning him back into his seat as he pushed the throttle forward.

At 3,000 feet, Shank fine-tuned his lock for the lead tank. The most forward T-14 in the square would get a big, fat Maverick through its turret as a reward for advancing first.

At 2,500 feet, he punched the button, launching one Raytheon AGM-65 precision-guided missile. The smoke and flame of the missile's booster rockets momentarily blinded him. Then the Maverick accelerated to 600 knots as Shank followed in its smoky trail.

Shank let rip with the 30mm main gun as he dove below 2,000 feet.

The tank's reactive armor fired an instant before the missile hit in order to destroy it, but it didn't save the big Armata. A spout of flame and a large fireball told him the Maverick had penetrated the turret and blown everything inside to bits. Holding down the trigger, he could see the impacts of his gun in the middle of the company. He shifted his feet to slew the aircraft left and right, peppering the target area with high-explosive rounds. The bursts looked to have caught the second T-14 in the blast.

At 1,000 feet Shank pulled back on the stick, sinking deep into his seat as the g-forces counteracted the dive. He checked his altitude and leveled off. Coming off the target area, he would power glide flat to lessen the chance of any MANPADS lock ons, skimming the building tops to mask his egress and foil any antiair attack.

He keyed the radio and called out the position of the Russian tanks, then looked over his left shoulder as he began climbing back into the circle to watch another of his A-10s diving onto the target.

He smiled as he pushed the throttle up. Keying his radio, he said, "Keep up the heat!"

CHAPTER 55

President of the United States Jonathan Henry hung up the phone, placing it back on the cradle on the *Resolute* desk, which dominated the Oval Office. He then breathed out a slow sigh of relief.

He'd done it. He'd bought his forces some time.

The call to the Taiwanese president had been masterful in its subtext. Henry was friendly but persuasive, at once encouraging and supportive as well as faintly threatening while maintaining plausible deniability of being so.

He'd explained that he had been forced to redirect a carrier battle group that had been steaming toward Taiwan. Right now it was north of Jakarta, Indonesia, but it had just been ordered to turn 180 degrees and race at top speed to the African coast.

Removing this carrier battle group and all its firepower from Asia just at the moment when China was set to invade had been necessary, but it meant America's response to any Chinese aggression would be weakened.

The Taiwanese president simply inquired as to what he was being asked to do, and Jonathan Henry did not hesitate to extend his request.

"I need you to postpone your elections, just by one month. It's in your constitution: you can do it in the case of national crisis."

There was a long silence on the line after the translation was delivered. Finally the Taiwanese president said, "Postponing an election is a dramatic move in a democracy such as the Republic of China. This will make me appear weak to my supporters and enemies alike."

Henry had a good relationship with the president, and he hoped that would remain the case after he took the gloves off now. "Sir . . . not as weak as you will look if China conquers your island and puts you up against a wall to be shot."

The delay in the response this time was much longer than before—so long that Henry continued. "Mr. President, it's one month. You will take some heat for the decision, I agree, but I truly believe it is in your best interests."

"And what if your other carrier cannot return in a month? What if your forces are defeated by the Russians?"

To this Henry simply said, "Then God help us both, Mr. President."

There was no immediate commitment, and Henry put the odds at 50 percent, but within hours the Taiwanese president held a live televised address and postponed the election for thirty days.

The Chinese troopships turned back to ports on the mainland within hours. The soldiers had been at sea for months; conditions were miserable, and this bought them some time as well.

Henry was pleased with what he'd done, but geography and math were not in America's favor. The USS *John Warner*, tracking the Russian-Iranian flotilla in the Gulf of Aden, sent a flash message that the enemy ships had turned shortly after shooting down the B-1B Lancers, and they now appeared to be heading to port, not in Mombasa, but in Djibouti City. This would take nearly a day off their time on the water, and hinder the West from targeting them again from the air.

The Pentagon quickly calculated it would take the Russians two full days to get from Djibouti to southern Kenya. The Marines heading to the mine at Mrima Hill on board the USS *Boxer* would get there first, but they would be seriously outgunned and outmanned.

The carrier battle group on the way to the Marines' rescue, on the other hand, needed a full three and a half days to get close enough to begin air ops in Kenya.

No, Henry realized. If the Marines raced across the ocean and then up to Mrima Hill, they would have just enough time to dig in. And then, for at least an entire day, the Marines would be on their own as Boris Lazar attacked.

WROCŁAW, POLAND
27 DECEMBER

The battle around the Old Town of Wrocław was finally over, but Paulina Tobiasz could still hear explosions off to the east and northeast. The fighting moved farther and farther away each minute, and this was comforting, but the occasional sounds of fighter aircraft over the city were much less so.

She'd been involved in three more brief engagements since she'd fired from the window of the office building next to the town hall, each time when retreating Russian scout cars had raced back through Market Square, alone and frantic to get away from the attack. She hadn't destroyed another vehicle, but she'd fired her RPG at a group of dismounts fleeing a downed GAZ Tigr while a dozen AKs simultaneously opened up on the young men, and she felt reasonably certain her rocket killed at least one or two of them.

Only now, after nine in the evening, did the Polish Land Forces move through the wrecked streets of the Old Town and declare over loudspeakers that the danger had passed, other than continued potential for Russian aerial attacks. Paulina left her position and crossed the road between the city hall and the bank, walking through the smoke and stench and utter chaos. She'd been handed a radio by a section commander of the militia, and on it she was told the militia was to be picked up by school buses in the next hour. But she'd left her purple backpack with her personal belongings in it at her initial fighting position in the bank, and she needed to go back and retrieve it and whoever remained, if anyone did, from her small squad.

Fires burned all around, smoke and the smell of burned rubber choked her, and she had to stop suddenly as an ambulance raced past along the sidewalk to get around the wreckage of a Tigr utility vehicle lying on its side.

There were bodies in the street; she hadn't been counting but she'd passed two dozen at least. Some dead Russian soldiers, their burned skin black, more than a few with appendages missing.

She walked past a handsome Polish soldier in the uniform of a special forces sergeant, slumped against the wall on the sidewalk. His positioning made it appear as if he were sleeping, but Paulina could see death in his pallid face.

It wasn't until she was halfway up the stairs to the bank that she remembered the girl she'd met just before the battle began. She wondered if she'd made it, but from the broken masonry and smoke-filled hallway of the bank offices, she thought the chances were slim.

She entered the room in the corner and saw bloody handprints on the wall. The windows that looked out to the town hall were blown in, office furniture smoldered still, and a group of militia sat huddled together, although Paulina was too far away to hear any talking.

A pair of bodies lay just inside the door; they were already covered with vinyl ponchos, and from the small boots of one of them she could tell a female corpse lay on its back.

Paulina Tobiasz had no idea why she was still alive when so many around her had died.

Again.

A voice spoke to her from behind.

"Not today."

She turned. The small dark-haired girl from her team sat there, back against the wall. Her face was black, smeared with weapon grease and smoke and bits of burned paper.

Paulina nodded. "Not today. I'm glad to see you."

"We lost two."

Just two? Paulina thought but did not say. "Can you walk?" she asked.

"Yes."

"Good. Let me help you downstairs. Buses are coming to pick us up."

"Where are we going?"

Paulina shrugged, aggravating her two-day-old shoulder wound yet again. "Don't know. I guess we chase the Russians."

DJIBOUTI CITY, DJIBOUTI
28 DECEMBER

French special forces captain Apollo Arc-Blanchette was seated near enough to the front window to look out of the Airbus A400M Atlas as it descended through the clouds. The dark brown rocks of the northern mountains of Djibouti were visible to the west, but in front of them was a seemingly endless expanse of brown flatlands interspersed here and there with tiny villages. It was a wholly different terrain, weather, and population from where he had been fighting just days earlier, and he found it surreal to be in Africa while there was a war going on in Europe.

After his two firefights with Russian Spetsnaz forces, Apollo had been recalled to Brussels and then ordered to attach to the Troupes de Marine, the former colonial troops of the French army, now the French Expeditionary Forces Command in Africa.

The Dragoons were the most eligible and best-trained unit to go to the tiny African nation of Djibouti, now the presumed landing port of the Russian forces that the West felt certain were on their way to the rare-earth mine in Kenya.

A minute before landing, Apollo saw the coastline and the azure waters of the Gulf of Aden, and he scanned until he found what he was looking for. It was the new Chinese naval port facility. The Chinese had a military base here in Djibouti, but they didn't have much in the way of infantry forces, so Apollo assumed the Russians weren't worried about landing here.

Plus, China didn't have much of a stake in this fight. The discovery of the massive rare-earth deposits in Kenya was bad news for China no matter who ran the mine. They'd be forced to pay either the West or the Russians for the metals, and it would drive down prices of their own REMs, so there was no use getting in the middle of a superpower war and picking a side whose victory wouldn't make much beneficial difference to them but could cause a deepening of hostilities with the other power.

Furthermore, China had its eye fixed firmly on another prize now: Taiwan.

The Airbus bounced once on touchdown; then the pilot hit the brakes and reversed the engines, slowing the big machine. It taxied to the airport's service apron on the French military side and slowly came to a stop.

The sixty-four men of the French special forces, 13th Parachute Dragoons, stood simultaneously, shouldered their packs and weapons, and began preparing to move the heavier equipment off the big aircraft.

As the hatch opened, Apollo was slammed in the face by the oppressive heat, like a blast from a furnace. He squinted into the brightness, marveling at the fact that he'd been fighting for his life in deep snow less than seventy-two hours earlier.

As he reached for his sunglasses, he was met at the open hatch by the French military attaché, a commandant in rank, which was equivalent to major. Behind him stood an overtly perspiring diplomat in a tropic-weight tan suit. Both men looked harried, panicked.

Apollo stepped up to them.

"*Vous êtes Capitaine Arc-Blanchette?*" the major asked.

"*Oui, mon commandant.*"

The commandant extended a hand with a sealed file in it. "Your orders. I am not authorized to talk to you about the contents. Now, get your men and their gear off the plane, because we need to get on. We've been ordered to evacuate all consular personnel immediately." The commandant gestured outside, and through the open hatch Apollo saw a long line of civilians, all sweating profusely and carrying their possessions in backpacks and roller luggage. They poured across the tarmac toward the aircraft, jostling one another in the process.

Apollo turned to the cabin, and loudly ordered his men to get their gear and get off as quickly as possible. Before they hit the bottom of the ramp, several men tried to squeeze around Apollo's heavily laden troopers.

They were unsuccessful.

Once on the tarmac, Apollo pulled his men off to the side and out of the way. Here Sergent-Chef Dariel called them to order. When the men were at attention, Dariel saluted Apollo, who returned the salute. Dariel then gave the booming command to pivot to the right and marched the men in as sharp a column as they could maintain, given the heavy bags, right past the scrum of French civilians.

The commandant remained at Apollo's side. "Thank you, Captain. It's been a hell of a day. Two ladies threatened me this morning. One hit me with her bag across the face." He pointed to a large red welt; clearly the bag had a metal buckle. "The other was the wife of an oil CEO. Apparently she knows the prime minister's wife pretty well. At least, that's what I understand after the four phone calls I received from Paris."

Apollo saluted the superior officer, uninterested in the man's situation. He had his own issues to concern himself with, and he prioritized them higher than this man's getting hit with a handbag.

He turned to the diplomat. "I might ask you, sir: Do you know a man named Pascal Arc-Blanchette?"

"Yes, I know him. He's not here. He was told he could leave, but he didn't show up at the airport, and we're not waiting around."

"He's my father. I just want to know if he's reachable via mobile phone."

"I don't know, young man. Call him and see. But word is—and you didn't hear this from me, *Capitaine*—that the Russians have been hacking into the cell networks. They have been more unreliable than ever, and sometimes you can hear strange clicks on the line."

"Thank you, sir," said Apollo.

Both the diplomat and the commandant left the Dragoons behind as they rushed toward the aircraft stairs, eager to get themselves on the turn-around flight to France.

DJIBOUTI CITY, DJIBOUTI
28 DECEMBER

The flotilla of Russian and Iranian warships and the remaining commercial cargo and fuel haulers arrived in port in Djibouti City at eight a.m.

While the frigates patrolled the mouth of the harbor, the other ships docked so they could off-load their men, fuel, and stores.

By nine the off-loading of Iranian transport and cargo containers was going smoothly. Colonel General Lazar watched from the pier side, flanked by Colonel Kir, as the huge cargo crane swept back on board the big Iranian vessel in front of them and then lowered its boom and began unspooling its braided steel cable.

The Iranians were particularly harsh to the Djiboutian dockworkers, working them on double-quick time, presumably to impress their Russian leadership. Shouts in Arabic, French, Farsi, and English echoed across the water in the bustling Djiboutian industrial harbor. The Iranian naval personnel now seemed bent on meeting the off-loading deadline they had promised.

Lazar watched the crane come up from the hold with three BTR-82A armored personnel carriers marked for and guarded by Colonel Borbikov's Spetsnaz personnel. The vehicles were braced next to one another on the ends of the cables and the strain made the crane's winches squeal. He was pretty sure they were maxing out the allowable weight to get three off at a time, but the crane held, and moments later it placed them gently on the pier.

Lazar knew that a half dozen nuclear artillery shells would be secured in one of the vehicles, and he tried to determine exactly which one by the number of hulking special forces soldiers guarding the massive machines on the dock. Just behind the two command vehicles tasked to Borbikov, a third BTR was virtually surrounded by Spetsnaz once it was unhooked

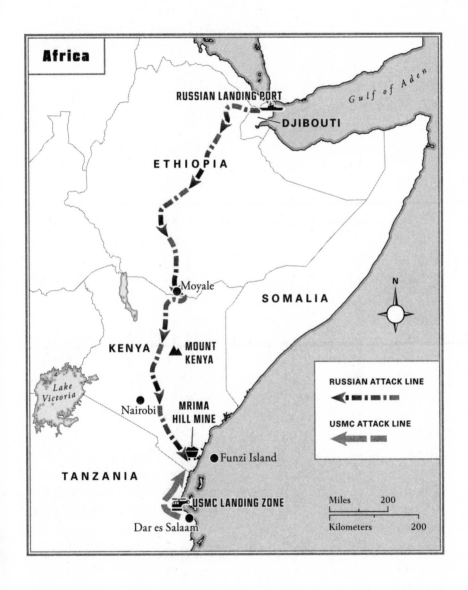

from the hoists, and Lazar could see Borbikov, still on the ship, looking down at it.

Well, there you are. Borbikov's nukes, Lazar told himself.

The whole idea of bringing nuclear ordnance to Africa was insane as far as Lazar was concerned. He understood that it would be an important bargaining chip once he took the mines, a way to get the rest of the world to hesitate before making any attempt to retake Mrima Hill for fear of causing the Russians to fire on approaching forces at distance—or, worse from an economic standpoint, to set fuses and vacate the area, leaving behind nuclear devastation that would render the entire mine unusable for centuries.

But Lazar was a conventional soldier, and he did not like this escalation from his side, because he suspected that it would lead only to an escalation from the other side.

Lazar told himself for the hundredth time in the past four months that he must be successful in taking and holding the mine so that there would never be any detonation that could start a full-scale nuclear war.

The general's own BTR command-and-control vehicles came out of the hold next. Unlike the fighting variant of BTR, which carried troops and a 30mm cannon, Lazar's C2 variant had an extendable communications mast and an array of antennas. Without satellite phones or a spot to set up a long-wire high-frequency radio, he would be able to talk to his own brigade for a limited time, but he would feel immeasurably more comfortable once aboard, on the move, and surrounded by his maps, with Colonel Kir directing traffic. They would stop periodically to throw up the bigger antennas, and about halfway through their drive south they'd get satellite comms up again and begin making regular reports back to the Kremlin.

Lazar signaled to Colonel Kir to mount up and take the three vehicles to the staging area. The general had decided to walk instead. He would be cramped in the BTR on the drive south to Kenya, and he felt the walk might be his last stroll for a while.

Along the way, he spoke with pockets of Russian soldiers marching in platoons toward the head of the pier. Stretching his legs and chatting with the boys raised his spirits. He hailed familiar faces as he went and received a few cheers in response. With a smile on his face, he reached the end of the pier and spotted Kir and the assembling troops and lines of vehicles. They were about halfway done; in another few hours they'd be fully offloaded.

CHAPTER 56

"Helm, come to one-two-nine degrees. Depth, thirty feet. Speed, four knots," whispered the navigator.

"One-two-nine, and thirty feet, aye," answered the pilot.

"Confirm heading and depth, aye," said the copilot.

Commander Diana DelVecchio watched the two men at the controls. The two young men sat next to each other, working in perfect harmony with her boat to keep the submarine level and on course.

The XO leaned over to her and spoke softly, out of the earshot of others. "Ma'am. We're doing this? We're going to attack the port of a nation we're not at war with?"

"I prefer to think of it as us attacking hostile forces who are in the process of invading the nation we're not at war with."

"Yes, ma'am," he said, but DelVecchio acknowledged his concern.

"The area commander opened ROE when the shooting started in Germany. Having said that, some locals around the port are going to die if we hit one or two of those oil tankers. It will be devastating." She remained silent for a moment, then spoke up in a louder voice.

"Weapons, status report."

The weapons control officer responded with "All tubes loaded. Tubes two and four are still awaiting confirmation. Outer muzzle door is causing them some trouble."

"What's the issue?"

"Captain, we don't know—might be barnacles crusting the outer hatch, portside. Torpedo room wants permission to flush it with air to see if they can jar the hinges."

"No," she said. "Get the targeting solution finished. When we fire the starboard tubes, tell them to pop air in on the portside, then immediately fire the other spread. That way we'll only give away our position to anyone listening when the first fish are already in the water."

"Aye, Captain," said the weapons control officer, who turned quickly back to the two men at the digital targeting computers.

"Up scope," she said to the weapons station officer.

With stealth and cunning and supremely accurate navigational charts, the *John Warner* had managed to slip through the phalanx of Russian submarines and the Iranian and Russian frigates, and was now within range of the harbor of Djibouti City. Only silent running here would keep herself and her crew alive, and she knew they'd have time to fire only one spread of torpedoes at the big ships now at dock before they'd have to turn and run.

DelVecchio now knew what everyone above the surface knew: the Russians were going for that rare-earth-mineral mine that had been such a big story in the news for a few months three and a half years earlier. She'd received word that a mechanized brigade was on board the flotilla, as well as a warning that there was almost no way to stop them once they were on land. A few companies of the French Foreign Legion and a battalion of the Kenya Defence Forces protected the mine itself, and French and American military leaders were scrambling to get assets into play; but with the shooting down of the four B-1B Lancers the day before, nobody wanted to fly anywhere near the Russians.

It was up to DelVecchio, here, now, to thin the ranks of the enemy, or there would be nothing to stop them from winning the mines and destroying everyone and everything in their way.

DJIBOUTI CITY, DJIBOUTI
28 DECEMBER

French spy Pascal Arc-Blanchette watched the activity at the port through his binoculars from over a kilometer away, standing outside a press box at the Stade Hassan Gouled, the largest soccer stadium in the East African nation. He had a decent if distant vantage point from here and he could determine only two things: there were a *lot* of Russians, and they had brought some toys.

It had been a hell of a morning. The sixty-four-year-old had spent the previous evening at the French embassy learning details about the fleet and the destruction of four U.S. bombers over the Gulf of Aden, and he'd been on the phone and met in person with local contacts, doing his best to set up lines of communication so they could stay in touch and report in when the streets were clogged with Russian armor, Russian guns, and Russian eyes.

He truly wished Paris had paid closer attention to his warning that Russian special forces were operating in Djibouti, and he blamed himself for not raising a louder alarm. But not for long. He understood that his little corner of the world here was on no one's radar more than twenty-four hours ago, and with everything else going on, there was no alarm he could have sounded that would have allowed Paris to stop a Russian invasion.

No, this attack had been coming for some time—it was inevitable—and now all Pascal could do was that thing he did best: spy on his adversary.

To this end he turned away and left his high perch at the Stade Gouled, heading downstairs for his car. He'd relocate to the far edge of the city to put himself in position to monitor the Russians when they left town on their way to Kenya.

As he made his way down the poured-concrete staircase, his phone rang. He snatched it up, thinking it might be one of the dockworkers he'd been trying desperately to reach for the past few hours.

"*Allo?*"

"Hi, Papa. It's me."

Arc-Blanchette usually beamed from ear to ear upon hearing his son's voice, but not now. "You're here, aren't you?"

"How did you know?"

"Not much goes on around here I don't know about, but in your case I got a call from a friend at the ministry involved with the evacuation. He mentioned a group that sounded a lot like yours was flying in, and then the plane would fill with those French flying out."

"I was hoping to see you getting on that plane."

Pascal laughed softly. "I've spent years down here with nothing much going on. I'm certainly not leaving now while there is some real excitement." His tone turned serious. "I'm more concerned about you. What can you and your tiny band of lightly armed soldiers do against all that pouring off those ships?"

"The less you know, the better."

There was silence for a moment. "Ah, my brave, brave boy. The Arc-Blanchettes have fought for France in every capacity since the time of—"

"Yes, I know—since the Battle of Montebello. You tell us all the time. Where are you? I'd like to see you."

Pascal thought for a moment. "There is a place I use from time to time. The owner and his family are trusted friends. La Mer Rouge. It's a kilometer south of the highway as you leave the city. But beware: Russian eyes and ears are everywhere."

"I will, Papa. Be safe yourself."

PORT OF DJIBOUTI
DJIBOUTI CITY, DJIBOUTI
28 DECEMBER

On the pier adjacent to where General Lazar now conferred with his staff, Colonel Borbikov was not happy. His Tigrs were just now slowly rolling off the gangway, and the Djiboutian dockworkers seemed intent on banging every crate and cargo net full of equipment during the off-loading. He told himself he'd be lucky if half his ammunition and equipment was operational after such rough treatment.

The longshoremen were being paid a considerable sum, Borbikov knew, and he wasn't getting much out of them in his estimation. He told himself these Third World wretches would quickly start working a hell of a lot harder if he started shooting the laziest in their ranks, but he did not pull his pistol.

Instead he let the thought pass. There was a strong possibility Russia would need the use of this port again in the future to bring more equipment or troops to the rare-earth mine.

The local men passed him without a word; most looked the other way when they noticed his angry glare.

Suddenly an ugly noise jarred him out of his thoughts. The vessel's Klaxon alarm began sounding.

What the fuck are these Iranian assholes up to now?

He ran up the gangplank as dockworkers filed past him, looking around in mild curiosity. Some Iranian sailors and Russian troops peered up into the morning sky, worried about an attack from the air.

Borbikov pushed through them. "Make way! Move your asses!"

A man he recognized as one of the junior Iranian deck officers ran onto the bridge wing above him, leaned over, and yelled down through a bullhorn.

"Hujum tuwrbid! Hujum tuwrbid!"

"Speak Russian, you fool!" he yelled back up.

The ship's loudspeakers were already doing the job of translating, and an Iranian-accented voice yelled out in Russian, "Torpedo! Torpedo! All men brace for impact! Torpedo in the water!"

Borbikov looked out to sea. *How could there be a torpedo?* The mouth of the port was supposed to be filled with antisubmarine ships and three prowling Russian subs. *Could the Americans really be so stealthy that they could slip through?*

All around Colonel Borbikov, men began to panic, running toward the gangway to get off the ship. A GAZ Tigr, midway down the ramp, smashed into the railing, its front wheels falling off the edge, wedging it there as the driver jumped out of the vehicle and took off for the pier.

Undeterred, Borbikov ran toward the ship's water side and looked over. A thin white sheet of wake approached at high speed. To his left, he heard two other ships' klaxons wail.

Borbikov watched the incoming torpedo with detachment for a moment; then self-preservation kicked in and he grabbed a railing. He had just done so when a muffled boom rocked the vessel and an enormous spray of water erupted into the sky farther down the hull. Borbikov's body shook as the explosion below the waterline vibrated throughout the ship, and then a secondary explosion rocketed him off his feet and smashed him against the deck.

More explosions came from farther down the pier as other ships were struck with torpedoes.

His brain, rattled and slowed by the impact, forced him to lie still for a moment, all but deafened. Then the sounds of bedlam erupted slowly as the ship began listing slightly to one side.

Borbikov, touching his hand to his forehead, felt a slight trickle of blood. Angered and stunned by this latest turn of events, he climbed back to his feet and grabbed an armor sergeant running by him toward the gangway.

"Halt there, trooper! Grab two men and slow the others down. No panic!"

The man looked at him with crazed eyes.

Seeing that he wasn't getting through to the panic-stricken soldier, he reached out a hand. "Give me your *fucking* rifle, you idiot!"

The man handed it over reluctantly, expecting to be shot on the spot. Borbikov flicked off the safety and racked the bolt back, aimed the AK-47 skyward, and fired a burst of fifteen rounds into the air. All around him men dropped to the deck.

The blast of gunfire was a sound of destruction they all recognized. Everyone on the deck of *Sabalan* stared at Colonel Borbikov.

"Listen to me! If you make order, you'll have time to get yourselves and the equipment off. I will not tolerate any more panic. You are Russian soldiers, on a mission vital to your nation. Every man is your comrade!" Either the burst of fire or his sharp words did the trick, and the sergeants and junior officers took charge and began a firm but more orderly evacuation of the ship.

Borbikov made his way to the bridge to see how long they had before the *Sabalan* went down. He glanced back at the gangplank, where a group of men was trying to straighten the Tigr that had halfway fallen off the ramp. An incredible explosion some way down the pier signaled another hit. He could feel a heat wave and guessed it was an oil tanker going up in flames.

The U.S. submarine chose wisely, he thought as he climbed to the bridge. Two oil tankers, the command ship, and a cargo vessel carrying tanks and ammunition. The torpedo hits on the tankers had been calculated to severely degrade his task force before it even assembled on land. The Iranian frigates were already racing out of the mouth of the bay to search for the enemy submarine, but the damage had been done.

USS *JOHN WARNER*
GULF OF TADJOURA

On board the *John Warner*, the sonarman called out to DelVecchio. "Captain, full spread has hit. Active ping sounding now. Those frigates are coming out after us. Still more than five nautical miles distant. From their tracks, they are uncoordinated and searching blind."

Diana DelVecchio said, "Let them come. XO, I want more than twelve nautical miles distance within the hour, but keep a good sweep searching for their subs, because you can be sure they'll be converging on our location. Calculate course and speed to get us there. Hydrophones, confirm ship's noise—I want silence en route. Then I want you to pick a nice sandbar. We'll wait for them to pass over us, and only then will we go for deep water."

A murmur of assent and pride quietly went around the *John Warner* as word was passed in low tones from stem to stern that Captain DelVecchio had sent four vessels to the bottom of the Djiboutian harbor.

The boat snuck along just above the seafloor as ships in all directions began hunting for it.

CHAPTER 57

After thirty-eight miserable hours of constant travel, Lieutenant Colonel Dan Connolly landed at the civilian airfield in the city of Victoria, the Seychelles. When he disembarked from the C-130, two CH-53E Super Stallion helicopters from the USS *Boxer* were on the tarmac waiting to pick him up.

A Marine captain, dressed in a spotless green flight suit and sporting a khaki flight jacket bedecked with his unit patch, the Marine Heavy Helicopter Squadron 465, strode up and saluted smartly.

His leather name tag said his rank, last name, and call sign: "Booger."

"Are you Colonel Connolly?" asked Booger politely but with a tone of surprise. Connolly looked awful, smelled worse, and was so tired he couldn't even muster the strength to be professionally embarrassed for not shaving.

"That's me."

"Sir, you look like shit. The regimental commander isn't expecting us to get you aboard the *Boxer* until we get a flight check from ground personnel here. If you want, I'm sure one of the crew has some spare toiletries, and back behind the cargo terminal there's a duty hut with a head. If you can shit, shower, and shave in less than fifteen, we can keep our timeline and take you to the *Boxer* to meet your new boss."

"Thanks for taking pity on an old, dirty grunt."

"Sir, we've all been there before. We're a long way from anything, but I hear you came from D.C., and D.C. is the other side of the earth."

Fifteen minutes later the Marine lieutenant colonel was clean and refreshed and ready to report into a combat zone.

One and a half hours later, he touched down aboard the USS *Boxer*, the command deck of the 15th Marine Expeditionary Unit, and now also the headquarters of Regimental Combat Team 5.

Colonel Kenneth Caster stood ready to greet him on the big, flat deck, and Connolly recognized him instantly. The Marine Corps was a pretty small place for men who had been in as long as the two of them, and Connolly had worked with Caster on many occasions.

Connolly stepped out of the helo, his legs weary from so many hours aboard cramped aircraft, and they wobbled, unused to the pitching deck. The colonel approached the open helicopter door and yelled above the rotor wash in a Texas drawl, "Welcome aboard, Dan. Grab your shit and follow me down to the CiC. We don't have a second to waste."

The CiC of the USS *Boxer*, the command ship of the six-ship flotilla, was a spacious Navy gray–painted room littered with computers, phones, and radio sets. Whiteboards hung on every open bulkhead, and the ceiling was a mass of cables, wires, and pipes common to Navy ships. The room was oddly lit by overhead fluorescent lights that gave the space a dim and drab quality.

There were a few digital maps on the two big LED screens, but the paper maps on the big table were the center of attention. They depicted all six ships in the flotilla. Dan Connolly looked over the chart table; dryerase marker on acetate overlays showed the latest data.

A single blue rectangle sat off the coast of Tanzania near Dar es Salaam. This was the symbol for Marine Corps units here on *Boxer*, ready for the "go code" to off-load.

Caster stepped up to the table now and put his hand on the shoulder of the new arrival. "Okay, folks, this is Lieutenant Colonel Connolly. He's been sent here from the Pentagon, from the Director's Office for Strategic Plans. He's got some words for us on how we are to prosecute this mission, and he's our link to the national decisions being made about this whole thing.

"Dan, what have you got for us?"

"Well, sir, I can say a few things about what we're up against and what this is all about."

"Anything you got, Marine. We've been pretty much flying blind. Seems all the relevant background is being kept close back in D.C."

"Yes, sir. Here's the situation. I'm sure everyone is tracking what's going on around the world. The movements in Taiwan and the . . . *issue* with the admiral and the general—the Russians orchestrated that, and it was the opening salvo. That set PACOM back, and we deployed the entire Global Response Force to PACOM expecting we were going to have to support our friends in Taiwan. Next came Europe, Christmas Day. A huge deal, and seemingly unrelated, but now it looks like that was just the second punch of the fight. The attack on AFRICOM and EUCOM left those commands in tatters and the majority of our remaining quick-response forces were sent to clear Russia out of Europe. That's still ongoing, but we're making good progress.

"The Russians banked on a limited or nonexistent U.S. response here, in Africa. In a sense it was a one-two fake out."

"So the landing of Russians in Africa is the third punch in that metaphor?" asked the colonel.

"Yes, sir, we believe so."

"And their ultimate objective is this mine outside of Mombasa?"

"That's right. They feel like if they don't grab it now, while the West is involved with China, soon enough they'll have to buy all their rare-earth metals from the West. Metals needed in things like missiles, guidance packages, computers, et cetera. At any time we could embargo them back to the Stone Age, so to speak, technology-wise. They would have to grovel to the West or China and behave at all times or suffer our economic wrath. It would constitute a worse threat than they faced during the Cold War."

Caster said, "So this is Russia's big bid for success. And that means they're in it to win it."

"Yes, sir. This is their attempt to secure a future free from Western influence. An independent economy in the computer age."

"Then why not send their entire army?" He pointed to the Russian icons on the map. "I mean, surely there's more stuff in the Russian arsenal than this."

"They were hoping to hide a smaller, faster force. Remember, they are retreating from Europe—they anticipated NATO would think right about now they'd fought the Russians back into a box. Besides, they helped distract pretty much everything in the U.S. arsenal over to the Pacific. There isn't much left that will be here before they can take over the mine."

"How will they hold it? I mean . . . sooner or later we can get a force arrayed to dislodge them, even with AFRICOM in tatters."

"I haven't figured that out yet. I *will* say I think they must have a plan. More forces on the way, a political deal in the works with Kenya once they own Mrima Hill . . . something else. I just don't know."

The colonel clearly did not like this one unknown element in the situation. He let it go and said, "How long until we can expect reinforcements?"

"The *Vinson*, along with the rest of its carrier strike group, are on the way, but they won't be offshore for three days. Till then, you're it, sir."

Colonel Caster looked back to the map. "From the sat images over Iran, it looks like the Russians are a reinforced mech brigade. We don't have anything like the bang to go up against that kind of armor. One of our subs took out a sizable portion of their fuel in the harbor in Djibouti, but there's still plenty of armor that *can* make it down to the mine."

Connolly said, "We do have airpower on our side. Navy and Marine Corps attack aviation."

"Yes, but I'm betting they thought of that. Are we guessing they have more than just a little antiair?"

"Well, yes, sir. We believe some of it is the newest Chinese stuff. Bought presumably so we wouldn't notice the increased production at facilities in Russia."

"Looks like we're facing about four-to-one odds. And no cavalry coming over the hills anytime soon," said Colonel Caster. Then a faint smile crossed his lips. "Just the kind of odds that the Marine Corps dreams of."

The men pored over charts and maps, looked at timetables, and came up with solutions. Assembling men from each of their commands, Connolly was now the de facto chief plans officer for both the Navy and Marine Corps units and ships. Fortunately, he'd had plenty of experience organizing campaigns. The only catch was most of his planning experience had been in Afghanistan and Iraq against insurgents. Fighting Russians, the planning team agreed, was going to be a whole new ball game. They took their best crack at it and came up with both a landing and a subsequent assault plan.

An hour later Connolly and the new planning team gave the commanders a solid walk-through. They would steam to port at Dar es Salaam, in Tanzania. There they would bring the regiment ashore, and once all the gear and vehicles were off-loaded, they'd begin their movement north to Kenya, where they would defend the mine.

The captain said, "Navigation? What's our time to get to Dar es Salaam?"

"Sir, sixteen hours until we can make pier side."

Caster asked, "How long do you figure it will take to off-load pier side?"

"We calculate it'll take about ten to twelve hours to get your rolling stock ashore, Colonel."

Connolly added, "Then another sixteen to get up to Mrima Hill."

Caster whistled. "Damn, that's cuttin' it close. One mistake or some bad weather and Lazar beats us there. Once he gets into those mines, he'll be like a tick on a deer in December."

Connolly said, "That's true, sir."

Caster put a finger on the map at Mrima Hill and then drew it north. "We have some air mobility; they do not. That means we have the advantage of speed and surprise. I want to use it. I want a spoiling attack mounted in the next twenty-four hours. Find me a piece of terrain along their route. Someplace where they are forced to slow down, a choke point where they can't spread wide."

The colonel continued. "Use the light-armored reconnaissance guys and some Force Recon JTACs to get up north fast and pound the Russians one time in the snout. I want them to know they're headin' for a fight with the Marine Corps."

Connolly said, "I'd like to request permission to join that fight, sir. We can make an amphibious landing and take the LAV-25s; they'll move a lot faster than anything else we have, so while the main element moves to the mines, we can race ahead in the LAVs and meet the Russians"—he looked at the map quickly—"at Moyale. It's on the Ethiopian-Kenyan border. I can be there in twenty-four hours, just before Lazar's force arrives."

Caster thought it over. "Permission granted."

Now Connolly said, "I just wish we knew more about the makeup of Lazar's forces."

CHAPTER 58

Three immense spouts of flame burned skyward in great chimneys of fire from the stricken Iranian ships. The flames topped more than one hundred feet high, casting flickering light across Djibouti City.

The two split oil tankers had disgorged their liquid cargo and coated the bay in a sea of fire. The burning oil drifted against the pier, waves of flame washing over the concrete and utterly destroying what had been a calm and orderly port only hours before.

Occasionally ammunition would blast from the ongoing conflagration aboard the ammo ship, flipping and spinning like fireworks, detonating in the air or crashing inland or out to sea as the bunkers of rockets or missiles cooked off.

The ammunition ship, tied next to one of Lazar's cargo vessels, had sunk halfway, settling onto the sand in the shallow draft of the inner harbor. The burning pieces stuck out like flaming broken bones reaching up from a flooded graveyard.

The destruction was otherworldly, and local citizens and foreigners alike made signs of the cross or said prayers in either Arabic or French.

On the horizon beyond the mouth of the bay, Iranian and Russian *Tarantul*-class warships crisscrossed rapidly, frantically searching for the culprit in the attack.

Colonel General Boris Lazar sat atop his command-and-control BTR on the road just in front of the pier and watched the continuing debacle impassively. He had seen destruction on a large scale before. He'd seen bodies stacked like firewood outside a Dagestani mosque, artillery work over a Ukrainian hamlet until it was nothing but a smoking hole, and airpower decimate a hillside full of brave but hopelessly overmatched Afghan mujahideen. As then, he was detached now, but as he watched the colors dance across the horizon, he remembered the pain of battles from before.

He rubbed his chin and watched the fire splitting the ships apart. Another explosion; this time it might have been an anti-tank round aboard the munitions ship. Streams of smoke corkscrewed up and outward as missiles lit off and fired erratically.

He had taken his vehicle helmet off so he could avoid the frantic radio transmissions for a while. All the chatter between his commanders and his chief of staff, Colonel Kir, had been too much for him. The damage reports kept flooding in.

He'd heard radio traffic like that before, in other lands, other times, other battles. He'd listened to the calls of desperate men at the edge of their wits more than he cared to remember.

War did seem to have familiar echoes.

His big chest heaved in a large sigh as his brain worked over the meaning of this mess.

A suboptimal way to begin the attack phase of this mission, he thought with understatement.

Colonel Borbikov stormed up alongside Lazar's vehicle. The general spotted him instantly out of the corner of his eye but ignored him until the younger man climbed up the side of the BTR and knelt next to the open top hatches. Even then Lazar fixed his gaze on Colonel Kir, sitting just in front of him in the BTR. Kir had a notepad in his hand and was jotting down numbers while listening to the radio, trying to consolidate the damage reports and create a comprehensive picture of what they had lost and its impact on the mission.

Colonel Borbikov cleared his throat. "Colonel General?"

"Wait a moment," said Lazar as he continued to look over Colonel Kir's shoulder.

"Sir," Borbikov persisted. "We need to move out of the harbor area. We are a target for American bombers here."

Now Lazar turned to him slowly. "Colonel, do you wish to tell me how to run my command? You will wait a moment as we process the reports and determine what is recoverable and what is lost."

"Colonel General, I am *certain* you have an appreciation for the situation, but we have a timeline, and I need you to adhere to it. The European actions have succeeded, so in spite of your setbacks here, you *must* rally your troops and get going."

Borbikov's language was carefully chosen. He'd intended to prod the general into action, instead of leaving him just sitting there, licking his wounds. He was cautious not to cross too many lines of military protocol, but wanted to be clear about distancing himself from the losses Lazar had taken.

Lazar replied, "Colonel Borbikov, once the damage assessments are in, we will know how to proceed. Moving out sooner would be foolish." Then he added, "I trust your 'special cargo' is undamaged."

No one but Lazar was supposed to know about the backup plan to use the threat of nuclear artillery to hold the mine, so Borbikov did not like the general stating this in front of Kir and the other men around them. With a steely gaze that could have earned a less well-connected colonel a trip to the stockade, he said, "All *my* equipment is intact, sir."

"Excellent. And now perhaps you should go back to your Spetsnaz men and leave me to my infantry, because I have work to do." Colonel General Lazar dismissed Borbikov with a wave of his hand and turned back to Kir and his notepad.

Borbikov seethed at his mistreatment by Lazar but knew this was a catastrophe that the regular army needed to sort out. He'd said his piece and the general would be well aware that Borbikov, although just a colonel, had back channels open to the Kremlin and President Anatoly Rivkin himself.

The special forces colonel dismounted the command BTR and walked down the narrow pier to his own GAZ Tigr, where his small contingent of men awaited his return.

Kir turned to Lazar while he continued speaking on the radio and underlined the word "tanks" on his notepad, then crossed the word out with a big red X. Next to it he wrote "ZSUs?" He glanced over at the general, who nodded in understanding and agreement. Kir's meaning was clear—the task force's ZSUs would go, but the forty-one T-90 tanks they'd brought along for the operation would have to remain here at the Djiboutian harbor until more fuel could be arranged. The tanks drained more fuel than any of his other vehicles or equipment, and Colonel Kir had run the numbers: there was now simply not enough remaining for the hulking metal beasts of battle to cross Ethiopia and Kenya to make it to the mines.

Lazar said, "Contact Moscow. I want more fuel brought down from Iran. I don't care how they do it, but we need our tanks at the mine. We can take Mrima Hill without the T-90s, but we won't be able to hold it without them."

"I'll contact them as soon as I finish with damage reports, Comrade General." Colonel Kir then immediately got back on the radio, responding to one of the regiment's logistics officers who was in the process of detailing his list of vehicles now at the bottom of the Djiboutian harbor.

Handpicked by Borbikov, the Spetsnaz men kept a keen eye around them, sometimes sighting their rifles in on the few Djiboutians looking out the windows and doors of nearby warehouses, surveying the destruction. The Russians had taken on a new attitude, a grim, no-nonsense demeanor. The war, for these men, was now on, and any who crossed their path would likely die before many questions were asked.

A wry smile returned to Borbikov's face as he approached the men and sensed their renewed sense of the stakes of this endeavor.

He realized that there was a benefit to all this destruction. He felt it would now be easier to get the men moving. He told himself he could harness this anger with his bold leadership and drive them more easily toward the purpose of the mission.

The men were ready to lay down their lives for the task if necessary. That was the kind of loyalty he expected, from both subordinates and superiors alike. No doubt his actions to promote calm on the pier showed them what he was made of.

Good, he thought. *I will need steel nerves to complete this operation. No more sitting here and licking our wounds.*

Crates were broken open and Lazar's men began removing the weapons, but Borbikov's men pushed into the melee and took what they wanted.

The colonel watched the action for a while. Most of the soldiers eyed him and his Spetsnaz troops with some fear in their eyes.

Borbikov stepped forward into the group and hefted a 9K333 Verba antiair missile, checking its weight in his hands and carefully inspecting the sight system. The Verba, or "Willow" in Russian, used a multispectral optical seeker combining three sensors: ultraviolet, near-infrared, and mid-infrared. This allowed the missile's computer brain to look across three means and discriminate targets, making them much less susceptible to flares and chaff.

Borbikov grabbed the nearest infantryman being issued the modern missile.

"You there: Do you know how to fire the Verba?"

"Yes, sir, Colonel Borbikov," the soldier answered quickly. *Good,* thought Borbikov, *the rank and file here know who I am by sight.*

"What are the six components of the weapon?" he asked.

The soldier looked down at the ground in concentration. "There are six components, sir. The thermal battery, the self-contained day-and-night sight system, the grip stock, the launch tube and missile housing, the launcher system, and the . . . the . . ."

"You have not been properly trained." Borbikov turned to another man, a sergeant who met his gaze confidently. "You there: What is the sixth component?"

"The friend-or-foe radar antenna," replied the man.

Borbikov handed him the missile. "Good. Ensure only men with the proper training receive this weapon. We will need them in the upcoming fight with the American aircraft. You men will be the guardians of the ground forces. Do not forget that."

Colonel Kir appeared beside him. "Yuri, we are ready to send the scouting and reconnaissance parties. Still not enough fuel for the tanks. Shame. We could have used them, and you know the boss is a solid armor officer."

Borbikov said, "We have more than enough light and medium armor to take the mines, and Moscow will get more fuel across somehow. Our subs will find whoever is responsible for today's debacle and blow them out of the water before the next tanker sets sail."

U.S. AIR FORCE EXPEDITIONARY AIRFIELD
NEAR GÖRLITZ, GERMANY
28 DECEMBER

Senior Airman Jones gave the briefing of the maintenance-readiness status of each of the remaining aircraft in the squadron. Out of eighteen original, workable, and flyable Warthogs, they were now left with only eight.

Fallen Air Force men were laid out in front of the plans tent. It was cold enough outside that they could remain there, sealed in black body bags, awaiting the Graves Registration personnel who would come to Görlitz and collect their remains.

Higher headquarters remained in chaos, so there was no telling how long it would take GR to unscrew things and make their way here.

Bullet holes and tears from shrapnel let the light into the field tent.

The Russian special forces surprise ground attack early in the day had cost the Air Force the lives of nearly a dozen airmen plus several ground crew, including one of the most experienced senior enlisted leaders in the unit.

The attack had been repelled, but it had also reinforced the fact that Russian special operators were still here at the German border, far behind the now-disorganized Russian armor force, and the Spetsnaz troop had orders to ruthlessly eliminate any NATO advantage they could find.

Two aircraft had been destroyed in the fighting, and one of these was still smoldering on the edge of the highway the Americans had been using as a runway.

The ground crew had spent the last hours since the attack working on both their aircraft and their expeditionary airfield. Stripping parts off the planes damaged beyond repair, through the freezing rain and the wind that bit right through them, they had worked nonstop to get these eight A-10s back to flight status.

When Jones finished, the colonel closed the brief by giving some encouragement in the face of the bleak circumstances. "Men, you know your purpose. You understand the equation on the ground. That mixed U.S. and German regiment in pursuit of the enemy is counting on you to support them in kicking the shit out of the Russians before they escape into

Belarus. The Poles are—wisely, I suspect—holding their own armor close to Warsaw to fight off anything else that might come over the border, so they're counting on you to help minimize the loss of lives they've already endured.

"Your country expects you to do your job to the hilt until we get that call to pull off the dogs of war, and that's just exactly what we're going to do.

"Keep your heart, keep your strength, and for God's sake keep your shit together. No individual heroics. Now . . . join me outside and we'll say a few words for the men we've lost and ask them to watch over us and provide their blessing as we continue our mission."

Once the memorial was over, Shank and seven other pilots now under his command jogged out to the flight line and boarded their aircraft. The long, flat stretch of autobahn that ran off to the east in front of them and served as their runway was plainly pockmarked, but it had been hastily repaired and deemed safe enough for the stalwart A-10s to take off from.

The aircraft themselves didn't look much better than the banged-up stretch of concrete the Warthogs had available for a runway. Patched bullet holes in the fuselages, newly riveted panels made from hand-cut metal, replaced ailerons. Every one of the eight ships looked like it had taken hits, but none of the pilots cared. They trusted their flight crews with their lives, and as long the wrench turners said the planes were safe to fly, that was good enough for them.

Shank climbed the retractable ladder and swung his legs into the cockpit, then patted the side of his aircraft and buckled himself in. He lowered the bullet-resistant canopy and sealed it tight with a snap. He hit the power cycles and increased the throttle a touch.

He looked out his left window and returned the salute from Airman Jones, who used his left hand to do so, because his right arm was in a sling. Then Shank opened the throttle, keyed the radio signaling his takeoff to the expeditionary air controllers, and began rolling down the S217 highway. In moments he climbed into the low gray sky, his small wing of seven more aircraft following him aloft one by one.

DJIBOUTI CITY, DJIBOUTI
28 DECEMBER

Pascal Arc-Blanchette climbed the narrow concrete stairs to the roof of La Mer Rouge. The pool deck was quiet. He didn't expect to see anyone around, but Tristan, the French proprietor, was at the top of the stairs behind the steel gate, staring down at him as he climbed up.

"To what do I owe the pleasure?" he asked as Pascal puffed from the climb.

"Ah, Tristan, my old friend," Pascal said, then stopped at the metal gate and grabbed onto it for balance. "Do you really keep the gate locked on me today?"

"Well, when you call me 'old friend,' I know I should think twice before unlocking it."

"No time to play. I need you to let me in."

Tristan looked into the eyes of his friend and compatriot. "What are you getting me into?" he asked as he unlocked the creaky old gate.

"Izzîla and the girls are not here?" Pascal asked.

"No. I have eyes, don't I? We watched the Russians come in and I heard about their rough treatment at the dock after the American torpedoes. I sent my girls away a half hour ago."

"You always get information at the speed of sound."

"Many still whisper in my ears. But my guess is I have sent them away for good reason, because you and I are about to engage in something truly rotten . . . on behalf of our country."

"Yes . . . truly rotten," said Pascal, "but on behalf of our country, as you say."

Tristan had deployed to Djibouti with the Foreign Legion long ago and he never went home to France after having his heart stolen by a gorgeous Djiboutian woman. A supermodel hidden as a shepherd's daughter. He had fallen deeply in love, wooed her, then made promises to return when his unit was moved away. She had doubted him, believing his honor was a fool to his passion. Years passed and then he retired from the legion and returned to Africa to resume the courtship. A conversion to Islam appeased her father. A healthy dowry appeased the tribe. A wedding, then four beautiful children. Now the owner of La Mer Rouge and a French expat,

Tristan was one of the happiest men Pascal knew. A loving father to two sons and two daughters. The sons were now old enough to run the business, and the daughters, in the mold of their mother, were old enough to tear at the hearts of every weary and dusty traveler who frequented the restaurant. Many returned often just to get a glimpse of them.

Ten minutes later, Pascal Arc-Blanchette embraced his son as tightly as he could through the bigger, younger man's body armor and other equipment strapped to him. Apollo returned the embrace, holding his father for a long time. The two men hadn't seen each other in person since Christmas just over a year ago now, although they made it a habit to speak on the phone each week.

They sat down at a bistro table on the balcony of the restaurant. In the distance a haze of smoke hung over the port.

Pascal already had a coffee tray set up, brought upstairs by one of Tristan's sons, and Apollo took no time pouring himself a cup and drinking it in gulps.

There was a ridiculous incongruity to the two men as they sat at the little table and sipped coffee. The silver-maned older gentleman in a tweed coat across from a powerfully built young soldier wearing a helmet, body armor, and desert camouflage, with a rifle across his chest and a radio headset and microphone on his head.

Apollo put his cup down and said, "Papa, I cannot remain with you. The Russian advance will be leaving the city soon. They have their reconnaissance scouting the way."

"I understand, son. You have men counting on you."

"I really wish you'd gotten on that flight to Paris."

Pascal shrugged. "This is home now. I'm not leaving."

"It's not safe."

"I still have a satellite phone. If it gains reception soon, I can keep NATO abreast of the Russians' departure, the damage caused, and what force they leave with."

"You don't think you are in danger here?"

"*Non, pas du tout.* ("No, not at all.") I am worried about you, though."

"I know what I'm doing."

Pascal put his hand on his son's muscular shoulder. *"Mult ad apris ki bien conuist ahan."*

Apollo fought an urge to roll his eyes. "You *do* know that I *don't* know ancient French, Dad."

"Yes, but you know the sentiment. 'He has learned much who knows the pain of struggle.'"

Apollo finished his coffee. "Sorry, but I have to go."

But Pascal was not finished quoting ancient writing. "'He has conquered his way across so many lands / He has taken so many blows from good sharp spears / He has slain and vanquished in battle so many powerful kings: When will he ever forsake waging war?'"

Apollo stood. "Not until I beat those Russian asses all the way back to Siberia." Apollo smiled behind his boom mic. "Papa, you do love your Charlemagne."

"You know, your sister may be the one with the better education, but I am so proud of my warrior son."

"They're calling me in my earpiece, Papa. Please be careful." He kissed his father on both cheeks in the customary French fashion and turned for the stairs.

"You, too, my boy."

The father watched his son leave, then gathered his binoculars, the satellite phone, and the cell phone. Neither phone was working, thanks to the Russian Spetsnaz teams' efficiency in taking down towers and jamming sat signals, but Pascal knew he had to first record the size and equipment of the Russians leaving the city and then, somehow, find a way to transmit the data back to Paris.

When Apollo appeared downstairs he re-formed with his men by their vehicles, a pair of rugged Toyota Hilux pickups left for them by French embassy security. The rest of the Dragoons went to load into three helicopters, flown up from Addis Ababa by contractor pilots.

Apollo's small force here at the restaurant was armed to the teeth and alert to every corner of the adjacent market as they loaded back up into the two Hiluxes. The captain climbed into the backseat of the rear vehicle, where Caporal Konstantine was waiting for him with a radio receiver in hand.

"Boss, Sergent-Chef Dariel says one of the SA330 Puma helicopters isn't operational: maintenance problems. He wants to know if you want to commandeer the two that remain."

"Two Pumas are not enough to lift all the men, and I don't want to split up. Tell him to grab any pickups or Bongo trucks they can find. We can even buy them from the Djiboutians that work at the airport if we need to. But they need to get extra cans of fuel, and they need to hurry. We'll be there in thirty minutes, and I want the men ready to leave immediately."

"Copy, sir. Transmitting now."

Apollo looked back once more at the four-story building his father had commandeered to use as a lookout post. La Mer Rouge. Clearly his father knew the lay of the land. The Russians could move south only on one of three roads, and crafty Pascal would be able to see all three from his perch.

Hopefully, the Russians wouldn't realize the advantage this building gave to a spotter and send a team to check it out. Apollo had no doubt there were Spetsnaz teams working around the city; he couldn't even be sure he himself wasn't under observation right now.

The two trucks rumbled off toward the airport, their occupants knowing they were racing against the clock to get out of town before they found themselves face-to-face with Russian armor.

CHAPTER 59

The USS *John Warner* had spent hours on the shallow, sandy bottom just south of Moucha Island and north of Djibouti City. She now turned to the urgent task of making best speed, heading for open sea. The Tadjoura Trough was a deepwater cut that ran west to east and would give *John Warner* a fair run straight into the Gulf of Aden and away from the sweeping sonar of the searching Russian ships, which were closing on the *Warner* by the minute.

DelVecchio was all business now, giving rapid-fire orders to her crew. "Helm, focus on the cavitation bubble. OOD, I need max speed, but run silent. Sonar, keep us alert to any boat noise. And, Quartermaster, I want a depth beneath the keel every five minutes or by exception."

The quartermaster was the first to respond. "Yes, ma'am. Depth is one hundred eighty feet under keel."

The officer of the deck said, "Noise is limited. Divisions report all hands at QSO—at this time." Quiet ship operations had been invented for times like this.

The helmsman spoke up last. "Ma'am, steady at six knots. I am holding speed and depth."

"Very well," DelVecchio responded mechanically, her mind racing as she tried desperately to think a few moves ahead.

They had just over seven and a half nautical miles to the Tadjoura Trough. At six knots that was almost an hour to reach the outlet to the deep sea. But she knew they didn't have that kind of time. The Russian vessels were sweeping in too quickly. If she ordered a faster speed, the *John Warner*'s screws would cavitate: a bubble of air would form behind the sub's screw, and the sucking noise would be audible to everyone with sonar equipment for miles around.

There has to be a way. The various algorithms she'd memorized over the years danced in her mind; the numbers arrayed themselves as she searched for the mathematical solution. The numbers represented speed, distance, depth, current, and noise—all the factors submariners had pined over since the inception of the first military sub.

The sonarman said, "Ma'am, contact three, bearing two-three-eight has picked up an active ping. She's at eight nautical miles."

The XO added, "She either thinks she's got something or they are going to try to drive us out of cover."

"Yes. The shadow of the island will give us some time, but it won't be long before they converge on us."

A hollow boom permeated the hull, and a jarring impulse made the *John Warner* shudder, chattering the crew's teeth, making pens skitter across the map boards. Everyone knew the sound.

The sonarman threw off his earphones and rubbed his ears in pain.

"Depth charge," the XO said, putting words to everyone's speculations. "You okay, sonar?"

"Yes, sir . . . just didn't expect that. I had gain and pitch all the way up, trying to differentiate ship noises. Thought I heard a fucking splash."

"Guess you did."

Commander DelVecchio turned to face the crew. It was clear she'd made a decision. "XO, I want to line up the closest Russians with this Moucha Island, and we'll use the shadow of the landmass against them. We round the island, and then I want you to kick us up to full speed and follow the bottom down as it falls away. The sound waves from the screws will refract around the island. It will give the Russians two false signals to our location, as the sound waves will bend around in opposite directions and they'll steam full speed off after one of the signatures. I've read about this being done before, but I've never been caught in shallow enough water to actually try it. It won't fool them for long, but if they're bombing the shit out of the south side of the island, it'll at least give them some false vectors to chase."

"Got it, ma'am," said the XO. "Sonar, line up the two nearest Russian ships, then give me an azimuth. Helm, stand by for a course correction. Once we get the cardinal direction, we kick it into high gear."

DelVecchio gripped the railing in front of her. Fooling the Russians with a false acoustic shadow, speeding into the trough, then diving deep enough to get below the thermocline and race for the Gulf of Aden.

DJIBOUTI CITY, DJIBOUTI
28 DECEMBER

Pascal watched through his Vortex binoculars as the last Russian vehicle drove out of Djibouti City; then he lowered the binoculars and closed his eyes, resting them with supreme relief.

It had taken more than eight hours for the entire Russian brigade to drive south from the still-smoldering harbor, down the Rue de Venice, onto the RN1, then the RN5, and finally out of town to the south. And Pascal had been there to watch every last piece of equipment, every single soldier visible.

The units had left the Djiboutian harbor warehouses interspersed by thirty minutes, organized in three separate fighting columns, likely for their own protection, because moving in one long column would have made them more vulnerable to air reconnaissance and air attack.

Unit by unit, in tactically ordered clumps, they seemed mainly centered around the motorized rifle regiments with some independent forces, mainly reconnaissance, Pascal surmised.

He had been furiously scribbling notes the entire day. While he was neither a military vet nor a Russia expert, he was perfect for this surveillance and reporting work. He was an old African hand, but he possessed intimate knowledge of Russian military equipment. It was no surprise, considering how many nations on this continent the Russians supplied with weapons of war.

He'd counted the equivalent of three motorized rifle regiments of Russian BTR-82As, a headquarters unit including medical companies, two battalions of artillery, a large battery of antiair vehicles, and a full battalion of anti-tank weapons. All told, about the size of a Russian rifle brigade.

Mon dieu, he thought, looking down at his notepad. *A massive force. I have to send in a final report to the Direction Générale,* he thought, *and Apollo . . .* The notes were all enciphered by Pascal and full of neat, hand-drawn tables filled with rows and rows of codes that symbolized and characterized Russian vehicles.

The most interesting thing to Pascal was actually not something apparent in the vast Russian arsenal but something missing: tanks. There was a distinct absence of any heavy armor. Pascal couldn't imagine a Russian brigade forgoing their tanks. He understood speed and surprise, but certainly the Russians did not expect to maintain surprise once they landed in Djibouti. This was a major weakness he'd have to ensure his superiors understood. The rest of the regiment was about what he'd expected: loads of BTR-82As, BRDM-2M reconnaissance vehicles, Kornet-D anti-tank trucks, a unit of Pantsir-S1 antiaircraft vehicles, and some BM-30 Smerch multiple-launch rocket systems. He also counted twenty big ZSU-23 tracked antiaircraft vehicles.

Those tracked machines will slow them down. Probably no faster than forty kilometers per hour, thought Pascal.

Pascal assessed, all told, that he'd seen more than two thousand troops riding on light-armored vehicles or in heavy trucks, and he presumed there were thousands more inside the hundreds of BTRs and other armored vehicles.

He checked the Inmarsat satellite phone to see if he'd received any news from his son. He had not, but it had a strong signal now, and two messages had been left while his attention had been on the column. One was a coded note from Direction Générale requesting his status, and the other was from one of his contacts in Djibouti requesting a meeting to share intelligence.

While he'd been watching the column, Pascal had received a visitor about every half hour here at his rooftop observation post. A gas station attendant, a truck driver, several employees from the docks. All contacts of his.

For the first time in a long while, Pascal felt relevant.

He read the contact's message first, and sent a reply agreeing to meet him here at La Mer Rouge at ten p.m. The message from Direction Générale was a simple series of code words ordering him to report in, which he responded to as well, telling them he had picture messages to send to them and would do so immediately.

More than anything in the world, however, Pascal wanted to call his son. But this would have to wait for now. *Business first,* he thought.

He started to take pictures of his notebook with the sat phone's built-in camera so he could send them digitally over the satellite. It was all written in a shorthand code he'd been trained to use many years before. The young field agents used digital encoding—Pascal doubted anyone under the age of forty could understand what he was photographing—but he knew they still had old-timers around at Direction Générale who could translate the codes.

He flipped the pages in the notebook and took one picture after another, storing them in the sat phone's onboard memory module. It had taken him the better part of a year to learn how to use the device. Even when direction came down for all field agents to refrain from using cables and encrypted letters, he had resisted until he received a stern warning from the Direction Générale to cut it out and get on board with the modern era.

Finally, when he was finished photographing all his notes on the sat phone, he began transmitting them up into space and then back down to Paris.

This process always took several minutes, so he put the phone on the table by the balcony railing. He was exhausted from the hours of careful surveillance, meeting with contacts, and recording his notes.

He could still see the joint French and American base at Camp Lemonnier on the horizon. Smoke continued to rise from the buildings and Pascal could only imagine the fate suffered by any of his compatriots who'd still been there when the Russians arrived. The Russians' first order of battle, clearly, after mustering up their forces and leaving the harbor, had been to send a regiment to destroy the base and the airfield.

He stepped to the edge of the balcony railing now and looked over at the traffic passing below. A rush hour had begun after the departure of the Russians. Setting his tea and binos down on the wide wooden railing, he sighed a heavy sigh and glanced at the Inmarsat phone. The phone's digital upload display read "66%."

"Allo," said a voice in stilted French behind him, startling Pascal from his thoughts.

He turned around to face a large man in a tan shirt and Bermuda shorts standing at the top of the stairwell. His relaxed apparel was more Western in design than anything common in Djibouti. At first glance he thought maybe Tristan had hired some new waiters at La Mer Rouge.

Then Pascal's heart sank and he began to perspire even more from the instant recognition. He knew this man. This was one of the young men he'd seen at Restaurant L'Historil.

He was a Russian special forces soldier.

Pascal slipped a hand behind his back, picked up the Inmarsat from the railing, and nonchalantly tucked it into his waistband under his jacket.

The high-end binos were right behind him on the railing. He kept them shielded with his body.

"Bonjour," said Pascal, trying to appear relaxed. Sometimes it just took a moment for his fieldcraft to kick in.

With a casual motion he backed up to the railing, tipping the binos over the edge with his butt. He'd angled the nudge just right to knock the binos onto the awning over a portion of the pool deck below. Without looking, he listened for the soft, almost noiseless bump and slide across the canvas surface confirming the optics had survived the fall and wouldn't alert any of this man's compatriots who might be downstairs.

Satisfied with his concealment of the sat phone and more than a little pleased with himself for his quick thinking with the binoculars, Pascal spoke to the man in fast and fluid French. "I'll have a wine—make it a Merlot. Something from Tuscany, if you please."

Seeing no response, he continued in a haughty and condescending French tone as he took his seat at the little table. "A glass of the Tenuta dell'Ornellaia is my choice. Actually, let's make it a bottle, shall we?"

Still no reaction. The man just stared at Pascal.

Then the man's attention turned to the stairs, and Pascal followed his gaze.

Another man appeared at the top of the staircase. This one wore the tan "Tetris"-style digital desert camouflage uniform of a Russian Spetsnaz soldier. His shoulder boards were large and adorned with three stars, denoting him a full colonel.

Pascal's face blanched. A cold sweat broke out across his brow.

Stay calm, he told himself.

For a fleeting second he considered trying to rush past the new man, to launch for the stairs and race down. Certainly the colonel was not as big and imposing as the other Russian.

The Frenchman stood calmly and took a step in that direction, but the colonel immediately held up a hand, stopping him from coming closer. "Yes. Tuscan Merlot would be nice," said the Russian colonel in heavily accented French. "I think I'll ask the proprietor to set out a glass. Or maybe two. But you may not be staying for the cheese, monsieur."

The man in civilian attire pulled a pistol from under his shirt, walked behind Pascal to the vacated table and chair, and started perusing Pascal's notebook.

The Frenchman's adrenaline was now pumping and he entertained three thoughts. One, jump. Two, push past the bigger man and leap for the adjacent roof. Three, push past the colonel. But he just stood still.

More cold sweat dripped down his neck, and he gripped the railing behind him. He cursed his old and overweight frame. A younger spy would just leap and probably land on the awning below and probably still have the energy and reflexes to scamper off.

But Pascal was not that man. He sighed lightly and his shoulders slumped.

Reading his mind, the Russian colonel spoke up. "Oh, I would not challenge Serzhánt Ketsov. He has an itchy trigger finger, and . . . you know what I just found out downstairs? He *really* hates the French."

This last statement made Pascal wonder what the Russian might have done to poor Tristan.

The colonel smiled, then signaled the man he had called Sergeant Ketsov to search Pascal.

Pascal raised his jacket with his free hand, fished the phone from his sweaty pants waistband, and took a quick glance at the screen. It read "75%." He handed it to Sergeant Ketsov with a smile.

He turned to the colonel. "I didn't catch your name?"

"My name is Colonel Borbikov."

"DeGuzzman," Pascal said. "François DeGuzzman."

"I see. And you are here on a military mission of some kind, watching my troops move through Djibouti? Perhaps for the French government? Maybe even for La Sécurité Extérieure?"

Pascal adopted a look of genuine humor. "A spy? *Non*, I am merely a diplomat." The big Russian handed the sat phone to the colonel, who took it and glanced at the screen. Pascal said, "I'm a member of the French diplomatic monetary fund mission with the Bank of France. We are here to supervise the transition of La Banque Centrale de Djibouti and offer support in stabilizing its currency against the euro."

"Good. I am thankful for that, because if I understand my Geneva conventions correctly, a man caught sending information to La Sécurité Extérieure while out of uniform would be . . . a spy, *non?*"

Pascal said, "I confess, I have no idea about that."

The colonel gently pressed the sat phone's off button. It emitted a familiar three beeps as it shut down. Then, just as carefully, he removed the plastic back cover and pulled the battery free, pocketing both phone and battery.

The sounds of others echoed up the narrow stairwell and three more Russian soldiers now joined the trio on the rooftop of La Mer Rouge hotel and restaurant. These troops all carried AKs and wore advanced military hardware and equipment but over civilian attire that was similar to Sergeant Ketsov's.

Pascal recognized another two of them, also from Nadal's restaurant. One man and one woman.

Their expressions looked severe now. No-nonsense. Gone were the calm, fun countenances they'd held while drinking coffee and socializing at Restaurant L'Historil.

Borbikov said, "You will not mind if we have a look at your credentials, though I'm certain they are all in order."

Pascal smiled and walked toward the woman, handing her his wallet. The identification and credit cards carried his false name, false addresses, all under the identity of Monsieur DeGuzzman, a legitimate banking cover he'd held for years in Djibouti.

Now we are getting somewhere, thought Pascal confidently. They would buy his cover story. It was elaborate enough and all the details in his wallet fit perfectly. If they needed more information, he had plenty of contacts in the city who could confirm his identity.

The colonel looked over the documents and waved him forward, stared into his eyes, and handed them back. Then, smiling, he pointed to the stairs and made a motion for him to go.

Well, that was easy, thought Pascal, stepping confidently to the stairs.

He made it one step from the stairs, when Colonel Borbikov spoke again. "Oh, one question before you go, Monsieur DeGuzzman. Are these yours?"

The woman handed the colonel a pair of high-definition Vortex VK binoculars from a tactical pouch on her waist.

He looked at the optics as though he'd never seen binoculars before. Not skipping a beat, Pascal answered hastily, "No."

"It is all just a misunderstanding, then," said the colonel, waving him away.

"Good. *Adieu*," Pascal said, and then feeling emboldened, he added, "I must have my phone back, if you please."

"That won't be necessary, Monsieur . . . *Pascal*, is it?"

"As I've said, my name is François DeGuzzman."

"You will first join me for a little discussion," said the colonel, and he drew his pistol from the holster on his hip. Leveling it at the Frenchman, he said, "Ariadne, take *Monsieur Pascal* downstairs; then tie him up next to the old man."

CHAPTER 60

Shank's underarms were soaked. Half-moons of sweat had stained his flight suit a dark green. He hadn't shifted in his seat in more than forty-five minutes. His crotch itched uncontrollably, but in the small A-10 cockpit he had no space to move and, with his current speed and attack angle, no inclination to do so either. He had tasked the rest of his flight with hunting for tanks, and now he and his wingman, Nooner, were scanning for deeper, more lucrative targets.

Beads of sweat dripped down his forearms and into his gloves as he gripped the throttle and stick controller. He did his best to ignore the annoyance and maintain focus on his heads-up display. He tuned out all sensations that weren't visual or auditory while searching the darkness for Russian armor on the ground and watching the low skies for the telltale pinpricks of light that indicated a SAM launch.

His ears were on high alert as he listened for his warning systems.

It was all about balance, he'd told his students back at Nellis. If a Warthog pilot concentrated too much on offense, he'd get killed; if he concentrated too much on defense, he'd be worthless to the troops on the ground he was out there to assist and protect . . . and *they* would get killed.

"No pressure," he would always joke, with a smile, back in the classroom.

But he wasn't smiling now.

The HUD had the last known locations for the Russian tanks plotted, and as long as the tanks hadn't moved too far since the last update, right now he should be screaming at top speed in a steep dive toward a cluster of T-14 Armatas that had been pounding the German and Polish forces pursuing them.

Shank used his keen eyesight to scan the wood lines, ridges, towns, and valleys. He concentrated on everything: any changes in color patterns denoting camouflage, lines, or tracks in the winter snow; smoke from exhaust rising in the frigid air; trees moving as heavy armor passed.

And then, as he dipped below one thousand feet, he saw it: movement in front of the wood line in the distance, about four kilometers away.

He adjusted his angle of attack slightly and focused on the area. What he at first thought was a column of trucks suddenly came into focus. It was a long, dark olive green shape. It blended with the trees at first, but as it emerged from the forest it snaked through the white snow, moving from southwest to northeast and growing longer and longer by the second.

Into his mic he said, "Holy shit, Nooner! Eleven o'clock low! I've got a train. A big-ass train moving without any lights."

"I tally," replied his wingman. "Could be the enemy train, but how do we know it's not some civilian cargo—"

Nooner stopped talking when smoke trails rose above the center of the train. Four surface-to-air missiles lifted up ahead of fat white columns, and before the two Americans' eyes, the smoke began angling in their direction.

Shank and Nooner both juked right, enacting a standard prearranged battle maneuver. Nothing was said between the men as they pulled a hard two-g turn. The twin General Electric TF34-GE-100 turbofan engines blasted them up to four hundred miles per hour; red flames issued in spouts from the engines as both pilots kicked on the afterburners. In unison they both dumped multiple chaff-and-flare pods, steering directly away from the launched missiles to provide a minimum profile to their heat-seeking warheads.

One of the inbound missiles fell away, banking toward the flares. Both men watched their radar closely, tracking the other warheads as they closed. They each launched another bank of flares and chaff.

The men juked their aircraft back hard to the left. Seconds later, relief washed over the men as the last three missiles went dumb, following the flares and chaff to the ground and crashing harmlessly into the trees.

"Shit," Nooner said into his mic. "If I'd been carrying a lump of coal up my ass, I'd have myself one hell of a diamond now."

But Shank was mission focused. "Nooner, we're attacking that bitch."

"Hey, sir . . . I'm just gonna say it once, but that train's probably got more than four missiles. We close the distance again, it'll reach out to say hello again."

Shank said, "Copy, but intel suspects that thing is the nerve center of this whole damn invasion. We have to light it up!"

"Understood. How you wanna play it?"

Shank replied, "Easy day, Captain. Here's what we're gonna do." Shank explained his plan, then asked, "You got it?"

"Copy all. I'm ready to close in, sir, but I may have to keep one hand on the ejector handle."

"I hear you, man. We need an attack heading of zero-one-four. Less than three minutes to target. Stay alert."

"You think she'll stop? Get into that next mass of forest and just sit and wait for us to come back around where they can take another shot?"

"Negative. I think in spite of all their firepower, they're racing against time to get across Poland. They know every hour they're in Western Europe, NATO will continue to bring in new flights of attack aircraft.

"We'll hit her on the far side of the woods. Let's take it even lower. Need to stay below the trees to block her radar. I want to crest them at our twelve o'clock and hammer down. You take lead—you've got two missiles left and I've only got one."

"Two copies," came the simple response from the number two airplane.

Both men concentrated hard on controlling the Warthogs; perfect stick-work demanded huge effort, especially with the throttles open at such a low altitude. The A-10 was not a nimble aircraft, and it had never been intended for precision flight. It had the nickname "the flying tank," and sometimes it drove like one. Heavy and slow, but powerful and dangerous.

Flying at just over two hundred feet, Shank and Nooner raced over a narrow village that wound along a two-lane road. The undulating landscape meant the two men were constantly pulling back and pushing down on their sticks, fighting for the right balance of low flight and avoiding the absolute worst nightmare of any pilot.

The anodyne official term was "controlled flight into terrain," but that was just a fancy way to say "crash."

Any military pilot would have much preferred getting blown out of the sky by a missile than going off into eternity with the rest of the flying community knowing he'd slammed his jet into the damn dirt.

They coursed over the fields now, still skimming the surface of the earth, the ground whipping below them in a blur. Ahead, the last wood line before the tracks rose above them.

At the last second, both Nooner and Shank pulled stick and barely crested the tall Polish pines; then they sank back on the other side over a wide clearing in the scattered but thick evergreen forests.

"Ten o'clock!" said Nooner.

Shank flicked his eyes to his left. "I tally." He banked slightly to line his nose up for the kill.

Across the field, just over two kilometers distant, the train slithered between snowy fields on the outskirts of a city. It moved due east now. More dense woods lay ahead of the train, and in seconds it would be back in cover, and the pilots would have the disadvantage of having to fly directly over the top of the train to look for the best shot.

"Fox Four!" Nooner said as he fired both his missiles.

Immediately two AGM-65 Mavericks bolted forward from Nooner's pylons, boosting and accelerating rapidly to six hundred knots per hour.

The enemy must have spotted the attacking aircraft at the exact same time.

More white smoke erupted above the train in the evening moonlight, turning into ten distinct plumes as ten missiles rose from ten antiair missile tubes right as Shank fired his lone remaining Maverick.

"Guns, guns, guns!" said Nooner as he let loose with a burst of extreme long-range cannon shot; then both pilots pulled a hard right pitch and gunned their engines to maximum. If they could dip back down on the far side of woods, they might send the missiles crashing into the tall pines instead of into their now-vulnerable tails.

The Warthog had one of the tightest turning radii of any jet, but every millisecond felt like an eternity as Shank and Nooner cranked the noses of their aircraft 180 degrees, grunting loudly against the g-forces.

The Russians had fired eight short-range SA-24 Grinch missiles and two of their longer-range S-400 Triumf batteries with 9M96E2 missiles. The 9Ms ejected from their launchers with a gas charge and popped up to a height of forty meters; then their booster rockets kicked in. The SA-24s rapidly acquired the two A-10s, and accelerated to their 1,200-miles-per-hour maximum speed in pursuit. In seconds they reached a frightening 2,200 miles per hour, nearly Mach 3.

Shank and Nooner were now flying beyond the recommended maximum speed. The Polish wood line rose in front of them and they closed the last two hundred meters in seconds. The 9M missiles quickly overtook their smaller, slower SA-24 brothers and reached Shank and Nooner just as they were cresting the trees.

The huge array of flares and chaff dumped by the pair of A-10s was not enough to stop the nearly three-meter-long missiles. At the last second one streaked through the cloud of decoys, detonating into a flare virtually right next to Nooner's left wing. The other smart missile, its advanced technology detecting its proximity to its intended targets and also their rapid down angle, instantly computed that there would be no room to turn and re-engage, so it detonated immediately.

Shank took shrapnel to virtually all of his aircraft; chunks of metal sprayed through his left engine, eviscerating a small portion of his left wing and cutting off a chunk of his tail.

He looked over at Nooner as they just leveled out below the wood line. Behind them none of the other missiles had been smart enough to avoid the trees, because their algorithms didn't account for obstructions. All but two detonated against the tall pines. One of the others tumbled into a farmer's field, where it detonated in the snow. The second spun wildly up in the air, careened around in a spiral, then tumbled, its stabilizer fins ripped off as it dropped through the hundred-year-old pines and exploded against the ground.

Nooner's voice was strained over the radio. "Shit, Shank, I gotta head back. This thing's not gonna hold together. I'm leaking fuel and I don't have full control."

Shank had been checking his own gauges. Thankfully he found they looked better than his view outside the windscreen of his fuselage and control surfaces suggested. "RTB, Nooner. I seem to be holding together, and I still have something I need to do."

"Sir, you *can't* go it alone. I can at least stay nearby. Find and report your position if you get hit."

"Dude, I'm looking right at your bird. You aren't leaking fuel—you are *gushing* fuel. You won't make it five minutes before you'll have to punch.

Plus, you've lost maneuverability. Don't give the enemy an easy kill. You get back; I'll take one more pass and join you."

"Copy that. Good luck, Ray," said Nooner. In his emotion he'd forgotten to use his flight leader's rank or call sign. Shank's wingman turned for a heading that would take him back in the direction of their expeditionary airfield on the old German highway.

Shank knew Nooner wouldn't make it anywhere near Germany, much less their airfield, but at least he'd be gone from here before he had to bail.

With his tail rudder damaged, Shank had less-than-optimal stick control. It felt heavy, sluggish, like a car riding on a flat tire. The A-10 responded, but every sweep to the left or right took a few moments and this had to be fitted into his mental calculus as he guided the bird.

He skimmed the fields and forests at four hundred feet now, mindful that his moves and any small rise in terrain would have to be anticipated and calculated well in advance.

He could see the woods in the distance at the edge of the town. If the train had accelerated, as he'd guessed it would, it would now be nearing Jelenia Góra. The map showed a very large industrial rail yard and switching station on the far side of the urban center. The train would have to slow to take a long curve to get around the town and then remain slow as it passed through the industrial yard.

He decided to try to time his attack on the train to hit it in the rail yard. It wouldn't be in the center of a populated area, and it was an easily identifiable landmark he could focus on as he approached.

But if his calculations were wrong, he might arrive before the train and then catch a flank shot from its missile batteries.

Shooting 30mm GAU-8/A Gatling guns at a stationary target was tricky. Shooting the gun at a train as it moved at an unknown speed away from him, while simultaneously watching out for another battery of missiles—all with a severely damaged aircraft—seemed utterly impossible.

But he flew on.

His integrated flight-and-fire-control computer, or IFFCC, calculated his aircraft's airspeed over the ground. The computer, intended to make it easier for the pilot to get bullet convergence, also calculated the bullet drop needed and depicted this in the HUD reticle.

But Shank knew he also had to mentally calculate the appropriate lead of this moving target in only seconds or else his rounds would fall harmlessly short. The computer was designed to provide an aiming point, like the sight on a rifle. The reticle placed the maximum number of rounds in the smallest possible diameter ellipse on the ground in order to kill a tank.

Shank flew over a dam and a hydroelectric power station, then over the Bóbr River.

He glanced down quickly at his joint operations graphic air map. The JOG-Air was useful, as it showed only landmarks and topography that could be seen from the air.

He checked the lead-in features—terrain landmarks he used to guide himself into the target area—on his kneeboard. The power station, a small hill, a bend in the Bóbr River, then a small lookout tower perched on a hill overlooking the city of Jelenia Góra. The river bend was now behind him as he passed low over the tower. He barely had a moment to notice a small throng of people in the tower below, all hitting the deck as his jet screamed by.

Ahead, the city rose in the night; the church steeples he'd seen on the JOG-Air map were just where they should have been. He ticked them off one by one. A castle tower, then another church to his right . . . He should spot the rail yard shortly.

His hands perspired through his gloves. His pounding pulse quickened.

The last church steeple. Then . . . *There it is.*

The rail line came into view, and there, skirting the city, he saw the massive green Russian military train, burning from multiple missile strikes but racing east at speed. He found himself aligned almost perfectly with its rear as it pulled along the long curve, picking up speed, following the banks of the Bóbr.

Shank pitched the aircraft down, trying to align the gunsight in his heads-up display. His aircraft responded lethargically. Parts of the broken tail assembly clattered against the empennage, making a loud clacking sound that threatened to break his concentration.

He put his reticle on the track running through the distant rail yard, well in front of the first engine of the massive train, and saw that he was one and a half miles from his target. This was within cannon range, so he put his finger against the red trigger.

A-10 pilots normally fire one-second bursts from their cannons, and to maintain a uniform length of firing time they often chant a mantra, dating back to the Cold War, out loud while pulling the trigger.

Shank pressed his trigger.

Through the gunfire he shouted, "Die, Commie, die!"

Firing shells the size of Coke bottles, the weapon roared, a cacophony and vibration in the cockpit. A burst of flames and white smoke spit from the nose of his aircraft as the GAU-8/A gun system's seven hydraulically driven barrels spun, launching a torrent of 30mm depleted-uranium and high-explosive rounds.

He let off the trigger and immediately pressed it again and again.

"Die, Commie, die! Die, Commie, die!" He was still lined up on the tracks, and each phrase uttered meant another squeeze of the trigger and another burst of 30-mike-mike from the gun. He didn't look at the round counter, just as he'd taught his students at the weapons school not to, but it clicked down at a rate of 3,900 rounds a minute.

Ahead of him the train raced on through the rail yard.

1,150 rounds . . .

Brrrrrrrrt!

1,030 rounds . . .

Brrrrrrrrt!

910 rounds . . .

He fired a fifth burst in time with "Die, Commie, die!" and watched the earlier shots hit, impacting in a narrow circle, spraying the tracks.

790 . . . The round counter clicked away with each squeeze.

Brrrrrrrrt!

Huge chunks of wood and metal blasted free from the train, careening skyward. The rail yard glowed with orange starbursts from the hundreds of explosions as he closed inside of 3,000 feet, still hammering the trigger for controlled bursts. Every ounce of his physical and mental skills poured into the stick and rudder to keep the fire on target.

Blasts of hatred, spitting forth from the bow end of his airplane onto the fleeing train.

Some odd stray rounds and ricocheting shrapnel from the exploding shells slammed into parked cargo trains loaded with wood and grain. The cars ripped apart, their contents spilling out and igniting.

Most of the rounds, however, raked down the length of the fleeing Russian train. Shank had been aiming for the six heavy-duty armored military engines plowing hard to pull the rest of the heavy cars through the town and to safety. The rounds fell short—Shank's estimate of the train's speed had been off—and the damage he did was farther back, along the open-backed cars.

But this did nothing good for the Russians. One of his bursts slammed into a fuel car, and immediately the bulk fuel and oil detonated; smoke and fire and shrapnel erupted right in front of the Warthog's windscreen.

Shank was forced to pull up and away from the massive fireball that rolled skyward in a glowing mushroom cloud. It took all his upper-body strength to yank the heavy, lumbering craft into a tight turn to avoid flying right into the tumult.

Damn it! he cursed to himself, because he knew instantly he'd have to make another pass to stop the train. He skimmed nap-of-the-earth over the city, flying between and below the tops of the tallest buildings, trying to place the big, disabled Warthog as far down into the streets of Jelenia Góra as he dared. His whining aircraft raced close enough to blast the snow off roofs, his wingtips just feet from the smokestacks that dotted the town.

This was incredibly perilous flying, but he needed to keep the buildings between himself and the train or he would receive another salvo of missiles, right up his ass.

He checked the mirror above him and saw the train in the distance to his rear, and was mollified that even though he hadn't blown the damn thing off the rails, his first pass had done some serious damage. The last four cars were a smoke-belching conflagration. Fuel stores were incinerated in huge jets of fire that shot into the night sky. Spouts of flame shot out like blood gushing from the ripped artery of a wounded animal.

The train continued to flee, increasing speed.

In order to get behind the train, Shank had to pull hard right and circle around again toward its vulnerable back side. The last railcars burned out of control, and this gave Shank an idea. The billowing black smoke would obscure his approach from the rear, and the Russians wouldn't be able to launch missiles through the burning fuel and launching debris.

He pushed his damaged bird to its limit, tightening the turn radius to get back onto his killing course. Again he passed the church steeples and the old castle; soon he was back over the rail yard, now burning uncontrollably. The train raced along toward the open countryside, where it could again fire on him with impunity, and where the low skies were not filled with the buildings of the town that masked his approach.

Lining up the gun, he positioned his HUD reticle much higher than before, acknowledging his earlier miscalculation and also the train's increasing velocity. He couldn't fully see the target in front of him through the roiling black smoke, but he knew by instinct where the engine and other cars lay along the tracks. He drew in a deep breath and then chanted again the fire-control saying.

"Die, Commie, die!"

640 rounds . . .

Eight thousand feet distance.

"Die, Commie, die!"

520 rounds . . .

Six thousand feet distance.

"Die, Commie, die!"

400 rounds . . .

Four thousand feet.

"Die, Comm—"

A loud *crack, crack, crack* blasted him from his concentration, and he paused in his trigger pull. Machine-gun rounds tore into the belly and nose of his aircraft, slamming against the titanium bathtub built around the cockpit.

Shank realized he should have assumed the Russians would have every gun on the train turned to the rear, firing wildly through the smoke. His approach angle and altitude had been so plainly obvious, he could have kicked himself for not thinking before flying himself into unnecessary danger.

But he didn't stop—he *couldn't* stop: he had them now and he knew it.

He pressed his gloved finger again, renewed his mantra: "Die, motherfuckers, die!"

But *brrrrrrrt* had turned into *thump, thump, thump.*

The GAU-8/A Gatling gun fired, but at a dramatically slower rate. He could hear an off, odd whine coming from the weapon below his left foot and a new unstable vibration throughout the cockpit.

He realized his one weapon had been hit and damaged.

He pulled the trigger anyway, letting loose a slow but steady stream of 30mm rounds. The gun counter was frozen at 370, but the weapon continued to pump out shells at a much-reduced rate.

His master caution light began flashing; a quick glance at the warning panel showed fluid was dangerously low in not one but both of his redundant hydraulic systems. If he didn't do something soon, the plane would be impossible to control.

Without releasing the stick, he reached behind to his left side and, just by feel, threw a switch to "manual reversion," then punched out the "master caution." Like a car switching from automatic steering to manual, the plane was now controlled exclusively by mechanical connections from the stick to the control surfaces. It felt like a ton of bricks weighed down the stick when he tried to move it. His ability to make fine-tuned movements would be even further compromised, but at least he was still airborne and in the fight.

He burst through the black smoke rising from the back of the burning train, skimming less than seventy-five feet above the roofs of the cars. He fired a constant, steady, but slow stream of rounds as he pulled back on the throttle to increase his brief time on target.

He could see the damage now. Whole cars were ripped open from his earlier bursts; tanks, Bumerangs, and antiair batteries burned. He even saw troops on the cars, every weapon they possessed blazing wildly skyward in hopes of beating back his oppressive fire. He continued to pound them, the train's engines now visible in front of his gunsights.

"Die, *motherfuckers*, die!" he said, although he did not let up on the trigger at all. Even with the slow firing of the Gatling gun, he managed to dump explosive shells into the row of heavy engines.

Dead ahead of him, all six engines high-order detonated, along with a car full of ammo, obviously tank rounds and 120mm mortars. The blast was so huge, he had to shove over his heavy stick to pull hard right so that the shrapnel wouldn't tear him from the sky. He felt a wave of intense heat over him in the cockpit as he flew through the edge of the volcano-like eruption from the front of the train.

The firing from below stopped immediately.

He turned his even more disabled aircraft 180 degrees around, getting lower again in case some trooper with a shoulder-fired missile wanted to give him a good-bye kiss. Looking again in the mirror, he saw the front of the train was off the tracks; cars slid and crashed into one another and flipped and burned.

Staying low, he flew to the west, concentrating on straight and level flight. He wasn't shooting for his air base; he was vying for distance. The last thing he wanted was to eject anywhere near the exploding train.

He hoped like hell he could find an airfield or even a flat, empty stretch of road so he wouldn't have to ditch his magnificent, wounded plane.

With a shaky hand he patted the control panel and gauges like he was acknowledging a good dog that had just rescued its master from a fire.

He had done it.

She had done it.

The man and the machine.

CENTRAL POLAND
28 DECEMBER

Four minutes after taking out the train, Captain Ray Vance climbed to 5,000 feet, fighting his A-10 with all the strength in his arms. The damage was incredible. The sounds, the shakes, the lack of response from the controls . . . The thirty-four-year-old pilot had no idea how the hell he was still in the air.

Suddenly he felt three hard jolts to his aircraft, and he knew he'd been hit by cannon fire. Both his seat and his stick shuddered and vibrated. He dropped the throttle back, slowing his wounded bird as quickly as he could, but with each passing second the flight characteristics deteriorated more and more.

He wrestled with the 25,000-pound monster as he fought the jerking stick in his hand.

He had no idea what had hit him, whether it was ground fire or a Russian aircraft up here in the dark sky, pursuing him from behind. He swiveled his head around to look behind him but couldn't see any attacker.

Wham! Wham! Wham!

Another three blasts struck Shank's Warthog, this time hitting the left side of the fuselage and the canopy just two feet in front of his face. Metal and glass ricocheted around the cockpit, slicing him across his left arm and right leg. One hot piece of shrapnel shattered his visor and struck him high on the left cheek.

With the broken canopy, Shank was now exposed to the whipping, freezing winter air. Blood blew up from his cheek and into his eyes, all but blinding him.

Shank had flown damaged aircraft multiple times in combat, but flying without a canopy, bleeding from multiple wounds, and blinded as the wind blew through his exposed cockpit were more than he'd ever imagined in his worst nightmares.

And then his plane began to spin out of control.

Working purely by the instincts gained from years of training, he reached beside his legs, his head thrashing around as he tried to see *anything* through the blood.

Where is the motherfucking ejection lever? He could feel the negative g's tossing him left and right as he tried blindly to grasp the controller that would punch him out of there.

Thunk! Thunk!

His aircraft was hit twice more, somewhere aft of his cockpit. There was definitely a Russian fighter up here, and the other pilot wasn't going to quit until Shank's A-10 cratered a smoking hole in some snow-covered field.

"Shit!" His aircraft corkscrewed down; he could only guess at the altitude because he couldn't see the gauges, but he was pretty sure that if he didn't find a way to punch in the next few seconds, then he wouldn't be ejecting at all. He caught himself starting to go into G-LOC, or gravity-induced loss of consciousness, and he grunted and flexed all the muscles in his body in an attempt to keep the blood in his brain so he could stay awake.

He found the side of the ejector with his left hand, but the hand seemed to be going numb and was no longer functioning properly. His right hand released the stick and reached over, as he still tried to get a hand on the redundant left- and right-side ACES II ejection controls.

"Eject! Eject!" he croaked, just to hear himself speak, to verify he was alive.

Finally, his right hand wrapped around the angled metal of the ejection handle and he pulled hard. Nothing. He yanked again. Nothing again. *"Punch! Punch!"*

He had grown too weak with the G-LOC.

Wham! Wham! Shank took two more blasts against the belly of his A-10. He felt searing heat grow all around him, even with the shattered canopy.

Christ almighty, I'm on fire!

The A-10 now fell like a sack of bricks toward the earth.

The enemy fighter continued pounding him mercilessly, and presumably would until he exploded into the ground.

This Russian pilot wanted Shank to die. It was as simple as that.

"Fuck you!" he yelled breathlessly through the clatter of metal ripping away from his once-perfect airship.

With every fiber of his being, with all his remaining strength, Shank yanked the ejection lever with his one good hand, throwing his back and shoulder into the movement with all the power remaining in his body.

He heard a loud *bang* and then a shock slammed his helmet back against the headrest. The rocket-assisted seat catapulted him out of the burning and spinning A-10, but as he was oriented upside down at the moment of ejection, he fired straight down at first before the onboard gyroscope righted the seat and he angled laterally, then launched upward on a plume of smoke.

Soon he felt a *pop* and a *whoosh* and suddenly all was slow and calm.

He began swinging gently. God knew how far he was from the ground, but he *was* under a canopy.

Thank God, he thought.

He assessed his wounds, feeling with his one good hand across his body. Both legs were there. He could feel blood on his chest and shoulders. He looked down at his left hand and saw it was there but bleeding. He was sure it had been broken somehow, but he wasn't going to worry about it.

His pain numbed in the frigid and still air as he drifted toward the earth. He lifted his right hand to wipe the blood off his face so he could see a little; in doing so, he felt his left eye swollen completely shut. Through his right eye he could see that the Nomex glove of his right hand was burned, but the hand itself seemed to be working properly.

Now running on adrenaline alone, he looked around for his aircraft, found it, and watched it fall away from him in the darkness, slipping below his feet at a steep downward angle, burning a fiery streak earthward. Soon came a blast and a shock wave as the fire reached the A-10's aviation fuel and the ship exploded while still dropping.

In the distance, with his one good eye, he saw an aircraft. Then another. They were heading his way.

He felt his consciousness slipping.

He saw the first plane race past, narrowly missing him. He could see the silhouette of the pilot in the low light, a black helmet and shiny face visor staring back. His pain-addled brain understood in an instant from the aircraft's profile that it was a Russian Su-57.

But what stuck him the most as he fell into unconsciousness, wounded and spiraling downward in a damaged parachute, was the red eagle talon on the tail of the aircraft.

Then his world went black.

CHAPTER 61

Forty-five minutes after the utter destruction of *Red Blizzard 2*, the wreckage continued to burn and smolder in the darkness, a long ribbon of stationary twisted metal, fire, and death that wound around desolate snowy farmland outside the Polish city of Jelenia Góra.

Thick black smoke raged from windows and jagged holes in the aluminum-shelled train cars and rose into the early-morning sky, disappearing into impossibly low gray cloud cover.

A column of Russian armor had appeared at the site just minutes after the attack, and by now it had arrayed itself in a defensive perimeter around what remained of the long train, their medium and heavy weapons all pointed skyward, ready to unleash a hail of gunfire if the Yankee aircraft returned. Troops had spilled out of the train, many wounded, and they joined their arriving compatriots, sought aid, picked through the wreckage for dead comrades, and smoked cigarettes uneasily, their weapons at the ready.

The number of Russian vehicles increased even more when a company of Bumerangs arrived from the west. They pulled up to the command car and its back hatches began to open. A dozen armed men leapt from the vehicles and adopted their own security barrier; many more carrying shoulder-fired antiair weapons fanned out and peered into the night sky; and then a man emerged from the rear of one of the armored vehicles.

Colonel General Eduard Sabaneyev climbed out in a crouch but quickly rose to his full height in order to survey the wreckage. He wore his heavy boot-length coat and a thick fur hat. He was surrounded by Colonel Smirnov and several other subordinates.

He turned to Smirnov now. "Go back and check on the prisoners. Give the generals a chance to get out and stretch their legs, too."

Smirnov began walking back to a cluster of APCs farther back in the line.

Sabaneyev and the others had left the train just twenty-five minutes before the attack from the air. It had been at Smirnov's urging that Sabaneyev agreed to move himself, a portion of his command force, and the prisoners into armored command vehicles heading east, under the assumption the train's chances for survival declined every hour it remained in NATO territory.

Western GPS satellites were back online; by now surely the Poles had figured out antiair missiles were being fired from someplace other than the main column, and if they hadn't already known that the Russians were using a modified train to egress through their territory, they certainly would have figured this out during the twelve-hour delay caused by Dryagin getting his armor out of Wrocław and heading back in the right direction.

The general had depended on the train as long as he dared, then acquiesced to Smirnov's urging.

And not a moment too soon.

Sabaneyev was shaken, but he was hiding it. Since the beginning of the attack in Wrocław he'd been in a state of fury and near disbelief, but he'd let nothing show other than confidence tinged with anger that his men weren't executing tactically in accordance with the strategic decisions he made.

Wrocław had been devastating to his forces: the Poles destroyed fully 21 percent of his armor, killed or severely wounded 335 of his men, and, even more critically, significantly slowed his exodus from Poland, because the once-organized column was now just dozens of groups of armor vehicles fending for themselves in small packs, often traveling overland, and the speedy highway travel had turned to a slow crawl over frozen fields. His thousands of men and hundreds of vehicles were scattered all over south-central Poland now, with some units engaged in combat at this very moment, and all his forces under danger from the air.

This had allowed American and German forces to flank them north of Wrocław and forced Sabaneyev and his still shell-shocked troops to engage with the Abrams and Leopard 2 tanks the moment they escaped from the death trap of the city.

It was total war here in southern Poland now. The cease-fire that Moscow had set up to ensure Sabaneyev's safe return was nowhere in sight.

"A fucking disaster," he said to himself. He'd planned to be crossing the border to Belarus about now, but the way the fight was going, he suspected he wouldn't see the Bug River, which formed part of the border between the two nations, until late the next evening.

He still possessed sufficient armor and ammo to fight his way to Belarus, but the delay meant there would be more coordinated attacks from the enemy, because they would have more time to find and fix the Russian forces. Already he'd been told that Russian fighters were battling NATO aircraft trying to make their way into the area, and he had no doubt that NATO's response would only increase by daylight tomorrow.

He'd radioed Moscow and demanded that *Red Blizzard 3*, the support train, be rushed this way. It had all the air defenses, tanks, troops, fuel, and ammunition to more than make up for Sabaneyev's losses in the past half day, but it would be leaving Minsk only now, and it wouldn't arrive in the area for several hours.

His triumphant mission for Russia had turned into something less triumphant, but, he told himself, he'd soldier on, destroy every bit of NATO personnel and weaponry he encountered, and make his way across the Bug River and into Belarus in less than twenty-four hours.

He'd still return to Moscow a hero of the *rodina*.

He looked up after being lost in these thoughts and found Colonel Smirnov standing there.

"We must leave, General," Smirnov said. "Your command-and-control Bumerang will give you everything you need. Certainly not all the visibility you had on the train, but the radio access crucial to coordinate the withdrawal."

Sabaneyev knew this, of course. He said, "I want our forces pressing east in company- and platoon-sized elements. We won't have to face a large frontage on our route, only harassing attacks from the air, a few PLF hits, and the occasional strike from those damned tanks that won't leave us be. Better we don't give the enemy long highways full of targets. Keep individual movements small: back roads and overland when able. I want everyone to the border by midnight tomorrow, and pass the word that the only excuse I will entertain for failure will be death."

"Yes, sir." Smirnov hesitated a moment, then said, "To your command vehicle, sir?"

The good-looking Russian general took one last look at the detritus of his once-beautiful train, then turned on his heels and headed back to his APC.

Today was NATO's day. But Red Blizzard 3 *will meet us soon, and tomorrow will be Russia's day.*

CENTRAL POLAND
29 DECEMBER

Paulina looked the new arrivals over with the help of her flashlight. The two pickups that just ground to a halt in the gravel meant her squad had grown in size but not necessarily in experience. Every one of the eight new members in her tiny unit looked as though they had just left their day jobs. Three of them were not even in uniform. She'd get an excuse from each of them: they had lost them; they were at the cleaners when they were called up; they didn't fit.

Most of the eight appeared terrified. She'd been told they had come straight in from Warsaw, so none of them had seen the fighting that had been going on here for the last several days, but on their way they would have passed some of the destruction in the wake of the Russian column: burned-out civilian vehicles on the side of the road, corpses of militia or PDF soldiers in body bags or left contorted in death along the snowy fields that lined the highway . . . They surely saw the glowing fires in the distance to the west, and now that they were out of their vehicles and standing on the gravel road, they could make out the distant booming of tank rounds and bombs dropping and even the chatter of heavy machine guns.

Paulina had heard on the radio that the Russians were all over the place now, in small groups, dozens of cells, all heading generally east but in a seemingly uncoordinated fashion. Their disciplined column had been stirred up on leaving Wrocław, and they had clearly decided they'd go wide with their formation to keep NATO aircraft guessing their locations.

This confusion meant Paulina could expect action at any time, so she concentrated on getting these new people folded into her unit quickly.

One of them, a youngish man, pulled Paulina aside as he got off the truck. "Hey, Sergeant . . . or whatever you are. I don't think I'm supposed to be here. I had, like, a college deferment. So . . . can I leave?"

"No. Get in line with the others," Paulina said impatiently.

"But I can show you—"

"In line!" Paulina shouted, surprising the young man. He was more surprised when she lifted her AK-47 and, using her rifle's butt, pushed him over to the sloppy line of militia forming next to her more orderly group of four, all veterans of Wrocław.

One of the new militia members was a youngish girl. Her shtick seemed to be pretending to be bored; she constantly checked her cell phone even though Paulina knew the service was still out. Paulina could see through her façade and sensed she was actually scared out of her wits. There was also an older man, somewhere in his fifties, in the group, and he looked as lost as the kids around him.

She had already begun to worry over which of them would be able to take orders, which would be the most likely to stick around should they find themselves in another fight, and which were most likely to flee in panic and get shot in the process.

The girl, thought Paulina. Her bored façade was masking her true horror over her new lot in life.

Funny how I now no longer take the time to learn people's names, she noted to herself.

She decided it was time to get their minds onto the task and convince them they could survive this if they'd just follow her orders.

She spoke with intensity, the edges of anger creeping into her voice.

"If you fail to listen to me or fail to look out for the man or woman to your left and right, you are going to die the first time we make contact with the Russians."

No one spoke. Their fear and dread only grew.

I'm no officer, Paulina thought, but she kept talking, forcing some authority into her voice even though she hadn't yet even made shift leader at her coffee shop.

And probably never would now.

"I and the rest of the squad must be able to count on you. We will rely on one another, or your families will bury you like many others I've served with over the past week. Complaining will not help you. Running will get you killed. Only determination and a resolve to work together will keep you alive. If you do what I say, I promise you that I will look out for you. Do you understand?"

Everyone nodded.

Paulina took a call on her radio and received an order to follow one of the train lines to the east and stop at every switching station she could find. She didn't really know why, but earlier in the day she heard someone say they heard that the enemy had rolled a train straight into Germany, so she figured she would be looking for anybody working with the Russians along the line. It seemed like a routine and boring mission; the Russian forces were still to the west, and she was being sent east.

But she and her fifteen squad members climbed into three pickup trucks, their rifles on their shoulders, and headed out.

The highways and side roads were barren, almost eerily so. Everyone had been ordered indoors. Houses had even doused their lights or blacked out their windows in an almost World War II throwback to prevent Russian bombing. Paulina was pretty certain that was overkill, but she knew the citizens were terrified. Invasion from the east had been Poland's national nightmare for a very long time.

In the first two hours they made stops at three different train-switching stations. Each time Paulina had her small force climb out of the trucks and patrol around. She critiqued them on how they walked and held their rifles at every opportunity. Each stop was a chance to teach them the few things she'd learned, both from Lieutenant Nowicki, the PLF officer who'd trained her before dying that first morning of the war, and from Paulina's own combat against Russians since that time.

She taught them to drive without headlights; to stop a few hundred meters away from their destination and go on foot; to make regular security halts, take a knee, listen, and look.

She switched up the boys and men in the point position regularly. She'd learned that from a war movie her brother and dad liked, but it seemed to work and made sense. She stayed in the middle of their formation and kept everyone equidistant from one another.

It was nearly two a.m. now, and they walked a dark, snowy path along the tracks toward their fourth location of the night.

This station stood just south of a town called Łuków. The switching stations were all small brick buildings, more or less colocated with the train stations along the tracks. The switches themselves were outside the switching stations, next to the tracks. Pulling a lever would physically move the track, the rails sliding laterally to another track so an incoming train could be sent over to another line to continue its journey.

When they were still half a kilometer away from Łuków, bright lights turned on ahead of them, surprising everyone. Paulina whistled and the loose column stopped and knelt down. She moved to the front, took a knee, and pulled out her map.

This switching station building at Łuków was about one hundred meters southeast of the actual civilian train station. Unlike those at the other stations the squad had been to that morning, and unlike those at the blacked-out houses nearby, the lights of the entire rail yard in Łuków shone now. Green and yellow bulbs blinked by the track.

The Łuków rail yard looked open for business.

Paulina shifted her rifle up, putting the wooden stock at the ready against her shoulder and peering toward the flickering lights.

She said, "We're going to check it out. Everyone keep silent." Paulina waved for everyone to move out.

She found it surreal to be patrolling a Polish neighborhood, walking through gardens, across driveways, and on the quiet streets.

At one hundred meters from the switching station building, she halted her squad and pulled everyone in closer. She had them all kneel in a semi-circle down behind a billboard for a local ballroom dance studio.

Flickering light from the rail station and switching station made shadows dance eerily. "I'm going ahead to check it out. You stay here and I'll see what I can see."

Paulina crept off, moving forward a few steps at a time. At fifty meters from the switching station building she slipped into a private yard so she wouldn't be as exposed to anyone looking out windows. She continued through back gardens, nearing her objective, then knelt down behind a wooden fence.

Now she saw movement inside the switching station shack. The outline of a man in the bright lights.

Paulina edged closer, now crawling on her right hand and knees, still favoring her wounded left arm and shoulder as she struggled to push her rifle through the snowfall in front of her. She found a place under a bush, right at the edge of the station grounds, and focused again on the man. He was young, somewhere in his twenties, and physically fit. After a few moments she noticed he wore the cap of an employee of PKP, the main railway operator here in Poland.

Relieved, she stood up and started to walk over to the building to tell him to turn his lights off and go home.

But as she began around the side of the shack, still in the darkness, she stopped cold. Four men with rifles stood there in front of the shack, lit up by the red and green lights flashing above them. They looked off intently in the opposite direction from her, to the east; otherwise they would have seen her.

They wore military uniforms of some kind. She wondered if they were another militia unit who'd been sent here to check the station.

Frozen, she watched and listened carefully. In the crisp winter night sound traveled clearly. A radio beeped. One of the men took a handset off another man, who wore a backpack radio.

Her militia unit didn't have anything like that.

Then the man answered the radio, and she could clearly hear him speaking Russian.

"Gówno," she breathed out, finally exhaling.

The door to the shack opened and the man in the PKP hat stepped out. She could see the AK-47 in his hand now, and he began talking to the others.

She backed away slowly, her eyes locked on the men bathed in the green and red lights; then, when she was back in the neighbor's garden, she turned around and ran.

Back with her squad, Paulina motioned for all of them to come in tightly to her. They obeyed.

She spoke in a quiet whisper. "Do not make a sound." They all nodded. "Russians," she said, and everyone's eyes grew wide, visible even in the darkness. "Five of them." She paused. "We're going to kill them all," she announced. "We will crawl into the yard adjacent to the switching station. Then I will assign each of you a target."

One of the men asked, "What if . . . what if they surrender?"

"We are going to shoot them. There will be no one surrendering."

That sank in a moment.

The men and women looked terrified, but there were nods all around. "Good. I will assign multiple shooters for each target; that way we cannot fail."

She motioned for all of them to rise and put their rifles to their shoulders. She led the squad to the far side of the yard, and then they dispersed under the snow-covered bushes.

The Russians were still there, peering to the east.

Paulina crawled to each person, verifying their target and making sure their safeties were off on their AKs. Four of the Russians would be targeted by three militia members apiece, and her two remaining "veterans" would shoot the fifth man.

Then, like the chief executioner of a firing squad, she sat up on her haunches, lifted her own weapon, and yelled, "Fire!"

Fourteen rifle shots rang out almost as one. Paulina watched five men fall, knocked back by the force of multiple impacts. The men and women kept shooting till all the Russians lay still.

"Reload," she said, and looked down the rail yard toward the station, half expecting more enemy to materialize out of the darkness or to hear the horrifying sound of the Russian machine gun or 30mm cannon she had learned to dread.

After a time she stood and motioned for the rest to follow. She walked forward, her weapon scanning in front of her, until she made it up to the dead men in front of the track. She kicked them all, checking for any signs of life.

There were none.

She went inside the shack now, looked over the dead man there, then came back outside.

She waved the rest forward, then ordered everyone to stay alert.

"What were they doing?" asked one of the new members of her squad.

"Waiting for something, I guess."

"They were here at the switching station. Do you suppose they were going to switch the tracks?"

Paulina looked at the waterproof panel outside the shack. It looked like the cover of the panel had been pried off. On it were five thick buttons. Three were unlit, black, but the other two were red and green, obviously corresponding to the lights above the station.

"Maybe," she said, "but there has been no rail traffic. I would say if they wanted to switch the track, they would have already done it. Why wait?"

Paulina rifled through the men's packs. Food, civilian clothing, ammunition, a few maps and radio booklets. In the red and green light Paulina went through it all. None of it made much sense to her.

Then she felt the rumble in her knees on the cold ground. Vibrations growing by the second.

"A train is coming from the east," she said.

She stood back up and looked at the blinking lights next to the station. *If green is go and red is stop, maybe we just switch the order,* she thought, looking up at the two solid red and two blinking green lights.

She wondered if reversing whatever the Russians had likely done would be better than keeping things as they were.

"Hey," said one of the new members. "Whatever we're doin', we have to do it and get out of here."

The sounds of the train were clearly audible now. It seemed huge and fast, and it was obviously running without lights.

She said, "Screw it. I'm switching this thing."

She pressed the green button, which began flashing yellow. She pressed the red button next; it, too, flashed yellow.

Suddenly she heard a loud whir and a clank a few meters down the rail yard. She watched the tracks move to their new alignment and slam into place.

The train closed at high speed.

"Everyone off the tracks! Grab the Russians and drag them away. Then get into the hedges or over here with me inside the switching shack." They did as instructed, and Paulina and the older man propped one of the dead Russians up against the wall of the shack, then hefted him, dropping him in the switch master's stool.

The train appeared in the station lights, barreling through at over one hundred kilometers an hour. The onrushing wave of cold air became a wall of wind just as Paulina shut the small metal door to the shack. The three militia members in there with her peered out the window as the train rushed by. Paulina watched, trying to count the cars. She gave up after forty. Heavy machinery, engineering equipment, tanks, armored personnel, rows and rows of troop cars. She could even make out the faces of

Russian soldiers in the windows. There were heavy antiaircraft machine guns on each car, the crew manning them bundled for the frigid temperatures and staring out into the night.

When the train was gone, Paulina and the others with her waited a few more moments, then emerged from the shack. The others came over from their hiding positions adjacent to the tracks and huddled together, all looking to Paulina for direction.

"Prepare to load back up. We will report this but continue our mission."

"Do we know where they are going now?"

"No," Paulina answered. "But if we're lucky, neither do they."

The young, waifish girl spoke up now. "Sergeant, is it okay if we take the dead guys' guns?"

Paulina smiled. This girl was getting the hang of it. "Hell yes, it is. They are nice ones."

CHAPTER 62

Lieutenant Colonel Connolly was just getting up from his bunk to go for a run aboard the big flat deck's exercise area, when a call came over the USS *Boxer*'s loudspeaker system. It was 0500, but still he heard the bosun's shrill whistle call, and then an announcement. "Lieutenant Colonel Connolly to combat, Lieutenant Colonel Connolly to combat."

It was always a little embarrassing being called across the entire ship. With a complement of over 900 sailors and an additional 2,000 embarked Marines, the USS *Boxer* was a living city and the centerpiece for the two Marine Expeditionary Units under Colonel Caster. A small aircraft carrier, it carried most of the Marines' all-weather AV-8 Harriers, its Cobra attack helicopters, the heavy-lift helicopters, and the light UH-1 Hueys, which had been in service with the Marines since before the Vietnam War.

Connolly put on his remaining sock and tennis shoes and stepped out of his stateroom. He'd been stuffed into a room with the regimental operations officer, a fellow lieutenant colonel friend of his whom he'd been glad to bunk with, or at least he was until he realized the man was going to snore all fucking night.

This, and the fact his body clock had been ravaged by flying around the world, accounted for Connolly's rough early start on the day.

He hustled into the combat information center and looked around. "Someone looking for me?"

"Yes, sir," said one of the Navy watch operators. "There's a call for you from the Vice Chairman of the Joint Chiefs' office on the secure satellite comms." He pointed to a bank of three satellite phones, one with a green light. Familiar with the setup, he sat at the radio terminal and checked his watch. All the eyes in "combat" watched him with curiosity.

"This is Lieutenant Colonel Connolly."

"Good to hear your voice, boss." It was Griggs.

"Hey, Bob. Likewise. Things are heating up out here, and by that I mean the temp is over ninety and we're about to fight the Russians."

"I picked up on the double entendre without the explanation, sir. Your jokes still suck."

Connolly said, "You woke up half the *Boxer* with your call direct to the ship. Let's legitimate the expensive call on the taxpayers' dime with something more than shit talking."

"I have some more for you on the Russians. French intelligence, the Direction Générale de la Sécurité Extérieure, has a man on the ground in Djibouti. He saw and cataloged all the Russian forces as they departed the port. He sent a pretty good update on the composition of the enemy forces."

"Just pretty good?"

"Yeah. Trouble is, his transmission back to their headquarters was cut short. They aren't sure what happened, but it seems he may have been compromised."

"Copy. Dangerous work."

"Here's the gist of it. It's a full brigade. Like, the equivalent of a Soviet-era brigade. Plenty of infantry, antiair, and a shit ton of artillery. I'll send over the partial report we got from the French."

"Tanks?"

"The *Virginia*-class sub that squeaked into the harbor wiped out two of the three refuelers. The Pentagon estimates they lost over 145,000 barrels. Right now their tanks are under guard by Russian forces just outside of Djibouti City. We think they just left them behind because they didn't have the gas."

Connolly whistled. "Damn, leave it to the Navy to take out more tanks in this conflict than the Army and Marine Corps combined."

"We figure they are trying to get more fuel sent in somehow. The Russians didn't bring them all the way here just to have all their tankers bask in the sun on the beach, and they have to figure that once they take the mine, they'll have to hold it by force. Maybe the Kremlin will make a deal with some other African nation to provide the fuel, or else they'll just take it. But that will take some time."

"How long?"

"Best guesstimate from up here is only about five days to refuel and reach you."

"Wonderful. So if we don't figure out how to counteract the advancing Russian force and build up defenses in the mine in five days, we'll be facing the Russian reinforcements in the form of heavy armor?"

"Yep, and we're talking a *lot* of armor. A battalion of tanks. And that's just part of it. Fronting the brigade moving south toward Kenya now is a Russian special forces unit led by a guy named Colonel Yuri Borbikov. All sorts of stories about this joker, and it turns out he has a history at the mine. He was the Spetsnaz commander at Mrima Hill when Moscow sent the order to surrender the mine three and a half years ago. He walked out of there with his tail between his legs, but now apparently he's heading back with a vengeance.

"I'm sending his digital dossier to your SIPR computer now. Got some tidbits from Melanopolis. They were able to dig up a lot of material on this guy from intel sources in Moscow. Connecting the dots . . . looks like this is the bastard who masterminded this whole operation, from the blitzkrieg across Europe to the capture of the mines."

"Bob, he hasn't captured the mines yet."

"Uh . . . that's right, and you won't let him, will you, boss?"

Connolly sighed. "Things would be better if AFRICOM was still up and running the show. There's a lot of confusion down here. Without that headquarters, we're kind of running blind. Also, all the preexisting contacts with the countries we need to work through are null and void. The word I'm getting about the Kenyan government in Nairobi is they sound ready to let the Russians have the mine because they want a good relationship with whoever's there. Guess they figure if you can't beat 'em, join 'em.'"

Griggs said, "We're hearing the same thing at the Pentagon. Everyone in Africa remembers us stepping on our crank in Somalia a while back. Shades of *Black Hawk Down* and all that. Kenya doesn't trust America to pull this off, so they're betting on the inevitable and staying out of the fight."

Connolly blew out another sigh. "Any progress back there?"

"Department of State is trying their best. They counted on AFRICOM as well when it came to liaising with African nations. Most of the military attachés didn't reside in those countries; they just went down for negotiations when necessary. I guess that was the whole reason for having AFRICOM up in Europe. Everyone always assumed EUCOM was the more important of the two missions. No one predicted that colocating the two headquarters endangered the AFRICOM mission as much as the EUCOM mission. I think it's going to take months before we have leadership cobbled together. In the meantime, Colonel Caster down there on the *Boxer* is in charge of the whole region's military affairs on behalf of the United States."

"I'll be sure to tell him."

"Just be careful you don't get squashed like the little road bumps you are on the strategic maps up here at the Pentagon."

Connolly chuckled. "Any more good news?"

"Let's see . . . Oh, yeah, Julie says you have to take the garbage out for a year once you get back."

"*What?*"

"Had dinner at your house last night. Man, you never told me about Julie's meat loaf. Frickin' heaven on a plate, boss."

"*Seriously?* You're eating at my house?"

"Yep, and taking Jack to baseball practice tonight."

"Well . . . thanks for that."

"You bet. Just get back home in one piece, okay, boss?"

"I'll do my best. Gotta run. We're landing in three hours."

"Kick ass, Marine," Griggs said, and Connolly smiled.

NORTHERN ETHIOPIA
29 DECEMBER

Caporal Konstantine crept up to his captain's position on the hill. His French special forces three-color, or "trico," desert camouflage was soaked with the sweat of exertion in the African heat, which made the red Ethiopian dust cake to his uniform like a thin layer of mud. All the Dragoons' locally acquired vehicles were parked down below the small, sandy hill in a line of heavy shrubs off the road, masking them from view from the north. Konstantine glanced down at the men, busy at their work cutting foliage for camouflage and setting up temporary barricades on the road.

As he made it to the top, he could see Apollo looking through his binoculars, fixated on Route 51. A small dust cloud had appeared in the morning light, but it looked like it came from a group of vehicles, just a few Bongo trucks. Bongo was actually a brand name for a vehicle manufactured by both Mazda and Kia. Light-duty trucks, they were ubiquitous in Africa as the best means to transport everything from people to khat, and they were often adorned with lace or colorful fabric and painted in bright colors.

Apollo put the binos down on the open flak jacket he was using to keep the dust off his gear. His FN SCAR-L carbine lay in front of him next to his body armor, which he'd taken off to remain low. The ejection port of his weapon was positioned up and out of the sand and dirt.

Konstantine said, "Sir, I have good news. We have comms back up."

"*Bon*, I could use some." Apollo pulled the binos up to his eyes again. Still no telltale columns of red in the sky. He knew a mechanized column would throw up a hell of a lot of dust. But he only saw the two covered Bongos making their way toward his position. He wasn't especially concerned; he'd seen several similar vehicles in the last half hour, mainly taking things to and from the market.

Apollo focused on the two Bongos. "Tell Sergent-Chef Dariel to stop those trucks. They might have some intel on the Russians' location."

"Yes, sir." Caporal Konstantine scrambled back down the scraggly hill toward the roadblock, positioned behind the hill so the vehicles approaching from the north could not see it.

Apollo looked to the distance again, well beyond the trucks and off toward the horizon. A change in hue in the low sky there sparked his interest. It wasn't more than a haze, slightly reddish brown, but he'd worked reconnaissance for years and his instincts told him this meant a large group of vehicles was on the horizon.

"Hey, Konstantine!" he yelled down, hoping to stop the *caporal* before he got too far. Hearing nothing, he took one last long look at the cloud, then peeled his eyes away from the eyecups and looked back down the hill.

The two trucks had made the turn, and now they drivers saw the barricade of oil drums blocking their path. They slowed and stopped.

Three Dragoons approached the simple vehicle barricade they'd constructed. Two stood watch from about fifteen meters away as the other continued forward.

Apollo was starting to turn away to redirect his attention back to the haze in the distance when he heard the loud and unmistakable sound of Kalashnikov fire.

He turned back to see smoking, firing gun barrels jutting from windows of both small trucks. The three Dragoons in the road fell immediately, but two of them were able to scramble back to a ditch full of dry brush on the near side of the road.

The third man had been closest to the truck and now he lay motionless in the dirt.

Fuck, thought Apollo. He realized this was a Spetsnaz unit conducting forward reconnaissance.

He kicked his legs around, braced his weapon on his body armor lying in the sand, and pointed the muzzle to the southwest, facing the action. He extended the bipod on the front of the SCAR and took a high-profile prone aiming position. Through his six-power scope he could see the Russians clambering out the opposite-side doors, likely just as surprised by Apollo's men as the Dragoons had been by the Russians.

The captain squeezed the trigger. The sharp report wasn't enough to make him take his eyes off the target. He could see where the round hit, as dust jumped off the top of the vehicle.

He squeezed off another shot.

This time he fired through the roof near the back door. He was rewarded by seeing a man fall over from behind the vehicle, his rifle tumbling down with him.

Men began bailing out of the far sides of both trucks.

Apollo pulled his rifle to the right, focusing on the second vehicle. Its driver was apparently still alive, and he jammed the truck into reverse. As he did so, four Russians who were using the truck for cover were exposed. They turned and ran alongside the vehicle, firing wildly at the troops by the vehicles next to the sandy hill.

Apollo dumped rounds at the moving truck, this time hitting the driver's window. The Russians behind it continued shooting through the windows and over the hood. A heavy staccato of gunfire continued between the French and Russians.

Apollo remained undetected for now, above the fray. He used this to his advantage as the Russians focused on Dariel and the men down by the French vehicles.

The captain lined up another shot into the driver's window of the rear vehicle.

Bang.

The Bongo truck veered backward off the road and came to rest 120 meters away from Apollo's perch.

The Russians behind the rear truck could tell they were getting hit from a different angle at the same time that one of the surviving Spetsnaz soldiers behind the first vehicle noticed the shooter on top of the hill. He dumped rounds from his AK-47 at Apollo.

Apollo shifted his aim to fire at the man.

Bullets whizzed over his head now and more impacted the dirt in front of him, kicking dust up into his riflescope. He took a breath and then exhaled slowly, counting silently, and on three he squeezed the trigger. The Russian by the front truck dropped, a dark red stain expanding on the white sand beneath him.

By now all the Russians were wise to Apollo's sniping from the hilltop and had taken up good concealment next to the engines of both vehicles and in a shallow ditch on the far side of the road. From his position Apollo tried to fire down into the ditch, but the angle wasn't right and the surviving Russians maintained their cover.

At the bottom of the hill, Sergent-Chef Dariel began ordering his men to slowly close in, using fire, and maneuver. Some continued shooting while a few bounded forward and took prone positions in the dirt. The French might not have picked the time of the attack, but they had carefully chosen the terrain to offer at least a small advantage. The Russians, even using their vehicles for cover, were on the downslope and stuck by the dual-laned dirt road with no natural cover available save for the runoff ditch.

A loud *pop* followed by a long *fizz* sound, along with a trail of white smoke that shot just over the heads of his men to his left, confirmed to Apollo the presence of an RPG.

Although they were outmatched by French manpower and firepower, these elite Russian soldiers were not going down without a fight.

Apollo increased his rate of fire. His men had by now brought the machine guns into the fight, and he knew this would keep the enemies' heads down.

It was unlikely these Spetsnaz men had a handheld radio that could effectively reach the main Russian column, which Apollo assessed would now be about twenty kilometers north and approaching fast. The telltale plume of dust he'd seen on the horizon and the presence of the special forces troops in his midst told him they were operating in a pretty standard Russian method: Spetsnaz out front scouting the way. They'd have light-armored mechanized forces next, then the heavy stuff. Tanks if they had them, or armored personnel carriers if not.

He wanted to quickly eliminate this small force in front of him, because he and his own unit wouldn't stand a chance against the light-mech forces that were almost certain to come next.

Apollo made a quick calculation in his head. If the Russians had not yet made solid radio contact, and his observations on their commanders making haste were accurate, they'd be driving pretty much full bore. On these roads that probably equated to fifty or sixty kilometers per hour, and at that rate and distance they'd be here in twenty minutes. There was no time to trade shots carefully, or very soon he and his men would be overrun by hundreds and then thousands of Russians. Also, if they didn't keep these surviving Spetsnaz men fully occupied, the Russians would be able to raise their antenna and radio a warning.

He had to somehow inform Sergent-Chef Dariel that they needed to assault the Russians in their cover, but he was nearly seventy-five meters to the east of the rest of his unit.

He decided he wouldn't tell him what he wanted to do; he would show them. If Apollo attempted to attack all the way into the Russians, his men would understand.

Surely they wouldn't let him go it alone.

He hoped.

Apollo climbed up to his knees, fully exposed to the enemy. He pulled his magazine out of his carbine and hefted it. *No more than ten rounds left,* he thought. He tossed the magazine into his drop pouch and slapped a fresh one into the magazine well. There was already a round in the chamber, so he just stood, sighted back in, and advanced down the hill in a crouch. His men kept their heavy fire up, so he decided to hold his own fire to try to flank the enemy and surprise them from the east.

In moments he was less than thirty meters from the rear truck and a little farther away from the ditch. From his position he could just barely see an AK-47 muzzle sticking out from the depression, facing in his direction. A single Russian was covering the rear flank.

These guys are no fools, he thought. Placing a man to cover the back was smart. A lesser force would have had everyone tucked in behind the trucks and focused on the French direct assault and machine guns.

If Apollo could just cover the distance, he might get the jump on this soldier, who had clearly not yet seen him.

He kept his rifle's scope centered on the nearest threat and waited for another long burst of machine-gun fire from his Dragoons. Once it came, he took off at a full sprint. Dariel and the men must have noticed him, because they all increased their volume of fire on the trucks.

Thirty meters.

Twenty.

Ten.

The Russian rear guard must have known the heavier volume meant something and he chanced a peek over the lip of the ditch. Apollo saw the AK's barrel rising and pivoting; he kept up his sprint but pulled his SCAR to his cheek. Forgoing his scope, he looked directly down the barrel. He put his finger on the trigger and continued to close the distance. At five meters Apollo could see the man coming up to his knees and the French captain let fly a volley from his carbine. A pull of the trigger on burst mode.

The carbine jerked up three times and Apollo tried to time the fire with his sprint.

Three rounds caught the Russian in the chest. The Spetsnaz soldier, unlike Apollo, wore body armor. Still, the impact forced the man off his feet and down onto his back. The AK flew up, but he was disciplined enough not to let go.

Apollo leapt into the ditch, stepped on top of the man's chest with one booted foot, pointed his SCAR in the man's exposed face, and pulled the trigger once more. The carbine was still in burst mode, and three rounds exploded from the muzzle, blasting the man's head into red pulp.

Apollo continued the advance; he was now behind the enemy's truck. As he did so, the gunfire from his men stopped abruptly.

He found four Russians alive behind each vehicle. Apollo dropped the nearly expended magazine and put in a fresh one. Using the lip of the ditch for a firing position, he pumped several rounds rapidly into the closest four enemy, aiming for their heads and upper torsos so he didn't waste rounds banging their armor. It was dirty business, but part of combat involved identifying and exploiting an enemy's weakness.

All four men spun and died where they stood.

The four men behind the lead truck turned to the exchange of frantic gunfire. They saw Apollo moving out of the ditch and toward the cover of the rear vehicle and then opened fire. A hail of incoming 7.62mm rounds blasted the side of the truck. Apollo dove to the ground and rolled behind the Bongo to avoid the incoming fire. About half the rounds penetrated the thin side of the truck above Apollo's head, driving him down tighter into the dirt just behind the vehicle.

The tires on both sides of the truck were blasted apart and the vehicle now rested on its rims, with inches of clearance from the ground. Apollo leaned under the truck, trying to get an angle on the Russians, but he couldn't see a thing.

Still, he emptied the rest of his magazine under the vehicle, hoping to get lucky.

He reached to his chest and realized his load-bearing vest with the rest of his ammo, along with his body armor, was back up on the hill.

"Merde."

Remembering the half-empty magazine in his drop pouch, he rolled slightly in the dirt to access it. He fished it out, ejected the spent mag, and loaded the partial into his SCAR.

It wasn't going to be enough. He could hear the Russians shouting to one another, which to him meant they were coming up with a plan on how to deal with him. He was caught behind a thin truck, with no body armor, less than half a magazine left in his carbine, and a brigade of armored Russians bearing down on him.

Maybe fifteen minutes until the Russian armored reconnaissance arrives, he thought.

"Merde," he said again softly, with his mouth pressed into the sandy red dirt.

Rounds cracked overhead and clanked through the thin skin of the Bongo as the Russians fired in his direction. Pieces of shrapnel and bullet fragments flew like a swarm of bees around him. He felt an impact and then a sting in his neck and two more in his upper back. His heavily muscled frame tightened as the rounds continued to penetrate the truck.

This is it, he thought. Apollo prepared to fire his last few rounds at the first asshole who rounded the rear of the truck.

"Mon capitaine!" came the familiar French voice of Sergent-Chef Dariel, shouting from Apollo's left, twenty or thirty meters away at least. *"Dans trois secondes, sortez en tirant!"* ("In three seconds, come out shooting!") Dariel was gambling none of the Russians spoke French, and this meant Apollo was now making the same gamble.

"D'accord!" ("Okay!") he yelled, then began counting to three.

"Un . . .

"Deux . . .

"Trois!" Apollo rolled right, out from behind the truck, tucked the carbine against his cheek, and let loose at the Russians, who were bounding from the front truck to the rear.

Two of them were just a few meters away, closer than he had anticipated, but a barrage of fire over and through the vehicle from Dariel and his squad caused the Russians to pivot in that direction.

Trying to use only one round per Russian, Apollo steadied for each rapid squeeze of the trigger.

Bang, bang, click. His magazine ran dry.

But there were two more threats, just ahead and swiveling to engage him now.

From his left a half dozen of his boys came around in front of the rear truck, guns blazing, spinning the last two Russians to the sand and raking the men Apollo shot with dozens more rounds, sending red mist and chunks of flesh spraying.

Apollo was on his stomach now, and when he saw the threats eliminated, he dropped his head onto the buttstock of his FN SCAR-L and let out a long sigh.

Sergent-Chef Dariel stepped up behind him and kicked him gently with his boot. *"Mon capitaine,* are you dead?"

Apollo let out a laugh as he slowly climbed up to his feet. "No, but thanks for 'corpse checking' me before you asked."

Dariel chuckled, too, then said with a wry smile, *"Mon capitaine,* next time you charge, I request you let me know, and at least have the courtesy to put your body armor on as an example to the young men. You know they look up to you for guidance."

"Trust me, I'll put on my body armor and I won't take it off till I'm back home on my sofa watching football."

Konstantine came up to the scene now and kicked a couple of dead Spetsnaz men. "*Capitaine* Rambo. That was an interesting tactic."

"Yeah . . . I don't recommend it," Apollo replied, checking over his carbine.

"Do you think they were able to transmit to the main column?"

"Not sure," Apollo said, taking a fresh SCAR magazine from the young corporal and feeding it into his weapon. "But we're not sticking around to find out. It's time to run like hell."

"Run where, *mon capitaine*?"

"South. We're going to stay ahead of these forward units, and harass them again."

CHAPTER 63

The four massive Vericor Power Systems ETF40B gas turbines shrieked as they came alive on the landing craft in the *Boxer*'s well deck. Called an LCAC, it was a flat hovercraft that rode the waves to the beach on a cushion of air. They had already made two trips ashore and back, dropping off a platoon of four tanks and an infantry company—nearly 140 Marines.

Pretty solid work, thought Connolly as he looked at the long line of Marines filing down the *Boxer*'s gangway behind him as another company prepared to go ashore along with the vehicle crewmen for four light-armored vehicles. All the Marines wore eighty-pound rucksacks and body armor and each carried either a rifle, a carbine, or a machine gun. The clatter of their boots was drowned out as the LCAC's turbines became the only noise anyone could hear. As with jet engines, the blast of hot exhaust from the adjustable propulsion systems filled the air, knocking any unwary Marine back a step.

The ship's crew chief beckoned Connolly and his small contingent of 5th Marines regimental headquarters personnel to board the craft. The wood planks of the *Boxer*'s well deck were slippery with seawater from the LCAC's second return from the beach, as well as with oil and grease. Connolly had spent plenty of time aboard U.S. Navy amphibs and was able to keep his feet as he moved along, but he and the men climbing aboard all watched as two headquarters guys slipped and fell, skidding toward the deck of the landing craft with the rolling of the ship, landing in a heap next to a cluster of nineteen- and twenty-year-old radio operators.

Connolly was extra careful, because given the laughs and catcalls the young men gave to the two junior officers who fell in front of him, he gathered these Marines would just *love* to see a lieutenant colonel take a spill, too.

On board the hovercraft he made his way past the two Humvees and over to the LAVs. The light-armored vehicle was the smaller and faster Marine equivalent of a Russian BTR or Bumerang. It had eight wheels, and the LAV-25s on the deck each had a 25mm cannon and carried six scouts in back trained in battlefield reconnaissance.

Since Connolly was to ride near Colonel Caster as one of the staff, he'd be in a LAV-C2, the command-and-control variant. These vehicles were beefed up with a ton of communications equipment: they had satellite and three types of radio bands necessary to speak to the rest of the task force, along with long-range communication back to the Navy ships or to USMC aircraft overhead, and computer assets tied into the NATO global communications grid to provide them with the basic satellite uplink with classified Internet.

Connolly found his ride, attached his pack on the side of the vehicle with a heavy steel shackle, and climbed aboard. He pushed past all the gear and tackle inside and took his seat.

The back steel hatches closed and the LCAC's engine shrieked to an even louder pitch. He picked up his crew helmet, pulled the built-in earphones over his ears, and settled in for the short trip to shore.

Exhaust blasted through every crack in the hatches of the LAV. There was no way to avoid the fumes, and soon everyone inside fought nausea.

After ten minutes the massive hovercraft began rising and falling dramatically, presumably as it rode the large waves of the shoal waters. Confirming this assumption, blasts of sand mixed with sea air came blowing through Connolly's LAV as the landing craft crossed from the surf zone and onto Bakhresa Beach, just south of the Dar es Salaam port facility.

There was a *whoosh* and one last great cloud of sand inside the LAV, and then the LCAC came to a halt.

Connolly stuck his head up and out of the hatch. Bright light off the sandy beach filled his vision. Just beyond the yellow sand he saw thick palm trees, and farther inland he could make out the edge of Dar es Salaam's urban sprawl.

The beach was already packed with Marine Corps equipment and men. A large staging area contained row upon row of seven-ton trucks and aluminum pallets of supplies.

The back hatch of the LAV opened and one of the sergeants motioned him off. "Sir, you need to head over there and grab your supplies."

Connolly lined up with the other Marines and picked up his MREs, enough water to fill his CamelBak, and six boxes of 5.56mm ammunition. He put it all in his pack, except for the ammo, which he took back to the LAV and loaded into his M4 carbine magazines.

Connolly watched the sergeants in the vehicle with him as they looked over their new windfall in ammunition, cataloging it like it was Halloween candy. AT-4 anti-tank rockets, M72 LAW light anti-tank rockets, Mk 153 SMAW bunker-busting rockets, 40mm under-rifle grenades, M67 hand grenades, and lots and lots of machine-gun ammo.

A Marine sergeant handed Connolly three grenades. Connolly took them and stuffed them in his pouch.

"You need a refresher course on how to make it go *boom*, sir?"

Connolly chuckled. "I know how to throw a grenade, Devil Dog."

"Check, sir. Figured you'd been behind a desk for a while."

Connolly sighed. It wasn't as if he'd never been teased by the smart-alecky and headstrong sergeants the Marine Corps was famous for, but the man's comment was a little too close to the truth these days.

"What's your name again, Marine?"

"Casillas, sir. Sergeant Casillas."

"All right, Casillas, let's make a deal. If I have to throw a grenade, you promise to lay down a really heavy base of fire so I get a good toss and don't catch a round through the running lights. Deal?"

"Sir, if you finally get me and the boys into a firefight like that, you won't have to ask. I'll have the hammer down so hard, the only thing you'll have to worry about is the next paper cut you'll get back in your office."

Connolly laughed. "Damn, Casillas, you got a thing for officers?"

"No, sir, I just know who does the real work in the regiment."

Marine sergeants had a way of squaring up to their bosses and getting away with it. They obeyed every legal order down to the letter; it was just their way of testing their bosses to see if they could hack it, assessing their leaders for any possible weakness.

Connolly watched a forklift shimmy down the gangplank, its operator driving a pallet over to a pool of waiting vehicles. On the side of the box was stenciled block lettering reading:

**AMMUNITION FOR CANNON
WITH EXPLOSIVE PROJECTILES.
M791, 25MM, APFSDS-T
3,000 CARTRIDGES**

-

**WARNING: THIS BOX CONTAINS
NOVEMBER ACCOUNT
LFORM AMMUNITION
FOR NATIONAL CONTINGENCIES ONLY**

Connolly had put the word up the Pentagon, and they'd authorized the regiment to break into the LFORM. This was short for "landing force operational reserve material," a war stock for the Marines on board in the bottom of the naval amphibious ship's holds that no one was allowed to touch without approval from the secretary of defense. There was definitely a "Break glass in case of war" aura around this ammunition. To the officers of the regiment, Connolly had already paid his dues when he placed a call back to the Pentagon to shorten the approval chain to use the ammo and equipment.

Now he just needed to earn the respect of the men.

Connolly and the rest of the 5th Marines began rolling to the north. He, Lieutenant Colonel McHale, and a unit of Force Recon would race ahead of the slower-moving equipment and meet the Russians in combat.

These Marines were loaded for bear and, for the first time in any of their lives, they were up against the Russian bear.

**SOUTHEASTERN POLAND
29 DECEMBER**

Colonel General Eduard Sabaneyev stood outside in the snow, next to the engine of his Bumerang command-and-control vehicle to keep him warm.

Standing with him was Colonel Danilo Dryagin, his assault force commander. The two men had not seen each other since before the raid into Western Europe began four days earlier, but in all the chaos of the last day the colonel and the general found themselves close enough to each other's locations to arrange a face-to-face meeting.

It was midmorning now, the temp was below freezing, and it looked like the low gray clouds would drop sleet or snow at any moment.

"This column of yours is a fucking *mess*, Dryagin," said the general.

"Admittedly, sir. My units exited the urban center of Wrocław via fourteen different routes. Some of them drove right into PLF dug in along the highway, and this split them into even more groups. I fully agree with your orders to keep the convoy split up to reduce NATO's ability to fix us to one position, but hundreds of vehicles separated by a hundred kilometers means that coordinating an effective response to each attack has become . . . a challenge."

"What percentage of the original attacking force has been eliminated?"

"Forty-four percent is the latest estimation from my XO. But it is a fluid battle space, as you clearly know."

Sabaneyev and the company of vehicles surrounding him had been pounded by jets just an hour earlier. None of the armor had been destroyed, but some troops riding on the hull of a T-14 had been killed and a scout car was damaged and left behind along with the wounded troops riding in it.

Sabaneyev replied with sarcasm. "Yes . . . I have noticed that our enemy continues to engage."

Dryagin said, "Did you receive an update about what happened to *Red Blizzard 3*?"

The general rubbed the back of his neck, a show of stress, but only for a moment, and only in front of Dryagin.

"Fucking Borbikov's hot-shit Spetsnaz boys were supposed to send the train to the southwest. Instead, the tracks never got switched, so it rolled on to the northwest. It traveled forty kilometers before they realized what happened. Forty kilometers closer to Warsaw. They tried to stop, to reverse, and to go back to the switching station, but in that time Polish tanks arrived and destroyed the train."

Dryagin nodded slowly without revealing emotion to his general. "We are growing short on munitions. We had counted on the cargo train delivering us supplies, troops, and armor, and we had counted on being together to receive and disseminate them. As it is now, Comrade General, we are like sixty or seventy roving bands of marauders, plus however many Spetsnaz teams Borbikov has kept in theater. It makes things more difficult from a logistical standpoint."

The general said, "So we press on. Hard. No stopping now. Not even to lick our wounds. The Poles might be arrayed at the border in numbers to threaten small groups of our vehicles. They might not know where we all are right now, but they certainly know where we are all going. Tighten everyone up and we'll punch through the border together. Mow down everything in your path. No remorse, Colonel. Do you understand? No remorse!"

Dryagin straightened up and nodded. "*Da*, Comrade General, but that means the forward units will have to pause for the rear elements to catch up. Could be a delay of another twenty-four hours."

Sabaneyev was surprised by this. "That long?"

"There is fighting to the west. Our forces there have to push through or go around. This will take time."

Sabaneyev looked around. "This forest is decent protection. We have plenty of antiair to keep the enemy aircraft reticent about mounting any large-scale attack. We will stay in the woods and have our scouts keeping an eye out for those American tanks that have been bedeviling us for days. When we get our force together, we'll continue."

Sabaneyev thought about being stuck yet even longer in Poland, and anger welled inside him. "I want air defense on full alert at all times. Tell your men."

"Of course, Comrade General."

RADOM, POLAND
29 DECEMBER

Captain Raymond "Shank" Vance rubbed the cast on his left hand and thought about ripping it off to scratch the maddening itch that had been growing by the hour. But the dressings were tight and there was no way he could slide a finger through to get to the source of the discomfort.

The one time he had been able to catch his reflection in a window on the way to the hospital, he saw his left eye swollen shut and the left side of his face pockmarked by three deep lacerations and innumerable smaller cuts from canopy glass turned to shrapnel by an Su-57's cannon.

His left hand was in the worst shape. It was broken and the doctors thought a fragment of a cannon round must have pierced it completely, but when they took him into surgery to remove shrapnel and set the bones, the surgeon said a visual inspection of the nerves around the damaged areas made him optimistic that Shank would regain full use of the hand.

For the time being, however, it hurt like hell.

His head ached behind his swollen eye now, but it wasn't as bad as the itching or the pain in his hand.

He could tell he was receiving special treatment here at this aid station set up by the Territorial Defense Force. Even with the Polish Land Forces moving out of the area a couple hours earlier, he continued to receive good medical care from doctors working with the militia. He didn't speak a word of Polish, but enough of them spoke English to make things work. Most referred to him simply as "Mr. Pilot," which he didn't mind.

He picked up from some of their discussions around him that the militia had watched as he destroyed the Russian train, only to see him get shot down by a Russian Sukhoi on his egress. A few dirty, war-ragged militia members, looking more like World War II anti-Nazi partisans than any modern-day military force, had come to the clinic to meet him in person. Some of the older Poles' English was nonexistent, but they seemed happy to just pat him on the head and offer him sips of vodka or some other, unusual-smelling liquor.

Shank was lying alone with his thoughts now, his mind addled by painkillers and booze but still wondering about the fate of Nooner and the rest of the pilots in his squadron, when a young girl with dirty-blond hair stepped into the room full of wounded men on hospital beds. She wore a militia uniform with mud-caked knees, an AK-47 over her shoulder and a black knit cap on her head. Her face was smudged with smoke but pink from the cold and her youth.

Shank thought she looked both like a kid who might pour him a latte at Starbucks and also like a battle-hardened soldier.

Shank tracked her as she looked around at the two dozen or so patients, then stepped over to a middle-aged man with his foot in a cast suspended over his bed. She talked to him a moment, rubbing a cast on her left fore-arm as she did so. She then scanned the room until, surprisingly to Shank, she locked eyes with him. She walked to him, picking her way around the other wounded and moaning men lying on mattresses, bed frames, cots, chairs, and any other furniture the Polish orderlies had dragged into the room to turn this small office supply store into a makeshift hospital.

The blonde stepped up to his full-sized hospital bed. There was no smile, no pat on the head. No greeting at all. "You are the American pilot?"

Shank had spent years in and out of combat zones, and he sized the young woman up instantly by her intense eyes. *This kid's been in the shit for the past few days, and she's lost friends.*

He smiled at her a little. "Yes, ma'am. I'm the Hog driver who got shot down," he said.

She was confused. "Hogs? Hogs . . . like pigs?"

"No . . . it's my plane. We call it the Hog."

"Yes. Your plane crash. It fly like pig."

Shank laughed and winced with fresh pain. "Right." He smiled, ex-tended his right hand. "I'm Ray. People call me Shank."

She took his hand but did not return the smile. "Tobiasz."

"You got a first name?"

"Of course. Doctor says you walk, yes?"

"Yeah, I can walk," Shank confirmed. He'd used the bedpan a couple of times, but just a few minutes earlier he'd walked across the room to the bathroom and had managed to put one foot in front of the other with a limp off his sore right ankle.

She looked over his swollen eye, the bandages on his cheek, and the cast on his hand and wrist. "You know to talk to the airplanes?" She shook her head quickly, clearly knowing her English was failing her. "You under-stand? You can talk to American planes in sky?"

"Not without a radio. A U.S. radio."

"*Wolniej* . . . slower, please," she said.

Shank pushed himself up in the bed with his right hand and spoke more slowly. "Yes, I can talk to American planes. But I would need the right radio."

"I have American radio. Come with me. You talk to planes. Kill more Russians."

Shank was confused. "There's still fighting? *Shit*, I figured the Russians would be back in Belarus by now."

"No. Russians not gone. Russians are all over south of Poland now, from Radom and Kraków to Belarus border. Polish Land Forces and militia follow Russians. Kill them. Push them from Poland. You understand?" She spoke slowly, but clearly she had paid attention in school; her vocabulary wasn't bad.

"Yes, I understand."

"You come now. We fight Russians. You talk to American planes for to help us. Is okay?"

Shank wanted to get back with his unit, but he knew this was a fluid situation, and the girl was insistent. He figured he could help them establish comms with NATO forces flying overhead, and then whoever he spoke with could alert his squadron of his location.

She told him to meet her outside; then she walked out of the room without looking behind her to see if he was even going to make it to his feet.

He pushed himself off the bed and rolled clumsily to his right side. He winced in pain, his left arm getting caught under him as he tried to sit. He pulled it up abruptly to hook it back into its sling. Shank threw off his blanket, climbed to his feet, and began getting dressed.

A few minutes later he headed for the door, leaning on the railing by the wooden steps to support his injured leg. The Polish field doctors watched him casually as he left; one caught up to him and handed him a crutch. Judging by the amount of dried blood Shank saw on it, he'd guessed the previous owner no longer needed it. Shank ran his right hand over his flight suit, an unthinking gesture to neaten his torn, filthy uniform, and, using the crutch, walked out into the winter air and blinding white landscape.

Shank had watched a lot of the landscape passing below him, but now that he had a chance to view it properly, he saw how picturesque it was. He doubted anyone in a thirty-mile radius had stopped to look at the snow-covered pine forests as a thing of beauty in a while—they would all be more preoccupied with the invasion of their nation—but to Shank it was so peaceful and serene. Even though he was wounded, the smell of fresh air reminded him how close he'd come to death and how lucky he was to be alive.

He hobbled over toward the militia members, about fourteen of them, all hanging out next to the mix of military and commandeered civilian vehicles.

None offered him a hand as he approached them. Trying to maintain his balance was a challenge, but he persisted, and arrived at the group. Clearly the stroll from the makeshift hospital to the vehicles constituted a sort of test. When he made it, one offered him a cigarette, which he declined.

Paulina reached into the back of a small cargo van and pulled out a white down coat. It looked like it had been used as a pillow for someone dying from a head wound, but the blood was now dry, and Shank had nothing else to keep him safe from the subfreezing temperature.

She held it out to him, and he took it.

"A friend of yours?"

Paulina shook her head. "No. A civilian." She looked out to the adjoining field. "We stripped the dead in Wrocław. We are the TDF; we don't have much equipment."

A man in his forties and dressed completely in civilian attire spoke up in perfectly fluent English. "Hey, man, glad to have you on our team. You know, some of us watched you strafing that train." He smiled and took a long drag from his cigarette, then did his impression of the sound made by the GAU cannon on Shank's aircraft.

Others started laughing.

Paulina did not laugh. She spoke rapidly in Polish to the man, and he looked up to Shank now. "We need to mount up. She wants us to get to a spot near Radom. The Reds have been doing a pretty good job sticking to the side roads and traveling in small clusters. We think they know that NATO airplanes are hunting for them, so they have changed their tactics and are moving in smaller groups."

Shank nodded. "Smart. I'll need a UHF radio if I am going to talk to NATO airplanes."

"No problem."

The man motioned Shank into the front passenger seat of a cargo van, and shut the door behind him after the American struggled to get his crutch inside. When the man climbed behind the wheel, Shank said, "The girl—she's in charge?"

The man just nodded as he fired up the van. "Paulina Tobiasz. She's our leader."

Shank saw her climbing into another vehicle. He couldn't get over how young she looked. "She's, like, a lieutenant or something?"

"A what?" the man asked, momentarily confused by an English word he didn't know. "Oh, like an officer. Good question." He asked another of the Polish militia members something, and when he answered, the English speaker said, "We don't know her rank in the militia. She's just our leader. She's famous. She has the . . . What's the word? The *odwaga*. Courage, I think."

"You don't know her rank? How did she get to be in charge?"

"She's a hero. There is a picture of her everywhere in Warsaw that shows her battling Russians on the first morning of the war. I think she killed, like, ten of them or something. The only thing she thinks about is killing Russians. That's all," the man said, then took a last drag and flicked the cigarette out the window as he started the truck and put it into gear.

CHAPTER 64

The woods were spotty but dense with a tangle of vines and thickets. Mostly low scrub, but plenty of moderate trees to make visibility of Ethiopia's Highway 80 difficult from here, five hundred meters to the east.

The Kaskazi winds blew constant dry air from the Persian Gulf across the sixty-one able-bodied men of the 13th Dragoons, and the sun baked any exposed skin as they sat there in the scrub of southern Ethiopia, swatting at mosquitoes and flies for more than two hours while awaiting the Russian column. They'd shooed off a group of curious tribesmen who'd approached on foot without a shred of fear of the heavily armed men, and a herd of ibex goats ambled through their position slowly, providing a humorous distraction.

Apollo and his men had planted explosives, all they had, on the highway, but also in the gullies and under dirt paths along it. The terrain was channelizing, and unless the Russians found the explosives before they got to them, they were going to be inconvenienced with the destruction of some of their lead elements and slowed by the need to check the area carefully before proceeding with the main column.

The lead units of the southbound column arrived in early afternoon. Apollo waited until the first four vehicles were directly in his kill zone before ordering the initiation of the first of the explosives. Four more BTRs, another platoon, raced up to protect their comrades, firing wildly in all directions. The Russians dismounted and Apollo detonated the rest of the charges.

It was a cold tactic, obliterating the response force. He'd seen it used to horrific effect by the insurgents in Afghanistan. But he also knew he could expect the exact same treatment from the Russians.

The Dragoons ran to their vehicles and raced south. Right now they were the only thing standing in the way of the brigade of Russians and they weren't going to get many more free ambushes like that one. The plan was to keep up the hit-and-run as long as they could until help arrived or they were told to quit.

He pulled out his satellite phone, first looking for a call from his father; when he saw no calls, he contacted the Hexagone Balard, the French Pentagon.

Five minutes later he disconnected the call, a little smile on his face. He'd been told to hit the Russians one more time and then contact a contingent of U.S. Marines who were now heading north through Kenya, planning their own harassing action against the Russian column.

American Marines are coming to join the fray. It's about time.

He decided to fall back to the border city of Moyale and try to take out a few more pieces of enemy armor to slow them down before contacting his new allies in the fight.

SOUTHERN ETHIOPIA
29 DECEMBER

The radio came alive in Colonel Kir's ears, pulling him out of the most restful few minutes of sleep he'd managed in a day. It was Colonel Nishkin, commander of 1st Regiment, some two hours ahead of the headquarters element. After his spearhead elements were attacked and destroyed passing the Yabelo Wildlife Sanctuary three hours earlier, he'd managed to press on toward Moyale at the border.

And now he was unclear on his orders.

He didn't explicitly say that over the radio, of course, but Kir inferred as much when Nishkin said he wanted to take "an operational security halt," to let his men stretch their legs and top off their fuel tanks.

General Lazar had been standing up in the open top hatch of the BTR— he heard the call himself—and he squatted down next to Colonel Kir.

"Ah, old 1st Regiment. What do you think, Kir? Are they lost?"

Kir lowered the scarf that had been keeping dust out of his throat. "Perhaps, sir. We should give him permission to halt."

"But if we do, we either require *everyone* to halt, which wastes time, or we continue driving and risk collapsing the distances between the regiments and bunching up, which will make us a juicy target for any Western friends flying around above us."

"What do you want me to tell him, sir?"

"I want *you* to think, Kir. What do *you* think we should do?"

"Well . . . I would say, we tell him to push onward. Deny his request. Tell him we have no time, and if he halts, he will likely be attacked."

"He is still lost, Dmitry. If he rushes forward now, he will only become more lost."

Kir thought a moment. "Perhaps tell him to use his damn GPS or even his compass."

Lazar gave a warm belly laugh at this. "Tempting, but that will do nothing but drive him off the radio. How about we just show some patience and coach him through his problem? We tell him he has only ten minutes to pause, and then remind him the sun is the correct direction of travel. He need only follow it to get out of the mountains and into Kenya."

Kir nodded thoughtfully. "*Da . . . da*, sir. That is the better response. If we get him to slow down for a few minutes, he will find his way, and it will be good for him to know he has our trust to continue."

"Good. Now send that transmission, but tell 1st Regiment to be more cautious. According to the map, Moyale is a tricky city to navigate. If I were a Yankee, I would confirm our routing by watching a regiment pass through Moyale; then I would hit the follow-on regiment. I would hope to spread discord by attacking the center of our advance."

"Sir . . . how can you know that?"

"Just my feeling, Colonel Kir. Tell 2nd Regiment to use the ten minutes to ensure his ZSU radars are up and ready."

"But what if we are wrong?"

"Then we are wrong and 2nd Regiment wastes a few minutes and they are more prepared for air defense. Also, when you tell Colonel Nishkin he has ten minutes, I know he will actually take thirty. Either way, we will be prepared if the regiments bunch up in Moyale."

Colonel Kir grabbed the radio and delivered the orders to 1st Regiment.

He received Colonel Nishkin's acknowledgment immediately. Kir was about to send the transmission to 2nd Regiment when he stopped, then looked back up at his boss. Lazar stared back down at him through the hatch. He smiled and winked at Kir, then stood up high in the turret, lost to Kir's view and into the whirling dust outside the vehicle.

The old son of a bitch. He knows the battlefield because he knows his men and he knows the enemy. Lazar has spent over forty years being both the hunted and the hunter.

Kir replaced the scarf around his mouth, choking on dust and marveling at his boss's intuition, then pulled the scarf down and transmitted the instructions to 2nd and 1st Regiment.

CENTRAL KENYA
29 DECEMBER

Connolly's force had been racing south, but they stopped to refuel on the highway, and the commanders took advantage of the break to check in with the *Boxer.* Connolly moved through the throngs of vehicles and men on the road surrounded by vast, open desert, searching for Lieutenant Colonel Eric McHale.

Dan Connolly had known the regimental operations officer for twenty years. They had been together at Marine Corps Officer Candidate School and even graduated in the same Infantry Officer course, but as was usually the case in the service, they hadn't had much time to get together in the intervening years. Career and family got in the way, usually in that order, and though the Corps was the smallest of the four U.S. military services, the two men had lost touch until now.

He worried McHale might be thinking he was trying to steal his job. Connolly was "Nick the New Guy" with this unit, and as such it was assumed he would keep his mouth shut. But Connolly was also here on a pressing mission, so it was crucial to him that he establish an amicable relationship with McHale from the start.

"Hey, man, hope I'm not getting in your way," said Connolly as the two men busied themselves putting up a long-range antenna.

"Hell no, brother," said McHale. "You're value added. Having a direct dial to the top and a shot at this mission is more than we could have asked for. If you hadn't pieced together all this crap, we'd be cutting Gator

Squares up in the Gulf." "Gator Squares" meant Marines on a ship at sea, sailing endlessly in a tight patrol sector and awaiting action.

Every Marine's worst nightmare.

Connolly said, "Any way I can help, I'm here for you."

Sergeant Casillas called out from the back of the LAV now. "Lieutenant Colonel Connolly, sir? There's a French officer on the radio for you. Says it's an emergency."

"*French* officer?" Connolly looked at the colonel, who shrugged. "Okay, put him through to my station."

Caster and McHale came over to listen in as Connolly got up in a seat next to the radios.

Casillas hit a switch on the communications board in the LAV-C2. "Okay, sir, toss on a crew helmet, flip the switch, and you're all set."

"Do we have a call sign for this guy?"

"He said it was Apollo, sir. Could be a unit call sign. Dunno."

Connolly put on the helmet as instructed, then flipped the switch. "Call sign Apollo, call sign Apollo. This is Marine Task Force Grizzly—do you receive me?"

McHale climbed in through the back hatch of the cramped vehicle and sat next to Connolly. He plugged in one of the speakers so everyone could hear the radio broadcast.

"*Allo*, Marines. This is French special forces captain Apollo Arc-Blanchette. We have made contact with a sizable Russian force. Do you copy?"

"Good copy, Captain."

"*Bon.* My government has told me to get in touch with a man named Colonel Daniel Connolly. We have taken some casualties and request assistance. We wish to collapse into your perimeter. Can you comply?"

"Sounds like his *name* is Apollo," said Connolly. McHale nodded and pulled out a notebook.

"Roger, Apollo. I receive you loud and clear. Can you give us a grid location for your casualties?" Connolly glanced at McHale, who nodded his approval. All NATO services treated one another's casualties as if they were their own.

Apollo called in his current location, a spot just southwest of Moyale, on the Kenyan-Ethiopian border. Connolly acknowledged and said he'd get right back to him and to stay close to his radio.

"What do you think, sir?"

McHale said, "Find out how many men he's got and we'll spin up and go get them. We'll have helos from the *Boxer* brought up." The regimental operations officer added, "Dan, you want to lead the group to fly in? You can get intel from him on the way back. I've got to keep us pushing south."

"Absolutely," Connolly replied, and he brought the radio back to his mouth.

CENTRAL POLAND
29 DECEMBER

Captain Raymond "Shank" Vance climbed out of the truck and stumbled into a snowbank along the road, accidentally reaching out with his bad arm to arrest his fall. He was rewarded with a jolt of pain in his hand even though he landed in nothing firmer than wet snow. He was helped back to his feet by a young militia member.

The younger man brushed the snow off Shank's coat.

"What was it like?"

"What was what like?" Shank asked.

"Getting shot down."

Shank had been trying not to think about it all, although it came back to him every few minutes. He said, "It sucked."

Paulina appeared in front of him with a radio in her hand. She used it to point to a faraway rolling pasture, a vista at least a mile distant and a mile wide.

She said, "Russians will be here in three hours. Only way east to stay out of city to north and not cross river to south." Then she added, "You get planes."

Shank shook his head. "We need to know what frequency the aircraft are operating on. I need to know what the AT is for the day and what sortie we're on. I mean, if there *are* even any A-10s up."

"No planes?" A look of disappointment crossed her otherwise emotionless face.

He sighed. "We'll figure something out. I kind of thought you had some resources, or were dialed into the NATO AT cycle, or *something.*"

"What you need?" she asked, a tone of frustration in her voice. He realized she and her group of about forty militia were effectively working alone.

Well, he asked himself, *what did I expect? A well-coordinated ground unit?*

This was the fucking civilian militia.

"If I had a NATO or U.S. UHF radio, maybe I could raise someone on the guard net."

Paulina turned away and walked off to one of the other vehicles. She returned a moment later and handed a wooden-stocked AK-47 to the American pilot.

Shank took it and slung it over his back. He'd fired an AK only once before, when he was goofing off in Afghanistan, and had no real training on the weapon.

"Okay, radio is coming. We make a camp here."

Shank followed her into the woods and immediately saw why the Poles had picked this site. They were actually on an escarpment that looked over a broad and open vista. But this prominence was the only one, which told Shank that if they were going to ambush the Russians from here, the Russians would put together very quickly what piece of ground the militia was using to overwatch their movements.

He thought for a moment about suggesting they move to a lesser hill, but he didn't see any other options. Besides, the immediate concerns were to get a radio and try to dial up someone—anyone—who might be scouting above.

Shank followed Paulina up to a position they had prepared out of a tangle of cut brush and some packed snow. There were already three Polish militia members there with a DShK, or Dushka, heavy machine gun. The barrel poked out from the brush, but otherwise it was well disguised.

The fluent English speaker who called himself Jahdek stepped up to him and handed him two different handheld radios. One was completely wrong for his needs. It looked Russian, but as Shank examined the dials, he could see from the numbers it was in the VHF range. Handy to have, but likely no one would be monitoring those nets unless instructed to do so.

The other radio was a NATO UHF. It looked like an Italian brand, but it certainly had the markings he was looking for.

"You can use?" Paulina asked.

"Yes, I think so. I doubt this thing has its encryption still encoded, but maybe I can try it."

"What you need?" she said.

He fiddled with the dial and the knobs, and the radio came to life with the sound of static.

Jahdek stepped up to the American. "The Polish Rifles—they are another militia group. They are thirty kilometers to our west. They stopped responding on the radio. We don't know, but maybe they were overrun by the Russians who are coming this way."

"Shit," Shank said, but he kept trying different radio frequencies.

"Paulina wants to set an ambush. She wants your planes to attack."

Shank said, "I get it. I think the radio is ready, but there's really no way to test it."

Now Jahdek said, "She will do the ambush even if there are no planes."

"With *what*? That Dushka? That's not enough. Even for just a Russian reconnaissance unit. Their infantry carriers have heavy armor. They'll kill you all in minutes."

"We have more than just that Dushka."

Paulina stepped up to the two men and pointed at the truck. "Does radio work, Mr. Shank?"

"Once we see or hear any aircraft, I will give it a try."

"It work?" she said, not fully comprehending.

"We'll see."

It had *to work,* Shank thought to himself. This was his job. His duty. Even if he wasn't in the cockpit himself, he could still do his part to put ordnance on targets.

CHAPTER 65

ETHIOPIAN-KENYAN BORDER
29 DECEMBER

The crew chief leaned out the side hatch and called out distances to trees and the ground. The big, fat CH-53 shook as the pilot slowly eased the collective to control the helicopter's rate of descent.

With a gentle bump the helo landed.

Connolly shouldered his M4 carbine, closed the Velcro on his heavy Kevlar body armor, and jogged off the back ramp where the rotor wash from all four aircraft flung dust and debris, causing a miniature sandstorm. It was hard to see through the haze of dirt and the darkness, but he could just make out four men running toward him. Connolly then watched as the equivalent of a reinforced platoon, about sixty soldiers in all, entered the landing zone from the wood line. No words or other sounds were audible above the din of the four giant helos, so the crew chiefs on each aircraft motioned for the wounded and dead to be carried onto one bird, and the able-bodied men to board the others.

The Frenchmen complied, carrying fallen Dragoons both on stretchers and in body bags up into one of the CH-53s. When the casualties had been delivered to the Navy corpsmen waiting there for them, the French troops all boarded the other helos.

Connolly walked between the CH-53s now, asking around for the French captain he had spoken with. He tried to call above the deafening rotor wash into the back of each helicopter. "Apollo?"

Several men pointed him to a big man already sitting in the last helo.

Connolly climbed aboard and beckoned the captain back to the other CH-53. There they both donned headsets, the rubber ear caps muffling the loud rotors and engines above.

Shaking hands finally, the American said, "I'm Lieutenant Colonel Dan Connolly."

"Captain Apollo Arc-Blanchette. Thirteenth Dragoons. We are very happy to see you, sir."

"How are your men?" The helo began to shudder as the pilot changed the pitch of the blades and added power.

"Eight wounded. Three KIA, unfortunately. We hit them just south of Yabelo, caused some damage, but they were quick to counterattack in force. You will take my casualties to your ship?"

The crew chief signaled for the two to fasten their safety harnesses, then went back to instruct the Frenchmen who were still strapping in, struggling to fit themselves and their big rucksacks in the relatively small space.

"Yes. We have full surgery aboard the USS *Boxer* and your men will be taken care of. The rest of you will fly back with me. Our forces are moving up from Tanzania to the mine, but we have a battalion-minus of light-armored vehicles just south of here. We're going to hit them as they leave Moyale."

The crew chief shut the side hatch; the pitch of the rotors turned louder, and the wide helicopter lifted into the air.

Apollo said, "Good. We faced the Russians three times now. They are *formidable*. The first hit was a small Spetsnaz force. No problem. The second was an ambush we set up against forward reconnaissance. We destroyed them but used all our explosives. Then we hit them at the border."

Connolly patted Apollo on the arm. "I think your information on the Russian task force is going to be valuable. Would you mind briefing our intelligence guys and the senior leaders once we get back to our forces?"

"I'll brief anything so long as we get after these bastards when I'm done." The Frenchman sighed. He said, "I was fighting them the other day in Germany, and now we're fighting down here."

Connolly stared in surprise. "Wait. You were in combat in Germany?"

"*Oui*. At the beginning of it all. The Russian Spetsnaz placed a laser navigation device on the tallest mountain in Germany, but we discovered it and wiped them out. Lost two men in the process, though. We had several more wounded hours later in Czechia. Again we were fighting Spetsnaz."

Connolly was amazed. Reports from Europe were still so spotty, he knew nothing about either of these engagements.

"You obviously have a lot of intel about how the Russian special forces are operating, in both Europe and Africa. We're a little thin on the actions of the rest of the brigade heading south."

The Frenchman looked at the American for a long time.

Connolly picked up on the man's reticence to say more. "What is it?"

Finally Apollo spoke. "My father. He's a . . . a diplomat stationed in Djibouti. He stayed behind to record every piece of armor and every troop he could see as the columns left the capital."

Connolly presumed this meant Apollo's dad was a spy, but he had the good manners not to mention it. "We received that intel. That was damn good work by your dad. Hope you'll tell him the U.S.A. appreciates him."

"I'd love to do that, Colonel, but I haven't been able to reach him. I'm a little worried."

"Yeah . . . I can understand why." Connolly put his hand on the younger man's shoulder again. "The quicker we end this thing, the better for your dad."

"Oui, bien sûr." He changed the subject. "To that end, what is your strength?"

"A regiment, roughly. With some air assets."

Apollo blinked in surprise. "The Russians have a *lot* more than that, just in their column. When are you being reinforced?"

"That's kind of the problem. We're it for now. A carrier battle group is on the way, and it will bring in a *lot* more air, but they won't get here till well after the Russians arrive at the mines. If Russia takes the territory, we won't be able to dislodge them without laying waste to the whole thing."

"It's a mine. You could bomb it and then just dig the rock out of the rubble, no?"

Connolly said, "The Russians have to know that, so I think they have a way to protect the mine once they take it. We need to prevent them doing so."

Apollo nodded. "Most in my command still believe the real show is Europe."

"Well, Apollo, for you and me, this fight down here is the only fight that matters right now, and even though the numbers are against us, we're going to *fucking* win it."

"*D'accord.*"

SOUTHERN POLAND
29 DECEMBER

Jahdek had brought Shank some pain pills, but the Pole couldn't tell him what they were other than prescription meds the forty-five-year-old had for his bad back.

Shank took them anyway. His broken hand throbbed like hell, and his facial wounds hurt like he was constantly being stung by bees around his left eye. He figured he wouldn't be able to make it through the evening with his wits intact without something to take away at least a quarter of the agony.

The two men sat on the hood of a truck. The cold air outside the vehicle helped Shank with his pain, and Jahdek didn't seem to mind, which Shank assumed came from a lifetime of harsh winters like this.

Shank said, "I'm not going to pretend to be much of a historian, but you guys have had to deal with a lot of assholes from other places marching around your nation."

"Truly," Jahdek said. "Before we gained our freedom, we were slaves to the Soviets. Before them, the Nazis, of course. And the Russians again before that. We experienced more than a hundred years of slavery to other nations. Nations who used us, used the people, and erased our history to exaggerate their own. So now we fight."

Shank raised his right hand and high-fived the man sitting next to him. "And I'm right here with you, brother."

Shank looked up to the sky suddenly, and Jahdek saw this and followed his eyes. After a few seconds both men could make out the sounds of jets somewhere off to the west but hidden above the low cloud cover.

Another man came running over now.

"Mr. Shank, we hear a plane!" he yelled, out of breath.

All three men moved over to the radio, which was positioned behind logs and sandbags a few meters back from the edge of the wood line.

Shank trained his students to memorize the guard frequency for just such an emergency. He could think of only two frequencies now, but he wasn't certain about either of them, perhaps due to the effects of the pills Jahdek had given him.

He dialed in the first radio net ID he remembered. "Any station this net, any station this net, this is call sign Shank on guard net ID three-four-eight decimal four-five-zero."

He felt rather than saw Paulina appear on his left side by the truck. He looked up at her as he tried again. "Any station, any station. Shank on guard net. Do you receive me?" There was some static on the line now, which was encouraging, because it indicated someone might be broadcasting, but he heard no voices.

He reached for the radio and punched in the numbers for the second frequency he remembered.

He tried again. "Any station this net, any station this net, this is call sign Shank on guard net ID three-niner-five decimal one hundred. Do you receive?"

Still he heard nothing but static.

Again he looked up at Paulina, who was now scanning through her binos out over the snowy fields in front of them. A small band of Polish militia was hoofing back to their spot from another wood line about three hundred meters away, and this made Paulina curse under her breath.

As he was about to transmit yet again, a voice suddenly came over the radio, speaking American-accented English. "Station calling. Say again call sign."

Paulina stepped in closer to listen.

"This is call sign Shank. I'm an American A-10 pilot. Shot down this morn—"

Was it really this morning? Was it yesterday? He decided to just give the area: "Shot down over Bełchatów. I'm with the Seventy-fifth Fighter Squadron."

"We copy," replied the phantom aircraft overhead.

Shank still had no idea who this guy was. All pilots were taught that the simplest ruses were common during war, so neither man would take the other's word that he was American, even though both men certainly *sounded* American.

"Stand by for verification," the voice over the radio said.

After a few minutes the pilot came back with authentication data. Information only Shank and his unit could know. "What was your first command as a lieutenant, sir?"

"I pushed papers at Andrews. I didn't have a command."

"Were you ever incarcerated?"

Shank smiled a little. "Arrested in Italy. Two nights in jail. It's where I got my call sign."

After this brief exchange, the pilot seemed to be more trusting of Shank. "Okay, we have your data. We'll pass along your location to the search-and-rescue folks."

"Uh . . . negative. I've linked up with Polish ground personnel. We believe we have Russian forces approaching our position. I need someone to prosecute targets for me."

There was a long pause now—so long that Paulina looked at Shank and pointed to the dial, indicating that perhaps he should adjust it. To this Shank just shook his head. These things took time. He had gone from the standard procedure of a downed pilot requesting evacuation to a downed pilot calling for close air support.

He pictured the pilots of the aircraft above radioing back to base or else just discussing it among themselves, trying to figure out what to do.

Then finally the radio crackled and the pilot said, "We copy all. We have your request and we'll send it back. Remain on this net and we'll check in."

"Understood. Here's the issue. We believe Russian forces will be here in"—he looked at Jahdek, who held up two fingers—"two hours. I need close air support at that time. Please pass along." It was dangerous to send up this information, but Shank was hoping the Russians were too far away to be listening in on him.

"Okay, we copy all, Shank. We'll pass along your request and will advise."

Shank turned to Paulina. "I told them the situation. Now we wait to see what they will do about it."

He stood up to stretch, careful to keep his wounded hand close to his body so he didn't bump it on the people and equipment around him. Paulina squeezed his good arm gently and smiled, the first time he'd seen her do so. "You do it, Shank! Very good."

NORTHERN KENYA
29 DECEMBER

The Cobra attack helicopters' twin Lycoming T53-L-703 turboshaft-driven blades chopped the air, thumping above the helicopter's pilot and the gunner, driving the machine at a breakneck 170 miles per hour.

"Stinger One-Six, this is Two-Six," said the twenty-five-year-old pilot, scanning the horizon for the lead flight of four attack helos lined up to the front of his own flight of Cobras.

"Go for One-Six," the response crackled back.

"I've pulled left from Route C80. Currently at grid 37 November 2059 6172. I am at the B.P. and inbound, time now," he said, referring to the preset battle position.

The pilot and his gunner in the front seat experienced momentary weightlessness as he pushed the stick hard forward and left and worked the rudder with his feet. He could see the flat desert landscape changing from the terrain he'd seen after taking off from USS *Boxer*.

"Clear through and forward from BP Jenna. Friendlies are LAVs and remain at given grid. Vicinity the 17 63. Confirm." Ahead of him the low Kenyan desert rose sharply in a series of rocky hills that separated it from Ethiopia. The escarpment that rose toward the city of Moyale was unmistakable from the maps they'd studied aboard ship, and the miniature map currently strapped to his kneeboard.

"Confirmed. About forty or fifty vics. I have positive identity. Requesting to go hot." The thermal camera mounted on the ball sensor assembly on the nose of the aircraft showed the white-hot outlines of several clusters—he supposed they were in platoon order—tucked in the lowlands, out of sight from the rising escarpment that led up to Moyale.

"Copy, Two-Six. I have the lead. You are cleared to click off safe. TOT remains one-eight."

"Copy. I confirm TOT is one-eight. Call sign for ground unit?"

"Call sign is Grizzly OPS. He's switched to net ID four-five."

"Understood, four-five. That is the unit?"

"Negative. That's OSC. Unit is call sign Highlanders."

"Copy, One-Six. Let me know when you are clear from the target."

"Affirm. I have my guys doing right pull. Then I'll call you clear onto target. Time is one-seven. Commencing TOT in one mike. Off the net. Out."

The *whump-whump* of the rotor blades on the AH-1 Cobra attack helicopter filled the pilot's ears as the radio went silent for the one minute before all hell was scheduled to break loose. He flicked the master arm switch and watched as his instrument panel went from red to green on all weapons. He turned the forward sensors toward the spot where they were told to expect to see the Russians, the top of the shelf at Moyale. He could already see sixteen to twenty BTR-82s making their way down the winding road. It was a perfect place for an attack.

Then, in front, he saw the four Cobras from the first flight rise up from behind the tall hill clusters. Each aircraft quickly launched two missiles.

About half of the missiles appeared to impact their targets; then he heard the call.

"Two-Six, we're clear of the target. We'll fall in behind you for a re-attack off of BP Jenna with more PGM and a rocket-and-gun run. Your turn now."

The lead pilot called to the other aircraft, each pilot slipped his collective forward, and the aircraft raced just above the Marines on the ground. He could see the dismounted infantry, each clustered near the LAV vehicles, now firing rapidly at the distant targets.

Boom-boom-boom, came the throaty roar across the canyon dividing the Americans from the Russians. The Marine Corps LAV-25s unleashed a fury of 25mm cannon rounds. The Americans were firing at maximum range, but getting any closer to Lazar's armored column would have been suicide. They had counted on surprise, and had achieved it, but it wouldn't last, and the BTR-82s' cannon outranged the Marine Corps' 25mm.

The pilots knew this needed to be a quick fight with a quick getaway, or the Marines would get slaughtered.

On the ground, Dan Connolly watched the LAVs firing their depleted-uranium armor penetrators at the enemy. The light-armored vehicles weren't getting as many precision hits as the Cobra pilots, but he saw one and then another of the BTRs in the kill zone hammered by the two LAV companies. The BTRs, in contrast, were having trouble fixing the source of the fire. Their cannons thundered out responding shells, but the shots went short, left, and right of the distant Marine vehicles.

The whole reason Connolly and the regimental operations officer had taken a bet on this being a good site for an attack was the fact that the Russians were forced into a vulnerable position on the road. Although the Marines were attacking from below the Russians, they had the advantage of being on terrain that allowed them to hit and run, while the Russians were forced to drive down the road single file due to the terrain around them.

A Cobra swept in from the southeast and pulled up directly over Connolly's position on the hill, then opened up with his 20mm gun and Hydra 2.75-inch rockets. Connolly could see the spread of ordnance across the battlefield; most missed as the pilot fought to keep the helo steady, but three or four caught the flanks of Russian vehicles winding their way down the mountain road from atop the high Ethiopian shelf.

Boom! Something detonated right next to Connolly, blasting him out of his thoughts and blowing him off his feet, sending shards of red flint rock into his face and sides. He hit the deck hard, then ran his hand over his face and even his body armor. A sharp red shard, more like a slice of crystalline glass, had penetrated the outer layer of his load-bearing vest.

In rapid succession, three more blasts impacted near him—enough to send him and the small group scrambling off the rocky promontory that gave them great sight lines but also made them one hell of a target.

Incoming 30mm rounds echoed off the canyon's walls, and blasts of return fire peppered the landscape in hundreds of small explosions.

The Russians had them spotted and in range.

Connolly ran to the LAV-C2, where he was met by Sergeant Casillas. "Sir, you okay?"

"All good, Marine. Those cannon are getting closer."

"Check, sir. The LAV company wants to fire for another five mikes. Then the commander wants to pull back. He just lost two vehicles."

Connolly nodded and loaded up. He knew the enemy commander was advancing. The Russians possibly sensed that this was a small ambush, and knew they could retain the upper hand if they attacked into and through the forces lined up in front of him.

It's what Connolly himself would have done, and what he had done in Afghanistan many times.

Connolly heard a new and unfamiliar noise, but when he looked into the sky he realized what it was.

A Cobra had been hit full force by cannon fire.

The helicopter burst into a ball of flame, breaking into tiny pieces, propelled through the sky behind burning fuel.

Another buzzing sound was followed by another explosion, and the downed Cobra gunship's wingman exploded like his leader.

Just like that, four men had been lost and two helicopters were down.

Connolly and the men around him dove into the open rear hatches of their armored vehicles as pieces of burning debris began raining down with a vengeance. Connolly's LAV driver jammed his vehicle into reverse, tossing the lieutenant colonel and the rest of the men back against the metal hull and down onto the grated floors in heaps as gear and heavy ammunition boxes flew around inside the armored personnel carrier.

Connolly looked up at Sergeant Casillas. "Is he trying to get us killed?" Punctuating his thought, the vehicle hit a huge bump, sending everyone in back flying into the air before slamming back down on the unyielding surfaces.

Connolly untangled himself from the communications cords, then stood up and opened the top hatch to look out.

Up on the mountain shelf leading from Ethiopia into Kenya, he counted roughly two dozen burning vehicles. What he now identified as Russian ZSU-23-4 self-propelled antiaircraft weapons were still firing their quad-barrel 23mm cannons into the skies in an effort to catch more of the now retreating Cobras. The Cobras were out of the fight now that their pilots had witnessed the capability of this awesome weapon; they just dropped flares and did their best to dodge the shots fired at them as they raced from danger.

Connolly couldn't see how many Marine Corps vehicles had been hit, but from the radio traffic he could hear through the headset in his crew helmet it sounded like casualties had been mostly one-sided, with the Russians taking the brunt of the damage.

Surely a few LAVs had been destroyed, along with the two Cobras, but the light-armored reconnaissance attack had likely accomplished its mission. The Russian advance would slow down to regroup, and with luck they might pick their way a little more carefully as they rolled south.

The heavy gunfire continued behind Connolly as they raced away along with the rest of the two LAV companies. The remaining Cobras escorted them out of the area and stayed ready to fire standoff missiles in case the Russians pursued at speed.

But the Russians remained in Moyale, licking their wounds and reassessing their movements toward Mrima Hill.

Connolly got on the radio and sent a situation report to Colonel Caster in the regimental command post. Connolly's mission had successfully bought Caster some time, hopefully enough time to get everyone up to the mines and dug in.

Caster's response came over the radio soon after. "Good work to you and the two LAR company commanders."

"Thank you, sir."

"Any idea where those ZSUs came from? I hadn't seen any intel on those things, and they sound like they're murderous."

"No, sir, didn't see any reports on the things, either, but they certainly have leveled our aerial advantage. I counted at least twelve of them just with this regiment."

Caster's Texas drawl rumbled over the radio. "That worries the shit out of me. Assuming Lazar's other forces have similar assets, it's going to mean the vast majority of this fight is going to be done on the ground." And then the colonel said, "I want you to fall back. We're sending some tanks up to Mount Kenya; it's a few hours north of here. The terrain is jungle and the highway passes close by, and Lazar won't be able to bypass it if he wants to get here to the mine before our carrier battle group arrives. We'll hit him with a bigger delaying action, really give our boys at Mrima Hill time to dig in and get ready for the Russians."

"Copy, sir. We're on the way."

Caster replied with "Grizzly Six, out."

CHAPTER 66

Shank woke to someone shaking him by the knee where he sat in the heated truck. He opened his eyes and saw Jahdek.

"You need more pills?"

Shank felt a little better. Not good, just better. "No, I'm okay. What time is it? I think I fell asleep."

"Yes, no trouble. It's almost nine o'clock. Paulina looked in here and saw you sleeping. She ordered everyone to leave you alone."

Shank asked, "What about the Russians?"

"A company of tanks and some troop carriers are coming this way. PLF has seen them just to the west, but that unit doesn't have anti-armor weapons, and our air force is down to our last F-16s. There will be no chance if your pilots don't come help."

Shank quickly went about trying to raise anyone on the radio. Five minutes, nothing. Ten, still no one.

After a few more tries he heard a distant voice. It was weak, but clearly it was calling for him. His antenna was simply not enough. He needed them to fly closer.

Paulina came by. "Radio working? You have plane?"

"I can hear them; they just can't hear me. Still trying."

"Please," she said. "Not too much time."

Shank continued calling out on the radio. Behind the lines, where he sat in the truck, was a bustle of frenzied activity, and Shank just sat there, rubbing his cast gently.

Paulina watched him a moment, then heaved a heavy sigh. She was disappointed in him, and it made him feel like shit.

She began to turn away, when a voice came over the radio.

"Shank? Shank, this is Nooner. You receiving me?" The broadcast was loud and clear.

Shank grabbed the mic. "Hot damn, Nooner, you bastard! I've got you Lima Charlie."

Paulina smiled. She understood enough to realize Shank knew the pilot he was talking to.

"Roger, sir. Same, same. We thought you were dead until we got word back at . . . well, you know . . . back at our airfield." Nooner was cautious with his words over the unencrypted radio channel. "You all right?"

"I look like shit but I'm operational. I've linked up with a Polish militia unit. We are forward of the Russian advance, which has split into smaller elements."

"Yeah, they have. They're all over the damn place down there."

"Roger that. We have eyes on some roads and fields that are going to be rotten with Russkies in the next few minutes." Shank ran his finger over the map. "A town called Kraśnik is about twelve kilometers west of my position."

"Copy. We're a four-gun flight, ready for work. Let me know what you want to do."

"I want to integrate you into the Polish militia ambush. You'll kick it off. I need you to set a battle position in the vicinity of a place called Zamość. We'll call that BP Raiders. I need you then to fly along Route 74, heading west, then veer hard north at Frampol. From there I want you to run in two craft sections, one every five mikes, then back to BP Raiders and then along that route again. We'll start there, then see what effect we achieve and shoot up another nine-line brief for changes as needed. Good?"

"Nooner copies all. What's the TOT?"

"Copy. TOT is . . ." Shank checked his watch; it was 2210 hours. "Can you make twenty-two-thirty hours?"

"Roger. We copy. First TOT is set for two-two-thirty hours."

Paulina stood near Shank again, right at his shoulder, listening intently. "All okay?" she asked.

"Yes, all okay." He smiled back. She held up his left arm and examined the bandage carefully. She unwound it a few feet and then retied it more neatly.

She gave him a pat on the back. "We need planes."

"Yes, ma'am," Shank said.

Paulina walked off into the night while unslinging the rifle from her shoulder.

Minutes later Shank could tell the Poles had spotted the Russians. The first of a series of hushed whispers arose from the position nearest him. It was a little earlier than he'd anticipated, so he snatched up the radio handset again. "Nooner, this is Shank. Need you to accelerate TOT. Can you make a new TOT? Two-two-two-five?"

There was a pause, then: "Copy, Shank. We can make that TOT."

"Good man. Lean into that throttle, brother."

Shank trudged through the snow on his crutch toward the Polish lines. He found himself pleasantly surprised to see a mountain of anti-tank rockets, grenades, and boxes of machine-gun ammunition. Slit trenches had been dug into the frozen earth, and the Poles were protected enough to stay safe from all but airbursts and overhead hits.

Pretty good, thought Shank.

The operator of the massive DShK machine gun waved him over and motioned for him to look through the starlight scope of his weapon. Doing so, Shank immediately saw a line of tanks. It took only seconds to ID them as T-14s.

He turned away from the scope without a word and rushed back to the truck as fast as his crutch would take him. When he got back, Nooner was already broadcasting, declaring himself ready to attack.

"Shank, this is Nooner. BP inbound. I can see a row of tanks. They're right where you said, sir. I have clear line of sight."

Shank's heart pounded as if he was about to deliver ordnance on target himself. "Roger. I need you to clear our gun target line. Pull right off target. There will be a lot of shooting going on down here, and your chances of getting hit are high if you don't fire your ordnance and climb immediately."

"Copy all," Nooner said. "Let your people know we're starting our attack run now. PGM first, then second passes with guns."

"Copy all. Clear to prosecute targets."

Shank heard the unmistakable whine of the A-10s above on their attack runs, then the terrific sounds of two missiles shrieking through the air. This was followed seconds later by the rolling explosion of destroyed Russian armor. Fireballs lit up the night sky and now machine-gun tracer fire lanced across the open field from the wood line, pounding into the approaching vehicles.

The gunners blazed away, lighting up the night. Shank looked up and down the line and saw six other heavy weapons pouring fire into the Russian column.

The Russians quickly determined the source of the fire from the incoming tracer rounds emanating from the woods on the hilltop, and in moments Shank heard a spinning, whirring noise as 120mm tank gunfire rolled across the open farmland and toward them, passing overhead.

This was followed quickly by more incoming tank rounds. Again, most were high and arced over the hilltop only to cause devastation kilometers behind the Polish force, but a few hit just in front of the militia, shook the ground, and dumped what snow was still clumped in the pine trees above after the jackhammer assault of the machine-gun and cannon fire.

Someone shouted over the crashing sounds: "They're moving through the field in our direction! Four hundred meters!"

Fuck, thought Shank, *they'll assault right through. These little trenches and felled trees aren't enough to protect us from a full-on attack.*

He moved back over to the radio. Above him he could hear limbs snapping as the coaxial machine guns on the Russian tanks peppered the wood line with heavy fire.

He ducked low and reached for the handset.

Before he could broadcast, his wingman came over the radio. "Shank, this is Nooner. I've got eyes on armor headed toward your position."

"Nooner, this is Shank. Set up for an immediate reattack. Bring the BP to just west of my position and cycle on target. The Russians will be on top of us in minutes if you can't hit them hard and fast right now."

"Can do. Am I clear onto the target?"

"Yeah, ASAP. Pull right stick off target and gain to six thousand."

Before Shank had finished speaking the night erupted with a loud and inordinately long *Brrrrrrrrrrt.* By the sounds of things, Shank estimated Nooner had dumped over a hundred rounds onto the Russians in one blast.

A second after the first sound ended, there was another long burst as Nooner's wingman fired his cannon.

Racing jets flew low, just overhead but invisible in the darkness.

The Poles at the wood line erupted in cheers, and they continued pouring their own fire down at the approaching enemy.

Shank keyed the radio. "Nooner, Shank. You're making friends down here. What's your time left on station?"

"I can push past war limits, but I still only have another fifteen mikes left. We burned a lot of fuel looking for you."

Shank pointed to his watch and then held up one and then five fingers to Paulina. She nodded and ran forward to another of her machine-gun positions.

Shank watched her a moment as she went, then pulled up the mic again. "Roger. Let's get to work. Be advised, we are still in danger of being overrun."

"Copy all. Bringing it in tight. Make sure your guys are keeping their heads down. We're going to crisscross that kill zone with everything we've got."

For the next fifteen minutes Shank coordinated the air-to-ground battle. The direct fire from the Russians continued closing in on the Polish positions. As the enemy got closer, the sounds of smaller- and smaller-caliber weapons added to the mix told Shank that dismounted infantry was nearing the woods. He gave Nooner some more guidance, then decided he couldn't stand it any longer.

He had to get another firsthand look at the fight to get a better view. He climbed behind the wheel of the truck next to the radio, then put the vehicle into drive. He drove forward toward the machine-gun position with the lights off. He knew the Russians would be looking for thermal signatures, so he didn't move too close to the wood line before putting the truck in park.

A Russian tank round slammed into the trees just twenty meters off his ten o'clock position, and a spinning branch spider-webbed his windshield.

"Fuck!" he shouted. He fell out the door of the truck, reached back in for his crutch, and then moved as fast as he could toward a machine-gun emplacement. The cuts on his legs had all split open and he could feel blood oozing out.

Looking out over the Polish valley now, he could see the Russian tanks and BTRs. Ten pieces of armor burned, but another ten sprinted up the hill, moving in pairs forward, while another two shot volleys of suppressive fire. The closest vehicles were now less than one hundred meters away, clearly desperate to make it into the trees and among the Poles so that the NATO aircraft above couldn't continue whittling down their ranks.

In front of Shank's eyes a precision-guided missile drilled the lead tank as an A-10 passed low under the cloud cover. A second Hog followed only three seconds behind, its 30mm cannon spewing fire. The tracers blazed through the night in a long and continuous red and yellow streak across the blackness, directly onto a BTR. At least half of the rounds penetrated the vehicle. They were more than enough; the crew had no chance. The vehicle burst into flames; then the ammunition cooked off, sending sparks and flares into the night. Brilliant flames licked thirty feet into the air from the blasted open top hatches of the vehicle.

"Good work, Nooner!" Shank shouted, though he wasn't on the radio.

The assistant gunner of the Dushka spun about, hearing Shank. His face was covered in blood. One of the tank blasts had sent shrapnel into his position.

Now Shank did return to the radio and grab the handset. "Pour it on, Nooner!"

The level of incoming fire began to slacken.

"Nooner, Shank. Do you see signs of withdrawal?"

"Affirmative. I see vehicles turning back to the road. They are headed due east. Looks like they're bookin' it. I think you're just fighting their rearguard now. Want us to hit them in the ass on the way out?"

"Negative. Please remain on station here. If these positions show signs of slackening, they could still overrun us. We're so lightly manned, I think a platoon of Russians with night-vision equipment could kick our asses."

"Copy all. We'll keep an eye on your flanks and let you know. We have great thermal pictures with the temps so low."

Shank put the radio handset down. He could see the outline of Paulina approaching him, her AK-47 up at the ready. He stepped out of the truck again. "Hey, looks like . . . ," he began, but she raced forward and threw her arms around him and hugged him hard. It was painful on his wounds—he imagined it was painful to her injured arm as well—but he hugged her back. He laughed, happy that she was happy. Then he noticed she was sobbing. He pulled back and looked at her. She turned away but then back to him again, wiping tears that left streaks on her dirty cheeks as she smiled brightly. He reached up with his good hand and brushed the tears away. It didn't do more than smudge the dirt around, but she leaned into his hand, enjoying the personal gesture.

"You save many Polish today. You kill many Russians today."

"I just got my guys in the sky to do the work," he said, and she hugged him again.

CHAPTER 67

Commander Diana DelVecchio sat with her XO in the wardroom; before them were laptops, charts, papers, and laminated maps.

Both of them were dog tired.

The *John Warner*'s journey through the Tadjoura Trough had been a harrowing experience for all on board, and the crew was utterly exhausted. The acoustic-shadow trick at Moucha Island had worked to an extent. But the hot pursuit of Russian naval vessels, the seemingly endless cat and mouse, the active sonar sweeps and screens, had taken a toll that showed in everyone's face. Commander DelVecchio had led them through the hours of tense creeping along the bottom without any great incident. A few more distant depth charges had been fired to flush them out, but otherwise the *John Warner* had popped up unscathed. Perhaps wiser and more trusting of their captain's and their own abilities to run a gauntlet of hunter-killers. A Cold War skill that had become increasingly rusty with the U.S. Navy's perceived dominance of the seas in the intervening years in submarine warfare.

After a full day of slow, silent running and virtually no sleep for the crew or command, the *John Warner* had managed to sneak away from its Russian pursuers and into the open waters of the Gulf of Aden. But the rapidity with which the ships and subs hunting them broke off contact immediately made DelVecchio suspicious that the Russians had been called away for either a tactical or a strategic reason. She decided to chance an ascent to raise the UMM and communicate with Fleet, and when she did so her suspicions were confirmed.

The entire surface and undersea force arrayed against her had turned away and was now steaming into the Indian Ocean, presumably, said Fleet, to stand watch off the African coast. The Russians would know the American *Virginia*-class was somewhere out there in the deep, and the last thing they would do would be to allow the American sub to come close enough to shore to effectively fire its cruise missiles in support of the Marine contingent forming at Mrima Hill.

And Diana DelVecchio had been sitting there for the past hour, trying to find a way to do just that.

Maybe the exhaustion she and her team were experiencing was partially to blame, she told herself as she reached for her thermos of coffee.

And maybe, she also considered, this was just an impossible equation to solve.

The USS *John Warner* had a dozen Tomahawk land-attack missiles on board, and the TLAM was an incredibly potent weapon. It could deliver either a 1,000-pound high-explosive warhead or a similarly sized cluster bomb with pinpoint accuracy.

But TLAMs worked best against stationary targets. GPS-guided munitions flew to a fixed point on the map and then detonated; this was not the way to combat a brigade of attacking armor rolling toward friendly forces. Sure, DelVecchio could launch salvos of TLAMs willy-nilly at coordinates north of Mrima Hill and hope she got fortunate in taking out armor, troops, or the like, but it would take one hell of a lucky shot to do any real damage.

And even if the Marines could give her the exact coordinates, the Tomahawks would still be ineffective from out in the Indian Ocean. They had an impressive range—over 1,300 miles—but they traveled subsonically, no more than 550 miles an hour, and to be utilized in the most time-efficient way would have them flying near enough to the enemy surface force arrayed off the coast.

If DelVecchio launched from hundreds of miles away, the Russians would have time to move fixed-position forces or equipment to safety before the TLAMs arrived.

No . . . firing a dozen two-million-dollar missiles into the plains and jungles of Kenya would do nothing for the Marines, and it would imperil her crew unnecessarily by revealing their location to the enemy.

She raised her thermos to her mouth, hoping like hell the next jolt of caffeine would be the one to help her see the answer to this riddle.

Finally, reluctantly, DelVecchio looked up at her XO with bloodshot eyes. "I'd do anything in the world to help those boys, but I don't see any way without putting the *John Warner* in absolute peril."

The XO nodded at her. "I concur. If we could slip in like we did in the port in Djibouti, then I'd be the first to say so. But we'd have to get so close to the coast to be effective with the TLAMs, there would be virtually no chance of survival."

Commander DelVecchio's tiny frame deflated, and she put her elbows on the table. "All right. We'll go to a position three hundred miles from the coast. Flight time of the TLAMs will be well over a half hour from there if they fly in a straight line, a lot more if we send them around the Russian fleet. It's the best we can do, but it's not good enough, because it won't do a damn thing to help the Marines."

"You can't win them all. We helped by knocking out the fuel for their tanks."

DelVecchio did not respond.

The XO stood. "I'll give the command. Please, Commander, get some rest."

She didn't look up or answer verbally; she only nodded with her head still buried in her hands.

SOUTHERN POLAND
30 DECEMBER

Shank, Paulina, and the small unit withdrew from the battlefield at one a.m. and drove to a nearby village. With a swagger born of their time together and a heady confidence taken from a successful fight, they knocked on the doors of a couple of adjoining houses and asked if they could stay the night. Both families were happy to oblige and took them all in.

Paulina left the house for a meeting with TDF leadership and to check on the wounded, but Shank stayed with a group of seven militia in the kitchen. The family brought them cold meats and cheese and wine, and the talk at the dinner table was robust.

A bottle of vodka came out, and Jahdek looked to the American. "Shank, we say *Twoje zdrowie!* Then we thump the glass and drink."

Shank was exhausted. He'd taken another pain pill and really just wanted to lie flat and sleep. But Jahdek was insistent.

"Okay, maybe just one." He held up the glass and butchered the toast. *"Tow-jaw, drove-away!"* He downed it in one gulp and gagged from the harshness of the vodka going down his throat, and the others laughed while Jahdek patted him on the back.

Another bottle was brought out and soon everyone was singing.

After a time, Shank's eyes began to droop, while the men and women around him kept drinking. The lady of the house saw her celebrity was tired, so she guided Shank to a private bedroom on the second floor.

Soon he was sound asleep.

He woke sometime in the night—his hand itched under its cast. He figured he wouldn't be sleeping well for a long time.

He opened his eyes; shafts of soft moonlight reached into the room, and in the light he could see Paulina sitting on the edge of the bed and looking at him.

"You sleep?" she asked.

He blinked his good eye and stared at her, unsure if he was dreaming. Sensing his confusion, she took his left arm in her hands and felt the bandages.

"We must change, okay?" She reached to the floor and retrieved a small medical kit. Putting his arm in her lap, he felt her soft skin as she unraveled the wraps one at a time. "I change. You rest. Okay?"

He tried to lay his head back, and he watched her in the moonlight as she first unraveled the old bandage and then rewrapped his arm.

While she worked, she said, "You like family?"

He was surprised by the question till he figured out she was asking if he liked the family hosting him that evening. He replied, "Yes, they were very kind. So are you, Paulina."

She smiled a little, focusing on her work. "Tomorrow men will take you to Warsaw. You return to your Americans from there. Not safe to travel through south. Still too many Russians."

"What will you be doing?"

"I stay in south. Go east. Look for more Russians."

Soon she tied off the bandage around his hand and then examined the dressing over his left eye.

She felt his face and traced the lines of the bandage with her fingers. "Must change, too. This one hurt, okay?"

"Can't wait," he answered.

She seemed confused for a moment, then smiled again.

She worked gently in the moonlight—slowly, not like an expert; he doubted she'd ever done this before. But she seemed surprisingly tender, like she cared enough to put effort into doing it right.

He could tell this war had made her do ugly things, but he could also tell that, underneath, she was full of kindness and caring. A tenderhearted girl tossed into combat unprepared but doing her best by steeling her heart against damage.

Shank was no psychologist, but he'd been involved in war his entire military career. He had the sudden impression that she had lost someone extremely close to her in all this.

He reached up and touched her cheek. Again, as when he had rubbed away some tears out on the battlefield, she leaned into his hand, almost like a cat. This time she added her hand to his, clutching it and pulling it into her face.

Shank blinked his right eye in surprise.

Something changed in the room. Shank felt as though this had been planned. This wasn't about changing his bandages. Maybe she was just a girl, lost in the hate and terror and wanting an escape, even if it was just for a night. An escape she would never allow her squad to see—*couldn't* let them see.

Paulina swept aside the covers, and with gentleness she threw a leg over him and laid herself against him. She lowered her lips slowly toward his, her warm breath against his face, and she kissed him.

She leaned into his ear and whispered, "Captain Vance, you are . . . you were much *odwaga* today." She brought her hands up to his face and held it as she placed her elbows on the bed, careful not to put any weight on his wounds but resting atop his supine frame.

He'd heard that word before. *Odwaga.*

The one her troops had used for her.

"Courage." He hadn't thought of it, but coming from her—a natural leader, a woman warrior—it was the finest compliment he'd ever received.

Downstairs the militia laughed and sang as the celebrations continued, louder and more boisterous than before with the arrival of more wine. And both downstairs and up, the night was electrified with the joy of being alive.

MOUNT KENYA
30 DECEMBER

Mount Kenya was a massive 17,000-foot mountain, beautiful and green around the sides and dense with trees that continued halfway up its slopes, but the top of the mountain itself was bald, craggy, and covered in snow.

Colonel General Lazar looked from inside the BTR-82A turret up at its impressive peaks in the distance. In another life he would have loved to climb them and enjoy their majesty.

The reports had been coming in for hours from his reconnaissance forces claiming the Americans were arrayed in and among the foothills of the mountain. He could envision this American game with ease. They were goading him into a fight, knowing that he would determine that these forces would simply attack his rear if he tried to bypass them.

And, obvious to Lazar, there would be more defenses set up at the mine to the south. He had satellites working to determine their positioning and strength now.

Well played, Marines, he thought.

Dark clouds surrounded the distant peak, suggesting rain was imminent. He reached inside the vehicle and felt for his poncho.

"Dmitry, order the artillery into position. We will blast those Marines out of our path."

Colonel Kir nodded. "Yes, sir."

"And make sure all our air defenses are lined up. These Americans think a lot of their air units, but we will hit them hard and send them running as we did up in Moyale."

Just over six kilometers away, Apollo spit on his hands and rubbed them together, his energy renewed by the strenuous work. He hefted the pickax and swung it down, dislodging another large chunk of the hard-packed red earth. Up and down the line, other tools clawed into the earth as the men hastily improved their positions.

Clods of red dirt had been packed into sandbags, three wide at each position. Brush and greenery had been cut and set up in front of the positions.

Apollo's unit had come to Africa vastly underarmed in comparison with the hulking Marines working around them. Every Marine, it seemed, carried an anti-tank weapon, and there were medium and heavy machine guns every ten to twelve meters along the rocky jungle ridgeline.

Lieutenant Colonel Connolly came over to his position to check up on him. "Captain? Are you okay? Ready for this?"

"I am, sir. We all are."

The buzz of something overhead caught Connolly's ear and he looked up. It took a moment to find it; he and Apollo saw it at the same time. A drone. First one, then at least four more. No bigger than a few feet in size, they came from out of the sky and buzzed north to south, then began circling. This was the first time either the Americans or the French had seen an enemy drone. Many stopped digging in and began looking skyward.

"Oh shit," said Connolly.

"Merde," Apollo added. "That's not your guys?"

"That's the other guys. Take cover!"

The men heard a boom somewhere in the distance, followed by another and then a third.

"Incoming!" came the yells from both American and French NCOs up and down the lines as a fresh shrill shriek of incoming artillery filled the air.

The men raced to their fighting holes. Those Iraq and Afghanistan veterans among the French Dragoons and U.S. Marines got as low as possible, opening their mouths but holding their ears. Experience had taught them that "overpressure" caused by multiple heavy, concussive blasts could cause their eardrums to rupture and noses to bleed.

The ground shook as the accurate incoming Russian artillery fire slammed into the rocky earth around them. An earsplitting noise and blast waves washed over the men and in some locations the earth ruptured and fighting holes evaporated.

The drones had done their job, providing accurate target information for their well-drilled artillerymen.

Dense, dry thickets in the foothills at the base of the mountain began to smolder and burn.

General Lazar called the gun line to congratulate them on their accurate barrage.

"The firing data we received for the targets' coordinates was exceedingly accurate," said one of the artillery captains.

Colonel Borbikov sat next to Lazar, watching and listening, a smug smile on his face.

"Well done. How is the round count?" asked Lazar.

"We will use twenty percent of our allotment—unless you wish us to fire more?"

Lazar said, "No, save some for the next event, and good work."

Borbikov turned to him. "Sir, that's a sizable force there in the foothills. If you allowed thirty-three percent of ordnance expenditure, I am certain we could destroy these battalions, which will greatly diminish the defense of the mines when we—"

Lazar turned to Borbikov. "Who is in charge of the tactical plan, Colonel Borbikov?"

"Sir, you are. I just—"

"And are you suggesting you know more about artillery fires in your Spetsnaz outfit? Tell me, what sort of artillery pieces do you and your boys wear on your backs when you jump out of airplanes or slide down rappelling ropes?"

Borbikov fumed. "I merely suggest we take advantage of—"

Lazar turned to the artillery captain, who looked straight ahead, terrified to be in the middle of an argument between President Rivkin's favorite officer and Russia's most decorated general.

"Captain," Lazar said, "you have your orders."

"Sir. Twenty percent and then we cease firing."

He left the command post. Borbikov turned on his heel and left as well.

As soon as the artillery barrage was complete, a long column of Russian BTR-82s hurtled south along a rocky dirt road, then broke left and right, bouncing up onto the rough terrain while maintaining an impressive clip.

A Marine LAV TOW gunner was the first to spot them, and he radioed to the company command post. He and his TOW section had a clear line of sight, and they requested permission to fire.

The LAV company XO looked to Connolly for instructions. Both men were kneeling in the sandbagged dugout quickly built as a command post. The last hour of artillery had deafened every one of the two dozen men in the trench considerably, and several were dazed from the barrage. But most of the Russian fires had landed near the front line, and this small CP had avoided any heavy casualties aside from some shell shock.

"They are clear to fire," Connolly said; then the LAV company XO issued the approval. In seconds a massive salvo of TOW-II missiles streaked over the lush green hills toward their targets approaching on the lower ground.

And seconds after that, five BTR-82s had been blasted to bits.

When confirmation came, Connolly keyed the radio. "Oddball, this is Grizzly. You are clear to launch into the attack."

When the Russian forces had barreled south down the Kenyan route A2, they had sent their drones forward to investigate the Marines' positions. The obvious dust clouds of moving vehicles and spoiled earth of hurriedly built fortifications were easy to detect at the base of Mount Kenya, and very quickly the images of the positions were used to build the Russians' battle plans. But what the Russian drones had not been able to detect from the air was the deep wadi snaking along the flatlands in front of the foothills. An intermittent riverbed, it was dry now but covered with a thick canopy of vegetation, and the sandy streambed was the perfect depth and width to serve as a hiding place for a company of Marine Corps M1A2 tanks.

The mobile LAV companies at higher elevation had been the bait, and now, as the BTRs raced into range to destroy the force there, the tanks rumbled out of their positions of concealment on the enemy's western flank and opened up with a devastating salvo of 120mm cannon fire. The Marine tanks were not as modern or high-tech as the U.S. Army versions, but the Russians were caught focusing on the dug-in Marine defensive line ahead, unaware of the heavily concealed armor to their west until the first massive rounds began striking targets.

The initial salvo from the fourteen American tanks caught Lazar's 1st Regiment in the flank; ten BTRs burst into flames as high-explosive shells blasted directly into the smaller, lighter-skinned vehicles' troop compartments. The Marine Abrams tanks reloaded and fired again, this time while moving forward toward the Russian position. The main-gun fire was markedly less accurate bouncing over the broken and rugged terrain west of Mount Kenya, but they still scored six hits and five kills with their second salvo.

Watching through a spotting scope from ten kilometers' distance, Colonel General Boris Lazar quickly realized that he'd moved forces directly into a trap, but his leadership and tactical sense were equally quick to find a solution. He sent in his second brigade, still traveling south on the A2. They pulled off road in their BTRs and, in a well-rehearsed battle maneuver, lined abreast of one another, rolling and bouncing over the rough terrain even faster than the U.S. tanks. In near unison, every second vehicle fired one of the newly mounted "saddleback" 9M133 Kornet anti-tank missiles mounted on its modified turret, sending jerking, sputtering pinpricks of light across the long, open ground toward the Marine tanks, while the Russian vehicles in between fired smoke dischargers, screening and obscuring the Marines' view of the enemy advance.

Three of the Marine Corps M1A2s took direct hits to their flanks from the Russian anti-tank missiles. Two of the stricken vehicles erupted as the ammunition on board began to detonate through the open top hatches. The third took a strike to the turret, which immediately jammed, its barrel dangling, practically blasted free from the hull. The tank sped on with the rest of its pack, but it was out of the fight.

The rest of the armor weathered the salvo, and the company continued driving and firing, pushing directly into Lazar's 1st Regiment, taking out armored personnel carriers with each salvo.

Eight Cobra attack helicopters swooped in from the west, flying just above the growth of the jungle flatlands, firing missiles, rockets, and guns as they approached, holding off any would-be attackers in 1st Regiment and allowing the M1A2s to break away from the attack at their rear and race away at top speed to the southeast, away from Lazar's 2nd Regiment, which continued in pursuit.

"Hit their defenses with more artillery, Kir!" shouted Lazar, as he stormed toward the colonel and the headquarters command unit, standing in the open next to the field radios.

Kir stood up from where he'd been leaning over a map and looked for his general in the group of men. Seeing Lazar approaching, he said, "The Americans are fleeing. The reports we have from reconnaissance and drones are that the Marine defensive line has crumbled. They are driving south, back in the direction of the mines."

Lazar arrived at the table and cocked his head. "Are they fleeing? Or was this their plan? A hit-and-run. Tell 2nd Regiment to keep up the pressure."

"I will, sir, but the farther they get from the main body, the more effective those Cobra gunships will be. They are picking some of 1st Regiment off as we speak."

"I understand. Pursue as best as 2nd Regiment is able. We will follow. Tell the ZSU batteries to get as far forward as they can. Take out more of those Cobras. One more attack helicopter destroyed today is one less we'll need to fight tomorrow at the mine. These Marines do not have an unending supply of them."

"Yes, sir. What then?"

"Then . . . then we stop and lick our wounds. We walked into a trap with those tanks. We must carefully consider our next moves."

Connolly watched the Marine M1s following him and the rest of the LAVs as they sped south through a narrow but well-maintained jungle road toward the mines and the Marine Corps' final defensive line. Sporadic long-range Kornet missiles fired from the Russian BTRs slammed into trees, the road, and occasionally American vehicles while those Marine tanks that were still operational, their turrets to the rear, kept launching 120mm return fire at the pursuers.

Russian artillery dropped in and around the American tanks, but the M1s somehow managed to drive through the waves of heavy fire unscathed.

After twenty harrowing minutes of close retreat, the Americans worked their way clear of their pursuers and made it to the B6 highway, where they sped south even faster en route to the mine.

Connolly heard from Caster's intelligence officer that the Russians had ceased their pursuit at the edge of the jungle. But this wouldn't last long. He knew Lazar would only pause to regroup before beginning an orderly approach to Mrima Hill.

CHAPTER 68

Colonel General Sabaneyev stood outside his GAZ Tigr all-terrain infantry mobility vehicle, snowfall covering his shoulders and his helmet, as the last T-14 tank crossed the Polish border into Belarus. It was difficult not to breathe a sigh of relief, although he hid his emotions from his subordinates.

The tanks from the fighting battalions had shown their effectiveness in combat, they had accomplished the mission, and now virtually all of the once brightly painted and new precision instruments bore the effects of battle: scratches and giant dents from the hard combat in the concrete jungle of Wrocław; layers of mud churned up from battle across the Polish fields; and, on virtually every piece of armor, small pockmarks and large, jagged scars exposing bare steel, gained from strikes from RPGs, machine-gun fire, and 120mm tank fire.

A long line of BTRs crossed the bridge next, weary infantry mounted atop them, glad to be catching a ride from their armored brothers.

Sabaneyev and his staff had already crossed, and now they observed the movement from the crest of a small hill outside Brest as the columns of armor and men drove past. As they watched the column, a T-14 missing its entire turret drove past, a crew of infantrymen hanging off the top, the vehicle's function transformed from battlewagon to a simple but overengineered tracked cart for moving personnel. The turret of this tank had been blown off in combat in what was called the jack-in-the-box effect, a result of enormous overpressure, usually caused by a detonation inside the vehicle. Often this killed the entire crew instantly, but sometimes, as was the case here, the vehicle remained roadworthy, just lacking a turret. Often, within its cramped quarters, the gruesome remnants of its former occupants bore witness to their final horrible moments.

But for the group of exhausted infantrymen sitting on the vehicle, men who'd seen enough of combat, this battered tank was just another way to get home.

Upon watching the sad sight roll on a few seconds more, Sabaneyev realized this tank was an obvious symbol that they were no longer the attackers, the wolves on the prowl. Now they were fleeing, the victims of a series of battles that had left them crippled and worn.

He reached out and took Colonel Smirnov by the arm.

"Feliks, tell that unit to abandon that tank; it will have a terrible effect on the men if they see it."

"Sir . . . for them that is now a viable alternative to walking. If I ask them to abandon that tank, those men will be forced to continue on foot, and it will slow their company's rate of march."

"I don't care if they crawl to Moscow from here, Feliks. We are in friendly territory and we must consider our next stage. We will throw up a line at the border. I want those Yankees and their Polish dogs to pay a final price. We will fire across the border when the enemy arrives, cause maximum damage with whatever munitions we have remaining, then continue our march back to Russia. Do you understand?"

"*Da*, sir," said the operations officer, sensing that now was not the time for any dissent. "I will make the necessary arrangements to fight once more, then withdraw."

"Good. And have that damaged tank driven into the woods and left. It's bad for morale."

Eduard Sabaneyev stormed off toward his Bumerang to give new orders to Colonel Dryagin.

"Walking through the snow is bad for morale, too, General," Smirnov muttered to himself.

One of the Russian tank platoons that was still fully intact, four T-14 Armatas in all, formed a line abreast in thick trees on the eastern side of the

Bug River. The metal beasts were covered in dark black mud and snow. The platoon commander for this particular section, a lieutenant, enjoyed a cup of coffee the crew had brewed by putting their steel pot on the engine's exhaust. The coffee wasn't the usual military-issue junk but rather something his platoon mechanic had stolen from a Polish house when they'd been driving over frozen farmland between Görlitz and Wrocław.

Fucking Wrocław! the platoon commander thought as he sipped the coffee and picked at chunks of moss covering a section of his vehicle under the turret.

His platoon sergeant walked over, interrupting his thoughts. The commander dropped the moss and picked up some of the black mud and squeezed it between his fingers, not wanting to be caught idling like a girl.

The sergeant said, "That crap Polish mud will be damn hard to wash out from the turret ring, sir."

The commander agreed. "*Da.* We'll need to put a hose to it once we're back in the heated tank ramps in Smolensk."

"Any idea how long we're to be here, sir?"

"Orders are to fire at the Americans and Poles as they approach the border and the west side of the bridge. We are to engage targets from here as long as there are targets to engage and we have ammunition with which to engage them. With a little luck the fucking Americans will want to stand and fight, and we'll kick their asses. Here we give them one final taste of what it means to be up against the Russian army, unlike the pigs they're used to fighting in the sands of the Middle East."

The platoon commander looked behind him as another tank crew moved a tank hulk missing its turret into the trees. They were from an adjacent company he'd trained with before, and he'd known the men on board. He hadn't seen them get hit in Wrocław, but he'd heard about it. A Polish militia unit had attacked them from an upper story in a building with an AT-4, and the blast had blown the turret sky-high. He supposed the turret would become some kind of monument to the Polish people's resistance to their attack.

The turretless tank hulk was depressing to look at. *At least it might afford the infantry some protection,* he thought.

The crew fired up his vehicle again. The platoon sergeant had been given their exact location to set up their defense, about two hundred meters away, concealed among the pines. He scrambled to the back deck of the T-14 to grab the coffeepot before it fell off the tank and deposited its contents into the snow.

They rolled up to the bank of the Bug River on the Belarusian side near the raised automobile bridge. There they had a clear line of sight over the ice-covered water to the fields and forests on the eastern edge of Poland.

When the tanks stopped, the lieutenant clambered up onto the slippery steel of his Armata, while around him the men began gathering branches and brush to camouflage the platoon. He slid down into the open turret and clicked several switches; then a whir started up on the infrared sight's cooling system. Behind him, the tank's backup generator hummed as it kicked in, providing holdup power. He pushed his face onto the tank's eyecups and yelled, "Turret rotating!" to forewarn anyone close by as he began to turn the main gun and the sight to scan the horizon.

This terrain was perfect for a tank battle. He zoomed in the T-14s' sight system and scanned slowly across the Polish landscape. He saw a Czech Škoda Octavia some three kilometers away on the Polish highway 698, its driver unaware of what was soon to take place here.

He put his padded Russian winter tanker's helmet on and called through the intercom: "Driver."

He heard some clunks as the driver fumbled around and keyed his microphone. "Yes, sir?"

"I want you to fire up the engines for fifteen minutes, then cut them off. We need them to cool long enough to be invisible to the enemy IR systems. We'll button up and turn up the heaters so we can maintain a bit of warmth, but it's going to get cold in here while we wait."

"Yes, sir."

"Gunner, you copy?"

"Yes, sir," said the gunner from outside the turret. He jumped in through the top hatch; snow came off his boots in clumps and fell on the metal decking. He pulled his helmet on and switched channels to pass the lieutenant's instructions over the radio to the rest of the platoon.

The lieutenant heard a rough rumble and the tank shook as the powerful Chelyabinsk Tractor Plant 360 engine came to life. He reached into the emptied machine-gun ammo can he had bolted to the back of his tank commander's seat and pulled out a pad and pen.

"Gunner, get out a notepad and write our tank's range card. See that frozen pond at about two kilometers at two-four-zero degrees?"

"Yes, sir. I see it."

"Call that center and find me a reference point to the left and right. I expect the enemy to arrive on the main east-west highway, then spread out onto the fields. I'm going to walk our line and get the platoon's position diagram and have the other three working on their range cards, too."

"Yes, sir," said the gunner, who took over the controls from his boss on the dual-pad turret and stared through the sights, making himself even more familiar with the terrain.

The lieutenant stood from his seat and pulled himself out of the turret, back into the cold air. He climbed down into the snow and walked over to his three other tanks in succession. Each time he climbed aboard, knocked on the hatch, and then leaned in to confer with the tank commander.

Each man passed over his range card, including a diagram of his tank and its relationship to the other tanks in the platoon and its frontage.

The lieutenant then went back to his tank, where he combined the small diagrams into a fire plan sketch, which he reviewed with the company commander when he came down the line a few minutes later. The commander brought it up to his battalion commander, and the final consolidation of everyone's drawings across the battalion gave the unit its full defensive fire plan.

The final product was a diagram of a location crisscrossed with trigger lines, alternate positions, reinforcement and resupply lanes, and a host of other military data required for the commander to make decisions and hopefully maximize the potential of his unit against the enemy.

When they were done, when all the tanks up and down the river were emplaced and ready, the men looked out to the west and waited for the arrival of the Americans and Germans who'd caused them so much grief over the past several days.

MRIMA HILL, KENYA
30 DECEMBER

Sergeant Casillas directed the driver of the light-armored vehicle up the dirt road leading to the regiment's command headquarters. The LAV-C2 antennas slapped the branches of the dense jungle foliage as they made their way up the steep slope. Connolly stood in the turret, ducking constantly to avoid getting smacked on the helmet. He silently cursed Casillas for trying to take his head off.

Sensing his lieutenant colonel's frustration, Casillas spoke over the vehicle intercom. "Sir, I told the driver to hit as many branches as possible on the way up."

Connolly relaxed, the sergeant's gibe reminding him that all the men on the LAV were just doing their jobs. The instructions he'd given them had been to "get me to the regimental CP as quick as possible," and, he had to admit, they were doing a damn fine job at that.

This rutted dirt road had seen better days. Cut some years back to allow heavy equipment up to an old copper mine shaft on the northern slope of the hill, the road went into disrepair when the shaft stopped producing ore. Now other roads had been improved that led to the main rare-earth-metal pit, and the Kenyan jungle was hard at work reclaiming its territory here on the route to the disused shaft.

And it didn't help the surface of the road that the regimental vehicles had all come this way, ripping down big limbs and leaving sizable obstacles and torn-out sections of the dirt track in the process.

If it ain't the Russians, it's gonna be these crazy roads that kill us, thought Connolly.

The Mrima Hill mine complex was at the top of the thickest part of the woods in a naturally made and human-enhanced terrain feature called a "saddle." A bowl or crater had formed between the two hilltops from hundreds of years of erosion, the constant digging, and piles of wasted mine tailings. This double crest afforded some protection to the area where the regiment had set its command post. The greenery, like much of the East African landscape, was a mishmash of low and dense thickets, scrub plants, and tightly packed broad-leaved trees.

The mine itself was now practically abandoned. Word of the impending Russian attack had spread like wildfire, and all the employees and local villagers for many miles around had cleared out.

Ditto the Kenyan military. The French Foreign Legion troops who had been protecting the mine had remained, while the Kenyans had taken off to Mombasa. There was politics in play here: Kenya's very real desire to maintain a good relationship with the Russians when, in the minds of many, they inevitably took over the mine. Many of the Kenyan soldiers wanted to stay and fight, but just like with Borbikov and his unit three and a half years earlier, orders were orders.

The Foreign Legion contingent was only two hundred men, but they were most helpful to the Marines because they knew their way around the area, and were adept at giving advice on how to best fortify the location's defenses.

Three Marine infantry battalions were now dug in around the base on the northern, eastern, and western sides. To the south lay a swamp determined to be uncrossable except by venomous snakes, huge flocks of cranes, and some hippos, but the Foreign Legion troops had been positioned there to keep an eye out, anyway.

Mrima had two sister hills nearby: Marenje, six kilometers to the southwest, and Jombo, seven kilometers to the northwest. Mrima was the biggest of the three, but the others would certainly be key terrain in the upcoming fight, so the Marines posted units on both of these adjacent hilltops.

As Sergeant Casillas pulled into a parking area by the mine shaft, the row of Humvees and LAVs and a pair of dug-in artillery batteries indicated to Connolly that the regiment had been exceedingly busy while he had been slowing the Russian attack up north.

As he stepped down from the big armored vehicle, he watched and listened to the sounds of Marines around him preparing for the impending battle. Improvements to the regiment's defenses were constant, as were the shouts from angry NCOs, unhappy with the Marines' speed, skill, or both as they dug in, cut limbs, vines, and brush, prepared their machine-gun bunkers, and disguised their positions. The men had clearly not received a break since they arrived. The corporals and sergeants knew the Americans and French would force Lazar's brigade to discover the hidden positions only when they had closed to within a lethal distance so the Americans could fight them toe-to-toe.

Connolly left his LAV and walked toward the entrance to a horizontal mine shaft two-thirds up the hill on the northern side. Copper had been extracted there long before anyone knew what a rare-earth mineral was, but the copper had dried up and this part of the hill had been abandoned, and now REMs were mined out of a massive open pit on the top and back side of the saddle.

Outside the entrance to the old copper mine shaft sat a scattering of one- and two-story shacks. The 5th Marine Regiment had converted the shacks and the area just inside the cavelike shaft into its headquarters. When the Russians commanded this ground years earlier, they'd set their headquarters up in the cinder-block buildings of the REM mine itself, almost a kilometer behind and high above where the Marine HQ was now positioned. It was hoped Lazar would assume his enemy would simply move into and fortify these buildings, as his countrymen had done before, and that this would allow the Marine regimental HQ to remain hidden, at least for a while.

Rusted mine machinery and a few heavy-duty cranes, abandoned for years, had now become host to a small cohort of Sykes's monkeys. They scurried across the tops of the equipment and sat observing the Americans as they worked. Some scavenged food from the young Marines, who, though warned not to play with the animals, couldn't help themselves. Connolly knew it would inevitably be some young kid who would try to pet one and get bitten. Of course, this was probably preferable to what could happen if the regiment remained at the mine more than a few weeks. Then, in Connolly's experience, the men would try to domesticate a few, turning them into platoon mascots and pets.

In Iraq, Connolly once broke up a Marine-constructed fighting pit for snakes versus scorpions, but these things only happened once boredom set in, and from the looks of things around here, the NCOs kept boredom in check by giving their Marines plenty to do.

He spotted the guidon, a small pennant, this one representing the Fighting Fifth Marine Regiment. It flapped gently in the breeze in full view, indicating that Colonel Caster was here and not out touring the battalions.

Dan asked a group of passing Marines if they knew the whereabouts of the command post. They slowed just enough to salute and pointed to the entrance to the shaft, but they kept moving. Dan soon saw why. Just astride the rocky entrance to the mine, a regimental supply section had set up a full chow line. The men quickly hurried off to grab trays and get in line, and Connolly entered the horizontal shaft.

Ten feet into the mine, the temperature dropped significantly. It was a relief, but it was still hot: the air was thick, damp, and muggy. Still, the shaft was dug into hard rock and looked like an incredibly durable position.

Nevertheless, Connolly couldn't help but remember the fate of the Marines, sailors, and soldiers on Corregidor during World War II. They, too, had holed up in a tunnel. He hoped the outcome would be a bit better than that of the brave men who fought that fateful battle, when the men were eventually surrounded, cut off from supply, and forced to surrender to the Japanese.

A steady flow of water leaked into the cave from the roof, making the floor wet and muddy, with rank smells. The stench of bat guano hit Connolly full in the face as he walked deeper into the huge space.

Swarms of black fruit bats flew by above, their rest disturbed by whatever the Marines were doing deeper within. They moved en masse to the entrance, then, sensing it was still daytime, turned around to go back. Soon they were swirling in an odd dance just below the rocky ceiling.

Two hundred feet or so into the mine shaft, a wide section had been cleared of debris and the headquarters NCOs had put out folding tables and chairs for the many officers and staff NCOs. Battle boards, covered with maps dividing up the surrounding terrain by sectors, were hung against the rock. The regimental fires officer, in conjunction with the battalion fires leaders, had marked their maps up with strike-aviation attack vectors, holding areas, battle positions, and preplanned artillery targets in spots where the Marines expected the Russians would most likely muster before or during an assault on the mines.

At another row of tables, a line of radiomen worked busily. The beeping, humming, and crackling of the multitude of speakers echoed in the dark, cavernous space. Thick knots of antenna cables and communications wires banded together with tape stretched up toward the cave mouth and then outside to antennas positioned high on the rocky, jungle-covered hill. Adding to the din of radios squawking with patrol reports and readiness data from the battalions was the noise of the battery of Marine Corps M777 155mm howitzers being set up and dug in not far from the cave. No better location could be found as an ammo bunker for the artillery shells, so Marines walked back and forth, hauling the ammo into the mines so that it would be ready when needed.

Dan took it all in, then dropped his pack on the periphery and out of everyone's way. He was uncomfortably aware he was still something of an outsider.

He sighted Colonel Caster and headed over to him.

"Hey, Dan." The colonel clapped him on the shoulder in a genuinely friendly manner. "Glad to get ya back in one piece. You bought us some time and the battalions here did a pretty good job getting set up. Now is when the real work begins."

"Thanks, sir. The LAR and tank guys did all the heavy lifting. How are things looking back here?"

"Me and the sergeant major toured each of the battalions and they are about as ready as they can be."

"Hope you still have a use for me in the upcoming battle, sir."

"Yep, right here. I need you supporting the fight by helping me and McHale coordinate the battle. Sit down and we'll read you in on the game plan."

Connolly sat at the map table with Eric McHale. Both of them looked older than their years at the moment, due to the effects of battle and lack of sleep.

McHale smiled at Connolly. "You look like shit, Devil Dog."

Connolly used a green towel to wipe a layer of grime and sweat off his face and neck while McHale explained the plan, its execution, and Colonel Caster's intent: to defend each sector using the might of all his combined arms. The defense was well laid out, but it was clear to Connolly the Marines and French forces were stretched thin.

Connolly listened to McHale describe what could only be considered a fight-or-die situation, and he thought of the Alamo for a moment.

He then quickly told himself, *This is a terrible time to remember the Alamo.*

CHAPTER 69

Twenty-two Antonov An-26 propeller aircraft swept in low and slow over Tsavo West National Park, but no one besides a few game wardens and curious tourists at the massive wild animal preserve noticed. Their flight in had been through Uganda and over Lake Victoria. In Entebbe the aircraft received a quick refueling and this gave the 880 Russian paratroopers of the 23rd Air Assault Regiment of the 76th Guards Air Assault Division a chance to stretch their legs after their nearly twelve hours of flying.

Now the red lights in the back of the first aircraft switched to green, and forty men hooked up their parachute static line hooks to the long steel cable running the length of the plane. Every soldier checked the gear of the man in front of him. Then the green light flashed, and the paratroopers knew they were now over their landing zone just two hours' drive northwest of Mrima Hill.

The men dove out, one by one, the broad green plains below them. The battalion commander, a lieutenant colonel of paratroopers named Fedulov, jumped with the second assault wave, and could clearly see the terrain he'd been memorizing ever since being given this mission. As his feet swung back and forth he pulled his hands off the risers and felt for his radio and map pouch. He couldn't see any of the U.S. Marines or French special forces units he'd been briefed about, but he knew they were digging in somewhere to the south.

The foolish Yankees again assumed no one else in the world could match them with airpower and assault force projection. But the 76th Guards had more than enough combat power to pack a punch. Lieutenant Colonel Fedulov wore a patch on his shoulder showing a lion and a golden-winged parachute, and it was reassuring to him to wear the symbol of his magnificent unit, born in the cauldron of fire that was the Battle of Stalingrad.

He looked at the other men slowly descending through the scant and light puffs of low clouds as they drifted quietly toward the dark green African earth.

Fighting the Americans had been a dream of most of these men their entire careers. All the officers of the Guards Division had studied American doctrine voraciously in their military academies and schools, awaiting an opportunity to test their mettle against the West's supposedly superior forces.

Meeting and then beating the U.S. Marines was what Fedulov and his men had trained for.

Fedulov watched his first wave already touching down, but he was still 150 meters up. He swung his rifle forward, aiming it down in case of incoming ground fire as he had been taught during his training. With his free hand he felt for his radio, then tried the call sign he'd been given for the Spetsnaz officer who had requested the Russian paratroopers. "Tsentr One, this is Kilovat One-One. How do you read me?"

The response was immediate. "Kilovat One-One, this is Tsentr One. I read you loud and clear. We are receiving your first wave. Any trouble?"

"Negative, Tsentr. I am landing in the second wave." The ground was only fifty meters from his feet now. He calmly pocketed the radio handset and shifted his rifle, then pulled the release cord on his gear bag. The huge bag, now untethered, fell freely to earth. He experienced the bounce of weightlessness, a momentary updraft felt upon releasing the heavy fighting gear. It churned the stomachs of the new men, causing many to lose their meals just ten or twenty meters up. The experienced paratroopers clenched their stomachs on releasing their bags to prevent the nausea caused by these "*rvotnyye karman,*" or puke pockets. They also learned to avoid the "*rvotnyye rakety,*" or vomit rockets, that rained down on the unsuspecting from men above.

The Russian paratrooper commander collapsed at his knees as he impacted the ground. He, along with all the other men of the second wave, unbuckled their chutes, rolled the suspension lines, and tucked them into the canopies.

A man wearing the collar devices of a Russian Spetsnaz colonel made his way over to him as he unbuckled his helmet and pulled out the side straps of the heavy gear bag he'd jettisoned above.

Fedulov shouldered the pack and snapped to attention at just the right moment, cocking his head as he saluted. "Comrade Colonel."

Colonel Borbikov saluted back. "Welcome to Africa. As was explained to you, you won't be needed for the initial attack on the mine, but your men will be brought in once the American defenses have been overrun and their heavy weapons are silenced. You'll do the close-quarters mopping up, and then your battalion will assist with security."

"Understood, Comrade Colonel. We are ready."

"*Khorosho.* Now, have your men fall in. Once you have assembled your forces we're off. I look forward to my return to Mrima Hill."

"A *triumphant* return, sir. We will not fail."

POLISH-BELARUSIAN BORDER
30 DECEMBER

Lieutenant Colonel Tom Grant had hoped to arrive at the border when there was still some light so he could see the Russians heading east in the distance, but it was pitch-black now, at seven in the evening. His tank was three back from the lead as they neared the border crossing and then the automobile bridge over the Bug River, and he stood high in the turret, scanning left and right, looking for trouble.

They were still a kilometer away, but he worried the past week had made him paranoid. All indications by the Russians were that they wanted nothing more than to limp back across the Belarusian border and get the hell away from the fighting, but for some reason Grant worried there might be some parting gift: a mined road, a few mortars or even tank rounds popped back over the border—something else to give him trouble.

He clicked his mic so he could ask Anderson if he had anything on thermals on the far side of the river, but just as he did so, the night turned bright in front of his eyes.

The lead tank exploded in a ball of flames, the turret rocketing up into the sky.

"Holy fuck! It's Parsons's tank, sir!" screamed his driver, Sergeant Franco.

All the explosives on board Parsons's destroyed Abrams began high-order detonating.

"Driver, reverse the tank—*now*! Don't look at Parsons's tank! Focus on getting us the hell out of here!"

Franco dropped the M1A2 into reverse and the tank quickly began to back up.

"Pull behind the hill, near that pond to the front left."

Franco moved the massive piece of steel expertly off the road and through the rolling, snow-covered fields, following Grant's direction.

More Russian tank main gun fire slammed into the hard earth around them. Grant ducked low, looking out with his head only a few inches above the turret hatch as the sky lit up with streaking tracers of various colors. He was grossly exposed to enemy fire here, so close to the front of his column.

This was an egregious mistake for a commander.

The radio was alive with chatter as the M1s that had been driving orderly up Route 2 all peeled hastily left and right to avoid the incoming enemy fire. Grant shouted orders into his radio, sending them north and south, trying to get them to the woods or hills or anything that would serve as cover.

Franco kept driving at a breakneck pace, zigging and zagging to the pond and a small hill that afforded some protection from the incoming rounds.

The cannon fire from the east was unceasing. Snow and dirt flew into the air under a flash just thirty meters in front of Grant's vehicle as a tank round narrowly missed him.

Trying to control his own vehicle in the fray, Grant listened as his operations officer took initial damage reports from the companies that included three K-kills: totally destroyed tanks.

Suddenly, a pounding crash shook Grant's own tank. He ducked down but quickly realized an enemy HEAT round had skipped off the hull on the armored forward slope of his vehicle just as they drove behind the hill. Two other M1s launched over the crest and then stopped just behind Grant's.

Sergeant Anderson looked through the main gun sights and reported that the hill now masked his sight line.

"Could you see any of those enemy positions before we made it to cover?" Grant asked.

"No, sir. They were too well camouflaged. But they were definitely in the woods on the Belarusian side of the river."

"*Shit!* How the *fuck* did we drive into an ambush?"

Grant's gunner waited for a pause in the incoming transmissions as the lead company called out their temporary defensive positions. "Sir, they know we won't pursue them into Belarus, so they set up on the far side and waited for us."

Grant looked out to his right flank and behind him at the crossroads of Route 698 and Route 2. Three vehicles burned. The big main gun on an M1A2 tank was now elevated at a ridiculous angle and the barrel was split in half, which indicated that a round must have detonated inside the gun barrel. Flames engulfed the other two vehicles, and explosives cooked off every few seconds.

Grant was furious with himself for not staying back with his command-and-control vehicles, because their comms were more solid. From his lead tank he'd be lucky to reach half the regiment via radio.

He looked around at the part of the terrain he could see, then ducked back down into his tank.

"Sergeant Anderson, hand me the map."

The map came up to the commander's position, and he began looking it over. After a few seconds he said, "If these fuckers want a fight, we'll give them one." Then Grant turned the dial on his radio and called the regimental operations officer. "Brad, it's the CO. Are you receiving me?"

The reply came through faintly. "I am, sir. We're getting the regimental CP put together. Radios are up and running; tents and maps are up when you need 'em. Just receiving casualty reports now."

"Copy. Send up a Humvee to bring me back to the CP. I'm all the way up at the river. We'll come up with a game plan."

"Roger, sir. I'll get a vic on the way."

Grant ran into the makeshift command post of Humvees parked together with tarps pulled over the tops, antennas poking out on all sides, and the men manning the radios and maps. He stepped up next to his operations officer, who hurriedly took maps out of a large case. He watched as the man tossed maps of Poland aside and opened his map of Belarus. Grant saw it was no tactical map; it was out of a Michelin guide.

A continuous exchange of tank and cannon fire thundered in the distance, a constant reminder that the clash of U.S. and Russian armor continued, although the Americans were somewhat protected behind low hills and forests on the Polish side of the river.

The radios in the makeshift tactical operations center were alive with reports from the battalion commanders. Grant listened in as the headquarters men processed requests and moved pins on the map as units conducted micro-maneuvers to gain better positional advantage.

A radio operator rushed over. "Sir, we have satcom back to NATO." He had a small military speaker with him. "Unsure who it is on the other end of the radio."

Grant looked at the speaker for a moment, then said something that stunned every man within earshot. "Unplug that shit."

The radioman did not understand. "Sir . . . it's someone from NATO HQ. They requested to speak to you."

"I know . . . Unplug it." The young man did as instructed, a stunned look on his face.

Grant turned to Brad Spillane. "You and me have got a few minutes to get this right. I want it laid out in an organized manner, so I need your thoughts and input."

"Copy, sir. But what about NATO?"

"They aren't going to like what I'm about to do, and I'm not going to give them the opportunity to shoot me down."

Grant next conferred on the radio with his scout company commanders; then he stepped back over to the map table, walking into his circle of leaders, who had all been summoned from their individual commands. He looked nothing at all like an Army regimental commander—more like an exhausted mechanic who had been working on an impossibly broken-down car and had come to share bad news with the owners.

"Gentlemen, I've made a decision, one that will mean my court-martial when we return." His shoulders were slumped and his Nomex tank suit, covered in blood, grease, dried mud, and salty sweat, made him look as dejected as his attitude and lack of sleep suggested. "I need your input . . . I need your permission . . . or your disavowal." He stopped, clearly unsure of how to proceed.

Captain Spillane interrupted: "You are asking us to pursue, boss. To go into Belarus. To finish the job we started."

Grant nodded. "I am. They violated the cease-fire . . . *again*, when they fired on us from over the border. I'm going to return the favor and chase those motherfuckers back to Moscow if I have to."

German major Blaz Ott was astonished by this. "You will attack? Into Belarus?"

"Damn right, Blaz, into Belarus. They won't stop firing, so neither will we. I'd say we're in hot pursuit right now, and I'm not going to break it off."

It was quiet for a moment. Then Ott said, "You are my commander. You give the order, and I will obey." A small smile appeared on his face. "Let's get going. If the Russians decide to break contact, this will be harder to justify."

The others all nodded in assent.

Grant said, "I've been talking to my scouts. I think we have a way over that river to the north that will let us get behind the Russians."

CHAPTER 70

General Lazar's headquarters tent had been erected twenty kilometers north of Mrima Hill in a dry, shallow streambed that intersected the jungle here on the flatlands. After he woke from a nap in the back of his command vehicle, he climbed out and walked over to the tent, already a hive of activity.

He entered and was offered tea by a young sergeant, which he took and sipped molten-hot, even though the nighttime temperature was eighty degrees and the humid jungle air kept him covered in sweat.

He saw Colonel Kir talking to the radio section. "Dmitry. Where is Colonel Borbikov?"

Kir said, "He just left with a contingent of his Spetsnaz. They said they were heading to inspect the new artillery firing park that's being set up now."

Lazar stood in silence for a moment. Then he uttered something between a statement and a question: "Special forces is going to inspect artillery."

"I admit, I was confused, sir. He asked for the location on the map and left with his men."

"I tell you, Dmitry, there is no good to come from this latest news."

"Yes, Comrade General," Kir replied, then: "Forgive me. I'm not sure what you mean."

"Come with me outside the tent." For a very public leader like Colonel General Lazar, taking one of his senior subordinates aside to speak with him in private was an unusual move, enough to gain looks from the men in the command post.

Out in the darkness and away from others, Lazar said, "We were bloodied at the port and lost much of our armored punch. The damnable flank attack gouged out a sizable part of 1st Regiment. We are left now with three understrength infantry regiments. We still outnumber and out-gun the Americans, but they have the defensive positions."

Kir countered, "Our estimates are they're nothing more than a single reinforced regiment. We have three—damaged, but still we have three. And our BTRs are superior to the bulk of their power, their LAVs. Only their few tanks pose any real—"

Lazar interrupted. "I know all this, of course. My concern is not the Americans."

"Then what *is* your concern, sir?"

"I cannot control Yuri Borbikov. He has a benefactor in Anatoly Rivkin. I don't trust the colonel, and I'm sure he has something planned."

Kir cocked his head. "He has airborne troops to bolster the final phase of the attack, but you knew that already."

"I'm speaking of the nuclear devices. In order to serve as a deterrent to counterattack once we take the mine, they must be placed at the center and wired together so they can be activated with a timed detonator."

Kir knew about the artillery shells—Lazar had told him—but he'd been ordered to keep it to himself.

When he made no reply, the general said, "We take the mine, Borbikov sets up his ridiculous nuclear brinkmanship, and then we are safe and sound, or so the plan goes." He paused, then said, "But if we are unsuccessful in capturing the mines . . . *then* what will he do?"

"I . . . I don't know."

"If all you have is a hammer, Dmitry, every problem becomes a nail."

Kir blinked in surprise. "You are suggesting that if we fail to take the mines, he will detonate?"

Lazar shrugged. "He'd have to be able to deliver the nuclear warheads deep within the Marines' lines to render Mrima Hill inoperable for generations. But if failure is at hand, I know he will launch the shells on the Americans from distance."

Kir never cussed in front of his general, but now he said, "Shit. *That's* why a Spetsnaz colonel is inspecting the artillery."

With a solemn look, Lazar slapped the younger man on the shoulder. "So . . . we must be victorious—to save the world." He smiled a little, but the impact of his previous comments remained.

The general continued. "The Americans have a carrier battle group that will be in range in less than two days. So we attack immediately from three directions. We blast the enemy with artillery on one side, then advance on the two other fronts. They may have good firepower, some air coverage, but we are the attacker and they the defender. They are static and we are mobile. In a battle of fixed frontages, the defender loses.

"Didn't I teach this to you in school?"

"You did, Comrade General, only . . . this is different."

"Not at all. We will split his attention. In my estimation, the Americans no longer know how to fight a conventional force. They have been fighting insurgency for years.

"We place the Marines and their French allies in the horns of a dilemma. How will the enemy commander divide his few aircraft? Until the carrier arrives, he has only the few planes the Marines have on board the *Boxer*. He does not have the sortie generation rate, and if he brings them in small numbers, our antiaircraft fire will smash them. Where does he place his anti-armor missile systems? We identify them and take them out. Then we look to see which side of his defense is breaking and we attack there with everything in the reserve."

Kir said, "We penetrate and we annihilate."

"*Da,*" said Lazar.

POLISH-BELARUSIAN BORDER
31 DECEMBER

Nearly fifty M1A2s hid behind the various hills on the western bank of the Bug River. The air sparked with continued sporadic fire, but the battle was at a stalemate. To Grant, it seemed the Russians planned to stay at the border and lob shells as long as they knew there were targets within range, and this had bought him the time he needed to put his plan into action.

The radio in his M1's headset crackled with the call from the commander of 1st Battalion. "Courage Six, this is Bandits Six."

Grant keyed his radio while standing in the turret and looking out into the snowy night. "Bandits, Courage. Go."

"Copy. We're set. Time now."

"Understood. Awaiting the call from Dukes. Once they are in position, we will commence the attack."

Instantly a new voice crackled. It was the 2nd Battalion Commander. "Courage, this is Dukes. We're in our cold positions. All ready to go here."

"Copy, Dukes. Commence your support by fire."

"Courage, this is Dukes. We're commencing our fires, time now." Within seconds of his radio call, the sharp blasts of thirty U.S. tanks firing their 120mm main guns erupted, and simultaneously coaxial .50-caliber machine guns began chattering all over the Polish side of the river. The cacophony of the U.S. suppression fire and the arc of tracer fire electrified the night. The Russians were slow to respond, but soon they began firing back with their own guns. Occasionally an anti-tank missile crossed the open terrain and rocketed over the narrow river.

But Grant wasn't watching the tanks. Instead he was eight miles to the north, peering through his night-vision optics at a distant rail bridge that crossed the river into Belarus. To the south he heard the battle resume with new vitality, but on the far side of the Bug here he counted only four Russian tanks, a single platoon, guarding the bridge.

He assumed they would have wired the iron-and-timber trestle bridge to blow sky-high in the event the Americans tried to cross, but he suspected the Russians weren't expecting any crossings.

Especially not here. This bridge was old, and it didn't look heavy enough to accommodate more than one piece of armor at a time. It was, Grant's scouts determined, a passenger-train-only bridge, unable to handle the much heavier loads of rail cargo.

The lieutenant colonel peered through his thermal sights as a small group of his scouts crept through the fields on the Polish side, then began shimmying under the bridge. His heart threatened to beat out of his chest as he watched the men crawling along, clinging precariously to the undersides of the spans. Their gear and equipment plainly visible in his thermals, they made their way in silence and in darkness, hoping like hell the Russians were scanning deeper into Polish territory for tanks and Humvees, and not looking under the bridge for individual sappers.

Grant checked yet again into Belarus, but still there was no reaction in this sector. Either his plan to paralyze their headquarters with an immense fusillade was working, or any second he would watch a platoon of his best scouts evaporate in a ball of fire.

He held his breath when a soldier's foot slipped on ice, and the man nearly fell forty feet to the hard, frozen river below. He managed to get caught in rigging attached to two other men as he fell, and the other young soldiers were forced to grab tight on their own spans, holding on for dear life as the man hung there for a moment before pulling himself back onto a lower metal beam. Quickly, Grant scanned the four tanks in their dug-in emplacements to the north and saw no evidence that his men had been spotted.

The team radioed back that they had discovered multiple explosive charges. Grant didn't have the resolution in his night optic to see them clipping the wires, but they stopped at different points along the bridge, worked intently for a moment, and then moved farther down.

The distant sound of heavy cannon fire and the flashes and flames lighting up the night to the south were incessant.

After what seemed like an eternity to Grant, the scouts radioed that they had clipped the wires at all five charges under the span.

Now the second squad, their Javelin missiles clearly visible in the thermal contrast on his goggles, crept slowly across the ice covering the Bug River on the northern side of the bridge, out of the view of the tanks, which were positioned on the train tracks as well as to the south. The squad was well led, and in minutes they were across the frozen expanse.

Finally the third team moved out, following the first, only this one crawled along the top of the bridge, and some of the men hauled the big Javelins along with them. The men were dressed head to toe in white, and with the snowfall all around and their careful movements they remained undetected. Soon they reached their position and lay prone, hidden behind the wooden beams over the bridge.

Grant breathed a sigh of relief.

The firing to the south intensified, low reverberations of cannon reports and explosions continuing, but here, in the snowy woods miles to the north, all was still.

Then Grant heard a faint rumbling behind him that grew in volume by the second. The ground began to vibrate, and snow fell in clumps from the trees.

Grant called over his radio.

"Hit 'em."

An instant later six FGM-148 Javelin anti-tank missiles rocketed atop fiery blasts from the dense brush and high reeds of the far bank. A second later six more were fired from the middle spans of the bridge, where the second scout team had crawled.

The strike got the job done, but in the end it was massive overkill. The platoon of four Russian tanks dug in across the river never knew what hit them. The T-14 reactive armor fired to diminish the damage done by the Javelins, but the missiles rained down from such a high angle that several of them penetrated the turret hatches.

All four Armatas exploded in fireballs.

Watching and listening to the beginning of the supporting fire attack from 2nd Battalion, Grant transmitted to 1st Battalion, "Bandits, you're clear. Launch your forces into the attack. The bridge is open."

"Roger." An Abrams lurched from deep in the Polish forest and began heading toward the rail bridge spanning the Bug River and then onto the territory of Russia's vassal state of Belarus.

Behind them the increasing rumble turned into the unmistakable sound of more tanks, and a dozen massive M1s rolled at their top speed of forty-five miles per hour along the cleared forest next to the train tracks, racing to get behind the first to cross the bridge.

And to the south, dozens more American tanks unleashed a continuous hell as the radio call reporting the success of the scouts went out, keeping the main force of Russian tanks heavily occupied.

The first M1 slowed as it arrived at the train bridge, then rolled gingerly onto the span. Keeping his speed down, the commander bravely continued all the way across.

Only when he was completely clear of the bridge on the Belarusian side did the second tank begin its crossing.

More American armor broke cover out of the forest and drove at top speed for the bridge. Again they received massive suppression fire from the south while they, one by one, rolled onto the bridge, each M1 trying the crossing a little faster than the one that went before.

The four tanks on the far side moved to cover as another two and then two more M1s made for the bridge.

Grant had an understrength regiment of U.S. armor, depleted by the fighting against the Russians over the past several days, but by now these tanks were operated by incredibly experienced drivers, gunners, loaders, and commanders, and they re-formed into platoons and companies easily in the darkness over the border.

Lieutenant Colonel Grant watched from the wood line as all twenty-eight tanks that crossed the bridge made it to cover.

Grant turned to his S3. "I didn't think we'd make it this far before the Russians figured us out."

"You and me both, sir. Looks like 2nd Battalion's fires are keeping them pinned down, but the scouts did a damn good job wiping out anybody who could report in."

"Let's mount up and head for that rickety bridge that just had to go through the stress of two dozen M1 crossings."

"Sounds like a hell of a plan, boss." Both men began moving for their vehicles.

Boom! A U.S. tank round fired just beyond the bridge on the Belarusian side of the river. This told him his armor had found the flank of the Russian tanks past the now-dead bridge guard platoon.

More pounding erupted seconds later, and within moments heavy cannon fire rippled through the forest from across the Bug, joining the sounds of the continuous fire from 2nd Battalion to the south.

Grant climbed into his Humvee and looked through the advanced optics of his SPI IR 360 surveillance camera system. He could see his cavalry company making their way back over the bridge and finding cover near the bank on the Polish side. Their mission had been a dangerous one. He would talk to the master sergeants later. *These guys deserve to be the ones with the big, fat medals,* he thought.

Grant's tank lurched forward now and began racing for the bridge.

He'd just ordered an invasion of another country, and he wanted to get his licks in before he was thrown into the stockade.

CHAPTER 71

WESTERN BELARUS
31 DECEMBER

General Eduard Sabaneyev and his headquarters staff had taken over a medieval castle just south of Brest, five kilometers from the Bug River and the Polish border. It had once been a stately residence of a local prince, but now it was rented out as event space for corporate retreats and the like, and all the furniture looked old and shabby.

But it was a beautiful, comfortable building, so he was in no great rush to break contact with the Americans over the border in Poland. His men had enough ammunition for another hour or two of combat, so fifteen minutes earlier Sabaneyev had poured himself a glass of the Hungarian red wine one of his subordinates found on a rack in the basement, and he sat back on a worn leather couch with it.

He'd listened to the intense American and German barrage and over the radio he heard his forces near the river engaging with the enemy.

He expected the NATO tanks to retaliate for a few minutes, and then he presumed they would withdraw. He assumed his own armor along the river would soon have no more targets to prosecute.

But then new crashes of heavy tank fire reverberated through the ancient stones of the castle, and Sabaneyev rose quickly to his feet. The fighting wasn't terribly close, was still a few kilometers away, but this new fire was most definitely coming from due north, not west—the direction of the border. He looked over at the radio operators, who were already sending out calls to Dryagin to find out what the hell was going on.

"What the fuck is that?" the general demanded. "That sounded like it came from east of the river. I did *not* give the order to volley fire again. Find out the unit that broke the protocol. Call Dryagin. He and his forces should not be wasting ammunition!"

The operations officer said, "We're checking now, Comrade General." After a pause to listen to the response he said, "The chatter between the companies coming through over the net makes it sound like the Americans have launched an attack."

The general cocked his head. "They cannot attack with a river in their way."

Smirnov leaned over the radio table now, trying to listen to a multitude of reports coming in and simultaneously appease his boss's thirst for answers.

The sounds of a triple detonation rattled the old castle.

Smirnov held his hand to his earpiece, then spun up to look at Sabaneyev. "Report coming in that the front line is collapsing at the border! The Americans are across the river, eight kilometers north!"

Sabaneyev was stunned. "How did they . . . They have invaded a sovereign nation! Do they wish to start a full-fledged war? Contact Moscow right away. We need air support immediately."

Sabaneyev had not counted on the Americans being so brazen as to continue hostilities against him once he made it into Belarus. Moscow and the general had both relied on the West's reluctance to cross the border into a country that most certainly would follow Russia's lead.

Over the next few minutes the fighting intensified outside, and Smirnov received more reports. "They used a rail bridge. We had assessed it unsuitable for tanks. It is just north of—"

Sabaneyev said, "I know the *damned* bridge! I ordered it guarded and wired with explosives. I ordered Dryagin to cover it with tank fire and drop it into the river as necessary."

"Sir, I believe he had done so—wired it, that is. The Americans sent scouts over the river, eliminated the guard force there, and cut the explosives on the east side."

"But *tanks*! Tanks, man—how did the Yankees cross with tanks?

Where was Dryagin's observation post? Where were his tank crews guarding the bridge?"

Smirnov said, "Dryagin had limited forces. He placed a platoon of T-14s at the train bridge, but they were wiped out. The colonel believed it wiser to dig in the bulk of the heavy armor farther south, thinking most of the Americans were arrayed there."

Sabaneyev stormed around the floor of the command center. "Then he's a fool! He may have cost us today's fight, but I will guarantee he will not lose us even more. Get him up here. And send word to his forces: I am now *directly* in command of the unit. The commanders will only take orders from me and my headquarters. Is that understood, Colonel Smirnov?"

"I am clear, sir. I am understanding the general has just relieved Colonel Dryagin of his command."

"Yes, I will tell him in person."

A radio operator looked up to him. "Sir, reports from the 2nd Battalion, to the northwest. They have American tanks mixed within their position. He is requesting permission to turn his tanks away from the M1 road bridge so he can face the attackers."

"Damn it! Is there no one left with the stomach for this? Tell him to get off the damn radio and turn his ass around and fight! What's 1st Battalion doing?"

"He has made no reports, sir."

"Tell him he is to mount a force to support 2nd Battalion immediately. We'll pummel these bastards back to fucking Poland!"

The message was relayed, and when the reply came, the radio operator said, "Sir, 1st Battalion is still pinned by direct and accurate fires from the Americans on the other side of the river. His dug-in positions are the only things keeping him intact. He cannot move or he will lose tanks. Also, sir, he says his men see Western air units overhead. They have been hit twice by accurate bombing runs by F-35 jets."

The radios broadcast constant transmissions as reports came in rapidly, one after another. The exact location of the Americans was still presumed, but 2nd Battalion continued to report heavy contact by Abrams tanks. Additionally, all up and down the line, they reported accurate attacks from U.S. Apache helicopters.

The parting shot back over the border into Poland had been a mistake,

Sabaneyev now saw. But he wasn't going to take the blame for it. No, none of this was his fault, he told himself. He'd place the blame for all this on those below him, like Dryagin, and those above him, the ones who overestimated the American desire to negotiate peace.

And Dryagin wasn't the only one on the general's mind. He shouted, "I will flog that bastard Borbikov myself when I see him. He gave me assurances about this operation!"

Minutes later, Colonel Dryagin stormed into the bustling command post almost at a run. Pulling off his snow-covered hat and his thick gloves, he looked around the room.

Sabaneyev stood by the roaring fireplace, still listening to the radio reports coming in from the action now four kilometers to the north.

"Colonel General, I must protest! This is the worst timing. We are in the middle of—"

Sabaneyev spun around to him. "You are relieved for incompetence, Colonel. Move to the supply headquarters and make yourself useful organizing my logistics. Our forces are now divided due to *your* lack of attention to *my* orders. I made it clear to guard the passenger rail bridge as well as the heavy-vehicle bridges and by your failing to do so we now are faced with a flood of American tanks."

"But, sir, we had . . . that is, the American tanks are heavier than ours, and we determined—"

"Leave now, Colonel, or you will return to Moscow in chains!" Sabaneyev shouted, then turned his attention away from his former senior commander and back to the radiomen.

Dryagin stared a moment at the general's back. Seeing the futility in protesting, he saluted out of habit and then turned about, drained and empty. He walked in silence to the door, the radios alive with reports of his men in the fight, who were his men no longer.

A radio operator looked up to Sabaneyev. "Sir, I have Moscow. The deputy commander orders you to withdraw into the interior of Belarus, then back to Smolensk. He says to make no more delays."

"Give the command for withdrawal, Smirnov. It will take the Americans some time yet to cross the river in any great numbers, and we will be gone by then. If the Yankees will not respect the soft border of Belarus, they will certainly respect the hard border of Mother Russia. We'll drop a curtain behind us once we receive air cover. Tell the deputy I want Russian jets to line my path as we head out of this mess. If the enemy continues to pursue, we will choke him to death in the Belarusian interior."

Colonel General Sabaneyev packed his leather map case, helmet, and pistol. He had been planning a leisurely movement across Belarus, but now he was steeling himself for further action.

As he stepped outside into the frozen night, he glanced to the east. Several flashes of light flickered behind a distant wood line, and then, three seconds later, tank rounds slammed into the rolling pastureland just south of the castle. The closest was no more than two hundred meters from where Sabaneyev stood.

Smirnov grabbed his general by the arm, swung him around, and pulled him back into the castle. He shouted to the radio operators, "Order the general's Bumerang to pull up to the door! The Americans have us on three sides now!"

Sabaneyev was slow to put this together, still utterly stunned by his change of fortune. After a moment he said, "South is clear. South is still clear." He looked up at Smirnov. "What's to the south?"

"The Ukrainian border, Colonel General."

Sabaneyev was not going to invade Ukraine to escape a motley collection of American armor and a few aircraft. He shook his head. "Withdraw to the east. They can't have gotten much armor behind us this quickly. We'll punch out and kill Americans in the process. Get moving!"

NORTH OF MRIMA HILL, KENYA
31 DECEMBER

Lazar held the encrypted military satellite phone to his ear, and the message came in clear. It was Army general Korotkov, the commander of all southern forces, under whose command Lazar now fell for the conduct of his mission in Africa.

Korotkov said, "Comrade General, I must inform you that the West has crossed into Belarus and currently has Sabaneyev's forces partially surrounded."

Lazar closed his eyes in utter frustration. He looked over at Colonel Borbikov, who seemed to already be aware of that information.

Lazar wondered to himself about Borbikov's magic trains, which were supposed to protect Sabaneyev, but he said nothing.

Korotkov continued. "We're trying to get Eduard reinforced, but the Kremlin is losing its mettle in all this. They are worried about the loss of tanks, and they are worried about the fact that Eduard was stuck in Poland for two days on the return. They are talking about a political solution while Eduard is under fire from main tank rounds. The Belarusian army—what there is of it, anyway—so far has not provided any help."

Lazar realized the European portion of Red Metal had turned into a disaster. An American invasion of Belarus threatened a wider war, and the Kremlin *surely* must have realized a large-scale counterattack from NATO right now could be repelled only with nuclear weapons, because a large portion of Russian armor was otherwise engaged.

Nuclear war on two continents seemed entirely possible now, and Lazar put all the blame for this on the Spetsnaz colonel in the corner, conferring with his men.

The older general kept his tone even as he spoke into the sat phone. "I understand you, General. What are your orders?"

"Boris, we are out of bargaining chips here. Things have just gotten very ugly, my old friend. Get us that mine. No matter what."

"How does our seizure of the mine change the equation, General?"

"We have *nothing* now. Nothing to broker with except that mine and its impact on coming generations. Nothing will settle the West down like the knowledge they'll have to be our business partners. Sure, Sabaneyev still possesses a handful of American and NATO superior officers as prisoners, but we do not occupy any ground with which to trade."

Korotkov added, "I must tell you, Boris, the Central Committee has been talking of launching tactical nuclear weapons to stave off the attack. Things are at a critical state here."

Lazar closed his eyes slowly. *Utter madness.*

"So here it is, my final word: Boris, take . . . that . . . fucking . . . mine."

"I understand, sir," Lazar said, and hung up the receiver.

Colonel Borbikov stared at him a moment. Soon the younger man began speaking in a slow, measured, if not condescending, tone. "Comrade General Lazar—"

Lazar saw it coming and held up a hand and cut him off. "This was *your* plan, and it is turning into shit on every possible front."

Lazar and the men would fight, and many more would likely die, and then, if he interpreted General Korotkov's words correctly, the Russians might give the mine or a portion of its bounty to the Yankees for political concessions. Lazar was not sure Borbikov had fully registered that yet.

General Lazar turned to Colonel Kir, who had been standing behind them, listening intently to everything Lazar said.

Kir threw his shoulders back. "Your orders, General?"

NEAR BREST, BELARUS
31 DECEMBER

Sixty minutes after Sabaneyev and his HQ section left the castle, Tom Grant's command vehicles rolled up the drive toward the stately structure. Grant saw that Captain Brad Spillane had climbed off his vehicle and was running up toward the lieutenant colonel's tank.

Grant could hear the fight raging in the forests to the east. The Russians were probing up different roads, trying to move past the Americans who had flanked them. He knew his battalion positioned in that direction wouldn't be able to hold off the regiment of Russians, but Grant was pleased to hear new reports every few minutes about his force taking out individual enemy vehicles. And the Russians were doing more running than fighting at the moment, which was saving his tanks from weathering a full-on battle.

The one advantage for Grant so far had been a distinct lack of Belarusian resistance; the local forces seemed content to stay the hell out of this fight, although Grant figured the diplomatic fallout of this for Minsk in its relations with Russia would probably exceed any military damage done to the tiny nation in battle.

He had just pulled off his helmet, when Spillane arrived. "Brad, whatcha got?"

Spillane clambered up the side of his commander's Abrams so he could be heard more clearly above the high whine of the big tank's gas turbine engine. "Sir, what about using that castle as a temporary CP? It was the Russian HQ just an hour ago."

"Watch it," warned Grant as the turret began rotating, threatening to knock Captain Spillane off. "Anderson is still scanning those trees for stragglers." Spillane climbed onto the bustle rack at the back of the turret to continue speaking while the huge steel and depleted-uranium turret moved freely left and right.

Grant peered out into the night, looking at the stone fortress just ahead. It was clearly something from medieval times, and it was also clear from the tracks in the snow and mud that the Russians had been there very recently.

Grant said, "If it's good enough for a Russian general, it's good enough for a tanker like me."

The political decision for NATO to enter Belarus was not made without a tremendous amount of trepidation on the part of the West. When they learned that U.S. forces had pursued attacking Russian forces over the border, they realized they needed to deliver a clear ultimatum via open diplomatic channels. NATO stated that Belarus had knowingly and deliberately allowed an aggressive Russian force to depart its country to attack NATO, and the combined forces of NATO, bar none, collectively held Belarus accountable. They demanded right of passage through Belarus in pursuit of the Russian force.

Belarus was caught in the middle. If they denied allowing the Americans in, the West would call them complicit and the consequences could be dire. They could not afford to go to war alone with the West, and Russia seemed unwilling to place any further forces in their country.

On the other hand, if Belarus complied with the NATO demands to let them pursue the Russians, they could never count on support from Russia again.

In the end, they decided to do nothing.

The government in Minsk didn't respond to political demands from Russia to defend their fleeing forces, and they didn't tell the West it could not pursue: they merely told their citizens to stay off the major east-west-running highway for their own safety.

And this was enough of a signal to the West.

Air support for Grant's forces came quickly, and ground support was ordered forward. Two brigades from NATO's immediate response forces had taken days to come online, but they entered the fight now: an Italian light infantry regiment and a composite Belgian and British medium-armored regiment.

The two units crossed the undamaged bridges over the Bug River sixty kilometers north of where the Russians had disabled the other crossing points, and they raced to catch up to the American and German tank force led by Lieutenant Colonel Grant.

And the Belarusians did nothing to intervene.

CHAPTER 72

MRIMA HILL, KENYA
31 DECEMBER

Lieutenant Colonel Dan Connolly, Captain Apollo Arc-Blanchette, Colonel Caster, and Lieutenant Colonel McHale ducked into the command tent of 3rd Battalion, 5th Marines, while touring the northern perimeter defenses of the Mrima Hill mine. A light breeze floated through the open side flaps. Marines outside were busy filling sandbags and cutting branches to further conceal the battalion headquarters' location from enemy drones and reconnaissance forces.

The Darkhorse command post was a hive of activity as each officer and staff NCO labored to get the defenses organized. Maps were laid all over the center tables. On the edges of the tent were more tables full of radios, plotting boards, sketches, and timetables for the battalion's mortars and regimental artillery.

"Ben," Colonel Caster said to the commander of the 3rd Battalion, 5th Marines. "Talk me through your defenses."

The Darkhorse commander pulled out an acetate overlay and placed it carefully onto the primary battle map in the center of the table. It showed a detailed graphic depiction of his forces down to the squad and machine-gun levels.

"Sir, here's us in the northern third. You can see that I've tied my western flank in with 1st Battalion and my eastern flank with 2nd. I've got a layered defense in depth to deal with most contingencies the Russians decide to toss at us." He pointed to the symbols for the tanks and LAVs well out in front of his positions.

For the next thirty minutes the Darkhorse operations officer and operations chief briefed Colonel Caster, Apollo, Connolly, and Lieutenant Colonel McHale, describing their intent for a layered, ringed defensive tactic. If it worked, it would force the Russians to advance through "kill boxes" where the Marines would surgically take out the attacking heavy weapons until Lazar had mostly just infantry left. Then the Marine infantry would do what they did best: kill what remained.

The first layer of their defense was the Marine reconnaissance units. These were also the farthest away from the battalion's headquarters high on Mrima Hill. There were several different flavors of reconnaissance scouting for Russians in front of the battalion's lines.

Marine Force Reconnaissance, called simply "Force," had been dropped by helicopter to the farthest layer, about sixteen kilometers away. These teams would identify the incoming Russians, obtaining an understanding of how they amassed and attacked. Force would radio this data back to the Darkhorse command post so the Marines could fine-tune their defenses. The specially trained men of Force would then go to ground, remaining concealed behind the enemy as they passed. Then they'd pop out and hit unguarded vital enemy formations: an artillery section, supply trucks, a radio terminus, or, if they were exceedingly lucky, a headquarters.

The next layer in the defense, fourteen kilometers away, was the hand-selected and elite men of the light-armored reconnaissance companies. They lived like the cavalry on their armored mounts, and were one of the fastest reconnaissance forces in the world. They had 25mm guns, TOW anti-tank missiles, and their own mortar section. Trained to "shoot 'n' scoot," they used a medium array of firepower and worked to flank their opponent. If the Russians chased them, they would remain elusive and then request a sheaf of artillery to be dropped behind them to "close the door" as they withdrew. Overhead throughout the operation the Marines had their own mini Air Force: AV-8B Harrier II strike jets. Also, thanks to the Marine VMFA-121, the Green Knights squadron, a host of F/A-18s had flown over in advance of their carrier, which was still too far to support directly.

The next defensive line was the heavy firepower of six Javelin missile crews and a platoon of four Abrams tanks. The operations chief briefed that teams were still digging in eight kilometers away with the support of the regiment's engineers. The anti-tank missile teams and the M1A2s would work together to take out as many of the Russian BTRs as they could.

Each tank had one "cold" position, where it would remain concealed until the right time. Then it would drive up to its "hot" position, a dugout where only the turret was exposed so the crew could fire freely. They'd send two or three rounds, then reverse back to the "cold" position, where, even if they were spotted, they would have some defense from Russian missiles.

The last line of defense was the hard-core, disciplined fighting men of the Marine Corps infantry, armed to the teeth with AT-4 and SMAW anti-tank rockets; the reliable, heavy Browning .50-cal machine guns, capable of penetrating light armor; medium 7.62mm FN M240s; and the light 5.56mm M249 SAW and M27 IAR machine guns.

The Marine infantrymen were heavily concealed in the thickest parts of the woods at the base of Mrima Hill. They dug vehicle ditches and laced the roads with explosives, claymore mines, and barbed wire designed to halt Russian vehicles and snare the Russian dismounts. Every obstacle was covered by a machine gun so that when the BTRs were bottlenecked or halted, the Marines could blow the explosives, then cut the infantry in half with machine-gun fire.

Behind them on the hill were Darkhorse's heavy 81mm M252 mortars, dug into pits in clearings in the woods. The M252s were ready to rain down steel explosives the size of whiskey bottles onto the enemy. They also possessed illumination rounds to light up the skies in the likely case of a nighttime attack, and high-concentrate smoke to obscure the movements of the Marines.

As the briefing wrapped up, Apollo felt a buzzing in the cargo pocket of his uniform pants. He felt inside his pocket and found his phone was ringing.

Apollo looked down at the number. It was his father.

Finally!

He leapt up from his little chair, excused himself, and stepped outside the tent.

He answered with, "Papa?"

There was a brief pause on the line; then an unfamiliar male voice spoke in French. *"Bonjour, monsieur.* Am I speaking with the son of Pascal Arc-Blanchette?"

Apollo felt his legs weaken. He continued walking away from the command tent. *"Oui."*

"Monsieur, my name is Arthur Caron. I am calling you from Djibouti City. I am a cultural attaché at the embassy here."

The French captain's mind knew exactly where this was going, but his heart tried to tell him he was wrong. Still, his face morphed into a mask of pain, and tears welled in his eyes.

"I am afraid," Caron continued, "that I am calling with terrible news. I don't know how else to put it."

Apollo sniffed now, lifted his chin, forced his eyes to sharpen as he blinked out the tears. "I will spare you of the need, monsieur. You are calling to tell me that my father is dead."

Caron hesitated—perhaps he was surprised—but finally he said, "I am afraid that is so."

Apollo's jaw muscles flexed.

"His body was found with those of three other French nationals in a restaurant at the edge of town. He has been brought back to the embassy, and will be returned to France immediately."

"How did he die?"

"Well . . . I . . ."

"How . . . did . . . he . . . die?"

"He was tortured and then shot. I am sorry."

Apollo closed his eyes a moment, then said, "I assume you worked with my father." The French embassy had cleared out days ago. If there was someone claiming to be a French cultural attaché in Djibouti now, then Apollo was certain he was *not* a French cultural attaché.

"Well . . . as I said, I am an employee here at the embassy. I knew him in passing only. A very fine man. I am truly sorry for your loss."

Apollo lowered his voice an octave. He spoke now not as a heartbroken child of a deceased father but as a military officer on a mission. "I assume you *worked* with my father, monsieur." Apollo knew Caron would be loath to admit this to anyone.

But the situation and the captain's tone both compelled him. *"Oui.* That is correct. We both work for the same department."

Apollo knew this was DGSE. French foreign intelligence.

"My father was a hero of our nation," Apollo declared, the pride and the sadness welling up within him in equal measures.

"Unquestionably," Caron said immediately. "I cannot speak more about this, you understand. But he worked diligently until the very end."

Apollo was certain he was talking about the transmission of data on the Russian brigade.

Caron added, "He has done much more than I during the current conflict, than any of of us—that I freely admit."

Apollo nodded at the phone. "Well . . . at least you're there, which means you didn't get on that plane full of French government personnel that left my father behind the other day. You have my respect. Thank you for your call, Monsieur Caron."

Apollo hung up the phone and looked down the hill. It was dark now, but he could picture the jungle that went on for kilometers before turning into reddish brown arid land. He closed his eyes again but opened them when he felt someone walk up beside him.

"Hey, Captain. Any news about your dad?" It was Connolly, the American lieutenant colonel.

Apollo's eyes searched the distance, but it was too dark to see the enemy. "The Russians tortured and murdered him."

"Jesus Christ." Connolly put an arm on Apollo's shoulder and squeezed it tight. "I'm sorry, Captain. I'm *really* sorry." Apollo did not respond. "Look, you should probably go to medical and take a few minutes to—"

The Frenchman turned to the American. "I came here to stop those men, down this hill, from killing my men, and your men. Right now, Lieutenant Colonel, nothing else matters."

He squeezed the hand on his shoulder, nodded his appreciation to Connolly, and said, "I need to check on my Javelin crews at the front."

He turned and walked off into the darkness.

SOUTH OF WARSAW, POLAND
31 DECEMBER

The four Polish Land Forces vehicles stopped at the gas station just before two a.m. While men began pumping gas into the Honker Skorpion 3 all-purpose pickups, others who were awake and felt like stretching their legs climbed out to smoke or just stand around. More than half the men remained in the beds of their vehicles, sleeping against their huge military field rucksacks.

The pickups had machine guns and all the men carried rifles, but the war was over, in Poland anyway, so no one was on any real guard. The Russian armored column, fractured and diminished as it was, was well inside Belarus and running through the night.

These men were all weary from fighting, glad it was over, and looking forward to their first real rest in a week.

The night was well below freezing, but the air was clear and the stars shone brightly. A train passed a few hundred meters away, heading west, the clickety-clack of its steel wheels the only sounds in the still winter night. It was clearly a local passenger train; the lights were on inside the cars, and the soldiers watched it drive past absentmindedly as they smoked.

It was a nice reminder that things would someday return to normal.

Ray Vance hobbled out of a truck behind them, and when they offered him a smoke, he accepted. Shank didn't look much like a smoker. More a clean-living guy. The bandages over his eye and hand couldn't mask his keen features. He was youthful looking and handsome.

The turret machine gunner on the lieutenant's Skorpion 3 spoke enough English to understand the pilot and to be understood himself.

The pilot had been handed over to this small group of regular army forces for transport up to Warsaw. He would go to the hospital there to be checked out and then fly back to his unit in Germany.

For the motor transport lieutenant and his drivers, this was actually the fifth stop. Their most recent was at a jeweler's in the town of Grójec. It was an unofficial detour because the American had asked if he could run into the store for a few minutes, and the young PLF lieutenant had no problem with a little break, especially because the American offered to buy all the men lunch at McDonald's.

The American spent nearly a half hour in the jewelry store browsing through rings.

The Poles came back from McDonald's to find the American holding a small shopping bag. Of course they were curious, and they prodded him a bit, with the gunner translating, but he wouldn't tell them what was inside the bag.

Hours had passed since then, but Shank had remained tight-lipped about his purchase. But now, as he stood with the others near the wall of the gas station, smoking and huddling deep in their coats to ward off a cold breeze, the turret gunner asked him again, "What did you buy?"

Shank smiled. "You boys are gonna keep asking till I tell you, aren't you?"

"Yes. The guys want to know what was so important."

After a pause he said, "A ring."

"For mother?"

"No. For a girl."

The gunner translated and the men all laughed. They spoke more to the young gunner, and he looked back at Shank.

"They want to know if it is a Polish girl. Someone you met here."

"As matter of fact, yes," he answered with a grin.

His words needed no translation, and the others all laughed some more. More cigarettes came out; he demurred on a second. But when the lieutenant brought out a flask of Polish vodka, he took a sip along with the men.

Shank had gotten his first taste of ground combat and he hoped like hell it would be his last. The worry was constant. The threats were constant. But it was good to be around others. In the air he was alone. Here, the camaraderie was ever present. Strengthening their resolve. Bonding the men and women of the ground combat arms.

The lieutenant said some words to the gunner, who translated yet again. "He says that vodka warms the belly on a cold night like this. But that maybe your heart is already warmed by this *Sasza* of yours."

"Oh . . . ," said the American captain, blushing a little under the scrutiny. "Actually, her name is Paulina."

More laughter as all the men repeated "Paulina," clapping him on the shoulder and back.

The lieutenant looked at his watch, then smiled. In English he said, "Happy New Year, Shank," and he offered him another drink.

Shank smiled as well as he took the flask. "Happy New Year."

As he finished swallowing his gulp, a flash of light and a concussive crash enveloped the gas station. One of the Polish Land Forces pickups went up in a ball of fire, blasting debris in all directions just fifty feet from where Shank stood.

The men near the store turned to find cover, but the gunfire of a dozen fully automatic rifles began jackhammering from the trees to the west, the whipcrack of AK rounds snapping through the air around the men standing there by the wall.

Shank began to race through the front door of the gas station, but a rifle round caught him under the chin. He raised both arms and clutched his throat with his right hand and the cast on his left.

Blood shot out of the wound; an artery was severed.

The second, third, and fourth bullets hit him in the back and legs.

Shank pitched forward and fell facedown on the sidewalk in front of the door.

As the others spun and fell, the lieutenant's gunner, wounded, managed to scramble to the door of his Skorpion 3. He was just leaning in to grab his rifle when a burst of rounds caught him in the abdomen. He fell to the frozen concrete, the lit cigarette still dangling from his mouth.

The bulk of the firing lasted no more than fifteen seconds, and in that span the American pilot and all sixteen Polish soldiers were killed, their bodies perforated by gunfire or torn by explosions. Some of the men died while sleeping against their packs in the truck beds.

The Spetsnaz troop reloaded their magazines in the trees, then approached the gas station with weapons held high. They had spent the last two days on foot, moving east only at night. The plan had been to rejoin the main column as it passed through Poland, but the routes changed after Wrocław, and this team had been missed by the Russian forces on the way out.

So tonight, hungry, cold, and tired, Major Lyosha Rochenkov decided they would steal some vehicles for warmth and mobility.

It had been pure luck to find the Polish Land Forces Skorpions filled with and surrounded by soldiers who looked like they had no idea there were still Russian military inside Poland. Rochenkov had carefully moved his men into the trees near the gas station, then ordered them to open fire.

The Russians walked among the bodies now, kicking the still forms lying on the ground and poking with their rifles at the men in the trucks, checking to see if any remained alive.

They were all dead.

A young Spetsnaz soldier said, "Major, this one over here is an officer. Do you want his uniform?"

"*Da*. Everyone, change quickly into their uniforms."

"Sir," said the NCO of the unit, "if we are caught in Polish uniforms, we will be shot."

Rochenkov said, "What the fuck do you think they will do with us now that we've slaughtered half a platoon of men without quarter? We can move easier in their vehicles with their uniforms on, and we're just as dead either way if we don't make it into Belarus by sunrise."

The Spetsnaz major removed the coat from the lieutenant and put it on over his own uniform. It fit, for the most part, though the front was still wet and red with blood.

A special forces sergeant called from over by the door to the gas station. "Major? This one over here . . . I think this guy is an American."

The Spetsnaz major walked over and looked at the body on the sidewalk in front of the door to the gas station. He knelt and rolled the man over on his back. Rochenkov nodded. "That's an American air force flight suit. Look at the cast on his arm and the bandage around his face. He must have been shot down."

"This was not his lucky week, then," laughed the junior NCO. "Next time, stay at home, Yankee," he said, staring at the body.

Others gathered around, fascinated to see the dead American.

"Look," said the NCO. "He's got a flask next to him."

"Not a bad way to go," mumbled another. "A little drink in your gut is better than most get."

Major Rochenkov said, "All right, mount up in the three remaining pickups." They all moved toward the vehicles, some still buttoning up their Polish uniforms. "We have to make it to the border before daybreak or we'll have to lay up another day. Man the turret guns and everyone stand at the ready with your weapons."

The NCO added, "No sleeping. Look around you—you see what sleeping will get you."

The Russian soldiers climbed into the Polish vehicles and headed east toward Belarus, leaving the corpses behind in the frigid night.

CHAPTER 73

MRIMA HILL, KENYA
31 DECEMBER

Connolly had been dozing uncomfortably in a folding camping chair just inside the entrance to the horizontal shaft. He snapped awake as loud radio chatter came in, and he looked at his watch. It was four a.m. and instantly he knew he was going to have to dig deep into a reserve of energy to stay alert this early morning.

He rubbed his stiff knees as the Force Recon radioman's snap report echoed throughout the cavernous mine shaft.

"Grizzly, Grizzly, Black Diamond One, over."

"Go, Black Diamond."

"Roger. SPOTREP follows."

"Black Diamond, go with SPOTREP."

"Roger. I have eyes on, time now. Be advised, enemy is approximately a regiment-sized unit of BTR-82s. Unit travels north to south along highway Charlie one-zero-six. Speed is about four-five kilo-papa-hotel, now crossing phase line 'Chesty.' Enemy unit is arrayed in traveling formation."

Lieutenant Colonel McHale was up on the net instantly. "Black Diamond, Grizzly Main. We copy all. Continue to observe and report." He ran his finger down the map from the enemy's position and south about eight kilometers. He looked over to Apollo Arc-Blanchette, who had been dozing while lying against a backpack. The Frenchman was on his feet in a second. "Captain, at present direction and speed, I estimate the enemy will be on your Dragoons in about ten minutes."

"Understood," said Apollo. He hurried over to a table, then confirmed on his own map lying there.

Caporal Konstantine handed Apollo the French radio handset and he transmitted to the men of Three Team. "Dragoon Three, are you copying the Marine report?"

"Dragoon actual, this is Dragoon Three. We copy all. Ambush position set," they responded.

Apollo gave McHale the thumbs-up. "They'll punch them in the nose, sir. They've been at it for days now, on two continents."

The half-moon glowed high in the cloudless Kenyan sky, offering plenty of light for the eight men of Dragoon Three Team. With their night optics they could easily discern the shapes of the distant Russian BTRs still driving in a traveling formation, rolling straight down the road, maximizing their speed but making themselves excellent targets for the French special forces men.

"How many do you count?" Sergent Coronett asked his missileman, who was looking through the thermal sight system of his anti-tank Missile Moyenne Portée. The young Dragoon's hands cupped the twin grips, slowly rotating the massive launcher on its tripod mount as he tracked the approaching Russian vehicles.

"I count twenty." He pulled back a bit to address his team leader. A green glow illuminated two circles around his eyes where the eyecups leaked light from his thermal sight system. "Maybe more, boss. Too many to see the back of the column. I see no tanks, just BTRs." The man leaned back to the scope and continued tracking.

Sergent Coronett grabbed his squad radio to talk to the rest of his missilemen. "All teams, prepare to launch on my mark."

The missileman with Coronett said, "Ready to fire."

After a few seconds Coronett patted him on the back. "Fire."

The Dragoon flipped off the thumb safety and squeezed the trigger on the butterfly grip.

There was a loud, hollow *pop* as the missile ejected six feet from the launch tube; then a massive *whoosh* filled the quiet night as the rocket motor kicked in, jetting the missile hundreds of meters into the air.

To Sergent Coronett's left and right, six other missilemen took their cue and fired their Moyennes.

In just under four seconds, five of seven tandem HEAT warheads blasted into the lead BTRs. The missiles peeled open the tops like tin cans, destroying the vehicles and the occupants instantly.

Without a word, all seven crews collapsed their missile launchers and gear, hefted everything onto their backs, and sprinted fifty meters back to their waiting pickups.

Four kilometers to the north the Russian lead battalion quickly fanned out into combat formation and began firing wildly, clearly shocked by the impact of losing most of a platoon without warning, this far north of Mrima Hill. By the time some semblance of fighting order had been established in the Russian ranks, the Dragoons were racing south at full speed.

At the regimental command post, the radio crackled. "Dragoon Six, this is Dragoon Three. Five enemy BTRs KIA. We are executing bump, back to our next anti-armor ambush position."

Apollo keyed his radio. "Good work, Three Team. Reload and get ready for another salvo." He looked over at Lieutenant Colonel McHale to see if he was tracking. McHale was talking on another radio but signaled that he was following the successful French first hits with a thumbs-up.

Apollo finished his transmission to Three Team. "The southern Marine Force Recon team is set and wants you to make haste driving through their positions at the bridge."

A few minutes later a whispering voice came over the Marine radio. "Grizzly Three, Grizzly Three, this is Black Diamond. I have the lead unit of the Russians passing me now. We estimate six minutes until the center of the regiment."

"Copy. I show all friendly forces south of your position. You are clear to demo the bridge on your timeline."

"Black Diamond copies all. Out."

Sixteen kilometers from the command post, the Force team now lay in wait, watching Russian BTRs stream past. Five detonators, five lines of det cord, and five wires led to their concealed positions in the dry riverbed east of the heavy bridge on the C106. Camouflaged by cut foliage, their faces painted, the team leader counted vehicles quietly while the assaultman, a specially trained demolitions expert, made a final check on the explosive initiators.

The radio operator inched up to his team leader and whispered into his ear. "Sir, word from Grizzly Main. We're clear to initiate."

The Force Recon team leader, a Marine Corps staff sergeant with eleven years' experience, just nodded.

He felt for the handset of his squad radio without pulling his eyes from the night optic he used to track the approaching forces. He pressed the button and spoke softly. "Spotter, you have eyes on?"

The whispered response came back. "Affirm. Center mass of the regiment is two-zero-zero meters. One platoon . . . They're slowing. They're gonna inspect the bridge."

The Force Recon staff sergeant responded with a calm that belied the danger he was in. "Copy." He put the handset down and reached over, tapping the assaultman's back with his free hand. "Safety off. I'll give the signal. On my mark." He kept his eyes in the night optic, watching while a row of BTRs closed on the bridge.

"Understood," came the hushed response, and the assaultman connected the wires to his detonator. He folded the plastic cover back and held his thumb above the trigger switch.

Two of the big Russian armored personnel carriers drove over to the south side of the bridge while the other two remained on the north side. In their night-vision goggles the Marines could see Russian soldiers pouring out of the backs of the BTRs. They immediately fanned out and began looking around. A dozen men climbed over the metal railing and began moving down the spans.

He could tell by their speed and haste that they had been ordered to proceed as fast as possible. Even while the soldiers were still below the span, another platoon of BTRs began rolling over it.

He watched the Russian soldiers crawl around the spans. After another platoon of BTRs started to cross the top of the bridge, the team leader tapped his assaultman.

The Marine placed his thumb firmly on the control switch and in one quick motion pulled it back, initiating the electronic trigger.

A flash followed by a thunderous explosion, and the bridge disintegrated. Steel and wood whirled into the night sky.

The BTR platoon burned in the twisted wreckage of the bridge. The vehicles turned to red and yellow glowing heaps; then, as they lay on their sides in the shallow, muddy river, their ammunition ignited, shooting bright white flames and sparks.

The Marines fitted their NVGs back on their helmets, shouldered their rifles, and ran south into the inky darkness.

The call came into the Grizzly command center. The bridge was down and the attacking Russian regiment in the west was now split almost in half, one half trapped on the northern side of the bridge, the other half on the southern side. They would certainly figure out how to circumvent the downed bridge, but there would be a lot of confusion in the Russians' western regiment as they sorted out the destruction and mayhem caused by the Marines and French Dragoons.

The radio operator looked up at McHale. "Sir, you'll want to take this. Radio call incoming from 2nd Battalion in the eastern sector."

McHale took the radio. "Warlords, this is Grizzly. Send traffic."

"Copy, Grizzly. Our LAR platoon reports enemy vehicles coming into their zone. They don't have good visibility in the broken terrain to the east but believe it's more than a battalion. The enemy are coming through the eastern boundary, down route C108, moving fast. LAR is going to take some shots and retrograde. Requesting immediate air support to cover their withdrawal."

"Understood, Warlords. Confirming now. Get ready to receive close air. I'll check them in on station and pass them to your FAC." Lieutenant Colonel McHale radioed over to the USS *Boxer* and initiated the call for close air support. They were going to have to use their air judiciously in the coming hours, but this situation definitely warranted it, as far as McHale was concerned.

Aboard the USS *Boxer*, the six pilots of VMFA-122, who had been waiting strapped into their F-35B Lightning II fighters, now began blasting off the deck. Just twelve minutes later they were passed to the light attack reconnaissance forward air controllers. All six made a single pass, each launching two air-to-ground attack missiles, but in the broken, hilly, and wooded terrain to the east of Mrima Hill, only a few met their marks. Four BTRs were destroyed, but many times that number continued forward.

The Russians had been waiting for the Marines to start using their aircraft. Just after the attack run, sixteen Russian ZSU-23-4 antiaircraft vehicles launched streams of Igla 9K38 missiles. The Iglas were better used on helicopters, but the Marines brought the fighters in too close in order to pick out targets in the rough terrain. Two F-35s succumbed to the fast-flying missile systems, taking direct hits and exploding in fireballs. The remaining F-35s were forced to climb to a higher altitude to stay clear, and this limited their ability to accurately support the Marines on the ground.

Losing an aircraft was an almost unimaginable event for the Marines. Before the pair of F-35s augered into the African dirt, the Marines had not lost a jet aircraft to ground fire since Vietnam.

The Cobra gunships from HMLA-267, called the "Stingers," lined up to assist the LAR platoon withdrawing in the east. The Cobras had suffered two losses at the hands of the Russians up north at Moyale, and with only six gunships remaining, they were forced to use caution.

The quad-23mm cannons on the ZSUs sprayed a wall of bullets every time the Cobras attempted to approach, and one helo was hit within minutes of arriving on station but was able to limp out to sea and back to the *Boxer*. A second helicopter took a direct hit to its main rotor by an Igla missile and exploded five hundred feet above the earth. A few Cobra TOWs hit their marks, killing three Russian BTRs, but, running low on fuel and flares, the attack helos were forced to pull back.

At six a.m., 2nd Battalion, 2nd Marines, reported in. Their lead Javelin gunners were engaging approaching Russian BTRs in their sector. In the east the Russians, working their way through restrictive canyons and hills, had closed the distance to just over eleven kilometers from the mines.

Transmissions back to the Grizzly headquarters from 1st Battalion in the western sector reported that the Russians had found a bypass around the blown bridge by using a portion of the river where there was less than a meter of water and the gradient of the banks was not as sheer, and now they were less than fourteen kilometers from the Marine defensive lines.

The mood in the regimental CP seemed to change from guarded optimism to tense desperation in a matter of moments. The Russians' incredible antiair resources had all but eliminated the effect of aircraft from the *Boxer*, and the enemy advance continued.

Colonel Caster and Lieutenant Colonel McHale discussed shifting 3rd Battalion to support the other two if they remained unengaged in their sector, and there was talk of bringing the Foreign Legion forces around to the northern side of the hill, but the Marines had more and superior antiarmor weapons.

McHale turned to Caster. "Sir, if the Russians attack in the north now, we will be stretched to the max."

"Work on keeping air in the fight. Cycle them back to the flat deck as needed. Keep the battery firing. We can fly in more ammo later if needed, so direct them to use everything they've got."

"Aye, aye, sir."

Colonel General Boris Lazar sat in the command position in a BTR-82A atop Jombo Hill, looking south, toward Mrima through the vehicle's night-vision system, scanning the lowlands that lay before him between the two hills. By the light of the predawn half-moon, he could see terrain dotted with a light growth of trees, open fields, and a few small clusters of buildings and farms.

His own reconnaissance forces had successfully jammed the Force Recon Marines' radios as they slipped quietly up Jombo, fully expecting to find Americans hiding there. His special reconnaissance men then attacked the Marines, killing four and driving the others off after a frantic, close-in firefight.

Lazar now held this high ground, and he visualized the chaos inside the 5th Marines' regimental headquarters as he tightened the noose encircling their defenses.

It was to be expected that he'd lose men and machines fighting in this manner. He, too, had divided his forces, and the Marines had been careful in their preparations. But he watched as his forces in both the west and the east peeled back each layer of the Marine defenses. He knew this would mean a quickening pace in the Marine headquarters. The Americans' tasking of their aircraft, their use of artillery—their reactions in general—were becoming slightly more sluggish now as Lazar's predictions unfolded.

Kir was able to learn this himself in the headquarters tent as reports came in from individual sections and he checked over the map. But Lazar just felt it by instinct, his mind carefully absorbing all the information coming in and then picturing the battle space in his mind.

He could almost hear the increasingly anxious combat reports, the casualty figures mounting, the tension heightening as the Marine commander tried to send forces to react to each new Russian attack. The American was placing his fingers in a leaky dam, and he didn't have many fingers left.

Lazar, a colonel general, was equivalent to an American three-star general. He was fighting against a simple colonel, and although the American had likely seen combat in Iraq and Afghanistan, he was already demonstrating his lack of practice at dealing with the higher orders of battle Lazar was throwing at him now. The Marine colonel's experience chasing the Taliban, tracking how many goats each mountain village had, and combating poppy cultivation would provide him no great advantage today, the general thought to himself.

And now it was time for Lazar's third attack. This onslaught, he'd calculated, would grossly overextend the Marine regiment's ability to command and control and provide fire support. And without coordinated artillery fire, the Marines were outnumbered against an organized system of combat power.

He expected that the Marine battalion defending to the north of the mine would fight hard, since they had not yet taken enemy contact. But he would watch carefully for a slower response from their regiment. He had told Colonels Kir and Glatsky to look for a slackening or heavily reduced response in artillery. This would be the first test to see if he was right.

Lazar confidently ordered Kir to unleash a massed heavy artillery barrage onto the hapless Marine battalion defending the north side of Mrima Hill.

An hour later the first hues of dawn broke, and Boris Lazar could finally see the valley below him. The battle in the west raged on. He observed rockets and missile launches every few minutes, with return fire from the Americans. The Marines were fighting with everything they had. A few of 1st Regiment's BTRs had been hit by the deadly American Javelins; Lazar watched the flashes of light and listened to the delayed sounds of explosions as his young men in the distance died fiery deaths.

The Javelin was an accursedly accurate weapon, but the general knew it'd be in limited supply.

Simply put, Lazar had more boys and armor than the Marines had missiles.

He had told Colonel Nishkin to make all haste, bypass any small pockets of Marines, and put pressure on their center. The latest report from Nishkin was that they had successfully broken past the demolished bridge and were advancing at a good clip. Red tracer fire from 30mm cannons and 7.62mm machine guns continued in heavy bursts, cascading across the landscape in long beads, ricochets launching up into the early-morning sky. The thumping from twenty or thirty weapons firing cyclic remained virtually constant now as 1st Regiment broke through the smaller French and U.S. forces.

In the east, Russia's 3rd Regiment was still being harassed by a few Marine helicopters, though in limited numbers. Colonel Klava was using the ZSUs to good effect, hiding them carefully, then launching massive barrages of fire once the Marine helos tried to approach.

As Lazar watched now, four Cobras moved forward again in the distance. They launched missiles at Russian armor; then the attack helicopters began circling, firing their 20mm Gatling guns at long range.

The answer from Klava came swiftly. Igla missiles were launched in unison, followed by the heavy chatter of 23mm cannon fire. The air was alight with green tracers, a deadly fireworks show that enraptured the sixty-four-year-old general.

Two American helos were hit almost simultaneously. Lazar saw the bursts of yellow-orange and watched while they spun back down to earth, their fuel burning out of control.

Both aircraft crashed into the hillside.

Bravo, Klava, he thought.

Lazar looked over his maps and conferred with Colonel Kir over the radio back at his command post. Then he turned and signaled to his second regimental commander that he was now clear to attack.

Lazar would watch this for a few more minutes; then he would personally accompany 3rd Regiment in their assault on the enemy's northern battalion.

CHAPTER 74

The frigid weather made the image in General Sabaneyev's binoculars stand out crisply and clearly. He drew in a deep breath, the cold air filling his lungs, then held the breath to steady the binoculars. He rolled the dial with his forefinger, trying to make out any sign of the enemy.

Colonel Smirnov stepped up next to him. "Colonel General, Moscow has sent a digital combat message response to your last transmission. They said to continue with all haste to the Russian border."

Sabaneyev listened but held still. He took another deep breath of the freezing air, remaining sighted in on a small speck on the highway in the distance. It could easily be just another commercial tractor trailer, except for the fact that the Belarusian government had halted all civilian traffic earlier in the morning.

Then he saw another speck, and then another. They were definitely large vehicles and definitely moving in his direction. With his eyes still pressed firmly into the binos he said, "Did Command say anything about Belarusian military coming to our aid?"

More vehicles approached.

"He did not, sir. He gave us assurances the Kremlin was negotiating, but Belarus had their hands tied. He said NATO had given them an ultimatum to stay neutral and at the moment Minsk seems to be complying with it."

"Damn it," Sabaneyev hissed to himself, vapor clouds rising around him. "It's just one lone tank brigade that's on our tail. The rest of the NATO forces are hours behind us and well to the north. We've beaten this attacking brigade and battered it and certainly forced it to expend most of its ammunition. The Belarusian forces could coordinate with me, and we'd slaughter them in an hour."

"Command gave no further guidance, General," said Smirnov, wrapping his greatcoat around his face. The Belarusian plains were colder than the Russian hills and wooded countryside. Open and wind whipped, the country was probably nice in summer, but now there was hardly a tree to shield them and everything south of Minsk they'd passed had been open farmland.

Sabaneyev slewed the binos to the left of the specks that were growing in his vision to compare their size with a few buildings. They were nearing the off-ramp, where the rearguard would intercept them if they were, in fact, American tanks.

"Any word from 3rd Battalion?"

"They are on the radio now giving a report, but I thought you would want to hear the message from Moscow."

"To hell with Moscow. Go and listen to 3rd. I need to know if this new traffic I see is the Americans continuing to advance from the west."

The sun warmed the pavement, causing heat lines to blur his image of the distant vehicles.

He shifted his gaze nearer, and now he could see the Bumerangs of the 3rd Battalion staged on his side of the overpass, just over a kilometer away. They were in the process of rotating their turrets around in the direction of the approaching vehicles.

Explosions of flame and dirt kicked up around 3rd Battalion before Sabaneyev's eyes.

American guns were firing on them.

Sabaneyev said, "This tank commander—he's clearly insane, out of his mind with rage, desperate for revenge."

"Yes, sir."

"Doesn't he see this is just war? Why is this so fucking important to him?"

"I don't know, sir," said Smirnov. "It's madness."

Eduard Sabaneyev watched the fight a few moments more. The

Bumerangs were no match for the heavier M1 tanks with their longer-range guns. Several Kornet missiles were launched by the Russians, and some struck their targets, but soon the surviving Bumerangs of 3rd Battalion were in full retreat, racing down the E30 highway toward Sabaneyev and the headquarters group.

The general released his iron grip on the binos, wiping cold sweat from his brow. Now, as he relaxed his concentration, he felt the wind whipping his face again and the chill settling into his bones.

The Americans and the Germans were *still* coming.

He walked down to his vehicle and gave the signal for the unit to move out.

In his memoirs he'd have to justify running from the small but seemingly unstoppable force of NATO tanks, but, he told himself, that was a problem for another day.

For now it was all about staying alive.

MRIMA HILL, KENYA
1 JANUARY

A deafening roar echoed through the mine, and dust and small stones fell from the ceiling. Everyone in the HQ looked up nervously, worried the damn roof would collapse. This wasn't incoming but rather outgoing artillery, fired in desperate support of 1st and 2nd Battalions in both the east and west. Connolly heard urgent requests for fire over the radio every few minutes; then the gun line would calculate the trajectories and the artillery boys would go to work.

Lieutenant Colonel McHale's response to the attack on two fronts had been to split the firing batteries. Caster had been out of the mine shaft checking on his troops, but as soon as he returned he agreed with McHale. This lessened the firepower in either direction, but there was no alternative anyone could see.

Despite the limited number of artillery pieces, the sounds of booming 155mm M777 howitzers ripping out into the early morning were comforting to Connolly and the men with him. But while it was good for the Marines to hear outbound fire, it also signaled that the enemy was within artillery range now, and that meant the Russians were closing in.

Marine radio operators fought to be understood as well as to understand the incoming transmissions. Pressing their handsets tight against their ears, they spoke between the terrific sounds of the nearby guns.

"Apache Red One, say again your last!" shouted a radio operator when there was a brief respite in the artillery fire.

The response was immediate and the tone urgent. "Roger. I say again, Force Recon, north of my position, has been overrun on Jombo Hill." There was a pause. The call sign identified the transmitter as an LAR platoon commander, a lieutenant, fighting to get his transmission back as he bounced over the terrain. "We have extracted the remnant of the Force team." He was interrupted by the sounds of cannon fire on the radio, then the pounding of machine-gun fire close to the radio handset. "We're withdrawing south. Let Darkhorse Battalion know we're coming in hot. The Russians are six hundred meters back, right on our ass!"

Another voice on the radio, probably the man's gunner, could be heard yelling in the background, "Four hundred meters, sir! Engaging." The transmission was cut short again as the sound of more 25mm cannon fire drowned out whatever the lieutenant was trying to say.

The radio operator next to Connolly tried to sound calm. "We copy. Call off a grid. We'll work up a fire mission and close that door behind you."

"Copy. I am the trail victor in my platoon. My grid . . ." There was a pause, a loud explosion, then momentary silence. Then the voice of the platoon commander came back on. "Be advised, we are hit . . . still mobile . . . trying to get south. My northing is at the two-five-six. All north of my poz is enemy."

The radio broke off again, and there was another long pause.

The regimental CP was silent, all men hanging on to the one broadcast from the Marine in distress. He sounded like a younger officer, likely a second lieutenant. Connolly stared at the radio with everyone else in the HQ, trying to picture the desperate scene.

Then there was a screech of noise and the lieutenant's voice returned, but in a bloodcurdling scream. "We're on fire!"

The radio went dead.

Connolly didn't hesitate; he grabbed the field phone tied into the artillery batteries outside. "Patriot, fire mission. Immediate suppression. HE and WP mix. Battery Six, target location two-five-six, zero-niner-three. Lineal sheaf east to west. Over."

The response came back acknowledging the mission, and the firing battery read back the coordinates but told him there'd be a delay. They had to "shift trails," or pick up the heavy howitzers' rear legs, known as the spades, and physically rotate the weapon ninety degrees. They knew when they received an immediate suppression mission that the shit was hitting the fan and the infantry, or in this case the LAR unit, was in desperate need.

It took time, but soon the Marine artillery began firing into the grid. A wall of flame brightened the morning sky to the north as a Marine platoon raced to the south. It came too late to save the young officer, but his dying act was slowing the Russians just enough to protect what was left of his platoon.

A Marine tank platoon commander lay in the dirt, looking through his binos, watching the artillery fire and the flames spewing from a demolished Marine light-armored vehicle on the winding dirt road.

Behind the young officer and down the hill, the loader on the platoon commander's tank shouted out, "Hey, Lieutenant, the LAR guys say they are hell-for-leather with Russians on their heels! He's a reduced platoon of three LAV Two-Fives, coming in fast. You should see them any second."

Sure enough, through the lieutenant's binos, three shapes materialized in the near distance, traveling off-road now. He grabbed his map case, binos, and carbine, then scrambled back down the hill to his tank. There, he climbed onto the armor hull, donned his helmet, and leapt down the tank's hatch, sitting down hard in the commander's chair.

He keyed the intercom. "Driver, into the hot position. Now!"

The tank, two more to the left, and one more to the right, all revved up instantly and then lurched forward, driving just a dozen meters and then down into the dugout created by the Marine engineers. The gunner immediately swiveled the turret in the direction of the LAV-25s.

The light-armored vehicles screamed past, one of them almost running into a half-buried M1A2 tank in the process.

The four tanks' heavy 120mm main guns then picked targets among the pursuing Russians and fired, reloaded, then repeated the process as fast as the crews could operate. Each time the tanks fired at a BTR, a haze of dust billowed around them. Their fields of fire gave the tanks the advantage as they picked off Russian armored personnel carriers one at a time.

But the BTR crews were able to see where the fire was coming from, and their missiles were accurate. They snuffed out first one, then two of the four tanks.

Eight Marines died with the first salvos.

The last two American tanks continued firing until they'd taken a half dozen missile strikes in and around their positions. The near misses left their turrets damaged, but they managed to pull out of their positions in an attempt to escape, driving through preselected routes of gullies and ravines that led back to the south.

One of the big M1 Abrams tanks succumbed to its earlier hits from a fast-flanking BTR and threw a track. The Marine tankers grabbed their rifles and whatever gear they could carry, climbed out of the big, dead piece of armor, and then sprinted to the sole surviving tank. They clambered aboard and held on when it lurched forward, resuming its frantic escape from the attacking Russian forces.

Twelve kilometers from the mines, 3rd Battalion's Javelin gunners prepared to fire. Through the thermal imagers attached to the launchers, they watched the three American LAVs, then the damaged M1 with surviving tankers clinging to it, retreating in their direction.

The Marine weapons company executive officer was in charge of the Javelin teams, and he and the company gunnery sergeant called back and forth on their radio net now, dividing up targets.

After a signal from the XO, the first Javelin belched out from a team lying on the roof of a farmhouse. The gray puff of smoke was barely visible, and then the missile jetted from the launch tube ahead of a spear of fire.

The instant the missile was away, the Marines grabbed their gear, jumped off the roof, and ran to their next position, a clump of trees two hundred meters back in the direction of the hill.

The Javelin "fire-and-forget" missile continued skyward. The advanced munition would fly in an arc, level out for a second, then drop to strike the target where it was most vulnerable, on the less armored top.

The Javelins were built to destroy tanks, so using them on the more lightly armored and less powerful BTRs was overkill, but none of the Marines gave a damn about the expense of each launch. The red trace of three other missiles now joined the first, all darting across the early-morning sky.

The Russian armored personnel carriers had no way to avoid them; they could do nothing more than fire in the general direction of the launches in a last act of defiance before they were destroyed.

The Marine missilemen crews and a crew from One Team of the French Dragoons each fired a Javelin, then fell back to another concealed position. Fire, run, get to a new location, reload the weapon, and prepare to fire again at an enemy who was gaining ground by the second.

Lieutenant Colonel McHale took Connolly and Colonel Caster aside. Addressing the colonel, he said, "Sir, enemy is ten kilometers north of Darkhorse's final defensive lines, and Darkhorse is down to his last tank in his sector."

"I'm tracking," said Caster, standing over the map, watching as the small red pins were moved in closer to the mine.

Things to the north were bad—the line seemed to be slowly but steadily collapsing—but that didn't mean the situation in the east and west was that much better. That said, it looked like the break 1st Battalion got in splitting the Russians was playing to their favor. They still had all four of their tanks and a full LAV platoon.

The broken terrain to the east had meant the BTRs could approach only three abreast, so 2nd Battalion was still more or less in control of their fight, though they, too, were falling back slowly.

In Darkhorse's zone, though, the Russians were closing in quickly.

"What do you think, Dan?" the colonel asked.

"Sir, I could tell you a whole lot better if you'd let me go down there and lend Darkhorse a hand."

"You think you can do something for them there you can't do here?"

"Maybe. A spare officer who knows how to call for fire might come in handy. Worst case, I'm still shooting high expert with my rifle." Connolly smiled and hefted his carbine up.

Colonel Caster didn't return the smile. "No shit? Well, all Marines are riflemen first, regardless of rank." He looked around. "And we might all be tested on that before this day is through." Rubbing his stubbly gray hair, he said, "Eric, if you don't need Dan right now, let's send him down to Darkhorse. He can give Darkhorse Six a chance to focus on his fight and let us know how we can help them from up here."

McHale agreed, and Connolly was moving in under a second. He grabbed his kit and the expensive radios he'd been lugging around and slung them onto his shoulder. He pointed to Sergeant Casillas, who had been standing along the wall of the mine shaft, awaiting orders. "Let's go, Sergeant."

"Yes, sir!"

"One thing, though, Dan," Caster called out as Connolly headed for the exit. "Darkhorse Six is the best, a top-notch officer, but if his line is cracking, he'll be the last to admit it. He's a real fighter. So if things look really bad and I need to shift over a company from 2nd or some tanks or LAVs from 1st Battalion, you let me know."

"Aye, sir." Connolly and Casillas raced out the door.

Sergeant Casillas directed his LAV's driver down to Darkhorse Battalion's position along a steep, winding stretch of mining road that had a thick jungle canopy covering it. During the few times they could catch a view to the north, however, they watched tracer fire and missiles streaking across the battlefield in the darkness. The sounds of booming artillery and tank main gun fire had become a constant orchestra of low, rumbling explosions, higher-pitched pops, and whizzes racing overhead.

The light-armored vehicle passed the two artillery batteries, which had by now moved to a new firing position. Called a "survivability move," the relocation was an admission that the Russians would soon be inside the range where they could pound the source of the artillery that had been pounding them. It would be assumed that the location of the big Marine guns had been approximated by the enemy, so moving them a few hundred meters away, though arduous and time-consuming, was the only way to keep them in the fight.

The cannoneers had reset their weapons, and the guns were once again firing furiously: grabbing the heavy, nearly hundred-pound shells by hand, hoisting them onto the sled, ramrodding them into the breech, and then packing powder bags in behind. As his vehicle raced past, Connolly watched one of the split batteries in the morning light as the men closed the breeches and yanked the lanyards all in unison. He also saw that they were now divided into thirds; just four M777 artillery pieces covered each of the cardinal directions.

Less concentrated fire. Much less, he thought.

Soon there would likely be a gunfight between the two sides' artillery forces, since the Russians would probably creep their big 152s in behind the infantry. It was an old tactic, but Connolly figured if anyone was going to use it, it would be the crafty old general.

Penetrate and obliterate, Connolly said to himself.

CHAPTER 75

Casillas's LAV made it to the Darkhorse command post. Connolly climbed out of the back hatch and ran toward the tent, which was well protected in a small natural gully reinforced with timber and sandbags.

When he entered the CP, he could feel the tension instantly. A few red lights were hung up here and there, but they barely illuminated the dim interior. Marines ran in and out carrying messages to and from company defensive positions.

Maps and command boards hung on the tent walls, and men huddled around them; radio sets, just like back at regimental command, broadcast a constant traffic of voices of men in combat.

The CP was a hive of activity, but activity conducted in whispers and low light.

All but one of the Darkhorse Javelin teams had made it back from their forward positions, married up with their companies, and were now integrated into the final defensive lines. The one surviving tank had been given a spot near Kilo Company, where the engineers had prepared another firing position for it. The tankers and the infantrymen there knew the M1 was now a fixed part of the lines; there was nowhere farther to fall back to.

Connolly stepped over to speak with the commander, a short but thickly built lieutenant colonel with a big wad of chewing tobacco puffing out his lower left cheek. As had been the case with McHale, Connolly and Dickenson knew each other from way back.

The lieutenant colonel turned and saw Connolly. "You here to support me or to relieve me?"

"Here to work for you if you can use me, Ben. Put me in, coach."

A smile broke out on the man's chapped lips and tanned face. "Can you work my fires?"

"If your men will take me."

"Shit yeah, they'll be happy to have you. I had to send my weapons company CO down to help his boys lay in new positions for the .50-cals once the Javelin teams came in." He spit tobacco juice onto the ground with a scowl. "Honestly, I didn't think they'd be on us so quick. We've been hitting them hard, but the fuckers broke through the LAR screen like butter and waved my fucking tanks aside."

Connolly said, "Boris Lazar's got a lifetime of combat experience. He's not going to roll over. We have to destroy his ability to advance."

Dickenson turned to grab a radio handset from a communications sergeant; then, covering the mic, he turned back to Connolly. "Wait. Did the old man tell you to watch over me in case I got in too deep?"

Connolly gave a half shrug. "Yeah, something like that. He's ready to send you a company or tanks from 1st and 2nd if you need 'em."

"I'd ask for them now, but it'd be more trouble than help trying to set them with everything else going on. If it gets to that, we'll make the call together."

Connolly nodded as Dickenson pulled out another big wad of tobacco and stuck it on top of the first one.

Seeing his old buddy deep in the fray and hearing firsthand that the Russians were bearing down were unsettling, but Connolly was glad to be closer to the fight. The dark mine shaft was not where he needed to be.

He moved over to confer with his new team: the air officer, the artillery liaison officer, and the mortar team leader. Together, they made up the battalion's fire support section.

Connolly was in his element now; he was an expert in the use of combined-arms fire, a system of mathematics and maps, of trajectories and timing, of calculating depth, and, most of all, of combat intuition. It was a balance of estimating the risks and weighing the needs and urgency of each unit in the fight based on a best estimate of the enemy situation now, a minute from now, ten minutes from now, and beyond.

A new transmission on the Darkhorse net from the front lines reported the sounds of loud buzzing in the sky. The infantrymen were unsure what they were hearing.

But Connolly knew instantly. It would be the Russian drones, judging from the observation that the noise was like that of multiple lawn mowers. He had seen them at Mount Kenya and knew the three-meter-wingspan UAVs had pinpointed the Americans' positions.

Immediately, reports came in from frontline companies confirming his suspicion. They had seen them flying over their heads.

Connolly said, "The companies there can expect incoming artillery soon."

He gave directions to his fires coordination cell, or fires team, to call back to the artillery battery. If those drones really did presage a Russian artillery attack, he wanted to make sure the Marine counter-battery radar was up and searching to the north. If the radar could catch the trajectory of the incoming rounds, they could triangulate the back azimuths, letting Connolly know where the Russian batteries were firing from.

In less than five minutes the whizzing sounds of incoming artillery filled the air. At first it sounded like a kid's whistle, then more like a symphony of whistles, but immediately the explosions began, slamming into the hill to the southeast of Connolly's position. Either the battalion command post hadn't been spotted, or else it had simply been spared the first barrage.

But within a minute it was clear that rounds were falling closer.

A radio officer looked up at Connolly. "Sir, counter-battery radar has a fix on the artillery. It's not certain, but it might be enough."

Connolly grabbed a slip of paper from the radio operator and checked the coordinates on his map. He carefully plotted the location. It was a thick jungle area about fifteen kilometers from his current position.

"What do you think, guys?" he asked his fires team.

The artillery liaison was the first to respond. "If it were me I'd fire from there. Looks to be a good location we wouldn't be able to spot from higher up on the hill behind us."

The rest of the team agreed.

Connolly said, "Work up a fire mission. Call it up to the guns. Let's hit that target now. If my guess is right, the really heavy stuff hasn't come yet."

The fires team went to work, calling the data over to the artillery fire direction center. In minutes they heard the Marine Corps' big guns on top of the hill thumping out return fire. It wasn't a large amount of outgoing, maybe ten or twelve rounds, but Connolly guessed the batteries were now trying to conserve ammunition for targets that were more certain than the speculative fix they'd gotten from the counter-battery radar.

Still, the incoming Russian artillery stopped almost immediately.

Just as the men began congratulating themselves, word came in near simultaneously from the three rifle companies on the defensive lines. The enemy had been spotted five kilometers from the leading edge of the battle space.

And they were advancing in swarms.

Connolly leaned into the radios to listen to every broadcast. The companies were engaging at their maximum effective range. SMAW anti-tank rockets could be heard going out in earsplitting cracks. Browning M2 .50-cals cracked automatic fire, loud even here in the HQ.

And the noise increased by the minute.

Connolly stepped out of the tent now and looked toward the bottom of the hill. He could see mortars impacting and pillars of black smoke rising from burning fuel, indicating destroyed armor.

Tracer rounds burst from the Marines' lines in reds, ambers, and yellows. The incoming fire came in the form of green tracers. Russian weapons sprayed at first from twenty or thirty points in the distance, then forty or fifty. In less than ten minutes, the exchange of deadly fire on Darkhorse's frontage turned into a constant, violent fireworks display of horror.

Dan Connolly watched, one hand pressed against his ear to lessen the noise, the other firmly against the radio, listening for the calls for fire from the line companies.

New reporting came in that Russian soldiers had made it to the edge of the Marine barbed-wire-and-obstacles perimeter.

Soon Connolly could make out the blasts from claymore mines detonating within the cacophony.

He looked over at Darkhorse Six; Ben Dickenson was desperately talking to his line commanders through the radio, ordering them to hold. He moved a few platoons around to plug gaps in the lines created by the slackening of outgoing fires resulting from the Russian vehicles' pounding the Marines' positions.

Connolly briefly considered calling Colonel Caster but decided instead to up the ante and begin forcing fire support to those areas that needed it most but might be too busy to request it. He conferred with his cell and they all called back to the regiment, using the terms they knew would garner all the support they could get.

The air officer called the 9-line requests over the UHF radio. In moments he was told he'd get two passes from the Harriers and one pass from the F/A-18s.

It wouldn't be nearly enough, but it was a start.

The mortar leader directed the 81mm mortars to fire at coordinates to the north, everywhere a thinning in the American lines had been reported.

Darkhorse Six yelled over to Connolly now. "India Company has Russians in the wire! What can you give me right now, Dan?"

"Get me a grid and I'll get the battery to fire an immediate suppression mission."

The commander passed on the coordinates, then went back to his radio to reassure India Company's captain they were about to get close artillery.

"Patriot, Patriot, this is Darkhorse fires," the artillery officer called into his mic next. "Fire mission. Immediate suppression. All guns fire. Danger close. I say again, danger close!"

Seconds later, the speakers crackled. A voice said, "Station calling. This is Patriot. Need authentication. Over."

"Damn it," muttered Connolly. Without higher authority, the artillerymen would not fire and risk hitting friendly troops.

The voice of Colonel Caster, back in the mine shaft higher on the hill, boomed over the regimental command net. "Dan, you have my authorization if you think it's worth the risk."

"Yes, sir, I do."

Connolly picked up the radio from the artillery liaison. "Patriot, initials Bravo Charlie."

"Patriot copies. On Grizzly Six approval, stand by for danger-close mission."

"Acknowledged. Sending target location," replied Connolly as the artillery officer relayed the grid.

From the sounds of things over the battalion radio sets, Russian soldiers were less than three hundred meters away from where Connolly now stood. He could easily make out the rapid *snap-snap* of rifle fire in the cacophony of jolting noise. The entire line of Marine infantrymen engaged with all the arms in their arsenal in a fierce battle to keep the Russians off the hill.

As a battery of outbound artillery shells shrieked overhead, a small cheer went up in the tent. They didn't fire for long, but Connolly hoped it would have a pulverizing effect on the Russian attackers.

And then, when the shooting slackened for a moment, the sounds of drones outside the tent could be heard. First one, then another and another. They seemed to be buzzing right overhead.

Lazar had zeroed in on the Darkhorse command post.

"Everybody out! Everybody out!" screamed Connolly.

He helped the fireteam grab their radios, and in seconds Marines were racing out through the tent flaps, trying to get far enough away from the command position before the inevitable.

Connolly and his crew dove into slit trenches dug for just this contingency under thick trees fifty meters away. Seconds later a 152mm artillery round slammed into the hillside, just seventy meters short of the HQ. Men fell to their knees; shrapnel whistled through the air. The second and third rounds all fell less than twenty meters from the tent; then a fourth hit just ten meters from the timber wall on the northern side of the tent. Connolly heard the screams from the men who had not made it to the trenches before shrapnel ripped through them.

Connolly watched three more rounds land in rapid succession. Four Marines caught out in the open vanished in the fire and flame. There was nothing he could do for them—nothing *anyone* could do.

"Sir!" yelled the mortar team leader over the noise. "The counter-battery system is picking up the data on those incoming rounds!"

"You're kidding me. They're still up and working?"

"Yes, sir, they called it in. Here's the grid." He handed Connolly a torn slip of paper with the grid on it.

More incoming as four heavy artillery shells blasted the now-vacated battalion command post to shreds. Tables, tarps, and radio equipment launched through the air, adding to the shrapnel. Farther down the slit trench, Connolly could see Darkhorse Six surrounded by Marines. He was the epitome of the fearless Marine Corps commander, standing in the trench, trying to see everything for himself, a radio held to his ear. The clerks and radio operators around him all had their rifles at the ready, scanning the trees down the hill to the north.

Connolly grabbed the regimental fires coordination cell radio from the artillery liaison. "Grizzly Fires, Grizzly Fires, this is Darkhorse Fires. How copy?"

Higher on the hill, shells and missiles rained down around Colonel Caster's regimental command post. The horrific screaming wail of the multiple-launch rocket systems, one of the Russians' favorite shock weapons ever since they were called "Stalin's Organs" during World War II, pummeled an area the size of several football fields at the top of Mrima Hill, and the shaft where Caster and his men were hunkered down shook violently with each impact. The concussions entered the tunnel, making work and even clear thought challenging. Dust fell in cascades with each impact.

The barrage slackened for a moment, and more than fifty men from the regimental logistics section stumbled in from the outside, seeking shelter. Wounded and dead were carried in as well. The mine was now cramped, filled with sweating, stinking, and bleeding men.

The Russian artillery resumed in earnest, raining death outside.

Caster knew his northern line was failing; the enemy had his HQ pinpointed, and there were a hell of a lot more of them than there were of his Marines.

This could well be over in a couple of hours, he caught himself thinking, but he shook the thought away and began shouting out new orders.

CHAPTER 76

Only twenty-one miles off the coast of Mombasa, Kenya, a small black shaft of metal, little more than a wire, broke the surface of the sea. It was the antenna of a Raytheon HDR (high data rate) multiband-satellite communications system, and it was mounted to the mast of the American *Virginia*-class submarine that lurked just below the waves.

The USS *John Warner.*

Commander Diana DelVecchio stood at the helm, eyes on the communications officer as she broadcast a digital transmission that would fire up to the Milstar satellite network and inform Fleet Operations of the submarine's current location and disposition.

It was this disposition that DelVecchio and the others on board were concerned about now.

After telling herself days earlier she had no chance of slipping through the Iranian and Russian ships and subs that would be arrayed in a picket line in the waters off Mombasa, searching for her specific acoustic signature, she'd set about finding some sort of patrol area far out to sea where she could both protect her crew and at least have *some* chance to affect events on the ground at Mrima Hill. But as the *John Warner* moved toward its patrol area, DelVecchio's confidence grew. A particularly wily Russian sub that they had just barely escaped days earlier up north had sprinted down into the area to wait for their arrival, but the *John Warner*'s radar operators found her when she surfaced, presumably to send and receive messages, and the American boat slipped around her undetected.

And it was at this point DelVecchio told herself to go for it. If she moved slowly, took care to stay in the right thermocline to make it harder to be detected by sonar, and had her own sonar team working tirelessly to find and fix all threats, then maybe, just *maybe*, she could get her boat somewhere closer to the action, where they would be exponentially more useful.

So she did just that, and for thirty-one hours all hands on the *John Warner* worked virtually without rest or breaks. Now they found themselves just twelve nautical miles south of an Iranian frigate with antisub rockets and depth charges, and nine nautical miles northwest of a Russian frigate with even more counter-submarine abilities. Also, there were other subs in the water; the *John Warner* had detected them intermittently, although right now she had no idea where the hell they all were.

The *John Warner* was in position to launch a single salvo of cruise missiles if the Marines needed them, but they'd have to be sent to targets that would be in the exact same location for sixteen minutes, the flight time from the *John Warner's* current position to the Mrima Hill area.

Plus, after firing this single salvo, the *John Warner* would have to somehow slip the noose yet again and find a way out to sea as the enemy all around closed in.

DelVecchio and her XO had been working the charts for most of the past thirty-one hours, and they thought they'd found their escape route. A trench that would help mask them zigzagged to the southeast; they would have to dive into it and race through it, relying on nothing more than their nautical charts to tell them when to turn to port and starboard to avoid colliding with the trench walls.

But if they could do this, DelVecchio felt good about her chances.

Now it was all up to the U.S. Marines to give her targets and to make this entire endeavor worthwhile.

Eight minutes after sending the transmission, the SATCOM monitors broadcast a reply. The Marines were in desperate straits at Mrima Hill. The battle had been raging for half a day, and some Russian units were inside the lines. Fleet had sent word to the *Boxer*, and the LHD was in the process of setting up radio communication between the *John Warner* and the Regimental HQ on the top of Mrima Hill so that there would be less delay in comms between the customer of the weapons and the supplier of the weapons.

DelVecchio nodded slowly as she read the transmission.

To the bridge she said, "All this wasn't for nothing. Our forces need help, and we're only going to get one shot at this." She added, "And then we're going to run like hell."

MRIMA HILL, KENYA
1 JANUARY

Connolly looked over the lip of the trench to the north and saw fire and smoke and explosions, dead lying on open ground between his position and the wood line, and mangled wreckage of Marine Corps vehicles, and it occurred to him that he'd never seen combat like this in his life. But he was not alone. None of the Marines had.

Nor had the Russians, for that matter.

One of the radiomen turned to the lieutenant colonel. "We're going to get overrun with the next wave down here, sir, and the regimental command post is under threat of complete destruction behind us. That arty is too intense for us to fight; all we can do is hunker down and wait for the BTRs to come up the hill and kill us in our trenches."

Dan Connolly had to admit that this twenty-two-year-old Marine had as accurate a take on this battle as any working group at the Pentagon ever would.

He kept looking over the top of the slit trench, his eyes just barely high enough to see the continuing explosions at the front of India Company. There had been reports that the Russians had broken through in platoon-sized elements, but the last series of strikes from the F/A-18s took out six or seven BTRs, with the loss of one of the aircraft.

He was about to task the last two Cobras when a call came from a battalion radio operator. An unknown number of Russian BTRs had indeed made it inside the defensive lines, and they were now marauding in the rear.

Damn it, he thought. *They've broken through.*

He looked over the air officer's attack data and thumped him on the helmet, giving him the approval for the Cobra run. Then he looked down the line in the direction of the battalion commander. Everyone in the trench was low to the ground, and one of them yelled and pointed to the north. Connolly turned his head to see three figures coming from his right. They were Russian infantrymen racing through the trees, obviously dismounts from a BTR.

A grenade bounced along the dirt and rolled across the front of Connolly's trench.

"Watch it, sir!" Casillas stood up on the top of his LAV just behind the trench and cut loose with the M240 machine gun. He laid into the trigger, spraying rounds into the approaching Russian soldiers.

Connolly dropped down now, falling on top of the rest of the fires team.

The grenade made a deafening crack less than a dozen feet from the lip of the trench. He heard the shrapnel beating the dirt above his head like steel rain.

The men in the slit trench next to Connolly popped up, firing their rifles as yet another group of Russians appeared soon after. Casillas fired from atop the LAV, and the enemy scrambled for cover.

A BTR burst from the shattered trees at the northeastern side of the clearing, and raced into the open, veering between the wrecked hulks of LAVs and other vehicles. It fired wildly into what remained of the battalion headquarters, destroying vehicles, generators, aid station tents, and the seven-ton trucks parked in the wood line behind Connolly's position. The Russian APC's cannon peppered the area, sweeping a wide arc left, then right, shooting at anything in sight.

Connolly heard the agonized cries of men caught up in the blasts.

His group ducked down into the trench again to avoid the incoming 30mm fire as it passed close, and then Marines left and right popped up to fire with their rifles. It forced the Russian soldiers to duck down but it could not penetrate the BTR; its armor was too thick, even for Casillas's heavy weaponry.

The Russian machine advanced slowly with soldiers crouched behind it, using it as a shield and firing to their flanks.

Connolly hefted his carbine, thumbed off the safety, and rose above the trench line. He only managed to squeeze off a few rounds in anger at the BTR fifty meters away before his position was raked by 7.62mm fire.

Dropping back below the lip of the trench, he looked behind him. There was nowhere to go. If he and his team jumped out, the BTR would cut them in half. If they stayed, eventually the soldiers closing in on them would take the trench.

They were completely pinned.

Without warning, an incredible screaming sound shot right over him. He heard an explosion just to the north, and then heat and flame shot over the top of the trench.

The incoming fire stopped immediately.

Connolly poked his head up and saw the BTR, a gaping hole in its side, smoke pouring out of its top. The Russians behind it were either dead, wounded, or scrambling for cover back down the hill.

"Get some!" came a shout from behind, and Connolly turned to see Sergeant Casillas off his LAV, on his knees in the dirt with an empty AT-4 rocket tube in his hands.

He tossed it aside and started to climb back aboard his LAV. His uniform was shredded at his right thigh and completely coated in shiny, slick blood.

Men cheered and poured fire into the surviving Russian dismounts.

Connolly yelled for the two nearest men from his fires team to race out to grab the Marine sergeant. Casillas had made it halfway back to the top of his LAV and was trying to man his machine gun in case of further attack. They reached him quickly and coaxed him back down despite his protests, and corpsmen were called over to carry him to the makeshift medical station in another slit trench in the clearing.

Connolly worked on getting the aircraft back on his radio for confirmation and another run, then shook his head in amazement. *Only a Marine sergeant would get shot, then try to climb back to his post to continue his duty.*

The radioman next to Connolly had wicked cuts to his face, and blood was smeared around it like war paint, but he was still doing his job.

"Call from the *Boxer*, sir!"

Connolly couldn't imagine what the hell the *Boxer* would have to tell him that would do him any good right now. "Unless they came across an extra squadron of F/A-18s down in their hold, I don't have time to talk with the damn ship."

The radioman handed Connolly the hook, too overwhelmed by events to laugh at the joke. "They said it's urgent, sir."

Connolly brought the hook to his ear with annoyance. "Grizzly Five, fired. Over."

The voice on the other end said, *"John Warner* is in range and on station and offering to help. They have cruise missiles but a very short window before they'll have to turn and run once they expose themselves. Flight time to estimated Russian positions is sixteen minutes, but they'll need coordinates from you. Not sure how effective they'll be, seeing how we don't have the Russian forces locked into one area."

A shell crashed less than twenty-five meters away from the trench. Dirt, stones, and branches flew inches over Connolly's head while he squatted with the hook at his ear.

But despite this his eyes widened and he broke into a smile.

"Sixteen minutes' flight time? Hell yeah, I can work with that! Wait one." He looked to the men around him and shouted over the sound of the incoming. "TLAMs!" The men knew he was referring to the Tomahawk Land Attack Missile.

The men squatting in the trench next to Connolly gave him a puzzled look. Then a young captain said, *"Sub*-launched Tomahawks, sir?"

"Yes. If we can just silence the Russian artillery we can help break the attack on the battalion. I want you guys coordinating the close air support and hitting everything in front of India Company. The Russians picked 3/5, India Company in particular, as their through point, and if I read their general correctly, he's about to turn up the heat. Get a full package ready to fire on my signal."

The men began working up the necessary equations while huddled together on their knees in the slit trench, which looked like it was about to collapse around them.

Connolly radioed up to Caster; it took a full minute to get him off another radio and onto Connolly's net.

"You guys holding the line, Dan?"

"Sir, the command post's been destroyed and we're in the trenches now. India Company is about to be in a real shit sandwich. But the *John Warner* is in range and ready to prosecute stationary targets with Tomahawks. If we can neutralize that Russian arty with the cruise missiles, we can take the pressure off India, and then Darkhorse can adjust his lines to deal with any attempted breakthrough."

"You tried to take out those Russian cannons once before, but it seems to me like they still have plenty of fight left in them."

"Yes, sir. But we have an accurate grid, and based on the Russian rates of fire, they're pouring it all on. They have *not* moved their guns, sir. Lazar should have, but he's too confident they're about to break through to slacken the fire. Those artillery pieces are in the same place where they were an hour ago. I bet they'll be there in sixteen minutes. If Lazar keeps up the heat on us, the TLAMs can hit that grid and shut them down."

"How sure are you on the grid?"

"Solid intel, sir. My map says they're in an open spot."

Caster and the CP were clearly under withering fire at the moment; Connolly could barely hear the colonel over the sound of artillery. "Then let's put that sub to work. Send the coordinates. I'll get McHale and his fires coordination cell to look over the firing data and deconflict the Tomahawks' path with the converging fires from artillery, mortars, and the helicopters and jets already converging on Darkhorse's frontage."

"Roger that, sir."

CHAPTER 77

The direness of the situation just thirty miles inland wasn't lost on Commander DelVecchio. She could hear the urgency in the tones from the Marines' radio transmissions at the regimental fires coordination cell. She could even make out booms and crashes in the background as the request was called in. Hearing the explosions had electrified all the others on the bridge as well.

DelVecchio said, "Weaps, fire eight Toms on those coordinates. We'll hold four missiles in reserve, but keep them in ready-to-fire status. Let the Marines know that if they need 'em, they can have 'em, but we can't wait around all day."

"Aye, Captain," he said, turning to the men at the fire control computers.

The weapons men punched the data into the computer. They triple-checked the computer's launch criteria and trajectory paths requested by the Marines.

"Captain, I show all TLAMs ready to launch," the weapons officer said.

Commander DelVecchio didn't hesitate. "Fire."

A tremendous *whoosh* shook the submarine.

The men's ears felt the pressure change. Rushing sounds as the vertical launch tubes were flooded with air, then a shock as the air blasted the hatch open, ejecting the huge missile up and into the water.

Next came the booster motor. The missile forced water against the sub's hull as it rapidly ascended fifty feet, then breached the surface of the Indian Ocean. There it dropped its launch brackets and the rocket motor kicked in. Yellow flames poured out of the bottom of the BGM-109C missile as it raced skyward, rapidly attaining its maximum speed of 550 miles per hour. In seconds it was joined by seven more, for a total mix of four BGM-109Cs and four BGM-109Ds, the cluster-munition variant.

NORTH OF MRIMA HILL, KENYA
1 JANUARY

General Lazar stood in a BTR turret, directly behind the advancing lead battalion in his 3rd Regiment, and listened to the casualty reports as they came in. The damage was heavy—much heavier than he'd anticipated. Still, he ordered his forces forward, because he could feel the Americans' lines cracking in the center.

Getting his soldiers in this close, this fast, had been a part of his design. It was now time for the well-trained men in Colonel Glatsky's regiment to finish off the Marines protecting the northern side of the hill. Once this was done, the Russians would be inside the American defenses en masse and they would attack the other battalions from behind, rendering their defensive positions ineffective. At that point the battle would be all but won.

He'd then task the paratroopers with moving in and doing the dirty work of mopping up the trenches, mine shafts, and the like, and this battle would be over by midnight.

He'd taken some calculated risks to keep the intensity up on the overworked Marines, not the least of which was retaining his artillery batteries in one position for longer than he would have liked. The F-35s hadn't pinpointed them, and Lazar's antiair batteries were doing a fine job keeping them at bay.

Lazar called to Kir, whom the general had sent to the artillery park behind Jombo Hill to check personally on the situation there, and to encourage the artillerymen to continue to pound the enemy headquarters they'd discovered. If they could keep the American HQ busy, the Americans would not be able to react to this assault.

A minute later Kir came back on the radio for him. "Sir, I just received word: 2nd Regiment needs to halt. They have taken heavy casualties."

Lazar felt frustration. He knew pressing the attack would wear the Marines down quickly, but he also knew to trust his commander. "All right. Tell Klava he can pause his advance for the time being. But order him to continue firing on the enemy positions. I don't want to let up on the pressure."

"Yes, sir. Also, sir, did you receive the reports from Glatsky? He says there are a few platoons that are in and among the Marines. He says the breakthrough is imminent."

It was odd to have a report go all the way back to Colonel Kir at Jombo Hill, then out to Lazar just behind the spearhead. Lazar was deep in and among Glatsky's lead battalion. But often in combat the reporting chain remained the same even when commanders themselves moved to the leading units.

"This is good news," he said, pulling up his binoculars to look ahead. He could see the close fighting on the jungle roads heading up the hill. The sounds were always the same, but the spraying of machine guns seemed louder every minute, the chatter of rifle fire constant. He saw hand grenades explode, which told him the two forces were just meters apart now.

Yes, Lazar thought. *Very good.*

"Something else I need to report, sir. The artillery commander here informs me Colonel Borbikov has ordered that—"

Lazar pulled off his helmet to listen to a noise he'd detected over the BTR's engines. He looked up toward a buzzing sound that seemed to be coming from overhead. At first he thought it was coming from one of the UAVs his artillery forces used to identify American positions, but this sounded different somehow.

It wasn't like a lawn mower engine; this was a race car rounding a track. Searching skyward in the African sun, he saw three, then four, then six slender, dark, cigar-shaped objects flying low and parallel to his position. They passed overhead and quickly behind him to the north.

He recognized them as Tomahawks and knew they'd be heading for his artillery.

He spun backward in the hatch, watching the missiles coursing rapidly toward their targets on the northern side of Jombo Hill.

He fought to get his helmet back on. "Kir! Take cover!"

Before the general's eyes, the first missile descended behind Jombo, and seconds later a huge shock wave made its way forward to Lazar's position, over two kilometers to the south. This was repeated three times in rapid succession. Trailing Tomahawk missiles broke open and dropped cluster munitions over the same area, sending hundreds of tiny bomblets falling free.

More shock waves passed through Lazar's position and the booms continued, reaching an incredible crescendo.

The sky to the north ruptured.

The firing at the front ceased as friend and foe alike stopped to look at the spectacle. But the rolling explosions, sprays of incendiaries, and heavy white smoke told General Boris Lazar all his artillery ammunition, and likely the majority of his artillery batteries, had just been destroyed.

Lazar keyed the radio. "Kir? Kir? Damage?"

The reply took several seconds. Finally the colonel answered in a disoriented and dazed voice. "Comrade General, all the guns have disappeared . . . vanished. There are dead everywhere."

"Damn it, Kir! Shift the trailing battery up; we can still break through."

Kir coughed several times. "Sir, as I tried to tell you, we have only one battery of six guns left, and Colonel Borbikov has requested it be held in reserve."

"Borbikov has requested *what*? Listen to me. Fucking *Spetsnaz* does not command our 152s!" Kir did not reply, so Lazar said, "There are to be no reserves, Kir! Do you hear me? *No reserves!* Every man and every piece of equipment into the fight—*now*! We have the enemy at the point of cracking."

When the colonel did not respond, Lazar shouted again. "Kir? Are you there?"

Lazar heard a weak cough over the radio. "Dmitry? Are you injured?" he asked.

"*Da* . . . It's nothing. I just—"

Lazar had been yelling over the radio so loudly, he had not noticed what was happening around his BTR. He turned forward in the turret, toward the hill and the fight, just in time to see four U.S. jets shrieking out of the high clouds and directly toward his pack of vehicles.

They were lined up perfectly on this narrow road. There was no way the jets could miss their targets.

"Damn it to hell!" he yelled. But he had only seconds to react. Tossing his helmet, scrambling out of his hatch, and kicking himself free of the BTR, the burly General Lazar tumbled down onto the dirt road, then rolled into a drainage ditch and covered his head, doing so just as the first missile struck the vehicles, blasting his BTR and the one ahead of it into balls of flame.

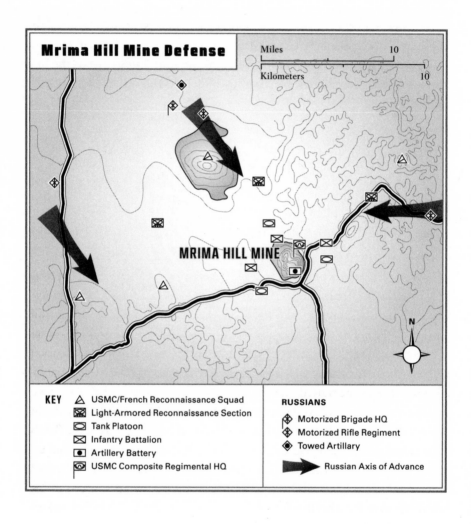

Mrima Hill Mine Defense

Miles 10

Kilometers 10

MRIMA HILL MINE

N

KEY
- △ USMC/French Reconnaissance Squad
- ▨ Light-Armored Reconnaissance Section
- ▭ Tank Platoon
- ⊠ Infantry Battalion
- ◉ Artillery Battery
- ⊡ USMC Composite Regimental HQ

RUSSIANS
- ◈ Motorized Brigade HQ
- ◈ Motorized Rifle Regiment
- ◆ Towed Artillary

➤ Russian Axis of Advance

CHAPTER 78

General Sabaneyev's once-formidable armor-and-infantry regiment was now running on fumes. Six of the fuel-thirsty T-14 tanks and eight Bumerangs had been left on the side of the highway in what amounted to a trail of tears, evidence of the armor column's woes as they fled east. Two more T-14 Armatas stalled soon after; two Bumerangs were parked off the road and siphoned dry so that their fuel could be transferred to the tanks, thereby allowing them to be moved out of the way to let the rest of the column pass.

The headquarters of the Belarusian 11th Guards Mechanized Brigade, in the city of Slonim, Belarus, was over one hundred kilometers from the Polish border, and getting here had taken virtually the rest of the column's fuel reserves. In the line of the Russian retreat, General Eduard Sabaneyev had pinpointed the brigade HQ on his map and ordered what was left of his battalions to make a beeline for the base, their only chance to refuel and rearm. The Russian general knew from experience that there would be several battalions of older T-80 tanks at the 11th Guards' base, so he knew they could get most everything they needed, both to resume their movement eastward and to fend off the Americans, who continued to nip at their heels.

The Russians' arrival at the gate of the 11th Guards right at dusk was met with hesitation, even some hostility, by the forces there. All local Belarusian military forces had been ordered into garrison and given specific orders not to meddle with either the Americans or the Russians.

"Stay out of it. Do not help or hinder" had been the command from Minsk.

At first the gate guards refused entry to the long line of ominous-looking Russian armor, citing the orders they had received from their leadership.

Then Colonel Smirnov dismounted, strode rapidly up to the front of the column, and reprimanded the guards, demanding they open the gates. His anger mounting, he next ordered the shocked troopers to ferret out the NCO with the keys to the fuel farm. The men, familiar with working with their Russian partners but unfamiliar with the current politics of the situation and the Russian brigade in their country, obeyed the colonel's command and flung up the exterior barricade, then sent someone scrambling to find the sergeant with the keys. The procession of still-mobile tanks and Bumerangs rolled in, then lined up around the corner and down the base's main thoroughfare.

Fuel keys were found and the slow process of refreshing the beleaguered Russian column began.

The Belarusian guards had, of course, informed everyone up the chain of command as to what was happening, and then they feigned complete surprise as the colonel serving as the mechanized brigade's logistics officer arrived suddenly. He raced to the front of the fuel farm in his personal vehicle, halting in the middle of the road, and then stormed up to the scene.

"Sergeant Volesky, turn off the pumps this instant!"

The sergeant complied, then backed away. He had no way of knowing if the Russians and his logistics colonel were going to shoot each other, but it certainly seemed that things were about to get ugly.

"By what authority do you steal my gasoline, Colonel?" demanded the officer from the 11th Guards.

Colonel Smirnov had expected something like this. "Get your fucking ass away from the fuel, comrade," he hissed, his hand working its way to his leather pistol holster.

An immediate look of fear washed over the Belarusian officer's face—the Russian masters had always been feared and respected—but it was also clear to Colonel Smirnov that he was probably buying time for someone with more authority to come and handle the situation.

Soon military police vehicles arrived and turned on their squad lights, the policemen dismounting and walking toward the gathering in the dying light of day. Colonel Smirnov signaled to the closest group of men. In moments they trotted back along the line and directed a platoon or more of the men to scramble up to the front of the line of Russian vehicles.

The Belarusian colonel conferred with the MPs and then pointed at Colonel Smirnov, gesticulating in an animated fashion. He was clearly at his wits' end and did not see this as ending well for himself. His anguish sparked the MPs, who drew their pistols. The gathering squads of Russians pointed their AKs at the Belarusians and lined up alongside Colonel Smirnov.

Before things could escalate any further, General Sabaneyev dismounted from his command Bumerang in the middle of the Russian column, smacked his heavy winter gloves against his fine wool general officer's greatcoat, and strode confidently over to the group by the pumps. He waded directly into the throng. His soldiers parted obediently and quieted upon his arrival.

Sabaneyev walked directly up to the diminutive Belarusian base commander and poked him in the chest with his finger. "Colonel," Sabaneyev said slowly, "open the petcocks on your fuel farm right now or I'll have you shot for violation of the Regional Forces Group orders." He was referring to the mutual-defense agreement between Russia and its smaller partner Belarus.

The shock of his words, as much as the sudden appearance of a general officer in their midst, cowed the Belarusian side into silence. They stared wide-eyed at the handsome and confident Sabaneyev, unsure just how to react. Seizing on their uncertainty, Sabaneyev pressed. "You will support us immediately per the order: that an attack on any nation in the RGF allows Moscow—which for your purposes today is me—to take the initiative and protect both states.

"And you, Colonel, whether you recognize it or not, are in a state of war with NATO."

The general's quoting of the rules of the loose military agreement between Belarus and Russia was specifically at odds with the orders the colonel had received not to aid the retrograding Russian attack forces. The orders declared that the Russians had violated all agreements between Minsk and Moscow by staging an attack against the West through Belarus without sending notification to the central government.

But whatever mental gymnastics he was performing were soon interrupted by a sharp and resounding crack, followed by a blast, and suddenly the decision had been made for them all.

A T-14 at the front gate fired its main gun. The first shot was followed quickly by another and another as more tanks fired and maneuvered.

"What the fuck are they doing?" Sabaneyev demanded of those standing around.

A head popped up from the turret of the closest Bumerang. "Comrade General, American M1s and German Leopards approaching from the west!"

Incoming shells slammed into a nearby street, rocketing a Belarusian armored car high into the air.

Sabaneyev grabbed the commander by the shoulder and together they ran up the steps and inside the nearest building.

The Russians in line for fuel began turning their vehicles and rolling off in different directions. Order evaporated as Russian soldiers variously ran back to their vehicles or mimicked their leaders, looking for shelter. The advancing American fire, in spite of the Russian defensive volleys, blasted overhead.

Tanks and Bumerangs dashed for copses of trees, behind decorative brick parapets, and in a few cases behind or into the brick buildings themselves, seeking shelter from the American guns.

Too many Russian tanks were unfit for battle, and too many of the Bumerangs had already fired off the last of their anti-tank missiles. They needed fuel and rearmament, right this moment, or they ran the real risk of being overrun by the invaders from the West.

Once inside the building, Sabaneyev grasped the collar of the Belarusian colonel. "Where are your war stocks?"

The Belarusian officer shook his head, his mind still racing to comprehend that his base was under attack. "I am sorry, comrade. I am not authorized to—"

"I don't *need* your fucking authorization. I need an answer—now! Where are they?"

"They are not here."

"*Lies!* This base is full of munitions given to you by Russia to be accessed in a time of critical need for our region. I know the weapons are here. Where the fuck *are* they?"

More crashing tank rounds impacted outside. Outgoing fire boomed in a chaotic fury.

The colonel said, "They *were* here, but everything was trucked off to Minsk this morning."

"What the hell are you talking about?"

"An order came from Command. My government does not choose to be a participant in this failed military attack of the West. Russian forces are not to use Belarusian—"

A high-explosive tank round slammed into the side of the building, shattering glass, shaking walls, and knocking men to the floor. Old masonry crumbled and dust filled the air.

Sabaneyev stood his ground, as did the Belarusian colonel. They could barely see each other for a moment through the haze.

"What *do* you have?" the general asked.

When the colonel did not immediately answer, Eduard Sabaneyev shoved the smaller man up against the wall and pulled his pistol from its holster. Jabbing it under the man's chin, he shouted, "I will shoot you myself this instant if you don't answer me!"

The man shielded his face in terror as he answered. "A couple hundred high-explosive rounds for our T-72s and T-80s, Comrade General. That's it. I swear it. The live shells are crated and secured in accordance with the protocol for the combined exercises, in an ammunition bunker a kilometer from here."

The T-80's main armament was the 125mm smoothbore cannon, the same size as Sabaneyev's T-14s' guns.

After another round hit the building, the general let go of the colonel's tunic and lowered his weapon, but kept his pistol at the ready by his side. "You will personally lead my XO, Colonel Smirnov, and whatever tanks I still have mobile to the ammo stores. We'll fight off the Yankees from inside the base until we can get fuel and leave. Your men will cover our withdrawal. Do you understand me?"

Several more loud explosions, all incoming tank rounds, hit in front of the building. Shrapnel tore through the hallway where the general and the colonel stood, sending them both diving to the ground. A young radioman who'd dove into the building for cover was immediately hit in the arm by a fragment, ripping flesh from the elbow to the hand, and he began rolling on the floor in agony as blood drained from his arm.

Sabaneyev ignored the soldier's wound and pulled the radio handset from where it was hooked on his load-bearing vest. "Smirnov? I've got ammunition but it's one kilometer away. What the hell is happening out there?"

No reply came for several seconds. And then: "The command vehicle has been destroyed!" came an unknown voice over the radio. A pause. "I don't see the colonel . . . but no one could have survived!"

"Shit!" shouted Sabaneyev. Into the radio he said, "Get me another APC and drive it to the front door of the command building. I'm coming out in thirty seconds, and all tanks not engaged now will follow my vehicles to the ammunition!"

He tossed the radio handset on the ground beside the writhing young man, grabbed the Belarusian by the shoulder, and pulled him back up to his feet. "You will take me to the main gun rounds now, Colonel."

Another salvo from the American Abrams tanks hit the building, but Sabaneyev ignored the debris and more fallen men in his path and ran for the door, still holding the colonel by the sleeve of his tunic.

They burst through the building's entrance, out into a smoke-filled gloom. They ran down the steps to the road in front of the fueling area, and only then did the smoke clear enough that they could see their way forward. In front of them were six destroyed Russian vehicles. More tanks engaged distant enemy targets over and through the metal fencing at the edge of the base. The whine of tank engines and the rumble of racing Bumerangs filled the air. Vehicles jockeyed for position to shoot back at the Americans.

This normally sleepy Belarusian base, with its carefully winterized lawns, neat brick façades, and orderly streets, was now a chaos of smoke and fire.

Sabaneyev saw only his own vehicles inside the wire. No Belarusian armor. "Where the fuck are *your* forces, Colonel?"

The Belarusian simply said, "We've been ordered not to assist. I . . . I . . . Comrade General, what will you have me do?"

The general had experienced many forms of combat before but realized this man in front of him had never heard a shot fired in anger.

Dropping the man's sleeve like one would a piece of garbage, the general turned and looked for the vehicles that were supposed to pick him up. The Belarusian colonel, his usefulness no longer required, raced back into the dust-filled building.

Standing amid the explosions of incoming and the boom of outgoing, his pistol drawn, General Sabaneyev glared angrily into the smoke, his last order apparently being disobeyed as the remnants of his regiment fought individual battles of survival.

In seconds he heard a growing rumble from his left, then another from his right. The high-pitched whine sounded different from the diesel engines of his own armor. From both directions, American Abrams tanks of the U.S. Army rolled into view, their main guns trained on Russian targets near the base entrance.

Sabaneyev spun around to run back inside, but the horrific ripping-canvas sound of a .50-caliber machine gun stopped him in his tracks. The automatic fire tore into the doorway, just ten meters up the stone steps from him.

The firing stopped, and the general turned back to the horror around him. In claps of thunder several T-14s down the block went up in flames, but with their magazine compartments dry of any ammo, so Sabaneyev was spared the roiling blasts of secondary explosions that he'd grown accustomed to in the past days.

A pair of German Leopard 2 tanks flashed by in pursuit of the retreating Russians, firing their cannons as they went.

Sabaneyev looked up and down the war-torn streets, disoriented by the smoke and debris on the unfamiliar Belarusian base. Could he link back up with some remnant of his fighting force? He tried to think clearly about what to do next.

But before he could decide, the hulking form of a U.S. M1A2 SEP Abrams rounded the corner of the building he stood in front of. The giant metal treads clanked along, half on the sidewalk and half in the street. Hugging the side of the building, pointing its 120mm barrel down the street a mere twenty feet away, it then pivoted in place, gouging the concrete until its full mass and its main gun pointed directly at Sabaneyev. A Yankee tank commander was up in the turret, a weathered and grim expression across his face, his pintle-mounted M240 machine gun trained on the general's chest. The young tanker seemed to be debating whether it was better to gun him down with the machine gun or just slice him in half with a main gun round.

Colonel General Sabaneyev dropped his pistol onto the frozen steps and raised his hands, a bewildered expression on his handsome but exhausted face.

CHAPTER 79

The tent flaps burst open as the three men entered, a gust of hot evening wind followed them in.

The Russian headquarters staff turned to see a wounded Colonel Kir flanked by two medics holding him up, one on each shoulder. The colonel's face was covered with blood and dirt; he had a shell-shocked expression and his mouth hung open. His left leg bled freely.

Several majors and captains rushed to him.

One of the medics said, "He would not allow us to take him to the medical shelter. The colonel insisted on coming here even though he is badly wounded." The man's frustration with his orders was evident.

Kir was helped over to a folding chair and he collapsed into it. His breathing was labored; he gripped his knee where the uniform pants had been torn off. Blood seeped through his fingers. Soon he looked away from the wound, put his head in his bloody hands, and rubbed his eyes.

One of the majors handed him a canteen of water, which he drank from while a medic knelt and began dressing his knee.

Kir looked up from the canteen. "You men there . . . have you heard from the general?"

A radioman shook his head. "We have not, sir. Glatsky's XO has reported that the lead company of 3rd Regiment has been practically wiped out. The general was with 1st Company. That is all that has been reported at this time, sir."

Kir just sat there a moment. Finally he said, "Tell Glatsky to suspend the attack. Pull back and reconsolidate his forces. And tell him to find General Lazar."

Colonel Yuri Borbikov, flanked by four Spetsnaz officers, stormed into the command tent while Kir spoke. All five wore body armor and weapons.

"Belay that command!" He looked around the room quickly. "Where's General Lazar?"

No one answered at first; then a major said, "He went with 3rd Regiment. He is not reporting in."

"So . . . he's dead?"

"We do not know. We haven't been able to raise him since American aircraft attacked Glatsky's advance."

Borbikov stood near the flap to the tent, taking in the dimly lit space in front of him. He turned to Kir. "Colonel, you are wounded. I insist you go to the medical shelter immediately."

Kir looked up at Borbikov, his daze quickly fading. "I will do nothing of the sort."

The Spetsnaz colonel boomed in a deep and commanding voice, "Colonel Kir, you are relieved of your responsibilities, now and on this spot! You are in shock and your actions are causing panic in the ranks. This is unforgivable in the face of the enemy."

Without waiting, he turned to the radioman. "Tell Glatsky he can take a brief tactical pause to reconsolidate his forces and to search for the general's body. We will reinstitute the surge on the north side of the hill shortly. Inform him that I am sending him a battalion of paratroopers."

Lieutenant Colonel Fedulov, the airborne battalion commander, stood at a map table with a cluster of captains. He looked up at Borbikov in surprise at this. He'd been told they'd be used only in close quarters, for "mopping up" on the hill, and defending the mine once it was taken.

Fedulov said, "Sir, the infantry's BTRs are armored and are better suited to punching through the American lines than my paratroopers."

"The arrival of you and your men will embolden Glatsky and his soldiers forward."

"Respectfully, Comrade Colonel, providing inspiration to the infantry is not our role."

Kir stood up on his wounded leg now; the medic had not finished tying off his bloody bandage, and the wrappings unwound and fell to the floor. Pointing a finger at Borbikov, he said, "Under what authority do you issue such a command, Colonel? Your only role here is as a headquarters advisor, and *only* an advisor."

Borbikov replied, "You are the one who no longer has authority, Kir. Your commander is lost and you are wounded and unfit for command."

Kir wiped blood from his eye and shouted in a loud and agitated voice, "Watch officer!"

"Here, Colonel," said the captain, just meters away.

"What is the report? Do we have any unit commanders in the northern sector responding after the American strikes?"

"We do, sir. Two of the commanders report present. Second Regiment has halted their attack but is firing onto the Marines as the general ordered. First Regiment is making slow progress, and they continue to receive attacks on their BTRs from dismounted anti-tank weapons. Both regiments have suffered heavy casualties. Nothing further at all from 3rd Regiment yet. The commander reported the lead company destroyed, then went off the air."

Kir turned to Borbikov. "There you have it: the next field commander is 1st Regiment's colonel. He will come and take command of the brigade while I receive treatment."

Borbikov shook his head. "Nonsense. Captain, call the medical orderlies back and have this man escorted from the tent. Note in the logbook that under the authority from the Group South commander, I am taking command of the brigade at this time."

The captain looked back and forth with wide eyes at the two senior officers; he was clearly conflicted and momentarily unsure about his chain of command.

Borbikov didn't wait for further debate; he signaled to the Spetsnaz in the tent, one of whom radioed to others outside. In moments, four more of Borbikov's men with AK-12s entered, making eight in all. Two grabbed Colonel Kir by the arms and led him from the tent, muscling him out despite his loud protestations.

None of the headquarters staff got in the way of the big special forces soldiers.

Borbikov grabbed the radio from the stupefied twenty-four-year-old watch officer and began a broadcast. "All stations, all stations, this is Colonel Yuri Borbikov. It is with great regret that I announce the death on the battlefield of comrade Colonel General Boris Lazar. I have assumed command of the brigade. We must now come together, comrades. We shall mourn the passing of our great leader and friend when this is all done. In the meanwhile, Moscow and Mother Russia expect every man to complete his mission. Acknowledge."

The officers of the headquarters section just stood there looking at the radio. For a moment the only sounds were those of the distant battle; Glatsky's forces intermixed in the Marine lines remained in heavy contact.

Soon, one by one, responses came over the radio.

"First Regiment acknowledges," came the strained voice of Colonel Nishkin.

"Colonel Klava acknowledges the order," came the subdued response from the 2nd Regimental commander.

"Third Regiment acknowledges receipt. This is the operations officer. Colonel Glatsky has just been confirmed dead on the front lines, but as yet we still have not found General—"

Borbikov interrupted. "I understand. Everyone now has sacrificed deeply, but it is time to fight. To accomplish the task at hand so these sacrifices are not in vain. I will provide instructions in a moment, but expect the offensive to resume within two hours. We will use our elite paratroopers to assault the enemy's position, timed with reattack against all frontages, by all regiments, to pin the enemy down."

Colonel Borbikov put the radio down and turned to the men of the command post.

"You have heard the plan for this evening's attack. I want you to prepare all forces. Get me a count of casualties." He turned to the paratroop commander. "Lieutenant Colonel Fedulov, you have your orders."

The square-jawed thirty-eight-year-old held his ground against the senior officer. "Colonel, the reports from the front are dire. Third Regiment has been badly battered. Do you really believe we can make the progress you require to seize the mines?"

"The situation is not dire and you will not use such terms."

"I only mean that the other regiments—"

Borbikov cut him off. "The other regiments will hold and pour fire onto the Marines. You will then be clear to advance."

"But—"

"Enough of this! Do you not understand the simple advantage we have? Even just in numbers?"

"I'm not questioning the mission, but the tactics appear questionable. I have been told the other regiments are severely depleted as far as the light armor necessary to close the distances successfully goes. Our artillery has been all but wiped out."

Borbikov glared at the paratroop commander, and he knew what the man was thinking. He was insinuating that Borbikov did not understand the master workings of tactics as well as General Lazar had.

Borbikov did not confront his allegation head-on. He just said, "The Americans will have another carrier battle group here in a day, and they will fill the skies with ground-attack aircraft. Once we take the mine, they won't be able to dislodge us, but we must take the mine.

"You and your men are to be my shock troops for the final assault. If you can't handle that mission, Lieutenant Colonel, I'll take over command of your men just like I did with Colonel Kir's troops."

The battalion commander from the 23rd Air Assault Regiment of the 76th Guards Air Assault Division knew the conversation was over. He nodded and reached for the radio to send the logistics forward into pre-assault positions to support the paratroopers' attack.

Borbikov sighed. Now even the most loyal men were questioning their orders. It was time for the final push, to hit these Marines with everything, and if these paratroopers failed to make the gains he demanded—failed to penetrate the Marines' perimeter—then he would have to resort to more drastic measures to defeat the enemy.

Lieutenant Colonel Dan Connolly's fires team had zip-tied two wounded Russian survivors of the attack on the Darkhorse command post. The battalion commander passed the word that India Company had taken heavy casualties, but they'd been able to wipe out the remainder of the BTRs that had crossed into the perimeter. They were still being hit by Russian 30mm cannon and 82mm mortar fire, but their own snipers, their Javelin teams, the LAVs, and the remaining tank seemed to be holding back any new attempts at a renewed attack.

This would not last long. They were almost out of Javelins: more had been transferred over from the eastern and western sectors, where the Russian contact was lighter, but the next concerted push by the Russians would use up the last of the Marines' best anti-tank systems.

Connolly pulled out his remaining canteen and upended it into his mouth. It was dry. He looked around for any water close by, because he didn't want to leave his position next to the radios in the slit trench for an instant.

He found a half-empty bottle and drank while he watched Navy corpsmen pick their way through the wrecked headquarters, treating the injured and carefully marking fallen Marines for later retrieval.

An air officer handed Connolly a dehydrated coffee packet. He ripped it open and swallowed the acidic dry crystals to give himself some needed energy before the next enemy wave appeared from the ripped and smoldering woods. More packets were passed out to other men nearby in the trench, and everyone took advantage of them.

The headquarters men, along with Connolly and his team, remained in the trench, eyes still fixed on the area to the north. Several here had been hurt, but they all deferred any treatment to the guys more severely wounded.

Connolly tasked a man with listening to the radio for the regimental commander and walked over to confer with the Darkhorse commander. Lieutenant Colonel Ben Dickenson stood in his trench. One of his sleeves had been ripped off, and dried blood was caked up and down his arm and across the back of his hand. He'd wrapped a field dressing around his elbow to stanch the bleeding, but it had soaked through and was now covered in dirt, leaves, and bits of splintered wood. A small pile of red-stained bandages lay stacked in front of him.

"Jesus, Ben, you need to get that arm looked after," Connolly said, kneeling next to the trench, eyes facing to the north as if another BTR might dart into the clearing at any moment.

"I asked the old man for a platoon of tanks to sweep out front and send some long-range fires to the Russian APCs."

Connolly noted the fact that his medical advice had been ignored, but he let it go. He understood. The commander of 1,200 men wouldn't give a damn about his elbow with danger to his Marines all around. "Hope he gives it to you, Ben. How's Darkhorse holding up?"

"We're beat to shit, but still rock-solid in our defense. I'm headed out to tour the front lines to check them out in a few. Hey, Dan. When you radio back to Caster, tell him Darkhorse can't be broken."

Connolly smiled at his old friend. "I agree with that statement, brother, and I'll ask him to hustle those tanks your way."

For the next two hours the exhausted Marines of Darkhorse prepared for the next assault. Connolly wiped fatigue from his eyes and peered out into the darkness around the command post. After digging slit trenches and fighting holes, the men had now mostly gone underground. The rest of the men in Connolly's small forward-fires liaison team were half-asleep on their feet, leaning against the dirt wall.

A commotion behind Connolly drew his attention away from the fires support maps he was trying to study. He pivoted in time to see the big French special forces officer walking toward his position with three other filthy but strong and heavily armed Dragoons.

Connolly called out in a hushed tone, "Captain Apollo, over here."

Apollo led his men over to Connolly's trench. *"Mon col-o-nel,"* he said. "Good to see you."

"You, too. What are you doing here?"

"We are to perform reconnaissance on enemy staging locations and then attack forward of Darkhorse battalion defenses. If the Russians start their advance, I am to call artillery on them, and hit them hard."

"Christ, Captain. We don't really have a good bead on the Russians' positions. Since their last attack, they are spread out all in front of Darkhorse, some six or eight kilometers wide. There's been a pause in fighting since we hit their artillery park, but now there's a no-man's-land between us, a crisscross of machine-gun fire, razor wire, tank ditches, and mines."

"Oui, that is why we will plot in all the Russian staging areas so you can fire artillery upon them. We have instructions to link up with a squad from India Company. They will proceed with us as guides and security."

"Okay, I can coordinate with India. I'll tell them to have a squad of their best waiting for you."

The French captain asked, "Do you have any intelligence as to why the Russians paused the attack?"

"Not really, but we grabbed a couple of prisoners. They told us there is a battalion-sized element of paratroopers waiting to be sent forward into the attack." Connolly looked down at his watch. "Don't know if they'll be in the next wave or not, but I'm guessing the attack will come around dawn, less than eight hours from now. Watch your ass, Captain, and don't get caught out there in no-man's-land when their final assault comes. I can pretty much guarantee Darkhorse will hammer the area with everything they've got."

"Always careful, *Col-o-nel.*" Apollo signaled back to the rest of his platoon, who emerged from the dark wood line.

Including Apollo and the three men with him, there were fifty-six able-bodied Dragoons remaining in the unit. Connolly saw AT-4 rockets, heavy machine guns, and light weapons on display. They would be a formidible force for a recon element, especially when augmented with a Marine rifle squad.

Connolly added, "If you're able to get the locations of each of their staging areas—if you spot the infantry, fuel trucks, ammunition stores, and such—I'll fire a 'shake-and-bake' strike."

Apollo gave a smile, barely visible in the darkness, understanding the military phrase. If Apollo succeeded in the reconnaissance portion of his mission, Connolly would hit the Russian infantry with a mix of high-explosive and white phosphorus artillery shells before they could step off in their final push against Darkhorse. The high-explosive shells, coupled with the burning phosphorus, were a cruel mix of indirect fires to use against troops. If successful, the shock and destruction could stop infantry and light vehicles caught in the hellish mix of razor-sharp shrapnel and the inferno of phosphorous fires that burned at over 5,000 degrees Fahrenheit.

Connolly watched Apollo and his men disappear into the broken foliage in front of the Darkhorse command post area and shook his head, recognizing anew that this venture might just become a tragedy of epic proportions.

Who knows? It might actually work. He tried to think positively, although he found optimism to be damn difficult to come by at the moment.

CHAPTER 80

Captain Apollo Arc-Blanchette and his men made their way down the hill, past the Darkhorse staging areas, and out to India Company's lines. Along the way they paused to ask permission to pass through each layer of the defense, and they waited until each senior officer directed them to proceed farther.

Finally, the French Dragoons found themselves with the forwardmost fireteam in the forwardmost squad in the forwardmost platoon of the Marine lines. The landscape changed dramatically, from heavy woods and thickets in the rear to earth pockmarked from heavy artillery and rockets closer to the front; burned and broken trees and brush and a mix of derelict and abandoned U.S. and Russian vehicles. Some still smoldered as burning gas, oil, or tires gave off thick black smoke into the night above flames sputtering like a dying man's last breaths. The apocalyptic war zone served as a gruesome reminder of the ever-present possibility of death to everyone here at the front.

Apollo and his men crouched with a young lieutenant in a trench just twenty-five yards from the razor wire signifying the extent of the Marines' control, with the shredded jungle just beyond. Movement to their left turned heads as a short, wiry Marine sergeant climbed down into the trench. In seconds the rest of the sergeant's thirteen-man squad climbed down with him, making the already tight space almost claustrophobic.

The lieutenant grabbed a thick wad of chewing tobacco from a pouch and stuck it in his cheek. He brushed off his hands and said, "Captain, meet Sergeant Cruz," slapping one of the dirt- and sweat-covered young men on the shoulder. "He's my best squad leader . . . Fuck, he's my last squad leader *alive*, so bring him back in one piece. He and his men will lead you through our minefield, help you with your recon, and then kick ass alongside you on your raid. Then they'll lead you back up here."

The *whizz* and *pop* of parachute flares overhead turned most of the men's eyes to the sky. They watched quietly while the illumination devices drifted over no-man's-land. Apollo took the opportunity to get a look at his newest troops. The Marines appeared war-weary, like everyone on Mrima Hill, but alert enough.

He also saw that Sergeant Cruz had a four-inch scar from the crease in his lip to his cheekbone. It had been badly stitched and it oozed blood.

These are the right kind of men for this mission, thought Apollo.

Sergeant Cruz spoke in an aggressive, heavy Bronx accent over the sound of a machine gun a few hundred yards away. "So, what are we supposed to call you, sir?"

"Captain Apollo is fine."

"Right. Now, what the hell is the plan . . . Captain Apollo?"

"We are going down the hill to fight the Russians before they come to us."

One of the squad said, "Fuck yeah," and another added, " 'Bout fuckin' time," and then Apollo briefed them on their mission.

Fifteen minutes later the men walked cautiously through the darkened, torn jungle, past the barbed-wire entanglements. Then Cruz skillfully maneuvered both his squad and the fifty-six Frenchmen around a network of claymore mines and booby traps.

Infiltration of the Russian lines by the Dragoons and the Marines was only possible because the Russians were there to attack, not to defend. The nearly seventy-man force sneaking through the shredded jungle was able to take advantage of the Russian plan to crack the American lines with everything they had as quickly as possible. The Russians had been sending their forces in pounding waves, and had not erected defenses like their adversaries. While the Marines held their desperate line with barbed wire, anti-tank ditches, and machine-gun slit trenches, the Russians followed offensive doctrine and intentionally guarded only their most rearward areas from conventional assaults, leaving more forces with which to attack. The tactic, of course, was not about seizing or holding terrain but about crushing the static Marines.

It was working in that regard, and the Russians were supremely confident that the defenders of the mine didn't have the forces to engage in any sort of meaningful counterattack, but this confidence left them vulnerable to smaller infiltrations.

Colonel Caster had banked on this when he sent Apollo and his men forward, and Apollo's slow, careful, and stealthy infiltration of the enemy lines was effected like a thing of beauty.

At the first gray of dawn, Apollo sat exhausted in waist-high elephant grass, kneeling back on his haunches so only his head was exposed. A group of panting Marines and French special forces was positioned loosely around him, their weapons pointed outboard in a 360-degree defense. Throughout the night, the sixty-eight men had crept in and around and through the Russian front lines with great skill, remaining undetected as they identified several fuel and ammunition stockpiles, all stored under infrared-concealing camouflage to protect them from any Marine Corps aerial detection. These were clearly staging areas for the upcoming attack. Apollo found them lightly defended but he recognized them for what they were, and knew they would soon fill with troops and armor.

The Marines gridded in the locations on maps and radioed the coordinates to Lieutenant Colonel Connolly.

Apollo was under no illusion that they had found *all* of the hidden positions, but they had found all they could before the dawn without exposing themselves.

Apollo brought his leaders and the Marine sergeant close enough to whisper, "Men, we've done our night's work; now we must prepare, with whatever darkness is left, for our final task." Apollo pointed with the infrared laser pointer on his carbine to a spot of level terrain about three hundred meters away. "There is a road network right here that leads to the easternmost Russian staging areas. So that is where the Russian right flank will pass."

The men sat in silence, staring at their new leader.

Sergeant Cruz said, "And you want to hit that when the troops move into staging."

"*Oui.*"

"We're almost totally exposed," said Sergeant Cruz.

Sergent-Chef Dariel said, "*Mon capitaine*, I must agree with the sergeant: this location, it is virtually suicide."

"I see no better concealment than this tall grass. It will provide no cover itself, but we can use the time we have to quietly dig in."

When no one replied to this, Apollo said, "Look, men, we *have* to attack. If the artillery can focus on the other five staging areas, we can batter this one. If we need support, we will call it in." He looked at the sky. "Sometime in the next half hour a force of Russian infantry will fill up that clearing. If we don't hit them here, then they and their mates will overrun Darkhorse. We have to give our defenses a chance."

"What happens if we don't? I mean, what happens if they just barrel over us?" Sergeant Cruz asked.

Apollo's voice slowed and deepened in pitch, to the point of anger. "Then we die, Marine. We will die the most ghastly death an infantryman can imagine, ground to meat under the tracks and wheels of the advancing enemy." He stared into Sergeant Cruz's now-visible eyes and saw his slashed cheek glistening with blood, as the wound had reopened. "Is that what you are wanting to hear, Sergeant Cruz?"

After a pause, Cruz said, "Yeah, Cap. That's all you had to say, sir. We Marines just like to know the odds. Tell us straight. And as long as we get to pop a bunch of those Russkies, death ain't but a thing.

"Let me go brief the boys," Cruz added, and then he was off to gather his men.

"Weren't you laying into him a bit, *mon capitaine*?" said Sergent-Chef Dariel.

"Yes, but that's what Marines want from their officers. They push back on everything and then listen for certainty from their leaders. Lie to them about the odds, and they won't believe another thing you say, but tell them they are going to die in a hail of glory, and they will advance toward hell."

"I am beginning to like these Marines, *mon capitaine*," said the sergent-chef.

"Me, too. Now, get the men digging in, and go ensure that all the rockets are prepped. Our first volley must count, because we may not get a second."

The men took what little time they had to prepare their ambush. They spread out in a loose line from north to south, oriented to the west, covering about 150 yards, and dug shallow pits hidden in the high grass.

Apollo would have liked another fifteen minutes to better coordinate the action to come, but the rumble of engines starting up reached their position from the north, and this told him the enemy would appear en masse sooner than he hoped.

Apollo chanced one last spot check, sprinting in a low crouch up and down the ambush line. The northern sector was led by Sergent-Chef Dariel, the southern sector by Sergeant Cruz. He checked to see that each of the dozen men charged with firing the AT-4s had two anti-tank rockets laid out, the shipping safeties off. He made sure each of the dozen or so machine gunners had four or five belts of ammunition neatly organized so he could grab the tail of a belt and feed it rapidly into his gun.

He then returned to his position in the center of the ambush and leapt into the foot-deep trench next to the Marine radio operator, who whispered into his headset, listened to the radio a moment, and then turned to the French captain.

"Artillery all set?" Apollo asked.

"Yes, sir. Grizzly fires has the five locations you asked for plotted. He says there is little chance he can get any air for us, and he did say our drones confirmed a dozen Russian vehicles are coming down the road now."

"Good. Get ready. Keep low."

"Aye, sir." The radioman put his headset back to his ear.

The men lay there for ten minutes, staring through binos and riflescopes at the staging area in the distance, where they could see a small cluster of BTRs, tents, ammo crates, and fuel bladders. A dozen men worked feverishly now around the area, making it clear to Apollo that the attack was imminent.

And then the sound of racing engines increased. The first wave of Russian troop transports dashed into view: six BTRs with one tracked ZSU-23-4 "Shilka" antiaircraft gun.

"Hold it," Apollo ordered through his headset.

Two trucks followed the first group; these were both open-topped and full of troops, some paratroopers hanging off the sides.

"Wait," said Apollo softly.

Six more BTRs appeared on the road, then followed the others into the clearing, where the staging area was ready to receive them.

When they were clustered together as tightly as he had hoped, Apollo yelled, "Fire!"

Eight AT-4 gunners rose to their knees and launched eight rockets, their weapons' backblasts thundering. The munitions streaked through the blue-gray light, across the high grass, and toward the staging area off the dirt track three hundred meters away.

Four rockets found their marks, catching the Russians by complete surprise.

Three of the BTRs were destroyed, and a heavily laden troop transport erupted in a ball of fire. Bodies were tossed like rag dolls into the air along with the flying wreckage.

Without pause, another six rockets were launched, with two BTRs taking hits. A white jet of molten fire poured into the closed vehicles, literally cooking the men inside alive. Secondary explosions only made the situation worse for those who had already dismounted vehicles in the staging area.

Now the Marine and Dragoon machine gunners began firing at dozens of troops in the open. Everyone with a rifle followed suit.

Another row of vehicles appeared on the road from the north—nearly a company of APCs—and these Russians immediately saw that their staging area was taking accurate fire from the high grasses to the east. Weapons in the APCs swung in that direction as the convoy bumped off the dirt track and began approaching.

A gun battle raged, and another pair of French AT-4s rocketed across the field and slammed into an APC, but more armor appeared out of the north in the predawn.

The incoming fire was withering, and Apollo was forced to bury his face in the dirt as rounds bit into the ground around him, blasting chunks of earth and tufts of grass into the air.

Apollo looked up and down the French and Marine line. All the men were similarly pinned; only a few were firing rifles and machine guns now as they tried to weather the heavy guns of the APCs and the increasingly accurate rifle fire from the dismounts near the dirt road.

Merde! Apollo thought. *So this is how we will die.*

When he heard more vehicles approaching his position, he took grim satisfaction, even without being able to look up, that the Russians had peeled off another group of APCs to come and rout out Apollo and his men. By now it seemed a full company had halted their advance to focus on the ambush.

In the distance he heard the Darkhorse artillery pulverizing the other five staging areas.

Oui, we will all die in this African dirt, he thought to himself, but the plan was working.

Apollo chanced a glance above the grass and behind him, looking for any escape for him and his men, but the terrain was flat in all directions. There was nowhere to go but down. Again he buried his helmet in the dirt.

The chirps, whizzes, and pings of incoming bullets made the air alive like a hornet's nest.

Apollo felt intense heat behind him. He looked back; the grass had caught fire from the Russian onslaught.

The Marine radioman defied death to inch over to Apollo. "Sir! Sir! I have the Grizzly fires officer on the net. Colonel Connolly says for us to keep our heads down."

"I don't think we can get much lower, Private."

"He said, 'Danger close,' and it's *corporal,* sir."

Jesus, thought Apollo, *only a U.S. Marine would quibble over his rank in the face of certain death.* But it was a short-lived thought, because an AT-4 took out another APC just one hundred meters away, and this caused the line of armor to pour more fire on the ambush line.

Someone to his left shouted, "Dismounts approaching!"

Apollo looked in the direction of a pointed finger and he saw a platoon of men assaulting forward through the grass, almost even with the Russian APCs. He knew if he didn't elimate these troops, he'd have enemy in his ambush line in under a minute.

Just after another AT-4 raced toward the Russians on his right, slamming into the tires of one of the APCs and causing a mobility kill, a loud screech came from the sky behind him.

Apollo understood what it was immediately.

"Fast movers," he said out loud.

Sergeant Cruz's shout from fifty yards away could be heard by Apollo a second later. "Motherfucking fast goddamned movers!"

The Russians didn't have any aircraft. The screeching of racing jet engines sounded like angels from heaven to Apollo.

The rest of the men seemed to realize the same thing, and a muffled yell erupted from the pinned-down defensive line.

A last hope, Apollo thought. *But we have to eliminate those dismounts before they get into the line.*

He looked over his shoulder and saw a Marine F-35 bearing down on them at an exceedingly deep dive angle, its underbelly alight from its four-barreled 25mm GAU-12 Equalizer cannon. Apollo watched the steady stream of tracer fire lancing over his position, then turned as it blasted into the Russians less than one hundred meters away.

The earth shook.

Enemy vehicles began to scatter across the field, and more BTRs approaching on the dirt road heading south left the track to distance themselves from the other vehicles, hoping to make a small and less enticing target for the American aircraft.

Two missiles blasted from the wings of the F-35 and streaked groundward, quickly followed by a pair of GBU-39 bombs. Apollo spun away, slamming his face down into the shallow trench shielding his view, but two quick thunderclaps told him the Marine pilot had hit his mark. The bombs landed only a hundred meters in front of Apollo—close enough that shrapnel fell through the air around the trench, peppering the lines with falling fragments.

A second jet, wingman to the first, followed just seconds behind with both guns and bombs. Apollo heard more thunderstrikes as targets were hit; then he lifted his head above the grass to see the black columns of smoke and showers of sparks from the secondary detonations.

Apollo's hope rose. But it was too soon.

A third aircraft was not as lucky.

The Russians rapidly attuned themselves to the new threat. Across the battlefield, eight or ten Russian ZSU radars locked, and their heavy-barreled, rapid-fire machine guns opened up.

The ZSUs had been mixed into the advance columns in true Russian fashion for just this very reason.

Apollo could only watch what happened next.

Streams of tracer bullets played across the sky like fire hoses, each spraying wide at first, but then they converged nearly simultaneously as the heavy antiaircraft guns found their range and accuracy.

The third diving Marine F-35 pilot tried to pull wide, recognizing the trap he'd entered, but it was too late. Heavy rounds slammed into his fuselage.

A wing tore free.

The aircraft entered a hellacious corkscrew and continued uncontrollably on its original trajectory, spinning faster and faster as it tumbled earthward. Flames spewed out of the torn wing like a red spiraling comet.

There was no time. No parachute pop. No way for the pilot to escape his fate.

The aircraft disappeared over the jungle to the east, and a roiling ball of yellow-orange fire rose into the morning sky.

All the APCs that had been advancing one minute earlier were now either destroyed, damaged and immobile, or racing back toward the dirt road.

But in all the smoke and fire in the area ahead, Apollo continued to worry about the dismounts he'd seen. He assumed they were now hidden down in the grass, or perhaps they found some gully he hadn't detected. He didn't believe it possible that they all had been killed by the F-35s.

He called over his radio, ordering his men to hurl grenades.

But just as he did so, he heard AK fire just forward of his position, and more of it to his south.

"Enemy in the lines!" he shouted into his mic, just as a Russian appeared in the firelight, a rifle at his shoulder. Apollo swung his carbine up and shot him a half dozen times, knocking him back into the grass. As the man fell Apollo had the presence of mind to realize the soldier was wearing the uniform of a Russian paratrooper.

More Russians appeared through the burning grasses. A few leapt down into the tiny trench, and gunfights broke out at contact distance. Apollo spun to aim at a big paratrooper twenty meters to his right, but he couldn't get a bead on him because Dragoons and Marines were in his line of fire.

Up and down the ambush line, medium machine guns, carbines, and rifles poured fire. He heard shouts and yelling all around, while above, the F-35s made another attack run on the APCs.

Apollo gave up on the enemy to his right, then spun back to his left just in time to see a Russian leap out of the smoldering grass and bayonet an American in the throat. Apollo raised his rifle to kill the attacker, but from the other direction gunfire ripped into the man and sent bullets whizzing past Apollo's position.

The gunfight in the trench lasted only a minute before it devolved into hand-to-hand combat as the frantic Russian paratroopers tried desperately to get away from both the APCs taking fire from above and the burning grasses all around. They'd deemed their enemy lines to be the safest place for them, and it created utter pandemonium in the fight.

But Apollo battled through the terror of the moment, personally eliminating another paratrooper just as the man lined his weapon up on a Dragoon who was dealing with a closer threat. He shouted orders into his squad radio for the men to stay focused and keep their fire discipline intact, and in another minute there was no more AK fire in close.

Just like that, as quickly as it had begun, the Russian attack of the shallow trenches stalled. Even so, there were still troops near the road, still APCs functional but retreating, and certainly more enemy troops in the smoldering grassland.

Dariel leapt to his feet and began moving forward, firing first left, then right, swearing bloody murder as he advanced, bursts from his carbine targeting any Russian that moved. Men would stand up amid the burning grass to return fire, but Dariel pumped burst after burst into each of them mercilessly.

One by one, the French special forces and Marines rose out of the shallow trenches and began moving forward, following the brave *sergent-chef.*

Two Marine medium machine gunners held their guns at the hip, opening up and concentrating fire on a group of Russians who appeared from behind a wrecked BTR. Belts of ammo tore through their guns as they fought the recoil to walk slowly forward. One of the Marines dropped, felled by an AK blast, but the other kept moving.

After twenty meters Apollo yelled for the men to cease firing. The last of the Russians were in full retreat back to the road, diving behind wreckage there.

The men looked at him as if he were insane. *We're winning!* they thought. But Apollo knew better. They were outgunned and outnumbered in enemy territory. They had the chance to withdraw, and Apollo knew getting as many of these men as possible back to the American lines alive was his mission now.

He gave the order to withdraw.

The men kept up a brisk fire and fell back. Hoisting the wounded and the dead up on their shoulders, they ran through the grass fires, a mass of destruction in their wake. A few shots rang out behind them, but the sounds of heavy explosions to the east and big plumes of smoke just visible in the growing light meant they had done their job. The Russians had been rocked by the preplanned American artillery strikes in the five staging areas. Additionally, the ambush here at the right flank had routed the enemy, and the only Russian paratroopers Apollo saw now through the haze of smoke in the morning were in vehicles racing back to the north, in full retreat.

Exhaustion hit the French captain like a mallet, but he shook it away and went to help some Marines struggling to run while carrying a man on a litter.

Apollo had won; he could feel it in his bones. But he also could feel the loss. He had no idea how many of his Dragoons were dead or wounded now. His father had been among the first Frenchmen to fall in this short but fierce Africa campaign, and he wondered if one of his brave men might end up being the last.

Just then, a voice came over the radio. It was Dariel. "Sir, Konstantine is dead."

"Merde," Apollo said softly as he took hold of a litter.

CHAPTER 81

Yuri Borbikov left the command tent and marched to the BTR logistics vehicle.

The special Spetsnaz force there greeted him. These men had guarded the vehicle all the way from Russia, through Azerbaijan, and Iran, and then to Africa, and they had been hand selected for this mission for two characteristics: their elite skills and their absolute, unwavering dedication to Borbikov.

The logistics vehicle was guarded by two other BTRs, also stacked with big, talented Spetsnaz soldiers, and this three-APC convoy had remained well to the rear of Lazar's main force, safely behind any fighting.

"Are you ready?" Borbikov asked the sergeant atop the vehicle.

"We are ready, Comrade Colonel."

"Good, let us drive to the reserve-artillery park."

All three BTRs advanced with a big roar of their perfectly maintained engines.

Borbikov knew Lazar's plan had failed. The armored forces at the front were nearly out of ammunition, the artillery was all but gone, and the paratroopers he'd sent forward had been slaughtered in their staging areas.

But Borbikov had one more card to play. He would not return to Russia in glory as he had hoped, but he would damn well make the West pay for the insult they'd caused him and his country by taking this mine away three years earlier.

America would pay one hell of a huge price for what had happened here, and while this would not translate into a victory for Russia's military or economy, it would constitute a victory for Borbikov himself.

He would win today.

The small Russian reserve artillery park was well hidden in a jungle clearing next to a rocky, dusty road. All the weapons and vehicles were camouflaged from above, and the gun barrels themselves were hidden inside the foliage at the clearing's edge.

The officer here had command of a battery of the huge 2A65 Msta-B 152mm artillery pieces. His six massive weapons had remained in reserve, and the men had been filled with jealousy as their brothers had consolidated and rumbled forward, taking almost all the ammunition with them.

But now all the other artillery forces were dead, their weapons destroyed, devastated by air attacks, and Tomahawk missiles apparently fired from a submarine off the coast.

The commander had assumed his unit would be ordered forward immediately, but the call never came.

For now he could only sit and wait and worry and hope that if he was tasked forward, the Americans would be out of *fucking* planes and *fucking* cruise missiles by the time he got there.

As the men stood there smoking and listening to the radios in the fire direction center, it was clear the latest attack was faltering as well. The Marines were holding their ground, or most of it anyway, and the bald-headed artillery commander did not understand why the *fuck* he wasn't firing his shells up onto the hillside and blasting the rare-earth minerals out of that mine.

A pair of BTRs rolled up the gravel road from the south, parked next to the fire direction center, and Colonel Yuri Borbikov climbed out and began marching quickly up to the twenty men standing there in the overalls of artillery forces.

The dust- and sweat-covered artillery captain walked over and greeted Borbikov.

"Good morning, Colonel. Thank you for coming in to visit the ass end of the brigade."

The colonel said, "You are no longer the ass end. How many rounds have you put through your guns so far?"

"Hundreds in Moyale and Mount Kenya, Comrade Colonel, but none here. We are ready to serve the attack."

Borbikov looked the artillery commander over for a few moments; then he inspected his men. "Follow me," he said to the captain, and then he walked to the rear of the logistics BTR-80.

Four Spetsnaz soldiers clad in the latest Russian body armor and carrying the new Kalashnikov AK-12 assault rifles stood guard at the back hatches. Borbikov signaled to the men and they pulled the metal doors open.

Three heavy steel crates were stacked one on top of the other near the rear hatches, a canvas sheet partially covering them, making it impossible for the captain to read any writing on the cases themselves.

He recognized each box as being the size of a standard two-count crate of artillery ammunition; he'd seen enough of those in his career to know that much, although those crates were normally constructed of wood.

The captain looked up at the colonel in confusion. "They look like crates that would hold shells for the 152s. Thank you, sir, but we have plenty of ammo."

Borbikov reached in and grabbed the canvas, then yanked it free of the BTR and tossed it behind him. "Go ahead—take a look."

The artillery commander looked at the crates, and immediately saw the unmistakable symbol for radiological devices.

Borbikov himself opened the lid on the top case and the captain let out a soft gasp.

Inside were two nuclear-tipped artillery shells. He presumed there would be four more in the two crates below the top one.

"Sir?" the captain croaked out now, because he did not know what else to say.

"Today, Captain, you will make history. You will order a shell loaded into each weapon. Your coordinates are the center of the mine. Fire for effect on my command."

"But . . . I am not trained on nuclear artillery. Don't we have to . . . arm them or something? I have no idea how to—"

"The weapons have been armed and readied. Proceed."

The artillery commander nodded, a dazed look on his face, and he began shouting orders to the young men in the crews behind him.

Five minutes later the breeches of the six weapons were loaded, and the crews were in position. The coordinates had been set on the artillery pieces, and the pattern of impacts was designed to hit the northern side of Mrima Hill at the very top, with a pair of nuclear devices to slam into the mine itself from above.

This was overkill for the task at hand. Every living thing on or in the mine and the hill itself would be wiped out, a radioactive cloud would hang over the area, and radioactive isotopes would cover the hill, the rubble, and the rock itself.

Borbikov took the handset of the fire control radio and had a radioman tune it so he could transmit to all Russian forces in theater. When this was done, he pressed the talk button. "All forces, this is Colonel Yuri Borbikov, acting commander. All units are to withdraw to initial staging positions as quickly as possible. Make haste—inbound Russian attack aircraft are fifteen minutes out. Confirm."

All three regiments responded that they understood the order.

Borbikov put the handset down and stood there, looking to the south. He couldn't see the hill in the darkness but, he told himself in a moment of dark humor, he sure as hell would very soon.

The artillery captain walked up to him. "Sir . . . will fifteen minutes be enough time for our forces to get clear of the fallout zone?"

"Plenty of time," he said, still looking into the night hanging over the jungle around him.

"Shall we wait for confirmation that all forces have returned to staging areas before firing?"

In a dismissive tone Borbikov said, "No time for that. The Yankees will suspect danger the moment we go into full retreat from the hill. They won't know *what's* coming for them, but they'll know *something's* coming for them. I'd love to let them sweat that out longer, but I don't want them to harden their defenses."

"But, respectfully, sir, how the hell can they build enough sandbags to stop a nuclear fire?"

Borbikov turned to the shorter man now. "In thirteen minutes I will give the order to fire your guns, Captain. If you won't comply, I'll have my Spetsnaz men pull the fucking lanyards, and you'll return to Russia in shackles."

The captain seemed to mull this over. Finally he said, "We will, of course, comply with your order."

A long row of BTRs appeared out of the jungle to the east, then rolled to a stop just behind the three Spetsnaz vehicles parked in the middle of the road. Men climbed out and began walking over toward the fire control area at the center of the six guns.

Borbikov said, "The rest of my men," then turned away, ambled over to one of the artillery pieces, put his hand on the warm steel of the open breech, and looked at the shell lying there, ready for its short flight south.

Finally he turned back to the new arrivals.

The first man to step into the fire control area, just twenty meters away from Borbikov, was Colonel General Boris Lazar. The sixty-four-year-old stormed up into the grouping of massive weapons of war, with several bandages around his face and neck and an arm in a splint. The wounds only served to amplify the anger on his face. He looked around, his eyes searching until he spotted Colonel Borbikov, who remained at the open breech of the 152, staring in the general's direction.

Borbikov looked like he'd been poleaxed. After a few breaths he said, "General, good to see you, sir."

Lazar said, "Back from the dead, you might say."

Borbikov stammered something unintelligible, melting under the general's gaze. Colonel Kir stepped up next to Lazar. He limped heavily off his right leg; white bandages covered his forehead and left leg.

Kir and Lazar both eyed Borbikov a moment more, surveyed the situation, and immediately walked closer.

As soon as Lazar stepped up to Borbikov, he said, "You're insane. You'd shell your own countrymen?"

Borbikov said, "I gave the order to withdraw."

Lazar shook his head in utter disgust. "You will surrender yourself immediately, Colonel. You are under house arrest."

Borbikov stood tall, looming over the smaller general. "*Nyet.* You have no cause. I had every right to assume command." Then he yelled for one of the Spetsnaz security men. "Captain Osolodkin!"

Men appeared from the darkness, but they were not Spetsnaz. They were the paratroop commander and survivors of his unit, all armed with weapons at the ready.

Lieutenant Colonel Fedulov was filthy from combat. Blood was smeared across the ammo rack on his chest, and his eyes showed nothing but malevolence at the Spetsnaz officer in front of him.

"Ah, good. Fedulov," Borbikov said, a little confused but hiding it. "Lieutenant Colonel, you will arrest Kir and Lazar immediately."

"On what charge?"

"They have failed to reach the objectives established for them by the southern command headquarters."

"Pytor," the general said to Fedulov now. "Do you remember when I first took you to the range? When we went to learn assault tactics with your new platoon?"

"Yes, Comrade General."

"What did I teach you about loyalty?"

"Sir, you said, 'Loyalty to the men comes first. Loyalty to the unit is next. Loyalty to Russia is the last hope when the other two have failed.'"

"Good. Pytor, I need you and your men to seize Colonel Borbikov, just as you did the other Spetsnaz forces. He will be returned to Moscow and charged with insubordination."

"Very well, Comrade General."

Borbikov turned to Lazar now. "Sir. We can win this! Right now! We shell that hill with these rounds and wipe out all the defenders, and destroy the West's ability to exploit the site."

"*Everyone's* ability to exploit the site, you mean."

Borbikov nodded. "If you like, yes! It is not optimal, but it will be a tactical improvement over our comparative relationship with the West. Even *you* must see that, General!"

"I'm not starting a nuclear war over African rocks."

"The Americans won't engage in nuclear war just because we use tactical nucle—"

Lazar shouted, his voice pounding even the deadened ears of the artillery crews. "Tell me all about what the Americans will do, Borbikov! Please! Your track record for predicting their actions has been exemplary. Tell me, young Yuri, was the American invasion of Belarus all part of a master plan about which I was unaware? Do you even know that Sabaneyev has been taken into custody by the United States Army? He's finished. He'll be tried for war crimes, no doubt, and convicted, no doubt, and every dirty thing we've done in Europe to achieve victory here in Africa will be revealed."

Before Borbikov could answer, Lazar turned to the artillery commander. "Remove the device from the breech, Captain."

"Yes, Comrade General." The man began doing so, while the paratroopers moved toward Borbikov.

Red Metal had been the perfect plan; Borbikov still believed this fully. If the two generals had just obeyed their orders, if Sabaneyev had skirted around Wrocław, and if Lazar had sped up his movement from the port, then the situation would be totally different.

The colonel shouted, "You will be arrested as soon as we return, Comrade General! You have failed in your mission. I will speak to Anatoly Rivkin personally about what has happened here. You will be shot for not implementing your orders."

Lazar smiled, surprising everyone. "They can shoot me. But not until I end this madness. I will reach out to the Americans and sue for peace."

Eyes turned back to Borbikov, everyone expecting anger, fury, or at least some sort of rejoinder, but he merely stared at the burly general. No words came, but the rage in his eyes was penetrating.

Lazar looked at the paratroopers. "Take him away." He turned to confer with the artillery captain and Colonel Kir.

The Spetsnaz colonel's shoulders slumped, and he was braced by two paratroopers who knew better than to put their hands on him. He began walking toward their vehicle, and they remained at his sides, their rifles hanging in front of their torsos with the barrels pointed down.

After no more than three or four steps, Yuri Borbikov reached out and grabbed the rifle on his right with both hands. He yanked the sling over the head of the younger man and swung it around toward the general and the men standing with him, no more than ten meters away.

Lazar was facing Kir and the captain, but they both saw the movement, though only Colonel Kir responded to the danger.

He lunged forward on his good leg, threw himself between the AK-12 rifle and Colonel General Boris Lazar.

A burst of automatic gunfire pounded the air. Kir took the brunt of the 7.62mm rounds, his body bucking and his arms flying up.

The second paratrooper swung his weapon around and opened fire into

Borbikov's back at contact distance. The first rounds slammed into the colonel's body armor, but the last few took him in the lower back and hips. Exit wounds blew out his front and he dropped the rifle and fell on his face.

Colonel Dmitry Kir lay dead, and the artillery captain had been shot in the left forearm and was rolling in the trampled grass.

General Boris Lazar stood there, with no new injuries, although he was momentarily dazed by what had just happened.

He knelt down and took Kir's head in his hands. "My poor Dmitry." After seconds of silence, he looked up to the paratroopers. "Secure the artillery shells. I want them placed back in their cases and put in my command vehicle. You will accompany me back to the command post."

The artillery crews followed their orders without question or hesitation. Boris Lazar had that effect on his men.

CHAPTER 82

Lieutenant Colonel Tom Grant slouched back in the large leather office chair and kicked his feet up on the huge oak desk. His boots were filthy, caked with mud that flaked off and soiled the documents and map over-lays. His tanker uniform was covered in oil, grease, and gunpowder, and stiff with sweat and bloodstains. Grant had not looked in a mirror in a week, and he purposefully avoided his reflection, worried that his haggard appearance might only serve to exhaust him even more. But even without looking, he knew his face would be completely smeared with carbon dust from the gas discharge emitted every time his tank had fired its main gun.

He looked around the well-appointed office. Someone had said this building was the command post for the Belarusian 11th Guards Mecha-nized Brigade, but all the soldiers had melted away during and just after the fighting here.

He kicked his feet off the broad wooden desk and leaned forward now, his eyes locking on a silver box on the desktop. A Belarusian armored unit symbol was emblazoned on the front above an inscription in Cyrillic, in-decipherable to the American from Ohio. He flipped it open and found an ornamental lined-cloth interior and twenty cigars. He drew one out of the humidor; the sweet scent of aged brandy and tobacco instantly filled the air. He held the cigar to his nose.

Master Sergeants Kellogg and Wolfram almost didn't stop as they walked down the hallway of the captured garrison headquarters. They saw the lieutenant colonel as they passed the doorway, then backed up and entered the room, looking around in amazement at the elegant office.

"Hey, boss," Kellogg said. Grant didn't look up; he was pulling open desk drawers, looking for a lighter. "The NATO prisoners are all getting checked out in the infirmary here. They want you to come down so they can thank you personally. Lots of generals and admirals in that mix, so . . ."

Grant still searched the desk.

". . . you might want to think about doing that."

Still no response from the lieutenant colonel.

"Or not." Kellogg waited a moment, cleared his throat, then said, "Also, we have a final tally on the captured Russian equipment. The Bumerangs and tanks are all operational, but half the shit is out of gas, and more than half the vehicles were Winchester on ammo." He paused to smile. "These bastards did *not* predict us chasin' their asses into Belarus."

Wolfram laughed at this, but Grant made no reply. Instead he just bit the end off the cigar crudely and spit it on the floor.

"We have the rest of the reports when you're ready to come and review them." Again Grant made no response. Kellogg looked around the room in the silence for a second, then said, "Of course, you might just want to hang out in here for a bit. This office is pretty cool."

Grant found a heavy steel lighter in a drawer and hefted it with a little smile, then flicked the flint wheel. The carefully crafted lighter's wick burst in a soft red and yellow flame.

Kellogg now said, "And that general is downstairs. Sabadudad . . . something like that. Have you seen that asshole? Looks like a movie star. Course, he also looks scared shitless, though he's putting on a tough face. Anyway, his translator says he's ready to surrender to you."

Grant touched the flame of the lighter to the tip of the cigar and leaned back in the chair. His Army-issue M9 bayonet scraped along the leather, cutting a deep gash. Uncaring, he looked up at the ceiling and puffed the cigar, savoring the richness of the brandy flavoring. He pointed to the silver box and only now did he speak.

"Gents, help yourselves. There's enough in there to pass around to some of our NCOs. God knows they deserve it."

Grant pocketed the lighter in the breast pocket of his winter tanker jacket as both master sergeants rushed forward, grabbed fistfuls of cigars out of the humidor, and stuffed them in their drop pouches.

Tom Grant said, "Tell that general I'll accept his surrender when I'm good and ready. And let him know he'll be flown to NATO HQ in Brussels to be tried for fucking *war crimes*. Let that shit sink in a bit. I'll be down when I'm done with this cigar."

NORTH OF MRIMA HILL, KENYA
1 JANUARY

The sixteen LAVs rolled north down the hill in the late-morning sun along a dirt road cratered by war and littered with the burned-out hulks of Russian medium armor, shrapnel holes, and thin copper wires floating in the air, the detritus from fired Russian and U.S. anti-tank missiles. BTRs lay split open, all twisted metal, their insides spilling out onto the dirt-and-brush landscape.

Smoke rose from vehicles and burning foliage, and a thick, ugly haze hung in the hot air.

Several areas had already been marked by locals who returned after dawn this morning, trying in vain to reclaim their war-torn land. T-shirt flags and crooked sticks and other markings warned of where munitions had landed but not exploded.

There were bodies on the road, and hanging out of vehicles, too; Connolly even saw two mangled Russian soldiers suspended in trees. Many corpses were burned beyond recognition.

Connolly and Caster sat in the hatches of the LAV-C2 looking out at the wreckage strewn across the African plain.

"What a fucking mess," Connolly muttered to himself.

He imagined nature would reclaim the land in just a few years, as it had done on battlefields throughout history. Not many would see it the way he saw it today, and he figured that was probably for the best.

Now Caster spoke up. "What a fucking mess."

They passed the remains of a Marine M1A2 tank. Its turret had been blown off and a team of young Marines stripped down to their bare chests was trying to recover the crew's remains to send back to their families.

It took over forty-five minutes of driving through a horror show of destruction before the American convoy made it up to Jombo Hill.

Connolly had to fight the urge to lift his carbine as they passed into the Russian perimeter at the base of the hill. Dozens of BTRs, all apparently still in fighting shape, were parked in clearings just off the road, and hundreds of troops could be seen among the trees. There were wounded among them, lying on the ground or on litters, or just standing there bandaged and shell-shocked.

Most of the young men whom Connolly saw looked much the same as the young Marines at the front lines he'd seen behind him.

The LAVs passed sandbagged machine-gun emplacements and a medical aid station, then stopped short of the Russian command tent. The general's guidon hung out front and flapped in the early-morning breeze.

Apollo Arc-Blanchette climbed out of his LAV and walked stiffly over to Connolly as the American exited his own vehicle. The Frenchman pointed at the rows of armored personnel carriers. "Those would make a nice target."

Connolly replied, "Yeah. If this doesn't go as planned, then we'll get right back to work blowing those motherfuckers up."

Apollo chuckled, then spoke softly. "Really? With what?"

Both men knew the Americans and French were virtually out of tanks, helos, attack aircraft, and missiles.

Connolly winked. Softly he said, "We're bluffing here, Captain. I'm just trying to get into character."

A contingent of Russian junior officers approached Arc-Blanchette, Caster, Connolly, and the rest of the contingent of Americans, then ushered them into the large tent.

It was dark inside, and all the radios and maps were covered with blankets, presumably to shield them from Western eyes. Connolly was pretty sure Major Griggs and his buddies at the NSA had detailed diagrams of every piece of equipment in here, but Connolly knew he would cover *his* gear if this meeting were taking place at the Marine regimental CP.

A barrel-chested bald man in a field-worn camouflage uniform with the stars of a Russian colonel general sat at a table on the far side of the tent. Connolly recognized Boris Lazar from the photos in his dossier. Three colonels sat on either side of him, and Connolly checked the Cyrillic name tapes on all the uniforms to see if one was Borbikov.

He couldn't find the infamous colonel among them, and found himself disappointed he couldn't look the bastard in the eye.

A young translator, an infantry captain, stood at the end of the table and beckoned the Americans to sit. Caster was in the middle, with McHale on his left, Connolly and Apollo on his right.

The general spoke in Russian, although Connolly had read that the man spoke fluent English.

The translator said, "You are here to surrender to our forces?" There was a faint smile on Lazar's lips, while the colonels sitting next to him sat stone-faced.

Colonel Caster saw no humor in Lazar's joke, either. "No."

Lazar spoke Russian again. "Well, then," said the translator, "what shall we talk about?"

"*You* called *me*, General."

Lazar nodded and replied at length, and his words were translated into English. "Ah, yes. I did. You and your men fought valiantly. But I know you are low on ammunition, virtually devoid of armor, and weak at every point of the compass. I am told you have a carrier battle group steaming over from Asia, but they won't be in range until long after I take those mines and make it impossible for them to dislodge us. We have other tricks up our sleeve, Colonel, and orders to achieve nothing less than victory here.

"I propose we stop the bloodshed. You and your men vacate the mine— *our* mine—and in return I can offer you safe passage to Mombasa."

Caster did not respond favorably to the general's request. In his Texas drawl he said, "*You* will quit Kenya, and *you* will quit Africa . . . or we will annihilate every last one of you."

The general began speaking before the translator was even finished relaying Caster's comments to him. The captain quickly switched to English. "So, it is the time for threats, then, is it?"

Caster replied, "Not threats. Facts. You leave or you die. You killed a lot of my boys and I sure as hell didn't come up here for your jokes or your games."

The general remained stoic as the captain replied.

The captain at the end of the table said, "No more young men should die on either side."

"On that one item, you and I agree," Caster said.

The translator began to say this in Russian, but Lazar just nodded and waved a hand. As Connolly had thought, the old man understood English.

Lazar drummed his fingers on the table a moment in silence.

Everything he said and did, Connolly observed, was calculated. He was a shrewd, savvy son of a bitch. One who had likely experienced much more on the battlefield than anyone else in this room.

Caster said, "You halted your attack because you could not break my lines. My Marines withstood all the pressure you could throw at us, and now your army is weakened to the point where you are unable to continue the attack.

"But *I*, on the other hand, have received reinforcements."

Lazar smiled at this and looked around the room. "Really? I don't see them."

"That's because you can't see what's sitting off the coast. Our carrier strike group has arrived to within striking range. And if I can hold back your entire force with a Marine rifle regiment, imagine what I can do now with dozens of Navy F-18s."

After Lazar spoke animatedly, the translator relayed the message with similar enthusiasm. "A rifle regiment? You had more forces than that, Colonel. Those Tomahawk missiles fired from your submarine didn't help you at all—is that it? What about the aircraft from your ship?"

Caster shrugged. "I brought along friends. And *more* friends have arrived. Where are *your* friends, today, General Lazar?"

Dust swept in under the tent flaps. Bugs crawled on the table and buzzed in the warm morning air.

The general leaned forward and spoke slowly, his voice metered and steady. "You, Colonel, must be quite a poker player, because I have been a professional soldier for forty-two years and I cannot tell if you are bluffing." He smiled. "Are you? Because I don't believe there are any more forces out there yet. My units have kept you under constant watch, and there is no movement from the coast, none of your LCACs crossing the marshes, none of your famous Ospreys in the air bringing in hundreds more troops. You might have your carrier coming, but it's not here yet, despite what you say, or the skies would be full of your warplanes. I believe you are still nothing but a reduced regiment guarding a small clump of clay and trillions of dollars of damn bits of metal."

The tone was cold, almost sinister.

The carrier strike group was, in fact, another seven and a half hours from being in position to deploy its F-18s, and then only at their maximum range, and the Russians could probably take the mines in half that time if they threw all those BTRs Connolly and the entourage had seen on the way in at the hill right now. Lazar must have suspected this, Connolly thought, and while he certainly hated the general for what he'd done, he had to respect Lazar's ability to read his adversary.

Caster waited a moment. The room was so quiet now Connolly could hear the muffled sounds of the Russian radios hidden from view under blankets.

Then the colonel leaned forward and said, "If you don't believe me, little froggy . . . then jump."

He waited a minute as the interpreter translated the curious phrase. There were puzzled expressions on the faces of Lazar and his colonels, and then the Russian side of the table erupted with anger.

Everyone looked at the general. He remained still a moment; then he began to chuckle. His laugh grew. He had to clutch his side with an arm that Connolly only now noticed he was in a splint, half hidden under the table.

Caster remained emotionless.

To Connolly's surprise, Lazar switched to English. "Okay . . . little froggy." His smile drifted away. "I must tell you something that is relevant to our meeting. I have here"—he handed a piece of paper to Colonel Caster—"a direct order from General of Russian Federation Forces Ketsov instructing my army to retire to Djibouti for some resupply and refit. There we will join our tanks, which have been refueled by friendly African nations—I cannot say which. You understand. And then we will decide whether we will come back and seize the mine or return to Russia.

"I will tell you . . . you must not interfere with us as we return to Djibouti. If you do, I will not hesitate to defend myself with the significant forces and munitions I have available.

"Am I clear, Colonel?"

Caster didn't blink. "General, you can take all the time you want to head back north. But if you take *one . . . more . . . step* to the south, it'll be your last."

A murmur went around the room. One of the Russian colonels leaned in and whispered in the general's ear. Lazar listened while sitting back in his chair.

He switched back into Russian and spoke to Caster, who waited for the translation. "Then it is settled. We will begin preparations to withdraw immediately. There is nothing further for us to discuss. Thank you, Colonel Caster."

Caster stood and started to walk out, followed by Connolly and the others. When he stopped and turned back around, the men around him did the same. Caster said, "If your forces are still here tomorrow morning, I will consider it a further act of aggression." He nodded at the general and touched his Marine Corps cover as if it were a Stetson.

Then he pivoted and walked out.

Connolly, McHale, Apollo, and the rest of the Marines followed.

Dan Connolly's last view was of Colonel General Lazar sitting still at the table, narrow eyes following the Americans as they left.

Five minutes later Connolly again rode with McHale in his LAV, on the way back to Mrima Hill. "Borbikov wasn't there," Connolly said. "And he was the mastermind behind this whole thing. The one guy who would be there, front and center, if they still intended to attack. His absence means he's been killed, wounded, or . . . relieved. Either way, I'll bet you a hundred dollars—no, make that a mine full of rare-earth minerals—they *will* be gone by tomorrow.

McHale said, "Lazar just wanted to see if we would blink. Caster didn't, so now Lazar's more concerned about getting what's left of his boys home." He added, "You're probably right about Borbikov. You think Caster got all that?"

Connolly shrugged, looking out at the devastated landscape. "Doesn't matter. He played it like a true Texan. 'Get off my land or I'll fuck you and your whole posse up' was all those Russkies heard."

They passed again through the graveyard of American and Russian vehicles. Several crews of Russians were scattered on the battlefield, along with American Marines in Humvees and French soldiers in trucks gathering what remained of fallen comrades. Connolly watched a tank recovery crew stopping to assist a Russian unit pulling a missile-and-flame-ravaged BTR out of a wet, swampy irrigation canal.

McHale said, "A few hours ago we were killing each other." He shook his head. "War is fucking insane, Dan."

Connolly nodded. "You're preaching to the choir, Eric."

CHAPTER 83

Lazar's departing army was tracked from above by no fewer than three satellites and two Air Force reconnaissance planes, and round-the-clock Marine Corps aircraft from the USS *America*. The Marines weren't taking any chances on the Russians reconstituting and popping up somewhere else. Theirs was a remnant of an army now, heading north to Djibouti, a trip that would take them days, as they dragged with them whatever vehicles and equipment were still working.

General Boris Lazar walked on the road alongside his command vehicle, surrounded by dismounted troops. Like his men, he looked terribly bedraggled; his uniform was torn, and his boots were caked with dark red clumps of earth. His broken arm hung in a sling, and his face was an almost impenetrable mask of dirt, with giant circles left from where his goggles had covered his eyes before he took them off to let the sweat dry out of them.

While hundreds of men rode in the armored vehicles, thousands more walked, limping back north at just a few kilometers an hour. The Kenyan government was in the process of rounding up buses to help with the lift back to Djibouti, but no one knew when the transports would materialize. The Kenyans did have an incentive to get the vanquished Russians the hell out of their country, but they weren't operating with much real enthusiasm.

If the Russian forces dropped dead in the heat while walking the length of their nation, well, then the Kenyans would be well rid of them.

Major Ustinov, Colonel Kir's adjutant, had taken over for his fallen superior. He stood up in the turret of Lazar's BTR now and called down to him over the noise of the long row of vehicles. "General? First Regiment says they have confiscated some fuel and are making a good pace."

"And 2nd and 3rd?"

"Both report the men are tired, but they have the strength to continue. I told them that once we get back to Moyale, we will give them a rest and perhaps confiscate more fuel, food, and water."

"Yes. We will do that." He was so used to having these conversations with Kir, it was surreal to be dealing with someone else working in Kir's capacity.

Ustinov said, "General, do you wish to ride awhile?"

Kir would have known better than to ask, he thought to himself. "No. The wounded need the space in there. And I would rather walk with the men." He smiled in spite of the situation; his coffee- and tobacco-stained teeth seemed to be covered in a layer of dirt and grit. "I will go back and visit with the men of 3rd Regiment for a bit now."

"Yes, sir."

Colonel Ustinov nodded. He'd been around long enough to know the general wasn't just making small talk with the soldiers; he really enjoyed the men's company.

The general stopped in the road, turned, and went off looking for what remained of 3rd Regiment.

LANDSTUHL REGIONAL MEDICAL CENTER
LANDSTUHL, GERMANY
4 JANUARY

"Watch this little maneuver," said Sandra Glisson with a wry smile. She held the video game controller with her right hand and pushed the "X" button repeatedly. On the TV screen her Apache helicopter spun around 180 degrees; rockets launched from the pods and slammed into Jesse's Russian Mil Mi-24 assault helicopter. Jesse dropped his PlayStation controller on his bed in a fit of rage as his helicopter spun toward the ground, burning and smoking.

"That's bullshit!" he said.

"Face it. I kicked your ass."

"Whatever, Glitter. It's just because you cheated and stole the only Apache."

She leaned over, straining to get her mouth on the straw sticking out of the can of Coke laced with Jack Daniel's that Lieutenant Thomas had brought her. Bourbon and Coke wasn't her favorite, but this is what Thomas had been able to slip past the watchful U.S. Army guards here at Landstuhl, so that made it good enough.

Her body cast kept her in a near-rigid state. She was covered from her ankles to just above her waist. One arm was in a cast and held up and out by a plastic bar. She gulped down the drink and reached over with her good arm to pull the copy of the English-language newspaper from under two vases of flowers. She propped it up on the traction machine that connected her with pulleys and steel wires to the big bed frame.

She sighed to herself as she flipped the pages, looking at the articles and ads, her mind and body restless from being cooped up. Another three weeks in the hospital, and then, she'd been told, the *real* pain would begin. Rehab to get her back aligned and, eventually, to get her walking again.

Permanent injury was a very real possibility, the docs had told her. But she had ignored their warnings. They didn't know what she was made of. She planned on blowing their minds with her progress.

Still, it was depressing when she thought about it, so she did everything she could not to think about it.

And the Jack was helping with that.

She leafed through the paper, stopping to read an article about the Marine Corps action in Africa. "Hey, Jesse, did you see this article about all this Marine crap in Kenya?"

Her copilot wasn't as badly injured, but a broken femur would keep him virtually bedridden for a few weeks.

"Whatever," he said. "Marines fighting their little sideshow doesn't interest me. The big battle was up here."

"They interview a few of these Marines who talk about fighting the Russians with close to nothing. Little armor, dwindling ammunition, just like hanging on by the skin of their teeth."

"Sounds like bad planning from the Marines. Someone should have packed more ammo."

"Here's an interview with a Marine tanker; says they lost almost their whole company."

"Thirty-seventh Armored lost over a battalion's worth of tanks. What we did, and those tank guys from the 37th did, and the pilots, the French special forces—*that* is the real shit. I even heard about some Polish civilians who aced, like, five or ten tanks using just RPGs and rocks and shit. Pretty badass."

Sandra Glisson laughed, but it hurt her from head to toe to do so. After a moment she closed her eyes, ignoring the pain and itching, and told herself that she was tough enough to fight the Russians, so she was more than tough enough to endure the next year or more of rehab.

WARSAW, POLAND

4 JANUARY

The band struck up "Mazurek Dąbrowskiego": "Poland is not lost . . . whilst we still live." The national anthem, it was meant to boost the morale of Polish soldiers serving with Napoleon and symbolized their nation's longing to remain free from oppression. The army men's choir sang the tune with verve and pride as Paulina Tobiasz, along with eight men, stood at attention. Two of the men were on crutches and one had been in a wheelchair but had pulled himself to his feet with Paulina's help; he leaned on her during the anthem.

All wore various uniforms of the Republic of Poland.

A wave of guilt passed over Paulina as she glanced at these men, a few now crippled for life.

After all, what had she done? All she did was survive.

No, she did something more. The simple act of switching the train tracks had made a difference, or at least someone told her it had.

She knew she should be proud, but the intense melancholy she felt would not allow her any positive emotions right now.

Paulina had to keep reminding herself that she was now an officer in the Polish Land Forces. Too valuable a commodity to be let go from active service, she'd received a personal warrant from the president the evening before. She didn't really want to be a leader, but the president had been insistent, so Paulina had been coerced into becoming one of Poland's newest second lieutenants.

A week and a half ago her aspirations ran only as high as the assistant manager's position at House Café Warszawa, leading a team of baristas.

She looked out into the crowd, finally found her father and brother, and looked away self-consciously when she realized her dad was openly weeping.

The band fell silent and President Zielinski stepped forward and faced the gathered crowd in the center of Warsaw's Old Town, just half a block from Paulina's coffee shop. A few people hissed—rumors had just gotten out about Zielinski's decision to draw the Russians into Wrocław—but the gathering was mostly respectful.

The massive crowd was huddled together as light snow fell, their steaming breath rising in the chill winter air.

The president said, "Behind me stand some heroes we wish to thank for their services to the nation. They will graciously accept these honors because they know that the honors they receive today represent the courage and bravery of many others, whom we also honor, but who instead lie now in peace beneath our feet."

President Zielinski paused, then said, "General, present those to be awarded."

The general, crisp in his sharply starched dress uniform, belted out the order: "Personnel to be decorated . . . front and center, march."

In unison Paulina and the others walked and hobbled forward. They saluted together and remained at attention.

Cameras flashed.

The president stepped up to each honoree and pinned the gold Virtuti Militari medal, the second-highest military honor in the nation, upon his or her chest. They each saluted in turn and shook the president's hand.

Paulina was last. She was not nervous or scared; she just hoped to get this over with as fast as possible. She didn't want the attention, and anyway, she had somewhere else to be.

The band struck up again and Paulina and the men made an about-face and moved away. She helped the wounded man back into his wheelchair and then stepped down the stairs to the street. News crews clamored for an interview with her: the image of her being shot by a Russian soldier taken the first morning of the battle had been printed in every paper in Poland by now, and it had gone around the world on the Internet as a symbol of the fighting, but no one had heard a word from her.

Nor would they. She walked by the press without speaking.

The group was soon led into a dressing room and they changed back into their civilian attire. The PLF captain appointed as their handler gave them stiff instructions for the dinner in their honor. "Do not even think of being late," he said. "We will have your uniforms pressed and ready for you. Now you are free until 1900 hours. Dismissed."

Paulina, her hair still tucked into a centerline braid, pulled a sparkly silver stocking cap over her ears and ducked out the underground passageway they'd been instructed to use to avoid the media.

She boarded the M1 subway, then stepped off at Plac Wilsona, named in honor of U.S. president Woodrow Wilson after World War I. The Communists had, of course, renamed it when they held Poland under their thumb, but in a ceremony after the fall of the Soviet Union it was changed back to its original name.

She walked awhile in the snow, stopping only once, at a small florist shop on Słowackiego Street to pick out two bouquets. One was an upbeat assortment of sunflowers and daisies. The other was a big arrangement tied together with colorful pink ribbons and bows with blue forget-me-nots, white lilies, and two beautiful red roses. It had been hard to get the flowers in winter with all the wartime disruptions, but Paulina found her name was now good for something.

The walk was cold but pleasant enough. Paulina watched life shifting back to some semblance of normality here in the capital.

She was certain things looked very different in Wrocław.

The backfire of a delivery truck made her drop the two bouquets. She picked them up and brushed them both off lovingly and continued down Powązkowska Street, turning through the iron gates of Wojskowy Military Cemetery. As she entered, she could see the many dark brown cuts in the earth where fresh graves had been laid. Many families in somber moods wearing black also walked the footpaths among the tombstones, visiting relatives recently lost in the conflict.

She walked to the center of the cemetery. There stood a black artillery caisson, a large wagon that would normally be pulled by horses. On top of the wagon was a casket, but there were no horses in sight.

Two Polish soldiers and two U.S. airmen at attention guarded the casket. The Polish soldiers recognized Paulina in spite of her low-key appearance. They spoke in hushed tones to the USAF men, who glanced at Paulina with curiosity. All the men then moved off together a respectful distance and shooed a few onlookers back to give her some privacy.

Paulina ascended the leather rungs of the wagon, the caisson's metal leaf springs squeaking as she did so. She pulled her heavy down coat around her, gathering the fur lining closer to her face and neck, and she sat in the seat, facing the U.S. flag–draped casket.

She put her hands out and touched the flag and placed the red, white, and blue flowers on top.

Paulina sighed for a moment and thought silently; then her eyes fell to the little silver promissory ring on her finger. She twirled it in her fingers, pulling it off and reading the inscription for the hundredth time since it was handed to her the previous day by a TDF militia officer who immediately suspected who it belonged to when he was told about its discovery next to the body of an American pilot.

The inscription read: "Bonded by fire. With love, Ray."

She wept openly there for several minutes.

Finally she descended the creaky carriage, its protestations louder now, as if begging her not to leave. She took one last glance at the casket holding Captain Raymond "Shank" Vance's body, then turned and walked back to the metro, the eyes of the four sentries following her.

CHAPTER 84

It was just after three p.m. when the wheels on the military train came to a halt at the Nuremberg Hauptbahnhof. Lieutenant Colonel Tom Grant pulled back the closed curtain on the window and looked at the drab grays that hung over the city.

He turned and eyed the men around him in the car. His two acting battalion commanders; his operations officer, Captain Brad Spillane; and Major Blaz Ott of the German army were themselves all looking out the windows.

They stood as one, then grabbed their rucks.

A minute later Grant assembled with Ott and a few of their men, both officers and NCOs.

An Army lieutenant with a sidearm stepped up to the lieutenant colonel. "You Colonel Grant?"

"I am."

"Copy. You need to sign for these." The lieutenant handed him a sealed manila folder and a routing form, and Grant signed for the envelope. The lieutenant took it, wheeled around without a word, and left.

Kellogg and Wolfram stepped up. "What is it, boss?" Kellogg asked.

"Either an arrest warrant or some orders, judging by the envelope."

Grant took out his bayonet, sliced the envelope open, and pulled out the single-sheet signed and dated message inside.

He scanned it quickly, then folded it and put it in the zippered top pocket of his tanker suit.

"Well, you gonna tell us, sir?" asked Master Sergeant Kellogg.

"Orders."

"To jail?"

"Nope, back to Fort Bliss. There are planes waiting for us at the airport."

"How about us, sir?" asked Major Ott.

"Nothing about you, Blaz. I'm sure you'll get your own orders soon."

"Then this is good-bye?"

"I guess it is. For now."

"Wait a moment," Master Sergeant Wolfram said. "Kellogg, come with me." Both men ran off into the train station and returned in under a minute with several bottles of beer. Wolfram said, "Let's drink a real German beer instead of any long good-byes. *Ja?*"

"*Ja!*" they all responded.

The men stood around sipping their cold beer on the frigid afternoon. There was much to say, yet no one had any words.

Soon the Americans shook hands with their German counterparts again and boarded trucks waiting for them outside the station for the drive to the airport.

USS *BOXER*
4 JANUARY

Rows on rows of aluminum caskets draped with American flags filled the hangar deck of the *Boxer*. Colonel Caster walked slowly among them, looking them over with reverence, ensuring the flags were set in military order and reading the name tags. He said the names quietly to himself. The sergeant major waited as he finished walking the final row. Soon both men would assemble the Marines of their task force up on the flight deck for what they hoped would be a joyful ceremony: a chance to award the Marines and sailors who had survived the fighting, and to pin on a few medals for heroic acts of bravery on the battlefield.

Every one of the men in the task force deserved a medal, Caster thought as he touched each flag-draped casket. He felt the fabric of the American flags, coarse on his fingertips, each stitch made by hand back home.

These fallen men would also get medals today, he thought. A medal he'd wished in his twenty-six years he'd never had to give out to men wounded or, worse, killed, in battle. The Purple Heart. He would sign the rest of the endorsements later that evening, then forward them up the chain all the way to the president, who had sent word that he wished to sign each personally. Then, in a separate ceremony tonight, after taps was sounded, he and a group of men would attach the medals to the caskets before they were flown off the ship and onto a larger military transport plane.

Two hundred forty-two caskets.

Two hundred forty-two medals.

Two hundred forty-two letters home.

Caster knew the number by heart, although he hadn't known every man. The number was burned into his consciousness, and he wanted to remember the names and fought to remember some of the faces.

These were my boys.

And he was sending them all home soon.

These men are going home the wrong way, he thought as he walked somberly among them. Lives cut short. Brave men, every one of them, fallen for a piece of dirt on the other side of the planet from their homes and loved ones.

It had always been thus for the United States Marine Corps.

Three decks above, the Navy band was practicing "Anchors Aweigh," the Navy's fight song. The morning sun filtered through the clouds and came in through the giant hydraulic elevator door. The Indian Ocean swept by at twenty knots, a clear and deep blue that sparkled in the sunshine. Two rows over from Caster, a group of three Marine sergeants sat around a casket, talking in low tones.

A favorite squad member? A fallen fellow NCO?

Caster didn't intrude and instead looked down to the casket on his left. As he'd done for all the others, he whispered the man's name: "Gunnery Sergeant Christopher Hall."

Caster stopped in midstride and placed his hand on the casket, as much out of respect as to steady himself. He knew some of the men by name. But this one in particular halted his advance across the metal deck. This was the son of the 2nd Marine Division's sergeant major. He would write the sergeant major a personal note tonight, one of hundreds, but he'd add a few more lines. He knew the sergeant major would already have been informed of his son's death. Word like that traveled fast in the digital age, even if the Corps tried to contain the news.

"Don't worry, Sergeant Major Hall. We'll get your brave son home to you soon," Caster said quietly.

Colonel Caster, the 5th Marine Regimental Combat Team commander, steadied himself. Neatened his camouflage uniform. Stood up straight, pushing the terrible emotions deeper inside.

He nodded to his sergeant major and together they marched toward the ladder well that led to the flight deck. Above them the band, still practicing for the ceremony, struck up the "Marines' Hymn." A fresh sea breeze blew down the hatch from above and greeted them as they ascended the metal rungs to the flight deck.

Caster had honored the dead a moment. Now he would honor the living.

"Sergeant Casillas, front and center . . . march!" yelled Lieutenant Colonel Dan Connolly in his best battlefield voice.

The young sergeant swung forward slowly on his crutches, the cast up past his knee, concealing his wounds. There was a moment when all the assembled men let out a brief gasp as he almost fell over, misjudging the pitch of the deck of the USS *Boxer* as she bore forward at twenty knots through the waves of the Indian Ocean. But the Marine recovered and steadied himself against an aluminum crutch, showing his determination despite the wounds left by three Russian-made 7.62mm rounds the Navy surgeons had excised from his leg.

Once Casillas was ready, the sergeant major shouted, "Attention to orders!" He then boomed out the award citation.

"The president of the United States takes pleasure in presenting the Silver Star Medal to Victor Humberto Casillas Ortega, Sergeant, U.S. Marine Corps, for conspicuous gallantry and intrepidity in action while serving with Task Force Grizzly, 5th Marines, 1st Marine Division, during combat operations in support of Operation Minotaur Forge, on the thirty-first of December, near Mombasa, Kenya. Sergeant Casillas destroyed a Russian BTR-82A infantry fighting vehicle and several combatants through the use of hand grenades and an AT-4 rocket. Additionally he laid down a base of automatic fire, killing six more Russian soldiers, and saving the lives of the regimental commander, the regimental plans officer, multiple headquarters staff, and the four crewmen assigned to his vehicle. His actions were instrumental in securing the regiment's objective at Mrima Hill, Kenya. By his bold leadership, courageous actions, and loyal devotion to duty, Sergeant Casillas reflected great credit upon himself and upheld the highest traditions of the Marine Corps and the United States Naval Service."

While the sergeant major read aloud, Connolly pinned the Silver Star on the sergeant's chest. Under his breath he said, *"Minotaur Forge?"* No one at Mrima Hill had heard the name of the operation until now. In fact, the Pentagon hadn't even gotten the operation name generator to spit it out until the day before, days *after* the battle was over. Connolly and the men had been too distracted to even notice until now.

Connolly spoke up with his officer's voice. "You honor us all, Devil Dog. You are a credit to our beloved Corps and to our great country."

"Hoorah, sir!" belted out the wounded sergeant. He leaned into the crutches and saluted. The sergeant major dismissed Casillas, and Connolly marched off the flight deck as one of the battalion commanders came up next to present awards to his men.

Colonel Caster met Connolly at the edge of the flight deck, behind the formation, with a grin on his face. Connolly saluted the colonel and he saluted back, then extended a hearty handshake.

"Way to go, Dan."

"Sir, thanks for letting me do that, even though I'm just attached to your command. He's a hell of a fighter."

"I wouldn't have had it any other way," the colonel said in his familiar drawl. "Glad to have you in the ranks of the Fighting 5th Marines."

Connolly smiled and turned to go down below to grab his seabag. He only had twenty minutes before the flight off the *Boxer* that would begin his long journey back home.

PARIS, FRANCE
6 JANUARY

Apollo Arc-Blanchette hoisted his father's coffin onto his shoulder and, along with the seven other pallbearers, carried him through a light snow to the hearse that would lead him to his final resting place at Paris's Saint-Vincent Cemetery.

The big captain wore his full dress uniform along with the new Legion of Merit medallion around his neck, given to him by the president of France the day before.

The French president was here today as well, and he and his wife had spoken briefly with Apollo and his sister to express their condolences and the thanks of their nation.

Apollo and Claudette both wished their father could have seen them.

As he and the others slid the shiny maple coffin into the back of the hearse, Apollo fought tears. He was sad—and angry. While he hoped the anger would subside in time, he was certain the sadness would stay with him.

He knew the way to get through the anger was by seeing that justice be done for his father's killing, as well as the deaths of nineteen of Apollo's sixty-four Dragoons.

And that was why he was pleased to see in the news this same day as his father's funeral that the president of the Russian Federation, Anatoly Rivkin, had been forced from power by the Duma. The utter military, political, and economic failure of *Krasnyi Metal* came more and more to light with each passing day, and Rivkin was catching virtually all the blame.

A leak out of the Russian Ministry of Defense revealed the Russians had brought nuclear devices with them to Africa on order of Rivkin himself, but the commander of the forces attacking the mine refused to employ them.

And in Europe, General Eduard Sabaneyev had already made his first appearance in The Hague at the International Criminal Court while Russian diplomats worked diligently to get him back and sweep the war crimes committed under the rug.

So far, at least, they'd been unsuccessful.

Apollo would love to watch the Russian general swing from a noose, but he knew that would never happen. Still, the invasion and the criminal acts were at the forefront of newscasts around the world, and the French special forces captain knew he needed to appreciate the focus on this while it lasted, because something else would take over the world's attention soon enough, and this whole awful escapade would fade from view.

He held the door for his sister and they both climbed into the back of the limousine; then they followed the hearse away from the church and toward the cemetery.

———

Two hours later Apollo drove through a snowy afternoon. The Oüi FM radio station played "Je te le donne," a duet by two popular Parisian singers.

Sergent-Chef Dariel, sitting next to his captain, turned down the radio. "What do you think Caporal Konstantine's family will be like, sir?"

"I don't know," said Apollo absently, flicking the turn signal as he compared the printed instructions from the Ministry of Defense with the GPS embedded in the Citroën's dashboard.

"You think they'll scream at us like Private Paquet's family did?"

Apollo felt the bandage on his neck where Paquet's mother had scratched him bloody. He hadn't minded it. If it helped her at all, he would willingly take ten more gashes just like it.

He said, "As long as nobody else pulls a shotgun like Fournier's dad did."

Sergent-Chef Dariel fell silent, remembering the incident from the previous day. "We'll need to visit them again in a few months. Once they calm down a bit, sir." There were good visits and there were bad visits. The bad ones stood out as they did their final duty to the men and bore the brunt of the families' anger. The good ones—really the sad ones—would be remembered much, much longer and only deepen the heartache.

"Agreed," said Apollo, turning the music up a few notches on the steering wheel, hoping to signal to his sergent-chef that he didn't wish to speak about it further.

The men drove in silence the last five kilometers. The GPS pinged their arrival at a small country farmhouse, the name "Konstantine" painted on the fence. Apollo parked the car on the opposite side of the dirt road. It was a sad precaution, but in the event they were attacked again, it would make it easier to get away. The two men climbed out and paused at an old, rusted iron gate overgrown with vines.

Instinctively the men looked over each other's dress uniforms, straightening each other's ribbons, and donning their white gloves.

Apollo nodded to Dariel. "Ready?"

"Is it possible to be ready for this?"

"Non, pas du tout," said Apollo, and the two marched toward the heavy oak crossbeam door.

EPILOGUE

The noise in Siné Irish Pub in Crystal City was almost out of control, which shouldn't have been a surprise, because it seemed the entire Pentagon had taken over the small establishment. The old wooden bar was packed with pitchers of beer, and men and women squeezed into every square inch of space.

Newly promoted Colonel Dan Connolly sipped a half-full beer in a booth in the back, and newly promoted Lieutenant Colonel Bob Griggs had a black and tan clutched close to him across the table.

Griggs held Connolly's new eagle insignia, turning it over in his hands.

After a time Connolly said, "That's enough, Bob. You're gonna get french fry grease all over it."

"But . . . this eagle is awesome, boss."

"So awesome, I'm worried next time I look up from my beer I'll find you've sauntered off with it in your pocket." He turned serious for a moment. "An officer should never worry about rank. The men pay dearly for idiots who chase after adornments."

Griggs nodded solemnly, then looked back down to the eagle. "Still, this is as close as I'll ever get to one of these babies."

At this Connolly laughed. "What are you talking about? You're shooting up the ranks yourself now that you saved the world."

Griggs laughed and handed back the insignia. "No, boss, I'm the flavor of the month, but I'll piss off the wrong person again before too long. I'll leave the spotlight and go back to a desk surrounded by file cabinets in the bowels of the Pentagon." He looked up at the Marine across from him. "Beats getting shot at for a living."

Connolly nodded and sipped his beer. "I'm inclined to agree."

A Navy commander they knew was hoisted on the shoulders of several younger officers and carried over to the bar. From the sound of things he'd refused any more alcohol, and the throng of officers' punitive measure was for him to sing "Anchors Aweigh" on top of the bar or drink a shot of rum.

He chose the rum, and Connolly appreciated him for it. There was enough bad singing in this room packed full of drunks, he thought.

Seeing the Navy commander made him think of the captain of the *John Warner*. She had been a hero, likely saving those Marines and French men who survived the siege of Mrima Hill, and then somehow managing to successfully sneak away from a picket of enemy ships to find safety in the Indian Ocean.

Commander Diana DelVecchio was still at sea, still weeks away from port, still lurking below the waves, but Connolly looked forward to the day he'd meet her, shake her hand, and fight the urge to hoist her onto his shoulders just like the commander across the bar.

Connolly sipped his drink in silence a moment while Griggs talked to a passing Army major. Connolly wanted to get back home to Julie and the kids, and he would do so just as soon as he could break away. Just three days earlier he'd surpised them, showing up unannounced after his trip to Africa, with flowers for his wife and chocolates bought in the airport for his kids, and with the grit, grime, and dirty clothes of war and days of travel.

The kids had been ecstatic; he played with them and then went into dad mode, getting them off to bed. And then, when they were finally alone, Dan and Julie shared a bottle of red wine in the living room.

Right in the middle of one of his stories about his week, she put down her glass, took his from his hand, and placed it on the coffee table as well. Then she climbed onto his lap and kissed him like they had kissed after all his dangerous deployments over the past twenty years, and he loved it as much now as he had back then.

No. He loved it *more* now.

"Can I see the other one again?" Griggs said now, interrupting Connolly's happy thoughts of home.

With a long sigh Connolly took the Navy Cross out of his pocket. He'd hidden it there before walking into the bar, not wanting to draw attention to himself, but it hadn't really helped. He'd had to pull it out four times already to show it off to half-drunk colleagues demanding to see it.

So for the fifth time he retrieved it and handed it over to Griggs, but just as his Army buddy took it, Connolly felt the buzzing of his cell phone in his pocket.

"Hold up," he said, looking at the caller ID. His phone's screen read "TX-185." An agreement with the U.S. cell phone companies allowed them to freely send senior military personnel alert signals. "Shit, it's the office. Something's up."

Griggs pulled out his own cell and began staring at it.

"Yeah, same here."

The two looked up at each other.

"What the hell is it now?" Connolly asked.

But Griggs just put his face in his hands. "We both know exactly what it is, don't we?"

Connolly stood up from the table. "Oh shit."

TAIWAN
15 JANUARY

The election in Taiwan had the world holding its collective breath, and although the results had seemed a foregone conclusion from the beginning, when they came in, they still caused Asian markets to plummet.

The hard-liners won, as expected, although only by a couple of points. Still, the Chinese immediately declared the vote to be illegal because of their accusation of the Taiwanese government's assassination of the pro-unification candidate.

Within hours of the polls closing, U.S. satellites noticed Chinese troops amassing near ports across the Strait of Taiwan from the tiny island.

U.S. intelligence analysts quickly came to a consensus.

The Chinese were coming. Not today, perhaps . . . but they were coming.

———

Captain Chen picked the NVGs out of the mesh bag on his waist and looked along the placid shoreline of the coast of Taiwan. From his perch aboard the Type 039 *Yuan*-class submarine's sail, he could clearly see the trees swaying gently in the offshore breeze that gusted in from behind him in the strait.

He looked down from the submarine's superstructure at a Chinese special forces sergeant and nodded. The soldier signaled down a hatch and in seconds the deck was flooded with forty elite Sea Dragons. They climbed into waiting inflatable boats, their dark camouflage uniforms almost imperceptible in the predawn darkness. Hardly a clatter from the rifles and equipment slung onto their backs.

Captain Chen leaned over to the ship's captain to gain his agreement to depart. Once granted, he climbed down the salt water– and seaweed-covered metal rungs and stepped easily into the lead rubber craft to begin his return to the shores of his enemy.